Life-Kill

Saniyi Thao

Cover by Magpie Designs, LTD

Printed in the United States of America

First Printing, 2018

ISBN 978-0-9997954-0-8

saniyithao@gmail.com

Contents

THE MAROON BOYS ACADEMY

KONGSAMPONG SUPARAT (KOSA)...the laid-back dean to the boys' academy, unless provoked.

GABE SHIBA...the doctor for the boys' academy.

RAELO FUJIWARA...the boys' homeroom teacher who despises his first name.

RAIN...the eldest of the boys, and a sharpshooting archer.

SHADOW...powers unknown, but his scarred right eye holds many secrets.

NARUYUKI...a healer whose weapon of choice is flowers.

KEI...envies his friends who have Soulmates, also the strongest healer amongst the boys.

POE...able to manipulate his energy rod into anything he wants.

DARK...controls shadows.

TAIKI...adores Umeko who hates him, also a healer who specializes in medicine.

KING...the swordsman who's constantly vying for first place with Hotaka.

HOTAKA KATSURA...has angelic wings.

YUUDAI...an electric user who's in a hate-love relationship with his best friend and own Soulmate.

TAIYOU...a healer who manipulates energy to fasten the self-heal process.

AOI...a foolish and carefree fire elemental.

TASUKU...the shyest of the boys who doesn't use his powers often.

TAKAHIKO...has Superman-like strength.

SASUKE...controls the forces of nature.

NOAH LI...scouted from the southern islands, also a water elemental.

TEO...able to speak to animals, has no other talents.

LOUIS...the only one in Life-Kill history with the ability to see the future, loves to meddle in others' affairs.

ARATA KAKINOUCHI...an ice elemental who despises his rival, Azuma.

ARATA AZUMA...able to move through mirrors, despises his rival, Kakinouchi.

TURQUOISE DOME

NICHOLAS TRIHEART...seems like a carefree soul, who's harboring a secret, able to jump through space.

LIZ...a shape-shifter who enjoys her cat form more than her human form.

THE SECRET SOCIETY MEMBERS

ICORA...the leader to the SS's Asian branch, currently overseas.

HOLLY...third-in-command, can see others' tear colors and use their powers if in the form of pearls.

LIST OF MAJOR CHARACTERS

FROM THE GOLDEN PALACE

THE GOLDEN GOD...the ultimate ruler who saved the world from extinction.

FRANZ...the Golden God's representative.

THE MAROON GIRLS ACADEMY

KIERA BROUSSARD...the girls' academy's dean, originally from the Violet Dome.

UMI OKA...doctor for the girls' academy, specializes in energy manipulation, and despises her last name.

JUNKO TANAKA...homeroom/history teacher for the girls.

NATSUKO 'GENERAL' KOGA...the girls' combat teacher.

LUCIA LIMA...originally from the Fuchsia Dome, and the dean's secretary.

MIO...the eldest of the girls, but a natural klutz who manipulates air energy.

JENNIFER MOORE...scouted from Canada. Her weapons are her bracelets that allows her to manipulate energy into a bow and arrows.

YEVE...pronounced Eve, the "Empress" who wields a silver katana, and can run at the speed of light.

UMEKO...the "Poison Princess" whose touch is lethal, Jennifer's best friend.

ALICE...the gun slinging girl.

CAMMIE...able to manipulate light energy into strings.

SORIA...a water elemental who prefers to sleep and make jokes.

HANABI...the wisest of the girls. Her powers allow her to see the past, if someone's emotions are strong enough.

SHAYLA OLOPOTO...scouted from Samoa, Yeve's disciple and Verse's eating buddy. She can also see the past, but her powers aren't as well-defined.

LOVE...a spell caster who prefers textbooks to people.

MORGANA...an ice elemental, unconditionally in love with Aoi.

REMI...originally a healer but neglected her ability to learn fire energy manipulation, also Soria's best friend.

CRYSTAL CHANDRAN...scouted from Malaysia, able to use her third eye.

VERSE...best friends with Yeve and Soria, her ability allows her to kill with sadness.

MAY...an electric user who isn't honest with her feelings.

HANA...the shy and beautiful one who fears her own powers: darkness.

MIDNIGHT MATSUOKA...the fearless youngest who adores her powers of nature.

YANA REINHARDT…a German-Russian girl from Germany who vows to use the Domes' own technology against them to bring down the Golden God.

SHIN…a young boy who's been burdened for being the Book's keeper.

HANAZONO…Shin's caretaker.

MICHIO…the genius who betrayed the Maroon Dome.

SEVERN…Michio's trusted friend.

HEIDI JENSEN…Michio's wife who will give birth to the first ever, Life-Kill-human child.

MERE MATSUOKA…Midnight's younger brother who was separated from her at a young age.

MISAKI SHIZOMIYA…next in line to inherit the Shizomiya Clan.

HEI…a loyal bodyguard to the Shizomiya Clan.

SYLVESTER…a Shizomiya bodyguard and Misaki's boyfriend.

PIA ICHIKAWA…a girl who was kidnapped from her home and sold, before being scouted to the Dome. Her life's ambition is to destroy the Shizomiya Clan.

Word Meanings

San – commonplace honorific, title of respect (equivalent to "Mr." "Mrs." "Miss" or "Ms.")

Chan – generally used for babies, young children, close friends, lovers, and is often regarded to as "cute", those who are often seen as childish will sometimes use this term to refer to themselves

Sama – significantly more respectful than san. Used to address people higher in rank or towards people one greatly admires

Sensei –used to address a teacher, other professionals, or persons of authority

Senpai – used to address one's senior colleagues

Kun – generally used by people of senior status, or anyone addressing men in general, male children, teenagers, or friends

Oye – equivalent to 'hey'

Yo – an easy-going greeting, usually used amongst close friends

Onii-san – older brother

Onee-san – older sister

Shinigami – Death God (soul reaper)

The Beginning of the End...

IT WAS PREDICTED that in the year 2000, technology would fail mankind and the end of days would begin. Many called it, Y2K, the Millennium bug.

But man, lived past that year and made it towards the 21st Century. Then, a discovery was made: the Mayan Calendar.

Many believed that earth and its inhabitants would undergo a positive or spiritual transformation on December 21, 2012, while others believed it dated another day in time the earth would meet its end. Fault lines would break, and volcanoes would erupt. Water would flow onto land and sink it. The wind would become so fierce; it would knock trees, houses, and buildings off their roots. Since man had made it through Y2K, they expected to survive the year 2012 as well.

And indeed, they continued to live.

The years following, no one could truly come to fathom.

Man, was too proud, too lustful, too gluttonous, and too deceitful. They couldn't see. The earth could no longer support them. They were overpopulating and ignoring the signs given unto them. They took and took, but never in return gave back to Mother Nature.

War quickly broke loose due to greed and power, causing great devastation. Weapons of mass destruction were used in all parts of the world. Manmade diseases were unleashed unto the unsuspecting citizens. It was an overwhelming phenomenon. Friends betrayed one another. Neighbors killed each other. Families were torn apart. It was every man for himself. Even in the richest of countries, those with wealth couldn't be saved from the famine.

But before humanity could be wiped off the face of the earth, a man appeared before the people who had lost hope and faith.

He claimed to be God, the Golden God who would bring peace. He did as he preached and stopped the Third World War.

He killed off the powers of the world and made himself the strongest being. There was no one who could oppose him, let alone match up to his powers. He was God. And by his side he had the strongest Army.

It is now a calm spring of the year 302, the Golden Era, 567 years after the calamity of World War III.

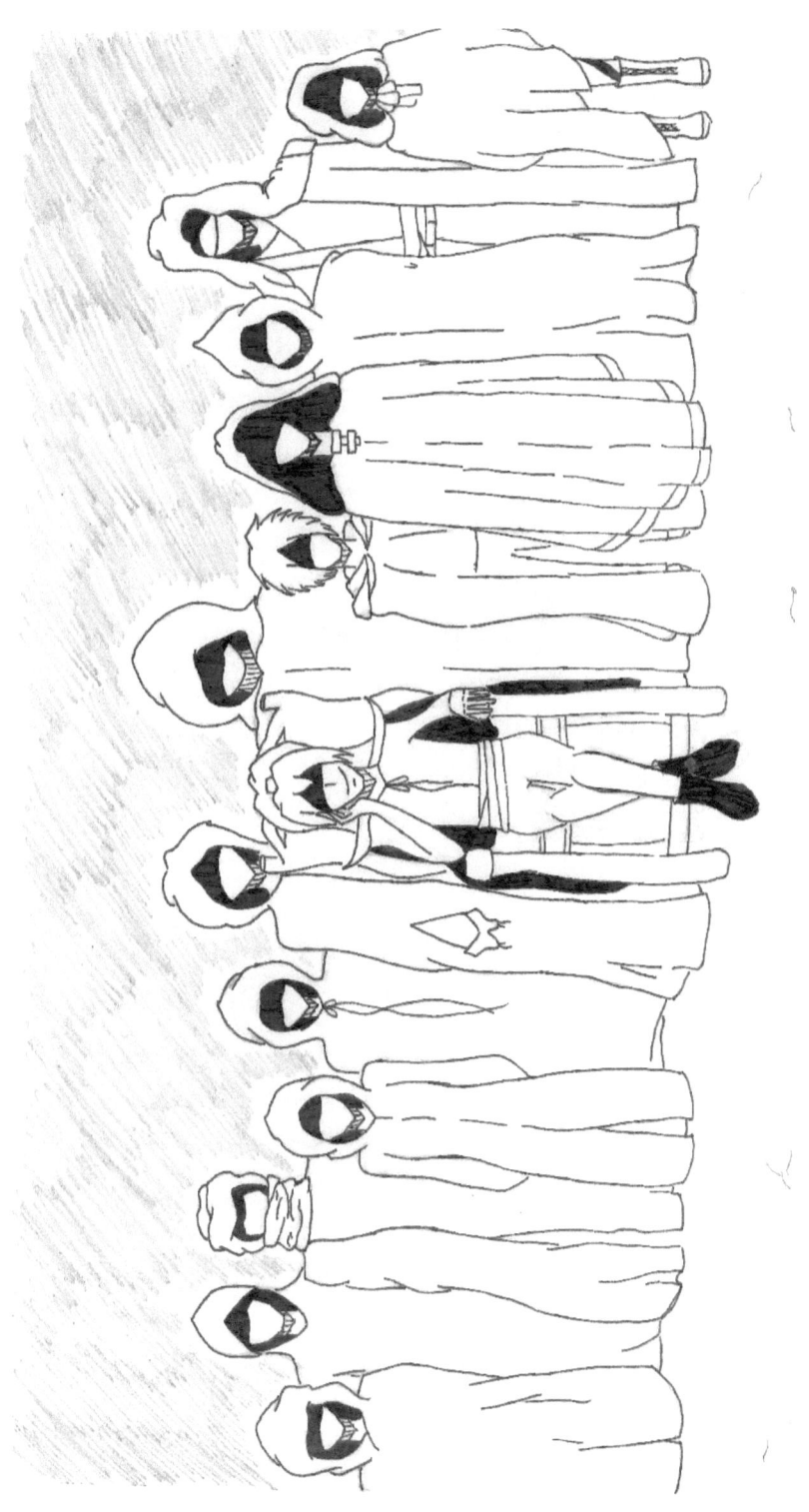

Part One
The Angels

1st Lie

IN THE BEGINNING, the Golden God saw how corrupt humans were, and so, he sought out immortality.

During his first century of living, he killed off his emotions and buried his past.

During his second century, he entered the medical field and experimented on his own body.

During his third century, he underwent extensive training under the strongest government agency, becoming their deadliest agent.

During his fourth century, he died and rose from the dead.

During his fifth century, he transcended into a being not of this world. Seeing that his dream was within reach, he set out to conquer the world.

During his sixth century, he recruited his soldiers. Satisfied, he called them, Life-Kills.

During his seventh century, he became God.

After perfecting his craft and becoming the supreme ruler, he sent his soldiers to do his bidding, by instilling fear and obedience unto the citizens of earth. His power and influence are felt, no matter where, so that no person or organization would dare to rebel against him.

Even now, the harsh experiments and intensive training continue, to train the new generations of Life-Kills.

∞

Where Mei Island and all of Higashi Port once existed in the Pacific Ocean, the grand Dome of Maroon now sits. In total, there are seven Domes situated for the seven continents. Each one is named after a color and made from the finest glass and steel.

Inside the Maroon Dome live the 200 children who're used as experiments. The girls reside on the west side, separated from the boys on the east. Situated between the two sides is a grand mansion where the staff and two deans live.

Unlike the real world, the Dome's weather is controlled. Summer is always hot, and the downpour begins in autumn when the leaves change colors. When winter comes, the ground becomes blanketed in white snow. During spring, flowers bloom and wild animals can be seen scampering about the forests.

During the holidays, the staff sometimes take the students on a cruise out to sea, but never to land where the humans reside.

From the 200 children, only fifty-one managed to survive. From there, it dropped to thirty-seven. Twenty boys. Seventeen girls.

Ms. Tanaka, the history and homeroom teacher for the girls stood before the grand window overlooking into the back court. Her meeting with Dean Kiera had finished minutes ago, but the laughter from the group of sixteen girls had caught her attention. They were screaming and playing a game of water polo in the swimming pool with their maroon colored bathing suits. Only one girl wasn't swimming or dressed down, and that was Soria who slept on a beach chair with an open novel lying on her lap.

With a sigh Ms. Tanaka smoothed out her gray hair pinned into a bun, not a strand out of place. Even her gray suit and matching heels seemed grim. It wasn't in her nature to joke and go easy on the girls. As their teacher, it was her duty to discipline and prepare them for the outside world, not be their friend. Which was why Ms. Tanaka thought that Dean Kiera was being too lenient with the girls. Just because they were leaving the Dome tomorrow, didn't mean they could slack off.

Overhearing the sigh, Dean Kiera glanced up from her paperwork. She wore a Sunday dress as usual with a straw hat sitting on her peach hair, though she was indoors. Standing beside her was her secretary, Miss Lima, who had naturally dark curled hair and long thick lashes. It was thanks to her Brazilian heritage that she had such amazing curves and strong facial features.

Miss Lima poured the dean a cup of freshly brewed tea and set it down.

"Thank you, Lucia," Dean Kiera said, taking a sip.

"You're welcome," responded Miss Lima.

"Ah, youth," she said, listening to the distant laughter. Her green eyes sparkled as she recalled her own adolescence.

"They should be training is what," Ms. Tanaka replied.

Chuckling, Dean Kiera set her teacup down and walked over to join Ms. Tanaka. There was no need to keep training, since Dean Kosa was probably also allowing the boys to play to their hearts' content. "They've worked hard. They deserved these two weeks of playtime."

No use in arguing with the dean who had made up her mind, Ms. Tanaka bowed and turned to leave. There was much work to be done still.

Dean Kiera turned back to her desk and noticed Miss Lima's mixed expression of sadness and joy. Knowing the reason all too well, she recalled the day Yeve and her secretary had met for the first time.

It was thirteen years ago when Soria snuck out of detention after falling asleep during the dean's assembly speech. That was the first gathering of the one hundred girls who would be attending school together. As Soria ran across the dean's tulip garden, she stopped to trample it. Miss Lima had witnessed from the office window and jumped out to punish Soria. The dean too had seen from her meeting room with the teachers.

Before anyone reached Soria, Yeve tackled her from out of nowhere. Standing off to the side was Verse who had tattled. After noticing the ruined tulip garden, Yeve turned to bow and apologize at Miss Lima before dragging a crying Soria back to detention. Verse stayed quiet and followed from behind, munching on chips and smiling. This was her payback.

The next day, the tulip garden had been replanted. Greeting them on the desk as they entered the office was a single tulip inside a vase. Dean Kiera took a seat and smiled, knowing who put it there. As she looked up, her robotic poker-faced secretary was actually smiling. It was quite a fright. Since the day Miss Lima was brought to Maroon from the South American Branch, the Fuchsia Dome, the dean had never seen her smile until then.

Ever since, whenever Yeve was around making a ruckus, Miss Lima's gloomy aura would be replaced with a cheery and smiley exterior. It was a change, and only Yeve could manage to do it.

"Lucia," Dean Kiera spoke, sitting at her desk.

"Yes, madam?" Miss Lima answered, retreating from her memory.

"Please cut some flowers for the room. It feels…dreary suddenly."

"Of course, madam."

∞

When the sixteen girls finished changing into their maroon colored school uniforms, they came out from the locker room, laughing. From ahead, the clumsy, blonde-haired Mio was dragging Hana with her noticeably pink hair down the hallway. They were returning to the dorm building to clean out their rooms before night fell. After tomorrow morning, they wouldn't be staying at the dorms anymore. The time had finally come for them to venture into the real world on their own.

"That was a good game," Crystal said, stretching her sore tan arms.

"It's too bad we never scored once," Alice said with a groan, while Crystal grimaced. Their game of water polo had been one-sided. Even though Yeve had taken the weakest girls to be on her team, she still somehow won as usual.

"Let's hurry and return so I can sleep," Soria said with a yawn.

"We have to clean," Midnight reminded.

Out of energy suddenly, Soria slowed her pace. She just wanted to kick up her legs and lay back without having to worry about working.

"Just be cooperative for today, Soria," Jennifer pleaded and shook her head full of orange curls.

Laughing, Remi linked arms with Soria. "If you quickly clean, you can probably find time to sleep."

"You know, you and Morgana have stalker tendencies," Verse joked with a straight face. Remi's attachment to the three of them was downright terrifying. It sometimes left Verse questioning why Soria had chosen Remi to be her best friend.

"Not true!" Remi and Morgana shouted in unison.

"But it is true. Remi's attached to Soria's hip, and you, Morgana, you're obsessed with Aoi."

"It's not an obsession!" Morgana shouted and glared. Her love for Aoi was pure and genuine. The first time they met on the boys' side, eight years ago, she had fallen in love at first sight. Then, there was the time when they had entered Blair to take on Leviathan, and Aoi jumped off the cliff to save her from the boiling lava. After their joint training began, Morgana only fell deeper and harder.

But no matter how much she showed her affections towards Aoi, he didn't notice. And it didn't help that Dean Kiera had assigned Yuudai, Aoi's best friend to be her Soulmate.

"Verse, my little piggy, you sure are talkative today," Soria insulted.

"Die," Verse hissed, attempting to smack Soria who dodged and ran off, laughing. While Verse chased her to pummel, Remi was right behind, playing peacemaker.

"Geez, those two," Love said.

"Maybe I should help Verse kick Soria's ass again," Morgana offered, a sly smile spreading across her lips.

"When have you ever bested that damn turtle?" Umeko asked.

"I will! One day!"

"Let's just hurry," Yeve said as they followed behind the five. The mile and a half walk back to the dorm was going to be a long one.

∞

While cleaning her dorm room, Hanabi sat on the floor, going through her belongings. Nearby was a trash bag as she tossed almost everything away. She wouldn't be needing these things while going on missions. Their time would be spent on the road and at hotels. There would be no more cozy nights to joke with the girls.

Smiling, Hanabi came across an old school photo. It was taken when they were ten and nine years old, except Midnight, who was eight. In it, they were wearing their yellow and lime green summer uniforms.

When Hanabi's eyes fell on the chubby Shayla with grape-like haircut in the front row, she chuckled. It felt like yesterday when Miss Umi, the girls' doctor, and Jennifer had forced Shayla through countless diets and workouts, though it never panned out. Then, when the girls had lost their duels to the boys, three years ago, Yeve took Shayla under her wing and did the impossible. It was only natural that she'd succeed when the girls feared her, except Soria, Verse, and Hanabi herself.

Tears filled Hanabi's purple eyes without her knowing. She gently thumbed the photograph and put it in the small pile of clothes that she would be taking with her to the outside world.

"Need your trash taken out?" Cammie asked, poking her head full of long blue hair into Hanabi's room. "Yeve's forcing Soria to take out the trash, since she's lazing around."

"I'm good." Hanabi shook her head as her white hair covered her face, hiding the tears.

"Okay then." Cammie nodded and left the room to see if Alice needed her trash taken out, not noticing how Hanabi's voice broke.

"Yes, I do." Alice nodded and pointed to a pile of trash bags. She grinned while Cammie chuckled. Soria was going to get a kick out of this.

"Be back." Cammie quickly left for Soria's room and found her snoring in bed while Remi cleaned. "What's going on here?"

"She said she was tired. So I'm helping." Remi smiled.

"Geez, Remi. This is exactly what Verse was talking about."

"I'm just being a good friend."

"Soria, I need-" Mio shouted, entering the room with a bag of trash. When her eyes fell on Soria's sleeping figure, she shook her head. "Seriously."

"Seriously what?" Midnight asked, passing by in the hallway. When she glanced inside and saw the situation, she sighed. If they didn't do something fast, Yeve would materialize out of thin air and lecture them for letting Soria slack off. "Soria," Midnight said, entering the room to shake her awake. "If you don't wake up this instant, Yeve's going to make you minced meat."

11

From top row (left to right): General Koga, Mio, Jennifer, Yeve, Umeko, Alice, Cammie, Soria, Hanabi
From bottom row (left to right): Ms. Tanaka, Miss Umi, Shayla, Love, Morgana, Remi, Cammie, Verse, May, Ilana, Midnight, Dean Kiera, Miss Lima

"I don't care," Soria grumbled and turned away.

"You're not even asleep."

"I am."

"What a liar." Midnight shook her head and looked to Mio for help. "Why are you just standing there? Help me."

"Do you seriously think that poop-head will listen to me?" Mio asked. Even if she was the eldest, it was only a title she was privileged to have. No one ever took her seriously. Only Remi and the shy Hana did.

"And you wonder why Yeve gets mad at you."

"Hah, she can pretend to be older than me all she wants, but it'll never happen."

"Soria, wake up. I don't wanna have to tattle on you to Yeve," Cammie said, coming to Midnight's aide.

"Fine, fine," Soria said, sitting up and yawning.

"We come bearing gifts!" Umeko shouted, entering Soria's room alongside Jennifer and May. They were each holding trash bags and smiling, making sure to overwork her.

"Ugh, all this cleaning makes me want to poop." Rubbing her stomach, Soria stood to finish her task.

"I'll help," May offered and smiled.

Annoyed, Soria walked over to snatch Umeko and Jennifer's trash bags before May could touch it. "I don't need your help. Also, take out your own shit."

Flinching, May backed into the hallway, holding her trash bag in-between them like it could vanquish Soria's rage.

"Soria, not now," pleaded Jennifer while Remi fretted from the floor. With a sneer, Soria stormed out.

Without realizing that she was holding her breath, Mio exhaled deeply. Though they were comrades, Soria really hated May and didn't bother masking it. "I hate it when Soria-chan's like that," Mio said and shuddered. "I wish she could stay as the lazy poop-turtle that we all know and find annoying."

"Let's get back to cleaning," Midnight suggested as each girl left for their respective rooms, except Remi who waited.

∞

With the moon high in the sky, all seventeen girls left the dorm building to hike into the dense forest for one last camping trip. It had come at the suggestion of Hana while they were eating dinner. At first, the girls were shocked that she'd suggest such a thing, given her nyctophobia, but they quickly jumped onboard.

After setting up camp, they sat around the campfire, reminiscing on old times.

"It's only been two weeks since we last saw the guys, but it feels like a century," Mio said with a sigh. She wondered what the guys were doing and how they were coping with this brief separation.

The rest rolled their eyes. Like when they had been kids, Mio was still boy-crazy to this day. Though she was assigned with a Soulmate already, her sights were set on Hotaka. The first time she met him inside the forest when they had been fighting the T-Rex, she became infatuated. Though Mio was the plainest of the girls in terms of looks, her cheerfulness and doe-like eyes made up for her lack of beauty.

"You'll see them tomorrow," Midnight said.

"I can't wait."

Groaning, Umeko slumped over while roasting a new marshmallow to make a s'more.

"What's with you?" asked Love. She took a drink of her juice while the light from the fire made her red hair look like it too was in flames. Sitting beside her was a black book with rune symbols and unrecognizable etches. After studying her butt off for the past eight years, she could finally understand and use magic, though she wasn't strong enough to summon spells without her book around. It was a weakness and she knew it.

"I don't want to see that damn Taiki Boy tomorrow. Even being with Yeve is better," answered Umeko.

"Did you just insult me?" growled Yeve.

"I—I dare not, Your Highness." Umeko quickly took the marshmallow off the stick to make a s'more. Crawling over, she bowed her head and held out the s'more as a peace offering.

Satisfied, Yeve took the s'more to eat. At least now, she didn't have to go through the trouble of making one herself.

The rest of the girls watched on and shook their heads. Those two were at it again, acting like Empress and servant. Then again, that was their real relationship. Yeve's goal in life was to usurp the Golden God, the holder of life-essence, and become Empress. Meanwhile, Umeko's bad luck had made her Yeve's target since they were kids.

Nervous about tomorrow's meeting, May chowed down her sandwich and quickly made a s'more. She didn't know how to act around Kakinouchi without the others around. Their duel three years ago had been intense. Ever since, she couldn't be honest with her feelings and treated him more brutally than how Umeko treated Taiki.

Also not looking towards tomorrow, Midnight glanced away to the starry sky. Like with Umeko, Midnight also didn't like her Soulmate the dean had assigned. Hotaka was cocky and arrogant, two traits she despised. Even their first meeting had gotten off on the wrong foot when Mio decided on a whim to infiltrate the boys' side because she wanted to see how they looked like. The infiltration had been a success, but chaos had ensued. Only Yeve, Soria, Verse, and Alice had refused to participate in the infiltration. Though the four didn't get to meet the boys then, they would soon enough, when the boys infiltrated their side and had accidentally been thrown into Blair alongside them.

"Let's go around the circle and tell ghost stories like the good ole days," Yeve suggested, drawing Midnight back to the present. She licked her sticky fingers before wiping it on a napkin.

"Let's not," Crystal objected, her gray hair shining like silver from the fire.

"Who wants to go first?" Yeve asked, doing as she pleased.

Hana raised her hand to offer, but not before Morgana piped up, "I'll go first!" Embarrassed, Hana lowered her hand. It was an instinct to raise her hand when she wanted to talk, like she was still back in Ms. Tanaka's class.

"Hana raised her hand first. She gets to go first," spoke Midnight. She winked at Hana and nodded encouragingly.

"Thanks." Hana smiled and began her story.

As each girl took turns, when it came to Verse who was last like usual, she told the scariest story. And as usual, the girls, too fearful to sleep alone, ended up sleeping together in a puddle of mess. Bodies sprawled about and blankets and sleeping bags piled on top of each other. Still, they didn't dare stray from the pack.

2nd Lie

ALL SEVENTEEN GUYS sat around the lounge room of the boys'
dorm building, reminiscing on old times. They laughed and ate junk food,
none of them bothering to sleep, though they had one last school assembly
with the dean and staff to attend.

"Yeah, remember Taiki and Umeko's first meeting? Man, talk about a cat
and mouse couple," Yuudai joked, tossing his blond hair back. He laughed
at the distant memory replaying in his mind.

"Don't remind me," Taiki hissed, but eventually smiled. It was true that
they had gotten into an argument, but he didn't hate her like how she did.
Instead, he was enraptured by her loneliness of not being able to touch
anyone or anything for fear of killing it.

"Shadow's eye," Takahiko remembered. He guiltily looked over at
Shadow who had an eyepatch covering his right eye. It was because of
Takahiko, losing his cool that day that Shadow had been severely injured.
Though Gabe, the boys' doctor had saved the eye, he wasn't a real doctor or
healer, and couldn't save Shadow's sight.

Able to sense Takahiko and Taiki's disappointment, Shadow smiled,
hitting each of them on the arm. "At least I'm not dead, right?" he joked.

"Not funny," the two growled.

"Bathroom break," the two Aratas spoke in unison. They even stood and
growled in unison. As if sharing the same first name wasn't bad enough, did
they now have to compete with going to the bathroom also? Though they
claimed to be bitter rivals, they were more like brothers.

From top row (left to right): Rain, Shadow, Naruyuki, Kei, Poe, Dark, Taiki, King, Hotaka, Yuudai

From bottom row (left to right): Gabe, Mr. Fujiwara, Taiyou, Aoi, Tasuku, Takahiko, Sasuke, Noah, Teo, Louis, Kakimachi, Azuma, Dean Kosa

17

Louis glanced at each Arata, neither of them daring to blink. Tired of watching them play a boring game, he stood up to go use the bathroom. "In that case, I'll go first."

"You two," King said, tired of watching Arata and Kakinouchi bicker as well. "Knock it off already. It gets tiring."

"It sure does." Hotaka nodded and grinned while King glared over.

"It sure does," Rain agreed and laughed as the two guys glared at him.

Teo who had been ignoring them and looking elsewhere giddily turned around, his eyes glittering. "The girls are camping out in the forest!"

The guys turned to look at him, eyebrows raised. It was mighty creepy for him to know something that shouldn't be known when they were miles away from each other.

"Oye, don't give me that look like I'm a creepy stalker!"

"You sure sound like one," answered Noah.

"I was just saying," Teo said in defense.

"Stalker," the guys accused amongst themselves while Teo cursed.

"Are you that in love with Crystal?" Sasuke joked and grinned.

"I was just saying! Sheesh, and anyway, Crystal still holds a grudge against me! Besides, the real lovers around here are Azuma and Shayla, and Shadow and Hana!"

Azuma choked on his saliva while Shadow simply laughed.

"I—we—it's not like that!" Azuma shouted, his cheeks blazing from being singled out. The guys laughed at his reaction. Even Kakinouchi sneered. Glaring, Azuma turned to point at Naruyuki with his long white hair tied into a high ponytail, exposing his tattoo on his nape that branded him as a Maroon Life-Kill. In fact, all Life-Kills were branded with tattoos by their respective Domes to signify where they came from. Some were harder to spot.

Eyebrow raised, Naruyuki stared at Azuma who was staring. "Why are you pointing at me for?"

"You're the same as me."

Not expecting that, Naruyuki pointed right back. It was all because of Louis for outing him during their duels. If he had kept his mouth shut, none of the guys would know that Naruyuki had a thing for Verse who never took anything seriously.

Turning, Naruyuki began singling out the others too. If he was being thrown into the same boat as Teo, Azuma, and Shadow, he was sure to bring the rest down with him.

"How the hell did this happy reminiscing turn into arguing about Soulmate couples?" Dark asked, shaking his head. Maybe it was as Yeve had said all those years ago. The foolish boys were lucky to have survived for this long, considering their personalities.

"Jealous because you aren't lovey-dovey with Cammie?" Poe joked.

Twitching, Dark smiled, trying not to let Poe get under his skin. He clenched his fists on his lap and turned away. "Are you kidding me right now?"

Poe laughed, hitting Dark on the arm. He could tell how much it bothered Dark that Cammie avoided him like the plague. "Sorry, sorry," he apologized and glanced around at the circle of guys. "But hey, look on the bright side, there's a few of us who aren't in lovey-dovey relationships."

"Was that supposed to cheer me up?"

"I did a damn good job, didn't I?" joked Poe as the two shared a laugh.

"What's going on here?" Louis asked, rejoining them after using the bathroom. Everywhere he looked, the guys were arguing.

"Just talking about relationships," Aoi answered.

"Oh yeah?" Louis' eyes lit up at the mentioning of relationships. Whenever the girls were involved, he was always hyped up. "I wanna know, I wanna know. Fill me in, fill me in."

"You, it's all your fault," Naruyuki accused with a finger.

"Still angry?" Louis asked, disappointed that Naruyuki would hold a grudge against him. It was thanks to his meddling that Naruyuki even stood a chance in wooing Verse, seeing as how she only cared about eating with Shayla, and making Soria and Remi's lives hell on earth. Then again, Louis' efforts of setting the two up on "dates" were always in vain. Naruyuki would run away or force others to join in on the "dates." Sometimes, he even hung out with Umeko to avoid everyone altogether.

"Everyone would've known even if I hadn't mentioned it. You and Morgana are bad at hiding your true feelings," Louis pointed out. "Besides, I saw the future with this genius brain of mine."

"Shut up with the future crap already," Naruyuki said as the two got into a tussle.

"Eh? Morgana?" Aoi asked, eyes widening. This was his first-time hearing such a thing. Aoi had always assumed that when the Soulmate Program started three years ago, after their duels, each couple was assigned as lovers. But the way Louis worded his last sentence made it seem as though Morgana didn't like Yuudai whatsoever. Turning, Aoi gave his best friend the saddest look. Was the reason why Yuudai had been so cold towards him because of Morgana's love towards one of the other guys?

With a groan, Yuudai turned away. It was a given that only his slow-witted best friend, and rival-in-love-without-knowing-it would be this dense.

Lips trembling, Aoi burst into tears and hugged his best friend with all his might. "Don't you worry, Yuu! I'll help you win Morgana's heart! I won't let whoever she loves win!" he shouted, turning to snarl and glare at Rain, Shadow, and Hotaka. From the guys, only those three would dare steal Morgana's heart.

"Why do you keep staring?" Hotaka asked, annoyed.

"You three womanizer."

"First of all, Morgana would never fall for me. I'm not her type."

"I'm Yeve' Soulmate," Rain chimed in and smiled, hoping to clear his name. "Morgana would probably be too intimidated."

"Then that leaves only one culprit," Aoi said, zoning in on Shadow who stared back, wide-eyed.

"Wait a minute here. Why is it me?"

"*Everyone* just loves you, don't they?"

"That's not necessarily true," denied Shadow.

"You do realize that the problem is *you,* right?" Takahiko blamed.

"Eh? How?! What'd I do?! I never did anything! All I've done is love Soria!" defended Aoi.

"That's exactly the reason," spoke Sasuke.

"I don't understand how my loving Soria is the reason for Yuu's woes."

"I have a fool for a best friend," Yuudai said, feeling sorry for himself.

"Agreed," the rest said in unison and burst into laughter. Even Yuudai cracked a smile. Aoi and Louis were so slow-witted it was fun teasing them.

"It's rude to laugh at someone who doesn't understand!"

"I hope we can always be like this," Rain said as the others nodded in agreement. Again, they went back to reminiscing, then played a few rounds of drinking grape juice shots as punishment for losing at Poker. Before they knew it, it was already four in the morning. Deciding to get a few hours of sleep before they left the Dome for good, they slept out in the lounge room.

3rd Lie

WHO KNEW anyone could ever get a grape juice hangover? Last night, the guys had gone overboard with the drinking, causing them to sleep in. What made things worse was that they hadn't finished cleaning the day before. And so, they ran around the dorm building throwing trash out. By the time they were done cleaning, they rushed off to get dressed for the last assembly they'd be attending.

The doors to the building slid open as Mr. Fujiwara, the guys' homeroom teacher stepped in, clearly fuming. The guys were late by a whole hour, having made the staff and Dean Kosa wait, though the dean simply laughed it off. Even Gabe didn't seem to care about the guys' tardiness.

"Oye, you lot, hurry up and-" Rain shouted, running down the grand staircase. As soon as his eyes fell on Mr. Fujiwara's killer grin, he slipped and tumbled down the last five steps. Cursing and laughing it off, Rain stood, dusting his wrinkly shirt. "Y—yo, sensei!" he greeted and leaned against the railings to wave.

Without a word of greeting, Mr. Fujiwara continued shooting daggers into Rain with his eyes.

Gulping, Rain stood straight up and bowed, his smile fading.

"Oye, where-" Hotaka began as he descended the stairs slowly. When his eyes too fell on Rain's stiff back, then to Mr. Fujiwara, he was down within a flash and bowed in greeting. "Fujiwara-sensei, good morning."

"Shit!" King shouted at the top of the staircase. He was so sure he had beaten Rain and Hotaka to the front lobby. "I was so sure that—oh fuck!

Sensei, what are you doing here?!" King descended the staircase by skipping two steps and bowed once he reached the landing.

"I don't remember teaching you to curse," said Mr. Fujiwara.

Sorry for being careless, King bowed again and gulped. "I'm sorry."

"Where are the others?"

"Still-"

"Ya-hoo!" Louis shouted, leading the pack of guys. He waved excitedly and stopped, his body suddenly turning to stone. His hand fell to his side, tears welling in his eyes. Before he could get to greet the outside world, he was going to get killed by Mr. Fujiwara.

"Shit," the others grumbled from behind Louis. They knew how much Mr. Fujiwara hated being held up. He found tardy people to be disrespectful.

"Boys," Mr. Fujiwara growled, a murderous aura surrounding him as he sneered. "The guts of you for making us wait."

"We're sorry!" they apologized and bowed, staying that way.

"What's taking so long?" Gabe asked, entering the dorm building also. He yawned while wearing his white coat to signify his position. His gray hair reached his shoulders as he raised an eyebrow at the guys who weren't standing up. "Raelo-chan, did you scare them again?"

Turning, Mr. Fujiwara grabbed him by the collars. Had he been too lenient with Gabe also? "You have a death wish, don't you?"

Shaking his head, Gabe smiled. Like with the girls' doctor, Mr. Fujiwara was alike in that one aspect. While Miss Umi despised her surname, and preferred to be called by her given name, it was vice-versa for Mr. Fujiwara.

"Please remember that we have an assembly to get to," reminded Gabe.

Hating that he was right, Mr. Fujiwara let go and adjusted his glasses on the bridge of his nose. He didn't want to keep the dean waiting any longer. "Let's go," he said, taking the lead.

"Boys," Gabe said, smiling at the group who had just been saved.

∞

Once they reached the school gym, they stood in their original positions, oldest to youngest. The gym had been decorated in yellow and lime green, colors that brought back old memories. It was really happening. They were going to leave the Dome without any supervision. This was what the staff had been training them to do since the day they could walk and talk. Everything was so that they could faithfully serve their ruler and protect him from evil.

Standing on the stage was Dean Kosa who was smiling and doing his best not to break down. Again, he was parting with another generation of Life-Kills. It never got easier, though he should be used to this.

Dean Kosa quickly wiped his eye as his curly peach hair bounced. Clearing his throat, he recomposed himself to give his assembly speech. When he was done, the guys were given small pendants, certifying their graduation from the Maroon Dome. After taking photos and saying their goodbyes to the staff, they headed outside to find the dean standing there, hands behind his back. He had one last speech to give before parting.

"Dean," they greeted in unison and bowed.

"From now on," Dean Kosa began, "you are all men and no longer boys. You will take on the real world. As your second assignment, we will now present them." He nodded as Mr. Fujiwara walked over to hand out manila envelopes.

"Can I look?" asked Teo.

"Not yet," Dean Kosa answered, shaking his head.

"You said this was our second assignment?" asked Hotaka.

"Yes, inside that envelope is your second assignment. Your first is to take care of your Soulmate and not let harm befall her. Once you leave the gates of the Maroon Dome, you are on your own. The only one who will serve as your source of support and strength is your Soulmate. That's why, take care of her. Now, be off and take care." Dean Kosa and Mr. Fujiwara moved aside as the group inhaled and exhaled deeply. They got inside the black limousines that drove them down the paved road towards the main gates of the Dome.

Once they reached the pearly white gates, the limousines stopped. Each of them stepped out, feeling jittery from the cage of butterflies that had opened inside their stomachs.

After taking a few more breaths, the guys took the first step towards the gates that were starting to open. Greeting them was a long white tunnel. Bright LED lights lit the way as they walked down the smooth pavement. From behind, the gate was closing loudly. They didn't dare look back or stop walking. When they reached the exit, a steel gate opened. Then, a second and third gate opened. They walked past the three gates and stopped.

Standing before them were the seventeen girls, waiting with their bags. They had beaten the guys to the pier docks. It was hard to imagine that when they first met they hated each other. Now, they were comrades and even friends. Funny how things fell into place so effortlessly.

Smiling, the girls waved in greeting. Returning the greeting, the guys walked over to join them.

"About time, you boys are slow," teased Umeko. She grinned and made a peace sign. "Yo, it's been a while."

Taiki couldn't help but grin in return. He had missed her terribly but would never admit to it. So, instead of running over to hug her, he kept up his cool front. "Your way of talking doesn't change."

"Taiki Boy," Umeko hissed, readying for a brawl. She had assumed that their two weeks spent apart would change him and he'd lose his know-it-all attitude, but it was too good to be true.

"Knock it off," demanded Yeve.

At the sound of her voice, Umeko bowed and obediently stopped with the taunting.

The group of guys slowed their pace, not wanting to get any nearer while Yeve was in Killer Mode as they had dubbed it. This fear from when they were children, instead of it waning, it only grew.

"Let's go!" shouted an excited Mio who turned her back and ran off first.

"Mio!" shouted the girls. "Wait."

"Don't wanna."

"Mio," hissed Yeve. "If your clumsiness causes you to fall into the ocean, I'm not gonna fish your ass out. And neither is Soria."

"Alright, I'll wait," Mio complied with a pout.

"It's the devil in the flesh," the guys mumbled, making sure that Yeve couldn't make it out. Even the Demon Miss Umi at the girls' academy had nothing on Yeve.

"She's still so carefree." Sasuke smiled as they headed towards the ship docked on the pier. It would be taking them across the sea to mainland Japan.

From afar, a factory ship of cruisers wearing binoculars watched as the kids hopped onboard. The captain of the cruisers lowered his binoculars and frowned. Though the group seemed harmless, he knew better. They were Life-Kills sent by the Dome. The Sea Captain put his binoculars back to his eyes and zoomed in. Even though they were far away, with the advanced binoculars, it could zoom in on anything as far as forty miles away.

Kakinouchi and Azuma were messing around like usual while King was yelling at them to stop. The girls simply watched in amusement as Midnight raised an eyebrow and laughed. Hearing her laugh, Hotaka smiled. Laughing too, Umeko pointed a finger and threw Noah who was closest into a headlock.

Meanwhile, Hanabi was entranced by the sky. When she lowered her gaze, she turned her attention in the direction of the ship cruisers.

"Uh, captain, can she uh, see us?" asked the cruisers who were also observing.

"Impossible, we're too far for her to see."

"But uh, she's staring and not blinking."

Hanabi stared and stared as if trying to intimidate them. Suddenly, Mio threw her arms around Hanabi's shoulders and laughed, breaking her concentration.

"What is that girl?" whispered the Sea Captain. He lowered his binoculars, instructing his cruisers to set sail.

"What's the rush, captain?"

"Get back to fishing, everyone. I'm gonna go contact Holly-chan and let her know about the new generation's dispatch," the Sea Captain answered. He turned away, doing his best not to show how Hanabi's eyes had shook the core of his heart. But he couldn't help but shudder. "They must be annihilated. We can't take any chances."

∞

Miss Umi sat at her desk, staring at her holographic desktop. In her hand, she twirled a pack of cigarettes. She was staring intently at the screen where the girls' profiles were open. A knock came at her infirmary door as she blinked, closing her desktop.

"Come in," she granted, spinning around in her swivel chair.

"Yo," General Koga greeted. She waved and smiled, entering with a brown bag. Her sheer height and muscles was enough to make anyone intimidated, especially while wearing a red midriff tank top and blue jean shorts. Her thin orange hair was tied in a ponytail behind her head, while the front was spiked. On both arms, she had tattoos with snakes and symbols while an unlit cigar sat between her parted lips.

"What is it?" Miss Umi asked, fixing her green hair.

"Gabe told me to give this to you." She set the brown bag down on the desk, grinning this time.

Laughing, Miss Umi shook her head. Gabe was always trying to catch her off-guard. It was too bad she was practically immune to his advances. "Is he trying to score points?"

"No." General Koga shook her head and glanced around the empty infirmary. With the kids gone it felt hollow and dead. She missed their laughter and innocence. "Gabe thought you might be brooding because the girls had left." General Koga's expression softened as she turned to leave. "You have no idea how lucky you are, Umi."

After a few minutes to herself, Miss Umi opened the brown bag, pulling out a beautifully wrapped box with ribbons. There was no letter. She held her breath and slowly opened it. Sitting on top of the colorful shredded paper was a palm-sized glass fairy that glittered like the rainbow.

Miss Umi touched it gently, afraid to taint something so pure. Finding the courage, she lifted the fairy out to set on her desk. "Fool," she whispered. And indeed, he was.

∞

An old man with a gray beard knelt inside an underground church while wearing his crisp kimono. When the door opened with a loud bang, he opened his eyes and turned around. Running towards him was a young man as they conversed quietly. "What?" he asked in a raspy voice. His eyes widened, and his wrinkly hands trembled. These kinds of bad news weren't good for his old age.

"Hanazono-san?" called out a scrawny, pale boy about twelve years of age. "What's wrong?" He came out from a room in the back and stopped.

"Shin-sama," the young man greeted with a bow.

"Good evening," greeted Shin as he smiled and bowed too. He turned to look at Hanazono and noticed his wary look. He knew that look anywhere, but still asked, needing to hear it come from the old man's mouth. "What's wrong?"

"We must relocate at once," he answered. "They've found us and have sent new assassins."

Shin frowned, thinking about the new dispatch. If they were as strong as the past generation, the Society was in trouble. They were low on manpower and if they were to be found now, they stood no chance, especially with Icora abroad. No matter how much Shin wanted to end the Silent War with his own two hands, he was powerless and could only rely on those with powers: the Life-Kills.

Hitting himself mentally, Shin counted to ten silently. He couldn't resort to pessimistic thoughts. The safety of the Society came first. It always had.

"I understand." Shin nodded. Even though he was so young, he was cursed with such a heavy burden. The people in hiding rested their hopes on his shoulders. It was his responsibility to make sure they were safe from harm. Yet on the other hand, they'd gladly give their lives to keep him alive. "Go."

"Yes," said the young man. He wasted no time in carrying out the orders and ran out of the battered church to spread the news.

Shin took a seat on one of the cracked benches, gazing up at the wall. A man sent from heaven was nailed to the cross. His palms and ankles were pierced by nails to keep him there. On his head, he wore a crown of thorns. On his back were whip lash scars. For the world, he had died. Yet the world forgot about him. "The Golden God, is he not satisfied with his golden throne? Why does he hate us so?"

4th Lie

AFTER SPENDING THAT AFTERNOON walking amongst humans for the first time, the group was cautious and excited. They kept expecting the humans to attack and eat them. But nothing of the sort happened. Once they were finally able to calm down, they began marveling at everything that they came across. It felt like they had been let loose at an amusement park and was too overwhelmed by the variety of rides.

When they finished playing and eating to their hearts' content, they managed to find an abandoned two-story warehouse out in the countryside of Tokyo. The empty room was spacious, but with no electricity. It was up to Yuudai and May to use their powers to keep the place lit. Even Aoi and Remi had been tasked with burning a few torches. There was a moldy smell coming from the cracked walls.

Rats ran rampant, scaring the group who sat in a circle. They had never met such fearless creatures before. Even the creatures used for training back at the Dome were cautious towards them.

In each of their hands were the manila envelopes they had been tasked to accomplish. After opening it and reading the contents, the group groaned, almost in unity.

Dark slumped over. He knew it was too good to be true that the deans would allow them to work together on one mission. Each and every single one of the couples were required to go separate ways. "Here Aoi, burn mine along with yours."

"Huh?" said Aoi. He looked over as the guys each followed in Dark's lead, throwing their papers into the middle. "Eh? Wait a minute."

"Here's mine," said King. He too tossed his papers into the middle. The instructions at the bottom clearly told them to destroy all evidence of their mission after reading it.

"Ooh, me too, me too!" piped in Louis as he gathered his unorganized papers that were lying in his lap.

"I never offered to burn anything," protested Aoi.

"We're just having fun," Takahiko said with a light chuckle. Shadow smiled and tossed his papers at Aoi without a word.

"Come on guys, stop picking on me."

"Won't you please?" Hana asked, innocently batting her long lashes.

Unable to protest, Aoi gulped. He could feel his cheeks heating up. Her big doe-like eyes and angelic smile could make any man weak. No wonder Louis was infatuated with her and Shadow was protective of her.

Growling, Morgana glared at Hana for making Aoi blush. If the cute Hana became her rival, it wouldn't even be a competition. Morgana would lose before it began. But when it came down to feelings, she was confident that she'd win.

"I—I guess I'll start burning." Aoi stood to approach the papers lying on the ground to burn.

Smiling, Hanabi stood and made her way out. The night was still young. She didn't want to stay cooped inside a warehouse, knowing the emotional girls would start crying because of the separation.

"Where are you going?" asked Love.

"Taking a stroll," she answered and left.

Alice held up a hand and stood also. "I'll go after her," she volunteered.

"Please do," answered Jennifer. She nodded as Alice went after Hanabi to keep her company.

"I guess…" began Hana. She tightened her hold on the papers still in her hands as the rest looked over. There were tears in her eyes.

"Don't cry, Hana-chan." Mio did her best to smile and hugged Hana with all her might.

"After spending our entire lives together, we're really going to part."

"Don't say that." Mio sniffled and wiped her nose. "Even if we part now, we'll always carry a part of each other with us, no matter where we are."

"Idiot, if you say that Hana's going to-" Love began as Mio burst into a wail. Suddenly irritated, Love glared away. Instead of Hana being the first to cry, it was Mio. She should've known. "I'm kind of happy to be rid of you."

"That's so mean to say, Love-chan! At least show me some love! That's your name, isn't it?!"

"I love discriminately."

"Evil!"

"I don't want to part from you girls!" cried Hana.

"Me neither Hana-chan, even if the girls are mean to me, I still wanted us to be together longer!"

Tears welled in Louis' eyes and his nose ran while the guys pretended not to notice. They'd already suspected that he'd be the first to cry from their group.

"Stop," Azuma said, handing over a handkerchief. He could no longer pretend when Louis was sitting beside him, sniffling loudly and giving him puppy-eyes.

Bursting into a bawl, Louis threw himself on Azuma. "I don't want to part either!"

The guys shook their heads, not wanting to deal with him.

"So noisy," complained Yeve. She stuck two fingers into her ears and stood up.

"Where are you going?" asked Crystal.

"To a place where its dead silent," she answered and left.

"Someone, make them stop," pleaded Noah.

With no one volunteering, Verse stood and walked over to the two girls. She placed a hand on each of their heads as they went limp and fell over like straw dolls. A shriek escaped from Louis as his tears immediately dried and his body trembled.

"She killed them!" shouted Aoi, Teo, and Azuma in unison.

"Peace out," said Verse who left too.

Morgana chuckled and shook her head. "No, Verse just tapped into their minds and probably made them feel drowsy. They're just sleeping," she explained.

Naruyuki raised an eyebrow and watched Verse's back disappear out the door. His initial gut instinct from their duel resurfaced. When Verse first tapped into his mind, he felt like she had done something. Though he couldn't quite put his finger on it. All he knew was that both Verse and Umeko had the same power. Death.

Taking a stand also, Midnight headed towards the exit. "I'm going out to clear my head."

"I guess everyone wants some alone time, huh?" asked Poe.

"I guess," answered Dark.

"The rest of us would be better off waiting here. Those who left will return on their own," said King. "We don't want to disappear one by one, now do we?" He glanced at the others who nodded in agreement.

"Remi," Noah said, tapping his chin while inspecting her.

"Huh? Yeah?" she answered.

"You changed your hairstyle, didn't you?"

Remi smiled and touched her layered hair. The upper portion had been dyed black while the rest was red. She boastfully nodded and responded, "yep,

I changed my hairstyle two weeks ago. I didn't think any of you guys would notice."

"How can we not? It kind of looks like Soria's hairstyle."

"That's exactly what I was aiming for! I can't believe you got it right!"

"Oh, I see."

"He-he, it's because we're best friends."

"Speaking of similar hairstyles, you should change yours, Aoi," Yuudai spoke up. He looked annoyed that Morgana was sitting beside Aoi, giving him ogling eyes. "It's too similar to mine. I hate it."

"But I've always had this hairstyle," Aoi said in defense.

"Why don't you change *your* hairstyle, Yuudai?" Morgana redirected, coming to Aoi's defense.

"No one was talking to you," Yuudai hissed, pushing her away.

"You and Soria really are alike. No wonder I hate you two."

"What a coincidence, the feeling is mutual."

Gasping, Morgana got into another tussle with him while Aoi tried to break them apart. No one bothered to assist as they carried on with their own conversations.

∞

From the darkness, ninja stars shot out as Yeve swiftly dodged. A black whip zapped across the empty air, securing itself around her silver katana strapped to her side.

"Who the hell?" Yeve growled, spinning around to look at who had stolen her katana.

A girl, a few years older than Yeve stood before her. In her right hand was the whip. In the other hand was Yeve's katana. Standing beside her were four men. They stared at Yeve, not blinking. From head to toe, they were covered in black clothing. The girl had her hair slicked back into a ponytail. "Hey there," she greeted.

Yeve held out her hand, not in the mood to play around after a tiring day. Neither did she appreciate the surprise attack. "Give back my katana."

"Can't even greet your elders? What has the Dome been teaching the students these days?" she joked and grinned behind her mask. In the end, she grimaced at Yeve's grim attitude. "The name's Mana."

"Katana," demanded Yeve.

"Sorry sweetie. I can't hand over your pretty katana. Without this weapon, you probably won't be able to fight, right?"

Yeve grinned, getting into attack position. She was being underestimated because she wasn't carrying a weapon. Oh, how she loved proving people wrong. "Is that what you really think?"

"You think you can defeat us?"

"I don't think. I am. After defeating you I'm going to make you spill the beans about why the hell you're here."

"You're one cheeky brat. You should be calling me, 'senpai' or 'big sis'."

"In your dreams."

"Mana," one of the men spoke up.

She slightly turned to look at him and nodded. "Go assist the others. I'll handle this one."

"You sure?"

"One hundred percent."

"Okay," they said, taking their leave.

"You shouldn't have done that," warned Yeve.

Mana couldn't help but grin again at Yeve's confidence. New dispatches were always so cocky. No wonder they died young. Yeve would be no different. "Then, show me what you've got," she challenged as they ran at one another.

∞

Feeling drowsy from Morgana's pestering of how Soria needed to protect Aoi and stop picking on him, she was on the verge of collapsing but suddenly perked up. There was a disturbance in the air. She put a thumb to her mouth, almost biting her nail, but stopped. Remi was inspecting her. Slowly, without raising suspicion, Soria stood with a yawn. "Be back."

"Eh? Where are you going?" Aoi and Remi asked in unison. The two glanced at each other, then to Soria who was taking her leave.

"Poop."

"Let me go with you. It's my job to protect you," offered Aoi.

"Ew!" shouted Morgana. She reached out to stop Aoi from following Soria. This was their last night together. She wouldn't allow Soria to come in-between her and Aoi's time together. "Just let her go. She's a big girl. She doesn't need supervision just to poop."

"But-"

"Stay," ordered Rain. The others who didn't notice the disturbance became tense. He only used that tone when something bothered him.

Suddenly worried, Aoi frowned. That only gave him more reason to follow his Soulmate. "I'm going to-"

"I said to stay."

"I'm not going to sit here and do-"

"My orders are absolute."

Unable to argue, Aoi fell silent. Since Rain was the eldest, the predicament they were in was in his hands. If only Aoi had noticed earlier, he wouldn't have let Soria go alone.

"Uh, what's going on?" May asked.

"Shadow, you're in charge. Keep everyone here safe."

Also sensing the change from the beginning, Shadow nodded. "Got it."

"Hotaka, King, let's go," ordered Rain as the three ran towards the door.

"Is anyone going to answer me?" May asked, worried that the guys were forming a circle around the girls.

"We're under attack," Umeko answered and stood. The color of her left eye turned from a soft brown to a blood red, an effect from her poison.

"Eh?" the girls said, finally catching on. "The others who left-"

"They won't fall so easily." Umeko smiled reassuringly while Jennifer nodded in agreement.

∞

Rain, Hotaka, and King ran, blending in with their scenery, making sure not to be seen. They had to take the enemy by surprise. "King and I will defend the base," Rain instructed.

"What about me?" Hotaka asked.

"Go find Midnight."

"Eh?" said the two guys in shock. They hadn't expected Rain to give out such orders. It wasn't in his nature to place anything or anyone above his comrades' well-being.

"You're worried about her, aren't you?" Rain looked over, able to read Hotaka's frown. "Go. I don't need you here if you're going to be distracted the entire time."

Grateful, Hotaka bowed.

"Bring her back safe and sound," King said.

"I know, idiot. She's my Soulmate after all. It's my duty to protect her." Hotaka smiled and disappeared into the dark.

King turned towards Rain, a grin spreading across his lips. "That guy's totally head over heels for Midnight."

"You and Jennifer can be too," Rain teased with a grin.

"Not a chance in hell," snapped King.

"Whatever you say."

"Let's just find these goons and make them spill their guts."

"Don't worry, I plan on doing just that."

∞

"It's beautiful, isn't it?" Alice asked, sitting on a tree branch watching the moon hang in the sky. Hanabi smiled from where she sat, gazing at the moon also. "You think the girls started crying yet?"

"I know so." Hanabi nodded and closed her eyes, the gentle breeze rustling the leaves. She too couldn't help but think about tomorrow's inevitable parting. "But you know, even if we part, we'll always carry a part of each other with us."

"Yeah, I know." After a few seconds of silence, Alice jumped down, dusting her dress. Hanabi also stood from where she sat. "We know you're there. You mind as well show yourself," Alice hissed. "Or I can always start shooting."

"Not bad," snorted the stranger who came into view. He was wearing black clothes with a black mask hiding his face.

"What do you want?" Hanabi asked.

"It's as our Sea Captain said. You kids are good. Which is why we're going to nip you at the bud before you can bloom into poisonous flowers!" he shouted and attacked.

"I got this, Hanabi," Alice assured. She parted her dress and unhooked her brown gun from its holster. With nimble fingers, she was able to slip in a red colored magazine. While Alice fought, Hanabi stepped behind the trunk of the tree to not get involved.

Unable to see what was happening, Hanabi waited. She could hear gunshots going off. A stray bullet even hit the trunk, causing splinters to fly. Hanabi flinched but never screamed or ran. Two explosions occurred from the battlefield until someone hit the ground and grunted. Hanabi gulped and clung to the tree bark, breathing heavily. Even though she had faith in Alice's ability, this was a real death battle in the real world, not training back at the Dome.

"Hanabi," Alice said, coming around the trunk, dirty. She smiled, giving her friend a peace sign.

Relieved, Hanabi returned the smile.

"He was a weakling, and he dared to challenge us." Alice flicked her golden hair, putting her left hand to her hip, gun in her right hand.

Hanabi chuckled and shook her head. Yeve had somehow rubbed off on Alice without her realizing it. The smell of iron hit Hanabi's nose as she walked over to inspect the man who had just been killed. His blood ran, staining the grass. There were two bullets that had pierced his heart.

"What are you doing?" Alice raised an eyebrow, curious about why Hanabi was kneeling beside a man who had wanted them dead.

Hanabi's heart pounded inside her chest. An indescribable pain washed over her like a river. She couldn't stop her tears even if she wanted to. The feelings from the dead man was calling out to her.

"Hanabi," called out Alice. She put her gun away in its holster and ran over to hold her friend. "Whoa, hey there. What happened?"

"Why?" Hanabi asked. "Why is it that we can kill without a second thought? Aren't we still human? So then, why does it feel like I'm missing an essential piece of me somewhere?" No matter how she asked, she knew Alice didn't have the answers. The answers to her questions was something she'd have to seek on her own. Still, Hanabi wanted someone to try and understand her. Was that why she sought out Verse, because they were similar?

∞

Pain ate away at the core of his heart until he yielded and fell to the ground, crying. In his hand was a dagger, but he never got the chance to use it before Verse delivered the finishing blow. The silent breeze passed as she stood in the dark open field where five dead bodies lay. These men and women would never get the chance to return home to their loved ones. Neither would they get to smile or laugh again.

A strike of pain hit Verse as she grunted and hit both knees. Her head pounded like she was having one migraine after another. Unable to kneel straight, she slumped forward, placing her forehead to the ground.

A blinding white light flashed before Verse while she panted for air. Footsteps approached her as her heart jumped. She had to get up before the stranger could reach her. If it was an enemy, they could strike while she was down. Though she knew the dangers, she couldn't summon her iron-like legs to stand.

"Are you okay?" asked the familiar voice.

The blood flowing in Verse's body froze at the sound of his voice. With what strength she had left, she managed to lift her head off the ground to gaze at his silhouette that was hidden by darkness.

"I'll always protect you." He held out his hand and she could sense that he was smiling warmly at her. Verse couldn't help but smile in return. She nodded and closed her eyes, wanting to hold his hand also. But the pain from the back of her head caused her to slump forward again. After a few seconds, the light disappeared, and she was alone in the dark field. When the pounding and throbbing in her heart ceased, she stumbled to her feet.

"You're okay." From behind, Soria approached silently while staring at the dead bodies.

"What are you doing here?" Verse asked in alarm.

"Thought you might need my help," she answered and shrugged. "Guess not."

"You're way too slow. Of course I'll finish them before you get here." Verse smirked and turned to leave, but not before wiping her sweaty forehead. "Come on. Let's go find Yeve."

"Yeah," answered Soria. She stared at the dead bodies for a few seconds before following. Not even five assassins could take Verse down.

"So?"

"So what?" asked Soria.

"Did you guys get attacked too?"

"Dunno."

"What do you mean you don't know?"

"Like I said, dunno."

"Don't tell me you left them behind."

"I did."

Verse shook her head before letting out a light chuckle. Even out in the real world, Soria wasn't going to change. "And this is why the girls think you're more heartless than Yeve."

"I guess," Soria said without a care.

"You really ought to change that personality of yours."

"Take your own advice."

Verse sneered. She should've known better than to pick a fight with Soria of all people. "Thanks for coming," she whispered.

"It's my job to back you two up," Soria responded and smiled, bumping fists with Verse.

∞

The vines parted as Midnight stepped out from within. The man she had injured hung before her, entangled in vines. "Tell me. Who sent you?" she interrogated.

"Who in their right mind would answer to a child?" he said and grinned.

"Just for the record, this *child* did kick your ass, all by herself."

"Pure luck," he said, shaking his bleeding head.

"You know, you're on your deathbed. Shouldn't you at least tell me before dying?"

"I'll die, taking this with me to the grave."

"Stubborn, aren't you?" Midnight crossed her arms. She hated stubborn people, especially men. There was a specific person she had in mind and when she thought about him, it brought the worst out of her. "So?" she urged.

"You mind as well finish me off because I'm not speaking." The man shook his head again. Blood dripped from his torn pectoral. It was only a matter of minutes before he bled to death. Even his self-heal couldn't repair these injuries.

"I don't like stubborn men."

The man stared back, tears flowing from his eyes. He smiled the saddest smile, causing Midnight to waver. "You really are just a child."

Just like that, her resolve hardened again. "I'm not a child. I'm sixteen. I'm already an adult, despite my short stature."

"You, whom know nothing about pain or loss, will never become an adult."

"What did you say?" A spark of anger flared in her eyes as she glared at the man. He had said something infuriating. How dare he judge her when he knew nothing about her? She did understand the meaning of loss. Before entering the Dome as a recruit, she had lost the most important person to her. "You have no right to judge me."

"Pitiful child, when will your soul be liberated?"

"Shut up."

"I hope that day comes soon," he said, ignoring her.

"Damn you old man, shut up already!" The vines pierced the man straight through the heart without hesitation. He let out a grunt and slowly hung his head down low, bleeding out. His body no longer moved as the vines parted, dropping him to the earth like a rag doll.

"Midnight!" called out Hotaka as he ran towards her and stopped. He looked at the dead man, then to her back. Relieved, he smiled. He should've expected nothing less of his hot-blooded Soulmate. "Thank goodness you're okay."

"You're noisy," she hissed, turning to glare at him.

Hotaka stood, glued to the earth as she walked around him to return to the abandoned warehouse. Even if her expression was full of hate, he couldn't let her walk away and pulled her back to eye. "What happened?"

From everyone, he was the last person she wanted showing kindness to her. "Nothing," Midnight spoke, breaking away to briskly leave. She put a hand to her mouth, fighting back the tears. She didn't want to look weak, especially in front of her nemesis and Soulmate.

∞

"You're...good," complimented Mana. She smirked from where she knelt, gasping for air. It felt as though Yeve was toying with her. Not once was Mana able to get near. By the time she knew it, Yeve had vanished from one place to another, causing Mana to use up her energy. Yeve had even managed to retrieve her katana. If Mana had known what they were going against, she would've planned meticulously before attacking. But because she assumed that the new generation were newbies, they'd be easy to kill.

"I told you already, didn't I?" Yeve wiped her bloody katana with a handkerchief she always carried. "Give up yet?"

"You mind as well kill me because I won't give up."

"You leave me with no choice then."

"I guess I don't," agreed Mana. She gazed at the moon, wondering why it was so lonely even with the stars surrounding it. "Shin-chan's going to get mad at me again."

"Huh?" said Yeve. She raised an eyebrow, confused. "Are those your dying words or something?"

Mana snorted. "Yeah, I guess you can say it's something along those lines."

"Should I pass it on for you then?" offered Yeve.

"No need. My words will reach them all on its own."

"Tell me something before I kill you."

"If you're gonna ask who sent me and why I'm here to annihilate you, I won't answer." Mana shook her head as she staggered to her feet. "I won't rat out my comrades."

"I admire your loyalty. Because of it, I'll give you a quick, painless death."

Mana chuckled, pointing the tip of her sword at Yeve as well. She even considered spilling the beans but knew that no new dispatch ever believed. Even she had been the same. "If we had met under different circumstances, I'd have loved to be your friend."

"Is that so?" Yeve smiled and got into attack position.

"Let's end this." Mana closed her eyes and tightened her grip on her short sword. The breeze quietly passed as the trees rustled nearby. A smile overcame her. She knew, she couldn't win against Yeve and her killer katana but refused to go down without a fight. With the remainder of her life, she'd use it to protect what she believed was precious.

A leaf fell and landed on the ground as Mana flung her eyes open. Simultaneously, they ran at each other and slashed, putting their all into the last attack. With backs to each other, they stood, swords in hand.

Mana smiled before collapsing. Her initial assumption had been right. Yeve may be young and fresh from the Dome, but her skills were on par with the veterans. Blood gushed from the fatal wound Yeve had inflicted as Mana lay on the ground. Slowly, she turned onto her back to gaze at the starry sky. Her breaths came in gasps and her heartbeat quickened, trying to pump enough blood to sustain her life.

Yeve turned, noticing the smile on Mana's face, and walked over. "Why do you still smile?"

Mana chuckled. "It's beautiful."

"What is?"

"Death," she responded. "I never knew that death was so beautiful."

"How can such a thing be beautiful?"

"One day, you'll come to understand death's beauty."

"I won't ever."

Reflected in Mana's eyes was a face that Yeve didn't recognize. The feelings that overflowed from her were overwhelming and overpowering. Yeve hit her knees, suddenly finding it hard to breathe. She couldn't peel her eyes away from Mana's, her body feeling possessed.

"Mana...!" called out the man reflected in her eyes. "Mana...I'll always be with you. So, don't go and leave me, okay?"

"St—stop," pleaded Yeve.

"Mana, stop!" he shouted, trying to stop her from going Berserk.

"I said, stop it!" begged Yeve. Tears flowed from her eyes like a waterfall. She threw both hands to her head and screamed. It felt like someone had entered her mind, tormenting her repeatedly. For the first time in Yeve's life, she yielded, but Mana's feelings refused to let her off that easily. It was going to take her down as well.

A hand reached out to cover Yeve's eyes from gazing into the now dead Mana's. Slowly, Yeve's shivering body calmed down until it lost all energy from the inner battle.

"It'll take me a sec," said Verse.

"Yeah," answered Soria. She was holding onto a now unconscious Yeve while Verse knelt beside Mana and covered her eyes. Soon, she was inside Mana's inner mind, where stairs were inverted. Some doors led to dead ends, while others opened to pitfalls. For as long as Verse could remember, she always knew where the door she sought was located.

As she ran, searching for *the* door, she never double-guessed or glanced back. When she finally found it, she stopped. It was a teal colored door with no markings or cracks. It was so well-kept she raised an eyebrow.

Verse placed a hand on the knob and twisted it open, expecting to find a burden of sadness and pain. Instead, she was met with a field of globe amaranth flowers. Verse's eyes widened. The feeling was similar to Naruyuki's inner mind when she had entered it three years ago. The only difference were the flowers.

"Mana," he whispered as Verse watched someone walk towards her. "Let's go." He held out a hand as Mana came running past Verse. She fell into his arms, crying. It had been a long time since she last saw him—*touched* him. "Geez, you're crying again."

Unable to stop, Mana held on tightly. How could she not cry after being separated for so long? They were finally together again. "I'm sorry. I'm so sorry. Please forgive me."

"It's okay now." He smiled and held on tightly, then turned towards Verse. "Thank you for opening the door. If not for you, she wouldn't have found me."

"Eh?" said Verse. This was the first time someone had thanked her for opening a door that was meant to kill the host.

"Let's go, Mana."

Wiping her eyes, Mana nodded in response and smiled.

He held her hand and gave Verse one last glance before smiling. "You..." he whispered, leaving his sentence unfinished. He waved a hand farewell and left with Mana by his side.

Verse stood, watching them disappear into the blue horizon. Without understanding a single thing that just happened, she felt content. From a faraway place, Verse could hear a piano being played. The sun above was so warm, she closed her eyes and tilted her face towards it. It felt as though someone was embracing her lovingly, that it could break her heart in two.

"Verse," called out Soria. She reached a hand out and touched Verse's shoulder gently. "Did you finish the job?"

"Ah, yeah," answered Verse. She blinked and nodded, letting go of Mana now that Soria had interrupted her thoughts. That warm piece of memory she had experienced was forever lost to the world. To her though, it would live forever.

"She's smiling," said Soria in alarm.

Verse stared at Mana's smiling face and smiled too. "Yeah, I think right now, she's in a happy place, full of sunshine."

"Happiness?" repeated Soria. She raised an eyebrow, questioning the statement just then.

"Forget it. It's nothing." Verse stood and walked over to Yeve's side, attempting to carry her back to the warehouse.

"I got her. You grab the katana." Soria moved her hand as water encircled Yeve, lifting her off the ground. It was easier this way, so they didn't have to exert energy. "Let's go." The two girls walked away as the water carried Yeve beside them.

"Hey, Soria," said Verse. She wiped the bloody silver katana clean before putting it back inside its black scabbard. It was a peculiar color combo, but that was how it came out after being forged for Yeve, using her blood.

"What is it?"

"Why..." Verse turned to look at the moon hanging in the sky. In the end, she shook it off. If she were to ask, it would sound naïve and foolish. "It's nothing. Forget it."

Soria glimpsed at Verse's profile before answering, "I agree."

"Huh?" Verse stopped, dead in her tracks as Soria took a few steps before halting as well. Even the water carrying Yeve stopped. Verse blinked a few times, staring at Soria's back. She hadn't even finished her sentence, yet Soria had answered with an agreement.

"You didn't have to say it. I know already. I feel the same too." Soria smiled and turned back. She reached a hand out, patting Verse's head like she was still a child that needed to be consoled. "Don't think too much about it. It'll just hurt your head. I've already tried and started getting migraines. One day though, our questions will be answered."

Verse smiled, brushing her head where Soria had patted. She looked up to the moon and closed her eyes while Soria continued back to the warehouse with Yeve. "Yeah, you're right."

"Come on, let's hurry. I don't want to hear any lectures from the others."

"Yeah," Verse answered, chasing after the two. "You know," she said cheerfully, upon reaching Soria's side. "It really does feel like we're sisters."

Soria smiled and nodded in agreement. "I know what you mean."

"Maybe it's as Mio said, maybe, we really were sisters in our previous lives."

5th Lie

"WE'RE BACK!" Rain announced as he entered the abandoned warehouse with the others who were also returning. A few were dirty while the rest seemed to be in tip-top shape.

"Did you get any answers?" asked Dark.

Rain shook his head in response. After defeating the assassins alongside King, they questioned a few who stubbornly bit off their tongues before choking on their blood and dying.

"Well, doesn't that suck."

"Soria!" Aoi shouted, happy that she was safe.

In a snarl Morgana glared at Soria who didn't care to notice. If it was the last thing she did on this earth, she would defeat Soria.

Yuudai noticed Morgana's jealous expression and frowned. It felt like they were back at the Dome again. While he stood by her side, she was constantly chasing Aoi.

"You guys are still alive. Yippee," Soria said, clapping her hands monotonously while expressionless.

"I can't believe you just upped and left!" erupted Umeko.

"Ah, these two are still sleeping?" Not feeling up to arguing, Soria bent down to stare at Mio and Hana who continued sleeping during the commotion. "Whoa Verse, did you knock them out that badly?"

"I could've sworn I went lightly on them," said Verse in defense.

"Oye, are you listening to me?!" Umeko shouted to Soria.

"Ah, that's right." Soria picked her ear with her pinky and turned to look at the floating Yeve. With the motion of her hand, the water laid the unconscious Yeve down on the ground, before dispersing.

"You," hissed Umeko. She stood, raising a fist. It was amazing how the lazy turtle was such a genius at pissing off just about everyone, when no one could do the same to her. "Don't ignore me!"

"Shouldn't we get some sleep? We've got a long journey ahead tomorrow."

"Damn you!"

"Knock it off, damn it." With one punch, Jennifer knocked out her best friend. She had been silent long enough and could take no more.

"That was a little too much, don't you think?" asked Shayla.

"She was annoying, and loud."

"I agree." Soria nodded and held up a thumb.

"Same here," said Jennifer who also held up a thumb.

"Weirdoes," they said. It wasn't as if they had done a good deed that needed two thumbs up.

"So," Rain said, peering over at Yeve. "What happened to her?"

"She got tired and wanted to sleep," Verse answered with a yawn and took a seat on the ground. It was getting late and she wanted some shut eye.

"Really?" Rain asked, incredulous. He couldn't help but raise an eyebrow. If Verse wanted to tell a lie, she had to do better than that. They all knew Yeve well enough to say that she wouldn't fall asleep during a fight. It wasn't in her nature when she could be instilling fear into people.

"I speak nothing but the truth."

"I can't believe you just lied to my face again." Rain shook it off, no longer prying since Verse wasn't willing to tell him—or anyone else.

"Well, I'm glad that nothing major happened," said May.

"Me too," agreed Noah.

"Everyone's fine. Now we can all relax," said Takahiko. He plopped down on the ground in relief.

"We can't really assume that we're safe just yet," said King. He took a seat at his usual spot, his broadsword strapped to his back as he crossed his arms. "What if more assassins come while we're sleeping?"

"Then we'll need someone to volunteer and keep watch for the night while the others rest," suggested Louis. He smiled boastfully at the conclusion he had come to and puffed out his chest. The other guys glanced at one another and grinned.

"You're absolutely right," agreed Poe.

"Thanks for volunteering Louis," said Teo. He held up a thumb in encouragement.

"Eh?!" shouted Louis. "When did I-"

"Thanks Louis," said the other guys.

"W—wait, hold on!"

"Louis-kun, you're so kind," said Remi. She clasped her hands together and smiled, her eyes twinkling like gems at his act of selflessness.

"Eh? Ah, well uh, yeah, you're welcome." Louis laughed it off and scratched his head. How could he refuse when Remi was smiling at him in such a way that squeezed his heart?

"I know," Shayla declared with a snap of her fingers. "Since Hanabi is Louis-kun's Soulmate, I volunteer her to keep watch with him."

"Now wait a minute!" she protested, shocked to be brought into something that had nothing to do with her.

Cammie nodded without giving it much thought. "I agree."

"I second," Crystal said, holding up a hand.

"Why do I have to?" asked Hanabi. The girls were ganging up on her, which was unusual.

"Because you're his Soulmate," repeated Shayla.

"That doesn't matter."

"I agree," said Dark.

"Anyone who agrees, say 'I,'" said Shayla.

"I," spoke everyone except for the four sleeping girls.

"This can't be happening," grumbled Hanabi. She turned to look at Louis who was seeping out a pink aura and giving her a puppy-eyed look. If he had a tail, it'd be wagging back and forth excitedly. "Geh," she let out and turned away. Why did he remind her so much of Mio? If he had been born a girl, he'd get along perfectly with her.

"I feel better, now that someone is helping me keep watch," Louis said.

"You," she hissed.

"What?" he asked, innocently.

"It's all your fault."

"But I never offered to keep watch. They just pushed it on me."

"Well, you two, get out there and keep watch," shooed Takahiko.

"That's right. Go, go," Love said, shooing Hanabi.

"Gosh," complained Hanabi. She threw her hands into the air in defeat and walked out.

"Why are you mad at me for? I did nothing wrong," Louis said, chasing her from behind. All he'd done was suggest something friendly. If she hated him for that, his life would end, then and there. He couldn't stand to know that a girl could possibly hate him. Though Yeve was an exception, since she was too scary for him to deal with.

"Well, those two are getting along just fine," said Morgana as she smiled.

"I wonder if you can even say that," said Yuudai.

She turned to glare at him. "No one was talking to you."

"Why you," he hissed in return.

"Let's clean up a bit and get some rest for tomorrow's journey," interrupted Shadow as he looked around the dusty warehouse. In this condition, they wouldn't be able to get a proper good night's sleep.

"Ah," Midnight said, pointing a finger at Soria who had gone to sleep beside Mio and Hana. "Wasn't she awake just a minute ago?"

"That lazy ass turtle, I'm gonna kill her so she won't ever get to see the sun rise again," Verse threatened.

"Now, now," Remi intervened. "Let's just clean this place and sleep in peace, okay?" She smiled pleadingly. It was no joke that Verse had no problem with killing Soria in her sleep.

"Let's start cleaning then," Rain said as they each began tidying up.

∞

A pink pearl hanging from Holly's necklace broke into pieces and evaporated into thin air. She hung her head down low, crying silently. More than half of the colored pearls hanging on her necklace had disappeared. Only a few remained. Her comrades she had sent to annihilate the kids from Maroon, had been wiped out. Not one survived.

Holly knew it was too early to attack the group when they knew nothing about their abilities. But Mana had argued her way into getting the rest to go with her. The result was a loss, and it was a huge blow to their force.

Holly shouldn't have been persuaded so easily. Now what was she supposed to do when Icora returned? How could she explain to him?

"Holly," called out Shin. He was standing in the doorway, watching her weep alone. Slowly, he approached to kneel and soothe her. "What happened?"

"Everyone…" Holly shook her head, tears still falling. All their friends they had made, all the comrades they had gathered had been killed easily by the new dispatch. "Everyone is dead."

"Eh?" Shin stared, unable to believe that Mana and her group, consisting of the best had been wiped out. Who exactly did they come across that they couldn't win?

"All their tears have evaporated." Holly stared at her necklace. The remaining colored pearls were their last hope.

"Even Mana?"

"Hers was the last to evaporate."

"I don't believe it," gasped Shin. He tightened his fist and lowered his gaze, trying to be strong. But it was so hard when Life-Kills and Dome assassins were constantly trying to kill them. It was getting to the point where he was tired of running and hiding. "I hate this. I hate standing on the sideline, watching everyone get hurt. Can't I do anything to ease your pain?"

"Shin," Holly said, reaching out to hug him. She smiled behind her tears. "You being here, is more than we can ever hope for." Holly squeezed him then released. It was because Shin was always here, waiting and praying for their safe return, that they could continue walking down this treacherous path. He was the strength they needed to get through the day with when it felt like the world was crumbling in on them.

"What do we do now? We have no one to protect us."

"I got us into this mess. I'll clean it up."

"How?"

"I may not be the offensive type, but I can still do a thing or two with my powers." Holly took hold of Shin's bony hands and squeezed them. Just holding his hand calmed her broken soul. "Put your trust in me."

"I've always trusted you." Shin smiled and nodded.

∞

While standing outside taking watch, Hanabi stared at the moon and millions of stars shining from above. Back at the Dome, the sky they saw was artificial. Now that the real thing was before her, she couldn't stop gawking. It was truly mesmerizing.

Louis on the other hand kept peeking at Hanabi, wanting to say something. Every time he opened his mouth to speak, he'd decide against it and gaze to the moon also. After his repeated actions, Hanabi rubbed her temples.

"What is it?" she asked, finally having enough of his constant stares.

"Uh, well," Louis said, wondering how to explain the situation. He wasn't sure he could do it properly, but desperately wanted to tell someone.

"I'm not going to waste my entire life waiting for you. So, spit it out already."

"I can see the future!" Louis tensed and turned his gaze away from the moon to the ground. He held his breath and waited for her to laugh but there never came a laugh. In fact, she didn't make a sound. Louis peeked over, noticing that she'd turned her gaze away from the sky to him. Beneath the moonlight, she stole his breath away. It felt like Hanabi herself was the moon. "Uh, um," he said timidly.

"And?" she asked.

"Huh?" he said, blinking repeatedly.

"And?"

"Well," he said, scratching his head. "In one of my visions, I saw May. She…" Suddenly unsure, Louis bit his lower lip. It was pointless after all. He couldn't tell Hanabi that May was going to kill Noah for unknown reasons. Even if he did manage to say it, chances were, she wouldn't believe him, since none of the guys did. Even Kakinouchi, who was the only one who knew of that sight was skeptical.

"She what?"

"She's going to kill Noah."

Hanabi's eyes widened. Her mouth opened to object and shout, but nothing came out. If he was lying, there was nothing to gain. Besides, he had taken the chance of being accused as a liar when he expressed his honesty. "What are you going to do about it?" she asked softly.

Louis laughed it off and scratched his head again. "I can't really do anything when I know nothing of what I saw, or if it's even going to happen. But I wish I could do something, so that my premonition doesn't come true." Again, Louis laughed, mainly at himself. He knew he should've kept his mouth shut. "Sorry, I didn't mean to tell you something so disturbing. It's just that, I desperately wanted to tell someone."

"Why me and not your friends?"

Louis looked alarmed at her question but ended up smiling sheepishly. "Only Kakinouchi knows. Besides, you're my Soulmate. In one of the ancient books I read, it stated that soul mates were created to complete each other. So, whatever I lack in, you make up in. That's why I wanted to tell you. Although, now that I'm saying it out loud, it sounds corny, huh?"

Hanabi smiled and shook her head. "No, it sounds nice."

"I feel that if it's you, Hanabi, I'll be fine." Louis turned his gaze back to the moon and yawned tiredly as the breeze blew.

Hanabi looked away from him and down at her own two hands. "I finally understand why the deans gave us each other now," she whispered to herself.

"Come again?"

"Nothing." She shook it off as they continued stargazing.

∞

Before the sun rose that morning, all seventeen girls and guys stood outside the chilly warehouse, forming a circle. Each of them standing next to their respective Soulmates. No one spoke. Nor did any of them move as a few birds chirped from nearby.

"Well," Jennifer said, breaking the silence first. There was no use in prolonging the inevitable. "Seems like this is it."

"It's finally time for us to part," agreed Midnight.

"We'll definitely come back together again." Hotaka put his hand out and smiled. Not needing words, the others followed his lead and put their hands into the middle. "Even if we die trying, we'll return back."

"Yeah," they agreed.

"Three!"

"Together!" they shouted in unison and threw their hands into the air. After spending more than half their lives with each other, they were finally going separate ways. They waved to one another, cried, bid a farewell, and left with their Soulmates by their sides.

"Don't forget me now!" shouted Mio. She was crying a bucket of tears while waving at each girl. "Take care!"

"Mio, let's hurry," said Sasuke as he led the way.

"I'm going to miss them."

"Cheer up. You've got me," he said, messing up her hair and grinning.

"That doesn't make me happy."

"Oye," he growled, throwing her into a light headlock while she fought to get free, and he laughed.

∞

"Soria, don't you dare let anyone or anything harm Aoi-kun! Or else I'll make you regret it!" Morgana screamed and cried while Yuudai dragged her away. Big tears rolled down her face while Soria groaned, ignoring her altogether. "Don't you dare ignore me, you damn poop-head! I'll kick your ass again!"

"See ya guys!" Yuudai shouted, disappearing with Morgana who continued bawling.

"See ya," bid Rain, Naruyuki, Aoi, and Noah.

"That girl," Yeve said, shaking her head.

"Tell me about it," agreed Verse.

"Well," Yeve said, turning to point at Soria and Verse. "You two better come back in one piece."

Soria snorted at Yeve's statement. How could she die after finally leaving the Dome? She now had all the freedom in the world to do whatever she wanted and wasn't about to let anyone get in the way. "You don't need to tell me that. I intend to return in one piece." Soria grinned, bumping fists with the two before turning to leave with Aoi who was waiting.

"Soria!" Remi cried. "Come back safely!"

"Take care!"

"Take care," the two girls bid as they watched Soria disappear.

"I can't stop worrying," Remi said, blowing her nose on Noah's borrowed handkerchief. He stared in dismay, thinking that she was going to

51

use it to wipe her tears. Instead, she was blowing snot onto his beautiful handkerchief. In the end, Noah shook it off. It was useless to say anything now, when she had already used it.

"We don't care about that," said the two in unison as they turned to stare at Remi's crying face. "Why are you here again? We never invited you."

"Wah!" she shouted in their faces. "Cruel, so cruel, you two are so cruel! We grew up together! We're like family! Don't suddenly treat me like a stranger! It's already too late to get rid of me! I'll never leave!"

"Ugh," groaned the two. They plugged their ears and turned the other way. As usual Remi had taken their joke seriously.

"Uwah!" Remi cried harder. "I love you girls."

"Ew," Verse said in disgust.

"Verse-chan!" she shouted, throwing Verse into a hug. "Even if you're evil to me, I'll miss you the most!"

"Mr. Soulmate, please do something about her before I do."

"Let's go," said Noah as he dragged Remi away from the group. It was time that they got going also. "See ya."

"Bye," called back the others as they waved at the two.

"But, but!" Remi protested while Noah ignored her.

"Ready?" asked Rain.

Yeve nodded and eyed Verse. "As for you-"

"You just worry about yourself." Verse hit Yeve lightly on the arm and turned to leave.

"Ready to go?" asked Naruyuki.

"Yeah, let's go." Verse nodded and smiled.

Yeve too smiled from where she stood, watching until Verse disappeared. A lump formed in her throat until she had to swallow it down. It was painful knowing that when she looked on either side, the two wouldn't be there. It just didn't feel right without them. Once Yeve's emotions were under control, she turned to leave with a patient Rain. "Let's go," she whispered.

The forest was now silent. There wasn't a single soul to be found. They had separated from one another.

6th Lie

FOUR MONTHS LATER

Shadow and Hana sat inside the bullet train that was taking them south to Okinawa, where their second mission awaited. Their first mission had been completed and reports were written before being handed in to the deans. Now that they got the gist of what a real mission was like, the deans had assigned a tougher second mission for each Soulmate couple.

Shadow caught Hana's nervous glances and smiled. She had reacted the same during their first mission. "What's on your mind now?"

"The girls," Hana softly answered and fidgeted with her perfectly groomed fingers. "I thought we'd at least run into each other."

"I'm sure they're fine. The guys won't let harm befall them. Even if we were rivals in the beginning, we're on good terms with each other now." Shadow reached out to squeeze her hand in reassurance.

Hana nodded in response, her heart jumping at his sudden touch. She turned to look out the window again. The scenery was flashing before them at the speed of light. Everything was a blur. Nothing could be made out except the greenery and gray building rubbles. Ever since the end of the war, the world population of 7.5 billion significantly dropped to 400 million. Many cities were torn down to rebuild forests for the animals in hopes of keeping them from going extinct, though the damage had already been done.

Noticing that Hana had gone quiet, Shadow blushed and quickly withdrew his hand. He had unintentionally made things awkward. "Sorry. I won't touch you again without your permission."

Hana turned to look at him, eyes widening. He was blushing and more awkward than her that it caused her to giggle.

"Wh—what?" asked Shadow. He turned away, having said something embarrassing.

"If anyone should apologize, it's me. I didn't do much during our first mission, and I even let you shoulder most of the work. I'm sorry."

"Don't be. I'm here to make up for what you lack in."

"You're too soft on me." Hana giggled again as tears flooded her eyes. If he kept covering for her, she'd remain useless to him. And that was the last thing she wanted. "I'm not as smart as the other girls. Neither am I as strong. But even so, please don't leave me." Her voice trembled as she spoke the words slowly. Without the girls, she only had him to lean on now.

Shadow smiled, remembering the day he met the shy Hana inside Leviathan's lair. Though they didn't get a chance for self-introductions, they met again inside the girls' infirmary. Her shy nature and generosity had won him over. The times they spent together at the Dome, training with the others only built up the chemistry between them. Then, there was the day of their fated duel. When she summoned her powers, and had gotten scared by it, he went to save her. That moment, he would never forget. The look she gave him when he found her, it was brimming with hope and joy. Someone had found her in the darkness. "...to me, you're the flower beneath the moon."

Hana had heard about time coming to a standstill, but never experienced it until then. She held her breath and stared at his smiling face. The things she would do to keep him happy. After exhaling, Hana stood from her chair to sit beside him. She put her head against his shoulder and closed her eyes, listening to him breathe. He wore no cologne but smelt like a sunny spring day when the laundry gets put out to dry. To her, he was her light in the darkness. "I wonder sometimes."

"About?"

Hana tightened her hold on his arm. After inhaling deeply, she exhaled the same way. She could never tire of this. "I wonder when we started accepting one another without realizing it."

"I don't know myself."

"Probably, it was meant to be."

∞

Chiba

Naruyuki and Verse silently stood on the side of the street, watching people pass them by. Too nervous to start a conversation, Naruyuki's heart thumped so loudly he feared that she'd hear from where she stood. Not wanting to blabber like a fool, he kept his mouth shut and kept up with his cool appearance.

"I don't get it," Verse said, crossing her arms against her chest.

Naruyuki glanced over, surprised that she had finally spoken to him. Clearing his throat, he asked casually, "You don't get what?" Even after calming his nerves, his voice still shook.

"Why are we standing here doing nothing?"

"Well we-" Naruyuki began and stopped. He seriously reconsidered her question. Even he wasn't sure why they were standing there doing nothing.

Before he could finish his thoughts, Verse's stomach growled. She threw both hands over her stomach and looked away, cursing under her breath. They had just eaten dinner an hour ago. Not to mention, Verse had eaten four person's worth of food. Now suddenly she was hungry again. It was incredible that her metabolism could keep up with the things she put inside her stomach.

Naruyuki blinked a few times before erupting into laughter.

"Forget you heard that just now." Verse hit her stomach with both fists and smiled it off. She was beyond embarrassed, hoping for a hole to open up and swallow her. "I don't know what's wrong with my stomach suddenly."

"Geez," Naruyuki said, still laughing. She had made things so much simpler now. His nervousness had vanished altogether at the sound of her grumbling stomach.

"Don't mind, don't mind."

"I heard about this from your sisters."

"Eh?" said Verse as her smile faded. "My sisters?"

"Yeah, Yeve and Soria. They said you eat a lot and that I better be prepared to feed you no matter the hour." Naruyuki chuckled and messed up his own hair. "I didn't think they were serious though."

"Um," said Verse. "They're not my sisters."

"What? They're not? But I thought they were, since you three look alike and all," he said, alarmed. "Hmm, and you even act like sisters."

"Is that how it seems?" Verse asked, her smile returning. She could still recall the day her curiosity led her to enter the white room with wide open glass doors. The white cloths that hung from the ceiling swayed gently in the cool breeze while Yeve lay on the floor. Verse had entered through the front door while a humming Soria entered from the glass doors that led to the green courtyard. Ever since, they laid claim to that room. "Mio and the others constantly joke about how we must've been related in our previous lives."

"Isn't that a good thing?"

"Huh?"

"You're so close that others mistake you as siblings. Isn't that a good thing? It just goes to prove that you three know each other inside-out."

"I guess so."

"Well, I'll go buy some snacks." Naruyuki patted her on the head and walked away to find a food cart.

"You don't have to!" she shouted after him.

"It's my job as your Soulmate." He waved back and left.

"Soul…mate," repeated Verse as she laughed to herself. "What a convenient word."

Naruyuki had a big grin on his face as he headed towards a street vendor. "If I'd known that food was the secret to winning her over, I'd have done it a long time ago." He laughed and walked up to the cart, inspecting the menu.

"Good evening sir," greeted the vendor.

"Evening," greeted Naruyuki as he smiled back. After a few seconds of looking, he got three orders of takoyaki and pulled out some money to set on top of the counter.

"Coming right up," the vendor said, getting the food ready. When he finished cooking, he handed Naruyuki the food and took the money off the counter. "Have a good night sir. Come again."

"Thank you, you too." Naruyuki bowed, returning to Verse with the snack. "If it was Umeko-san I was with, she wouldn't eat this much." Naruyuki chuckled, wondering if he'd have to feed Verse in the next few hours again. Abruptly, his legs came to a halt.

Umeko.

Had he just said Umeko's name? Why for? It made no sense. Umeko was with Taiki. So why did he compare Verse to Umeko just then?

"Umeko-san," repeated Naruyuki. His head throbbed as he grunted and leaned against the side of the building for support. That reaction wasn't normal, no matter how he thought about it. How could a single name make his heart feel like bursting?

"Are you okay?" Holly asked, passing by and noticing him stagger.

"I—I'm fine." Naruyuki pulled himself upright and smiled weakly. He couldn't inconvenience others. "Thank you for your concern." He slightly bowed and walked away.

"Ah!" shouted Holly.

"What is it?" Naruyuki spun back around, alarmed. Did something happen?

"Your tears…"

"My tears?" repeated Naruyuki. He touched his eyes where it was moist. Sure enough, tears had formed without his knowing. "What the-" he said, quickly wiping them away. If he had continued this way towards Verse, she would've suspected something. "Sorry, I don't know what's gotten into me." He laughed it off while Holly smiled.

"Your tears are a jade color and it's super rare. I've only met two people who possessed that color. Counting you, that's three now." Holly put a hand to her mouth, inspecting Naruyuki. What made him so special that his tears would be such a clear jade color?

"I have no idea what you just said."

"Sorry, it's nothing," she answered and laughed it off. "That must've scared you a little."

"You can see the color of tears?"

"Something like that," said Holly. She scratched her head, trying to play it off cool. She couldn't get caught here.

"What a weird ability you have."

"It is, isn't it?"

"Naruyuki, what's taking you so long?!" shouted Verse as she headed towards him and stopped once she noticed Holly. One of her eyebrows rose, but she said nothing, except bow and stand back up.

All the while, Holly stared at Verse like she had seen a ghost, "You."

"Hmm? Do I know you?" Verse inspected Holly suspiciously, but gave up in the end. They had never met until then.

"No." Holly smiled and shook her head. Her pearl accessories jingled where they hung. It was reacting. Verse noticed and raised her other eyebrow. "I must be going now. It was a pleasure to meet." She slightly bowed and ran from the two. Just meeting was more than enough for her.

"What was that about?"

"Even I have no idea," replied Naruyuki.

"Were you flirting with her?" Verse teased as Naruyuki spun around, glaring.

"What an insane thing to say!"

"Whoa, don't get so defensive about it. It was a joke, a joke."

"Why would I flirt with her for? Idiot."

"Don't get so mad. I said it was a joke."

"Even as a joke, don't accuse me of doing things I haven't done."

"Geez," said Verse. "Here," she said, holding a hand out to him. It was time to change the topic, seeing how moody he was.

"What?"

"My food."

"Oh, right, here," said Naruyuki. He handed Verse two takoyaki and kept one for himself as they returned to their original spots to stand guard for the rest of the night, without exchanging a word.

∞

"Holly," called out a girl from within a dark alleyway.

"Yana," Holly said, running over to hug the girl standing behind the smelly dumpster. With no light reflecting off her dark brown hair, her orange eyes were the only thing that seemed to stand out. Not even her German-Russian features could be seen.

"What took you so long? The meeting's about to begin. Let's go," Yana said, pulling away to route them through the maze-like alleys to get to the underground meeting room. "Also, why are you smiling so much?"

"That's because I just met one of our future followers."

"Eh?" gasped Yana. She reached out to grab Holly by the shoulders. "Where did you meet him? Why didn't you recruit him? You know we're in desperate need of help."

"I know."

"Then why didn't you take him?"

"Because the time isn't right," answered Holly. She shook her head, still smiling. No one knew her powers like she did.

"Timing doesn't matter right now. We're desperate."

"Even if we're desperate, I won't force anyone to Awaken, especially since this one's the rarest I've ever encountered."

"You're too soft." Yana shook her head, leading the way again. Even if she were to argue, she wouldn't win. Holly was just as stubborn as Icora. When they came to a secure door, Yana scanned her fingerprint on the machine as it slid open. They walked down a few poorly lit hallways before entering a secure room. "Holly's here."

"Good evening," Holly greeted, smiling at the room full of people in cloaks. Tonight's rendezvous would be a long one. She wouldn't get home until late.

∞

Okinawa

Hana was in the bathroom, taking a shower after falling into the pond at the park. She had been feeding ducks when she leaned in too far and fell. Shadow burst into laughter before helping her out. She glared at him, tears in her eyes. She felt like a clumsy fool and it showed.

Now that they were back inside the hotel room, taking it easy, Shadow stood stiffly out on the balcony. In his hand was a red envelope that had new information regarding their mission.

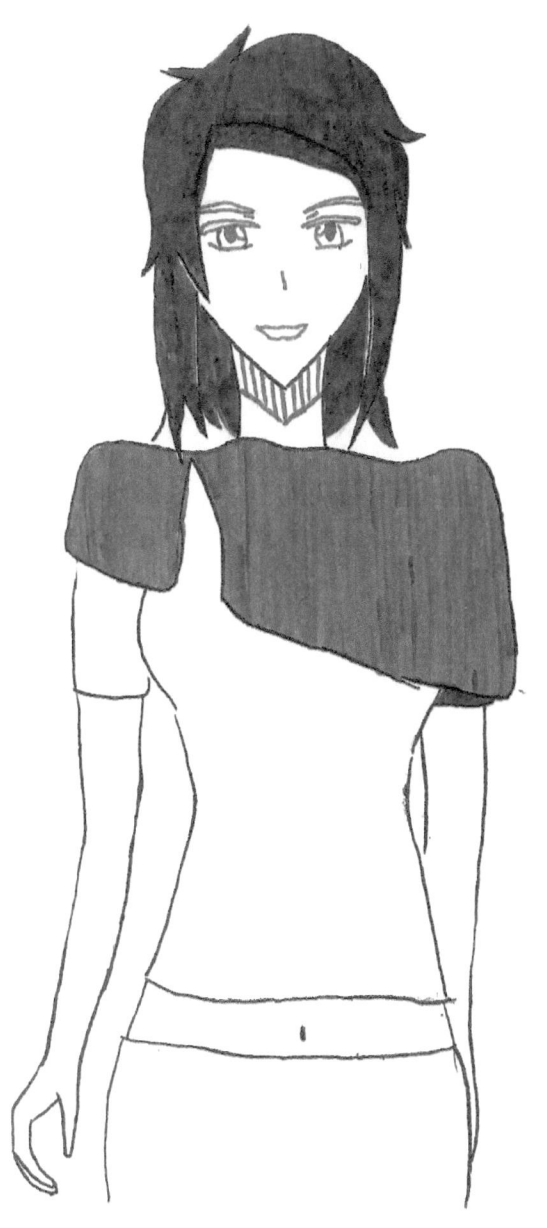

Shadow, there have been changes regarding your mission. You need to find a way to join a person named Zara's rebel group. Whatever happens, don't bring Hana with you. We can't risk her getting involved. Her power is too unstable. You'll be alone in this one.

Signed,

Dean Kosa

After reading, Shadow pressed on the red symbol as it burned into ashes, leaving no evidence.

He couldn't just up and leave Hana without a word. She'd worry to death. Determined to stay and disobey orders, Shadow stiffened.

"Orders are absolute," Mr. Fujiwara had told them the first time they had undergone training at the tender age of five. "The motto of all Life-Kills is: Serve the Golden God, die for the Golden God. Never forget."

Shadow clenched his fists by his side and grinded his teeth together. It felt like the stars above had disappeared and darkness had enveloped him.

He'd forgotten. Back at the Dome, they were taught that orders were absolute. They were never to question. Every task given required them to accomplish it, even if it meant dying. It was for the better of the world since they had been chosen to change it.

To defy orders meant extermination. Mr. Fujiwara always emphasized on that the most.

"Orders are absolute," Shadow repeated. He gulped and entered the room as the balcony door shut behind him. His palms became sweaty as he took a seat on the sofa, contemplating on how to carry out his new orders. In a few minutes Hana would come out. Shadow had to leave before then.

After gathering enough courage to stand, Shadow left the hotel room without turning back once.

"Shadow-kun?" Hana called out after taking her shower. Her hair was wrapped in a white towel as she entered the living room. When she didn't spot him, she tried calling his phone, but he'd left it behind. Not worried, Hana watched a bit of TV. Maybe Shadow had gone out to buy them some dinner. While watching TV, she fell asleep on the sofa. When the next morning came, she was still alone in the hotel room. Scared, Hana hugged her legs and cried. Had she been abandoned?

7th Lie

ZARA COMBED through her short choppy hair with her fingers, hoping that would make it look more presentable. Being stationed all the way out in Okinawa was uneventful and boring. She didn't understand why the boss wanted her there for. It wasn't like the gang in this city was a threat. Instead of being here, Zara should be stationed in Kochi, so she could destroy the Bat Angels' base once and for all. But orders were orders. Her job was to see to it that the boss was happy.

"Morning," greeted a few girls and guys who bowed in respect.

Zara waved in greeting and made her way out to her usual hangout with the others. When she got there, a few of her men were getting rowdy with a homeless man in an alleyway. She raised an eyebrow and took a seat, grabbing the nearest coke to gulp. "What's going on over there?" she asked and motioned to the commotion.

"We found some bum in there this morning," answered one of the girls.

"How long has that bum been there?"

"Don't know. Days. Weeks. Maybe months," she said with a shrug.

Zara raised an eyebrow and set the coke down. How could some homeless man get past their surveillance and camp out in their alleyway? She made it her top priority to know every single person who stepped foot onto their turf. From behind, there were a few grunts and yells as Zara turned back. Her men were being thrown to the ground. Whoever the homeless man was had given them a good beating.

Shadow stepped out from within the alleyway, wearing raggedy clothes. Even his long black hair was unkempt, and he smelled of garbage and urine.

His eyepatch had been taken away by one of Zara's men. "I warned you not to touch my eyepatch," Shadow growled and bent down, retrieving it. When he noticed someone staring intently at him, he turned and made eye contact with Zara.

As soon as she saw Shadow's right eye, she stopped breathing. It was the most beautiful and haunting thing she'd ever seen. Shadow's iris wasn't a natural circle. Instead, it was a crescent moon with an oval jutting through. The two shapes never touched but they glowed in two colors. The crescent was white while the oval, a blood red.

Shadow turned away and put his eyepatch back on before entering the alleyway. He hadn't gotten a good night's rest, tossing and turning from worrying about Hana. Having Zara's goons test him had been the last straw.

"Stop!" Zara commanded as her men and Shadow turned to look at her. She rushed over desperately and smiled. "What's your name?"

Instead of answering, Shadow turned away, hoping she'd take his bait.

"When I ask a question, I expect an answer." Zara caught him by the arm and squeezed, not used to getting ignored.

"Shadow."

"Shadow," she repeated. So, he was the one who had gotten past her men's surveillance without getting caught. If anyone was to stand by her side as an equal, it would be him. Only he had the potential to keep up. "Join me."

"Not interested," Shadow rejected and pulled free as Zara pulled him back again. "Let go."

"No one's ever rejected me before." Laughing, Zara let go of his arm. He was proving to be a real tease. But it was alright, she loved the chase more than anything. "Who are you running from, Shadow?"

"No one," he answered and returned to hiding behind the dumpster.

"Leave him be," instructed Zara as her men scowled and left. They could already see that she was smitten by a mere bum. "You'll become mine, sooner or later." She grinned and walked away, coming up with ideas on how to obtain Shadow.

His plan of playing hard to get was working. Shadow shivered and pulled the worn-out jacket closer to his body. It was a good thing he had exchanged clothes with a homeless man last night before coming. If he hadn't, he'd have been found out right away.

∞

Taiki and Umeko were returning to their hotel room after an uneventful night. They had been stationed in Kochi to cease the riots. For the past few weeks a group of rebels had been causing problems, claiming to take over the city. The two were sent to capture the leader and make the rebels stop.

"What a long night it's been," complained Umeko. She plopped onto her comfy bed and closed her eyes. "No wonder Soria loves sleeping so much."

"Don't get too comfy. We gotta go patrol some more," said Taiki. He took off his shirt and opened the drawer cabinet, pulling out a new shirt to slip on. When he noticed that Umeko wasn't answering, he glanced over. She had fallen asleep already. "Didn't I just tell her not to get comfy?" Taiki shook his head, unable to stop his smile. He brewed some tea and headed out to the balcony as Kochi's humid air hit him hard.

Inside, Umeko dreamt of standing in a field of flowers. The sun shone brightly as her pink flowery Sunday dress swayed. In one hand was a pair of matching sandals. On her head sat a straw hat. She was humming and walking down the lane of flowers reserved for her. Though she didn't remember this place, it felt as though she'd once walked down these paths with someone. She smiled, stopping her pace to let the sun beat down on her face.

"Umeko!" called out a voice from behind.

"Huh?" Turning, Umeko came face-to-face with an unknown baby-faced girl with blue shoulder length hair and gold eyes. While blinking, trying to pinpoint this mysterious girl, Umeko's gut feeling told her she was someone precious.

"Welcome back," she greeted.

"Ne-" Umeko began as a gunshot rang. Blood spurt out from the girl, staining Umeko's dress. Horror washed over her as she dropped her sandals to the grass. Her straw hat flew off from the fierce gust and she reached a hand out, all the while screaming, "No!"

"Umeko!" Taiki's voice broke through her dreams.

She woke up, gasping for air. Taiki hovered from her bedside, his chest heaving. "Taiki," whispered Umeko.

"Thank goodness you're okay." Taiki squeezed her gloved hand. Her screaming had given him a fright. "Did you have a nightmare just now?"

"Yeah," Umeko answered, blinking repeatedly. Once she managed to sit up with Taiki's assist, a loud buzzing began in her ears. She even felt like throwing up and grunted.

"What's wrong?"

"It's nothing," she whispered.

"Are you sure?"

"Yeah, I'm sure."

"What about your dream?"

Umeko raised an eyebrow, trying to remember. But her dream had mysteriously been deleted. "I—I can't remember."

"What do you mean you can't remember?"

"I don't know. I just can't."

Unsure if she was lying to him, Taiki draped his left arm around her, putting her head to his chest. This was all he could think of to calm her if she didn't want to talk about her dream.

Umeko's eyes widened. She opened her mouth to shout at him for acting out of character, given their history. Before she could speak, Taiki hummed a lullaby from his memories.

♩*Red bird red bird, don't cry*
Even if you are far away from home, I will bring you happiness
Red bird red bird, do not fear
Even if you are far away from home, I will always be with you
Red bird red bird, one day you will find your way home
You will fly far away from me and leave me
Red bird red bird, I love you
So please, do not ever forget me♩

Slowly but surely, Umeko's tense muscles relaxed. She was still perspiring, but her hard breathing was starting to stabilize. She held on to Taiki's shirt as the pounding in her head subsided. "Where'd you learn that song?" she whispered.

"I don't know," he answered and shook his head. "It just came to me."

Umeko chuckled at his answer and quickly frowned. The words that were about to come out of her mouth was something she detested saying. But it had to done. It was etiquette and respectful when someone was being helpful. This was a teaching that Yeve had enforced unto the disrespectful Umeko.

During her childhood at the Dome, Umeko used to get into trouble with the staff on a regular basis. On one particular day, she went to go hide out in the grand library, away from Miss Umi, thinking that no one was there. Little did she know, four girls were already inside playing a game, seeing who could get the highest book on the highest shelves and climb back down before the others. Umeko who was intrigued at the game watched from her hiding spot and eventually came out. As she did, Yeve, who was in the lead was climbing down the wooden ladder at full speed. Behind her was Verse, and behind Verse was Remi, who looked scared out of her wits. Soria who was dead last yawned tiredly and slipped.

"Uh-oh," Soria said, falling from her ladder like a star.

"Huh?" The three girls from their ladders glanced down, finally noticing Umeko who was like a deer standing before headlights. If she didn't move, she was going to receive a concussion from the ladder. Meanwhile, Soria continued falling, making no attempt to save herself. If this accident were to reach Ms. Tanaka, the girls would be forbidden to play in the library.

"Soria!" Remi shouted, clutching on tightly to her wooden ladder.

Without any time to speak or come up with a plan, Verse went to her right and Yeve, to her left.

Verse kicked the shelf where her ladder leaned against and toppled sideways. She made it in time and caught Soria by the left ankle. The ladder that Verse was desperately holding fell against the shelf on the opposite side of the room, stopping them from colliding into the floor. Relieved, Verse sighed while Remi let out a cry.

"Thanks Verse," Soria said, hanging upside down and smiling.

"I feel like dropping you into hell right now," Verse hissed back.

"If you did, you'd feel lonely without me," she laughed.

While Verse had saved Soria, Yeve went to Umeko's rescue. She kicked the shelf where her ladder leaned against and jumped off, tackling Umeko before rolling to safety. From above, Yeve and Soria's ladders collided before falling to the floor with a loud bang. Books fell from their shelves as Remi let out another cry.

"Well," Yeve said. "That was a close call." She stood, dusted her uniform and held out a hand.

Umeko grimaced, hitting Yeve's hand away to stand on her own. She had been saved by a stranger when she didn't need it. "I can stand by myself."

"Rude, aren't you?"

"Hmph," said Umeko as she dusted her uniform also. Turning on her heels, she attempted to leave the library, but not before Yeve took hold of her collar to force back. "What the hell?" Umeko said and glared.

"Ungrateful also," Yeve added in.

"Un-great full?" Umeko repeated, unsure of its meaning. It was surprising to hear a five-year-old kid talking and using such big adult words. "Whatever, let go."

"I believe a thank-you is necessary."

"Hah! In your damn dreams!"

"Uh-oh," said the three from behind Yeve. They had come down from their ladders to approach the two to see how the situation was holding up, only to find Umeko shouting in Yeve's face.

Umeko looked past Yeve to inspect the three. None of them looked special, yet they had somehow survived the last two harsh experiments. Remi looked ditzy and weak. Soria looked like she might collapse from tiredness. As for Verse, she miraculously found a lollipop and was now eating it. Umeko couldn't understand how these three weaklings had survived. Maybe Miss Umi was playing favorites with them, but that couldn't be true. Miss Umi was relentless when it came to her experiments. Which meant the three had survived by willpower alone.

"Oye," Umeko said, reaching out to grab Yeve's hand with her free gloved hand. If she didn't get out of there, a staff who had heard the noise would come and find her. "Let me go piggy. Or else I'll kill you with this poison eye," Umeko threatened as her left eye turned a blood red.

Yeve's eyes widened at the sight and loosened her grip.

Umeko grinned, shaking her off. It was as she had thought. Yeve was now scared. Everyone who knew what she was capable of always feared her. What she never saw coming, was Yeve's next expression.

"Oh?" she said, grinning in return.

"Uh-oh," the three said again, also not caring about Umeko's left eye that could change color. All they were worried about was Yeve's new murderous aura. "This is bad," they said in unison again, but made no attempt to step in.

"What the hell are you idiots-" began Umeko as Yeve threw her to the floor. It all happened so fast, she didn't have time to take any of it in. All she remembered was seeing Yeve's grin. Then, the next thing she knew, she was lying with her back on the floor, staring at the ceiling of the library, dizzy.

Hovering from above, Yeve crossed her arms and placed her heel on Umeko's flat chest. "You insolent little thing, you think that just because your eye can change colors it'll scare me? Hah! You're one hundred years too late to try that on me. In the presence of the Empress you better show some damn respect. The only one allowed to make threats is me. The next time I see you, you better bow to me. And if you don't learn how to thank others once they've helped you, then, consider yourself dead," threatened Yeve. She lifted her feet and bent down, smiling like a true devil. "Is that understood, Poison Princess?"

Having never met anyone who wasn't afraid of her powers, except the staff, Umeko was baffled. Also, she'd never been bested before, until then.

"Hey," Yeve hissed. "Is that understood my little Chihuahua slave?"

"I—I understand," she managed to say.

"Good," Yeve said, returning to her Empress-like pose. "That's more like it."

From behind, the three hit their foreheads. This was to be expected. No one called Yeve names or disrespected her and got away with it. No one.

Like that, Umeko encountered the Empress and became her first slave. Because of Yeve's nickname for Umeko that day, the rest of the other girls began calling her Poison Princess.

After Yeve finished threatening her, Ms. Tanaka who had heard the commotion came to inspect. The five girls were punished, and the four were banned from the library for an entire year. When they were allowed to return, they didn't, because of Remi's fear of heights.

"Thank you," Umeko said to Taiki and smiled.

"Hmm?" he said and laughed, not expecting such an unexpected thank-you from her.

"Shut up," she hissed, pushing him away. Embarrassed, Umeko turned the other way and glared. If it wasn't for Yeve and her sadistic ways Umeko wouldn't care to thank anyone for the remainder of her days. Scared for her life though, she had no choice but to obey. Even now, Yeve was still controlling her when they were no longer together.

Taiki, still laughing, patted her gently on the head. This felt better than having to bicker all the time. "Anytime," he replied, after calming his heart, "anytime."

∞

Naruyuki gasped and awoke from his sleep, reaching out to the white ceiling above. He blinked and lay still, staring at his outstretched hand. The nightmare he had just had, was slowly being chased from his mind, but the feelings lingered. It felt like he had lost someone or something precious. He lowered his hand and sat up on the sofa, chest aching.

Verse who was sitting on the second sofa, eating bread was curiously watching. While Naruyuki had been napping peacefully, he started tossing and turning, then awoke so dramatically. "Bad dream?" she asked.

Naruyuki looked over, then away. He rubbed his forehead and shook his head. "I can't remember clearly."

"If you don't want to tell me, just say so. There's no need to lie."

"It's not a lie. I'm telling you the truth. My head started hurting and then suddenly it was like my dream was deleted."

"Deleted?" she repeated suspiciously.

"Yeah, like with what you do to a computer. You delete the hard drive and get rid of all its dirty secrets."

Again, Verse raised an eyebrow at him and resumed to eating her second slice of bread. He was making weird analogies like Soria.

Naruyuki stood and headed for the balcony to get some fresh air, his head still pounding. All the while Verse silently watched. After a few seconds, she followed him out to the balcony. The wind was starting to pick up. From down below, cars could be heard. Lit billboards filled the streets. People were making their way about noisily.

"While you were having that nightmare, you were calling out to Umeko."

Not expecting that, Naruyuki kept his focus away, afraid that his eyes would give him away if he met her gaze. Truth be told, he was worried about Umeko, wherever she was, but couldn't tell Verse this. After all, she was his Soulmate. It was wrong of him to even worry about another girl when the one he should worry for was beside him. His heartbeat that had calmed raced again. This pain was different from the usual.

"Naruyuki," called out Verse.

He blinked and looked away from the city to smile at her. "Maybe you were hearing things. Why would I call out to her?"

"That's what I'd like to know. Why else would I tell you?"

Naruyuki remained staring at her. "You're my Soulmate," he confirmed.

If he was worried about Umeko, there was no need to lie. Verse would understand since back at the Dome he had been closest with her. "Here," she said, holding out a red note to him before heading back inside.

"What is this?" he asked and opened the note to read.

"It's our lead."

"Eh?" Naruyuki quickly opened the red note to skim its contents, then turned to look at Verse who was preparing to leave. "Wait for me, we can go together to investigate."

"I'll go alone."

"What do you mean? The note clearly says to go together," he said, entering the room.

Verse turned to eye Naruyuki, halting him from grabbing his jacket. He held his breath as he stared into her eyes that reflected nothing. There was no rage. No jealousy. No sadness. Nothing. It was empty. Void of all feelings. "I'll be fine, so just rest up." Verse smiled and waved a hand as the door closed itself behind her.

Whether it was from his guilt or not, Naruyuki couldn't find the courage to chase her. He stared at the red note in his hand again.

We've got a lead for you. Meet one of our spies at H Café. He'll relay the information he has about the group of rebels you're looking for. You are to arrest and interrogate them. If they resist, use force if necessary.

Signed,

Dean Rosa

Naruyuki touched the fire emblem at the bottom right hand corner as the note in his hand burned, covering its track. The ashes fell to the floor as he pulled at his ponytail, frustrated. If anything were to happen to Verse while he wasn't present, he'd never forgive himself. "Why do I keep thinking of Umeko-san for?"

8th Lie

A FEW DAYS had passed since Zara's encounter with Shadow. On some days he would mysteriously vanish, but always returned at night to sleep. Though Zara had made her men keep tabs on Shadow, it was impossible. They could never catch him in the act of leaving or returning. It was a real mystery and Zara loved it. Every chance she got, she would go sit with him in the alleyway and chat. Even though Shadow rarely spoke a word or two, she was glad that he was warming up to her.

A lot of her men didn't like her attachment to him, but she didn't care. She was the leader of the group and no one was to question her.

While humming and swinging the bag of food in her hand, Zara headed towards Shadow's alley and set it down. If he couldn't be bought with power and money, then she'd win him over with food.

"Let go," someone squeaked as Zara turned back to look. A girl with pink pigtails was surrounded by some of her men. There were tears in her eyes as she tried to fight back. Her powers were so weak, Zara was barely able to detect it. Maybe she was a failed experiment and had been deemed unworthy to keep. How she had survived this long was a mystery.

Not caring about what her men did to the cute girl, so long as they cleaned up their mess, Zara turned away.

Like a bolt of lightning, Shadow dashed out from the bright alley. Bewildered, Zara spun back in time to see him take down the five guys who had surrounded the pink-haired girl. The look on Shadow's face was more than enough to confirm Zara's inkling feeling.

So, the one Shadow had been trying to run away from was that girl.

"Shadow-kun," Hana gasped and cried, falling into his arms. He was thinner than she remembered. Was he not eating? And why was he wearing such torn clothes? Whatever the case was, she had found him and would do everything within her power to nurse him back to health. "You're okay."

Without a word, Shadow pushed Hana away as her big tears rolled down. "Leave," he said in a hoarse voice and turned away.

"Shadow-kun!" Running, Hana blocked his way. How could he leave her behind without a word? How could he be so cold and tell her to leave when she had been racking her brains trying to find him? Did he really not care for her anymore?

"I said leave."

"Am I really that unreliable?"

Unable to watch her cry, Shadow turned away, tears in his eyes. She shouldn't be crying for him. He wasn't worthy after hurting her in such an unbearable way.

Zara's clenched fists trembled by her side as her chest heaved. For a girl, he would show his weakness in plain sight. Someone like Hana wasn't worthy of someone like Shadow.

"Is it her?" Hana asked, reaching out to hold his hand. She could feel Zara's glare burning into her back. Shadow's actions were proof that he had left her for the mission. "Is she the one?"

"She is," he whispered and squeezed her hand.

Crying all over again, Hana squeezed his hand in return. She shook her head, unable to believe it. He'd made a promise to her. "She can't be more important than me."

Unsure of how else to make her leave, Shadow withdrew his hand and said the most hurtful words he could think of. "Isn't it obvious enough? I chose her over you. That's why I'm here, and not by your side." He walked around her and disappeared into the alley, a tear betraying his cruel insult. *Just walk away, Hana. I'm begging you.*

Instead of walking away, Hana stood on the street and wailed as loudly as possible. If Shadow could hear her cries, then maybe he'd return to comfort her like usual. But he didn't dare embrace her, for fear of jeopardizing the mission.

∞

Fukuoka

Dark and Cammie sat inside a family restaurant eating breakfast since they had skipped dinner last night. The two didn't bother to make any small talk since they were simply there to eat. That was all. It wasn't like they were friends catching up on old times. Besides, holding a conversation with Dark wasn't part of Cammie's to-do list. She couldn't get over the feeling that she might really hate him to death.

Every now and then, Dark would lift his head just a few centimeters to glance at Cammie. She was eating away without a care in the world. Even when he sighed or coughed on purpose, she didn't question it or lift her head to look at him. He was hated. That much he could tell. The reason? Unknown. Dark badly wanted to ask but was afraid if he uttered a word, he'd be hatred more than he already was. So, he kept quiet, waiting patiently for her to talk first. Being with her was already enough. Even if there was no hope in her ever talking to him, he still wanted to wait and see what might happen.

The door slid open to the noisy family restaurant as a rowdy gang entered. With one glance, the families inside the restaurant zipped their mouths and averted their gazes. Even the children who had been shouting and laughing became tamed. The group of guys joked and laughed hysterically as one of them pushed the other into a family sitting in a booth.

"Watch it," snapped the goon. The family bowed, apologizing for something they hadn't done. He glared at them some more before turning to joke with the gang once again.

Cammie threw her entire sausage into her mouth to chew vigorously, while Dark ate and drank his juice calmly.

"Oye!" shouted the leader of the four guys. They had confiscated a table from a family of five. "Where the hell are the waitresses?!"

"S—sir, please lower your voice," said a waiter as he ran over to bow.

"I didn't call for you. I called for a *waitress*. Get your ass out of my face." He kicked the waiter away as they laughed. Everyone watched but kept to themselves. "Hurry up and bring out the cute waitresses!"

"Sir-"

"Shut up and bring out the waitresses!" He stood, punching the waiter in the stomach as his friends cheered him on.

"Nice one, Ikuto!" they shouted.

"Don't!" three waitresses in sailor uniforms pleaded as they came running out from the back, not wanting any further trouble. They just wanted the gang out of their work place.

"There the cute gals are," said Ikuto. He pushed the waiter away and sat back down while his friends licked their lips, eyeing the waitresses up and down. "Keep us company, won't you?" Ikuto reached out to grab one of the waitresses who screamed and broke free.

Standing, the rowdy guys swarmed in on the three defenseless girls. Even when they pled for help, the families and other single customers didn't dare go to their rescue. More than half left before things got ugly.

"Don't-" began Dark. When he looked up, Cammie was already gone. "Damn it. She's so quick to jump into situations."

With all her force, Cammie struck the table where Ikuto sat with her fork and let go. It stood upright as the gang turned to stare at her, wondering who she was. No one had ever stood up to them before, especially a girl.

"What are you-" began one of the guys. Before he could finish his sentence, Cammie struck him down.

"What the-" began the other two as they backed away in shock.

"Insects," Cammie hissed, hitting the two to the floor. From behind, Ikuto stood, grabbing her and pinning her to an adjacent table. He wasn't going to sit still and watch a girl beat them. The waitresses who were now free ran over to the waiter's side to drag away from the fight. Though they were thankful for Cammie's help, they worried. Cammie was still just a girl. She couldn't possibly defeat Ikuto.

"Who the fuck do you think you are, messing with us Bat Angels, bitch?" he hissed into her ear before pulling her hair. She grunted but refused to show any signs of pain. "I'll fucking show you who owns your ass."

"If anyone owns anyone, then I own your ass," she redirected. A thread of light from the bulbs shot out to cut Ikuto's leg. He let out a surprise cry and faltered, letting her go. The light string had cut a tendon.

"Life-Kill!" screamed the remaining families inside the restaurant. Soon, they were up and running.

"Wh—why the hell is a Life-Kill here on our turf?"

"You don't need to know." Cammie smoothed out her blue hair and glared at him. Her hair was something she took pride in. Anyone other than herself was not allowed to touch it. "Did you know that the consequences for touching my hair is death?" Cammie raised a hand as threads of light shot out to attack.

"What are you doing here, Ikuto?" intervened a girl who walked by Cammie's threads of light, ignoring it. Her only interest was getting Ikuto to return to base. "I thought I told you to stay at the base."

"What the-" began Cammie.

The girl who had entered the fight, avoiding Cammie's detection, carried a wooden sword on her back. She was five feet and wore a plain high school uniform dress, with a white midriff cover-up. Her long, thin, black hair swayed as if a breeze had blown into the restaurant. Cammie couldn't help but frown. Even Dark seemed wary now.

"Pia," spoke Ikuto. He slightly bowed and spoke, "Sorry. We only came out to have some fun and eat."

"Don't apologize to me. Return," she instructed.

"Yeah," he said, dragging his goons away. Before exiting, he glared at Cammie one last time. The only ones still there were the workers, Cammie herself, Dark, and Pia.

"I'm sorry for the problems those guys caused," apologized Pia. She bowed at the workers and set some money on the counter. "That should be enough to cover any damages they caused." She bowed again and exited with a smile.

"Cammie-" Dark began as she dashed out. He hadn't bother to intervene in her fight with the guys, knowing she could take care of herself. However, that changed when Pia entered the picture. He had to get to Cammie before she did something stupid. Dark dug into his pocket and pulled out some money to slam down on the table he sat at. "Thank you for the food! Keep the change!" he shouted and ran out after the two.

"Oye!" called out Cammie as she got in Pia's way.

"Yes?" she replied, matter-of-fact. "How can I help you?"

"Who the hell are you? You walked right by my light threads without receiving one scratch. How is that possible?"

Pia raised an eyebrow, finally showing some emotion. "I see, so that was you."

"What are you-"

"What are you doing honey? Don't leave me by myself," interrupted Dark. When he caught up, he threw his arms around Cammie protectively, and pulled her away from Pia.

"Huh?" Cammie said in alarm and glared up. Why was he acting so weird? But he was the least of her problems. She wanted to know how Pia had gotten past her light strings so easily. "You, girl, who are-"

"Honey, love-bear, let's go back home."

"Huh? Why are you suddenly giving me weird lovey-dovey nicknames? Can't you see? I'm in the middle of a heated battle."

"Honey," Dark said, snuggling close to her and pouting like a child. "Why can't you be more honest with me?"

"Stop calling me honey. That sounds wrong."

"I see," said Pia as she interrupted their lover's quarrel.

"You see what?" demanded Cammie.

"So that's how it is. I see." Pia smiled and nodded like she knew the reason for them being there. "Well then, thank you and see you later." She bowed, taking her leave first.

"What the hell was that about?"

"She seems interested in you. That's what," answered Dark. He still had his arms wrapped around her, but now had his chin on top of her head.

Cammie tried lifting her head to look at him. That was when she noticed how much her head had suddenly weighed. "She's gone now. You can let me go." After waiting for a few seconds to no avail, Cammie elbowed Dark's ribs, forcing him to grunt and let go.

"Why'd you do that for? I still wanted to hold you some more." Dark rubbed his aching rib and threw her into another tight embrace, causing her to throw another fit.

Instead of worrying about her threats, Dark was looking to where Pia had been standing a while ago. *She's one of us, and she's dangerous. The way she deflected Cammie's light threads, wasn't normal. I better keep my eye on her from now on.*

∞

Zara stood inside the dark lonely alley by herself. Ever since Hana's appearance, Shadow had disappeared. Zara feared that he'd run off to find a new hiding place. If that was so, she'd lost him for good.

Scowling, she drove her fist into the dumpster, denting it as it skidded away. It was all because of Hana that Shadow had left her side.

"Zara," called out one of the girls with dreadlocks as she ran over.

"What is it?" she snapped.

"That Shadow guy was spotted on the other side of town."

Turning, Zara sprinted off. She didn't care if the other side of town belonged to the other gang. She was going to retrieve Shadow and that was final. Along the way, she saw Hana sitting beneath a lamp post, hugging her legs. When the two girls made eye contact, Hana flinched and looked away.

Without a word, Zara continued towards her destination. She fearlessly walked through the other gang's turf, killing anyone who dared to get in her way. When she found Shadow hiding out in a dark alleyway, holding a raggedy pink hair tie, she stopped. He kept staring at it with a forlorn look, that Zara was tempted to return to her side to dispose of Hana. But that would do her no good. She wanted Shadow, and there was only one sure way to accomplish that wish.

"Join me," Zara ordered as Shadow spun around. He hadn't been expecting her to find him so soon.

"I already said-"

"That babyish girlfriend that you ran from, I wonder how lovely her squeals are."

Shadow was up and about, ready to kill Zara. The look in her eyes was pure sinister. Though Shadow's task was to join her, this wasn't what he had in mind. He had made a meticulous plan, but Hana had unintentionally ruined it. Now, he had no choice but to join Zara then and there.

Grinning, Zara held out a hand. Shadow had a look of defeat on his face. He knew the consequences of going against her and would remember what was at stake, should he try to flee or betray her.

9th Lie

VERSE STOOD OUTSIDE a secret warehouse where a group of armed men were making their routine perimeter checks. After receiving the tip from the Dome's investigators, she had followed its lead for the past few days. It eventually led her to this place. It was only a matter of time until things started getting interesting around here.

Looking to the stars, Verse allowed her mind to wander to Naruyuki who wasn't there to back her up. Even during her information gathering, he seldom showed up to give a hand. It wasn't like she was mad at him or anything. So why was he avoiding her? "Geez, I even left a note."

"What note?" asked someone from the dark. He put a sword to Verse's throat and kept himself concealed.

Verse glanced at the tip of the sword and smiled. This was what she got for letting her mind wander.

"Why aren't you answering? Who are you? And what note?"

"May I ask who *you* are?" she asked calmly.

"Why would I give my name to you?"

"Because it's common courtesy to first state your name before asking another. Or are all humans these days lacking respect and common sense?"

He grinned from the dark and walked into the light where Verse could see. He was slightly taller than her by a mere three inches and had soft black spiky hair. "The name's Sylvester and now yours."

"Verse."

"Why are you here, Verse? You're trespassing on private property. If you don't want to die, I suggest you get out of here before the others come out

76

and skin you alive. They're not like me. They're fiercer and stronger. They won't go easy on you even if you're a girl."

"Thanks for the tip. I'll be sure to remember that."

"It wasn't meant as a tip. It was meant as a warning. Sheesh, what kind of girl are you?" asked Sylvester in disbelief.

"If you think I'm bad, you should meet Soria. That girl will seriously blow your brains out."

Sylvester raised an eyebrow. Though Verse was insulting this Soria person, she was smiling. "Who's that?"

"My sister," she answered intuitively and stopped.

"And you talk about your sister that way?"

"No." Verse shook it off and put a hand to her head. It was beginning to throb.

"No to what?"

"Soria…she-" Verse began and stopped, remembering a time when Soria had stolen her sandwich. She got so worked up; she refused to speak to her for the entire day.

"Are you still mad? I only took one bite," said the young Soria who smiled. Meanwhile, Verse continued ignoring her. "Well, I was going to ask if you wanted to share my burger with me. But since you don't want to talk to me, I guess not." Soria turned and waltzed away.

"Wait!" shouted Verse. She stood and chased Soria, wanting to eat the other half of the burger. But more than that, she wanted to stop the pointless fight and go back to how they normally were: sisters.

"It hurts!" Verse screamed, throwing both hands to her head. It felt like someone was hammering a nail into her brain. "It hurts, it hurts it hurts!" Tears slowly formed and fell. From the rod implanted into her brain, a liquid of some sort was released, rejecting the memory. "Stop, please stop."

"Oye!" shouted Sylvester who was kneeling beside Verse. Suddenly she had gone out of control, shouting and squirming about in pain. He sheathed his sword and reached out to hold her. "What's wrong with you?! Calm down!"

"Please don't take it." Verse reached a shaky hand out, trying to stop Soria's fading back. "Don't take it away!"

"Oye!" shouted Sylvester again as Verse knocked out in his arms. She had gotten so worked up that her body lost all energy. "What the hell just happened?" Sylvester said, contemplating on what to do next. His choices were to leave her to die in the forest or be a gentleman and carry her inside where it was safe. However he thought about it, both choices were bad.

"Sylvester," called out his comrade who had long purple hair and orange eyes. "What's taking you so damn long? Didn't we say to finish it off and come back?"

"Sorry Hei, she suddenly fainted on me."

When he noticed Verse unconscious in Sylvester's arms, he stopped and raised an eyebrow. "Are you finally cheating on Misaki?" Hei accused. "She'll murder you in your sleep, you know?"

"Shut up and help me take her inside!"

"Sheesh, I got it. Don't bite my head off." Hei walked over and took Verse from him to bring inside. Even though she was the enemy, they couldn't find it in themselves to leave her outside to die.

"You owe me one for saving your life," muttered Sylvester to the unconscious Verse.

"You act as if she can hear you," said Hei.

"Stop picking on me."

"But it's so fun!" Hei laughed while Sylvester cursed his luck for being the youngest amongst their group.

Off in the distance, hiding was Naruyuki. He was standing on a tree branch watching Hei carry an unconscious Verse inside. After reading her note and hoping to reconcile, Naruyuki had come on time to witness her being taken by the enemy. "Was I too late?"

∞

Dark and Cammie were taking the night off from night watching. They were sleeping inside their hotel room, but sleep wouldn't overcome her as she lay in bed staring at the dark ceiling. Glancing over at the peaceful Dark, Cammie sat up and threw the covers off. She slipped out of her pajamas and into some clothes. In the dark, she fumbled for her jacket along with shoes to leave. The door automatically locked itself behind her as she made her way down the extravagant hallway. She got inside the over-sized elevator and rode it down to the grand lobby. It was amazing that Dark could sleep soundly when she couldn't even close her eyes because he was so near. If only the hotel had had a two-bedroom suite, she wouldn't need to sneak out in the middle of the night like this.

Once Cammie exited the building, she walked around aimlessly, watching the night life bustle around her. When her stomach growled, she went in search of the closest street restaurant.

"Welcome," greeted the woman who was cooking behind the counter.

"Good evening," greeted Cammie as she bowed and sat down at an empty table. She was the only customer so far.

"Miho!" the woman shouted.

"Coming," answered the cheerful daughter as she came out from the back. She looked to be sixteen years or so, her short hair tied back by a blue bandana. She walked over to Cammie's table and smiled. "Hello, I'm Miho. What can I get started for you?"

"I have a friend named Miho too."

"Really?" Miho laughed as Cammie chuckled alongside. "What a coincidence."

"Yeah," said Cammie as she nodded and smiled. Just the thought of the girls being so far away saddened her.

"Will your friend Miho, be joining you tonight?"

Cammie looked up and shook her head. If only that was the case. "No, unfortunately it's just me for tonight," she said and ordered.

When Miho finished writing the order, she slightly bowed and left.

A little breeze picked up as Cammie shivered. For a summer night, it was chilly since that morning had been scorching. While waiting, her mind wandered to how the other girls were holding up. They had always dreamt of leaving the Dome to roam the outside world together. Instead of living that dream, they were tasked with missions to accomplish.

Homesickness settled in, making Cammie feel queasy. She wanted to run to where the others were, hating how she was separated from them.

After a good fifteen minutes, her food was served, hot and ready to eat. Cammie thanked Miho and broke her bamboo chopsticks to dig in. When she finished, she chatted with Miho for a bit before paying.

"Come back again," bid the mother-daughter duo.

"Thank you, I will." Cammie waved at them and left, stuffing her hands into her jacket pockets. She looked to the sky and exhaled. Two hours had passed since she left the hotel. Hopefully Dark hadn't woken up, or else she'd have a lot of explaining to do. "What a pain that would be," she said, rounding the corner and bumping into someone.

"Watch it!" shouted the other party.

"I'm sorry. I didn't-" Cammie began and stopped. She raised an eyebrow at the two crooks dressed in black. In the second crook's arms was an unconscious little girl whose wrists were bound together by ropes. "Please tell me this isn't what I think it is."

"Listen bitch, if you don't want to die, don't get in our way. We're the Thunderbolts. Hurry along and pretend like you didn't see a thing." The two crooks attempted to run around her as she blocked them off. "What the-"

"I can't allow you to take that sleeping child."

"You have no idea who you're dealing with!" shouted the first crook. He took out his bat and ran at her as a string of light from the street lamp shot across, cutting the bat into pieces. The crook stopped dead in his tracks and dropped the handle of the bat to the ground. The homeless folks sitting on the sidewalk witnessed and scurried into the dark alleys.

"I'll say this only once. Put down the girl and leave."

"Let her down!" shouted the first crook to his partner.

"But the boss-" protested the second crook. His knees were shaking so badly he didn't know what to do. It was either let down the girl and run for their lives, returning to the boss empty-handed. Or die trying to bring the girl to the boss while fighting Cammie. Both options were bad. They were bound to lose their lives one way or another.

"We'll think of something to say to the boss!" the first crook shouted, able to read his comrade's mind. "Or are you gonna take on a Life-Kill?!"

Gulping, the second crook set the sleeping girl down and ran off with the first crook.

Once they were out of sight, Cammie stooped beside the girl and touched her arm gently. Her body was still warm and she was still breathing. That was a good sign at least. "What were they trying to do with you? Child prostitution? Organ harvesting?"

From the shadows, a dagger shot across the empty air. Cammie spun, light strings cutting the dagger in half. A shadow shot out, pulling her towards the user, as a second dagger struck the spot she had been kneeling a while ago. Turning to see who had come to her rescue, Cammie grimaced. "Thanks," she said sourly.

"You're welcome," said Dark as he came into the clearing, eyeing the shadows where the enemy was hiding. "I can see you perfectly well."

The attacker came out from within the shadows, all the while keeping his eyes on them. The lower part of his face was concealed by a black face mask. Finally, he broke his gaze and glanced at the sleeping girl then to Cammie.

"Who the hell are you?" demanded Cammie.

"Let me speak," said Dark. "You've done enough for one night."

"What does that mean?"

"Are you with the Bat Angels?"

Without an answer, the stranger scooped the little girl up off the sidewalk.

"Wait a minute!" shouted Cammie.

"Rastus," called out Pia as she approached them. She glanced at the sleeping girl and touched her gently. She was still breathing. "Good job in retrieving her."

Rastus turned towards Pia and bowed, still without saying a word.

"You," Cammie snarled after seeing that Pia was involved.

"Oh?" Pia finally took notice of the two and smiled. It felt as though this was destiny. "You two again, what a nice surprise. It seems our paths just keep crossing."

"What hell are you going to do with that girl?"

"She's our treasure. Those idiot Thunderbolts tried to kidnap her from under our noses."

"What the hell are you talking about? Who exactly is she? Why are you two groups fighting over her? What's so special about her?"

"Shut your mouth. Your ranting is annoying me." Pia glared as the ends of Cammie's hair stood from the intensity.

"That's enough." Dark stepped in-between the two girls, halting them from having a staring contest. He took hold of Cammie's wrist to leave. "Let's go. This has nothing to do with us anyway."

"But-"

"I said, let's go." Dark pulled Cammie to go as she glanced back at Pia one last time. There was a sadistic smile on her face as Cammie shuddered and turned to face front. No matter how evil Yeve was, she always let them off easily because they were friends. Cammie could only imagine. If Yeve were to truly become an Evil Empress one day, she would be exactly like Pia—no, she'd be more ruthless.

Cammie broke into a cold sweat. She would never want to cross paths with an evil Yeve.

When they were far enough, Dark glanced at Cammie who had become eerily quiet. "What were you thinking coming out so late at night to start a fight?"

At the accusation, Cammie broke free from his hold. "I wasn't trying to start a fight on purpose. I was having a midnight snack when I ran into two goons kidnapping a girl."

"Sheesh, I just can't take my eyes off you even when I sleep," said Dark. "And what are you talking about a midnight snack? That was no snack. You ate three orders worth of food by yourself."

"Well sorry for being a pig!" Cammie glared at him, crossing her arms and turning the other way, then stopped. "Wait. How did you know I ate three orders worth of food?" she asked suspiciously and pointed a finger at him. The only way Dark could've gotten hold of that information was if he had been there himself.

"You told me just now." He tried to play it off cool, but his lie could easily be seen through. After all, he wasn't a good liar to begin with.

"You followed me!" Cammie couldn't believe that her own Soulmate would go as far as to stalk her in the dead of the night. He could've just come out and told her that he had been there all along.

"Well it's not my fault you just upped and left without telling me," he said in defense.

"That's because you were sleeping!"

"You only thought I was sleeping because I had my eyes closed."

"Then you shouldn't have lied about sleeping."

"Why are we even arguing? This is a pointless argument." Dark poked her forehead and walked away first. From the goodness of his heart he had followed her to make sure she'd be safe. He had even gone to her rescue after she failed to see the second dagger, yet she could only start an argument.

"I just can't seem to understand him." Cammie shook her head and followed him back to the hotel. This was enough excitement for one night.

∞

"Sylvester!" screamed an angry voice from the adjacent room.

"Wa—wait, wait, hold on a minute, Misaki!" shouted Sylvester's voice. There was crashing, yelling, and running, forcing Verse to awaken. She opened her eyes weakly and sat up on the sofa to look around. How had she gotten there? Hadn't she been outside talking to Sylvester a few minutes ago? The pounding in Verse's head returned as she winced. The side effects from the rod's drug hadn't subsided.

Slowly, she stood, heading towards the door that slid open. As soon as she stepped foot into the adjacent room, all eyes were on her. Only Sylvester and his girlfriend, Misaki weren't paying attention.

"How can I trust you ever again?!" she shouted while holding him by the shirt collar.

"How can you not? I'm your boyfriend and it's not like I cheated."

"Yes, you did!"

"How so?"

"You were courting another girl out at night. You were caring for her while she was unconscious, and never left her side. You were getting too chummy with her."

"You weren't even here to see what really happened. How can you assume that?"

"Hei told me!" Misaki shouted, pointing to Hei who sat near the corner, sipping tea. He even smiled like he had done a good deed.

"Hei, you jerk!" shouted a furious Sylvester. "Don't go around telling lies! You know that Misaki believes everything!"

"How could you? I trusted you." The tears that had welled in Misaki's eyes trailed down. She bawled that her boyfriend had been taking care of an unknown girl. It was unfair. Misaki was Sylvester's girlfriend. She should be the only one that he cared for, no one else. "Waa, I hate you!"

"Misaki, don't cry, please."

"Um, sorry to ruin your little love quarrel, but someone's awake," said Hei. He pointed a finger at Verse as the two turned to look.

"Evening," Verse greeted and waved.

"So that's the other woman?" Misaki let go of Sylvester, wiped her tears, and stalked over to inspect every inch of Verse's body. She stared and tapped her chin, finding nothing special about Verse that Sylvester needed to get so excited about.

"What are you doing?" Verse asked, staring back.

"So, we're both A's."

Verse twitched and sneered. She could already tell by that sentence alone that they were bound to butt heads. "I'm a B."

"How can Sylvester possibly think you're better than me? Is he blind?" Misaki insulted some more, ignoring Verse's comment just then. She flicked her short bob and went back to inspecting Verse's chest.

"Are you trying to piss me off?"

"I'm clearly the better choice."

"Would you stop that?" Sylvester groaned from nearby while the other guys laughed at his misery.

"Don't lie to me. I know exactly what you were thinking." Misaki finally looked away from Verse and over at Sylvester. She crossed her arms haughtily, still not forgiving him. "The moment you touched her you thought about cheating on me, right? You were probably thinking, 'oh my, what a cute girl, I'll probably lay her tonight!'"

"Um," Verse said, raising a hand to be called on so she could clear herself of all charges that Misaki had accused her of. Instead of caring about what she had to say, the couple drifted off into their own world again.

"You know what?" Sylvester snapped, having heard enough accusations. "You're right. I was thinking that. How did you read my mind?"

Gasping from the sudden confession, Misaki let out a sniffle as more tears welled in her eyes. "How could you say that?"

"You wanted me to say it!"

"I never said that!"

"Yes, you did!"

"No, I didn't!"

While watching the series of unfortunate events unfold before her, Verse found herself flexing the muscles in her arms. It was amazing that she'd encounter someone who could piss her off just as much as Soria did. Walking over, she smacked Misaki over on the head as she yelped, then kicked a shoe off at Sylvester. It hit him square between the eyes causing him to yelp and fall over on the floor. The other guys in the room simply watched, amazed at her accuracy. "Shut the hell up, you idiotic couple!"

After whimpering and massaging her head, Misaki turned to glare at Verse. The hit had been uncalled for and unnecessary. "What the hell Other Woman, you wanna fight?!" she challenged.

"Bring it on," Verse accepted by crossing her arms and glaring back.

"Don't I scare you?"

"I see nothing to fear."

"Don't you know who I am?"

"I could care less."

"You're really weird, did you know that?" Misaki raised an eyebrow and returned to inspecting Verse again.

"Eye Poking Technique." Verse reached two fingers out, poking Misaki's eyes without remorse.

"Ow, my eyes, my eyes!"

"Oye!" the guys shouted, running over to Misaki's side while glaring at Verse. They were ready to kill her for hurting their young mistress.

"You boys keep staring and I'll gauge your eyes out," Verse said as an ominous aura loomed about. Having no doubts that she'd carry out her threat, the guys shuddered from her stare.

Hei chuckled from where he sat. This little show he had forced Sylvester to participate in was turning out to be more entertaining than he initially thought, especially with Verse now involved. Hei finished drinking his tea and set the cup down. "I like her."

"Move," Misaki instructed to her men. Obediently, they moved as she narrowed her bloodshot eyes on Verse. Eventually, she cracked a smile. It was as Hei had said, there was something about Verse that she also liked. It wasn't often that Misaki got to meet such a frivolous girl. She had met her fair share of evil gold diggers and backstabbing goody-two-shoes, who gave girls a bad rap. Only a select few were genuinely loyal and kind in this day and age. "It's okay boys." Misaki waved at them to sit back down while Hei continued watching. "I like you."

"Am I supposed to be flattered?" Verse asked.

"You know, if it's you, I suppose I won't mind Sylvester cheating on me. But that can only happen when I die."

"What the hell?" She let out an exasperated sigh. "Man, if Soria doesn't kill me first, it'll be you."

"Huh?"

"Misaki," Hei said, brewing more tea, "if you don't introduce yourself properly to the poor girl, she won't know who you are."

Misaki nodded in agreement and pointed a finger to herself. She had forgotten all about self-introductions and went straight into arguing. "Listen here, girl-"

"Verse."

"Listen here, Verse, my name is Misaki Shizomiya. I'm the daughter of this clan's leader and I'm probably the strongest girl you'll ever get to meet in this lifetime."

Verse couldn't help but raise an eyebrow. She knew plenty of other strong girls. "Then, why'd you pick the weakest link to date?"

"Eh? Uh, well-" Misaki scratched her head, stumped by the question.

"I'm right here! I can hear!" Sylvester sat up on the sofa, rubbing his bruised forehead. Verse had insulted him even if she hadn't purposely meant to. He picked up her shoe and threw it back as she caught it

Verse put her shoe back on, unaffected and stood back up. "I'm just restating your words about how there were other stronger guys than you."

"I'm happy you think so highly of me," said a happy Hei.

"You're excluded!" shouted Sylvester.

"So," Misaki said, crossing her arms. The fun and games were over and done with. Now, it was time to get down to business. "Who are you and why are you here?"

"I'm here to handcuff you," Verse replied.

"She's a cop!" shouted the guys as they withdrew their weapons to point at her. They knew it was too good to be true that Verse would be a normal civilian who had wandered onto their territory. Even if she really was a normal civilian, she would've known who Misaki was when she stated her name.

"Stop," Misaki ordered to the group. She held up a hand to halt them from attacking. Even if Verse claimed to be there to handcuff them, she was too calm while outnumbered and made no attempts. Misaki couldn't act rashly without further investigation. "Are you really a cop?"

"As if," snorted Verse.

"Then, answer this simple question. Depending on your answer, it'll either lead to your demise or your freedom."

"Well," Verse said, contemplating for a minute. She took one last glance around the room. From the feel, it didn't seem like a meeting had taken place yet. But she couldn't be too sure, especially since there was no clock inside the room and she had no watch to tell the time. "Let me ask you a question first," Verse said, looking in Misaki's direction again.

"I'm the one doing the interrogation here."

"Depending on how you answer my question, it'll either lead you to my answer or to *your* demise."

Misaki smirked and crossed her arms. Even the way Verse spoke was to her liking. "I really do like you. Which is why, it'd be a pity to see you die so young."

"What are you talking about? You and I seem to be the same age."

"Spill it," Misaki instructed, not wanting to admit that she really was just seventeen.

"Your little meeting here, is it already over?"

"What meeting?"

"Don't feign ignorance, Misaki-san. Did you already hold your secret meeting with the other clans while I was unconscious or not?" Verse asked with a shrug. "It's a simple question, really."

Misaki nodded. "Yeah, we finished already."

"I see." Verse too nodded and thought about it for a while. "How long did I sleep?"

"For almost two hours."

"Then, forgive me," said Verse as she bowed.

"What are you-" Before Misaki could finish her sentence Verse pushed her down.

"Oye!" shouted the group. They withdrew their weapons again to rush at her while Hei set his teacup down and reached for his sword.

"Get down!" ordered Verse. She ran forward to steal Sylvester's sword and slashed at the air. The speeding bullet split in half as its trajectory changed, piercing the wall and door behind her. Standing nearby was Hei who had also slashed at the bullets with his own sword. The two exchanged glances and grinned.

"What the hell is going on here, Hei?!" demanded Misaki as the group helped her to stand.

"Sylvester," instructed Hei.

"I got it." Sylvester nodded and ran over to Misaki's side.

"What's going on here?!"

"Here," Verse said, handing Sylvester's sword back.

"Thank you for saving Misaki." Sylvester bowed and retrieved his sword before dragging Misaki out towards the secret passageway. They had at least three minutes to get away before the shooters entered. He had to get as far away as possible.

"Go with them," Hei ordered to the remaining guys.

"Take care of yourself," they bid and ran after the couple. Even if they hated leaving Hei by himself, they knew that Misaki was their top priority.

"Sylvester, what's going on?!" shouted Misaki.

"Those two noticed it first. We're surrounded by the enemy," explained Sylvester as he tightened his hold on Misaki's hand. He opened the door to the secret passageway two rooms down and descended the dirt tunnel that would lead them up to the fresh air in a few minutes.

"You mean, that girl brought the enemy to us?"

"No." Sylvester shook his head and ran around the corner. From behind, he could hear his comrades following. "I think the enemy is one of the other clans that's supposed to join us for the meeting."

"But-" Misaki said in disbelief. She squeezed his hand and gulped, afraid. "My dad-"

"I fear the worst has happened to him."

∞

"Sorry for the late introduction, my name's Hei, one of the Shizomiya bodyguards. It's a pleasure meeting you, Verse-san," greeted Hei as he smiled.

"Same here," responded Verse.

"Here they come," he said, turning towards the entrance with Verse. It came crashing down as a group of men came running in, pointing their guns at the two. The one they wanted, Misaki, was missing.

"Where's Misaki?" asked the short skinny middle-aged man who starting to bald. He glanced around the empty room with his beady eyes and huffed.

"Misaki's out on a stroll with her beloved," answered Hei.

"Is that so? What a pity when I came specially to see her."

"I also agree. It's a pity that you had to meet me instead." Hei tightened his sweaty grip on his hilt and gulped. "Where's my master? Wasn't he with you, Ishikawa-san?"

"Why must you ask a question you know the answers to?" asked the middle-aged man. He clasped his hands together behind his back and smiled.

Hei's grin was replaced with abhor and guilt. He knew he should've gone with Mr. Shizomiya that afternoon. Now, it was too late. He only had one option left to choose. "I'll die before I give Misaki to you. I made a vow to protect her from harm."

"Is that so?" Ishikawa smiled, backing away to stand behind his men for safeguard. "I've always wanted you to join my clan. With your agility and strength, I could be at the top. That's why, give your undying loyalty to me. Why work for such a weakling as Shizomiya?"

"Someone like you, has no right to know my reasons."

Verse glanced at Hei and smiled. Though she had no clue about their internal affairs, it proved interesting to partake. "You know, I was gonna bail and leave you to this mess since it doesn't concern me. But after hearing how cool you sound, Hei-san, I can't leave anymore. Besides, I wanna see you in action after hearing the old man hype up your skills."

"Thanks for the compliment. Also, just call me Hei."

"Then, leave out the honorifics for me too."

"We're still here!" shouted Ishikawa. Ever since Verse spoke up, she had made Hei disregard him. Being ignored was Ishikawa's biggest pet peeve when he was made for the limelight.

"Flies should just buzz off," Verse snarled, making the men shiver under her intense stare.

"Say," said Hei. He turned to look at Verse who was barehanded after returning Sylvester's sword. "How are you gonna fight without a weapon? They have guns."

"I could say the same for you," Verse redirected. "You have a sword and you're going up against guns."

"Better than nothing."

"I have my hands. That's all I need."

Hei stared at her for some time before grinning. Now he really wanted to see her in action. "Alright then, don't go dying on me just yet. You too, have piqued my interest."

"Kill her," Ishikawa hissed to his men. Again, he was being ignored. "Kill the girl!"

"Seems like that's our cue," Verse said, reaching out to grab a pillow from the sofa to throw at the men who fired.

∞

"We should be safe here," said Sylvester as they stopped in the forest to take a breather. He glanced around in case someone had followed them. So far there was no sign of an enemy nearby.

After getting her breath back, Misaki turned to look at the group that followed them. "I want four of you to go back and assist Hei."

"Yes," they answered and turned to leave.

"Wait," called out Sylvester as the guys stopped. "Don't. They'll be fine."

"How can you say that?" Misaki asked, eyes widening. It was Hei against an unknown number of enemies. If they didn't send backup, he would die. Losing just one member of her clan would sadden her for the rest of her life. Her clan was her family. That was what her father had taught her. Now that he was no more, Misaki couldn't afford to lose anyone else. For Sylvester to say such a thing was infuriating. "Hei needs all the help he can get. If not all of us goes, then a few will do."

"No." Sylvester shook his head, holding Misaki's gaze. "Verse-san is strong. She was the first to notice that we were surrounded and saved you from that bullet."

"You mean she knew before Hei?"

"Believe it or not, that girl is no ordinary girl. She complements Hei really well."

Misaki stared at Sylvester some more before pinching his cheeks. He let out a yelp and stepped away, glaring at her. "You've really fallen for her, haven't you?" she accused again.

"Now isn't the time for that!"

"But it's true!"

"You're unbelievable!"

"Well, it's not my fault you're-"

"We're being followed," interrupted one of the guys as they spun around.

"What? I thought we escaped?"

"Guess not," they said, forming a protective front. Whoever was chasing them was coming at an incredible speed. "Sylvester, take Misaki and go, we'll handle them."

"What? I can't run and leave you guys behind! I'm your future clan leader! I've never run away from a fight before in my life, no matter how dire it was!" shouted Misaki in disbelief.

"Misaki!" the guys shouted, reassuring smiles on their faces. It was exactly as she had said. She was their future clan leader. That was why they were willing to give their lives, so she could live to fulfill their dreams. "Put more faith in us."

Tears welled in her eyes as her lips quivered. Of course she had faith in them. It was the thought of leaving that she couldn't stand.

"Please go."

"You guys..." she said softly. The group had turned their backs to face front again. There was no use in arguing any further. They wouldn't listen to her even if she gave an order. All she could do now was run with Sylvester as to not burden them. Hopefully they would return to her side, safe and sound. "Today, you've gone against your leader's orders! Your punishment is to return to my side! I won't ever forgive any of you if you die here, got it?! You've taken a pledge to serve me for life! You better live to fulfill that promise!"

"Yes, mistress!" the group shouted, their strong and courageous backs stood tall and proud.

"Let's go," whispered Sylvester as he took her hand and ran.

"Sylvester," Misaki whispered. "Why am I being protected like this? Usually in the past the guys would always allow me to fight, even if the odds were against me. So why today of all days?"

"It's true that you're strong, but you're our precious young miss that we have to protect."

Misaki squeezed his hand as unwilling tears fell. For the first time, she felt sheltered and weak for being unable to do anything.

∞

Ikuto came out from within a bedroom as the door automatically locked. In his hand was a tray of bloody cotton balls and a dirty wet towel. He nodded at the guard standing outside the door and headed towards the empty lounge hall to find Pia and Rastus eating. Everyone else had gone off to bed after a long fight with the Thunderbolts that had suddenly infiltrated their base. "So?" asked Ikuto as he set the tray down and sat as well. "How'd you manage to retrieve Anoka from those goons?"

"Rastus tracked her down," Pia answered while playing with the broccoli on her plate.

Ikuto raised an eyebrow and glanced over at Rastus. "I thought they got a head start on you? You still managed to catch up?"

Rastus looked up and nodded in reply.

"Ikuto," Pia said, "this is Rastus you're talking about. No one can outrun him. He's like the endless shadow."

"I was just wondering." Ikuto scratched his head and stood, grabbing the tray. It was late and it was time for bed. Cleaning and tending to Anoka had taken its toll on him, not to mention disposing of the dead bodies. "Well, I'm going to sleep. You two should too."

"We will, in a while."

"Oh," said Ikuto as he stopped halfway at the doorway. He had remembered something. "Tric said when he caught up to you, you were having a chat with the two at the diner."

Pia stopped playing with the broccoli to look up. Now that was something worth her time to talk about. "We certainly did." She couldn't help but smile and poke her fork into the broccoli to chew.

Noticing her smile, Rastus pulled his black mask that covered the lower half of his face off. On the right side of his chin was a deep burn scar. It wasn't every day that she smiled. In fact, she hated smiling. For the first time that night, he spoke in a deep raspy voice, "Why are you smiling?"

"I was just thinking."

Ikuto couldn't help but grin. Pia was easy to read. "Is it that interesting to mess with the girl?"

An abrupt laugh erupted from her as she threw her head back. The two guys glanced at one another, unsure of what was so funny. "No," Pia said, shaking her head. "I could care less about the girl. She's a weakling and a nuisance. The one I want to toy with is her Soulmate."

"What about him?" asked Rastus.

"He's handsome and strong, two traits I like. Also, he never flinched when I slightly used my powers." Pia poked her pork rib-let this time, holding it up to admire. She grinned and took a bite, wishing it was Dark she was taking a bite out of instead. Her eyes rolled back slightly, savoring not the flavor but the moment her teeth dug into the flesh. "It's been a long time since I've wanted someone this much."

10th Lie

"WHEW, that's over and done with," said Verse. She took a seat on the half-sofa that was now torn and broken from the fight. It sat slanted with bullet holes, but Verse didn't care as she crossed her legs.

"You were really serious," Hei said, sheathing his sword to look over.

"About what?" Verse wiped her forehead before turning to look at him. One of the men on the ground groaned as she kicked the back of his head with her heel, completely knocking him unconsciousness.

"When you said all you needed were your hands."

"When I say something, I'm usually serious."

The two grinned, exchanging a silent conversation. "It's good to know that there are still people like you out there in the world."

"Is that a compliment?"

"Yes."

"Then, thank you. I'm glad there are people like you as well."

"You're welcome. And thank you."

"Don't mention it," Verse said, waving it off.

"Mag—magnificent!" shouted Ichikawa as the two turned to look at him, having forgotten about him. He held up his trembling hands to clap at the show they had put on for him. After witnessing her skills first-hand, he no longer wanted her dead but instead to join his clan as well. With them by his side, Ichikawa could defeat anyone who dared to oppose him. "You two were magnificent! That was spectacular! Hei and the young miss, come work for me. You two will be greatly rewarded. With your powers, we can change the tides of this war."

"What war?" Verse asked, raising an eyebrow. In all her years of being alive, she'd never heard of a war that was still being fought. The war that had caused the great devastation was over and done with. Besides, the Dome had eyes everywhere. As a student from there, she knew everything. So exactly what war was Ichikawa talking about that she didn't know about?

"This pathetic Silent War," Ichikawa answered, his eyes reflecting the need for power and vengeance. "Say that you'll join me!"

"Yeve will kill me if I join you."

"With you we can go in search of my daughter and change this world!" Already picturing himself as a new god and ruling with an iron fist, Ichikawa laughed hysterically. Like with the Golden God, he too would shape this world into his own image and kill anyone who dare to usurp him.

"He's lost it," Hei said, withdrawing his sword again. "I'll put him out of his misery."

"Wait." Verse held out a hand, halting him from approaching Ichikawa and stood from the sofa.

"What is it?"

"I want to see something." Verse walked over to kneel before Ichikawa. Hei's revenge would have to wait. There was something about Ichikawa that piqued her as she touched him.

"Say that you'll join me, say that you'll join me," he kept repeating.

Verse closed her eyes. When she opened them, she was inside a traditional Japanese home, taking in the surrounding. There was a tatami mat placed not far away. Pictures of idols hung on the walls of the room. A drawer with dolls and school books sat nearby. From out in the dining room, laughter could be heard. Verse walked over to the door and slid it open. There was no sign that technology had taken over this household. It was still very traditional to its style.

She followed the laughter and stopped outside the dining room doorway. Sitting around the brown table with short legs was a happy family. They sat on thin pillows and were eating snacks. The man was Ichikawa himself, but he looked younger and happier. The woman sitting beside him was his wife, a true *yamato nadeshiko*. She wore a beautiful black and white camellia yukata with her hair pinned into a low side bun. Sitting opposite them was a little girl, her hair pinned in two small buns on either side of her head. It reminded Verse of Love's hairstyle when they were still kids. In the daughter's hand was a piece of mochi. White powder dirtied her yukata as she laughed while her mother shook her head and smiled, reaching out to clean it off.

Verse placed a hand on the doorway and smiled. "What the hell is this? How is this his sadness?"

"Oh?" said the wife. She glanced over at Verse and smiled. "You're finally awake. Pia's been waiting for you."

93

"Come sit," Ichikawa said, motioning for her.

"I-" began Verse.

"Heita-kun, come sit with me!" Pia set the treat down on the plate and stood, running over to drag a boy who had been standing beside Verse.

"When did-" Verse began as the room darkened and the happy family vanished. It was nighttime now.

"Heita-kun!" screamed Pia's voice from the bedroom of idol posters. At the sound of her scream, Verse spun and ran back. When she reached the room, the *shoji* screens were broken. A man dressed in black was running off with Pia in his arms. Lying on the floor of the bloody room was Heita, wounded from protecting her. "Hei-kun!" she screamed again and reached a hand out to him as tears streamed down.

"Pia," called out the wounded boy who could only watch as the most precious person to him was kidnapped.

"Pia!" shouted Ichikawa's voice from behind.

"Oye," said Hei. He placed a hand on Verse's shoulder as she flinched and turned to look at him. Concern was written all over his face. For a moment there, it felt like she'd drifted to a faraway place. "What's wrong?"

"Nothing," Verse answered and smiled. She let go of Ichikawa's unconscious body on the floor and wiped her sweaty forehead. Any further and she'd have killed him.

"What'd you do? Kill him?" Hei joked.

"Drain his energy," corrected Verse.

"Huh?"

"Forget it." She shook her head, taking a stand to glance at Hei. He was kicking the broken wood out of the way so they could leave.

Noticing her stare, Hei turned back, eyebrow raised. "What is it?"

"This is gonna sound random, but I wanna ask."

"Shoot," he said, heading towards the broken doorway.

"Do you know a person named Pia?"

After thinking about it, he shook his head. "Doesn't ring a bell."

"I see." Verse nodded, peering down at Ichikawa. His tears were drying and would soon leave stains. She had two assumptions, either Hei really didn't know a girl named Pia, or he was playing dumb.

"Why'd you ask for?"

"Just wanted to know."

"Well, anyway, let's get out of here and find the others. I'm sure they're being tailed right now as we speak."

"Yeah," Verse said, following from behind.

∞

After leaving the group to fight the enemy, the couple could still feel him chasing them. It was like the group hadn't even put up a fight. Not daring to look back for fear of finding the enemy on their tail, Sylvester and Misaki huffed and puffed, concentrating on running.

"Damn," said Sylvester as he scowled and let go of her hand.

"Sylvester," gasped Misaki as she stopped running to look at him. He was already withdrawing his weapon and turning his back to her.

"Run."

"No!" she screamed, shaking her head. Of everyone, he was the one person she'd never abandon. "If you're not coming with me, I'm not going!"

"This is no time to be stubborn! I can't protect you and fight at the same time!"

"Then I'll fight alongside you!"

"Just run!" ordered Sylvester. He gulped and stared at the path they had come from. He couldn't hear the trees rustling, but he could feel the pursuer desperately getting closer.

Misaki stared at Sylvester's back, tears welling in her eyes. He really wouldn't follow her to safety. In just one night, she was going to lose everything and everyone she cared for. "Look at me."

"Run, Misaki. I'm not joking around."

"Look at me!" she demanded, running over to throw her arms around his waist. With all her might, she held on, refusing to let go. Not expecting a back hug, Sylvester stood still, eyes wide open. "I'm not going to leave you to save myself. I'll never abandon you. What kind of girlfriend would I be?"

"Fool," he whispered and smiled. This was just like her. "We might die here, you know?"

"I know. Even so, I'd rather die by your side than alone."

"You really are a fool."

"I know that too."

"I love you."

"I love you too."

Sylvester tightened his hold on his short sword's hilt. He wanted so much to turn around and embrace her, but feared that he'd break down. It wasn't the time to get emotional when they were being hunted.

"What a loving couple. Why can't we be like that?" the enemy spoke from the dark after finally catching up.

"Show yourself!" ordered Sylvester as Misaki let go to take out her twin daggers from her boots. She too was ready to fight to the death.

"I guess I have no one to blame but myself. It's my fault that I keep calling out to Umeko-san," he said, coming out into the clearing where his white hair glowed brighter than ever before.

"Who are you? What clan are you from? State your name," Misaki instructed, trying to keep her voice level.

Naruyuki looked away from the moon to the two. He had just been ordered by a stranger to state who he was. It made him grin. They had no idea who or what they were dealing with. "I answer to no one."

"You're in the presence of Misaki Shizomiya. Know your place," growled Sylvester.

"I don't care who she is. I'm just here to retrieve my Soulmate," he said, reaching into his pocket to pull out a yellow rose.

"Soul mate?" repeated the two in confusion.

"If you won't tell me, I'll just have to make you."

∞

The morning sun broke in through the curtains as streams of light awoke Cammie from her sleep. She felt groggy and angry from last night still. It was only 5:30 a.m. and her alarm hadn't even come on yet. Getting out of bed, she made her way towards the bathroom, cursing. Why did the sun have to rise so early during the summer?

"Where're you going?" Dark asked hoarsely from his bed, curling tightly under his blanket. Even though Cammie had been quiet in waking and getting out of bed, Dark's ears were sharp.

"Taking a shower, so don't peek," she warned and entered the bathroom. "Pervert," she added in.

"There's nothing to see," he insulted and fell back asleep.

The motion sensor in the lights came on as Cammie yawned. She undressed and inspected her body in the mirror. *Nothing to see*, she scoffed. From all the girls, she had the most desirable curves, followed by Jennifer, and surprisingly Shayla. Love had made it clear when she enviously stated it out during their puberty phase. It always made Cammie self-conscious, but Jennifer had embraced hers with confidence. Shaking off Dark's words, Cammie entered the shower to press the ON and WARM buttons.

"Why's it so cold in here?" she grumbled, pressing the up button to raise the temperature. Soon, steam filled the bathroom. "Ah, much better," she said, washing her back. It wasn't long until she noticed something moving in the bathroom. At first, she thought it was a mouse and ignored it, but the thought occurred to her. There couldn't possibly be a mouse in such a high-tech hotel. If the rich folks who stayed here were to get word of mice running amok, this hotel would've shut down already. Cammie tensed and quickly washed the shampoo out from her hair. "Dark, is that you? Didn't I tell you not to enter?"

No response came as Cammie rinsed her face before hitting the OFF button. The water from the rain shower head ceased and Cammie stepped out onto the plush mat. She reached for her towel in the steam, spotting not a single soul inside the fancy bathroom.

"Hmm, was it just me?" she asked, draping the towel around herself. Before she could finish, someone reached out from behind to gag her.

The towel hit the floor as Cammie struggled with the intruder. She tried to use her light strings, but darkness enveloped them. Her eyes widened in horror. The intruder had a similar ability to Dark. Before she knew it, she lost consciousness and fell limp into her intruder's arms.

∞

"He's not dead," Verse said, kneeling beside an unconscious Sylvester, feeling his faint pulse while his sword lay nearby.

"How can you say that so nonchalantly?" asked Hei.

"So," said Verse as she stood up to investigate.

"So what?" asked Hei. After leaving the hideout and catching up to the unconscious group of guys, the two treated them before they could greet the underworld. Not seeing Sylvester and Misaki around, Verse went on ahead to find them while Hei tended to the last of the guys before following. He walked over to where Sylvester lay and put him on his back to return to where the others were waiting.

"Did the attacker kidnap Misaki-san?"

"Must have if Sylvester is lying here on the ground, obviously."

"Hmm," Verse said, inspecting the scene with a raised eyebrow. Everything was intact, and nothing seemed disturbed. If a fight really had broken out, there should be more blood. The trees should have a few slash marks and the ground should be trodden. Yet there was no evidence of any of that. "Who's this attacker and why'd he take Misaki-san?"

"Again, it's obvious, isn't it?"

"And that would be?" Verse asked, annoyed at Hei's know-it-all attitude. No wonder Sylvester got so irritated with him.

"He wants to take over our territory."

"Then why didn't he kill Sylvester-san? Why let him live?"

"To send us a message," replied Hei as he turned to leave first.

"I'm not too sure on your theory." Verse looked around some more before noticing a tiny sunflower lying on the ground. She walked over, touching it. It was a secret message meant only for her.

"What are you doing?" Hei asked, turning back to look at Verse who was no longer following. Instead, she was crouched down, examining something that he couldn't see.

"Nothing." Verse shook her head and stood, the sunflower now in her palm.

"Let's head back. You can tell me your theory along the way," Hei said, leaving again as Verse followed.

"My theory?" asked Verse as she smiled and clasped her fingers over the tiny flower. "My theory is that this kidnapper is searching for someone."

"And that person would be Misaki."

Verse shook her head. Again, Hei was wrong. "No."

"Then who is it?"

"Hopefully me."

"You?" he asked, bemused as Verse walked on ahead.

"I guess we'll just have to wait for Sylvester-san to wake up before we can confirm anything. In the meanwhile, we should find a place to rest." Verse yawned to the sky where the sun was rising higher. "What a long night."

11th Lie

"WAKE UP," ordered Naruyuki as he splashed cold water against Misaki's face.

She gasped for air and flung her eyes open, alarmed. Standing before her was Naruyuki. "You," she said, blinking and studying the room. They were inside some sort of dark basement. There was only one door leading in and out of the room. Other than that, the room was pretty much desolate except a table and two chairs. There weren't any windows to tell how late into the day it was. "Where am I?"

"I'm the one asking questions." Naruyuki pulled up the second chair to sit on while inspecting her. A few minutes passed before he broke the silence that made Misaki squirm, "Where's my Soulmate?"

"For the last time, I don't know who you're talking about." Misaki shook her head, wondering what it would take to get past him and escape through the only door.

Out of patience, Naruyuki rubbed his forehead. Even now she was still feigning ignorance. After defeating the couple and questioning them, they kept their lips tightly sealed. It had been a good decision to let Sylvester live so he could lead Naruyuki to Verse's whereabouts. Once he changed Misaki, he returned to the broken warehouse only to find dead bodies.

"I'm talking about the girl you kidnapped last night. I was standing watch outside, waiting for her to come out once she defeated you guys. Even after thirty minutes, she never came out. I was going to infiltrate your base when a group of men beat me to it. Now tell me, where is she?"

"I still don't know who you're talking about."

"Verse! I'm talking about Verse! Where is she? What'd you do with her? Why is it that only you and those guys came out from that secret passage?" Naruyuki asked, his glare intensifying.

"I—it's Verse you're looking for?"

"So, you do know who I'm talking about."

"If it's her, then yeah, I know. But it's not what you think. She stayed behind with Hei to take out the bad guys while we fled."

"Why would she do something so foolish?"

"I don't know either."

"Where's your proof?"

"I don't have any—but it's the truth! You have to believe me! Verse's okay, she's with Hei, I just know it! Those two make a good team, or at least that's what Sylvester believes anyway. They're both strong and complement one another." Misaki tried her best to please Naruyuki with her answers so she could get herself out of a sticky situation. Little did she know, the more she spoke, the more vexed Naruyuki became. It was an insult, hearing that Verse complemented another man.

Smirking, Naruyuki leaned back in his chair. "Do you know who I am? Do you know what it is you're saying to me?"

"Eh?" Misaki said, confused.

"Listen." Naruyuki leaned forward leaving only an inch between them. Taken aback, Misaki jerked away as Naruyuki sternly caught hold of her chin. Any tighter and he would break her jaw. She had no choice but to sit still. "Verse is my Soulmate. *I'm* the only one who can complement her. You'd be wise not to insult me the next time."

Misaki nodded in understanding, not daring to voice about his fierce grip.

"Good," he said, letting go to stand. "I'm gonna go find this Hei person you keep praising. If he does have Verse, we'll make an exchange."

When Naruyuki was out of the room, Misaki who had been holding her breath finally exhaled desperately. She had been too afraid to even breathe in his presence. "Verse sure has weird taste in men," said Misaki. She tried to break loose, but the ropes tightly bound her to the wooden chair. "And what's with this soul mate thing? Verse's married already? What the heck? She was trying to steal my man when she has her own? That two-timer."

∞

"Cammie, I need to use the bathroom!" Dark shouted, banging on the bathroom door. It was locked from the inside and the only way to open it was from the inside, or if front desk was notified. She had been inside for the past hour. In this hotel room, she wasn't the only one occupying it and needed to learn to share with him. "Cammie, why are you taking so long?"

Again, there was no answer as Dark stalked over to sit on his bed. It couldn't possibly take this long to take a shower and get dressed. Or was she purposefully taking her time to irk him? It wasn't like he had said or done anything to anger her, other than the joke he made before falling back asleep. Shaking it off, Dark decided to give her another fifteen minutes before trying again. When time was up, he stormed over to pound on the door again.

"Cammie!" shouted Dark. "Alright, that's it. I'm coming in!"

Still, there came no response. Usually such a threat would've gotten Cammie worked up. She'd come screaming, even butt naked if necessary just to call him a pervert. Dark moved the shadows in the room and shifted it beneath the door crack. The shadow rose up the white tiled floor and pressed the OPEN button on the wall. The door slid open as the shadow dispersed.

There was no need to call front desk when he was a Life-Kill with powers.

He entered the bathroom and stopped. The steam from her hot shower had vanished and she was nowhere to be found. All he saw was her white towel lying on the marble floor.

Dark walked over, gently touching it, then noticed the tub filled with water. Floating atop the water were three wooden toys. One of them was a boy floating by himself. The other two wooden toys were floating together, they were both girls. One of the girls had a sword on her back. The second had long smooth hair. Suddenly, the unthinkable happened; the second wooden girl's head came off and floated away.

Dark's heartbeat quickened as he grabbed the toys and turned to look at the towel again. Darkness filled the room, blocking out the light. He'd failed in protecting her. "Don't test me, woman."

∞

Pia whistled a cheery tune while carving figurines out of wood. Strapped to a nearby chair was an unconscious Cammie. A blindfold was wrapped around her eyes in case she woke up. Seeing as how Rastus had kidnapped her without any clothes, Pia dressed her in a sky blue see-through camisole and underwear that matched her hair color.

"Pia," called out Ikuto as he entered the room. One look at Cammie and he turned a bright red. She was being exposed in plain view. Clearing his throat, Ikuto turned the other way. "Can't you give her something better to wear?"

"Why? I think I've brought out her inner charm as a woman." Pia turned to smile at Ikuto and put her carving down. With such a body like Cammie's, she could entice any man she wanted with ease. "Oh? Could it be that you're turned on by her? After all, you just love women, don't you?"

"Don't be stupid. That woman's violent, there's nothing charming about her."

"Huh?" Pia said, her smile widening. "I never said anything about her being charming. You added that part in."

Ikuto coughed and cleared his throat again. He hadn't come here to be made fun of. "Whatever, are you going to give her better clothes to wear or not?"

"No. I want to see his face when he witnesses the humiliation we put his woman through." Pia giggled at the thought. It was so much fun to bring down another Life-Kill to her level of misery. She wanted Dark to be consumed by hate until he had nothing left to give or take.

"I've never seen you like this before."

"Like what?"

"Acting out of place or wanting someone this badly, he must've really caught your eye."

"He did indeed." Pia nodded and smiled. "He almost reminds me of Heita-kun."

"Your childhood boyfriend you keep mentioning?"

"Heita-kun isn't my boyfriend. Besides, he's dead to me." Pia's expression hardened, and she shooed him out, returning to her carving. She hated reminiscing on the past, only if it served the situation. And right now, it was useless. "Tell Rastus to go with you to greet our guest. He should be here soon. In the meanwhile, I'll fix his sweetheart up real nice."

Ikuto shook his head but obediently followed her orders. Dark would be arriving soon, since they'd given him the address of their location behind the wooden doll's back.

∞

Sylvester awoke in a jolt, reaching a hand out to the ceiling. "Misaki!" he called out. In his dream, she'd been taken away by a beautiful demon with white hair. The fact that Sylvester couldn't protect her lingered painfully. If he never wanted to lose her again, he'd have to get stronger.

Verse blinked from where she sat while peeling an orange and threw a piece into her mouth to chew. Sylvester was so lost in thought he didn't care about his surroundings. "Is that supposed to be the first person you call out to when you wake up?"

Flinching and jolting upright, Sylvester cursed while breathing heavily.

"If so, then I guess I should try it too." Verse finished chewing and closed her eyes, not caring that she'd scared him half to death.

"What are you-"

"Naruyuki!" Verse shouted, flinging her eyes open and reaching out to the empty air.

Sylvester jumped at her abrupt shouting. Again, he'd gotten scared. "Would you stop that?!"

"What the hell?" asked Hei as he entered the room with the other guys. They had gone out to grab some food, leaving Verse to guard Sylvester. That was turning out to be a huge mistake.

"Hmm," said Verse, "it's not working for me." She shook her head and went back to eating her orange. Maybe her theory was flawed. But that couldn't be it. "I might have to try a different name."

"What the hell is going on here?" Hei demanded to Sylvester.

"Not even I know," he answered.

"So, who was this attacker? Why'd he take Misaki for?" asked Hei as he sat down. One by one the others sat along with him, distributing the food they'd bought. They waited, not caring to let him fully recover before beginning their questioning.

"Well, good morning to you too," Sylvester said sarcastically before smiling at the others. "It's good to see you guys again."

"Yeah, if these two hadn't found us, we wouldn't have made it."

"So?" Hei interrupted, being a real mood killer.

"Never seen him before. But he was freakishly strong."

"We already told Hei that," said one of the guys.

"If he wanted our territory, all he had to do was kill Misaki. Why take her? It doesn't make any sense," said Hei as he thought about it. "What's his real aim?"

"I don't know. But he said we took his soul mate and that he wanted her back," Sylvester said, scratching his head. Even now after waking up, he still couldn't recall kidnapping someone's wife.

Verse perked at the mentioning of soul mate and smiled. Without bothering to explain, she tossed another piece of orange into her mouth. This could turn out to be a fun game.

"What soul mate?" demanded a confused Hei.

"Like I said, I don't know."

"Hei," called out Verse.

"Hmm?" he answered while thinking.

"Come here."

Abruptly, Hei stopped thinking to raise an eyebrow. Even the other guys were giving Verse suspicious looks. "Why?" he demanded, thinking she might pull a prank of some sort.

"Just come over here."

"Tell me why first."

"Hurry up."

"Alright, alright," Hei said, standing and walking over to stand before her. She wasn't leaving him with many choices. "What-" Before he could finish his sentence, Verse grabbed his hands to put around her neck. "Oye," said Hei in alarm.

"You were aiming for Hei the entire time?!" Sylvester pointed a finger in utter disbelief. If her aim had been Hei all along, there hadn't been a need to create a misunderstanding with Misaki.

"What are you doing?!" shouted the others. She was making it look like Hei was trying to strangle her. All the while, Hei stared at Verse suspiciously. So, she was plotting something after all.

"Sorry," Verse apologized and pushed him away. An arrow shot through the window, past the two, as it struck the wall opposite them.

"Shit!" shouted the guys as they took out their weapons. "Who the hell shot that?!"

Unsure of what was going on, Hei stood from the floor and cautiously made his way over to the broken window. Standing on the opposite building with a bow in his hand was Naruyuki. Though he was far away, Hei could feel his piercing gaze. "That must be him," he said as Naruyuki fled.

"Oye, Hei, look at this."

"What?" he asked, turning around.

The guys had taken the arrow out from within the wall. Stuck in it was a note of challenge they just finished reading. "He's requesting to make an exchange by tonight."

"And what exactly does he want in exchange for Misaki? Money?" Hei walked over to take the note away. Halfway through it, he stopped and raised an eyebrow. Soon, all eyes were on Verse. "*You?*"

"That guy's kind of hard to understand, huh? For now, let's just abide by his rules," she said, enjoying the turn of events so far.

"We can't," said the guys. "You've done so much for us."

"Then, do you want Misaki-san to get hurt?" Verse redirected, silencing them. "Since you guys are so hopeless in getting your precious missy back, I'll help with the exchange."

"Is it just me, or are you actually turning this into a game?" Sylvester suspected.

"Oh, whatever do you mean?" she asked and laughed.

"You really are," he concluded.

"Well then, let's go find some ropes so you guys can tie me with." Verse smiled and finished the rest of her orange. The guys glanced at one another. Their eyebrows raised at Verse's outrageous suggestion.

"Oye," Hei said, frowning. "Are you a masochist?"

Verse simply laughed while the guys fell over in disbelief. Was that really all he could think of? "I really hate pain. Now shut up and let's go."

"A sadist pretending to be a masochist it is."

∞

"It just feels weird if we're not together, you know?" Dark spoke from somewhere in the shadows.

"Dark?" Cammie called out hoarsely while tied on the floor, aching all over. The place she was lying in was dark and murky. It made her shiver. "Dark?" she called out a little louder this time.

"Even if time is cruel and we break apart, let's always remember each other." He reached out his hands to cup Cammie's face. Light flooded in as she blinked a few times to adjust her vision. Kneeling before her was Dark. He sweated from the running and had a soft warm smile on his face. Even his hands were hot and sweaty. "I found you," he whispered.

Hot tears streamed down Cammie's face as she stared at him. An unexpected warmth overflowed her heart. This wasn't the reaction she had been expecting upon seeing his face. She didn't like Dark in any way possible, not even as a friend, or rival. In fact, she detested him. So why cry?

Dark chuckled, wiping her tears. "Why are you crying for…?"

"Wake up," instructed Pia as she threw cold water against Cammie's face.

She awoke, gasping for air and noticed her eyes were blindfolded, disallowing her to see her surroundings.

"Finally."

"You…from the family restaurant." Though she couldn't see, she could recognize Pia's voice anywhere. Rage flared as Cammie struggled against the ropes. "Where am I? Why'd you kidnap me for?"

"You're in my lair," Pia said, answering only her first question. She pulled a chair to sit opposite of Cammie and smiled. "Say, don't you feel cold?"

Cammie sat and pondered on the question before realizing that whatever clothing she had on, was thin, because she could feel the chill from the AC. Then, it hit her. She never had the chance to slip on any clothes or a bathrobe. Before she could finish draping the towel around herself, someone gagged her from behind. Embarrassment took place of her rage. "What the hell are you making me wear?!"

"Oh my, you finally realize how indecent you are right now." Pia giggled and put a hand to her mouth.

"Change me, now!"

"Why? I see no reason. You look very seductive." Glancing over Cammie's curves with an approving nod, she gasped. "Oh my, could it be that you're conscious of what your Soulmate might think when he sees you dressed like this?"

"Shut up."

"What you should really worry about is when another man lays eyes on you and takes you without your consent."

Anger returning, Cammie clenched her fists that were bound behind. "When I get free, I'm going to make you pay."

"Even if you did, you couldn't possibly defeat me." Pia stood and leaned forward, inches away from Cammie's face. In a raspy voice, she spoke again, "by the way, what kind of nightmare were you having just now? You were desperately calling out to your Soulmate."

Cammie grew silent as she sat on her chair, motionless.

Pia smirked, though Cammie couldn't see, then headed for the door that slid open. "Excuse me while I go greet him first." She stepped out, letting Ikuto enter.

"Pia-" he began.

"Gotta go," she said, winking and walking away briskly. "Can't make our honored guest wait too long."

Shaking his head, Ikuto turned to look at Cammie. He gulped, feeling the heat in his cheeks rise again. Shoving his attraction towards her down the drain, he approached her. No matter how tempting she looked, he had to restrain himself. "Let's go greet your boyfriend."

"He's not my boyfriend," she denied and hung her head down low as strands of hair fell to either side. She felt like disappearing inside a hole.

"Doesn't matter, we gotta go." When Ikuto finished untying her, he took off his jacket to drape around her.

"What are you doing?" Cammie asked in alarm when she felt the warm jacket go around her shoulders.

"It's cold, isn't it?"

Cammie smiled and nodded, grateful. "Thank you."

"Don't. You're the enemy. I just feel bad watching Pia force you to wear something like this against your will." Ikuto put cuffs around her wrists before pushing her to start walking. He reached for his gun and turned the safety off. Even though the drugs were still in effect, he couldn't take the chances, knowing what she was.

∞

The sun hung high in the afternoon sky as the temperature steadily rose. Lost in thought, Verse gazed outside from her chair. In six hours, the exchange with Naruyuki would take place. The guys had left to buy some last-minute items while Sylvester stayed behind to recuperate. He sat in bed, reading a magazine. Every now and then his eyes would drift to Verse's lonely figure by the windowsill. With a huff, Sylvester set his magazine down and cleared his throat, waiting for Verse to answer. Not once did she turn to look.

Scowling, Sylvester got out of bed and limped over to her side. Even then, she didn't seem to notice his presence as he took a glance outside also. There wasn't much to see, yet Verse was intensely staring at the skyline.

Sylvester cursed under his breath at how little his meaning of existence was, then finally spoke, breaking in through her thoughts. "What are you looking so depressed about?"

"Huh?" Verse blinked, turning to look at him. "Sylvester," she said, "what are you doing out of bed?"

"I'm bored," he answered, crossing his arms. "So?" he urged. "What are you looking so depressed about?"

Verse smiled and turned to look outside again. "Trying to see if I can find a heart."

"Huh?"

Verse touched the warm pane with her fingertips, but it felt like ice. "I feel so far away from him, yet so near. It's confusing."

"It sure is," he agreed with a nod and parted the curtains some more. The heat from the broken window made him shrink back where it was cooler from the AC. "So, who's this person you're talking about?" Sylvester glanced down at her and opened his mouth to say something but decided against it. He didn't want to be nosy.

"I don't know. I wish I could give you a name," she finally answered and averted her gaze from the window to her callused hands, a result of her training days at the Dome. It suddenly made her feel self-conscious. What if he hated how rough her hands were when they met again? It made Verse blush. Hands were hands. What did it matter if someone's hands were soft or rough? That didn't determine a person's value. But deep down, she wondered how to make her hands soft again.

Sylvester stared at Verse, long and hard. So, it wasn't Hei she was after either. Neither was it Sylvester himself. It made him feel dejected. He thought he'd graduated from being an Average Joe to becoming the new woman magnet, outdoing Hei. He should've known better than to get his hopes up. "Oye," said Sylvester. "Why do you look so sad thinking about him? Shouldn't you be happy instead?"

"Am I really sad?" Verse looked up, doing her best to smile.

Eyes widening, Sylvester watched as tears trailed down her cheeks. "Why are you...crying?"

Verse touched her wet cheeks, not understanding the reason either. There was nothing to feel sad about, yet her heartbeat quickened. Slowly, the pain came. At first it didn't feel like much, until it became piercing. "Why?"

"How would I know?" redirected Sylvester. He limped over to the tissue box and returned to her side, holding it out in offering.

Not caring for the tissue box, Verse placed a hand over her chest. She bent over, tears hitting her lap. This unexplainable pain, it'd stolen and hidden a part of herself somewhere in the world.

"Don't you dare faint on me again. This time, I really won't know what to do," warned Sylvester as he knelt, trying to cheer her up. No matter what jokes he told or how many funny faces he made, Verse continued crying. "Damn it," Sylvester said, running a hand through his hair. "Hei, get your ass back here."

♫*Hum, hum, stay where you are*
I will spread my wings over you, protecting you
I will stay forever with you in this sky
Believe in this promise I make to you, hum, hum♫

At the sound of the melody, Verse's tears quickly ceased. She lowered her hand from her aching chest and lifted her head slightly to look out the window again. A dove's feather fell from the sky, gracefully floating by the window. The voice had penetrated through Verse's sadness, washing it away. Now, she no longer felt a need to cry. The pain had even been alleviated from a simple verse.

Noticing, Sylvester inspected her. She had abruptly stopped crying for no apparent reason. Now, she was staring out the window again. "What's wrong now?" Sylvester worriedly glanced out the window, then back to her.

Verse smiled. "What a soothing melody."

"What...melody?" Sylvester looked about the room. He couldn't hear a song being played. Neither could he hear anyone singing, outside the window, or in the hallway. Whatever Verse was hearing it was something he couldn't hear, and so, he gulped. "Don't tell me she can see and hear ghosts."

∞

♫*...Take my hand, never let go*
I will always be with you
Believe in this promise I make to you, hum, hum♫

The door to the Maroon Boys' Academy rooftop opened as Mr. Fujiwara stepped out and stopped. Taiyou was sitting on the ledge, singing again. Mr. Fujiwara smiled and shook his head. From all the boys, Taiyou and Dark were the ones who loved singing the most, other than *him*. "What are you doing up here, Taiyou? It's time to go."

Stopping, Taiyou spun around, his yellow spiky hair swaying in the gentle breeze. One look at his teacher and he smiled like the sun, just like his name.

"Come, the other two are waiting."

"Yeah," he said, getting off the ledge to follow Mr. Fujiwara inside. Once they reached the landing of the staircase and was nearing the exit, Mr. Fujiwara turned to glance at Taiyou, wondering about the song.

"Isn't that the same melody you used to hum when you were younger?"

Taiyou looked over with a sly smile. "It is."

Mr. Fujiwara couldn't help but smile in return. From all the boys, Taiyou was the secretive daydreamer. "But there used to be no lyrics. When did you create lyrics?"

"I didn't need to create it. It's always been there."

Shocked, Mr. Fujiwara could only blink.

Laughing, Taiyou took off down the hallway first. "I'll be taking my leave now, sensei!" he shouted, excited about leaving the Dome with the other two guys. Finally, they were going to follow the others out into the real world. And if he did well on his missions with the two, maybe, just maybe he might get to meet *her*.

12th Lie

VERSE WAS BOUND by ropes and gagged by the time the exchange was to take place. What was left was to blindfold her. She stared at the guys who stood before her, smiling proudly at their handiwork. Satisfied also, she nodded.

"Alright then, let's go," said Sylvester.

"Let's!" shouted the rest of the guys as they clambered inside the car. Meanwhile, Hei picked her up and threw her into the trunk. "Why am I getting such an uneasy feeling about this?" he asked, climbing into the passenger seat. The entire ride to the secluded plain was in silence, each of them anticipating the meet with Naruyuki, who had single-handedly taken them out. In order to regain their honor, they needed to defeat him.

After a good hour, they reached their destination and got out. The sun was starting to set as it painted the sky an orange-pink. Just over the hill was where they'd meet with Naruyuki and Misaki.

Hei opened the trunk as Verse blinked a few times. "Forgive me," he said, blindfolding and throwing her inside a brown sack. Once he secured the string, he turned to face the team. They each nodded, ready to get this over with. "Let's go."

Leading the way was the group of guys, while Hei dragged Verse from the middle. Last in line was Sylvester who kept an eye out in case they were walking straight into an ambush. Hei dragged Verse down the hill and accidentally ran her into a fist-sized rock. She grunted as Hei and Sylvester exchanged worried glances.

"Sorry," apologized Hei.

Verse responded by shuffling and muffling. Unsure of what it meant, the guys quivered, knowing it wasn't good. Once she got out, she would surely skin him alive for running her over a rock.

"There he is!" one of the guys shouted and pointed. They came to a complete halt to stare at Naruyuki who stood beside a tree, arms crossed against his chest. Meanwhile, Misaki hung from the tree, wrists and ankles bound together.

"Misaki!" Sylvester frantically leapt forward as Hei pulled him back.

"Sylvester, Hei, guys!" shouted Misaki while she dangled in midair, tears in her eyes. It was good to see them again. At least she knew that they hadn't abandoned her.

"Don't worry, Misaki! We'll get you down!"

"Yeah," she answered and nodded, never doubting his words. Once they got her down, they could return home together.

"Where's Verse?" demanded Naruyuki.

The guys gulped, knowing exactly why he was angry for.

"Crap," Hei hissed under his breath.

"What?" Sylvester whispered in response.

"Look at how nicely he's treating Misaki. He didn't gag or blindfold her. Now look at us, we gagged Verse, blindfolded her, and even threw her inside a sack. To make matters worse, we *dragged* her."

"O—oye, why do you sound so scared?" Sylvester asked, avoiding Naruyuki's intimidating glare. This exchange was already spelling trouble.

"Where's Verse?" Naruyuki repeated, uncrossing his arms.

"In—inside here," answered Hei as he pointed to the huge brown sack.

Dumbfounded, Naruyuki stared at the sack that Hei had been dragging. He'd been hoping that inside were weapons. Now that he knew his Soulmate was trapped within, a killer aura beyond recognition emitted around him. "You bastards," he hissed as the guys backed away. "I treat your princess here nicely and you treat my Soulmate so cruelly. She's not a sack of potatoes!" Grinning, Naruyuki cracked his knuckles. "I'll make you pay."

"His idea," Hei blamed and pointed to Sylvester.

"What?!" Sylvester shouted, glaring at Hei who shimmied away. "What are you-" He never saw Naruyuki's fist coming as his body flew off the ground before smacking the earth. Dizzy, Sylvester attempted to stand but fell back down, his lip bleeding. When he noticed a shadow falling over him, he looked up to find Naruyuki there. *He's gotten faster. Is that even possible?*

"That's gotta hurt," said Hei.

"Sylvester!" screamed Misaki.

"You have a lot of guts to suggest throwing Verse inside a sack," hissed Naruyuki.

"I—I didn't suggest anything. It was all Verse's id-" Before Sylvester could finish his sentence, Naruyuki hit him again. He didn't even get the chance to clear his name of any wrongdoing. "Crap. I'm not even healed yet." Sylvester forced his body upright as the guys came running to save him from Naruyuki's onslaught.

"You guys again. I thought I killed you."

"Well, we're pretty much alive!"

While Naruyuki was preoccupied with the guys, Hei withdrew his sword to deliver a surprise attack. Swiftly, he dodged, completely disregarding the others to turn his full attention on Hei.

"You're quick," Hei complimented with a smile.

"You," Naruyuki growled. "You were the one trying to strangle Verse."

"Eh?"

Naruyuki grinned again, popping his knuckles once more. "I never forget a face once I've seen it."

"Eh?"

"Don't play dumb with me. I saw you. You were trying to strangle her. If I hadn't shot that arrow on time, you'd have killed her."

"Eh?!" Hei shouted. Now that he was rerunning everything in his brain a second time, it all made so much sense. His eyes bulged from their sockets. Sylvester had been right. Verse was making a game out of their misery and she was enjoying every second of it. Now, Hei was going to pay the price for a simple misunderstanding.

"We've fallen into her trap!" Hei turned, glaring at the brown sack where Verse was still imprisoned. He could imagine her sneering from inside.

"Don't avert your eyes from me." Naruyuki ran at Hei and threw his fist. Dodging on time, Hei put his sword in-between them.

"This guy isn't letting me off the hook."

Naruyuki popped his neck and smiled. "It's been a while since I've last fought someone strong. This'll be fun, especially since you're a human too."

"Huh? Human? Aren't you one too?"

"If I told you the truth, it'd ruin the fun."

"Is that so?" Hei asked, uninterested. "So, who was the first person you fought that you considered to be strong?"

"Rain, Shadow, Kei, Yuudai, and Hotaka," answered Naruyuki.

"Who're they?"

"I don't expect you to know." Naruyuki looked away from him and over at the sack, rethinking Hei's question. Of course, Verse's name was included in that short list. Naruyuki had never dueled a Life-Kill like her before.

This time, it was Hei who went on the offense. As soon as he sliced the air where Naruyuki stood, rose petals burst from out of nowhere. "What the—where'd these petals come from? Is he a magician?"

"Careful, Hei! That's how he defeated us!" warned one of the guys.

"How do you like my flowers?" Naruyuki asked, standing not far away, a rose in his hand, almost as if posing for a photo shoot.

Hei raised an eyebrow and sweat a bit. The words that were about to come out of his mouth was going to infuriate Naruyuki. But he did ask, so Hei was going to answer truthfully. "Eh, well," he said, scratching his head. "Flowers aren't very…masculine for being a weapon of choice."

"Are you insulting my flowers?"

"You asked. I answered." Laughing it off, Hei smiled sheepishly. No excuse was going to get him out of the hell hole he'd dug himself into.

"I'll show you the full extent of my flowers."

"Then bring it," challenged Hei as the two ran at each other.

"Those guys are putting on quite a show." Awed by the fight that felt like something straight out from a video game, Misaki forgot about the fact that she'd been kidnapped and needed to be rescued.

Meanwhile, Verse who was still confined was getting deoxygenized.

∞

Standing in the center of the glass room was Dark and Rastus who were having a staring contest. Nothing could be seen through the glasses as Pia entered with a smile. As soon as Dark spotted her, he marched over, but Rastus stopped him with his sheathed sword.

"Move," snarled Dark.

Before Rastus could attempt to withdraw his sword, Pia gave orders to stand down as Dark whisked away.

"Good even-" she greeted but never finished as Dark smacked her as hard as he could across the face.

Rastus' eyes widened at what he'd just allowed to happen. Within a flash he was at the two's side, sword placed against Dark's throat. "You," hissed Rastus from behind his black mask.

Calmly, Dark stood, eyeing Pia without the slightest hint of blinking or flinching. She'd crossed the line when she kidnapped Cammie from under his nose. Rastus' sword dug into his skin as blood trickled down his throat. Even so, he didn't bother to retaliate or move.

Pia's heart beat so rapidly, she erupted in a hysterical laugh. In the entirety of her life, not once had anyone dared to lay a hand on her, for fear of the consequences. And if they had succeeded, she spared none. Some couldn't even come near her before being struck down. Dark was the first to not care about the consequences, or the fact that his life hung by a thread when he entered their hideout.

Worried, Rastus gave her a side-glance. "Pia."

"That was so much fun! I haven't had that much fun in a long time!"

"Pia."

She hung her head down low, her happy chuckle ceasing. Whatever the cost, Pia had to have him. He was everything she wanted and more. Flicking her black hair from her face, she gave him a lazy smile. "It's been a while since I've been so enticed by anyone. And you, Soulmate-san, have managed to stir my soul. That's why, won't you become mine?"

Not bothering to respond, Dark allowed his black irises to burn into the core of her soul.

"Rastus, withdraw," she ordered.

"But-"

"Withdraw."

Obediently, Rastus backed down and put his sword away, but never took his eyes off Dark. Pia inched closer to run her fingers through Dark's silky black hair. All the while he stared, standing his ground while she tiptoed and smiled, closing her face in on his. With the tips of her fingers, she traced the outline of his cheek and jaw. They were cold to the touch.

"Are you done playing? Give back Cammie," demanded Dark.

Pia shook her head, unable to comply. She ran her hand down Dark's arms, temptingly but he didn't give in to her charms. "I can feel every muscle in your arm."

"Where's Cammie? If you don't tell me, I'll kill you where you stand."

"Would you really?"

"Don't test me."

"Then I should."

"Where is she?"

"Really, can't you stop thinking about her for a second?"

"No."

"Don't make me jealous. I kill when I become jealous."

Dark peered into her acute eyes. She meant every word. He'd have to be careful, especially since he didn't know Cammie's whereabouts. "Why are you aiming for me? We don't even know each other."

"What kind of question is that? We may have been strangers, but now, we're acquaintances. Besides, if you think about it, the answer is quite simple."

"How so?"

"Because I'm better suited for you than that Cammie of yours, who's only eye candy," Pia whispered, planting a soft kiss on his chin. "You should let her go, before this pain ends up killing you both."

∞

A fierce gust of wind swept up from out of nowhere as Hei and the guys panted for air. Their duel with Naruyuki lingered with neither side willing to give up until the other fell first.

Misaki let out a shriek while swinging violently from the tree. The branches swayed and leaves fell. Though they were some good ways away, the gust still reached where she hung.

"Misaki," remembered Sylvester.

"Go," Hei instructed, turning to duel Naruyuki one-on-one.

When Sylvester and the guys reached Misaki, they attempted to cut her down from the tree.

"He got him!" shouted one of the guys as the rest turned their attentions back to the fight behind. Again, they forgot about Misaki and proudly high-five at Hei's achievement. This battle wasn't a lost cause after all.

Blood trickled down Naruyuki's forearm and blotched the ground as a storm of petals surrounded him. This was what he got for playing around. "You're good," he complimented from behind his storm of petals. When it dispersed and floated away Naruyuki stepped out from within, completely healed. There was no scar, no evidence of him ever being injured.

"What the-" gasped Hei. No ordinary human was capable of self-heal. Only Life-Kills could accomplish such a feat. After coming to that realization, Hei scowled. Now it made sense how the group and Sylvester had lost to Naruyuki. It also explained why he wanted to retrieve Verse, whose hand-to-hand combat was unrivaled. The pieces were all there, but he'd neglected to see it. "Shit," he cursed.

"Life-Kill," gasped the guys. Their assumption of Naruyuki wanting to be some wannabe magician with his flower act was completely wrong. They'd been fighting a Life-Kill who was toying with them.

"While I had fun, playtime's over," said Naruyuki.

Knowing that he wouldn't win, Hei clutched tightly to his hilt. "Let's," he agreed as they ran at each other.

"Too slow!" shouted Naruyuki as he spun around to counter Hei's surprise attack. Suddenly, his vision blurred and he missed his chance. Instead, it was Hei who delivered the blow as Naruyuki fell, bleeding again.

What the hell happened to him just now? Hei backed away quickly. Naruyuki should've been able to parry, but didn't.

"What just happened?" Sylvester asked while the guys cheered Hei on without realizing that something suspicious had just occurred.

"Shit," said Naruyuki who breathed hard. The air surrounding him felt compressed as his chest tightened.

"Oye," called out Hei.

Through dazed eyes, Naruyuki looked up to find Hei approaching worriedly, but cautiously. He even lowered his sword in hand. Somewhere inside, something sparked as Naruyuki's adrenaline kicked into high gear. It was his first time feeling such a rush, and he liked it. Naruyuki grinned as his eye color changed to yellow. He dashed forward, suddenly changing into a wild animal.

"Those eyes," whispered Misaki. All the blood flowing in her veins seemed to freeze. She had heard about Life-Kills going into Berserk Mode from her father, but never seen it in real life until then. With Naruyuki losing control of himself and his powers, none of them would survive. "Run, Hei!"

"What the-" Hei backed away and brought up his sword to defend as Naruyuki disappeared before his eyes.

"Behind!" shouted the guys and Sylvester.

"Eh?" Hei swung around to counter but was too late. Naruyuki got one hand on him, as fear struck his core. So, this was how it felt to greet death.

"Are you trying to kill him?" Verse intervened and reached out to break Naruyuki's grip on Hei. "Naru-" she began and stopped when she looked into his hateful eyes. A pink aura emitted from her hand and Naruyuki's forearm where they made skin contact. Without wasting time, she let go and hit him away, gasping for air. He'd been trying to steal her energy.

Standing, Hei caught the light-headed Verse before she could fall. "You okay?" he asked.

"I'm fine." Verse pushed herself off him to stand on her own.

"When and how did she get out of the sack?" asked the guys as they glanced at the empty sack and loose ropes. They had tied her up well. Her getting free on her own was a mystery. Not to mention, they'd been too engulfed in the fight to remember that she was still inside the sack, same with the hanging Misaki.

Dazed, Naruyuki sat up on the grass, shaking his head. Even after stealing a bit of Verse's energy, it still wasn't enough. But now that he was no longer Berserk, he could heal normally. "What happened?" he asked and glanced up to find Verse there, arms crossed with a pissed look. "Verse," he gasped.

"Are you sane now?" she asked.

"What?"

"You idiot," she snapped. "You just went into Berserk Mode!"

While receiving an earful, Naruyuki continued gazing. She could smack him, dice him up, and burn him into ashes all she wanted, so long as he got to see her again. He sniffled and smiled, tearing up now. "I'm so happy."

"Huh?"

"I'm so happy you're okay!" Naruyuki stood and ran over, throwing her into a bear hug so he could snuggle. "You're okay, you're okay!"

"Why wouldn't I be? Now, let me go." Verse pushed him away but he held on tightly. It was impossible to get him off.

"I thought they killed you when I saw the sack."

"You really think those fools can actually hurt me?"

"You never know."

"Why are you so emo today?"

"Because-"

"Let go," demanded Verse. "Now."

"Okay." Naruyuki let out another sniffle and let go as ordered. He didn't want her to suddenly disappear on him again.

Misaki gaped, amazed at Naruyuki's sudden change in personality. She didn't think such a vicious guy like him could have such a cute side as well. "No-no. No matter how I look at it, it's impossible."

"Guys, help me get Misaki down," Sylvester reminded his comrades.

"Right," they said, giving a hand.

"Don't even think it." Naruyuki was over within a flash, standing in their way, arms haughtily crossed. If they wanted to rescue their princess, they'd have to get through the big bad dragon first.

"Move out of the way so they can get her down," instructed Verse as she walked over to drag him away by the ear. The game had been enjoyable, but now it was officially over.

"Ow, ow."

"She's all yours," Verse said to the guys.

"Thanks," they said as Sylvester cut Misaki down into their arms.

"Sylvester," she said in relief and hugged him once she was on her own two feet. "I was so scared."

"It's okay. I'm here now."

"Well, all's well that ends well," Hei said, sheathing his sword and walking over to join them.

"I still got a score to settle with you," growled Naruyuki. If he hadn't been fooling around wasting energy, he would've won. No doubt about it. "You got lucky I didn't use my special finishing move."

"What special finishing move?" everyone asked except Verse.

"You're the enemy, why would I tell you its name?"

"Stingy," said Hei and Sylvester.

"Shut up."

"So?" Hei directed at Verse. "You promised to tell us the real reason behind all this once we did the exchange."

"Yeah, about that," Verse remembered, smiling from ear to ear. "This guy here is Naruyuki. He's my Soulmate. We're traveling companions," she introduced and pointed to Naruyuki.

"She knows him?!" shouted the guys who never expected that. In the end, she really was the enemy.

"Are you guys serious?" Sylvester said with a sigh.

"We had no idea."

"I had a gut feeling she knew him," spoke Hei.

"Well, now that Misaki-san is in good hands, we'll leave," said Verse as she pushed Naruyuki to go. Night would fall soon, and she was getting tired and hungry.

"What are you doing? We're supposed to finish them off," reminded Naruyuki who was correct. Their mission was to destroy the Shizomiya family and anyone associated with them. If they were to resist, the couple was to use force.

"Not today," answered Verse. "Besides, the head of Shizomiya has already been eliminated. There's no real emanate threat anymore."

Naruyuki opened his mouth to argue. It didn't feel right to not finish their mission when their targets were standing before them. Besides, he had never gone against orders before and didn't want to receive an earful from the deans. But no words came out from his parted lips.

"If you wanna stay and finish the mission, be my guest. I'm returning first to grab something to eat."

Frustrated by the ultimatum she'd given him, Naruyuki gave chase, not wanting to be left behind again. It was unfair that she'd make him choose, when she knew his answer.

"Oye," Misaki called out as Verse and Naruyuki both turned back. "How dare you make a fool of me? You knew this would happen, yet still let it continue like it was nothing."

"It was just to pass time," replied Verse.

"Demon," she concluded.

"Well, until we meet again."

"I thought you were supposed to cuff us?"

Smiling, Verse shook her head and chuckled. There was no need to kill someone who had provided her with some sort of entertainment in such a boring situation. "You guys put on a good show for me so I won't cuff you. But the next time we meet, I won't be so lenient."

"You really are weird."

"Just…" began Verse as she turned away, suddenly sad. "Prepare a fine funeral for your father." She waved a hand and walked away.

From behind, the group stood, watching as the couple left.

"If she'd explain everything from the beginning, we'd have resolved the issue in a more civilized manner without resorting to violence," said Hei.

"She was testing him."

"Huh? What does that mean?"

A calming breeze passed as Misaki smiled. For the rest of her life, she would remember the debt she owed Verse. Because they had been let off the hook, Misaki could return to give her father a proper burial. A tear trickled as she wiped it away. "Let's return home."

∞

The grassy plain stretched on for miles as did the dusky sky above. Soon, they would be completely engulfed in darkness, limiting their vision. But Naruyuki didn't mind if he were to get lost along these dark paths with Verse. As they walked side by side, neither one bothered to exchange pleasantries.

"Why'd you let them go?" he finally asked, breaking the heavy silence.

Verse shrugged and smiled. She didn't feel like explaining herself, so she kept quiet and stared straight ahead.

Unsure of what else to say to keep Verse talking, Naruyuki scratched his head. She'd been silent for far too long. Did their separation for 24 hours really have no effect on her whatsoever? Had she gotten caught on purpose to get away from him? Just the thought of that pinched his chest. Since when did Verse's existence become as important as the air he breathed? If he didn't find a way out soon, he'd be entrapped for the rest of his life. But even something like being her prisoner, he didn't mind.

"That guy, he's strong," said Naruyuki as he changed topics, hoping to get a reaction out of her.

"Hei," corrected Verse.

Not expecting a response, Naruyuki looked over, eyes wide open. Instead of being happy about her finally talking, he felt irritable and ignored her correction. "That guy, he's fast too."

"Hei."

"That guy has talent, despite being a regular human."

"Hei."

Having heard enough, Naruyuki turned to glare at her. She was repeating Hei's name like a broken record. He got in her way, erupting now. "Why do you keep saying that guy's name?!"

"It's because you keep calling him 'that guy' so I was correcting you," answered Verse as she pinched his cheeks. She didn't understand the reason for his anger and it pissed her off. How could he start an argument with her after reuniting?

"Ow, ow, I get the point."

"Sheesh," said Verse as she let go and walked on ahead.

Naruyuki massaged his cheek and smiled. From the corner of his eye, he spotted the first star in the sky. His smile faded, but eventually returned. Wanting to capture the twinkling mystery, he reached a hand up.

"Naruyuki," called out Verse as she glanced back.

"Huh?" he answered without turning to look at her.

Verse studied his profile long and hard, the light in her eyes dimming. He looked like he had been spirited away. The pang in her heart caused her to gasp as she quickly nullified it. "Nothing."

"What is it?" Naruyuki asked, chasing her to nudge gently. "Tell me."

"Why'd you come after me?"

Bewildered, Naruyuki stopped in his tracks. "What kind of question is that? You're my Soulmate. I have to protect you. It's my duty and pride. No matter how far you are from me, I'll find my way there."

He spoke the words with so much confidence Verse couldn't help but smile. But the moment she gazed into his eyes, her joy faded as fast as it had come. Again, he looked lost, and she knew the reason all too well. "You should save those words for Umeko."

Unable to respond, Naruyuki just laughed and shook his head in denial.

"I can see it in your eyes. You were thinking about her again."

There was a twinge in his chest. But he shoved the ache away, not wanting to admit that he'd indeed been thinking about Umeko when he spotted the first star. "I wasn't," he lied, hoping it was the truth.

"Lie."

"I'm not lying."

They stared at each other for some time before Verse broke her gaze, hoping not to start another controversy. And so, she switched topics, "So, what was the name of your special move that you refused to tell the others?"

Naruyuki noticed, but let it slide. He too didn't want to start an argument. Besides, Verse had gone out of her way to change the subject, he would go along with her. "You really want to know?" he asked with a smile.

"Yes."

"You really, *really* want to know?"

"Not really, I was just being nice by asking."

Naruyuki glared away. "Well, too bad, I'm gonna tell you anyway. It's called, Fiery Sunset of a Dragon's Breath from Beautiful Roses, an Instant Death Kill."

"That's such a freakishly long name. There's no way you can say it all before the enemy lands an attack on you. It also doesn't make sense."

"Not true, I've shortened it to, FiSuDraBreaBeRo Instant Death Kill from the East of Maroon Dome, NaYu." After saying all that, Naruyuki struck a pose with two roses. The first was in his hand, the other, he had bitten by the stem.

Verse twitched, fed up with his ridiculousness. Not only was Naruyuki's attack name foolish, but also the pose. None of it was necessary. He was asking to get killed in combat if he were to attempt such nonsense. "That's even longer than the first one! And it still doesn't make any sense!"

"Yes, it does!" he defended. "It's really unique and genius!"

"My goodness," groaned Verse. She shook her head, blowing steam. In the end, she laughed at his foolish attempt to lighten the mood. "But I guess, that's just like you, huh? Even back at the Dome you were quite foolish."

Thinking that his eyes were playing tricks on him, Naruyuki turned away and rubbed his eyes. When he glanced back, Verse was still laughing. For the first time since they left the others, she was laughing genuinely. His heart leapt at the sight of her twinkling eyes and he too burst into laughter. What a sweet feeling this was. "You finally laughed."

"Huh?" Verse said, her laughter fading.

Naruyuki too stopped, putting a hand on top of her head, his expression softening. "The entire time you were with me, you always looked so sad and wary like you hated being with me. It was painful, knowing I couldn't bring you joy. Now that you're smiling, I don't mind acting like a fool if it means keeping you happy."

Verse rested her forehead against his chest, causing him to hold his breath. His words held so much tenderness and didn't feel forced whatsoever. "Naruyuki," she whispered as the wind blew.

"What is it?"

"What kind of corny dialogue is that? We're not in some love drama," she joked, lightly jabbing him to lead the way. "I'm getting hungry. Let's hurry back to town."

Naruyuki watched as she tilted her face to the starry sky. He could picture her smiling. Glad that he was the cause, Naruyuki chased her. Wanting to cherish that precious smile, he'd vowed never to lose her.

∞

Cammie was once again strapped to a chair, inside a different room that Ikuto had led her to. After injecting her with something, he left. Her head spun as she gasped for air. Even her body burned, and she perspired, like she was coming down with the flu.

"…return her…" demanded Dark from afar.

The blindfold came off Cammie's eyes as she blinked a few times to adjust them to the light. Even then, everything was still a blur. Before her was a two-way mirror. Standing on the other side, she could make out Rastus, Pia, and Dark. At the sight of him, Cammie almost broke into tears. He had come for her.

After naturally running her hands through Dark's hair, Pia pulled away. She touched his throat where it had healed and leaned in to lick the blood that was starting to dry. Raising her head, she inched closer to Dark until they were locking lips.

Cammie's eyes widened as her brain pounded and her body quivered. It was sickening to watch the scene unfold as her blood froze in her veins. The ringing in both ears worsened. Even her heart throbbed to the point where she had to slouch over. Her tears she'd been fighting back, spilled out. Cammie tried to pull her gaze away, but it felt like someone was forcing her to look against her will. "Stop it," she pleaded.

It shouldn't matter who Dark kissed. Cammie had hated him since the day they met. The very core of her being detested his existence. So then why? Why did she hate seeing another woman kiss him?

The jealousy within ignited. She wanted to be the only one he would look at with affection.

No. She wanted to flee from the very thought of him.

She loved him.

No. She hated him to death.

But love, is it not the correct term for this pain in her heart?

No matter how Cammie tried to deny the feelings that washed over her, she cried bitterly. She just wanted this internal war to stop already. "Ah!"

At the sound of her scream, Dark pushed Pia away. With eyes that could see in the dark, he spun around, looking through every mirror until he found her tied inside a room. Cammie wore a thin see-through camisole, shivering and sweating at once. "Cammie!" shouted Dark as he attempted to run over.

"I wouldn't, if I were you." Pia pulled him back by the wrist and smiled.

"I'm through playing your games." He whisked around and glared, never having felt such hatred like this before.

Pia grinned, loving his expression. This was exactly what she had wanted and motioned to the window as Dark turned to look again. Standing behind Cammie was Ikuto. In his hand was a gun that was positioned to kill her with one bullet to the head. Now tamed, Dark's fighting spirit waned.

It was so much fun that Pia could hardly contain her excitement. "Much better," she whispered, forcing another kiss on him.

"Oye, why are you crying so much for? Is it that much of a shock?" asked Ikuto from behind. He slightly lowered his gun, but never tried to shoot or put it away. In his opinion, Cammie was overreacting to the kiss. It was nothing to get upset over. "Oye-" he began and stopped. Reflected in the mirror was Cammie's sullen face. Her eyes were filled with so much bitterness and affection, it could drive anyone insane.

"Why?" cried Cammie. "Why do you hurt me like this?!"

"What-"

The rays of light coming from the bulbs shot out, slashing everything in the room. Ikuto moved but was too slow as the threads cut him and threw him against the wall.

Dozens of light threads from the other room took form, indiscriminately attacking everything and everyone. Not caring that she'd lost control of her powers, Cammie aimed to erase Pia's existence from the earth.

When the glass to the mirror cracked, Pia pulled away from her kiss and spun around. "What-"

"Pia!" shouted Rastus as he dashed towards her.

Within seconds, the entire place went pitch black.

"Shit!" shouted Ikuto. He fumbled in the dark, feeling for his gun he'd dropped on the floor. Once his bloody hand touched the hard steel, he stood and unloaded the entire magazine in the direction of Cammie's chair. When no more bullets came out, he shimmied towards the broken window. "Pia, Rastus!" called out Ikuto as he stepped on the broken shards.

"Emergency lights, activated," announced the automated voice as the second generator kicked in.

From above, red lights came on, exposing the empty room. Ikuto spun around trying to find Dark who had also gone missing. While covering for Pia, Rastus had gotten injured.

"You two okay?"

"Oye, the emergency lights came on! What happened?!" shouted the rest of the Bat Angels as they ran into the room, weapons in hand. Once they witnessed the state of the room, they stopped. Shards lay everywhere. From above, the white fluorescent lights had been rendered useless. There were even markings left on the walls. "What happened in here?"

"I underestimated that girl." Angry, Pia glared at the open doorway that Dark had used to flee. For a moment, it almost felt like Cammie hadn't been herself when her powers went haywire. If they were to meet again, Pia had to permanently erase Cammie from the picture.

∞

Dark stuck to the dark alleys while fleeing with Cammie in his arms. Luckily, he'd gotten out of there without having to fight. Now, he had to find a safe hiding place. Without a doubt, Pia would be coming for Cammie after that incident. Returning to the hotel was out of the picture. They had to lay low until he could ascertain their safety. Not to mention, they also had a mission to carry out.

"...me," she whispered.

"What?" Dark lowered his ear to her mouth. She was mumbling incoherent words. "What are you saying?"

Weakly, she opened her eyes, her dried tears leaving marks. Dark smiled and stopped running, relieved that she was now awake. He opened his mouth to speak but Cammie was unable to make out his words as she looked past him to the billions of stars.

The crescent moon that hung in the sky looked so content. It was beside its beloved earth. There was nothing more it could ask for. Not even the sun could come in-between them. Again, tears welled in her eyes, refusing to disappear as it clouded her vision.

"Please don't leave me," she whispered as Dark stopped talking to stare. "I'm begging you. Stop hurting me when I love you so, so much." Closing her eyes now, Cammie fell into a slumber of unconsciousness. The last of her tears trickled.

Dark clutched her tightly to his beating chest, afraid to let go. He wanted to assure her even if she was asleep. "I'll never leave you. So don't ever say that again."

Whatever drug Ikuto had injected into Cammie's bloodstream was now ceasing its effects. The pounding in her brain started to lessen. When morning comes, she wouldn't remember the agony she'd been put through.

13th Lie

WHITE CLOUDS FLOATED on by as Umeko lay on the grass, humming Taiki's lullaby. It was surprisingly calming. Her opinion of him was starting to change day by day. Smiling now, she closed her eyes.

"Umeko," called out a nostalgic voice.

"What is it?" she answered and stopped humming, not giving a second thought about who this person was.

"Umeko," he called out again.

"What is it?" Umeko sat up on the grass and turned towards the voice. He was making his way towards her, his long black hair dancing in the breeze. It was impossible to make out his face.

"Umeko," he repeated and smiled.

Though she didn't know who he was, his presence felt so nostalgic it caused her to tear up. "Naru…yuki," she whispered.

"Wake up," ordered Taiki as he kicked her leg.

"Ow!" She yelped and sat up on the floor of the hotel room, holding her aching leg. After massaging it, she glared up. "What the hell was that for?!"

"Oh, I'm sorry for kicking you while you slept in the middle of the room," he said sarcastically and smiled.

"Taiki, you-" Umeko stood and pointed a finger. "What's your problem suddenly? I thought we were finally on good terms. Damn it. I knew it was too good to be true. You're always gonna remain a rival and one of the greatest people I hate."

"Yeah, yeah, I'm tired of hearing you say that. It's starting to get old. Let's hurry and go." Taiki turned, leaving the hotel room first while Umeko cursed and followed him out.

Once they were out on the sidewalk, Umeko spoke, "I could go for a strawberry ramune about now."

"Ramune?"

"Yep, summer's the best time of the year to drink ramune, don't you think?" She glanced over and smiled, showing her sparkly white teeth.

"Then, we let's go eat after our stakeout."

"Deal."

Silence settled in while Umeko cheerfully swung her arms by her side. Meanwhile, Taiki frowned, wondering how he wanted to word his concern. "Inside the hotel, you were having another nightmare."

"Nightmare?" Umeko thought about it before smiling. It was anything but a nightmare. She could still recall the calm air about the stranger who had appeared from out of nowhere. He was the only one in this world who could make her feel secure and loved. For him alone, she would travel to the ends of the universe. "It was actually a good dream," she corrected.

Taiki nodded, his frown deepening. Though he didn't want to nag, his curiosity got the best of him. "What were you dreaming about?"

"Someone."

"Who?"

"I don't know. I couldn't see his face. But one day…I'll find him."

Taiki gnashed his teeth together until his jaw ached. When he realized how uptight he was, he shook it off to relax again. After a few seconds, he finally spilled the beans, hoping Umeko would be truthful with him. "You were calling out for Naruyuki."

Umeko choked on her own saliva and laughed, shaking her head. That was the most absurd thing to say. While it was true that from the guys at Maroon she was closest to Naruyuki, they were friends, simply friends. Besides, he was Verse's Soulmate. How could Umeko dare to dream about her comrade's Soulmate? But if that were true, why did his name resound within her?

Reaching out, Taiki poked her head. He didn't like the idea of his Soulmate thinking of another man while in his presence. "You just stick to that dream guy. No one in their right mind will want you, especially Naru."

"You," she growled.

Taiki smiled, happy that his insult had done the trick. He just wanted to put this conversation behind them. Nothing good would come from this if he were to keep prying. Besides, the look on her face while thinking of Naruyuki scared him.

From around the corner, a cry erupted. "Help!"

Without exchanging any words, the couple dashed off. When they arrived at the scene, a pretty girl wearing a chef's uniform was being harassed by a group of goons. She cried, pleading for help from the passersby who carried on like they were in a different plane.

"Oye," Taiki called out as the group turned to look their way. "Leave her alone."

The leader, Mario looked them up and down before snickering. Even his cronies followed in his lead. How dare the couple try to ruin his fun? Did they not know who he was? "Don't try to play hero, kid. You don't wanna incur my wrath."

"Let her go while I'm still being nice."

"Why are we even talking?" Umeko asked, tightening her gloves around her hands. She sneered at the group who was underestimating her. "They obviously won't listen so let's just kick their asses already!" she shouted and charged to start the fun.

"Geez," Taiki complained. As usual, Umeko was rushing into things without thinking the consequences through. Following her lead, Taiki assisted in taking out the group.

One of the goons threw a punch and landed as Umeko grunted, hitting the ground. Laughing, she stood back up and wiped her bloody lip. There was a glint in her eye as the goon who hit her gulped, suddenly scared.

"You're gonna pay for that," Umeko said, hitting his Adam's apple. He choked and backed away as she advanced, kneeing him in the face. From behind, another of the goons tried to get her with a surprise hit. Having sensed him, she dodged and sent an uppercut, breaking his jaw.

When Taiki finished off the last of the group, he turned towards Mario who faltered backwards and scrambled away.

"Well, that was fun," Umeko said, clapping her hands of dust.

Taiki glanced over. She had a big grin on her face. He too smiled and shook his head. "If you love fighting so much, why don't you try rebelling against Yeve? Surely she'd give you a fight worth having."

Eyes widening, Umeko's grin faded. Her face became pale at the mentioning of Yeve while Taiki laughed at her reaction. "I'm not that desperate to greet the underworld."

"Um," spoke the maiden that the two had saved. She smiled and bowed, happy that someone had come to her rescue. "Thank you for saving me."

"No problem."

"I'm Lori. And you two?"

"I'm Umeko. This uptight guy is Taiki." Umeko pointed to Taiki and grinned again. She just couldn't waste any opportunity to tease him.

"Oye," Taiki growled.

"Um, as a thank-you gift for saving me, please come eat at my family's restaurant. It'll be on me." Before the two could respond, Lori ushered them to a tiny family restaurant to eat brunch. Once there, she explained the situation to her family who gratefully cooked up the best dishes to serve Taiki and Umeko's heroism.

"Shit, dis iz gud," Umeko said, spitting out a few crumbs. She was chowing down the free food like she was at a buffet. If Ms. Tanaka was present, she'd teach Umeko a lesson or two about mannerisms. Good thing she wasn't around any longer to discipline the girls.

Taiki and Lori both stared at Umeko, clearly disgusted but said nothing. This was to be expected of his Soulmate who didn't care about impressions. Smiling, Taiki slightly bowed his head at Lori. "She has no manners, forgive her."

"Hoo 'as non mannerz?" Umeko snapped with a mouthful of food.

"Obviously you." He brushed the crumbs away and wiped her dirty lips with a napkin. She was like a toddler who needed looking after.

Lori giggled. It was refreshing to be around Umeko who did as she pleased. "It's okay. I'm just happy that there are still good people like you out there willing to put themselves in danger to help others."

"Don't mention it." Taiki picked at his food and kept glancing out the window every now and then.

"What's wrong? Does the food not suit your palate?"

"No, that's not it." Taiki shook his head. The food was far from his worries, but his actions made him look ungrateful.

"Then you should give it a try. That's my signature dish." She pointed a finger at Taiki's plate and smiled.

"Really?"

"Yeah, my family kept saying that I had no talent in cooking. But I proved them wrong when I made that dish. It's become so popular they had no choice but to let me work in the kitchen with them." Lori laughed as Taiki joined in. Umeko on the other hand just ate away. There was no denying that there was some chemistry between Taiki and Lori.

"Well then, in that case, I have no choice but to taste your signature dish." Taiki poked a piece of chicken with his fork and ate. His eyes widened. It was a simple but succulent dish.

"How is it?" Lori asked eagerly.

"It's delicious. You're amazingly talented."

Umeko who had been quiet, raised an eyebrow. She couldn't believe that she was witnessing Taiki flirt with a girl. In the years of her knowing him, she'd always assumed that he was a Girl Hater, seeing as how he rarely interacted with the other girls at the Dome and was constantly picking fights with Umeko herself.

"The use of cilantro in the dish is superb. It complements the chicken perfectly," praised Taiki who was almost done eating.

"Thank you," Lori said proudly and blushed.

"When did you become a food critic?" joked Umeko. She finished eating and took a drink of water, then burped, not excusing herself.

"Just now," answered Taiki. "Here, you should try some too. It's good."

"Sure." Umeko reached over with her fork and poked at some meat to eat. Her eyes widened. She turned towards Lori and gave a thumbs-up for approval. The dish was on par with the Dome's.

"You like it?" Lori asked.

"It's amazing."

"Right?" agreed Taiki as he smiled.

After eating and chatting for a bit longer, the two called it a day, ready to return to their task.

"Thank you once again!" Lori shouted after them.

"Don't mention it," responded Taiki. He and Umeko waved a hand goodbye before exiting.

"That was a good meal," Umeko said, rubbing her stomach.

"It was, wasn't it?" he agreed and glanced over, wondering if she was jealous from his flirting with Lori. But as usual, Umeko was indifferent as she picked her teeth with a toothpick. Exactly how long did he have to pretend that he wasn't affected by her treatment towards him?

∞

Aomori

Fine silk linens and jeweled décor surrounded Jennifer as she sat before a vanity made of rare Redwood. She put on a matching drop diamante choker necklace and earrings made of white diamonds. A couple of weeks ago when she and King had first been brought to the mansion by the master, Jin, she nearly had a heart attack. Being a poor girl who grew up in the slums of Port McNeil, she'd never been this close to wealth or seen anything this extreme before. Although the Dome was extravagant itself, it was simple and refined. This mansion was downright wasteful in everything it did.

Jennifer stood from her vanity and adjusted her expensive gold silk dress that accentuated her curves. There was a slit to the right, exposing her leg. Her orange curls were pinned with a breathtaking flower ornament.

A knock came at the door as Jennifer turned around. The door slid open, allowing the head maid, Maria to enter. Though she was ten years older, her youthful appearance could make any college student envious. The day Jennifer was introduced to her, she almost expected to get hated on, but Maria had welcomed her with open arms. Bowing, Maria walked over to set the sakura-patterned kimono she'd been carrying at the foot of the silky king-sized bed.

"What's this for?" Jennifer asked, walking over to examine its intricate details. The moment she slid her fingertips across the silk material, she frowned. *Of course, silk again.*

In this day and age, silk was reserved only for the rich and powerful. Some cloth stores even discriminately chose who to sell to from the upper class, showing that not all rich folks were equal. Jin's way of flaunting that he could acquire silk whenever he wanted to, was like him painting a red and white target on his back.

"It's for tonight's occasion," answered Maria. "The master instructed me to give it to you. I'll assist you in putting it on when evening comes. In the meanwhile, King-san has requested to meet you in the back court." Maria bowed and left, having many things to tend to before the party.

When Maria was gone, Jennifer groaned, wanting to be anywhere but here. Every night someone was hosting a pointless party, trying to outdo the other. And Jin was no exception, now that he had Jennifer to show off.

Pushing the idea of another long night to the back of her mind, she left to go see what King wanted. For the past two weeks he rarely spoke to her because of Jin's strong dislike towards him.

When Jennifer was outside, the hot air hit her, almost forcing her to return indoors where the AC was blasting. The only thing keeping her from returning was the thought of King waiting. Almost immediately, she started sweating and wiped her face with her hands.

Wearing a simple servant's uniform, King sat beneath a tree, swinging a cattail in the air. When he saw her, he quickly stood and smiled, waving. In a rush, Jennifer jogged over. He chuckled, noticing her sweating and panting.

"Shut up," she growled and plopped down, happy to be out of the sun. "So, what's up?"

"There's a lake on the estate. I thought maybe you'd like to go out for a stroll," King offered, scratching his head. "It's beautiful weather."

Jennifer raised an eyebrow and smiled. It was unusual for King of all peoples to invite her on a stroll. But since he was doing his best to act the part of her "brother," she'd go. "Alright, let's go on our long overdue date."

"D—date?!" King stammered and bit his tongue. He cursed while Jennifer laughed. For being such a brute, he was unexpectedly clumsy and shy. "It's not a date," he grumbled.

"Sure, it's not," she joked some more while King helped her to stand.

"Come on, let's go," he said, leading the way.

"How'd you manage to find the lake?"

"I couldn't sleep last night and went for a stroll and came across it. It can be our private place to talk, just the two of us, about this mission."

"Yeah, I was thinking the same. Talking inside the mansion is a little dangerous, since we never know who'll be listening," agreed Jennifer.

If they wanted to accomplish this mission, they had to find a way into Jin's underground laboratory. Whatever he was experimenting or hiding, it was locked behind a five-coded password door that was considered one of the most high-tech locks. Since it didn't have dials, switches, or serial numbers, they had to acquire Jin's fingerprint, blood sample, eye and body scan, followed by two questions. If they failed any of them, they'd be killed on-spot, regardless if Jin was with them or not.

"We can always meet at night," she joked and winked.

King reached over, nudging her head as she laughed. Sometimes he wondered why she enjoyed toying with him so much. It couldn't be that much fun. "Let's race. The last one gets to obey the winner," he suggested and took off, unusually cheerful that morning.

"Cheater!" she accused, while King laughed.

When they reached the lakeside, they took a seat beneath a tree. The shade helped cool them down while they caught their breaths. Birds chirped from all around as they watched the water sparkle like millions of gems. It was so serene it didn't even feel like they were undercover.

"Did I ever tell you that I was recruited from Canada?" she asked, breaking the silence.

King looked over, shaking his head. He knew Jennifer was Caucasian since she had no hint of Asian in her, but he never knew where she came from. It made him happy that she was confiding in him. At that precise moment, the stupid necklace decided to sparkle, practically teasing him to run a finger along her smooth neck. Blushing, King quickly averted his gaze before it could travel any lower. Like usual, Jennifer was the one taking the initiative to start a conversation. Today, he had wanted to be the one to instigate it, since Rain had once teased him about being a herbivore that only thought about competition.

"I expected the world to change a bit, now that I'm a teenager, but it hasn't," she continued, not noticing King's squirming. "Everywhere you walk and look, there are rubbles left from the past war. The rich still live like kings while the poor still starve on the streets, begging and dying in the slums. The government has forsaken them, allowing them to believe that they're better off dead. But I want them to know that this world isn't all evil. There's still good and beauty, if they're willing to open their eyes to it."

A butterfly flew by as Jennifer closed her eyes. She inhaled deeply before exhaling. Even with King by her side, without the girls, she felt lonely. Mio, the annoying crybaby would make Jennifer feel right at home.

"As a child, I used to fear Life-Kills. They don't exactly have a good rap. But now that I've become a Life-Kill, my views have changed." Jennifer turned to look at King, tears in her eyes. She could still taste the salt of the sea and smell the fishy air of her hometown. On some nights she'd dream of starving inside the unsanitary alleyways, scavenging for food. When she awoke, she'd cry herself back to sleep, fearing that her life at the Dome wasn't real, but instead the one she'd escaped in Canada. "At one point in time I even believed that death was the answer for people like me. But after being saved and brought to the Maroon Dome, I want to continue living, for the girls, and for my future."

"I think," King said, keeping his eyes pinned on the water surface. It was hard to stomach her confession. How could she think of dying? Life was so precious. She should continue living for as long as possible. And if she couldn't find a reason, he'd find one for her. "I think the past should stay in the past," was all he said.

After a few seconds of silence, she burst into laughter. King turned to look, eyebrow raised. What was so funny that she'd laugh so hysterically?

"Your answers and comments are always so vague."

"That's all?" he said, turning away again. His cheeks turned pink while he ignored Jennifer who was starting to talk again. No matter what he did, he couldn't hide the smile that crept onto his face. She was rubbing off on him again. It was the same as back then, during their first joint training. He couldn't ignore her for long.

Jennifer sat, cross-legged, smiling like a fool. Something as simple as hearing him talk, delighted her to the point where she wanted to celebrate. "Let's eat sushi when we get back."

"Sushi?"

"Yeah, sushi. Back at the Dome, our head chef used to always make it for me. It's so good. Back in my hometown, sushi was reserved only for the rich, until I came here to Japan. Everyone eats it! Insane, isn't it?!"

Laughing, King shook his head. He stood and dragged her to follow him. "Where are you taking me?"

"We're gonna take a dip."

"What? No way! I'm in a dress! And besides-"

"You talk too much." King picked her up into his arms and tossed her into the water as she squealed. Laughing again, he jumped in after her. The lake was warmer than he thought as the two stood up, soaked.

Angry, Jennifer began splashing water at him. Soon, they were both laughing and playing, trying to dunk the other's head under the water.

∞

Umeko stood on the sidewalk, kicking the ground, bored. Taiki had left to buy a few drinks. The crescent moon hanging in the sky was so bright,

Umeko couldn't help but marvel in its beauty. Although she knew she couldn't catch it, she still reached a hand out. It felt as though someone was trying to catch her just on the other side.

When Taiki returned with two mochas, he handed one to her.

"Thanks." Umeko took the mocha to drink as they stood in silence, watching people pass them by. Again, it was a quiet night. "This mission is starting to bore me."

Smiling, Taiki nodded and took a drink of his mocha also. Even he couldn't understand the reason for watching people. It made no sense, unless there was an underlying message. Perking, Taiki spotted a group staring and pointing. They had tattoos, piercings, and were smoking like it was cool.

"Who do you think they are?" Umeko spoke, taking notice as well.

"Ignore them." Taiki went back to drinking his mocha.

"Oye," called out the leader of the group as he marched over.

The couple looked over without a word, simply inspecting the leader. There was nothing special about him. If he was to launch an attack, they could easily take him out.

"What is it?" Taiki finally answered, uninterested.

"You two were the ones who took out Mario and his boys, right?"

Taiki and Umeko glanced at each other. They blinked and shrugged, confused about what the leader was talking about.

"You know, the guy who was messing with that cute girl."

"Ah," the two said in unison. If that was the case, then yes, they were the ones who took out the goons who were harassing Lori that afternoon.

"Yeah, we took care of some punks, not sure of their names, but what of it?" Taiki asked, raising an eyebrow at the leader who was sizing him up.

"Not bad," he said in the end, "join us."

"What?" asked Umeko in disbelief.

"You two are strong. If you join us, you'll be rewarded greatly once we take over the city."

"Not int-"

Before she could finish her sentence, Taiki threw a hand over her mouth. Maybe, his hunch from a while ago was correct. Perhaps, this was the truth behind their mission. Taiki wouldn't miss the opportunity and wasn't about to let Umeko ruin their chances with her big mouth. "Sure."

Umeko glared, trying to get free, but he had a firm hold on her.

"Alright then, we're having a meeting tomorrow morning at seven. Meet us here at six. We'll take you to our base." He waved at the two and left with his group, happy to have recruited some strong fighters.

"We'll definitely show up."

As soon as the group was gone, Umeko punched Taiki square in the stomach. He let out a grunt and bent over. "What the hell were you thinking?

Those are the bad guys. Why are you getting involved with them for? Are you trying to be rebellious now?"

"That's not it." Taiki shook his head and stood up, coughing. She had given him a good punch.

"Then what is it, huh?"

"I was thinking that joining them could be our real mission."

"Huh?"

"Listen, the deans wouldn't just send us here to scout the area, making sure that peace is present. That's just too simple," explained Taiki. "I think we're supposed to find the boss behind all the crimes and stop him."

After thinking over Taiki's explanation, Umeko nodded. It made sense if they could find and stop the one pulling the strings from behind the curtains. Clasping her hands together, Umeko gave Taiki her most innocent look. "I see. How smart of you, Taiki-kun. Sorry about the punch just now." Umeko laughed it off and reached out to rub his aching stomach. "Forgive me?"

"No," he growled.

"Eh? Why not? I apologized." She pouted, giving him puppy eyes.

Taiki smiled at her efforts to get him to forgive her but quickly covered it up. He held up his index finger to make a bargain. "First, I must get even."

"You wanna punch me too?"

"What? No."

"Oh, well then—you plan on *slapping* me?" she accused and backed away, never been punched before—except by Yeve and a few bad guys. Slapping though, that was an entirely different subject on its own. She'd never allow anyone to slap her in this lifetime or the next.

"What? No." Angry, Taiki glared. What did she take him for?

"Oh, well then, what-"

Tired of listening to her rant, Taiki abruptly swept down to plant a kiss on her forehead. After withdrawing, he crossed his arms, proud that he'd frozen her into silence. "Now we're even." Laughing, Taiki got a head start before Umeko regained her senses.

It took a few seconds before she finally snapped out of her dumbfounded state to chase him down the street, angrily waving her fist in the air. Every word that left her mouth were threats about how she'd skin him alive when she caught him.

∞

In an hour the party would begin, and Jennifer was late to meet Maria, so she could change into her kimono. As the couple ran back to the mansion, laughing and playing another game, they came to an abrupt halt. Standing on the patio was the thirty-year-old Jin. Fidgeting beside him was Maria while the rest of the workers were inside the mansion, doing last-minute cleaning.

Wishing that her role as "Hime" could go to Mio or Hana, maybe even May and Remi, Jennifer tried straightening her partially dry hair that had gotten wet again. There was no use in making such a pointless wish when this was *her* mission. She'd see it through to the end.

"Hime," Jin called out, rushing over to embrace her. He breathed easy again, scared that she'd gotten kidnapped when he returned home and couldn't find her anywhere.

King averted his gaze down to the dark grass. He hated pretending to be Jennifer's older brother. Jin was constantly taking all kinds of advantages to touch her whenever possible, and King was powerless to stop it.

"M—Master Jin," she protested, feeling uncomfortable and pushing him away. His out-of-production Michael Kors tuxedo stank of vodka and tobacco. "Not in front of nii-sama," Jennifer said, appearing meek and mild.

Remembering that King was there, Jin turned to glare at him. Like the first time when he met the siblings on the side of the street, begging for money, King was attached to Jennifer at the hip. "You," he growled and lashed out.

"King!" Jennifer screamed, rushing over to his side on the ground. Even if this was an undercover mission, she wouldn't allow anyone to hurt her Soulmate. "Are you alright?"

"I'm fine." King smiled and nodded, though his head spun from the surprise attack.

"Jin-san!" she shouted, jumping to her feet and whipping around to glare at him. "That was too much just now!"

"He took you out all day and even got you dirty," blamed Jin.

"You think I care for this?" Jennifer asked, waving her hand to the mansion behind him. Was he trying to belittle her? Or did he really believe that she was easy to buy? How dare he pretend like he knew the real her. Rage rippled throughout her body as Jennifer tore the flower ornament from her hair to toss onto the ground along with the necklace and earrings. "All your money and riches in the world can never satisfy me."

A long-forgotten memory resurfaced to Jin's mind as her works shook his core. He fell to his knees and clung to her waist. "Don't, please don't hate me!" he pleaded. "Anything but that, anything but that!"

"What are you doing?" asked Jennifer in alarm.

"Please don't leave. Don't leave me again, Hime."

King stared at the desperate Jin from where he was kneeling. None of them expected him to snap so suddenly not even Maria who looked horrified.

"I love you, Hime. I won't allow you to leave me again. If you do, I'll kill you."

This time, it was Jennifer's turn to pale at the threat. King stared at her back long and hard, until she forced her arms to drape around Jin. "I'll be with you until your last breath. I won't be going anywhere. I promise."

"Hime, Hime," he called out like a possessed man.

King bit his tongue until blood ran. He hated how Jennifer had easily made a promise to another man even if it was a lie. They were Soulmates, destined to spend the rest of their lives together. If she wanted to make promises, they should be made to him.

14th Lie

IT WAS A QUARTER TO SIX as the two made their way to the designated meeting spot. Umeko yawned and rubbed her eyes as they crossed the street. Taiki talked while she listened, not keen on engaging in small talk so early in the morning. After a while, Taiki stopped and bonked her on the head.

"What the heck?" she growled.

"Now are you awake?"

"That's no excuse to hit me," she grumbled, yawning yet again.

"It's impossible to talk to you in the morning."

"Then why bother?"

"Fine, I won't, see how you like it."

"That'd make all my mornings."

As cruel as her comment was, Taiki laughed and threw her into a headlock. Umeko snarled, attempting to grab a fistful of his bright red hair to yank on. But the sound of a car engine interrupted their playful time. They turned to look, wondering what the driver was thinking so early in the morning when half the residents were still asleep. A car came zooming towards them at full speed.

"What the-" began Umeko.

"Shit," said Taiki. He drew her close to his chest and turned his back towards the speeding car. At its rate of acceleration, they wouldn't be able to avoid impact. The best thing to do was expand his energy shield for protection.

At the moment of impact, the car was cut in two as each half went skidding in different directions, hitting buildings and lamp posts. With the loud collision, the sleepy residents of the city were forced to awaken.

It was the worst moment to freeze up as Umeko's mind went completely blank, like that time inside the library. Taiki's arms that shielded her began shaking terribly as she blinked. Someone had come after them with the intent to kill. With that sudden realization, Umeko's wits returned.

"Umeko," Taiki whispered. "Are you okay?" Falling to his knees, she caught him in her arms. He was a pale color after using too much energy to expand his shield.

"You...why...?"

"Good. You're okay."

"You fool!"

"Don't shout. My ears are ringing."

Without a word, Umeko nodded in response. It was so surprising not seeing her argue in return that Taiki smiled. And were those tears for him? Suddenly, he felt so blessed. If he could guilt trip her into caring for him, he wouldn't mind putting his life on the line each time. Remembering about the incident, Taiki turned to look at the car that had split in two. There was no driver fleeing from the scene as Taiki squeezed Umeko's hand. She couldn't stay here while he was in a weakened state. The perpetrator could attack at any moment.

"Run," he demanded.

Umeko's eyes widened at his selflessness and quickly shook her head. "I'm not leaving."

"Umeko-"

"I'm not leaving. That's final." Regardless of her dislike towards him, he had saved her, and she would return the favor.

Hoping that she'd stay, Taiki smiled. "Alright," he said, his chest heaving. "Just let me rest I'll recover in a few minutes. Don't forget, I'm a healer."

"I know." She nodded and picked him up to hide in a nearby alleyway, as a blaze started from the two car halves. Once they were settled, she put his head on her lap. Surely, someone must've called the police to inform them about the situation. Just to be on the safe side, Umeko took off her right glove but kept it from contacting Taiki. If the person trying to assassinate them was scheming nearby, she was ready to attack and kill with no mercy. In response to her resolve, her left eye turned a blood red.

"Just like...a ruby," whispered Taiki. He reached out to touch her left eye. Before he could, Umeko pulled his hand away with her left hand. Taiki gave her a hurtful smile, then closed his eyes to sleep. She had denied him the right to touch her just once.

A smile played its way to Umeko's lips. She could feel his sincerity, but couldn't afford to hurt him after he had saved them. "Be more concerned about yourself."

Hidden from view stood two figures in black who had witnessed everything.

"We gotta inform the boss about this," said the first crook.

"Yeah, he needs to know that the Dome graduates are here," agreed the second as they ran off. They couldn't afford to waste any time, given how the Dome wanted to annihilate their group.

∞

As part of King's job description, his responsibilities were to check the perimeters of the estate and see to problems if need be. Though nothing dangerous ever happened, he took it seriously and double-checked his work. If he slacked off for just one second, it could cost Jennifer her life since Jin had powerful enemies with connections. And although Jin despised him, he couldn't deny that King was an exceptional fighter after witnessing him take out five of his guards.

From up ahead, there was shuffling as he stopped and cautiously approached the target. When he reached the intruder, he stopped. An orange tabby cat sat beneath a tree, licking its paw. When she noticed King, she meowed.

"What are you doing here, kitty?" King walked over, picking her up and scratching her behind the ear. "Where'd you come from?"

Already fond of him for finding her weak spot, she purred and licked his hand. Even his arms were warm and safe.

King chuckled and brought her back to the mansion. This was his first time getting attached to an animal after just meeting. Teo's animal friends had taken him some time to get used to. "We better find your owner."

The cat purred again and leaned upwards, licking his lips.

"Whoa there," King said, only able to laugh and withdraw. It was an obvious kiss from a cat and he blushed, unsure of how to respond.

She purred loudly, giving him a seductive look before jumping and scampering away.

"Oye!" King called out and chased her. Before he knew it, he lost her trail and she was gone. After a few failed attempts, he called it quits. "That's one fast cat. I wonder if she sensed her owner nearby and ran after him."

"King-san?" Maria called out from the patio.

"Ah, yes?" answered King as he ran over to join her.

"Master Jin called. He wants you to meet him at the restaurant with the car."

A wide grin over took him as he thanked Maria and ran off. It was boring without Jennifer who'd gone out shopping with Jin since that morning.

Amused by his enthusiastic response, Maria chuckled. Some would view his demeanor as an annoying overprotective brother, but to Maria, she only saw a boy who loved a girl. "I wonder if they're even real siblings."

∞

"Oh? Where'd you go this time? I was looking all over for you." The foreigner with sandy blond hair bent down, picking up the orange cat that purred. He smiled and scratched her behind the ears.

She smiled in return, snuggling close to his beating chest.

"There you go again, Liz, taking an interest in everyone that you meet. First, it was Yeve. Now, it's this bodyguard?" He shook his head and scratched her ear one last time before disappearing into thin air.

∞

♪Red bird red bird, don't cry
Even if you are far away from home, I will bring you happiness
Red bird red bird, do not fear
Even if you are far away from home, I will always be with you
Red bird red bird, one day you will find your way home
You will fly far away from me and leave me
Red bird red bird, I love you
So please, do not ever forget me♪

Despite the fact that she was singing a lullaby meant to lull him to sleep, her soothing and melodic voice actually woke Taiki from his slumber instead. He was lying back inside the hotel room of his bed. A lukewarm cloth sat on his forehead as the woman shrouded in darkness smiled and reached out to push it aside so she could feel his forehead. At the slight touch of her warm fingers, Taiki's heart tightened. How he missed her.

"Oh love, why are you crying?" She chuckled as Taiki squeezed his eyes shut, tears trailing.

"Mother."

"You're awake," Umeko intervened and entered the hotel room with a sack of groceries. She smiled and set it down on the counter, then approached. The ghost of the woman had disappeared with Umeko's appearance. She sat on the bed where the woman had been sitting a few seconds ago to check on Taiki's temperature also.

After hearing sirens, Umeko bolted from the scene with Taiki. It was as she had suspected, someone had notified the police about the accident. As to not get caught up in the mess, she thanked the Golden God for her powers and fled with Taiki on her back.

When they reached the hotel room, Taiki groaned from a nightmare. Umeko did all she could to ease him but to no avail, and so, she left to go buy a few ingredients to make rice porridge for when he awoke.

"You know," said Umeko. "I really thought you were gonna die."

He grimaced at her joke that was rude and uncalled for, especially at times like these. "You really have no faith in me whatsoever, do you?"

"Absolutely none," she joked.

"I thought so."

"But I'm glad that you're okay now. It would've been sad."

"That you lost your one and only Soulmate?"

"Huh? No. That I'd have to tell the guys you died pathetically."

"You," he hissed.

Umeko laughed at her joke. It was pretty funny, so Taiki grinned. After having her share of laughter, Umeko gazed down at her gloved hands. If only she was normal and could touch others without killing them, she'd have been able to share her energy with him. "Thank you for saving me."

This made it twice now that she'd unexpectedly thanked him. Just like the first time, Taiki was unprepared for the damages she'd done to his beating heart. It was foul play and he couldn't even call her out on it.

"If you hadn't been there, I don't know what I would've done." She laughed it off, embarrassed. After all her training at the Dome, she chose such a time to freeze up. If the girls were to get wind of this, they'd never let her live it down, especially Mio. "You must think I'm really lame. Given my powers, I couldn't do anything. Sorry."

"Why are you apologizing for?" Taiki asked when he noticed tears welling in Umeko's eyes. He reached a hand up to brush her hair, surprising her. If they couldn't touch, skin to skin, then touching her hair should be fine. "I've never once thought you were lame."

"Taiki."

"I'll never think that."

"Taiki," said Umeko again.

"What is it?"

"You're still touching me."

"Huh?" Taiki noticed and quickly withdrew, sitting up and scooting away. "Sorry!"

"Ah, it's fine." Umeko smiled it off and turned away. Her own face turned pink from the embarrassment of not moving away on her own accord.

"Uh," he said, putting a hand to his face before glancing over. If it was now, he could ask and maybe get the truth. "You hate me, right? Since you know, back then at the Dome, we didn't get along and all. Suddenly we got paired up with each other. You must've been troubled when you found out I was your Soulmate."

"Yeah, I-"

"But," Taiki interrupted. Even after asking, he couldn't handle the truth that would kill him emotionally. "I wanted you to know, I've never hated you." He stopped and lowered his hand, finally being honest. "When we first met inside the forest and you first showed your powers, I thought you were amazing. You were so strong, much stronger than me. In a sense, I was ashamed that I couldn't protect anyone and had to rely on you."

Umeko blinked, not expecting Taiki to suddenly disclose such a truth. All this time, she'd assumed their hate was mutual. It was supposed to be a give and take, but she was wrong. The hatred was one-sided.

"When you showed me that blood-colored eye and told me how you couldn't touch anyone without killing them, it broke me to pieces. That's why; I went to Gabe-sensei. I wanted him to teach me everything he knew about medicine. I wanted to cure you from that poison inside you. I took blood samples from that dead bird you killed and began experimenting. That's how I created the antibiotic.

"Knowing you, I knew the poison would only become stronger as we grew older. That's why I had to come up with a second plan of creating a barrier around myself. That way, you could touch someone, and I'd be that someone you couldn't hurt with your powers. I'd be the one to ease your pain and sadness. But I was wrong."

Mr. Fujiwara's words from the day of the duel had haunted Taiki since. Even when he found an antibiotic, it wasn't enough because it wasn't *the* cure. "If you try to draw out that poison from Umeko's body, she'll die…The poison coursing through her veins is what's keeping her alive."

The fifteen-year-old Taiki had been devastated to hear such a startling revelation from his instructor. No matter how hard he studied, time was running out. Umeko's poison had evolved, surpassing his ability to find *the* cure. Even if there was a cure, the consequences were high. If what Mr. Fujiwara said was true, then Taiki would be killing Umeko when he removed the poison.

"There is no cure. I can't save you." He admitted his own failures and hung his head down low, his hair covering his dim eyes. "I wanted to save you so badly, only to disappoint myself. I'm sorry, Umeko."

After a moment of silence, she crossed her arms. If he was being brutally honest with her, then she wanted in also. Maybe then she could finally move on from this hate. "You're right. I do hate you. Even now, I still do. I hate how you continue pretending to be strong when really you're just a weakling. Even the way you talk and hold yourself irks me."

"You," hissed Taiki. He was trying to have a heart to heart conversation, but it was impossible after all. They were bound to butt heads and argue until the day they died.

"I hated how you reminded me so much of myself, only the boy version." Umeko chuckled and stopped as Taiki grinned. They were so similar, the two of them. They hated relying on others and tried doing everything alone. The answers they sought they couldn't find. "Even though you were the spitting image of me, you could touch others. If we were so alike in personality, why weren't you in pain? Why weren't you suffering? Why was I the only one? That's how I've always thought. But you see, that's too selfish. If the ones I hold dear are safe I should be content. That's why, don't try and save me. You're not a superhero."

Taiki's grin faded as a broken smile took its place. He nodded and whispered an "I know" to himself. He looked down at his hands. Even now, his invisible shield was still in place. It had become a bad habit.

"But I'll leave it to you, Taiki." Umeko smiled and looked over. Her eyes sparkled from the tears that built up from their emotional talk. "I know that you won't stop trying, even if I discourage you. So, I'll leave it to you, to find a cure and save me."

Stunned, Taiki continued staring at his hands. What did she mean by that? Turning, he gazed into her soft brown eyes. How could something so beautiful become so deadly?

"Did you hear me? I won't forgive you if you give up so halfheartedly." Even if it took Taiki more than a life's century to find a cure, she would be waiting. Why? Because, Umeko wanted to know what warmth felt like. She wanted to touch without the fear of possibly hurting someone.

In that moment, Naruyuki's smiling face and white hair flashed before her eyes.

When it came down to wanting to touch someone—anyone, Umeko wanted to hold Naruyuki in her arms the most. It'd be a dream come true if she could touch him one day. Should that day ever come, Umeko feared she might not be able to hold back.

"Yeah," whispered Taiki. "I'll become that person to save you." He nodded and smiled, reaching a hand out to touch her, but stopped. It looked as though Umeko had been whisked away to a faraway land. He withdrew his hand to his lap, tears in his own eyes. Even though he had said those words, somewhere in his heart, he knew the truth. He could never touch her, now or forever. The place he was standing, it didn't belong to him.

15th Lie

SPAR, THE LEADER Taiki and Umeko had met the night before, sat with one leg perched. He had a scowl on his face and a cigarette wedged between his parted lips. Taiki and Umeko had somehow tracked his men and forcefully beaten them until they took them to his training grounds. "You two have a lot of guts showing up now after standing us up this morning."

"We're sorry we couldn't make it," Taiki apologized by bowing.

Spar let out a cackle and spit his half-finished cigarette to the ground, near Taiki's feet. Umeko raised an eyebrow, already losing her cool. Spar stood, walking over to stand before them. "If apologies could stop wars, there wouldn't be a need for a God."

"Oye," snapped Umeko who had heard enough.

Taiki glanced over, shaking his head. This was no time to start a fight. They had come with one goal in mind: to join Spar's team and accomplish their mission. If they blew their cover now it would be meaningless.

With a loud huff, Umeko crossed her arms and turned away. She suddenly wished that the hot-blooded King was her Soulmate, so they could beat everyone present.

"We kinda got into a brawl and couldn't make it," explained Taiki. "But we really do wish to join your group."

Spar raised an eyebrow. Sure enough, Taiki's forehead was bandaged. Other than that, everything else seemed to be fine. He suddenly became unsure if recruiting them had been a good thing or not. "Heh, he-he!" Spar laughed, throwing both hands to his stomach. Even his men laughed along. Umeko on the other hand returned to glaring. "You fool!" he shouted, his laughter abruptly ceasing. "I don't need weaklings like you!" He pointed a finger to Umeko and Taiki both. "A girl with an attitude problem and a weak boy who can't protect himself isn't worthy to join me."

"Oye," Umeko hissed, grabbing him by the collars.

"Umeko," protested Taiki as Spar's cronies reached for their weapons. As soon as they caught sight of Umeko's left eye, they froze.

"Wh—what the hell are you?!" Spar shouted and tried to claw away, but Umeko held on firmly. "Let go of me you freak!"

Maybe always having her gloves on was a good thing. Who knew what she would do to Spar, now that he was in her grasp. "If you become a corpse, you'll stop hurting my eardrums."

"Let go, let go!"

"Umeko, that's enough!" Taiki shouted, grabbing her from behind to pull away.

"What are you doing, Taiki?! I'm gonna kill him as punishment for insulting us!"

The way she was standing up for them was so genuine, it made Taiki smile. He gently squeezed her in his arms before throwing her over his shoulders. When Taiki returned his attention back to Spar, he flinched and backed away. "The next time you want to run your mouth about my Soulmate, make sure I don't hear, or else, your head is mine," he threatened and left.

"B—boss," stuttered the cronies.

"I know." Spar grinned, massaging his neck. Even though Umeko had been holding his collars, it felt more like a chokehold. Her immense power was something to fear. "If I'd known what they really were, I wouldn't have dismissed them so easily. We absolutely need their powers to win this battle." With two Life-Kill drifters, they could easily overtake this territory and wage war with the other groups. Now the problem was, how to re-recruit them.

∞

"You can let me go now!" Umeko instructed while slung over Taiki's shoulder.

"Don't wanna," he answered while smiling.

"Just let me down already!"

"You really aren't lady-like."

"You got a problem?"

"It's true. You really have an attitude problem," joked Taiki.

Growling, Umeko hit his back with her fist so he'd drop her, but he never did. Now that she thought about it, he was well-built. Shaking it off, Umeko glared. She wouldn't give him any benefits. Besides, she knew how awful her attitude was without Taiki or Spar having to telling her. She'd been punished several times for it. "So what if I've got an attitude problem? I know that I don't suit you. You deserve someone passive, sensitive, and calm who won't erupt like me. Someone, like Hanabi, Hana, Remi, or maybe even stupid Mio might do."

Stopping, Taiki set her down. She was still fuming from Spar's insult. He poked her forehead and smiled, his action catching her off-guard once more. "You're an idiot."

Umeko's bottom lip curled and her eyes moistened. Not a second too late, she was bawling, surprising Taiki. "I really am an idiot! So what? Don't make fun of me just because I'm not smart!"

So that was the reason behind her tears. It almost made him burst into laughter. For being such a hard-ass, she was irresistibly cute. He couldn't stop himself from pinching her cheeks. "What I meant was," he said, smiling, "you're an idiot for suggesting that I might suit someone other than you."

Umeko stopped crying to stare. Were these missions making Taiki soft? She wasn't sure if she should be scared, thankful, or angry that he was pinching her.

"Yo!" Mario greeted and approached with his group of cronies. After searching all day for the couple, he could finally start and finish the task given unto him.

"You again," Taiki said, sizing up the group. Mario had more men this time, but it wouldn't make a difference. All Taiki had to do was teach him another lesson.

"My boss wants to meet you two."

"And who would that be?" asked Umeko.

Mario shook his head, still smiling. "Sorry, I can't go around disclosing his identity. All you need to know is that he's taken a fancy to you and wants to meet."

"And what makes you think we'll go willingly?" Taiki asked, taking a step forward in challenge.

"I knew you wouldn't come willingly," Mario said, scratching his head. Now that his option for being civilized wasn't available, it no longer mattered what method he used so long as he returned to the base with the two in tow. "Alright then, you leave me with no choice. I'll just have to use our group's secret weapon." Mario and his group of cronies parted to reveal a tiny blonde-haired girl standing behind them. She wore a blue dress matching the color of her eyes. "Anoka," instructed Mario.

"Yes," she whispered and nodded, eyeing the couple.

"Why is-" Before Umeko could finish her sentence, she was knocked unconscious. Taiki too, who never saw it coming fell over beside her.

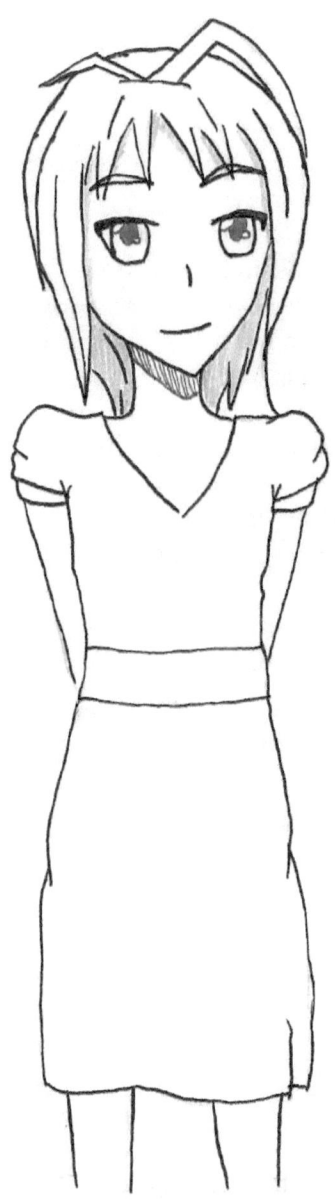

"Your brute force means nothing if you're unconscious, idiots. With Anoka on our side, we're practically invincible." It felt so exhilarating to finally have his payback that Mario laughed. He motioned for his men to capture the two before motioning for Anoka's hand. "Come, I'll treat you to some ice cream for a job well done."

"Okay," she said, taking his hand so they could leave. Their job for the day had been a success.

∞

Jennifer stood on the sidewalk outside the restaurant, waiting. While on her date with Jin, they ran into his colleagues and chatted for a bit until they began speaking a different language. Excusing themselves, they left to speak in private about the urgent matter.

Two of Jin's men had been tasked to stay behind and protect their pampered princess. And indeed, Jennifer looked the part with her hair curled, makeup done, expensive clothing, open-toe heels, and priceless jewelries. There was even a diamond tiara sitting atop her head. Her white dress that had been bought on a whim by Jin also had diamonds embroidered at the hem. Though she declined, he did as he pleased.

Even if Jennifer loved fashion, this wasn't remotely close to her style. Her overall appearance was too cutesy, and her face muscles ached from having to smile all-day long.

A black Mercedes now out of manufacturing pulled up as King stepped out. The two smiled at each other and waved. At the sight of her tiara, King laughed at how out of place it looked.

"Shut up," Jennifer groaned, embarrassed herself.

"Sorry, sorry." King did his best to stop but couldn't manage to do so. To take his mind off her cute image, he looked around. "Where's the master?"

"He's talking to some colleagues."

"How long now?"

"Maybe fifteen minutes."

"Should I let him know I'm here?"

Jennifer shook her head. There was no need. Jin would see him soon enough when he returned from his talk. Besides, if King were to show his face, Jin would only get angry. "He's talking business right now."

"Okay then."

Right on cue, Jin came strolling towards the siblings and two bodyguards with his colleagues. The moment he saw King playfully tug Jennifer's curls, his fists shook. "Hime!" he called out as Jennifer spun around to smile and King withdrew his hands to his sides. "Something came up at work. Can you go back home first?"

"Of course. Is everything alright?"

"It's nothing serious. Go back with your brother. I'll return after dealing with the problem." The moment she was within his reach, he hugged her and smiled. She needed to hurry and realize that the place she belonged was in his arms, nowhere else.

"Okay," Jennifer said, trying to ignore his possessive hold. She forced herself to return the hug, unable to push him away like normal. "I'll see you when you get back."

"Yeah, I won't take long." Jin let go and kissed her lips.

Uncertain about what the hell just happened, King froze. Since when did Jennifer and Jin advance to the next level in their fake relationship? King's face turned red and he clenched his fists, wanting to punch Jin, but held in that urge. He refused to yield, and watched no matter how sickening it was.

"There are people." Jennifer blushed uncontrollably, keeping her gaze away from King, whom she knew had questions.

"Ha-ha, it's okay!"

The colleagues simply smiled and coughed, feeling embarrassed for witnessing their affections. Jin was a stone-cold business man. Yet, when it came to his girlfriend, he became soft-hearted.

Turning his attention to King, Jin's look hardened. He had no choice but to yield for Jennifer's sake. "Protect your sister."

It was a given, without anyone having to tell him. "I know," King answered.

"Well then, I better get going." Jin pulled away and waved.

"Bye." Jennifer waved also and got into the backseat of the car, since she was forbidden to sit anywhere remotely close to King.

After a bow, King got inside the car and programmed it back to the mansion. He glanced at the rearview mirror to find Jin still standing on the sidewalk, talking to his colleagues. Something serious must've happened.

"What do you think happened?" Jennifer asked, taking off the tiara.

"Dunno," King answered, worry in his tone.

Jennifer twirled the tiara in her hands, admiring its beauty. She didn't understand the appeal but had nothing against it. While other girls dreamt of riches and a fairy tale ending with a Prince Charming, all she wanted was a simple life filled with smiles and warmth. Wiping her lips with her backhand, Jennifer could guess the reason for King's worry. It had to do with her. "I'll be fine. You just worry about yourself, got it?"

Grinning, King turned to face front. Funny how she knew him so well. They had somehow figured each other's personality out during their times together. "Why'd you take it off for?" he teased. "It suited you, Your Highness."

"Don't make fun of me."

Laughing, he shook his head. It was true though. If Jennifer wanted to, she really could pull off being a princess from a foreign kingdom.

Jennifer stared at him through the rearview mirror and slowly smiled too. The meaning of royalty had Yeve's name stamped all over it. She was the epitome of what a monarch was, unyielding and powerful. However, after hearing King call her royalty, it somehow didn't have the same feel as Yeve's. Strange. But beautiful.

Shaking her head also, Jennifer turned to look out the window. Now wasn't the time for jokes. If King was right and something big had happened with Jin and his colleagues, it was time for them to act. "I have a plan."

∞

Yamagata

May shifted in her chair, adjusting the glasses sitting on the bridge of her nose. She cleared her throat and glanced over at Kakinouchi. He was staring incessantly. She glared and turned the other way. They were waiting for the detectives that would be briefing them on the case. But the detectives were taking their sweet time getting there. Again, May stole another glance at Kakinouchi who continued staring. This time, she furrowed her brows. "What are you staring at?" she finally snapped.

"Nothing," was all he said.

"Weirdo," she muttered under her breath. The door to the office slid open as the chief of police entered. Beside him was a younger detective as all four greeted each other.

"It's been a while since the Dome last sent someone here to assist with a case," said the chief, Aikawa as he took off his hat and sat down with the younger detective, Shige.

"We'll do what we can to help," responded May as they sat back down.

"So, what's so special about this case?" Kakinouchi asked.

"Well," said Aikawa. He stood and clapped once as the lights dimmed. It would be faster to show than to tell why they were there. Aikawa pulled out a small switch from his pocket and pressed it as a white screen lowered from the ceiling. A light hit the screen and soon pictures of a crime scene showed.

"We have suspected this man," briefed Aikawa as a picture of a middle-aged man wearing a doctor's white coat, appeared, "to be the murderer of three victims, but haven't found any solid evidence to link him to the crimes whatsoever."

"Then why do you suspect him?"

"Before the three girls went missing and were found dead, they were last seen with Nishikawa-sensei. He treated them out to dinner. Every time we went to question him, he always had an alibi and they always checked out.

From what we've gathered on the victims, two of the girls were in high school and attended different schools. The third victim was a stay-at-home mother. Their looks ranged, along with their ages and personalities. We believe none of them has any prior connections to each other or Nishikawa-sensei."

"I don't get it," Kakinouchi said, scratching his head. "Why can't the Dome just step in and take over the case? As a rep from there, we don't need a plausible cause to arrest him. I'm sure that Gabe-sensei has some sort of truth serum to make him spit out the truth."

"There's something called the Golden Laws," Aikawa answered and chuckled. Though Kakinouchi had a point about the Domes being above the law, even they played by the rules set by the Golden God to not meddle in human affairs unless necessary.

"How troublesome," Kakinouchi complained. If the deans would just give him the okay sign, he'd haul in that psychotic doctor and be done with this mission. "I don't know how this benefits the Dome, but whatever, orders are orders." He glanced at May who stared at the pictures without blinking or making a sound. "May," he said.

"Huh?" She snapped her attention away from the screen towards him.

"You okay?"

"Yeah, I'm fine." She forced a smile and returned to the slideshow that was somehow beckoning for her.

"If you can help us solve this case we'd greatly appreciate it," Aikawa said, bowing his head.

"It's our job," responded Kakinouchi. He laughed it off and glanced at May once more, worried. She still couldn't peel her eyes away from the screen.

"Chief Aikawa," spoke May.

"What is it?"

"Why is each of the bodies missing a part?"

"About that," the chief said with a shake to the head and sigh. "We have no idea. The first female student we found, her hair had been shaved off and her legs had been surgically removed. The second female student we found, her eyes were missing. As for the mother, she was missing her breasts. We've been trying to figure out what he wants with those body parts but can't piece it together. We even got a warrant to search Nishikawa-sensei's house and lab but couldn't find any body parts or blood belonging to the victims. It's as if he's toying with us."

"Sounds like Frankenstein to me," said Kakinouchi.

"Franken-what?" asked Shige.

"It's a creature that—never mind. Forget it." Kakinouchi shook it off. To explain Frankenstein's origins would take too long, and he didn't want to stay another second now that he had information regarding his mission. Besides, it wasn't his duty to educate the outside world about literary works.

Aikawa clapped again as the lights turned back on and the slideshow ended. He turned towards the two and shook their hands. Deep down he despised anything and anyone associated with the Domes. It constantly felt like they were playing with human lives, but he couldn't deny that their help was essential to most of the cases he'd solved. "Thank you for coming in. We greatly appreciate your assistance."

"Not a problem."

"Then, we'll talk later."

"Of course." Kakinouchi nodded as he and May left the office together in silence. Once they were outside, he glanced at her. An odd sensation built inside him, but he wasn't particularly sure what it was. "You seem out of it," he said, trying to keep his mind off the bad feeling.

"I'm not." May shook it off and cleared her throat, her heart pounding inside her chest. Her palms were sweaty, and her eyes twinkled. She was getting psyched about this investigation. It was the most interesting thing to happen after parting from the girls.

16th Lie

STARGAZER LILY PETALS floated atop the water of the granite tub as a few candles lit nearby. Jennifer's hair was loosely pinned into a chignon while she stared at the ceiling, thinking about the mission. They had no leads or information to go off on, but at least she had this grand en-suite to drown her failures in.

After a few minutes, Jennifer finally stood and stepped out from the tub. She pushed a button to drain the water and petals before grabbing a silky peach robe off the table to drape on. When she finished blowing out the candles, she entered her master bedroom to find Maria sitting on the sofa. "Maria-san," said Jennifer in alarm.

Maria smiled and stood, bowing. "Good evening."

"Evening," Jennifer greeted, bowing also. "Is there something wrong?"

"Nothing's wrong." Maria shook her head and motioned to a tray of snacks she'd prepared on the coffee table. "I noticed that you and King-san didn't eat much tonight. I was a bit worried and decided to bring you both snacks. I already brought King-san his. You were still bathing so I waited."

Touched by her affections, Jennifer smiled. It was nice to have such a close female counterpart here inside the mansion. It reminded her so much of being with the girls back at the Dome again. During some nights, they would crowd around the lounge room where the fireplace blazed, eating the snacks Remi and Hana made. They'd talk about nonsense before falling asleep together. Those were the good old days. "Thank you."

"You're welcome." Maria smiled and bowed, turning to leave.

"Say, Maria-san," called out Jennifer.

"What is it?" she answered, turning back.

"Uh," Jennifer said, choosing her words carefully before speaking, "The master's previous lover, Hime-san, what happened to her?"

"Eh?"

"It's just that he sometimes mistakes me for her. I was curious to know what kind of girl she was." As soon as the words left her mouth, she immediately regretted it. Maybe it was a taboo subject. She couldn't afford to let her curiosity be the end of her. "Sorry, I shouldn't have asked. Forget it."

"Hime," Maria said, smiling and reminiscing, "was my best friend and a maid of this household."

"Eh?"

Maria chuckled at Jennifer's expression and walked over to sit on the sofa, motioning for Jennifer to sit with her. Obediently, she walked over to sit as Maria took her hand to hold. It'd been a long time since she last spoke Hime's name, considering how Jin prohibited any talks remotely related to her. "You must've heard the rumors about Master Jin being an illegitimate child of the previous master, correct?"

Though Jennifer hated rumors, she'd heard almost everything pertaining to Jin's life. A nod was her only reply as Maria continued.

"Master Jin's mother was a prostitute and had an affair with his father. When she found out she was with child, instead of getting an abortion, she bore and sold him to his own father for a hefty sum before leaving abroad. When the master brought Master Jin home for the first time, the mistress treated him horribly. She made him an outcast and tossed him to this mansion, so he couldn't vie for the position of heir to the company. Little would she know; her efforts were in vain." Maria chuckled, her eyes distant.

"The workers sent to care for him by the mistress resented him for taking them out of their comfy life at the main house. But only Hime treated him with kindness. Before anyone knew it, they were in love and spending all their time together.

"My dearest friend," she whispered, tears quickly welling in her eyes. "She was always smiling and laughing, kind of like you. Maybe that's why, the master took you in."

Tears too flooded Jennifer's eyes as she threw Maria into a tight hug. The reason for their similarity was because of her mission. None of it was genuine and it made her feel crappy for deceiving Maria. "You must miss her dearly," Jennifer whispered, knowing that if she lost one of the sixteen girls, her world would shatter too.

Maria nodded. Time hadn't been kind, but the healing process was beginning. "I do."

"So then, Maria-san...do you blame the master for her death?"

"No." Maria shook her head and pulled away, her eyes steadfast. Even her face didn't distort from hate or blame. It took Jennifer by surprise. Maria's faith in her master was strong. "Master blamed himself for Hime's death, but I never did."

"I see." Jennifer nodded and smiled. It all made sense now. "You must've loved the master too."

"Eh?" Maria gasped. How and why did Jennifer come to such a conclusion? It was so absurd she laughed.

"What is it? Did I say something weird again?"

"You most certainly did." Maria nodded, putting a hand to her mouth.

"Wh—what did I say?" Jennifer asked, feeling like a fool.

"You think I loved the master?"

Jennifer nodded then stopped. Maybe her imagination was running wild.

"Don't get me wrong." Maria shook her head, wiping the tears that welled in her eyes. "I'm here because I promised Hime to watch over the master for her. You see, I already have someone that I love dearly."

"I see." Jennifer's eyes lit up. She smiled again, relieved. "That's good to hear. It would be painful to see two friends falling in love with one man."

"That's what I used to say."

The two chuckled and chatted some more until Maria retired to her room, leaving Jennifer by herself. "As I thought, she isn't in on Jin-san's plans," she said, finishing up the snacks.

A light knock came at the large glass window, leading to the balcony as Jennifer turned to look. She stood and walked over to manually open the door, letting King slip in. "What brings you by?" she asked, quickly pulling the curtains closed before locking the door to her room. If anyone were to walk in on them, they'd be dead meat.

"Can't I drop by every now and then?" King redirected, taking a seat at the sofa. As soon as Jennifer plopped opposite him, he finally noticed that she was wearing only a robe. Blushing, he turned away and cleared his throat, not yet immune to her alluring charms. Then again, he'd never be. If this was her way of getting information out of Jin, she'd most likely succeed. "Why haven't you changed?"

"Hmm?" asked Jennifer. She looked at her robe and smiled, not bothered by it. "It's fine. We're Soulmates."

King did his best not to let her jerk him around too much and motioned to the empty tray. "I see that Maria-san brought you midnight snacks as well."

"She sure did. In fact, she just left," Jennifer said, crossing her legs to show some skin.

"Really? Why was she here so long?" King gulped and tapped his fingers on the armchair, avoiding the sight of her long legs.

"We were talking about girl things."

"Did you get anything useful out of her at least?"

"Only one thing, that Hime-san was a maid who once worked here."

King stopped inspecting the room to sit still. That was something new. "Didn't see that one coming."

"Tell me about it." Jennifer nodded, her mind wandering to their conversation inside the car that afternoon. "About my plan, do you agree?"

King stared at her for some time before responding, "Yeah."

Jennifer smiled. She could tell that King wasn't happy about it, but if they wanted to accomplish the mission, it was necessary. "Don't worry. I won't let anything happen."

Only able to pin his hopes on her, he nodded. "I know. I just hate the thought of his eyes on you."

Jennifer laughed, her cheeks flaring just a little. She uncrossed her legs and fixed her robe over them. Without a word, King laid down on the sofa and yawned, closing his eyes. It'd been a long day. "What are you doing? You can't sleep here. If Jin-san comes back tonight, you'll be in a heap of trouble."

"I won't get caught. Besides, it's only for tonight. Before you know it, I'll be gone." King opened one eye to wink. "Go on, go to sleep too."

"But it's danger-"

"Lights off," instructed King. The lights in the room dimmed and completely turned off.

"I haven't changed yet."

King chuckled in the dark while Jennifer walked over to turn on the bedside lamp. She grabbed her nightgown and quickly changed in the bathroom. When she returned, King was dead asleep. Shaking her head, Jennifer smiled and walked into the closet to grab a blanket to put over him. After making sure that he was comfortable, she unlocked the door to the room. It was one of Jin's mysterious orders, for all doors to remain unlocked, except bathrooms. Hopefully, he wouldn't return that night and enter her room like usual.

"Goodnight," Jennifer whispered, slipping beneath the covers. She turned off the lamp and went to sleep also. They had a long day ahead.

∞

May awoke from a nightmare, her chest heaving as she glanced around the furnished hotel room. After a few minutes of calming herself down, she sat up and wiped the sweat from her forehead. All last night, the couple had been investigating the crime scenes and files. Instead of making progress with the case, it felt like they were taking steps backwards.

May let out a sigh and ran a hand through her brown hair. Noticing her fake glasses were missing, she went in search of it.

157

"Looking for this?" Kakinouchi walked over, a pair of glasses in his hand.

"Why do you have them?" May grumbled and stormed over to snatch it.

Kakinouchi grimaced at her treatment and crossed his arms. There was no need to be hostile when he was being friendly. "You looked troubled while sleeping with it on, so I did you a favor."

"I don't need favors from you. It's just a waste of time."

Kakinouchi uncrossed his arms, opening his mouth to retaliate. In the end, he stopped himself. It was better not to start anything and have a calm day with her, rather than have her ignore and dog him. "Why are you wearing glasses anyway? You never wore them before. Only Love wears them," Kakinouchi said, walking over to sit on the sofa. He tossed the file he'd been looking through on the coffee table, stumped.

"You don't need to know."

"But I want to."

May stopped at the entrance of the bathroom and spun around, glaring. He wasn't going to let her off the hook that easily even if she were to give him attitude. "Anyone can wear glasses, not just Love."

"You know," Kakinouchi said, going through a different file. He was doing everything within his power to talk calmly, but she was testing his patience like usual. "I could've sworn back then you were a nice girl."

"I am nice. To everyone else, except *you*."

"And why is it only me who gets treated differently?" he asked, turning to stare at her.

May stiffened under his gaze and gulped, crossing her arms haughtily. She wouldn't allow a stare to intimidate her. "Can't you tell? It's because I hate you."

"You know," said Kakinouchi who didn't dare blink or look away.

"Wh—what?" stammered May. "Stop staring, it's rude."

Not caring to listen, he continued, "If this is about that time we fought three years ago, I'm sorry. It wasn't my intentions to insult or injure you on purpose. I just wanted to win."

At the mentioning, May uncrossed her arms. She knew it wasn't in his nature to be evil after watching him for the past few years. But instead of being honest, she gave him attitude. "What's been done is done. Don't bring it up."

"I know, but I still wanted to apologize. After all, we're Soulmates now."

"Whatever, I'm gonna shower," she said, ending the conversation and turning to enter the bathroom. Once inside, May leaned against the wall and withdrew the glasses that hurt her eyes. They were meant to make her look smarter, but instead she looked silly. May ran a hand through her hair. It wasn't just Kakinouchi that she treated differently. Soria was also an exception, but that was because she outright hated May to begin with. So,

May treated her in the same regards. If not for Yeve, she wouldn't care to put up with the detestable Soria.

Not wanting to ponder on things out of her control, May wanted to take a hot nice shower. It always cooled her down.

Meanwhile, Kakinouchi returned to the kitchen to pour himself a hot cup of tea. He ran a hand through his silky teal hair and groaned. May acted more like a rebellious little sister than a partner-in-crime. He was slowly starting to go crazy from her uncooperativeness. "I wonder if it's possible to trade Soulmates," he grumbled.

∞

Taiyou sat in his seat, watching as the train passed broken buildings and rubbles. The beautiful sun shone brightly from above as he smiled like it was the best day of his life. Until they were given Soulmates, the trio would be working as a team.

"What's with the creepy smile?" Kei asked, plopping into his chair opposite of Taiyou. His perfectly side-parted, slick hair bounced. In his hand was a cup of coffee.

"What? Is it a crime to smile now?"

"Whoa, bite off my head, why don't cha?" Kei said, taking a sip of his coffee. In a dejected sigh, he glanced out the window. Every time he remembered that he wasn't traveling with a girl, he wanted to scream for the world to hear. From all the guys, Kei had always been psyched about meeting the girls, even more so than Louis. It was unfair that he never got to meet them once while at the Dome. Even the infiltration to the girls' side, he hadn't been a part of. After finding out, he pressed the others for information, not allowing them to leave out a single detail. "I want to meet the girls."

"You met plenty of girls while we've been travelling."

"Yeah, but they're not the girls from the Dome."

"If the problem is that, then you'll get to meet your potential Soulmate soon."

"Potential," Kei repeated with disgust.

So, that was the reason why he was so angry. He didn't want a potential candidate. He wanted an official Soulmate to call his own.

"I wonder why we're the only three exempted. Did we wrong the dean somehow?" Kei leaned back in his chair, thinking until a grin slowly crept onto his face. "If Taiki dies on his mission, I'd be happy to meet my potential Soulmate."

Taiyou sweat a bit at the outrageous comment. Was Kei really this desperate? "If Taiki heard that just now, he'd skin you alive."

Taiyou

Tasuku

Kei

"Like I care." Kei scowled at how uncalled for it was to be placed behind Taiki, when clearly, he was older, the stronger fighter, and healer. "He can threaten me all he wants. He can fight me all he wants. In the end, I'm gonna be the victor."

"Where does all that cockiness come from?" Taiyou chuckled.

"Can't help it," Kei said, holding up a gleaming fist to the sun. "I NEED a Soulmate."

"No, you most definitely just *want* a Soulmate to show her off."

"Is there a problem with that too?"

"Uwah, you really are the worst."

"Um, you two," Tasuku said from behind his blue hoodie that hid his face. He even stared at the floor, refusing to look up. But it wasn't like they could see his face any way, since he was wearing a face mask bandana.

"What?" the two answered in unison and turned to look at Tasuku who was returning from using the bathroom.

"We're almost there," he said and pointed to a tall building in the distance.

"Ooh, we are!" Taiyou leaned over to get a better view.

"Even though the others got a few months' head start on us, let's beat them and accomplish more missions," Kei said, determined. If he could show how skilled he was, maybe the dean would make him Umeko's new official Soulmate instead of Taiki.

"That's right," Taiyou agreed and nodded. "So, we'll be counting on you, Tasuku."

"Um, well, if you think someone like me can be of any help." Tasuku shyly bowed and smiled from behind his bandana.

"Geez," said the two in unison. The overly shy Tasuku had just killed the atmosphere with his gloomy personality. "How many times do we have to tell you? Be more active like how you normally are when Aoi's around."

"Um, but it's difficult," answered Tasuku as he fidgeted with his fingers.

"Show your face! Stop hiding it!" The two guys lunged sideways, trying to catch him so they could force the hoodie and bandana off. Swiftly, Tasuku dodged and ran before they could get a chance. From behind, the two stood to chase him.

"We're gonna catch you, Tasuku!" shouted Taiyou.

"And when we do, we're gonna tickle you!" teased Kei.

"N—no way, you guys know I'm ticklish!"

"Even better!" shouted the two as they laughed, not caring about the ruckus they were causing on the train. It was a joyous day and they weren't about to let anyone ruin it.

17th Lie

IT WAS BRIGHT AND EARLY that morning as Jennifer sat on the terrace drinking tea by herself. The umbrella attached to the table blocked out the sun's rays as she took in the view of the estate. A flock of chirping birds flew by, but she didn't seem to hear, her mind focused on tonight's seduction.

"Jennifer," called out King as he approached her in a hurry.

"King," she said, choking on her tea. In the mornings he usually avoided her at all costs unless she approached him.

"We need to talk."

"Yeah, of course," she answered, setting her tea down and motioning to the chair opposite her. King thanked her and sat. "What's up?"

"I was doing a lot of thinking this morning."

"And?" asked Jennifer. Speaking of which, when she woke up, as promised, he'd disappeared like he hadn't spent the night with her.

"We can't go with your plan," King said, frowning and shaking his head. Anything could go wrong, and he wasn't about to take any chance. "Instead, I'll confront him directly. That way, we'll be guaranteed a way into the lab."

"That's-"

"Your plan is more reckless than mine. We can't be sure that he'll give you the information you want even if you seduce him."

"But it's possible to finish this mission without having to resort to violence."

Frustrated, King huffed and ran a hand through his hair. He knew she was going easy on Jin because of Maria. But if she wasn't careful, he'd blindside her when she least expected it.

"I know that you want to hurry and finish this mission. But I don't like the idea of you endangering yourself by forcing his hand."

"You think your plan is any better?"

"Well-"

"Do you really not see the way he looks at you? To him, you're not a person. You're simply a piece of property that he bought. And I'll be damned before I let him touch you." King had gotten so worked up, he unconsciously stood from his chair.

A soft fuzzy feeling sprung inside Jennifer's chest from King's lecture. He was worried for her and it caused her to grin a bit. This was nothing to be happy about, but she couldn't help it. "I-"

"Listen to me!" King shouted, causing Jennifer to jump and spill her tea. "Please, don't do it. No matter what, don't do it. I'm begging you," he whispered this time.

It was quiet for a few seconds until Jennifer nodded. If he was going to object this strongly, she'd obey. "Okay," she whispered. "We'll find a different solution."

"You didn't tell me *he* was here too," Jin said from behind.

At the sound of his voice, King turned around. Jennifer stood, forcing a smile. Standing beside Jin was Maria. He had returned home early, requesting to see Jennifer.

"I—I'm sorry," Maria apologized as she bowed at Jin's back.

"I don't want your apology. Leave," he ordered, stuffing his balled fists into his pockets. If he were to strike King again, Jennifer would never forgive him this time.

"Yes." Obediently, Maria turned to leave.

"Take the boy with you as well."

Maria stopped halfway and turned back to look at the siblings who stood side by side. She smiled weakly, unable to go against her master's wishes. King returned her smile and nodded in understanding.

"Take care," he bid to Jennifer and left with Maria.

All the while, Jin stood, staring at Jennifer, without blinking. Once the two were gone, he took out his hands and walked over.

"I-" began Jennifer. She had to clear up the misunderstanding before Jin threw a fit again and punished King.

"Thank goodness you're okay." He threw his arms around her, giving her a kiss on the forehead. "I was so worried when I heard him shouting. I thought he hurt you."

"Nii-sama would never hurt me."

"All men are animals, especially that brother of yours. If you didn't love him so much, I'd have killed him just now."

"He was only-"

"Today, you're coming with me to work," Jin interrupted and cupped her face into his palms. He smiled warmly as Jennifer forced another smile.

"But you never take me to work with you."

"Today's an exception. I want you beside me at all times."

"Alright, if you say so." Jennifer nodded and tiptoed, hugging him as he returned the gesture. She could see King's back that was fading in the corridor. Without a doubt, he was going to get angry. Jin was using King as an excuse to monopolize her again.

∞

"Don't fuck with me!" shouted Kakinouchi. He slammed both palms onto the table as the four glasses of water tipped and spilled across the edges. He stood from his chair so forcefully it skidded before toppling over. Kakinouchi glared at Aikawa for suggesting May to be bait to lure out Doctor Nishikawa. From an opening in the wall, electronic mice appeared to clean the mess.

"Kakinouchi-san, it was only a suggestion," said Aikawa in defense.

"Yeah, well I don't care if it's just a suggestion! May's not going to become your bait just because you can't catch this psychopath!"

Shige who didn't know what to do, looked back and forth at the two. He'd never met an irate Life-Kill and wasn't going to attempt to stop him. Then again, he was supposed to protect the chief.

Meanwhile, May adjusted her glasses and nodded. "I'll do it."

Stunned beyond words, Kakinouchi stared at her. Now what was going through May's head? He couldn't seem to understand, nor did he want to. Maybe the pressure from the mission had finally made her snap. Or maybe this was a new tactic to spite him again.

"I said I'll do it."

She agreed so calmly that it made Kakinouchi laugh. He shook his head at her offer. She was asking to get killed. "Stop joking around!"

"I'm not joking around." May eyed him, never once blinking. She was dead serious. If they didn't take this opportunity to catch the doctor, he might find a new target. This was the perfect plan. Knowing that she herself was a Life-Kill, she wouldn't die that easily. Was it so wrong to volunteer?

"There's no way in hell I'll-"

"Arata," May said sternly.

Kakinouchi stopped. He'd never heard her use his first name before until then. Saying it meant that May had set her mind on the idea. She would become the bait. Shaking his head, Kakinouchi snorted. Like before, they couldn't see eye to eye. Was their compatibility as partners this bad? "I'll never agree to it. You're like a sister to me. I can't have you getting hurt under my protection."

May's cheeks flamed at his use of words. "Then you can stand aside on this case. I'll handle it on my own." She stood, done here now, and bowed at Aikawa and Shige before exiting.

"Kakinouchi-san I-" began Aikawa. Before he could finish his sentence, Kakinouchi stormed out after May. Their talk was far from over. Aikawa watched, shaking his head. Teenagers were always a handful to handle. Throw in one who was a full-fledged Life-Kill, and the situation was beyond his control. "Kids these days, I can't comprehend them."

"Did you forget? I'm only two years older than Kakinouchi-san," he reminded.

"Yes, I was including you as well."

"Gee, thanks chief, I feel so honored," Shige said sarcastically and pouted. Aikawa was making fun of him again, even though he knew that Shige had graduated at the top of his class.

∞

"Sister. Hah! How unbelievable," May grumbled while stalking down the streets. How dare he call her his sister? They were anything but siblings. It made her blood curl just remembering. Did she not appeal to him as a woman? If so, that was the biggest insult in the world.

"What'd you say punk?!" shouted someone nearby as May turned to look. A group of thugs was bullying a middle school boy, who was doing his best to hold his own against them.

The thugs got rough and pushed him into the pole, breaking a small glass vase containing a single miniature rose. Before she knew it, she was running over. "Stop!" May commanded. "Let him go. Now."

The group turned to look her over while holding the teenage boy by the collar of his gray uniform. May hadn't been asking. She'd been ordering. It made them grin as they let go of the injured boy who fell to the ground, coughing. They didn't know who she was or what she wanted, but they wouldn't go easy after she'd interrupted their fun.

May gulped and backed away. She'd gotten herself into a sticky situation without thinking it through. "U—under the Golden Law, Line 23 of Criminal Punishment, it clearly states that if you were to lay a finger on an innocent person, such as myself, and if I was to get hurt, you'll be sentenced to jail for three years," May recited quickly and pointed a finger in warning. It had paid off to skim one of Love's many textbooks about the outside laws.

"Huh?" the guys said and stopped halfway from reaching her.

"And Line 55 of Sentencing clearly states that if I were to die after you hurt me, you'll be sentenced to a concentration camp, digging holes in a desert for the rest of your miserable lives."

"What the hell is she spouting?"

The teenage boy sitting on the ground stared at May, loss for words also.

Feeling like she had won this battle of smarts, she adjusted her glasses haughtily. If she kept this up, they'd get scared and leave her alone. If only Love was here to witness this, she'd give May some credit.

"We really don't care!" They ran at her again, fists up.

Not expecting that reaction, she turned and ran off screaming. Her plan had failed.

"Did she really think reciting The Golden Laws would scare those guys?" the teenage boy asked and stood up. He tried to chase them, but his aching ribs slowed him.

"Oye," Kakinouchi said, reaching out to stop the teenage boy.

Looking up, the boy gulped. Great, more trouble had found him. "Are you with those guys too?"

"What guys?"

"Those thugs."

"I'm not with any thugs."

Kakinouchi scowled and glanced around. He could've sworn he saw May standing here a while ago. Hoping that the teenage boy had seen where May had gone, Kakinouchi stopped him. "Well, *I'm* with someone. A stupid girl with brown hair, who likes to wear fake glasses, though she doesn't need it. She has a lousy attitude and personality and likes to get herself into a heap of trouble."

The teenage boy raised an eyebrow at how specific Kakinouchi was. It described May down to the very last detail. The boy held up a hand and pointed a finger. "Are you talking about that girl who was talking about The Golden Law?"

"Who?"

"Some girl helped me just now. She was wearing glasses, about my height with long brown hair."

"Yep, that's her," said Kakinouchi. He nodded, smiling a bit, then abruptly stopped. The teenage boy's words were reprocessing in his brain. "Wait, did you say she helped you just now?"

"Yes."

"That idiot, now what kind of trouble did she get herself into?"

"Uh, she ran that way," said the teenage boy. He was still pointing in the direction where the thugs and May had run off to.

Kakinouchi groaned from the extra work she was making him do again. He'd never get a quiet day to relax. "Since you know, you're coming." Kakinouchi picked up the teenage boy with one arm to sling over his shoulder like a rag doll before running off.

"Oye!" shouted the teenage boy. "Wait up, put me down! Why are you taking me to begin with?!"

"Because you're the only one who knows where May went. Now stop struggling before I drop you."

"All I wanted was to visit my dad. Why is this happening?" he asked in disbelief.

"Where'd they go?"

"I don't know. I just saw them running this way."

"You're useless to me then. Why'd I bring you?"

"I'm not useless!"

"You're loud. And annoying. Pretend you're a doll."

"Like I'm gonna do such a thing."

"I can always toss you into oncoming traffic for being useless to me," threatened Kakinouchi.

"I'll be a doll," he said, becoming motionless.

"Good," said Kakinouchi while he ran. If he didn't hurry, she'd probably cause more problems. "By the way, what's your name kid?"

"I'm not a kid. We're about the same age."

"You're super short. I thought you were still in middle school."

"Don't talk about my height!"

"Height complex much?"

"The name's Gon! Enough about my height!"

"Yeah, you've totally got a height complex."

"Bastard," hissed Gon. He threw a hand to his mouth, ready to puke. Kakinouchi was running too fast and too inhumanly. He'd never experienced this speed before. "I don't feel good suddenly."

∞

Wait a minute. Why the hell am I running? I have powers! May raised an eyebrow in remembrance that she was a Life-Kill, and that the group chasing her were ordinary human boys. There was no need to be afraid. Feeling foolish, she slapped herself mentally.

"Dead end, girly!"

May stopped running and came to a slow halt. Indeed, she'd run into a dead-end alleyway without knowing.

"Whatcha gonna do now, girly?" the thugs asked. They licked their lips and smiled, closing in. They were going to enjoy their time with her.

"Seems like I've got no choice." May took off her fake glasses and turned to eye the group. If push came to shove, she had no problem with using force, given that she loved fighting. "You boys are in for a big surprise."

"We're gonna tear you apart!" they shouted and charged.

"Let's do this!" May placed both hands together. When she separated them, instead of electricity zapping out, an ice wall appeared to protect her. "Eh?" May blinked at the wall of ice. Next, she looked down at her hands where electricity sparked. Again, she peered at the ice wall and scratched her head as the electricity ceased. "When did I learn ice without knowing it?"

"Whoa!" shouted the guys. They came to a halt, shocked as well.

"Hello there," Kakinouchi called out from on top of the concrete ledge. He stood, arms crossed like a superhero, coming to the damsel's rescue. The only thing missing was a cape and mask.

"Kakinouchi," said May. She turned to look at him in bewilderment. How did he find her?

Instead of paying her any attention, Kakinouchi was fixated on the group standing on the other side of his ice wall. "If you boys want to play so badly, how about I play with you instead? I'm game anytime."

It didn't take a genius to know who or what Kakinouchi was. He'd deliberately displayed his powers for them to see. "L—Life-Kill!" they shouted and ran away, afraid for their lives.

"I thought so."

"Oye, you," May said.

Kakinouchi peered down and smiled. He uncrossed his arms and made a peace sign. Did she see how cool he was just then? Was she finally going to acknowledge him and be nice? "Good to see you doing well."

"Eat this and die!" An electric current escaped from her fingertips, shooting him off the ledge to fall on the other side. She could hear a loud crash and Kakinouchi yelping.

"What the hell was that for?!" The concrete wall froze as he punched it into tiny pieces and glared. Could she really show no gratitude? "I came to save you and this is how you repay me?!"

"I didn't need you to save me." May glared right back and crossed her arms. Seeing his face reminded her of how he thought of her only as a sister and nothing more.

"You," Kakinouchi hissed, raising a fist to the air. If she wasn't his Soulmate, he would've knocked her out. In fact, he wouldn't care about her safety whatsoever. Any sane man would've left her ages ago. "You can't even spare me one ounce of gratitude?!"

"No," she answered flatly.

"Uh," Gon said from behind Kakinouchi, "you two." He pointed a finger at them, receiving the shock of his life.

"What?!" Kakinouchi snapped without turning around. He was still glaring at May with intense heat in his eyes. The next time he spoke with Dean Kosa he'd request for a new Soulmate.

"You're L—Life-Kill," he said and fainted.

"Ah," May said, looking away from Kakinouchi to Gon. She never thought such a thing as fainting from shock was possible until then. It was something she'd only seen in movies and read in books. "He just fainted."

"I don't care about him!" Kakinouchi refused to turn around and look. His eyes were still glued on May, but she seemed to have gotten over it. Like usual, she was disregarding his feelings without a second thought.

"He really fainted!" May pushed him aside and ran over to where Gon lay on the ground. If he died, the two of them would be in a heap of trouble.

"Don't ignore me!"

May rolled her eyes, but Kakinouchi couldn't see. "I'll deal with you later. Right now, we have to deal with this boy." She picked Gon up in her arms and stopped. He was heavier than she expected. Since she was a Life-Kill she assumed she could lift just about anything. That theory proved to be incorrect. She had no choice but to set him back down. "I am seriously weak. I need to start lifting. If being a Life-Kill means that I can't carry a simple boy, what's the use of becoming one?" May tried again but ended up grunting and laying him back down, ashamed and stunned at her weakness. It was so pathetic, it almost made her cry.

Kakinouchi walked over to yank Gon away. "Give him over." Once he had Gon on his back, he walked away with May beside him, patting Gon's back like he was a baby who needed to be soothed to sleep. She seemed more worried about Gon than the fact that she volunteered to become live bait. "May," he spoke.

Remembering about his presence, she asked, "What is it now?"

"You can hate me all you want. But just this once, listen to me. Don't be the bait." He gave her a stern look without blinking. Even if she drove him up the wall, she was still his Soulmate that he needed to protect.

Unable to find a snappy comeback, May came to a slow halt while Kakinouchi continued walking. He was filled with such defeat, and she was the reason. "Quiet down, heart. This isn't the time," May said, placing a hand over her chest where it ached.

18th Lie

GON AWOKE to an unfamiliar room that wasn't his. He sat up in the white bed and looked around. It was a hotel suite, a lavish one at it. He threw off the Egyptian cotton comforter and planted his feet firmly on the soft floor. From outside the room, he could hear two people arguing. One voice belonged to a girl and the second belonged to a gentleman. He recognized both voices; May, who had rescued him from the bullying and Kakinouchi who had come searching for May. They had both taken him back to their place since they didn't know where he lived.

"I wonder what they're arguing about." Gon tiptoed over to the door like a burglar and pressed the MANUAL button. He put one hand on the handle and slid the door open. Poking his head out, he looked down the empty hallway. The couple were in the kitchen as he followed their voices and stopped.

"Your cooking sucks," May insulted, no longer wearing her fake glasses. In her hand was a wooden spatula. Dripping from it was tomato sauce.

Soup, Gon guessed.

"I don't need to be told that by the likes of you," snapped Kakinouchi.

"But it's true. Anyone who eats your cooking will seriously suffer liver damage."

Kakinouchi glared at May who ignored him. That was enough insults for one day. "If you think you're so good, then you cook."

"I *was* cooking until you came and took over," May reminded, finally turning to glare his way. Once again, they were at each other's throats.

"That's because you were too slow."

"What the hell is with that reasoning?"

"It means that everything you do pisses me off." Kakinouchi reached out to flick her forehead. That was all he could do to physically hurt her.

"Ow!" yelped May. She put a hand to her forehead and kicked his leg.

"Ow!" yelled Kakinouchi as he glared right back.

The room was an eerie silence before May turned away, her face pink from losing control. "I bet the other Arata can cook." She had broken the silence with yet another insult.

"You really-"

"He-he," chuckled Gon from where he hid. When he caught them staring, he stopped and made a run for it. Before he knew it, Kakinouchi was already holding onto his back shirt. "Let me go, let me go!"

"Is that any way to talk to your savior?" he asked.

Gon stopped thrashing about to give Kakinouchi a look of disbelief. How could he say that when he made things so much worse? "How exactly did you save my life again?"

"I-" Kakinouchi began and stopped. He thought it over for a few seconds and ended up scratching his head. Truth was, he didn't save Gon at all. Instead, he brought Gon to more trouble by forcing him to go along in finding May. "Whatever, I brought you back. If not for me, you would've died out there."

"I could've brought him back," said May from behind.

"How about you just sit still and look like a pretty princess? Stop adding to my workload," he said, turning to look at her.

"Sexist, sexist!" she accused with the spatula.

"I'm not being sexist."

"Yes, you are! Girls are not inferior! We can do things just as equally!"

"Sheesh, no matter what I say, you always turn my words back on me. I give up."

"You're the one who started it."

"Really," he said, "can't we ever stop fighting and bickering?"

"Maybe when you're gone!"

"You," he hissed.

"Um, if I may," Gon said, raising a hand and smiling.

"What?" they snapped in unison.

"You two make for a dysfunctional couple."

"That's because this idiot can't even cook soup!" May insulted.

"Yeah, well, you're violent and can't acknowledge someone's help!" redirected Kakinouchi as he pointed a finger back.

Unable to intervene, Gon watched. He'd meant no harm in commenting how he saw them. Yet somehow, they turned it into a topic to argue about.

"Oye," May said, feeling her anger rise, "you just called me violent."

"And you called me an idiot who can't cook," said Kakinouchi.

"That's because it's true."

"Yeah, well, you do have a nasty temper."

"Um, I'm gonna leave now," said Gon as the two ignored him, still lost in their own world. "Okay then, bye." He waved at them and turned to leave just as the doorbell rang. The couple immediately stopped bickering as Gon turned to look at them. "You've got guests."

"Stay here," instructed Kakinouchi. He motioned for the two to stay and headed over to where the door entrance was.

"Come here." May motioned for Gon as they crept into the living room, close to the balcony door. For an unknown reason, he became scared. Usually when guests arrived, the hosts should be happy. The way they acted was like they'd been caught committing a crime.

"What's going on here?"

"Hopefully nothing," answered May.

From the doorway, they could hear Kakinouchi speaking to someone. A few minutes later, he returned with two people, Aikawa and Shige.

"Eh?" Aikawa halted, shocked to find Gon there with them.

"Ah," Shige said, shocked too, "Gon."

"You know the squirt?" Kakinouchi stopped walking to glance at them.

"Dad?!" shouted Gon.

"Dad?" repeated the couple in alarm.

"Gon, what are you doing here?!" Aikawa demanded, now knowing the reason why his son hadn't returned home, and why his wife freaked out.

"I should be asking *you* that." Gon stepped out from behind May, pointing a finger at his dad. How and when did his dad become acquainted with Life-Kills?

While father and son bickered, Kakinouchi inched closer to May. Even Shige stayed out of the quarrel. "Maybe we should step out."

"Don't wanna," she answered and crossed her arms.

Kakinouchi glared at her high and mighty attitude again. "You truly are hateful," he hissed.

∞

It was mid-noon as King tended to the stable, also part of his job, that housed the two horses that Jin owned. The first horse was a male, Smiles. He was colored brown with a white patch around his right eye, just like Shadow. The second horse was a female, Noel with a white coat. She was a shy racing horse who panicked when too many people crowded around.

The first time King met the two, they refused to acknowledge him. With patience and perseverance, he eventually won them over.

While brushing their manes, he retold a story from a book he once read at the boys' academy.

"…she managed to win over the wild tiger and eventually gained its trust, able to take a piece of its hair before leaving. After returning to the old man, she told him about her endless nights with the tiger. She handed the old man the tiger's hair. After examining the hair, the old man decided it was genuine. He turned towards the married woman and said to her, 'Like with the tiger, you must also show patience and-'"

The door to the stable opened as Jin entered with a few men in black. Trouble was written all over the four men, but King didn't dare raise suspicion unto himself after what happened that morning. Casually, he lowered the brush and bowed in greeting. "Good afternoon."

With one hand in his pocket and the other by his side, Jin cut to the chase, "Answer me truthfully. Don't you dare lie to me, boy."

King nodded. It really was impossible not to raise an eyebrow at Jin's suspicious behavior.

"Hime isn't your blood sister, is she?"

King stared back, wide-eyed. When had Jin figured it out? Had they been too careless and slipped up their real relationship? If so, he needed to find Jennifer and abort the mission. "What do you mean sir? I don't understand."

"Don't try to weasel your way out of this. Just answer the damn question. Is she your blood sister or not?"

King narrowed his eyes in on the men standing by Jin's side. He flexed his arm muscles, not daring to look away. Something was off here. Jin couldn't have come to ask about their brother-sister relationship. He came with a purpose, especially with these men by his side.

It was as Gabe had once taught the boys, "If you've been caught red-handed, don't try to feign ignorance, you'll only worsen the situation. Just admit it."

"That's correct," he admitted. "We're not related by blood."

Jin hung his head down low before looking up again. "Hime has no idea, does she?"

What? Confusion rose from within. *So, he only suspects that we're not blood-related. Thank goodness, I didn't reveal everything.*

King shook his head to answer, "No. Hime doesn't know."

Play it smooth. Don't let him suspect any more than he already does.

"That's more than enough confirmation for me." Jin cocked his head to one side and motioned for his men to move forward. Now that he had the answers to his questions, he could finally dispose of King. "Get him."

"What's this about?" King backed away with the horse's comb in hand.

"I can't have you hanging around Hime. You'll corrupt her. Besides, I know what you really are, monster. Did you really think you could hide your branded tattoo forever?"

King sneered. Indeed, he'd been reckless. It was a good thing Jennifer hadn't been found out yet, considering she spent most of her time with Jin. King turned towards the haystack not far away, attempting to make a run for it, but the men were hot on his tail, not letting him get a lead. He grabbed the pitchfork and attacked. In order to secure a victory, he had to retrieve his broadsword from its hiding place by the lake.

Smiles and Noel neighed loudly from the fight and tossed their manes. King who was too concentrated on the men in front never saw another coming down from above, knocking him out cold.

With a grunt, he dropped the pitchfork and hit the floor of the stable. Meanwhile, the attacker loomed over King's body, fully dressed from head to toe in black clothing.

"Bring him, Genji. Let's begin the experiment," instructed Jin as he led the way out of the stable. After so long, he finally had a Life-Kill within his possession.

"Yes, sir," answered the attacker who bowed and grabbed King to drag.

∞

The Next Day

"So, the squirt's father is the chief huh? What a shocker. Never saw that one coming," said Kakinouchi while he stood inside the kitchen with May. After meeting Gon at the Soulmate's hotel room yesterday, Chief Aikawa literally dragged his son home, forgetting that he needed to speak to the couple about an urgent matter. Kakinouchi turned to look at May who stood beside the counter, ignoring him. It was a brand-new day, and another brand-new way to anger him.

"What a day yesterday was, huh?" Kakinouchi turned, stirring his freshly made hot oatmeal.

Still, May ignored him, sipping her tea. She didn't have on her fake glasses and spun away. "See ya."

"What the hell do you mean by 'see ya'?!"

May stopped halfway and turned back. She blinked once and twice. Kakinouchi too blinked back, confused. "I have to go and become live bait."

"You're still on about that shit?"

"Please don't curse so early in the morning." And again, they were back at square one. May waved a hand and trotted away. She had a case to solve and didn't have time to argue with him. "I'm off."

"Oye!" shouted Kakinouchi as he followed her into the living room, forgetting about his oatmeal. She was setting her half-finished cup of tea down on the coffee table. "Wait up!" shouted Kakinouchi as he pulled her back to eye. "You're really serious, aren't you?"

"Aren't I always?"

"Don't be stupid!"

May broke free from his hold. Being called stupid and crazy was a pet peeve. "I'm not being stupid. I'm being serious. You're the one being stupid by refusing to cooperate."

"There are other ways to solve this case."

"Unfortunately, we don't have one. We've hit a dead end."

"Would you just-" Kakinouchi began and stopped. From the corner of his eye, a black sparrow dropped a red envelope on the balcony deck and flew off. With a grunt, Kakinouchi went out to grab the envelope before returning. He pressed his thumb on the seal to open the letter.

You have two weeks to wrap-up your mission. Regardless if you finish or not, return to the Dome. Your third mission is already underway.
 -Dean Kiera

"You've gotta be shitting me."

"There you have it," May said, reading the letter as well. "Even more reason for us to make haste."

"Please, just listen-"

May turned her back on him and headed out the door. There was no more time to waste by arguing.

Swirling around, he grabbed the teacup May had been sipping to toss across the room. It cracked against the white wall, staining it a greenish brown. The tea trickled down as the pieces of the cup fell to the floor.

"What kind of Soulmate is she? She won't even listen to me." Kakinouchi ran a hand through his hair and pulled on it. What did he have to do to make her see reason? It was so infuriating to have her as his Soulmate. "Damn it! What the hell?! Who does she think she is anyway?!"

∞

"Geez that guy," said May as she walked down the sidewalk, shaking her head. She was making her way to the police station to meet Aikawa and Shige to see what the plan was. "Why can't he ever cooperate nicely?"

"May-san!" someone called out from behind.

"Huh?" May turned around to find Gon there, huffing and puffing. He'd been running after her, but because her head was in the clouds, she didn't hear him calling out. "What are you doing here?"

"I wanted to talk."

"About?"

"About what you are," he answered. "I've never met your kind before."

"I met your kind only a few months ago too."

"I'm really interested." Gon smiled and peered at her like she was an exotic animal displayed at the zoo.

"Stop staring," she said, pushing him away by the face.

Gon simply chuckled. Life-Kills weren't so different from ordinary humans. "We're about the same age. Let's become friends."

"Aren't you fourteen?"

"Seventeen!"

"Oh," May said, snickering. "I didn't know. Given your small physique, who would've ever guessed?"

"Are you insulting me?"

"What do you want?" May asked, turning to leave. Gon was right on her tail, refusing to lose her. He had questions that only she could answer. "I have things to do. So if it's nothing important, save it for later."

"Are you heading to the police station?"

"Yes."

"Cool, can I come? Dad rarely lets me visit. And I hear that this time he's working on an intense case."

"If the chief doesn't want you going to the police station, he probably has his reasons."

"Yeah, right," scoffed Gon.

May looked over and smiled. He looked angry. "He probably wants to protect you."

"Yeah, right."

"I'm serious." May turned to face front as they headed to the station together. Once there, they went in search of Aikawa and Shige who found them first. One look at Gon, and Aikawa blew his stack. He didn't want his son associated with Life-Kills. Only trouble would occur.

"Escort him home this very second!" he ordered. Without delay, three officers ran over to escort Gon out while he kicked and yelled to get free.

"Should we go somewhere to talk about the plan?" May asked, not affected by Gon being hauled out.

After calming down, Aikawa nodded and led the way to his office. The three sat down, coming up with a plan. They would lure out the doctor tomorrow night, with or without Kakinouchi's approval or assistance. May's consent was all they needed. When they finished planning, it was close to three that afternoon.

"Well, I have a meeting with a few other directors in the next town. I'll be back tomorrow afternoon. In the meanwhile, get your nerves under control," Aikawa said as he left the station while Shige stayed behind, and May left to go buy lunch.

She went to a park and sat down on a bench to eat. Unable to stop thinking about Kakinouchi, she wondered what he was doing. He hadn't shown up at the station to protest, something May thought he'd do for sure. Was he still angry? It wasn't like she intentionally chose to hurt him. All she wanted was to complete this mission and not fall behind the others.

A flock of birds descended to where May sat and walked around, pecking on the grass. Smiling, she threw what remained of her rice near them.

"Found ya," Gon said, plopping beside her.

"Huh?" May turned, not expecting him. "I thought your father forced you back home. Why are you still here?"

"He can't make me do anything I don't wanna do," Gon retorted and crossed his arms.

May smiled, shaking her head at his rebellious phase. "You shouldn't have gone with me if you knew you'd end up getting mad."

"Mind you, I have a solid reason to be mad."

"That would be?"

"I'm not a kid anymore. That old man needs to stop shielding me. I can take care of myself. One day, I'm going to become a police officer too. So, he should just let me in on his cases."

"With that attitude, no one will take you seriously." May laughed and reached out to mess up his hair.

"Oye," he said, pulling away to fix his hair. "Like I said, we're the same age. If you agree that I'm a kid, then you're also a kid."

"But unlike you, I'm special."

Gon glared at her for rubbing the fact that she could assist with cases in his face. "Just you watch, one day I'll get to handle an important case too! Don't get conceited just because you're a Life-Kill!"

"You're so emotional."

"I'm not!"

"Excuse me," called out someone.

"Yes?" answered May as she and Gon turned to see who it was. At the sight of Doctor Nishikawa smiling and bowing before her, she jumped to her feet, fully alert.

Confused and surprised by May's reaction, Gon also bowed with no greeting.

Nishikawa-sensei, the man who's been murdering those girls and taking their body parts is here in the flesh. Why for? May gulped and glanced at Gon, her palms sweaty. *I gotta play this by ear and hopefully not get Gon involved.*

May smiled at the nice-looking doctor. Up close, he was tall and handsome for someone in his early forties. It didn't seem like Doctor Nishikawa was capable of murder. Surprisingly, May thought she'd be intimidated when meeting him, but she was calm and collected, almost excited. "Is there something I can help you with?"

"I would like to thank-you." Doctor Nishikawa held out a red rose he was holding and gave it to May. His eyes were glazed with tears, but he held them back.

"Oh," she said in alarm and reached out to take it. This was her first time receiving a flower. She was a bit flustered, even if that person was the enemy. She'd always hoped it was Kakinouchi who would bring her flowers. "Thank you."

"No. *Thank you.*"

"Oye, don't you think that old geezers like yourself should be picking up women your age instead?" Gon insulted, now standing beside May. The way she was blushing from the compliments of a man who was old enough to be her father made him want to puke. "May-san already has a boyfriend."

"Gon," she hissed, turning to kick his leg.

"Ow," he yelped, bending down to rub his leg.

Quickly, May returned her attention to Doctor Nishikawa and smiled. She couldn't blow her cover. And what was this about her having a boyfriend? May didn't remember ever having a boyfriend. "Sorry about him. He's got a bad tongue, but he's not a bad kid."

"I understand," Doctor Nishikawa answered.

"So, um, if you don't mind me asking. What is this rose for?"

"Well, a few days ago, some hoodlum rats broke a vase I set on the street as a memorial to my late wife. I was so angry, I could kill. Then, like an angel, you rushed to the scene and told those rats off. To think a stranger would go out of her way to do that really touched my heart. I wanted to find you and thank-you personally. It took me some time to locate you, but it was well worth the search. You're as sweet as you look. I'm sure my late wife is happy."

"Oh, well, it was really nothing," May said, shyly blushing. She couldn't remember a memorial vase on the side of the road but couldn't admit it.

"Oh no, really, what you've done is more than enough. Trust me."

"You're welcome."

All the while, Gon kept staring at the two. This situation was far too strange, but he couldn't quite put a finger on it. Why was May trying so hard to be girly for? And why did Gon have such a bad gut feeling about Doctor Nishikawa for? Was his instinct as a future cop kicking in?

"You should smell its fragrance," suggested Doctor Nishikawa.

"Oh, of course," said May. She nodded, lowering her nostrils to the red petals. As soon as she took a sniff, a spray emitted from the center of the rose. Dropping it, May shouted in shock, "What the-" She threw a hand to her nose and mouth, but was too late. Her head went blank as she fell over.

"May-san!" Gon shouted, catching her. "May-san!"

"That was easier than I thought."

Not strong enough to flee with May, Gon sank to his knees and clutched tightly to her. It was as he suspected, something had been wrong with the picture from the beginning. Now that he realized the truth, it was too late. He glanced up, sweating and gulping. Doctor Nishikawa adjusted his glasses, his eyes wild with delirium. "What have you done?" Gon asked, his voice breaking. "Who the hell are you?"

Doctor Nishikawa smiled. It was a good thing he'd tailed May secretly to the police station, then to the park. Overhearing Gon call her a Life-Kill made time freeze. She was the one he'd been searching for all this time. The girls he killed before now meant nothing in comparison. Even their body parts, he could feed to the piranhas. "Give the girl to me."

Gon shook his head. As a future policeman, he couldn't abandon her even if it meant he could possibly die. "No."

19th Lie

SPECKLE DOTTED PEOPLE and cars could be seen passing the corporate below while Jennifer stood in front of the large windows, glancing down. At Jin's request she'd gone to work with him that morning. Even yesterday, she'd been stuck here all day long, doing nothing. It was beginning to tire her out and not even the gorgeous scenery from the 600th floor could keep her attention.

Jennifer rubbed her forehead. The entire morning, she hadn't seen King. Even if he didn't eat breakfast with Jin and her, she always spotted him out by the stable with Smiles and Noel. When Jennifer couldn't find him, she asked Maria. Even Maria seemed worried when she went to wake King for breakfast and found him gone.

"Don't worry. I'm sure he's fine," Maria assured.

"Yeah, you're right." Jennifer nodded and forced a smile but could feel that something had happened. It was unlike King to disappear without telling her. "Please call me if you find him."

"I will," promised Maria.

Tears filled Jennifer's eyes as she wiped them away. If she had the time to cry, she also had the time to retrace King's whereabouts, starting from yesterday when she last saw him. The only thing standing in her way was Jin.

"Did you wait long?" Jin called out. He entered his office and smiled, a manila envelope in hand.

"No."

Sensing her unhappiness, Jin scrunched his brows and set the envelope down. He approached her and stroked her cheek gently. "What's wrong? You seem distant this morning."

"It's just," Jennifer said and sniffled.

"Tell me."

"I didn't see onii-sama this morning. I'm a little worried." Jennifer fidgeted with her fingers and looked down to the floor. Hopefully her little act would win her some pity points and he'd let her return to the mansion.

"He's a big boy. He can take care of himself."

Jennifer's eyes widened at his statement before looking up at him. After a few seconds, she smiled and wiped her eyes. So, Jin had something to do with King's disappearance. To ascertain her hunch, she would stick close by. "Yeah, you're right."

"When am I never right?" he joked, giving her a kiss. After withdrawing, he grabbed the envelope and took her hand to lead the way. "Come, let's go."

"Where are we going?"

Jin turned back and smiled, putting a finger to his lips while Jennifer giggled. They entered the elevator and rode it down to the lobby. Waiting outside was a limousine. Jin motioned to the worker to open the door as they both slid in and the driver inside started the engine.

"Alright," Jennifer said once the doors were locked. "The suspense is killing me. Tell me where we're going."

"It's a secret."

"What kind?"

"Once we get there you'll see." Jin smiled and handed the driver the manila envelope. *"Porta questi a Nishikawa* (Get these out to Nishikawa)," Jin spoke in Italian.

"Si, signore (Yes, sir)," the driver responded.

"Eh? What language was that?" Jennifer asked.

"Italian."

"How cool." She clapped her hands excitedly, his secrecy only added to her suspicions. "You're so talented, Jin-san."

"As the CEO to the corporation, it's only right that I know at least seven different languages."

"Wow," said Jennifer. "So, what did you say just now?"

"To make sure that the surprise is going to be a surprise," answered Jin. He took out a strip of cloth and held it up for her to see.

"You're going to blindfold me?"

"That's correct."

"But I don't want to," she whined.

"Come on. This has to be a surprise."

Jennifer pouted, but eventually gave in. "Okay," she said, turning her back to him so he could blindfold her. Whatever he had in store for her, she had a gut feeling she wasn't going to like it.

∞

Kakinouchi stormed into Aikawa's office breathlessly and glanced around. Shige who was the only one there looked up from his magazine. He set it down and sat up from his cozy position. Kakinouchi was over within a blink, forcing him to his feet by the collars.

"Whoa!" Shige shouted, not expecting that.

"Where the hell is Aikawa?"

"Uh, at a meeting."

"Where?"

"In the next town. He'll be back in a couple of hours. Why?"

"Where's May? Did you send her out on that undercover shit already?" he accused, his red eyes blazing.

Confused, Shige tired himself out from trying to break free. So, this was the strength of a Life-Kill. "What are you talking about? The plan isn't in effect until tonight."

"Then, where is she?!"

"Isn't she with you?"

"No. She never came back to the hotel. Why do you think I'm here, genius?"

"How would I know?"

"I suggest you find me some answers before I make you an iced man."

Shige stared into Kakinouchi's cold eyes. He was dead serious. "I—I understand. Let me go," he bargained. Compromising, Kakinouchi let go as Shige fixed his uniform. He walked over to Aikawa's desk to dial a number. Kakinouchi on the other hand watched every move Shige made in case he decided to make a run for it. After a few rings, someone answered from the other end. "Chief, we have a problem here."

"Shige!" Aikawa's tear-stained holographic face shouted.

"What's wrong?"

"Nishikawa, that bastard took Gon and May!"

"What?" Shige asked in disbelief. That was impossible. They made sure that the two wouldn't cross paths until the plan began. If Doctor Nishikawa had targeted May on his own accord, it only meant that they'd overlooked something crucial.

"May…" Kakinouchi gasped, all the strength in his body leaving. Maybe he'd misheard. Or maybe, this was all a bad dream and he just needed to wake up from it.

"…Gon was able to call my wife right before Nishikawa destroyed his phone!" Aikawa kept shouting from his end. "She's been trying to reach me all day and I finally just got back to her! That bastard had the guts to kidnap him and May in broad daylight!"

No matter how many times Kakinouchi pinched himself to wake up, he couldn't. This was no nightmare he was experiencing. It was real life, and he'd lost his Soulmate. It was the worst feeling in the world, to know he'd failed the first request the dean had given them.

"Are you sure it was him?"

"At this point, I don't care! Post some men at my house to protect my wife! You and I, and SWAT are taking that bastard in with or without a cause!"

"Understood!" Shige answered, ending the call and swirling around. "Kaki-" he began and stopped, the door to the room wide open. "Shit."

Kakinouchi ran down the hallways of the police bureau, as fast as his feet could carry him. His palms were sweaty, and his heartbeat spiked through the roof. All he could think about were the pictures of the crime scenes. Body parts of girls missing. Would that crazy doctor do the same to May? But what part of her was so valuable that he'd risk kidnapping her in broad daylight and exposing his true self?

Kakinouchi shook it off. He couldn't afford to be pessimistic. "May," he called out. "Wait for me. I'll come save you."

∞

Jennifer and Jin descended a pair of stairs and landed on the basement floor. Jin held her hand, leading the way down the bright white fluorescent hallway. This was the underground laboratory she'd been trying to infiltrate. Now suddenly, he was taking her there on his own accord.

When the driver had reached their destination, Jennifer could sense it was the mansion even with her eyes blindfolded. She could smell Maria's favorite candle scent in the air, before they made their way into the maze-like basement.

"Jin-san," Jennifer said, quivering from out of fear. "It's cold."

"Sorry," apologized Jin. He took off his coat to put over her purple strapless dress. "Better now?"

Jennifer smiled weakly and nodded, "Yeah."

"Good." When they reached the place he wanted to show her, they stopped.

The room they stood in looked exactly like a laboratory. There were beds used for experiments. There were microscopes, blood samples, and organs displayed in liquid-filled glass tubes. What was most disturbing was something hanging on the opposite wall, covered with a bloody white sheet.

Something or someone had just been made into a test subject. Even now blood still dripped.

"Are we there?" Jennifer asked, knowing fully well they had. She could smell chemicals and iron from the blood.

"Yes." Jin undid her blindfold as she blinked a few times, adjusting her eyes to the light of the laboratory.

After taking in everything, Jennifer was overwhelmed. She gulped and blinked again, trying to get her nerves under control. Now wasn't the time to freeze up. "What is this?"

"It's my laboratory."

"Why are we here?"

"My surprise," answered Jin. He smiled, pointing to the bloody sheet. "There," he said and walked over to pull the sheet down to reveal the surprise.

Jennifer gasped, forgetting how to breathe. Every single hair on her body stood on end. Hanging on the wall, bleeding was King. His shirt had been stripped off and his entire body was covered with slashes. The bleeding wouldn't stop as his breaths came in short gasps.

Jin backed away, admiring his masterpiece with a hysterical laugh. "Did you know, Hime? He's not your real blood brother! He's a monster, a Life-Kill who's been stealing your life-force!"

Gasping again, Jennifer took a step forward, slowly reaching out her shaky hand. Her lips trembled as tears flooded her eyes.

"Look at that monster. After an entire day of torture, he's still alive. His existence is a curse to this world." Jin stared at King, not realizing Jennifer's horror-filled expression.

She threw both hands to her head and pulled at her hair. "Ah!" she screamed at the top of her lungs. While she was busy getting cozy with Jin, his men were down here torturing King. Her heart wrenched from failing to protect him. Forget the mission. Forget succeeding. Forget everything. The most important thing was King. Only he mattered.

"Hime?" Jin spun around, alarmed at her scream. He ran over, holding her while she had a mental breakdown. "It's okay. He's not your real brother. He was deceiving you, trying to make you believe that you were related when you weren't. He was planning to do indecent things to you, but I stopped him by capturing him and revealing his true nature."

"King!" called out Jennifer. With all her might, she pushed Jin away to run towards her Soulmate. Her tears didn't know how to cease. "King!"

A stunned Jin watched as Jennifer clung to King. He'd done her a favor by getting rid of the beast. Yet she clung to him for dear life. It didn't matter to Jennifer that they weren't blood-related. Jin had hurt King, the person dearest to her. His anger flared at her rejection to him. Even now, he was still unloved. "Get her, Genji!" ordered Jin.

On-command, Genji appeared like a ninja and caught hold of Jennifer to pull back.

"Let me go! Let me go!" ordered Jennifer. "King!"

"Quiet down," instructed Genji.

Refusing to cooperate, Jennifer kept screaming and crying. She had to get him down. She had to share her life-force with him before he lost too much blood. Whatever torturous drug Jin had used, it was preventing King from self-healing. It was unbearable to see him in such a state. The resilient King she was used to seeing had been decimated.

"Sir," Genji spoke. He eyed the frantic Jennifer and let go. Jumping to safety, Genji got into a defensive stance, unsure of what her powers were. "She's also one of my kind."

"Eh?"

The reason King had been captured was because Jennifer was too weak. Everything she did was weak. It reminded her of that day two years ago when she made her resolve. They were training to become stronger after that shameful loss to the boys.

It was a blow to her pride. Jennifer bent over, panting. Somehow tears had welled in her eyes. She did her best not to cry but couldn't hold in the disappointment. Her lips trembled and soon the waterworks began. She had lost her duel against the shy Hana because she assumed she couldn't lose. Everyone also thought she'd win. But she didn't.

Umeko walked over and held out a hand. "Jen-"

"Get away!" screamed Jennifer. She hit her best friend's hand away and bolted out of the gym. From behind, the girls shouted after her, even Hana was worried.

Jennifer had been so confident about her match. In her mind, the victory was already hers before she even began. She never expected to lose. Out of the two, Jennifer was the stronger one. So why? Why did she lose to the weak Hana who was afraid of her own powers?

That day proved that Jennifer was all talk and no show.

She ran out to the stream in the back of the school and bawled her eyes out, refusing to stop after a humiliating defeat.

Shayla who had been training with Yeve and was now resting came after hearing the cries. She walked into the clearing and stopped. After becoming Yeve's disciple, Shayla was starting to slim down. Her grape-like hair had been cut and permed, per Yeve's orders. "Jennifer?" she called out. "Why are you crying? What happened?"

"Leave me alone!"

Shayla scratched her head, already able to diagnose the problem. The thing was, she didn't know what to do to soothe Jennifer. If anyone, Umeko would have the better shot.

"Shayla!" called out Yeve. It was time to return to training.

Shayla quickly turned to leave before Yeve could punish her for slacking off again. Unable to leave a depressed Jennifer without some words of comfort, she stopped and glanced back. "You know, being strong isn't about brawns, it's all about heart. If your heart is weak, you can never be strong. If protecting those who are important to you is your top priority, then you should strengthen your heart. Don't concentrate on powerful punches or laser beam eyes. Instead, concentrate on this," Shayla said, pointing a finger to her chest. She smiled and waved a hand to leave. "Remember it. Those are the words of my master."

Jennifer sniffled and turned around to find Shayla disappearing behind a thicket. When she was alone, she touched her beating chest. "The…heart."

Remembering that day, Jennifer reached for her accessories she always wore and turned, getting into attack position. Faint blue particles sparkled and began taking shape in the form of a bow in her hand. Even if her way of thinking was weak, even if her powers were weak, and even if her actions were weak, the one thing that wouldn't weaken was her resolve. With her life, she'd protect those who were most precious to her.

"Hime," called out Jin. He was shocked by the new aura that now surrounded her. It was as Genji had said, Jennifer was also a Life-Kill and had been tricking him. Her cuteness was now replaced with deadliness. "It can't be. Did the Dome send you too?"

"My name's Jennifer. Not Hime." Jennifer lifted her head, her eyes bloodshot as guilt and rage rose filled her chest. She pulled back the string of the bow as a blue energy arrow materialized. "I'll never forgive you for hurting my Soulmate."

"Hime," Jin whispered, trying to stop the past from resurfacing.

When it was decided that Maria was to be transferred to the main household, Hime cried. She didn't want to lose her best friend and offered to go along with Maria. Jin was so devastated by her decision. He locked her inside the underground basement that would soon become the laboratory. Each night Hime cried to be freed. She wanted to see Maria, to talk to her again. Hime loved Maria more than she loved him. Hime wanted to be by Maria's side more than she wanted to be with him.

Jin couldn't handle rejection from the only person he'd ever loved and killed her. If he couldn't have her, no one could. He encased her body inside a glass filled with liquid nitrogen to keep her body from decomposing. That way, she would always remain with him. Somewhere in the laboratory, Hime was still there, waiting to be set free.

"Why do you want to leave me so badly when all I want is to be with you, Hime?"

"Sir?" said Genji.

"Hime, my dear Hime."

"Jin-san," called out Genji.

All women were the same. They made empty promises and left the ones they supposedly "loved" behind. Now that Jin understood the true nature of women, he didn't need them in his life, or in this world. He'd eradicate every single one, and Jennifer was no exception. If she wouldn't choose him, then she couldn't be with anyone else. "Kill them. Kill them all."

"Understood." Genji nodded and attacked as Jennifer fired her energy arrows. He dodged and grinned. Jennifer was stronger than she let on. Maybe, she would give him a good fight. Genji stood with his sword in hand. "You and that boy," he said, "I'll enjoy killing."

"I'll never allow you," Jennifer snarled, going on the offense. Her hair that had been pinned nicely was now a mess.

Jin reached inside his jacket, all the while glaring at Jennifer. He took out a glowing red dagger of some sort that Jennifer had never seen before. "You take care of her, Genji. I'll take the boy and finish the operation."

"Yes, sir." Genji rushed at her again while she dodged and kicked her heels off at him. One of them hit his face as she ran towards Jin who was cutting King down from the wall.

"Get away from him!"

"Damn you," Genji growled, catching hold of her hair from behind to drag back. She let out a yelp and hit the floor, losing concentration as her energy bow and arrows disappeared, returning to mere accessories. "I was thinking of going easy on you since you were a girl. But it seems that option is out the window now."

"Don't underestimate me because I'm a girl."

"I don't plan on it anymore."

"Good." Jennifer watched as Jin dragged King into a dark hallway and disappeared. She had to chase them before Jin could finish his operation, whatever it was. But first, she had to take care of this ninja.

From above, Genji brought his sword down. Swiftly, Jennifer slid beneath his parted legs and winced. He still had a firm hold on her hair. At such a short distance, could she fire her arrows? She was never good at target practice, especially near-object targets. It was a pity. She should've trained harder and asked Rain to be her teacher, seeing as how he was so gifted with a traditional bow and arrows, while she had to rely on energy.

Genji was caught off guard from her slide and lost balance. When he turned around, Jennifer had taken a dagger out from under her dress. She brought it to her hair and cut it, now free from his hold.

Genji's eyes widened in shock. He'd heard that a woman's hair was everything to her, yet Jennifer easily chopped it off without hesitating. It only made him smile. She indeed proved to be different. It almost made him want to keep her for himself. "What a pity," said Genji. He tossed the long orange curls into the air as each luscious strand fell. "And to think you had such beautiful hair."

"If saving King means cutting my hair, I'll do it as many times as necessary."

"Even if it means cutting an arm or leg?"

Jennifer cut off the lower half of her dress and tossed Jin's jacket off as well. Once all the excess weight was gone, she ran at Genji and fended off his sword with her dagger. With her other hand, she grabbed a second dagger strapped to her thigh and slashed his abdomen.

Genji touched his bleeding side and laughed as the two stood opposite each other. "To think I would get injured by someone weaker than me, and a girl at it too!"

"You still dare to look down on girls?"

"This match just keeps getting interesting." Once again, they ran at each other. Instead of doing the cutting, Jennifer was the one to get injured. She stumbled backwards and put a hand to her side. "Ha-ha, what happened to your determination of defeating me?! If you don't hurry, Jin-san will take that boy's heart out and give it to Hime-san!"

"What?" gasped Jennifer.

"Haven't you heard the notorious story of a genius who came from the Maroon Dome? In his studies and experiments he took the heart of a Life-Kill and implanted it into a dead human body. Despite the differences, the heart revived the human."

"Maroon...Dome," Jennifer repeated, not believing that a genius had hailed from there. He wasn't even mentioned in their textbooks. How could someone so important not be taught by the teachers?

"His name is Abe Michio, nicknamed 'Genius of the Century.' It was rumored that he was as brilliant as Einstein himself. After stealing a valuable from the Maroon Dome thirty years ago, he disappeared with a trusted friend. Sources say, he's still on the run for his life."

Jennifer narrowed her eyes in on Genji and tightened her hold on both daggers. She couldn't allow herself to get distracted with the story, but if what Genji said was true, then King was in grave danger. "Are you done?"

"I was giving you a valuable history lesson."

"Ah, was that what your rambling was about?"

Laughing, Genji shook his head. He liked Jennifer. It was a pity she had to die. "Come." He motioned for her as they clashed head-on once more.

∞

Doctor Nishikawa entered the room where Gon was chained. His wrists were bound together but his mouth and eyes weren't covered. While Doctor Nishikawa moved about the room humming, Gon glared.

"Why aren't you killing me?" he asked.

"I need you as a hostage."

"If what you want is a ransom, I'll tell you now, my family doesn't have much money."

Smiling, Doctor Nishikawa shook his head. He glanced over. Was Gon serious? Or was he trying to play dumb? "Your father is Yamagata's chief of police, isn't he?"

Gon's face went dead at the mentioning of his dad. Of course. How could he possibly forget something so crucial? So, this was why Doctor Nishikawa had taken him also. It was all because of some grudge. "Don't you dare hurt my father!"

"I won't hurt anyone so long as you obey my every command." Doctor Nishikawa grabbed a few utensils from a top shelf and turned to leave.

"Where's May-san?"

Doctor Nishikawa stopped halfway from leaving to turn back. His smile was so sadistic it could be mistaken as the Devil's.

"Don't tell me, you killed her already?"

"I haven't done anything to her. Not yet, at least. Taking the heart of a Life-Kill takes considerate time and preparation. If I cut the muscles in the slightest wrong place or take too long with the surgery or go too quickly, the heart will bleed out and die. Or if not, it'll react violently when it gets put inside its host and kill it. You see," said Doctor Nishikawa as he walked over to crouch before him.

Gon gulped at the surgical utensils the doctor was carrying. He had to remember this was a madman he was trying to reason with.

"The heart of a Life-Kill is different from a normal human's. After centuries of evolution, it can grant the most desperate wishes. It will allow you to take blood straight from the heart and create magnificent weapons with it. It even allows you to replace hearts, regardless if its host and original owner's blood type don't match. It knows somehow and will conform to the host. Magnificent, wouldn't you agree?"

"Are you implying that you're going to take out May-san's heart to give to someone else?"

"Exactly." Doctor Nishikawa snapped his fingers, happy that Gon caught on quickly.

"And who are you trying to revive?"

"My late wife."

"Your-" Gon began. He thought back to yesterday's conversation when Doctor Nishikawa had first approached them. When Gon thought about it, it was because he had gotten into trouble with those guys that May had to pay the consequences. "I don't believe it."

"Don't fret so much. There are many Life-Kills still alive in the world. One heart won't matter to those bastards."

"You're wrong." Gon shook his head and glared again. The doctor's view of the world was incorrect. "One heart won't matter, you say? It makes all the difference. That heart belongs to May-san. You have no right to take it from her. There's only one of her in this world. If you take her heart, she'll die. She won't ever come back to life."

Amused, Doctor Nishikawa raised an eyebrow and let out a chuckle. "Boy," he said and stood. There was no more time to waste. The surgery needed to happen. Now. "You have no idea how scary that organization is. If they wanted, they can wipe all humans off the face of this earth. Heck, they can even imprison us and keep us as slaves. But because they like playing with their food, they let us run around this pen, just to suck our life-energy. As for that girl you're so concerned about, yes, it's true that she'll die when I take her heart. But if, oh, let's say, the organization came and found her, all they have to do is give her a new heart and she'll spring back to life, all her memories still intact. Or if not, they can always re-clone her."

"Impossible," Gon said, shaking his head. All the things Doctor Nishikawa was telling him sounded like a paranormal sci-fi movie. Under normal circumstances, none of it could be done. Even the most advanced hospitals couldn't do such things with their patients or test subjects.

"It's not impossible boy. There are plenty other scarier things they can do. But," he said, turning to leave. "My time with you is up. I gotta perform the surgery."

Gon curled his fingers into fists. He was useless and vulnerable. At this rate, he wouldn't be able to save May even if he wanted to. "There's that man!" he shouted, halting the doctor. "Kakinouchi, there's still him! He'll come and save her! I just know it!"

"*If* he can find this place on time." Doctor Nishikawa grinned and left with his tray.

All alone again, Gon stared at the four walls with no windows that cornered him in. He should've listened to his gut feeling when Doctor Nishikawa first approached them. "How can a beautiful thing such as love turn out to be so deadly?" Hanging his head down low, Gon blinked his tears away. "Kakinouchi-san, please hurry."

∞

Kakinouchi impatiently paced in the park, waiting for the black sparrow to deliver an important device to him. After running around town for the past two hours, trying to find May, he came up empty-handed. Even after obtaining information from the chief and infiltrating the doctor's office, Kakinouchi found no evidence of the two ever being there. For that one desperate moment, he wished to have Louis' random Future Sight instead. If he did, finding May would be no problem.

Having no other choice than to contact the Dome, Kakinouchi called, filling them in on the situation. They responded immediately and sent the sparrow out to his location, instead of a spy.

Kakinouchi kept staring at the sky and back down at his watch. It read: 4:39pm. In another minute, the sparrow would come bearing him a gift.

If he knew that the Dome had a tracking device beforehand, he would've contacted them about the situation from the beginning. Regardless if he was given an earful, so long as he didn't waste any time.

Kakinouchi stopped pacing with ten seconds remaining. He counted down those ten dreadful seconds and watched intently. There was no sign of the sparrow anywhere.

"Three…two…one."

The black sparrow flew into view and dropped a small box in its talons, along with a red envelope in its beak, before flying back to the Dome.

"Just on time," said Kakinouchi. He smiled. In its own way, having the Dome be so prompt was good. Grabbing the two things, he scanned his fingerprint and quickly skimmed through the note.

Inside the package is what you need to locate May. Go and save her by all means necessary. After saving her, you two will immediately return to the Dome and abort your mission. We have other backups.

-Dean Kosa

"Shit," said Kakinouchi. He knew the dean would be pissed, but not this pissed. The note burned into ashes and flew away in the wind as he tore open the box in his left hand. Inside was a tracking wrist device. He turned it on as a white holographic screen appeared with the word: NAME.

"Kakinouchi, Arata" he spoke.

The white screen disappeared and was replaced with a yellow one. It read: SOULMATE: MAY. CORRECT?

"Yes."

A new screen popped up as a 3D map showed the location of May's whereabouts. The place was where a church once stood, tall and proud. Due to the lingering wars, it was abandoned and was nothing more than rubble and stones.

"A church?" Shocked, Kakinouchi grinned. He should've known it would be the most inconspicuous place. Strapping on the device, Kakinouchi ran to his destination.

∞

Nemuro

A single water droplet fell from the spout and into the sink as a hand slightly brushed Soria's cheek. She flung her eyes open at his sudden touch as the droplet of water shot across the room. Before it could hit him, it evaporated into nothing but steam. Soria leapt from the sofa, getting into attack position.

"Whoa, whoa," said Aoi. He jumped away, hands up to surrender, not expecting that reaction.

"Was that you?" demanded Soria. She quickly scanned the room in case someone had entered the premises while she was napping.

"Yeah, it was. Your hair looked like it was bothering you. So I-"

"Don't ever do that again while I'm sleeping," warned Soria. She brushed her hair and cheek where Aoi had touched, standing from her attack position. "I could've killed you just now."

"Ah, sorry," he apologized hurtfully, but she didn't notice.

"It's morning already?" she asked and yawned.

"It's actually noon." He chuckled and watched as Soria walked over to the window, while he returned to the sofa, never taking his eyes off her.

"Is that so?" Smiling, she placed a hand against the cold surface of the pane and closed her eyes. Even though she wasn't standing outside, she could feel the wind from the sea brushing through her hair. "It feels nice."

"Ugh!" Aoi grunted, bumping into a table as Soria spun around to look at him. "That hurts." With a foolish smile, he rubbed his thigh. Even after four months of being alone together, Aoi's nerves wouldn't calm down. He always ended up looking like a fool. "Sorry, I'm a-"

"-klutz."

"Ah, yeah, but you didn't have to use that tone."

"You fool," she laughed.

"Huh?" Aoi stared, unable to look away. She was laughing, she was *actually* laughing. In the times they were together, she was either sleeping, bored, or busy fighting. This feeling, he wouldn't be able to get enough of it.

"That was a good laugh," said Soria as she wiped the tears that filled her eyes. When she realized that she hadn't eaten breakfast, she turned towards him. "Say, did you eat yet?"

"Not yet." Aoi shook his head, now smiling.

"Then, let's go get something to eat."

"R—really, the two of us?"

"Yeah, the two of us." Soria yawned again and headed for the door, wondering what she wanted for lunch. Maybe she'd spend the Dome's money on a gourmet meal. But that might not sit well with her stomach.

"It just comes as a shock that you'd invite me. Since you know, you hate me and all," Aoi answered coyly.

The door slid open as Soria stopped and turned back, eyebrow raised. "Whoever said I hated you?"

"You...don't?"

"Did I ever say I hated you?"

"Well, no...I just assumed." He blinked a few times still trying to process her words. So all this time everything had been in his mind. Just because she never acknowledged him didn't mean she hated him. Relief washed over Aoi as he sighed and bent over, tears in his eyes. He wasn't hated, which meant he still had a chance.

"Don't go assuming things without confirming it first. That's how misunderstandings occur, you hear?"

"Yep, I hear ya!" he shouted cheerfully and smiled.

Soria stared into his twinkling eyes and smiled as well. "Now come on, let's go. Or else you'll fall behind." She walked out of the room as Aoi ran after her. There was no need for her to tell him. He would've chased her even if she hadn't invited him.

20th Lie

JIN THREW KING'S BODY onto the operating table and yelled from out of frustration. After all the commotion, he still hadn't woken up. The anesthesia Jin had injected was stronger than he thought. The surgical tools were well prepared and laid out on the table nearby. He quickly washed and dried his hands then slipped on gloves to grab a scalpel. This operation required him to be quick, yet precise, in case Genji couldn't defeat Jennifer.

"Damn," he said, slamming the scalpel down as the table shook. His anger still wouldn't subside from Jennifer's act of betrayal. How could she use him when he'd been so good to her?

It took a few minutes for Jin to get his emotions under control before he picked up the scalpel to put to King's chest. The price for tricking him would be their deaths. Only then could he truly be happy.

"Stop right there," ordered Maria from the doorway. In her shaky hands was a gun. Her gut feeling about Jin being involved in King's mysterious disappearance was correct.

Not expecting to see her there, Jin stared, long and hard. He had ordered all staff personnel to leave the premise before he returned home with Jennifer. Had Maria disobeyed orders and secretly stayed behind? And how did she get into the laboratory? Had she been snuck in behind him while he was occupied with Jennifer?

"Put down the scalpel."

Obediently, Jin set it and held up his hands to surrender. They were master and servant. The nerves she had to raise a gun at him. "What do you think you're doing, Maria? I'm your master."

194

She nodded in understanding but couldn't stand aside and watch Jin kill an innocent person.

"And you still dare to point a gun at me, knowing that?"

"What are you doing to King-san?"

"I was going to cut out the monster's heart and give it to Hime."

"Hime?" Maria repeated, her voice shaking.

"That's right. Hime. She's still alive…well, technically speaking, she's dead."

"Wh—what are you talking about?"

Jin grinned as he lowered his arms. Maria was no eminent threat. If she wanted to, she would've shot him already. "Hime tried to leave me. I showed her the consequences of doing so."

His confession flooded Maria's eyes with tears. She couldn't believe that he'd been deceiving her the entire time. It wasn't because Hime had fallen ill that she'd died. It was because Jin had killed her and it made Maria sick to the pit of her stomach. "How could you?" she asked. "How could you do such a thing to Hime?! She loved you so much!"

"It was because of you!" Jin blamed as Maria stopped crying. "Because of your selfish desires to go to the main household, Hime wanted to chase you!"

"She would've returned to your side after seeing to it that I was fine! And it's not like I wanted to leave in the first place! I was forced to, by the Mistress, your step-mother! You know that better than anyone!"

"It's too late for your excuses now."

"What excuses?!"

"Don't get in my way, Maria. I've been waiting for this day for a long time. Nishikawa and I both, have been waiting to get our hands on a heart like this boy's. Once I put his heart inside Hime, she'll revive, and everything will be fine again. We'll be together forever, you, me, and Hime." Jin smiled like a madman and began laughing. Such a day as this wouldn't come by again. He couldn't waste such a golden opportunity. "Yes, everything will be fine again, even without the other Hime here."

"You've gone mad, Jin."

He stopped laughing to glare. "Since when did you start calling your Master by his first name? You insolent trash."

"You've gone mad, *master.*"

"If you wish to shoot, I suggest you do it now. You know how good I am at darts." Again, he smiled and grabbed the scalpel from the table to lick.

"Don't-"

Before Maria finished her sentence, Jin threw the scalpel across the room, striking her left shoulder. She let out a cry and fired at random as Jin ran over to unarm her. The gun skidded away as he pulled out the scalpel from her shoulder. Blood spurt and trickled as Maria hit the ground, trying to crawl towards the gun. Laughing at her feeble attempts, he struck her outstretched hand, making her scream again.

"You should've shot me when you had the chance." Jin grinned as Maria looked into his crazed eyes. What she saw caused her breathing to quicken.

"Don't do it."

"It's a pity," Jin said, slapping her and pulling out the scalpel by force. She shrieked as he stood and walked over to grab the gun. "Too bad you won't be here for the reunion when Hime wakes up. I'll tell her you died from an illness. She'll be devastated, but it'll be for the best." Jin raised the gun, aiming it at her forehead.

From behind, King tackled Jin to the floor. He hit the gun away as Jin stabbed him in the abdomen. Pain overtook King, as he fell over, grunting. Jin attempted to stab him again, but King punched him and groggily got to his feet.

Thanks to Maria for stalling, the anesthesia had worn off. Though he still couldn't keep his balance from the side-effects, or completely self-heal, this was better than nothing. It was a good thing Jin had been so concentrated on killing him he didn't strap him down. Holding onto his bleeding abdomen, King sneered. It'd been a long time since he was beaten to such a state. The last time was when he challenged Rain and was beaten to a pulp. It was fine though. King liked challenges. In fact, he thrived in them.

"Are you alright, Maria-san?"

"King-san," whispered Maria. She cried and nodded, happy to see him on his feet. "Yes, I am."

"Hurry and get out of here."

"But-"

"You bastard," Jin hissed, getting to his feet and wiping his bloody lip. The way to win was to grab the nearby gun, shoot King, and inject him with another shot of Nishikawa's anesthesia he'd created.

As if the two could read each other's minds, they lunged for the gun and fought for it. With no weapons, King relied solely on his brawns. This was the worst time to be without his broadsword. With the scalpel still in his hand, Jin stabbed King in the eye.

"AH!" Blood gushed out from King's eye as he took hold of Jin, doing his best to withstand the pain, and broke Jin's dominant arm.

Yelping, Jin scampered away while King fell to the floor again. "You piece of shit!"

While he was fixated on King, Maria stood and grabbed the nearest surgical tool to stab his throat with. Her forehead and lip continued bleeding as her hands trembled. When Maria realized what she'd done, she gasped and let go, backing away.

Jin turned to look at her, eyes wide open. He opened his mouth to speak as blood trickled down his neck, staining his suit. "Ma...ria," he gurgled out, "how...could you?" and fell to the floor.

Maria's knees buckled as she slid to the floor. She hung her head down low and cried. All she wanted was to stop him. "I always knew," she whispered with a shake to her head. "A part of me always knew you'd hurt Hime somehow. But I didn't want to believe it."

"Hi...me..." he called out before his heart gave way and darkness claimed him.

"It's enough. Go join Hime in the other world. That way, you can stop hurting in this one, master." After inhaling and exhaling, she quickly crawled over to King's side. The stabs that Jin had inflicted wouldn't stop bleeding. "Hold on," said Maria. She helped him to stand as they collapsed to the floor together. "King-san, hang on. I'll get you to a doctor."

"A doctor won't be able to help with this wound." He forced a chuckle and touched his left eye where the scalpel was still lodged. So, this was the world that Shadow lived in, half dark and light.

"Don't say that." Maria stumbled to her feet, helping King to stand again. He had saved her and she would return the favor somehow.

"Maria-san," said King as he stopped walking. "You came down here for a reason, right?"

Maria remained silent and simply nodded in response.

"Go find Hime. Set her free from her eternal prison."

"But you-"

"I'll be fine. I can sense Jennifer coming. So, go. Go to your best friend."

Maria nodded, propping him against the hallway wall and stood. "I'll be right back." Turning, she ran off to find Hime's body.

King slumped onto his side, his breathing coming in short gasps. He was losing too much blood and he could feel his life slipping away. "Damn," he said, grinning painfully. "Is this the end for me?" Chuckling, King thought back to his childhood. The first time he met the other guys, he called them out, only to lose miserably. After training together and becoming friends, they somehow banded together as a brotherhood. Then, there was King's first meeting with the girls inside the forest and the time they infiltrated the girls' side. Now, he had a Soulmate he needed to protect, who was more important than his ranking.

"...in...!"

"Jen...?" he called out weakly and reached a hand out to the empty air.

"...King!" Jennifer screamed, her voice closer now. She ran towards him, hand stretched out desperately. When she reached him, she fell to her knees and scooped his bloody body into her arms. At the sight of the scalpel in his eye, Jennifer cried. King's fight with Jin was worse than hers with Genji.

"Jennifer," he whispered and smiled. So, this was what a Soulmate was for, to have by his side until his last breath. His life had been a good run as contentment settled in. "Don't cry anymore." Though he couldn't see her tears, he could feel them falling.

"No, no!" screamed Jennifer. She looked around frantically, trying to find a way to save him, but there was nothing she could do. She wasn't skilled in medicine. Neither could her powers heal, like Naruyuki and Taiki. Even Remi, who had neglected her healing would be valuable right now. "How, how?" she asked desperately. There had to be a way to save King. She just had to calm down and think. "Umi-sensei."

Letting King down, Jennifer ran out of the laboratory and up to her room on the second floor. She scrimmaged for the device that the girls had been given before leaving the Dome. When Jennifer found the pocket-device, she called for help.

∞

A red-haired, pigtailed girl sat inside the infirmary as Miss Umi bandaged her arm. She'd gotten injured during training and wore the same uniform as the previous generations.

From the corner of her eye, a blinking red light on her desk caught her attention. Miss Umi frowned and stopped bandaging. Someone was making contact from the outside. Rolling her chair over, she tapped on the holographic screen. When Jennifer's picture appeared, her eyes widened.

The pigtailed girl raised her eyebrows, wondering who was calling and why Miss Umi looked so worried. "What's wrong, Miss Umi?"

"Leelee," she spoke without turning around. "Run along to class."

"But my injury-"

"Ask Tanaka to help you. I have urgent business to tend to." With her hand, she shooed the pigtailed girl out.

Unhappy, but complying, Leelee left the infirmary.

All the while, Miss Umi was typing at the speed of light. There was no time to waste. King was in a dire situation. Even if Miss Umi were to leave the Dome now to assist Jennifer, she wouldn't make it on time. The best bet was to call for help nearby.

∞

While still on their mission, the three guys had received orders to halt what they were doing to assist their fellow comrades, who were in deep trouble. Seeing as how it had been a long time since Kei last saw King, he separated from Taiyou and Tasuku to head up north. Meanwhile, the two guys headed southwest.

Kei infiltrated the mansion estate, making sure there were no guards. To his amazement, no one was around. "Hmm," he said, concerned. This was way too easy.

When Kei reached the front of the mansion, sitting off to the side, on the massive green lawn was Jennifer. Laying with his head down on her lap, was King. He was knocked out good. Kei stopped in his tracks. He couldn't take his eyes off Jennifer who kept staring at King.

Finally noticing that someone was there, Jennifer turned. One look at the fashionable Kei with slicked hair and she bawled.

Alarmed, Kei backed away. He'd never met one of the Dome girls before, or a crying girl until then.

"Are you...Kei-kun?"

With a gulp and nod, Kei inched closer. "Ah, yeah, that's me."

Letting go of King, Jennifer got on her knees to beg. "I've shared my energy with him, but it's not enough. Please, save him."

"Uh, well," Kei said, patting her unruly hair. Saving King was the reason he'd come. There was no need for her to plea like this. And why was he suddenly irritated? Was he suddenly coming down with the flu? "That's my job. So, lift your head."

Obeying, Jennifer lifted her head, but her tears continued streaming. "Thank you."

"Uh, yeah," Kei responded, feeling awkward under her gaze. He'd met a few human girls while out in the real world, but none of them had made a lasting impression. Even when he first saw a picture of Umeko, his potential candidate, he got excited, not nervous. His training too never made him nervous. Yet with Jennifer, he was being self-conscious.

After calming his heart, Kei pulled out the scalpel from King's eye and grabbed a pocketknife. He cut his left palm as blood ran. Meanwhile, Jennifer watched, horrified, yet intrigued. Kei opened King's bloody eye to let a few drops in. Next, he placed his bloody palm on King's chest to begin chanting. Seconds later, a pink aura rose from King's body.

When Kei was done with his healing ritual, his injured palm self-healed. Turning, he smiled at Jennifer. "He'll be-"

"You're amazing!" Jennifer threw herself on top of Kei and laughed. She couldn't believe that there was someone this magnificent amongst the boys.

"Eh?!" Kei shouted. His cheeks turned a bright red and his heart began beating irregularly. He wasn't sure what to do with this sudden development. He couldn't stray from the potential candidate the dean had assigned him, but Jennifer's wonderful curves and beautiful smile had stolen his heart. Was this the love that Louis always spoke of?

"If you're this amazing, how come you didn't heal Shadow's eye?"

"Ah, that," Kei said, disappointed. "Back then, our powers weren't fully developed. Gabe-sensei also isn't a real healer. That's why Shadow's eye is the way it is."

"I see. Sorry for asking."

From the mansion, there was a loud boom as smoke and fire arose. Hearing, Kei got to his feet and pushed Jennifer behind him.

"It's only Maria-san." Jennifer took hold of Kei's back shirt to squeeze. There were no enemies left to fight. He could relax.

"Huh?"

"Maria-san couldn't stand to be away from her best friend. Her guilt of hurting her master and best friend, made her stay behind. That fire is her way of atonement."

Kei turned to look at the sad Jennifer. There were tears in her eyes. At this rate, she would start crying a second time. "Don't cry anymore." Kei reached out to wipe her tears and smiled. "Keep smiling, got it? Tears aren't befitting of a beauty such as yourself. It's a waste if you continue crying."

Jennifer blushed and her eyes widened. Was Kei a natural lady-killer? If so, all women in the world had better watch out. He could probably break any heart without even trying. "You're so weird, just like Yeve," she said and chuckled.

"Huh? Who is that?"

"I guess you can call her our leader."

"Is that so?"

"Oye," hissed King. Now that he was fully recovered, he awoke to Kei, the last person he wanted to see, flirting with his Soulmate. With a glare, he pushed the two away from each other, not wanting Jennifer anywhere near this jerk. "Why the hell are you here?"

"Oh, King."

"You're all better now!" Jennifer exclaimed, happy to see him up and about. Even his eye was all better now too. Kei's abilities were top-notch, though they differed from Naruyuki's and Taiki's.

"Explain yourself, Kei," King ordered.

"Oh my," Kei said with a sneer. With King's presence, his giddy feeling faded. "I came to see how you were doing since it's been quite some time. When I got here, I found you near death's doorway. I thought such a hot-blooded guy like you would never be seen like that. This is gonna be an interesting story to tell Rain and Hotaka, wouldn't you agree?"

Gulping, King glared as the two friends got into a tussle. "Don't you dare, you bastard!"

"Oh yeah, watch me!"

"You two," Jennifer pleaded. She didn't want them fighting right after King had just awakened, but he seemed to be in such high spirits she couldn't intervene. It only proved that he had made a full recovery.

∞

Kakinouchi followed the 3D map as it led him to the rubble that was once a church. There were no signs of them as he tirelessly searched. From behind, a few mice were making their way above ground. As soon as they spotted Kakinouchi, they retreated. Quickly giving chase, he kicked some stones away to find a tiny tunnel.

"So that's where you're hiding." Kakinouchi smiled and placed both hands over the rat hole, freezing the entire ground. There was no need to find a formal underground passage when he had his powers. Taking form into his hand was an ice spear as he drove it into the ground.

∞

Doctor Nishikawa looked up at the trembling ceiling and set the bloody scalpel in his hand down. Someone had found his base. Sedated on the bed was May. Hooked to her were tubes and machines, monitoring her condition. There was a loud beeping sound coming from it, but he didn't care.

"Time to go." Doctor Nishikawa took off his bloody gloves to toss before washing his hands. He was calm about the entire ordeal, already prepared for this situation. He grabbed the beating heart that sat on a white toweled tray and carefully set it inside a metal cooler. Once Doctor Nishikawa locked it, he left the surgery room with his prized possession to retrieve Gon.

"I told you that Kakinouchi-san would come for his Soulmate!" Gon shouted and fought to get free. He had to stall for time.

"That goon's already too late." Doctor Nishikawa injected Gon with some sort of serum before unlocking his chains and cuffing him.

Alarmed by his words, Gon stared at the metal cooler sitting on the ground. His heartbeat fastened. He couldn't peel his eyes off the tiny cooler. It couldn't be true.

"It's the precious heart." Doctor Nishikawa smiled and took out a detonator from his pocket. "Start walking." He pushed an unsteady Gon forward and grabbed the cooler as they headed towards the exit. Along the way, they met Kakinouchi who had frozen his way underground to where they were. "Impatient, aren't you?"

"You," growled Kakinouchi. One look at the doctor's smug look nearly sent him Berserk. He wanted nothing more than to sink his teeth into Doctor Nishikawa's throat.

"Kakinouchi...san..." Gon said, barely able to form sentences.

"If you dare take one step, I'll kill the boy," threatened Doctor Nishikawa.

Without batting an eyelid, Kakinouchi sneered. "His life means nothing to me." Such a threat as that wouldn't work against him. His only concern was May.

"You don't care? You don't care if an innocent victim dies because of you?"

"No."

"You're crazy, just like me."

"You and I are nothing alike."

"Yes, yes," Doctor Nishikawa said with a nod and grin. "But you know, I did you a favor by killing your Soulmate."

"Huh?"

"Kakinouchi-san!" Gon shouted again. His mind couldn't focus on anything as the place spun, but he had to warn Kakinouchi of the doctor's plans. "Get May-san...! Psycho...took heart! If you not go... nothing left...! He...blow up!"

"What?" Kakinouchi lowered his gaze, finally noticing the cooler in Doctor Nishikawa's left hand. At the sight, his heart nearly stopped. "You-"

"Go!" ordered Gon.

"Shut up!" Doctor Nishikawa shouted, kicking Gon to his knees and pressing the button on the detonator. "So, what's it going to be?"

Both choices were horrible. It meant he was bound to lose one thing. But ultimately, he had to choose the most beneficial one, since time was of the essence. Kakinouchi glared at the doctor one last time before running to find May's body. "No matter how long it takes, I will find you."

"I'll be waiting." Without wasting a precious second, Doctor Nishikawa instructed Gon to start walking again while he set up C-4's behind them. When they reached a door, he punched in a password as it opened and they entered.

Gon looked about in a daze at the abandoned subway train they had boarded. "So," he said, "this how...we got underground."

"That's right." Doctor Nishikawa smiled and walked over, knocking Gon unconscious. After getting the train to move, he pressed a button to activate the C-4's. Now that they were safe, Doctor Nishikawa picked up the cooler to embrace with a breath of ecstasy. "Wait for me. I'm coming with your new heart, my beloved."

∞

"May!" called out Kakinouchi as he ran into the surgery room and stopped. She was lying on the bed, her chest exposed. Blood stained the bed and her hospital gown. Doctor Nishikawa didn't even bother to sew her back up after the surgery. Walking over, Kakinouchi tore the straps binding her. He grabbed the blanket and wrapped her with it, unable to stand the sight of her without a heart.

"May," he called out softly and picked her up to cradle.

From above, the ceiling shook uncontrollably. It was as Gon had said. The crazy doctor was planning to destroy May's body.

"I'm sorry. I let you out of my sight. I failed to protect you. Please wake up." He buried his face into her hair as the room crumbled in. Even then, he didn't bother to move.

Before the ceiling could bury them, someone fell in through, protecting them. All the while, Kakinouchi refused to move from where he was.

"Arata," spoke the protector, once the rumbling had stopped. Everything had been destroyed except for that one spot they stood in. "Arata," Tasuku said again, his hoodie and bandana still hiding his face from view.

Refusing to answer, Kakinouchi stood still.

Annoyed, Taiyou who was also present hit him over on the head and shouted, "Snap out of it, Kakinouchi!"

Slowly, Kakinouchi turned, tears in his eyes.

Feeling bad for hitting him after what had happened to his Soulmate, Taiyou scratched his head. "Geez, to think Gabe-sensei told us to take a detour to help you. It seems like you really do need our help. Just what the hell happened?"

"May," Kakinouchi whispered. He turned to look at May in his arms, his tears blinding his view of her. He fixed her hair and did his best to smile. If she were awake, she'd hate how her hair was out of place. Kakinouchi had to see to it that she always looked pretty.

"Here, let me," Taiyou said, attempting to feel May's pulse.

"Don't touch her."

"Oye, what the hell?" Taiyou said, stopping halfway from touching her.

"She's dead!" roared Kakinouchi. He let May down onto the bed and grabbed Taiyou by the collars, blood staining them both. Hatred was all that was left of him now. At this rate, he might even go Berserk if left alone. "What can you possibly do?! You're no necromancer!"

"Unhand me, buffoon."

"Come on you two," Tasuku said, playing peacemaker from behind. This was getting out of hand and he didn't know how to handle it.

Kakinouchi turned, glaring at Tasuku this time. "Stay out of this, wimp."

In a whimper, Tasuku cowered and fidgeted with his fingers. Meanwhile, Taiyou broke free and punched an unsuspecting Kakinouchi to the ground.

"Taiyou!" shouted Tasuku in alarm. Even if Kakinouchi deserved a good beating, now wasn't the time.

"Stand back." Taiyou pulled Tasuku away while he stood in-between them. Knowing Tasuku who hated violence, it was Taiyou's job to make Kakinouchi regain his senses. "You're right, she's dead, and I can't resurrect the dead. But at least I'm trying to help. Look at you. What are you doing to help? Nothing. You're just standing there, self-loathing. Get your head back into the game and do something," countered Taiyou. This time, it was his turn to glare at Kakinouchi's weakness. "If you can retrieve her heart and put it back where it belongs, she'll return."

Kakinouchi stared at the ground, unable to argue. He knew it was true but seeing May's state made him forget everything.

"Um," said Tasuku. He was staring at his device. Whatever he had to say seemed urgent.

"What is it?" answered Taiyou.

"It's Dean Kosa."

Kakinouchi's eyes widened. He knew what Dean Kosa wanted to say.

Still staring at Kakinouchi, Taiyou spoke, "Put it on speaker."

Nodding, Tasuku turned on his wrist-device. "Yes, dean?"

"Is Arata with you, Tasuku?" Dean Kosa asked from the other end. His usual playful voice was cold and stern.

"Yes, he is."

"Dean," Kakinouchi greeted, his voice cracking.

"Umi-sensei contacted me about May's sudden heartbeat disappearing from her monitor. Did you fail?" It was quiet amongst them as Kakinouchi nodded, unable to find his voice to respond. If he did, he might break down again. "I'm disappointed in you, Arata." Again, silence filled the air. "Return to the Dome as soon as possible with May's body."

Kakinouchi nodded obediently before whispering, "Yes, sir. I understand."

21st Lie

KAMIKATSU, TOKUSHIMA

The countryside was so calming that not even the loud cicadas or heat mattered.

Alice sat on the swing that hung from the old oak tree, wearing a green yukata. Poe and she had been sent there to investigate a small town with a total population of 1,253. They had stumbled upon the hot spring inn five nights ago with no food or money for shelter. The landlady of the inn decided to let them stay for free if they agreed to help with the chores, since her six-year-old son couldn't assist with the harder tasks. The couple quickly jumped at the offer, hoping to find out more information about the town.

After a little snooping around and asking questions, they were given a brief history. In the past, the town's population had once been around 3,000. However, as the years passed, a great and terrible storm threatened to wipe them off the map. Crops were lost, and homes were destroyed. Hundreds of their fellow townspeople died, leaving only 400 people. After many years of backbreaking labor and endless prayers, the town prospered, and the population skyrocketed to 1,000.

From behind, Poe approached with a loaf of freshly baked bread. He smiled and ran over to sit with her.

With a shriek of alarm, Alice nearly toppled over but caught her balance. She turned to glare at Poe who simply laughed it off, offering her some bread. If he weren't so darn cute, she'd give him a piece of her mind. "Thanks," she muttered, taking half the bread to eat.

"So?" he asked.

There was no need to ask. Poe probably heard the rumors circulating the small town and was teasing her by asking. "You already know. Why ask?"

Again, Poe laughed while eating his bread. "Don't you think it's so amusing though? The residents actually think we eloped."

"Why are you making a joke out of this?"

"Because it's funny," he answered and wiped his eyes.

"Gee, I wonder who's fault it is for putting that idea in their heads? Hmm, let me guess. It was probably because during our first night here you wouldn't let me take a bath *by myself*," she reminded and elbowed his ribs.

"Ow, okay, I admit it. I'm at fault." In Poe's defense, he had a good reason to be cautious. It was because their mission of investigating a small town with only one convenience store and one restaurant, where everyone knew everyone, sounded too fishy. That was why he didn't want Alice out of his sight and went as far as to hug and pull her back, crying and shouting, "Don't leave me! What if something happens to you?! No, no, no! I won't accept that! Let me go with you, Alice!"

Thus, began the rumors and raised eyebrows from those who had witnessed Poe's outrageous antics. Alice assured him she could take care of herself until he could no longer go argue and let her out of his sight for the first time since they parted from the others. After winning the argument, she embarrassedly rushed off to the baths with a few other giggling girls.

"But you know," he said cheerfully, "it does feel like we eloped huh?"

Alice choked on her bread to look over. "Don't you dare add any fuel to the fire."

It was true. Ever since they showed up, gossip started circulating about why two teenagers were traveling together, let alone a teenage boy and girl. Stories ranged from a master and servant, to a kidnapper and his hostage, to being star-crossed lovers. The story that garnered the most popularity amongst the small-town residents was the master and servant relationship.

Alice was the princess and Poe was her servant. They fell in love, but her wealthy family didn't approve and so they eloped to find their own happiness.

"Don't you enjoy the liveliness of the town? Remember when we first came? It was like a ghost town and no one was willing to talk to us," he reminded and glanced over while she continued eating in silence.

"I guess," she responded glumly.

Without a word, Poe reached out to brush her hair gently.

Surprised, Alice shimmied away on the wooden swing.

"Whoa, chill, crumbs," Poe answered and showed the crumbs he'd taken from her hair.

"You could've told me. I would've brushed it off myself," she said, turning the other way to eat.

"There's no need to get shy." Poe laughed again as Alice glared at him. As soon as they made eye contact, she looked the other way. "You're hurting my feelings here. I'm seriously going to start crying." He put a hand to his chest and let out a loud sniffle, but Alice continued ignoring him. Still smiling, Poe put his head down on her shoulder.

"What are you doing now?" she asked, his black hair tickling her cheek.

"Just for a little while. Let me rest my head on your shoulder."

"If you want a pillow, it's inside your room."

"Don't be so stingy."

"I'm not being stingy. This is my shoulder and arm, not yours. Don't use it as a pillow to your convenience."

Poe lifted his head to grasp her arm tightly. She winced but didn't utter a sound. "Did you know…?"

Alice stared, confused. She didn't quite understand why he was giving her such a pained expression.

"Did you know, people from the Godless Ages believed that if you were bound as soul mates, you were meant to be?" explained Poe. "That's why, don't be so stingy and lend me your shoulder for a while. I'm tired."

"Geez, there you go again. Why is it that you know so much about the Godless Ages anyway?" With that said, Alice closed her mouth. She didn't have any solid information or facts to back up her arguments if she decided to continue. It would only make her look silly. If it had been Love arguing with Poe, it would be a different story, since she was the most knowledgeable.

"Did you also know?"

"There's more?"

Poe let go of her arm, touching her cheek gently. It was so soft and silky, he didn't want to withdraw. "We are each other's reflection in a mirror. I am you, and you are me."

Alice sat still, not daring to move or breathe. Poe noticed and chuckled. Finally, she exhaled, her red face giving away exactly what she was thinking. "It's not funny! That was a cheap shot just now!"

"My sweet Alice," Poe whispered, caressing her face gently. He closed his eyes and put his forehead against hers, inhaling and exhaling deeply, her perfume surrounding him. He could die like this.

From behind, someone cleared their throat as the two swirled to look. Standing there was a worker from the hot spring who had a hand to her mouth. Her cheeks were flushed from witnessing their lovey-dovey act just then. "E—excuse me for interrupting you, love birds," she apologized.

"It—it's not what you think!" shouted Alice. She quickly stood and shook her head, trying to explain the situation.

"Breakfast is ready." The worker lady bowed and scampered away with a giggle. What she had witnessed was going to be the talk of the town. Once

Poe and Alice returned to the inn, everyone would he staring and pointing, whispering about the new rumor.

"What the hell just happened?" Alice said in dread. She hit her knees and pounded away at the earth. "Now she's going to tell, and everyone's going to think of more weird things to add to the story!"

"There's nothing wrong with the story. I kind of enjoy all this attention we're getting," chuckled Poe.

"Stop playing with me just because you find this situation amusing!" shouted Alice as she stood and ran off.

"Oye, wait for me!"

Alice turned back and stuck her tongue out at him, then turned around to run again. She'd done nothing wrong in this lifetime to deserve such an embarrassing punishment.

Her childish tantrum was so endearing, Poe laughed. The sky was so beautiful, he couldn't get enough of it either. From afar, Alice was shouting again about wanting to finish the mission in peace. "Run all you want. I'll always find you."

∞

Tokyo

A sleek, black private jet landed as an important figure stepped out from within. He wore a shiny gold and white robe uniform. Sitting on his glossy blond hair was a tall hat, also gold and white. Instead of looking like the Golden God's representative, he looked like a cult leader. As soon as he planted a foot on the concrete, a group of men in black rushed over to escort him to the white limousine.

Standing not far away was Takahiko and Love. They were part of his protection squadron, assigned to keep the peace on the streets. So far nothing had happened, which made it even more suspicious. With the representative, Franz's appearance in Japan, they knew something troublesome would be brewing soon.

Franz greeted the leaders of Japan who had personally come to see him. They shook hands and bowed. He turned to glance at the two kids amongst the adults and stared for a while.

"He's staring," Love whispered and adjusted her glasses. Being stared at by a complete stranger made her uncomfortable and fidgety.

"You're being overly self-conscious," said Takahiko in response.

"No, I'm not."

Franz finally smiled and bowed their way as Takahiko perked. So, Love hadn't been self-conscious after all.

"Bow," he ordered, forcing Love to bow with him.

"Why do I have to bow too? If you want to bow, you do it alone." She broke away from his grasp.

"It's called courtesy." He pinched her as she winced and glared. This was no place to be arguing. Again, he attempted to force her to bow.

"I can do it myself," she said and bowed unwillingly. When they stood, Franz was standing before them, smiling. "Whoa," Love said, jumping away. Why did it feel like he'd jumped the space between them?

"I'm sorry to surprise you like that," he apologized by chuckling.

"It's okay."

"It's a pleasure meeting you two. Seems like I'll be in your care." Franz bowed and stood as the two bowed again.

"Same here, pleasure meeting you as well," responded Takahiko.

"Well then, ciao," he bid, turning to leave with his group of men.

Once he was gone, Love hugged her spell book to her chest. She didn't like Franz, nor the aura he emitted. It was like staring at a snake who didn't know it was a snake. "Why do we have to escort him for? He has tons of reliable men serving him."

"Stop complaining."

"I'm just saying that this mission is stupid and boring. Oh, did I forget to mention, stupid?"

"Love," he snapped.

Love stared at him, noticing that he was losing his patience with her. "Fine," she said, dropping it.

"Orders are absolute. We must follow through with them," Takahiko said, watching as Franz entered the limousine.

Raising an eyebrow, Love turned towards Takahiko. This was her first time hearing such a thing. "Is that what your teachers drilled into your head back at the Dome?"

"It is."

"Well, I'd have hated to be part of your boys' school."

Takahiko turned, flicking her on the forehead. She was insulting his teachers and the way he was brought up.

"Ow! It was a joke, sheesh. You're no fun, did you know that?" Love rubbed her forehead and followed Takahiko, now that Franz had left in his limousine.

"I know. The guys tell me that all the time."

"What a coincidence, the girls tell me I'm no fun either because I'm always uptight."

"No wonder we're Soulmates, eh?" joked Takahiko as he laughed.

Love stared at his back, her cheeks flushed. She hated how he could get such a reaction out of her with just a few words. Now if she could find out his weakness.

∞

"What's on your mind?" asked the blond teenager who was sitting inside the limousine with Franz. He fixed his thin, red scarf around his neck while Liz, the sleeping cat lay in his lap. Takahiko and Love were so concentrated on Franz they didn't notice he had two other guests that had come out from the jet.

"Those two kids," Franz said, looking out the car window. "I could feel their strong connection to one another."

Not interested, he patted Liz who purred. "Liz says she's found two people who are far more interesting than the two you were talking about."

Raising an eyebrow, Franz turned away from the window. "Oh? Is that so, Liz?" He reached over, attempting to pat her also. Sensing his intentions, she woke up and hissed loudly as Franz withdrew.

"Be nice."

Liz purred obediently and put her head back down on his lap.

"So tell me, who are these two that Liz has her eyes on, Nicholas."

"Can't say."

"Why?"

"She doesn't want anyone to steal them from her." Nicholas smiled and glanced out the window. The reason he had volunteered to escort Franz to Japan in the first place was because he too had his eye on someone.

∞

The men reaping and sowing in the fields stopped what they were doing to glance up. The wind had picked up suddenly, swaying the long grass blades from side to side, while leaves were sent scattering from their twigs. Off in the distance, thunder could be heard.

"This one looks nasty," said one of the workers.

"Yeah, let's call it a day," agreed the others.

"Eh? Is it that bad?" Poe leaned against his hoe, watching the gray clouds roll closer to the small town.

The workers looked amongst themselves before cracking a smile. Poe was a city boy to the very core. He didn't know the dangers of the countryside. "Out here, the storm hits closer to home."

"For a newbie like you, you wouldn't understand until you've experienced it first-hand." Before long, they were laughing and packing up to head home early. None of them wanted to get caught.

Poe was the last to leave. All the while he held his gaze to the sky, wondering how such a cheerful morning and scorching afternoon could be ruined by a rainstorm. Before he knew it, his walking pace turned into a jog, and soon, he was desperately running back to the inn, his stomach churning.

∞

Even though Love was tired to death from the endless city patrolling, she had hallway duty that night. The top floor penthouse of the hotel had been reserved solely for Franz's stay in Japan.

After making her rounds, Love returned to standing a few feet away from the front door of the penthouse. She let out a yawn and flipped through her spell book, trying to learn higher spell levels while Takahiko had gone off with a coworker to inspect the lower levels of the hotel. An orange tabby cat trotted by like an elegant warhorse and purred as Love shut her book to watch. "A cat," she said, alarmed that Liz had gotten past her surveillance.

Liz turned to look at Love and haughtily trotted on by, not caring.

"Conceited."

Hearing, Liz turned back to hiss.

Love raised an eyebrow at its reaction. Did it understand human language? "What's with you, kitty?"

"Liz?" called out Nicholas as he entered the hallway and stopped. "There you are." He walked over, scooping her into his arms to scratch behind the ears as she purred. "Didn't I tell you to stop wandering off on your own? Geez, you never listen to anyone, do you? Should I put a bell around your neck?" he joked.

Liz let out another meow that sounded like a whimpering plea.

"I was just teasing." Nicholas smiled and turned to find Love staring. She clearly had a look on her face that said, "What the hell is with these two weirdoes?" "Oh, hello," he greeted.

"Hello," Love greeted with a slight bow.

"Did Liz cause you trouble by any chance?"

"No."

"That's good to hear at least. Well, thank you for finding her for me."

Love laughed off Nicholas' gratitude. She shook her head, turning a bright pink. He was awfully handsome for a foreigner. She almost couldn't find it in her to look him in the eye. This was the first time a boy was making her feel self-conscious. Was it because he was someone she didn't know, and she wasn't immune to his charms yet? "I didn't really do anything."

"You did, by not throwing her out when you saw her."

"Ha-ha, yeah," Love said, guiltily averting her gaze. She had been on the brink of summoning Liz away with her magic when he entered the picture.

Liz who was purring and rubbing her head against Nicholas' forearm, abruptly stopped. She hissed, able to sense Love's attraction towards Nicholas.

Love stopped smiling to raise an eyebrow. She adjusted her glasses on her nose, wanting to confirm her assumption. "Jealous women aren't beautiful, especially if they're cats."

With a glint in her eye, Liz jumped out from Nicholas' arms, trying to claw at Love who stood calmly without budging. Swiftly but elegantly, Nicholas caught her by the tail. Hissing and meowing, still trying to scratch Love, Liz didn't bother with the fact that Nicholas was holding her upside down by the tail.

"Sorry," Nicholas apologized. "Liz's attitude isn't the best in the world."

"Ah, that's quite alright. I know plenty of girls like that," Love said, smiling it off.

"Well then, please excuse us." Nicholas bowed and left with Liz by the tail. The night wasn't getting any younger, and he was jet-lagged.

When the two were gone, Love realized what a big blunder that was. She didn't know who they were or how they had gotten onto that floor without clearance. If they were spies or assassins, she'd be in big trouble. Then again, if they were trying to assassinate Franz, all they had to do was take out Love and enter the penthouse, seeing as how she was the only guard. "Damn, it's all that guy's fault for being so handsome."

"Who is?" asked Takahiko from behind.

"Whoa," Love said, jumping away. "Don't scare me like that."

"Sorry," apologized Takahiko. In his hand was a bag of take-out he'd ordered while patrolling downstairs. Though it was way past dinner, they needed to munch on something. "So," he said suspiciously, "who's this handsome person?"

"Someone," Love answered with a shrug. She was starving, and the aroma from the bag made her salivate.

Takahiko raised an eyebrow. It was unlike her to be so secretive. Now he *had to* know the mystery man who was making his Soulmate drool. "Is it one of the guys?" he asked, refusing to hand over the food. "Rain? Hotaka? *Shadow*?"

"What? No. It's some foreigner with a possessive cat," replied Love. She chuckled when she remembered how Nicholas had been holding Liz by the tail. It was too bad she didn't have a polaroid to snap a shot. Abruptly, Love stopped. Takahiko was glaring. "What?"

"It's breaktime. Let's go eat." He yanked Love by the wrist to drag down the hallway, knowing he shouldn't have left her unattended.

"What's with you suddenly?"

"Did you two do something for the cat to be jealous of?"

Love's cheeks heated at his accusation. Was he belittling her? Or was he hinting that she was untrustworthy? Was that how she appeared to him? Unfaithful? "What the hell does that mean?" she asked, breaking free.

"I was just asking."

"Yeah, well, your question sounded more like an accusation." Love briskly walked around him and left, no longer feeling hungry. She had to get away before their argument could get uglier. "Have someone help you keep watch. I'm going to bed."

"Love!" Takahiko called out, wanting to chase her to apologize, but didn't. The best thing to do was let her cool down and then apologize later. "Damn it." He pulled his red headband over his eyes and groaned. His timing for picking fights was the worst.

"You should really treasure her," said Franz. He was standing in the doorway of his hotel penthouse, smiling with his arms crossed. He had witnessed the entire ordeal.

Takahiko pulled his headband off his eyes and spun around, embarrassed about creating a scene. "Sorry for disturbing you."

"Isn't it a little late for dinner?" Franz eyed the bag of food Takahiko was holding, not caring about the apology.

"Yeah, it is."

Franz uncrossed his arms and motioned for Takahiko to enter. "Come, let's talk. I'm sure Love wants to be alone right now. All women are like that. They need time to cool down."

Takahiko smiled and nodded, his thoughts exactly. "Yeah."

"I'll pour us some tea. You can tell me what the situation is," he offered.

"Thank you." Takahiko bowed before following him inside.

∞

Soaked from the rain, Poe burst through the inn doors to find everyone panicking. No one paid him any attention as he set his things near the entry, then took off his wet shoes and rushed off to find Alice, not caring to change first.

"Poe-kun?" called out the innkeeper, Ms. Hirano.

Swirling around, Poe stopped. "Hirano-san."

"Thank goodness you're back!" She ran over to hug him, not minding that he was sopping, and that her yukata was getting dirty.

"What happened? Why is everyone up and about in this storm? And where's Alice?" Poe asked, pulling away.

"Oh, it's horrible. Alice-chan, Alice-chan," she wept.

"What about Alice?" he asked, holding his breath.

"While we were preparing for dinner, little Ben's father burst in. He was hysterical, saying that he'd lost little Ben while out fishing in the forest. Alice freaked out and ran out to find him. We're forming a search party now to-"

"Shit," Poe groaned, running out into the cold night with his shoes.

"Poe-kun, wait!"

Even though he could hear Ms. Hirano's frantic screams, he didn't dare stop. His legs kept moving and his adrenaline kept pumping. He had to find Alice in this horrible storm. If he let her stay outside for too long, she could catch pneumonia or get hurt somehow. Without a healer around, he couldn't afford for either one to happen.

From above, lightning zapped, and thunder clapped. Glancing up, Poe frowned. It was as the workers had said. The storm in the countryside really did strike closer to home.

∞

"Ben-kun!" called out Alice as she searched high up and down low for the missing boy in the forest. In her hand was a flashlight to shine the way. It was a good thing she'd grabbed it before leaving the inn. The rushing current ran before her as she stood at the fishing spot where the father-son had been.

After a while of searching, Alice came to a slow halt. The dark clouds and rain were hiding the stars. Drop after drop fell, soaking her from head to toe. Lightning zapped across the dark skies, making her feel like she was in a horror movie of some sort.

Alice touched her thigh where her gun holster sat. She shook her head and withdrew her hand. "That won't do me any good."

Following the current, she ran and ran until she heard a faint cry. In the middle of the rushing current was a boulder, and holding onto the boulder for dear life, was the green-haired boy.

"Ben-kun!" shouted Alice. She ran down the banks a little more and shone the flashlight out at him. His teeth chattered, and his forehead bled from hitting the rocks below after getting swept downstream. Exactly how far were they from the fishing spot now? Not even Alice could tell.

"O—onee-chan!" shouted Ben. He let go of the boulder with one hand to reach out. The moment he did, the water relentlessly threatened to carry him downstream. He let out a cry and quickly clung to the boulder again.

"Fool, don't let go!"

Ben nodded at her command and tightened his loose grip.

Alice stared at the boy who would soon pass out. His lips were turning a purplish blue. Tears flooded her eyes from being vulnerable. If she jumped in, she would get washed away with the current also. No matter how good a swimmer she was, the water was too strong for her to be testing.

"Nee-chan," Ben cried. "Save me."

Unable to stand and do nothing, Alice looked around. While she was being indecisive, Ben was barely holding on. The longer he stayed inside the freezing river, the more body heat he lost. Soon, he wouldn't be able to feel his body anymore and would eventually lose consciousness. It was already a miracle that he had held on for this long.

Frantically trying to find something—*anything* that could reach the boy, Alice began foraging. No matter what stick she found it was too short. She was running out of time. Where was Midnight and Soria when she needed them most?

"Damn it!" Alice screamed and turned to look at Ben again. He was slowly starting to close his eyes. "Ben-kun, keep your eyes open!"

Nodding in response, his teeth chattered uncontrollably.

"Damn it Alice, you still have time to save him. Think."

She scanned the area once more. All that surrounded them were rocks, thickets, and moss. There were no vines for her to try and create a rope. But there were trees. Tons of trees. Quickly, Alice withdrew her brown gun and unlocked the safety. She parted her yukata, revealing different colored magazines, all securely strapped. Her gun was unlike ordinary guns and bullets. These were custom made for Alice, using her blood. The different colored magazines were made for different purposes. As for the gun, it could be used in any kind of weather or condition.

She grabbed a green magazine and loaded it, aiming the muzzle at the tallest, biggest tree, on her side of the river. "Please," Alice whispered and unloaded her magazine at the trunk that chipped away.

"Onee…" Ben whispered, reaching his limit and letting go of the boulder.

"Ben-kun!" screamed Alice. She lowered her arms and ran down the banks to chase him. Just a few more rounds and she could have brought the tree down. With no other choices, Alice put her gun away and plunged into the freezing river.

When she came out from underneath, she gasped for air and swam towards Ben who floated away rapidly. Alice frantically kicked and pushed with all her might to grab him, but the rain above pelted the river, blinding her view. All she could see were her fingers poking out from the gray foam. Ben was so close, yet so far. It was painful to watch him slip further away.

Alice withdrew her gun again. This time, she took out a red bullet that was tucked under her bosom and clicked it into the gun. She'd been hoping to save her only red bullet for a fight but now needed its help. She aimed the muzzle down at the river bed and pulled the trigger. The red bullet shot out from the revolver and swirled through the water, hitting the rocks below. There was a brief quake and like a rocket, Alice jetted through the river.

After closing the distance, she smiled and reached out both arms to catch Ben's cold body. *Thank goodness.* Alice held on tightly and turned to look at where they were heading. The river went on and on, unending. But at the edge of the darkness, it would soon become a fall. If only she had another red bullet to blast her towards the banks she could have a chance to get them to safety. But it was useless to think about the *what ifs.*

"What a hassle you've caused." Poe slipped on two gloves and withdrew his palm-sized rod, that sparkled a blue. At his will, he manipulated the size and shape of the rod into an oversized scythe. With one fell slice, Poe cut the tree down as it fell across the river, crashing into other trees.

Alice looked back in alarm. They had swum past the tree, but something had caused it to crash down.

Running across the fallen tree was Poe. Once he reached the middle, he stopped and manipulated the scythe into a rope to secure around it. With the other end, he wrapped it around his waist and turned to face the river going downstream. With all his might, he dove as far as he could.

"Poe," Alice whispered and cried. Help was here.

He came out gasping for air and swam with all his strength to reach the two. "Alice, catch!" Poe shouted and threw a nylon rope as the water stretched it out. After desperately fighting the current to seize it, Poe lured them in with both hands. Once they were within reach, he secured an arm around Alice's waist while she held on to Ben with both arms.

"You came," she whispered.

"Once we're out of here, I'm gonna give you an earful," he snarled.

She smiled and nodded. Poe could lecture her all he wanted. All that mattered was that he had come when she needed him most. "Thanks for coming."

"What are you talking about? It's my job to keep you out of trouble."

"Yeah," she whispered, putting her forehead against his beating chest. It was warm even while inside the freezing river.

With Poe's free hand he pulled them towards the trunk in a hurry. The crashing of the tree had probably caught the attention of the townspeople who were searching for Ben. He didn't want to explain why he had a sparkly energy rod that could be manipulated.

"You know, they'll misunderstand us again," joked Alice as she chuckled.

"Dummy," Poe said, but eventually smiled. "They sure will."

When they reached the trunk and Poe hauled them up to safety, he put away his weapon as flashlights and shouts came from the forest.

Alice placed her chin on top of Ben's head, feeling exhausted. A tear trickled from the corner of her eye and fell into the river. She had succeeded in saving him.

∞

Poe slept beside Alice, holding her hand. They had returned a couple of hours ago when Ben was escorted home to recuperate. Though he wanted to voice out that the boy should seek immediate medical attention from the closest doctor living in the next town, he didn't, since his hands were full with Alice. When Ms. Hirano offered to tend to her instead, Poe refused. She was a Life-Kill, her body would automatically self-heal on its own, and he didn't want Ms. Hirano to witness it. Respecting his wishes, she let Poe take care of Alice while the rest went to sleep.

In a sudden jolt, Alice awoke on her futon, gasping for air.

Feeling her awaken, Poe bolted up. "Whoa, whoa," he said, cradling her trembling body. "Calm down. It's okay, I'm here."

"Poe?" she said in a broken voice.

"Yeah, it's me."

Alice closed her eyes, allowing him to rock her like a baby. She grabbed a fistful of his shirt, holding on for dear life. It felt like she was still stuck in that unforgiving storm that continued raging outside.

Once she calmed down, Poe rested his forehead against her beating chest and whispered, "Don't ever do that again. I thought I'd lost you."

Alice let out a weak chuckle as Poe flicked her forehead. "Ow."

"I'm being serious here."

"Okay." She nodded and opened her eyes fully to look at him. His silky black hair was so shiny, she couldn't help but touch it. It felt like centuries since she last saw him.

"What is it?" he asked as lightning zapped across the dark sky, lighting up the room. Thunder boomed right outside the room. For that instant, Poe's eyes changed from warm to cold. It was an illusion Alice was seeing, but it sent shivers down her spine and her body lost all warmth.

Wincing, Alice threw a hand to her pounding head. The pain was overwhelming.

"What's wrong?" Poe asked, touching her cheek, only to be taken by surprise when Alice slapped his hand away and yelled, "Don't touch me!" before scrambling away and withdrawing her gun.

"Alice," Poe whispered, the concern in his voice grew as well as the look on his face. They were Soulmates. There was no need to be so hostile. If she didn't want him to touch her, all she had to do was ask. Reaching a hand out, Poe pleaded, "put the gun down."

"Shut up!"

"Alice!" he shouted this time and lunged forward, trying to tackle her while she escaped into the back court through the sliding door to the room. Both her hands were on the gun, aimed at Poe. The rain came down in thick droplets, wetting her new yukata. From above, lightning zapped and thunder boomed again. This storm was far from over.

"Unforgivable, unforgivable," she kept repeating.

"Alice."

"Stop saying my name!" Alice clicked off the safety and pulled the trigger, a blue bullet blasting out. Poe dodged as it zoomed past him and hit the wall, sending splinters behind. It wouldn't take long before Ms. Hirano and the others came to see what the commotion was. Even so, it didn't stop the bullet. Instead, it circled back around to pierce Poe, its target.

"Shit." He stood and grabbed his rod to run at Alice who fired another bullet. Already expecting the second shot, Poe dodged in time, letting the two bullets collide. It let out a thunderous boom, blowing him away. His ears rang and his head bled, everything spun out of control. When he got his senses back and stood, Alice was gone. "Alice?" Poe called out, turning in full circles to find her. "Alice!"

22ⁿᵈ Lie

MS. HIRANO KNELT inside Poe's room with food tied inside a sack. It was morning and Alice still hadn't returned since last night's confrontation. Poe too sat on the floor, packing his belongings to depart since he'd finished Alice's bag already. Concerned, Ms. Hirano reached out to squeeze his hand, halting him from zipping up the bag. "Will you be alright on your own?"

"I'll be fine." He gave his best smile and zipped the bag. With a quick bow, he gave his gratitude, "Thank you for your hospitality up to now. After I find Alice, we'll be departing. Sorry for the inconveniences we've caused."

"Don't be so modest." Shaking it off, Ms. Hirano stood as did Poe. "It was my pleasure to have you as my guests. You even had to work here too." She chuckled and stopped when Poe didn't join her. With a tight hug, Ms. Hirano smiled. "I'm sure Alice-chan is fine."

Poe smiled and nodded, hoping that was true. "Well then, I'll be going." He withdrew and took Ms. Hirano's sack of food to leave.

The other workers watched him go and shouted their farewells. A few even waved as Poe returned the gesture. When he was approaching the edge of town, he slowed his pace. The villagers were already spreading rumors so early in the morning.

Funny how news traveled so fast in this small town.

"It was probably the old witch's doing," whispered some. "She probably possessed Alice-chan."

"I'm sure it was. Or else, why would she attack her lover?" They shook their heads and watched Poe walk by. He had his ears perked the entire time, eavesdropping. This tale, he'd never heard of while staying at the inn. It was a first and he was going to get to the bottom of it.

Before leaving town completely, he entered the only convenience store to loiter. Standing at the cash register was a peach haired girl named Hisoka. Unlike her name, she was the complete opposite. She loved spreading gossip like wildfire, regardless if it was true or false. Hisoka was in love with the outside world, dreaming of becoming an idol one day. Instead of getting to live that dream, she was stuck working at her parents' dead-end small convenience store.

Poe grabbed two water bottles and headed for the register. Hisoka looked up from filing her self-manicured nails and smiled. Her face was heavily dabbed with makeup from cheap manufacturers. Sooner or later, it would wash and she'd have to apply a second coat. Those kinds of cheap makeup never lasted too long. The kind that would stay on for hours were the expensive brands, ranging from Shiseido to Too-Faced to Mac. But all those names were rare to find in this day and age, unless you were a billionaire.

All it took was one look for Hisoka to feel bashful. Before Poe and Alice's arrival, she had never met anyone from the outside world. They felt like exotic creatures that weren't from this world. On some days she would sneak away from the store and go peep on the couple, though she never had the guts to strike up a conversation. "G—good morning."

"Good morning," he greeted and took out some money to pay.

"So uh, where you headed?"

"Home."

"Ah, I see, you're fleeing with the young mistress again, huh?"

Poe chuckled at the mentioning of the outrageous story. Still, he played along if he wanted to get some information out of her. "Yes."

"I'm so envious." She bagged the two water bottles and put it on the counter. "Your total is-"

"The change is your tip for being such a gorgeous woman." Poe put down more than enough money and smiled.

"Th—thank you." She took the money and put it into the register, blushing from his compliment. She wasn't used to city boys or any direct kind of flirting.

Poe grabbed the bag of water bottles and adjusted his pack on his back. "So," he said, not leaving. "I heard there's a witch living here, somewhere."

Hisoka's eyes bulged, almost falling from their sockets. She darted her gaze around in case something was eavesdropping.

"What's wrong?" Poe asked, taking interest.

Hisoka leaned over the counter, putting a finger to her red lips. "Don't speak of the witch so casually."

"Why not?" Poe asked calmly. "Is she someone to be feared?"

Nodding, Hisoka began her many stories and gossips she'd accumulated throughout the years. "Many believe that she's lived for tens, even hundreds of years. She feeds off young children, maidens, and wandering travelers. No one dares to speak her name aloud for fear that she might come to our houses at night and take us too."

Poe leaned against the counter as well. This was exactly what he expected. He knew Hisoka couldn't keep her mouth shut, even if it meant talking about a witch they all feared. "Where is she located?"

"To the south. Avoid her cottage at all costs. It's impossible to miss. She lives there with an ogre and hangs the bones of the ones she's eaten on trees, to wade off warriors. Her cottage smells of rotting flesh and blood. She's old and carries a walking cane. Some believe that on full moons, she turns into a beautiful maiden and lures humans into her web to eat."

"I see." Poe nodded and pulled away, ready to leave. "Thank you for the heads-up. I'll be sure not to cross the cottage down south."

"If she catches hold of you or your precious young miss, that's it for the both of you. No one's ever come back to tell the tale of that old heinous witch."

"I'll remember." Poe smiled one last time and left. He exited the town and headed south towards the cottage that Hisoka spoke of. If Alice had really been taken over by the witch, he was going to save her no matter the cost. But if Alice hadn't been taken over, and was acting on her own last night, he'd capture her and get the truth out of her. Only one obstacle stood in his way, he had no leads on her whereabouts after last night's rain washed away her tracks.

∞

By nightfall, Poe reached the old cottage to the south. He hid both his and Alice's belongings he'd been carrying to begin his investigation of the place. Unlike what Hisoka told him, there were no bones hanging from trees. Neither did the place smell of rotting flesh and blood. Instead, it smelled more like out-of-season peonies.

Like a predator, Poe silently stalked into the night to find a trace of Alice but came up empty-handed. He'd been so convinced that she was there. Now coming had been a waste of time. He'd have to contact the Dome about his situation and receive an earful. Turning to leave, Poe stopped. Someone was coming out from within the cottage. As he was taught at the academy from his instructors, it was crucial to never get caught on a mission.

Stealthily, Poe blended into his surroundings and watched from behind a bush. An old woman made her way out with an old walking stick. At least Hisoka got one thing correct from those rumors.

The old woman stopped right outside her mini garden and stooped down to pick some herbs. She smiled before returning indoors. Once she was gone, Poe came out from hiding. Who he saw coming out next from the cottage, made him hide again.

It was Alice. In her hand was a bowl of hot soup. "Granny, do I just put it on the porch?" she called back to the old woman.

"Yes, my dear, just leave it there. The stray cat will come and eat when he's ready to show himself." She chuckled from inside as Alice set the bowl on the porch, then turned to go inside.

"Alice," whispered Poe.

Just before closing the door, Alice glanced back into the dense forest. There was nothing there as she shook it off and shut the door.

"She's really here," Poe said in relief and smiled. The best part was that she was unharmed. "It wasn't a total waste of time."

There was a swooshing sound as Poe looked up, dodging the green bullet on time. It hit the tree behind him as he got into a defensive stance, energy rod in hand. Alice was walking towards him, gun in hand.

"Alice."

Her eyes widened. "How do you know my name?"

"Eh?" said Poe. How could he not know? They were Soulmates who grew up together. It was only right if he knew, but the look in Alice's eyes were different from usual. Standing, Poe put the energy rod away, cautiously approaching with both hands up. "Alice," he whispered.

At the sound of her name coming from his mouth, she backed away. "Stop! Don't come any nearer!"

"Why are you acting like that?!"

"Alice," called out the old woman from behind. She approached the two slowly and stopped. The air surrounding her was calm. She wasn't dangerous in the least bit. In fact, she was just an ordinary old woman living out in the wilderness. "Lower your gun."

"But-"

"That young man can never hurt you. Now be a good girl and lower that gun."

"Yes," Alice said, obediently putting her gun away. She slightly bowed at the old woman and gave Poe a wary look. It was as the old woman had said. Even after shooting him, not once did he try to counter. In fact, he put his weapon away and held up his hands to surrender. For now, she'd play along, but if he ended up being an enemy, she'd kill him in a heartbeat.

"Come, young man, let us go inside. For the night is still young." The old woman chuckled and headed inside with Alice first.

After debating, Poe finally followed them inside. He excused himself and sat down on a chair that the old woman beckoned to. Alice busied herself with cleaning as if this was her own home, and it was the most natural thing to do.

Poe glanced at Alice and caught her staring. She flicked her yellow hair at him and turned to leave. He smiled and turned to look at the old woman who also smiled, rocking back and forth on her rocking chair.

"That girl, she can tell," said the old woman.

"What do you mean?"

"She can tell that you mean her no harm. She's just scared because she can't remember."

"Who are you exactly? And why do you live in such a secluded place? Why is Alice here with you and what happened to her? What do you mean by she can't remember?" Poe had too many unanswered questions. He knew the old woman only had vague answers to give. Wasting time wasn't an option. He wanted things to quickly return to normal.

"I'm not sure what happened either. All I know is that she came here this morning, covered in dirt, crying, trying to flee from something. I took her in, and now here you are, claiming to know her. If possible, may I ask what happened?"

Poe bit his lower lip. Even he didn't understand, but in order to get the rest of the old woman's story, he needed to tell his half. "We saved a boy from drowning last night. I brought Alice back to the inn so she could recover. When she woke up, she freaked out and attacked me before fleeing." The old woman flinched slightly at the mentioning of the inn, catching Poe's eye. "May I ask why you reacted that way when I mentioned the inn?"

"That place," the old woman said with a shake to the head. The wrinkles on her face increased. "Is cursed."

"What do you mean?" Poe scrunched his brows, wondering how the village was cursed. He'd been there for almost a week yet found nothing worth noting. At one point in time, he even questioned why they had been sent there.

The old woman leaned back in her rocking chair. She stared at the ceiling, lost in her memories. "For as long as I could remember, every year, there was an offering made to the God of that village. His name is Devastation. They sent child after child, trying to please him, so that he'd allow them a good harvest and bring good fortune unto their families."

"Bogus." Poe shook his head in disbelief. That wasn't his perception on the villagers after getting to know them. They were good and honest people.

Not taking insult, she continued, "You see, not only did Devastation grant them good harvest and bring good fortunes, he also gave them eternal life. Those people are way past their prime. The village leader, owner of the inn, Hirano-san is much older than she looks."

"What? How is that possible?"

The old woman chuckled. She could tell, Ms. Hirano had done a good job in deceiving Poe into believing that the village was pure and innocent when it was the exact opposite. "When the population of the village plummeted from the sudden storms, the villagers lost all hope. Many evacuated, while some stayed behind. Hirano-san was one of those who refused to leave her beloved hometown. When she met Devastation, she struck a deal with him. By offering small sacrifices, Devastation granted their wishes. That included life. I too, became one of those small sacrifices."

"Then how is it possible that you're still alive?"

"I was made an offering forty years ago, thinking that I'd be eaten too. But Devastation doesn't eat humans like we initially thought. All he wanted was a friend to walk beside him. After becoming the offering, I stayed by his side, here in this cottage. I've been, ever since." The old woman smiled when she spoke about the town's god, making Poe even more suspicious.

The old woman was at least in her nineties. Was she trying to tell Poe that she was made an offering at the age of fifty?

"Did you...fall in love with him?"

The old woman chuckled again. In her lap was a handmade quilt. She nodded, a twinkle in her aging eyes. For a moment in the candle's light, she no longer seemed like an old woman, but instead a young woman in love. "Yes. Yes, I did."

Her story sounded so preposterous, but Poe couldn't wave it away. The old woman gained nothing from lying to him. So why was she telling him to begin with? "Does that mean he's still alive?"

"Yes."

"Hikaru?" called out a melodic voice.

"Yes?" answered the old woman as she sat up in her rocking chair and the two turned towards the front door.

In, stepped the most gorgeous man Poe had ever set eyes on, and stopped breathing. He was in his early twenties and had long silver hair with red eyes, like a demon. On his head sat a straw hat. He even carried a straw basket on his back. He wore a white kurta with faded blue jeans and strap sandals. His caramel skin glistened in the candlelight, and he smelt of jasmine.

"Were you feeding that stray cat again?" he asked and shut the door. "Oh," he said, alarmed at the sight of Poe. "I didn't know we had a visitor so late at night."

"Welcome home," she greeted with a big smile. "This is-"

"Poe," interrupted Poe as he stood and bowed, "nice to meet you."

"Pleasure is all mine," Devastation responded, smiling and bowing too.

"Alice made soup for dinner. We already ate. Go on into the kitchen and grab yourself a bowl," said Hikaru as she shooed him away.

"Okay," he said, obediently setting his things down to enter the kitchen.

Noticing that Poe was still staring at Devastation, Hikaru chuckled. She knew that look anywhere. Alice too had the same look when she first met Devastation. Everyone who met him was always left speechless, regardless if they were man or woman. "His beauty is surreal, isn't it?"

"Yeah, maybe a little too beautiful, if you ask me." Poe sat back down and turned to look at Hikaru in awe. So, that was Devastation, the god of the village. No wonder the villagers yearned for eternal youth. The god who could grant it was that beautiful.

"I," Poe began, "I don't think he's a god at all. He gives off the same vibe as me and Alice, a Life-Kill. Maybe his ability can grant youth, but not *life*," he concluded after thinking things through. "I've never heard of a Life-Kill who can grant life before. Not even the Golden God has that kind of power, even though he's the protector of life-essence. If Devastation did have that kind of power, he'd be considered a threat and be exterminated."

Hikaru nodded, impressed that Poe had figured it out in such a short amount of time. "What do you think?" she asked, looking past him.

"Huh?" Poe turned around to find Devastation standing nearby, smiling. In his hand was a bowl of steamy soup.

"You're correct," Devastation answered, impressed as well.

Poe scrunched his brows together. So, his suspicion was correct.

"I'm not a god. I can't grant life. Neither can I grant youth." Devastation shook his head and walked over to sit beside Hikaru. It was evident from the way he held himself, he was both elegant and deadly, like Naruyuki. Only in front of Hikaru did he remain composed. But what would happen if she was no longer on this planet? Would he lose control of his powers and go Berserk?

"How is it possible that you can keep those townspeople so young?"

Devastation looked up from his soup and smiled. He could lie. Then again, there was no need when Poe already knew the truth. "I control time."

"Eh?" Poe stared, not daring to blink. The ability to control time was about as powerful as the ability to grant life—maybe even deadlier. If what Devastation said was true, then he was a threat, to the Dome, to everyone, even the Golden God himself.

Chuckling, Devastation returned to eating his soup. He could easily decipher the look on Poe's face. He could even tell what Poe was thinking and lowered his spoon. "Though my ability is to control time, the Limiter my Dome's doctor put on me is rather harsh. They didn't want me to have such strong powers; for fear that I'd become a threat one day." Though he smiled, he seemed to be in pain.

Suddenly, it all made so much sense. The reason Poe and Alice had been sent to the village wasn't so they could blend in. The village and villagers were of no concern to the Dome. They had come for the sole purpose of

Devastation. He was their true objective. It only made Poe imagine what kinds of painful experiments Devastation had gone through to obtain such powers. Now that he had acquired such a fearsome ability, he was seen as a threat that needed to be annihilated. "What about the village?"

"I slowed the time flow in that town. They think they've stopped aging but that's incorrect. The crops that grow each year continue to grow fruitfully because its time too has slowed. Only the weather remains unaffected by my powers. Other than that, so long as I live, nothing will change in that town. However, if they dare step a single foot out of that village, they'll begin to age rapidly and die."

"How can you do that?"

Looking up, Devastation raised an eyebrow. "Beg your pardon?"

"How can you go around stopping time—granting wishes like that?" Poe asked, enraged that one of his own had gone rogue. Tweaking time was unforgivable. Everything had its order. It was in no one's hands to try and control time. No wonder the Dome had sent them. They either wanted Devastation dead or returned so they could repossess his rare ability.

Devastation and Hikaru exchanged smiles, neither of them feeling threatened enough to defend themselves from Poe. "I don't expect you to understand me. All I wanted was someone to walk beside me."

"Bullshit!"

Devastation shook his head. Poe was someone who could never understand his ideals and way of life, until Poe had lived for as long as he had. Even Devastation himself knew that he shouldn't have granted Ms. Hirano's wish to stay youthful. However, at the time, it didn't seem to hurt. "Alice-chan," called out Devastation.

"Yes?" she answered and came rushing.

"Hikaru is tired. Please help her to bed."

"Of course." Alice walked over and helped Hikaru up as they left. All the while she glared at Poe who had hurt their happy family of three.

After confirming that the two were gone, Devastation turned his attention to Poe. It was time to get down to business. "Did Gabe and Umi-chan send you?"

"Eh?" Poe gasped.

"We were in the same generation. So, I can only guess that it was them who sent you. They are still at the Dome, aren't they?"

Poe nodded, unsure of how to take in everything. What was with this cruel fate, that the two deans would give the order to track down an old student to kill? And why were Gabe and Miss Umi going along with the plan of killing an old comrade to steal his rare ability?

"Is Alice-chan your Soulmate?"

"Yes."

Devastation let out a cackle and set his unfinished soup on the table nearby. He always knew the Dome would hunt him down one day. He just never expected them to send Poe who knew nothing. Devastation picked up the warm quilt that Hikaru had been using and held it to his cheek.

"No way," whispered Poe. "You're in love with her too?"

"A long time ago, I once had a Soulmate too, but we were simply partners working together on missions. Nothing more. Nothing less. All the others developed something on an intimate level with their Soulmates, while others had affairs. When my Soulmate died in battle, it felt like I'd lost my sister. Even as I cried, I felt no love outside that of a brother's. I left the organization shortly and wandered aimlessly until I came across that small village. They worshipped me as a god and gave me child sacrifices to keep themselves from growing old and dying. It was Hirano-san who came to me with such a proposal."

Poe frowned. Ms. Hirano was a happy-go-lucky innkeeper with a mischievous son. The person Devastation was describing couldn't possibly be the same woman. Then again, did Poe really know her? He didn't even know his own teachers.

"I thought we could both benefit, so I agreed. But child after child she sent rejected me. They refused to come near me and tried to kill me. They even cried and cursed while trying to flee. It became such a tiring cycle that I stopped their time. I never meant for it to happen. It would always just happen. But that's no excuse." It was a painful memory to recall as regret washed over him. If he could turn back time, he'd have done it. "Even if I didn't love my Soulmate in such a way, she was always with me, through thick and thin. When I lost her, there was this void inside my heart. All I wanted was someone by my side again. I thought a child would be the best choice, given that they'd grow into adults. We could become best friends, maybe even family."

"That was when Hikaru-san came into your life?"

"Yes." Like his life was on the line, he whispered that single word. In that second, Devastation seemed to be nothing more than just an ordinary man, afraid to lose the love of his life. "I thought she would be like the rest, but I was wrong. Hikaru was an orphan from the village and had been preselected by Hirano-san to be the next offering. She never tried to kill me or run away. Instead, she decided to make this place her new home after having the villagers shun her. Do you know how happy I was? She accepted me for me. She wasn't afraid of my silver hair or red eyes."

Devastation smiled so happily that he tightened his hold on the quilt. "As you can see, Hikaru ages. I've offered to slow her time, but she refuses. She said when her time comes, it would come. She didn't want to be like the

228

villagers, greedy to keep their youth. 'Death is inevitable,' is what she told me."

Poe looked away from Devastation's pained expression. He knew that look all too well. It mirrored his own when Alice retaliated against him.

"Hikaru…is dying. Soon, she won't even be able to walk anymore. I want to slow her time so badly. Still, to the end, she refuses."

"She's dying?"

Devastation nodded. He wiped a tear from his eye and laughed. It felt like the two guys had bonded in those few minutes. Devastation had even spoken his true feelings and thoughts. "I'm happy I met you, Poe. You came at the right time."

"What do you mean?" Poe asked, confused. Why would he be happy? Then, it hit him like a ton of bricks. Devastation wanted to die with Hikaru. He couldn't live without her and he wanted Poe, a stranger to end his life for him. "No."

"I know why you were sent here, and I'm telling you now, I won't return to the Dome. Hikaru is my life and I can't picture it without her. So please, I beg you, don't tear us apart."

"You-"

"The same goes for you as well, right?" Devastation looked over at Poe, who could no longer retaliate. "I can tell. If Alice-chan were to die, you'd follow her. You wouldn't take on a new Soulmate, would you?"

"Well," began Poe as he thought about it. The answer was obvious. It was a definite no. "Wait," he said. Something Devastation had said struck his curiosity. "What do you mean by take on a new Soulmate?"

This time, it was Devastation who seemed curious at Poe's question. It was a given that should one's Soulmate die, they would be issued a new one. Even if they didn't want to, those were the rules. That was the main reason why Devastation had escaped. The deans and teachers back at the Dome should've told the new generation all this already. "Don't you know? If your current Soulmate dies, you get a new Soulmate."

"I didn't know."

"The higher-ups never told you?" Devastation seemed genuinely shocked at this news. "What's with the organization these days? Are they slacking off now?"

"A new Soulmate," repeated Poe.

"That's right. Whether you want to or not, those are the rules. Though some become an exception and get to fly solo."

After some time, Poe finally replied with a soft, "Why me?"

"When Hikaru leaves, I'm going to undo the time in the village. They'll all die and become nothing more than dust. The children whose times I haven't slowed will come to hate me. That's when you kill me, before their eyes. You'll be the hero to save their souls from an eternity of damnation."

"You're serious, aren't you?"

Devastation nodded. He had made up his mind long ago. He just didn't have someone to play the role of the hero. With Poe here, he wasn't about to waste the opportunity. "Yes, I'm serious."

"Why are you going so far for those children?"

"When I see them, I see...*us*. We grew up never knowing anything. At least in the wake of the truth, I want them to be free of pain and hatred. That's why, you must kill me to preserve their innocence. Don't let them become like us, filled with vengeance. Take them to the outside world so they can live their lives freely." Devastation chuckled and set the quilt down on the rocking chair before standing. "About Alice-chan," he said softly.

"Huh?" Poe said, looking up. He was too hung up on Devastation's sudden request he didn't hear anything else.

"The reason she can't remember you is because I tweaked her time."

"Eh?"

"When she first came here, she was crying uncontrollably. She even tried attacking Hikaru and I. To calm her, I've temporarily erased the reason for her worries, which would be you. But don't worry," he said, turning around to smile. "She'll return to normal in due time and her memories of you will resurface. In the meanwhile, please use the guest room. Ask Alice-chan where it is. I'll be going to sleep now." Devastation bowed at Poe, long and deep before leaving. He entered the hallway where Alice sat, silently crying. She looked up and spotted him, quickly wiping her tears. "He's waiting for you, Alice-chan." Devastation patted her head and left.

Alice sat still. After putting Hikaru to bed, she had returned only to walk in on Devastation's story. Somehow, the tears just fell. The last part about him temporarily erasing her memories of Poe caused her heart to ache more.

∞

Cars honked as neon lights lit the city skyline. People were trying to return home while others were just heading to work. Just a few streets down sat the red-light district where the rich went to forget their worries and reality. But that night, there was little evidence of them around this part of town. They had heard about Franz's visit and were sitting tightly at home, afraid to walk the streets. None of them wanted to accidentally bump into him and wake up to a red envelope sitting on their front porch. It only meant that Life-Kills or Dome assassins would soon be coming for their heads.

A few streets away from the red-light district sat the slums. Women, men, and children of all ages could be seen loitering the alleyways and dumpsters, searching for valuables and food. They were the ones the government had turned a blind eye to, the ones deemed as unfit to live in this new world order. In fact, just last month, a new law had been passed to enslave or kill the poor.

Laughter erupted from a group of teenagers as they passed Takahiko who stood in the middle of it all, waiting for Love to show up. Ever since their argument, they seldom spoke or even met up.

Takahiko watched the group enviously. He should also be enjoying his youth like them. Instead, he was stuck completing missions that would ensure the safety of their ruler. It was an honor to be chosen as a soldier, Takahiko knew, but sometimes he just wanted to be a regular teenager.

Sighing, he took out his red charm that Love had given him when they parted from the others. She'd been so nervous about giving him a gift that he teased her until she turned beet red. Tucked inside her spell book was a matching charm, its color blue. Though Love tried to hide it from Takahiko, he'd seen it on a couple of occasions.

A flashing red letter from a love hotel flickered, catching Takahiko's attention. He turned to look and put his charm away. After a few seconds of flickering, the red letter finally dimmed and stopped shining. Right when Takahiko turned away, a shadow moved from behind the shades.

Now *that*, was something to be suspicious about. Was he being spied on?

From out of nowhere, there was a loud explosion. A nearby street vendor's stall exploded. Debris blew towards Takahiko who threw his arms over his head for protection.

"What the hell was that?" he asked and quickly stood, running towards the chaos. People on the streets were screaming and running for safety. The street vendor and his customers had been killed. A few people were injured as Takahiko tried to find the perpetrator. Anyone who looked out of the ordinary, he would immediately chase.

"Love, you take care of the injured!" instructed Takahiko as he turned to his side to find Love absent. What a time to be without her. From the corner of his eye, the curtains from the love hotel room flapped. Someone really was watching him. "Bastard, I've got you now," he snarled and ran towards the love hotel.

23rd Lie

LOVE RAN DOWN THE STREET, fighting against the crowd to get to where Takahiko was stationed. It was where the explosion had occurred. Just then, a second explosion went off a few blocks away. The frantic pedestrians screamed, pushing her further away from her destination. "Move!" demanded Love.

The wails of a boy caught her attention as she glanced back. He was no older than eight and had been separated from his parents. Love looked away, having an internal debate. In the end, she ran over to the boy, scooping him into her arms. She couldn't turn a blind eye to a helpless child who could possibly die from the human stampede. Takahiko with his inhuman strength could defend himself until she got there.

"Stop crying."

"Uh, okay," the boy replied and nodded. He wasn't sure on how to react towards Love's snappy rescue.

After finding a safe place away from the crowd, Love stopped and put the boy down on his feet. "Now then, can you make it home on your own?"

The boy stood thinking before finally shaking his head. "No."

"Why not?"

"I don't know where we are."

What a hopeless kid. If he didn't know his way home, he was never going to survive in the world. "Geez," said Love, "I'm not from around here. And I also don't know where we are."

The boy gave her the saddest look and let out a sniffle. Was she going to abandon him after saving him?

Suddenly feeling crappy and incapable, Love sighed. She had no one to blame but herself. She'd taken on the task of saving him, and would see it through to the end. "Where do you live?"

"I live at Ever Tower, level 19, 9-12 Hayabusa, Shinjuku."

"Well, I'm not too sure about this, but it's worth a shot." Love opened her spell book, flipping to a certain page. She ripped it out and put it into the boy's palm.

"What's this for?" he asked, peering at the page with weird symbols.

"Shh," instructed Love. She put a finger to her lips to quiet him. Closing her eyes, she began a chant of some sort. Slowly, the symbols dissolved as a 3D map of the town appeared. Their location was marked with a blinking yellow circle while a green line showed the direction to the red X. "Well, I'll be darn," Love said proudly and smiled, "it actually worked."

"Wow!" the boy exclaimed, never having witnessed such a thing until then. "Magic!"

"Is it that amazing?"

"Yes!"

"Aw geez," Love said, feeling bashful. After remembering that there was work to be done, she snapped out of it and bent down, poking his nose. Even if she wanted to bask in the glory and praise, she had to hurry. So did the boy. It wasn't safe. "Well, now you have a map to guide you home. So, move along." Love pushed him to go and smiled. Her work here was done.

"Thank you so much! I'll remember this!" He bowed gratefully with the 3D map in his hand. "When I grow up I'm going to learn magic and be as cool as you!"

"Magic isn't all that exciting. Having superhuman strength or controlling elements is better."

"No way. If I learn magic, I can summon anything I want," he said, determined to learn magic. "You can summon people, right?"

She blushed like crazy from all the praise and scratched her head. "Well, summoning is beyond my level. I still need to work on it."

"So it is possible to summon then!"

"Yeah it is." Love smiled and nodded. With magic, anything was possible.

"How do I become a magician?!"

"You can't. Now go home." Love shooed him again as the boy thanked her one last time before running off. Kids were so full of ideas and vigor. Their minds weren't restricted, allowing them to think outside the box. It was what made them dreamers and optimists. Love wondered if she had been the same as a child, then remembered how the girls had called her straight-laced.

From behind, there was a clink as Love swirled around, only to be greeted by a whip. She did her best to dodge, but it lashed at her cheek.

"Well, hello there," greeted the owner of the whip. She twirled the rope above her head like some circus performer before stopping. Standing behind her was a group of rebels. "The name's Juel, nice meeting ya, comrade. We're here to make this place yours, your boyfriend's, and that damn puppet's burial ground."

"Don't dream on it." Love adjusted her glasses and wiped her bloody cheek as it slowly self-healed.

"Then bring-" Before Juel could finish her challenge, fire ignited through the whip, burning it to a crisp. She had no choice but to let go as Love ran over, throwing a fist. It connected, sending Juel tumbling sideways.

"That's what you get for underestimating your foe," she said, readying her next spell as the group of rebels ran at her.

"You cheeky bitch, I'll show you." Juel stood, spitting bloody saliva onto the ground. She sneered and rubbed her cheek. The thought of someone touching her beautiful face was uncalled for and she was going to make Love pay by putting her body inside a bag.

While dodging and attacking, Love huffed and puffed. Most of her spells had injured one-third of Juel's men, but without landing any of those hits directly, she did little damage. The one she had to worry about was Juel, another Life-Kill. "This is bad," Love grumbled. She wiped her bloody lip with the back of her hand. Her energy was quickly depleting.

"What's the matter, Wizard Girl? Weren't you acting all high and mighty just a while ago? Why do you look so sluggish now?" Juel teased, a new spiky whip in her hand. If that thing ever caught hold of Love, she was done for.

"Your jokes aren't very funny."

"Really, you!" Juel snarled as the rebels charged at Love with full strength.

"Damn it," Love said, opening her book to counter again. While busy dodging, she never saw Juel coming at her from behind.

She managed to snatch Love's spell book and scrape her throat with the spiked whip. With a cry, Love threw a hand to her bloody throat and hit the ground. There wasn't even time to curse as she leapt to her feet, already fending off the rebels with her bare hands. When she was able to get to safety, she heaved and stole energy nearby to self-heal as blue particles swarmed over. Meanwhile, Juel skimmed through the contents of the book and began tearing pages out, along with the blue charm.

Unable to stop her, Love watched in horror as Juel tossed the book to the ground and crushed it with her heel. "Stop!" Love begged.

"Pathetic," she insulted. "You need more training if you're still relying on a book. Anyone can tell with one glance that it's your weakness, even if it grants you power." Juel pointed her whip handle at Love and smiled, her rebels rushing in to deliver the finishing blow. "I'll be sure to give you a slow and torturous death. That way, when your boyfriend comes, he'll be filled with so much rage he'll go Berserk." She laughed hysterically and threw her head back. She could already imagine the distorted look on Takahiko's face when he saw what Juel had done to Love's body. Without a doubt, he would want revenge. "Ah," she said almost ecstatic. "Oh, I do love the sight of a Fallen One."

In Love's right hand was a single page from the book she'd ripped before losing it. One look at the symbols and she laughed. "Why'd it have to be this page of all pages?" Love blinked her tears away. She was losing more energy than she could replenish. Juel was too strong for her to take on. She should've fled when she had the chance.

With the rebels only ten feet away, Love placed the spell page onto the ground.

Back at the academy, Ms. Tanaka had once requested Love to perform a spell. Her task was to summon a tiger. She did the best she could but only managed to summon a worm. The girls exploded into laughter at her pathetic summoning. Embarrassed, Love nearly cried. The one to put the hysterical girls into line was Miss Umi who'd been present to watch. Knowing the devil that she was, the girls quickly settled down.

Ever since that day, Love trained and trained, honing her skills so she would be ready to do a summoning when asked again. After the second, third, and hundredth failed attempts of trying to summon a tiger, Ms. Tanaka gave up. Summoning was obviously out of Love's league. But she never gave up and even trained in secret.

Unlike those times, Love was in a real life and death situation. This wasn't leisure training back at the Dome.

Biting her right thumb until it bled, she placed it on top of the summoning circle. If she succeeded, she'd live to see another day. But if she failed, she'd die, then and there while unconscious.

"Please work," Love begged and cried. "I don't want to die yet." She used the last of her remaining energy and closed her eyes. When she reopened them, the rebels were only a few feet away now. Her heart hammered and her vision blurred. Just once more, she wanted to see the girls. "Summoning spell, I summon thee, Water Bearer!"

At her summoning, the rebels stopped shy. The last of Love's tears fell as she slumped down to the concrete, closing her eyes. Her summoning had failed yet again.

"Pathetic, how pathetic you are, Wizard Girl! Even until your dying breath you couldn't use your magic to his fullest potential!" laughed Juel. "Hurry and kill-"

A sudden gust of wind erupted, interrupting Juel who held up one arm to shield her eyes. A blinding white light lit the street as fog arose. A blue magic seal appeared from below and shone for a few seconds before fading.

"Love?" called out a voice that Juel didn't recognize.

Immediately, she froze and lowered her arm. Someone was standing within the fog, before Love's slumped body. "Who the hell?"

"Love?" called out Soria again. She got down on one knee and touched Love's cold body.

"Who the hell are you?"

Ignoring the question, Soria stared at the paper she was stepping on. There were rune symbols on it. In the center of the paper was Love's bloody thumb print. Soria stared some more before smiling. "You finally did it," she whispered and touched Love's bleeding thumb as a pink aura arose, healing the bite.

"Bitch, listen to me when I'm talking!" demanded Juel.

"Huh?" Standing, Soria turned to eye Juel and her rebels. She was dressed in a white satin robe, ready to take a shower, but that was no longer possible. Neither did she have on shoes. "Who exactly are you calling a bitch?"

Juel grinned and tightened her grip on the whip. "You've got a lot of nerves interfering in my fight."

"Your fight?"

"Yes, my fight, you dumbass. If you dare to interfere, I'll kill you also."

"Dumbass? Me, getting killed?"

Juel stopped grinning and glared at Soria who kept repeating everything she finished saying. "Are you a fucking retard? Why do you keep repeating my words? Just shut the fuck up and move or else I'll decimate you just like I did to your friend there," she boasted.

A grin overcame Soria. She had just been issued a challenge. "I highly doubt you'll scratch me." Soria shook her head, clenching and unclenching her fists. All the while she spoke through gritted teeth.

"You cheeky little shit."

"But if it's your doing that Love became like this, I won't forgive you." Soria lowered her head and stopped flexing her muscles.

"Who the hell are you to threaten me? You think I'm scared of you or something? I'm the Great Juel. Now step down and know your place, bitch."

Water bullets shot out from nowhere, striking Juel's rebels to the concrete.

"What the-" Juel took a few paces back, not expecting a one-hit kill. Soria's attack was so quick she didn't have time to take it in.

"I think you're the one who doesn't know your rightful place," corrected Soria. She looked up and smirked. If she had learned anything while living in the Dome, it was how to instill fear into people. "Shall I show you your rightful place?"

"You bitch!" shouted Juel as she ran at Soria with her whip.

"Your place is down here at my feet, groveling."

"Hah!" With a swift stroke, Juel whipped her spiky whip, trying to entangle it around Soria's throat as a spinning water sphere arose. It enclosed her from all sides to defend as Juel's whip was reduced to shreds.

"You made two mistakes today," Soria said, flying out from within the water sphere to punch Juel square in the face. Yelping, she tried to gain her footing, but not before Soria tossed her into a nearby building wall. Again, Juel yelped as the wall caved in on her. "The first, you caused Love to summon me here. The second, you caused her to become like that, and I won't let it slide."

She's quick, Juel thought, having no time to wipe her bloody lip. She pushed off the rubble and inched away while Soria continued advancing. There was no hesitation or fear in her strides.

"But I will thank-you on one occasion. Because of you, Love's summoning spell has been acquired. So, to show my appreciation, I'll give you a slow death," offered Soria. She raised one hand as the fire hydrant nearby burst.

Water spurt into the air as Juel watched in horror. She was way in over her head. "No, no!" screamed Juel as she turned to flee.

"Too late for that." Soria moved her finger as the water from the hydrant rushed over to encircle and penetrate Juel's body like a sponge.

"Help, help!"

Not wanting to watch, Soria turned her back and walked away. This fight was over. When she reached Love's side, water seeped under to carry her. The water from the hydrants had stopped. From behind, Juel continued screaming. Her body stretched so much, her skin began tearing from the pressure of the water.

"Stop, please stop! I'll give you any kind of information you want!" Juel screamed one last time before bursting into pieces. A water shield shot out from behind to cover them from the gruesome gore that splattered out.

"Now then, where do I go?" Soria mumbled and looked about. She had no idea where she was or how to get back to Love's hotel room. And where was Takahiko? From behind, someone came running as Soria spun back, summoning for a water sword in hand.

"Whoa!" shouted Takahiko. He stopped, dead in his tracks, both hands up to surrender. "Soria," he said in alarm.

"Takahiko."

"Love!" he shouted after taking one look at his unconscious, floating Soulmate. He ran over to her side worriedly. "What happened to her?"

"I don't really know myself. She got herself into one messy fight. I had to bail her out," she said, the water sword vanishing.

Takahiko reached out to touch Love before turning to look at Soria again. He raised an eyebrow, finally noticing that she was in a bathrobe, nothing else. "How did you get here again?"

"I'm guessing the idiot summoned me here."

"How-"

"Stop questioning me. I don't have any definite answers," interrupted Soria. "Let's go someplace safe."

"This way," said Takahiko as he led the way and attempted to carry Love himself.

"Hey," Soria objected by shaking her head. "Stop."

"But-"

"You look about as worn out as Love herself. Worry about yourself instead. I've got her."

"But-"

"I said no."

Takahiko gulped at her challenging tone and gave up. "I understand."

"Start walking."

"Yeah," he said, leading the way as Soria followed alongside. All those years, he and the rest of the guys grew up thinking Yeve was the only demon. Unfortunately, they had missed one along the way because of how well she played the part of the fool.

From high grounds, sitting on a building ledge watching were Nicholas and Liz. He smiled and dreamily planted his chin on his right palm. Liz hissed and glared. Reaching over, he scratched behind her ears, making her purr.

"She's good," Nicholas praised and stopped scratching, "better than I expected." He withdrew his hand back to his side while Liz hissed again at Soria's back. Chuckling, Nicholas picked her up. "Why are you mad? When you become interested in others, I don't object."

Liz purred loudly, her cat eyes gleaming. She wasn't going to let this slide easily but didn't want to start an argument after finishing their own fight against another rebel group.

Nicholas smiled one last time, his eyes never leaving Soria. They would meet soon enough, and he couldn't wait. But for now, he had to return to the hotel and report to Franz.

Soria spun around to look behind them and stopped walking.

"What is it?" asked Takahiko.

Confused about where the sudden disappearance of the onlookers had gone, Soria turned to face front. "Nothing, keep walking," she instructed.

Takahiko raised an eyebrow, wanting to ask, but was too afraid of getting lectured. So he continued walking and kept his mouth glued.

∞

It was close to midnight, but instead of sleeping, Devastation and Hikaru walked hand in hand, heading towards the field to watch the fireflies.

Standing in the doorway of the cottage watching was Poe. A smile played its way across his face. Just that afternoon, while in the fields, the two guys had had a heart to heart talk about life in general. Curious, Poe asked, "You two never wanted to have children?"

Devastation smiled and nodded, reminiscing on the past. "We did. But..."

"But what?"

"It's hard to believe now, but Hikaru is only forty-six years old."

Surprised, Poe stopped working. It was indeed hard to believe when his eyes told him otherwise.

"The first time we found out she was pregnant, the embryo already killed itself inside her womb. The second time, the embryo died again. But the third time...it survived. We were so excited and started preparing names and a room for it. Three months into the pregnancy, Hikaru bled and collapsed inside the kitchen. When I found her, she'd aged rapidly into her nineties.

"That was when I felt it. My unborn child had inherited my powers and without a Limiter, it was trying to kill its mother, the love of my life. I had no choice but to kill it."

Just hearing was unbearable as Poe turned away. "Hikaru-san...how'd she handle it?"

"She was furious at me for choosing to save her over our child. I told her, even if I was thrown into the situation a million times, my decision would remain the same. I'd always choose her, even over my own child."

"Limiter," Poe said, switching subjects. It was depressing. "That's the second time you've mentioned it. What is that?"

"So, they haven't taught you what a Limit is either, huh?" Devastation said with a sigh. Was the staff at the Dome trying to keep the new generations in the dark about everything? "A Limiter is a complex procedure that takes years to be put into place. It involves energy manipulation and blood fusion between you and your Dome's doctors, so that you can never rival the Golden God. When you go over your Limit, your powers will become neutralized, and you might even be killed."

"I'm envious of them," Alice said, joining Poe's side and interrupting his thoughts.

"Huh?" He turned to look at her while she watched the two disappear in the distance. "Why?"

"I want someone like that too."

"What are you talking about? You've got me," he said, nudging her.

She looked over and smiled. Though she couldn't remember him, knowing that he was willing to take the effort and time to find her, made her feel grateful and loved. "Thank you."

"It's my job as your Soulmate to keep you happy for as long as I live."

Alice stared at him long and hard before laughing. "What do you mean by it's your job? So, you're saying that if it wasn't your job, you wouldn't keep me happy for as long as you live?"

Not meaning to give her the wrong impression, Poe reached out to pull her closer. It had felt like centuries since he last saw her smile. He put his forehead against hers, theirs noses almost touching. Surprised, Alice tried to pull away, but Poe held on firmly. He closed his eyes and inhaled deeply. For her and her alone, he'd wait for as long as time allowed him. "Let me rephrase. Even if it wasn't my job as your Soulmate, as a man who loves you, I'll do whatever I can to keep you happy for as long as you live."

Alice stopped fighting to stay still. Tears flooded her eyes as she closed them. His words were so sincere she quickly wanted her memories to return.

∞

♪Hum, hum, stay where you are
I will spread my wings over you
I will stay forever with you in this sky
Believe in this promise I make to you, hum, hum
Take my hand, never let go
I will always be with you
Believe in this promise I make to you, hum, hum♪

"You're singing that song again?" complained Kei as he approached Taiyou. They were making their way back to the Dome as requested by the deans. It had been a long few days, and night had finally fallen.

Inside the ship recuperating were King and Jennifer. When she met the other two guys, she was curious about why they never got to meet while at the Dome. Not allowing the two to answer her questions, Kei hogged the spotlight and spoke until he tired her out. Now that she was sleeping, Kei had nothing else to do other than to bug Taiyou, since Tasuku was tending to Kakinouchi who refused to leave May's side inside one of the empty rooms.

"If you don't like my songs, don't listen," countered Taiyou. He turned to glare at Kei as the ocean breeze blew, swaying their hair. "How was King when you met him?"

Kei grinned. He was going to enjoy making fun of King while he had the chance. "He was beaten to a pulp. That wannabe-first-place was nearly dead if I hadn't arrived on time."

"You two just can't take it easy, can you?"

"Hell no." Kei grinned as it slowly faded. After some time, he cleared his throat. It was time to address the elephant in the room. "How's Kakinouchi's state of mind?"

"In shambles. He blames himself. Tasuku's inside, keeping him from going Berserk."

"I would too if my Soulmate's heart got taken."

"Yeah," agreed Taiyou. After a few minutes of silence, he spoke again. "So, are we gonna stay at the Dome also?"

"No." Kei shook his head, not feeling up to finishing their mission. He wanted to spend more quality time with Jennifer, but she was fast asleep. Maybe later, he'd sneak into her room and climb into bed with her. "According to the dean, we're only escorting the four back to the Dome's pier. Gabe-sensei and Umi-sensei will meet us there and take it from there. After that, we're to return to our original mission."

"Wow," Taiyou said. "To have Gabe-sensei come out himself, this is a serious matter."

"You said it yourself. Kakinouchi's state of mind is in shambles and Gabe-sensei is more knowledgeable in that department than me." Kei shook his head, unable to fathom Kakinouchi's situation. When he glanced over at the sullen Taiyou, he punched him on the arm.

"What was that for?"

"You looked like you needed it."

"How the hell so?" snapped Taiyou.

"You have that look on your face again."

"Huh?" Taiyou touched his face with his hand and laughed it off. "What are you talking about?" he asked, turning away. The only light in the darkness came from the ship. Other than that, the ocean was an eerie pitch black with no signs of life.

Kei too turned to look out the dark horizon. He placed his forearms on the railings and smiled. No matter how many times Taiyou denied it, the guys could see. He constantly had a yearning look in his eyes. "I hope you find her one day."

"Huh? Now what are you talking about?"

"Don't play dumb with me. Ever since we were kids, you used to have dreams about a mysterious person. You would always tell us at breakfast. Sometimes, Naruyuki would tease you. You'd get so pissed you'd punch him and get into a big brawl. It was always up to Rain, Shadow, and I to stop you two before the staff got involved. Even to this day, it still hasn't changed. That's why I hope—I really do wish and hope that you find her. Maybe when you do, she'll become your Soulmate."

Taiyou smiled and chuckled. "Idiot," he said softly. "How do you even know she's a love interest? What if that person is my sister or something?"

"Highly doubt it. The way you talk about her is too deep."

Tears came to Taiyou's eyes as he blinked them away.

"Well, I'm gonna go check on the others. I'm sure Tasuku's sweating bullets from being stuck inside a room with that emo Kakinouchi." Kei hit Taiyou lightly on the arm again before leaving him to his thoughts.

Taiyou closed his eyes and lifted his face towards the starry sky. He was trying to recall his dreams from when he was a child.

He was never able to see her face in any of his dreams. She was always shrouded in darkness. Even so, he always felt that she was smiling warmly at him. It was a mysterious thing. He didn't know the first thing about her yet felt she had been beside him his entire life. If he were to spontaneously meet her one day, would he recognize that she was the one?

Taiyou opened his eyes and glanced at the necklace the dean had given him when they left for their mission. Hanging from the necklace was a one-winged ring that seemed to be searching for its other half. "One day, I'll complete us."

24th Lie

LOVE AWOKE IN BED, head pounding to the point that everything spun out of control. Once it settled down, the fuzzy stars surrounding her started to lessen. Last night's match against Juel had taken its toll on her.

Love waited for a few minutes before kicking the covers off and sitting up in bed. She swung her legs over the side of the bed and noticed her glasses sitting on the drawer. She put them on and made her way over to the door. It opened automatically as she made her way into the living room. Sitting on the sofa, watching TV was Soria. Inside the kitchen, forced to cook breakfast was Takahiko. Neither of them had noticed her yet.

"You're slow, Takahiko. Hurry up. I'm hungry," complained Soria.

"I'm doing my best here," answered an annoyed Takahiko.

"Yeah, well, your best sucks."

Takahiko turned, glaring at her back. She was like a tyrant, commanding her troops on the battlefield. Of all the people on this earth to be cooking for, it had to be Soria. "Then why don't you come help me and stop ordering me around?"

"A great person such as I, never does such things."

"Just who exactly is she trying to kid?" he hissed and returned to cooking when he caught sight of Love. A big grin overtook him as he rushed over. "You're finally awake!"

"Huh?" Soria turned her attention away from the TV to the hallway. "About time," she said, almost annoyed.

"Are you okay? Should I get you something to drink or munch on?" he offered and guided her to the single sofa to sit.

243

"I'm fine," answered Love as she smiled. If he was this attentive when she was unwell, think of when they had kids. As soon as she thought that, she blushed and coughed, whispering a, "Thanks."

"Are you sure?"

"She's not pregnant," retorted Soria who grabbed a bowl of chips to eat.

"You're so inconsiderate."

Love smiled, happy that her wish had been granted. She'd survived to meet at least one of the girls "Really, I'm fine," she answered before Soria could really blow her fuse. She didn't want to hear an argument the first thing in the morning after waking up.

"You sure?" asked Takahiko again.

"I'm fine."

"Hey," said Soria from behind. "Breakfast can't cook itself."

"You," he hissed.

"Please go." Love smiled sympathetically, knowing the feeling of having to be bossed around by Soria all too well.

Takahiko nodded. Standing to go, he entered the kitchen to resume his cooking. "Just let me know if you need anything."

"I will," Soria answered while eating her chips.

"I wasn't talking to you!"

"Oh, well, you didn't specify who, so I answered."

"I feel for you, Aoi," Takahiko hissed, unsure if he should kick her out or stay silent and put up with her brutality. But if he were to treat her rudely, he'd have to answer to Yeve. Just thinking of her made him shudder. He'd rather deal with Soria.

Love shook her head again, smiling still. "What are you doing here, Soria?"

At that, Soria looked over and set the bowl of chips down on the coffee table. She pulled out a paper from her pocket for proof, in case Love didn't believe her. "You summoned me last night with this."

"I did?"

"You don't remember?"

"Well," Love said, unsure. She remembered fighting Juel who'd stolen her spell book. The only thing in her possession was the torn page for a summoning. After using all her energy on that spell, she fainted. "I remember fighting and desperately trying to summon something, but why you?"

"How would I know?" Soria snapped. She reached over and hit Love on the head as she yelped. "And I'm not *something*, I'm *someone*."

"Ah, sorry," apologized Love.

"Anyway, how do I return?"

"Huh?"

"How do I return?"

"Uh, well," Love said, scratching her head.

"You don't know, do you?"

Love smiled and shook her head. She hadn't the slightest clue. "Nope."

Soria flung herself across the room, landing on top of Love to headlock. She had wasted an entire night and morning waiting to be told that magic couldn't return her back. If she'd known, she would've left last night. "How dare you summon me here without knowing how to return me back?!"

"I'm sorry!"

"Oye, oye, off, off!" shouted Takahiko who had been listening and watching. He ran into the living room to pry Soria off, knowing a fight would break out. "She just woke up. Be more patient. Maybe she needs time to recover to remember how to send you back."

"Even if you say that Takahiko, I have absolutely no idea."

Angry, Soria reached out with both hands to wring Love's neck. "I'll kill her first, then return to Kiska Island!"

"Calm down, calm down," Takahiko said, continuing to hold her back.

"I'm sorry. This is my first summoning and I don't know how it works." Love laughed it off, not even worried at Soria's threat. Now that she knew she could summon, she had to learn its advantages and disadvantages, as well as a reversal.

"You better watch your back, Love. I'm gonna come for you like a reaper."

"I apologized already!"

"Like that's gonna do me any good. Aoi is probably worrying himself to death."

"He probably is." Takahiko agreed without a moment's hesitance. Aoi was a klutz, who needed constant supervising. Hence the reason he was best friends with Yuudai, a solemn guy. "He probably won't be able to finish the mission diligently if you're not there."

"He won't." Soria agreed without a tone of hope in her voice either.

"You two are being awfully rude, don't you think?" asked Love.

"It's the truth," the two said in unison.

"Well," Love said, "you two are nice."

"We are."

"Sarcasm, sarcasm," she hissed but they ignored her. "Anyway," said Love as she switched topics, arms now crossed. "Where were you last night Takahiko? I needed your help."

"Ah, well," he said, letting go of Soria.

"Yeah, where were you?" Soria agreed, crossing her arms also. "Don't tell me you were cheating on your Soulmate?"

"I would never!" he gasped and glared.

"Don't shout, I get it. So, where were you?" Soria asked in annoyance. Before Takahiko could open his mouth to reply, she interrupted. "Cheating?" she accused again and chuckled.

"Soria," groaned Love.

"You're still no fun," complained Soria. Once again, her wanting to have fun was being denied.

"So?"

"I was waiting for you at our usual spot when an explosion occurred. While trying to find the ones who set up the explosion, I noticed someone staring at me from a love hotel across the street," explained Takahiko.

"Oh-ho," said Soria. She put a finger to her chin as a devious grin appeared. Her intuition had been correct. "So, you *were* cheating."

"I said I wasn't!"

"Was she bodacious and curvy? What size was her cup? Was she better than Love? Come on. You can tell me the truth. I won't judge."

"Why are you still here?" Love hissed, her cheeks flaming from the insulting questions.

"I wonder who summoned me here without my permission."

"You sure know how to hold grudges."

Having Soria accuse him only added to Love's skepticism. He had to prove what a faithful man he was by continuing his story. "I ran into the love hotel room where the perpetrator had been watching me. When I entered, all I found was a little blonde girl with blue eyes, wearing a blue dress, eating ice cream."

"What's a child doing at a love hotel?" Love asked.

"I have no idea either, but while I was taking her away to safety, I encountered some hostile guys that needed to be taught a lesson. When I came to find you, Soria had already bailed you out."

"That sounds too suspicious."

"Yeah, tell me about it." Takahiko nodded in agreement, trying to come up with a reason why a little girl was at a love hotel. Were the perpetrators smuggling children?

"Takahiko," spoke Soria, who had been quiet for some time.

He turned her way and glared. "What is it? Are you going to say something sarcastic again?"

"Not right now, maybe later when I feel like it," she answered with a straight face.

"Geh, you're unbelievable."

"You said something about a blonde-haired girl with blue eyes and a blue dress, right?"

"Yeah."

"Where'd you take her?"

"About three miles away from the chaos."

"Why'd you go so damn far?"

"I was making sure she was out of harm's way!"

"Anyway," said Soria. "Was she one of us?"

"Now that you mention it," said Takahiko as he thought it over. The first time he laid eyes on the little girl, he had an inkling feeling they were of the same flock. "She probably is."

Love turned towards Soria. It was unlike her to take an interest in a little kid she'd never met, let alone ask so many questions. Now it made Love curious as well. "Why are you asking?"

"Forget breakfast." Soria stood abruptly, her dilly-dallying coming to an end. "I want a first-class ticket out of here to Sapporo, pronto."

"Why?" asked the two in unison.

"Aoi's in danger."

"What?"

"Think you two can book me a ticket while I run to the airport?"

"That's kind of impossible," they answered in unison again.

"Why not? Explain yourselves," demanded Soria.

"Well," said Love. "We can probably get you a ticket but it'll probably take a few hours before you board. I doubt they'll have last second tickets available for flying out right now, not to mention, first class at it. Even if they did, it'd be super expensive. We don't have that kind of cash laying around."

"Get the funds from the Dome. They're rich."

"True. But who knows how long that would take, especially since the deans and teachers have their hands full with the new students."

"What's the rush anyway?" asked Takahiko.

"Aoi and I are tracking down the girl you saw last night. We're supposed to rendezvous with those kidnappers on Kiska Island and make an exchange. But if what you said is true and if that girl is here in town, we've been set up," explained Soria.

Love was up and out of her seat, just as quick. If Soria was serious, then she needed to get back as quickly as possible. "Why are you still here talking?! You need to leave, now!"

"Haven't I been saying that?" hissed Soria.

"You could try the trains, or maybe even take a ship out there," suggested Takahiko.

"I could, but I'm worried I won't make it on time." Soria turned to leave. If she didn't hurry, Aoi would get ambushed. Knowing him, he probably wouldn't even suspect a thing.

"Where are you going?"

"I didn't want to have to use this last resort."

"What last resort?" asked Love.

Before completely exiting, Soria turned back. "Is there any lake or waterfall nearby?"

"Not that I know of."

"I know a place," answered Takahiko. "Yesterday afternoon, Franz-san and I took a stroll there."

"Show me," ordered Soria.

"What do you plan on doing?"

"You'll see once we get there."

"Sometimes she scares me," Love muttered to herself as she and Takahiko ran after her.

∞

Birds chirped as the rays of the sun lit the room Hikaru laid in. A light breeze blew into the room as she inhaled and exhaled deeply, a slight pain in her chest. She grunted, knowing this day would come, but still tried to fight it off. Beads of sweat rolled down her forehead, and soon it was getting hard to breathe. "Alice," she called out weakly, but no one answered. "Alice," Hikaru called out a bit louder.

"Yes?" answered Alice when she heard the faint call. She came running into the open room with her hair pinned into a bun and a dirty towel in hand.

"Call...for Devastation."

Alice's eyes widened, and she ran out without a word.

Poe had gone out to the fields to tend to the grain while Devastation was in Hikaru's garden, taking out the weeds that had sprouted again. When he noticed Alice bursting out from within the cottage, he turned to smile at her.

"Granny, she-"

Without waiting to hear the rest, Devastation dropped the tools he was holding and stripped off his straw hat before rushing inside. Alice's look said it all. When he reached Hikaru, she did her best to smile and shakily reached out. Devastation rushed over, clasping her wrinkly hand in his.

Unable to do anything except cry by the doorway, Alice took a step back and closed the door, giving them privacy. She couldn't insert herself into such an emotional situation. Hikaru's last moments on this earth belonged to Devastation and Devastation alone. Taking a seat in the hallway, Alice hugged her legs.

"Hikaru," whispered Devastation.

"Do you still remember that song you sang to me?" she whispered.

Devastation smiled and nodded, placing her backhand to his cheek. "How can I forget?" His lips trembled as her warmth slowly faded.

"Will you sing me that song again?"

"Anything for you, my love." He nodded again and squeezed her hand, before singing the same song he always sung.

♫ *When I shout out for help, the world ignores me*

248

And when I try to find a place to call my own, I am shunned
You, my beautiful light became my source of strength
When I cry and need to run, you will be the one I lean on
My beautiful light, I love you
Shine your rays down on me forever
I wish to always walk alongside you
But not being able to say, 'I love you'
Who knew such a thing could be so painful?
Oh, my beautiful light, I love you, remember this even in the next life♪

When Devastation finished singing, Hikaru cried and squeezed his hand in hers, afraid to part. In that moment, she transformed from an old woman into a young Hikaru who was bedridden. Their moments and memories seemed to spring to life. The first time they met, the first time they fell in love, the first time they kissed, and the first time they made love. This love, it had given them a reason to live. Now, it was giving them a reason to die for as well.

"I love you," she whispered.

"I love you more."

"You romantic." Hikaru chuckled and stroked his cheek. She could never tire from watching him. "Please live, for me."

Devastation shook his head in refusal. How could he continue living the next hundred years without her? Just one second would be hell itself already. "Forty years," he whispered, "wasn't enough. I need a thousand—no, I need every lifetime."

"Then, every lifetime it'll be, until you tire of me," she whispered.

"I'll never."

"Wherever I go, I'll take these precious memories with me. That way...I'll always remember to come back to you." Hikaru gasped, slowly closing her eyes. Her time had finally come. "...my only love." Her hand became limp in Devastation's as his tears fell like rain.

"Hikaru," he called out, but she no longer moved nor breathed. He stood and laid beside her, his heart feeling as though it had died as well. So, this was the pain his comrades had all gone through after losing their Soulmates. No wonder it drove them mad. "My angel," Devastation whispered, stroking her cheek. "Rest for now. I'll be there soon."

Alice who sat out in the hallway sobbed endlessly. She had both hands to her mouth, preventing any screams from escaping. The two inside, their love story had come to an end.

∞

Hands on her hips, Soria stared at the dinky pond sitting before her. When Takahiko offered to show her a place that had water, she'd been expecting a waterfall, or great lake. Not a pond at a park. "This is it?" she asked, glancing at a sheepish Takahiko.

"Unfortunately, yes."

"This should do," Soria said with a smile.

"Really?" Takahiko let out a breath of air. He'd been worried that she'd erupt and drown him. Fortunately, she was content.

"Remember what I told you two, try to get into contact with Aoi and tell him the situation."

"That's the hundredth time now," groaned Love.

"Oh, and one more thing," Soria said, disregarding her comment. "The next time you dare to summon me, make sure you know a way of reversal."

Love gulped and nodded. That one, she wouldn't argue with. "Okay."

"Well then," said Soria as she turned to face front, then stopped. "Ah, another thing," she added in, turning to look at Takahiko this time. "If you see that little girl again, kidnap her. If you let her go a second time, I'll wring your neck."

Takahiko too gulped and nodded. "Okay."

"Well, that's all for now." Soria stepped out onto the pond and walked across the water.

Eyes bulging, the two stared and pointed fingers. "EH?!" they shouted.

"How is that possible?!" shouted Takahiko.

"Is it a new magic spell that I haven't yet perfected?!" shouted Love. "How can you do that but not me?! I'm so disappointed in myself!"

Annoyed at their exaggeration, Soria rolled her eyes and continued walking until she reached the middle. The few people close by saw and pointed fingers. They whispered, wondering how someone—*anyone*—could stand on water without falling in.

After inhaling, Soria closed her eyes to concentrate on the water below. Little by little water particles rose into the air, forming a tight circle around her. Then suddenly, like geysers, the remaining pond water shot her towards the ocean where she would be able to control a larger amount of water. The swimming ducks and fishes fell to the bottom of the now dry pond. When Soria was gone, the floating water fell, sending splashes everywhere.

"Ah!" screamed Love as she backed away with Takahiko.

"Wow," he said, still watching the sky where Soria had disappeared to.

"Yeah, I know. Wow, right?" Love agreed, wiping the water off her face. With the remaining water left in the pond, the fishes swam again, while the ducks paddled along like nothing had happened.

"Amazing!" shouted Nicholas from behind. He clapped his hands excitedly and approached the two. Walking haughtily down by his feet was

Liz who swished and swooshed her tail from side to side, clearly upset about something.

"Nicholas-san," said Takahiko in alarm.

"Nicholas-kun," said Love. She looked down at the orange cat and sneered. "Cat-chan," she greeted, "we meet again."

Liz looked up, hissing loudly.

"Liz," warned Nicholas. He gave her a warning look, then smiled at the two. From below, Liz purred and rubbed her cheek against his leg, but he didn't bother.

"I've been meaning to ask," said Love. "That cat, she's also a Life-Kill, isn't she?"

Baffled, Takahiko could only stare. Love's theory sounded off the charts. There was no such thing as a shapeshifting Life-Kill. Or was there? He'd never met one before, and there was always a first for everything.

Nicholas smiled while Liz stared at Love. "She is."

"What?" choked out Takahiko.

"I thought so," said Love.

"How did you guess?" asked Nicholas.

"That cat doesn't act like a normal cat."

"Is that so?"

"She's really a person?" Takahiko turned, pointing a finger at Liz. So, a shapeshifting Life-Kill really did exist. He was going to enjoy telling the guys.

"Yes, she is. When she reverts to her human form, I'll introduce you again. Right now, she wishes to stay in cat form," answered Nicholas. He turned to leave and stopped, remembering why he'd approached them. "Ah, that's right. There's a meeting in an hour."

"Okay, thanks."

"Also, if I may inquire, next time Soria's around, please introduce us. I want to talk with her." Nicholas smiled one last time before leaving with Liz.

"Hmm?" Love said, staring intently at Nicholas.

Takahiko noticed and popped his face in hers, angry that she was staring at Nicholas for so long. What was so good about a foreigner like him? If Love had an affinity for guys with blond hair, there was King, Yuudai, and Taiyou. Then again, Nicholas was the one who'd made Love drool. "Why are you staring at him like that for?"

"How'd he know Soria's name?"

"Huh?"

"We never once mentioned her name. So how did he know?"

"Uh," said Takahiko as he thought about it. It was true that neither of them ever mentioned Soria, yet Nicholas magically called her by name. There was no answer to their question unless they asked him directly. But after getting to know Nicholas for these past few days, he'd probably avoid their question. Sensing Love's worry, Takahiko dragged her away and smiled. "Who cares? Let's go grab a quick snack before heading to the meeting."

Love nodded in agreement, suddenly hungry. After grabbing a quick bite, they headed to the hotel for the meeting. When they finished, Takahiko left to chat with Franz while Love snuck off to a shady pawn shop. After talking for a few minutes, the owner led her towards a secret passage.

Love looked around the dungeon-like black market. It had a moldy smell with little to no light. She could barely see where she was walking. When she reached the stall she was looking for, she stopped and peered at the books on display.

Love flipped through them, carefully examining their spines and spell pages. Each and every single one was lacking. None of these had the same depth as her old spell book. After hearing high praises about black market goods, she'd expected something over the top only to be let down.

The old stall attendant with a crooked smile and hunched back, slowly made her way towards Love. She could be mistaken to be a witch. "See anything you like, missy?"

"I'll take this one," Love answered, choosing the best book.

"That'll be 1,000 golden dollars."

"That's mighty expensive."

"I've got to make a living. Besides, spell books are rare to come by these days with the Domes cracking down on the merchants selling them."

Defeated, Love paid and left with her new book. Once out in the open air, she sifted through it again, feeling cheated. The book was half the size of her old one. "If I'd known these would be lacking, I'd have contacted the Dome for a new one." After thinking about it, Love shook it off. Waiting for the Dome to send a new spell book meant she would have to go without any form of attack. It was better to have something than to have nothing.

"Ugh," someone groaned as Love stopped and glanced back. A little girl with blonde hair and green eyes, wearing a matching green plaited dress was trying to climb a tree. Trapped in the branches was a blue balloon.

Smiling, Love walked over. "Need some help?"

The little girl immediately stopped trying to climb and scrunched her brows. At least she was wary of talking to strangers.

"I just want to help."

With a shy nod, the girl attempted a weak smile. "Yes, please."

"Alright then," Love said, opening her spell book, excited to be using magic again. "Black Magic, Level One, Tickles."

A group of palm-sized, white creatures appeared from the book and laughed. They were fluffy with big black eyes and tiny mouths, but no noses. The group of Tickles flew towards the balloon string to bring down, not needing orders. They knew exactly why they'd been summoned. Once Love took hold of the string, the group of Tickles laughed and disappeared.

"Here you go." Love handed the blue string over and smiled.

"Thank you," the little girl said, reaching out to retrieve her balloon.

"Are you lost by chance? Need me to take you home?"

"No." The little girl shook her head, trying to tie the string around her wrist, but was having no luck with it.

"Let me." Love crouched to help. When she secured the string around the girl's tiny wrist, she stood and smiled. "There you go. Now it won't fly off anymore."

"Thank you."

"You're welcome."

"Anoka!" called out Ikuto. He approached the two with his hands in his pockets and stopped. Pursed between his lips was an unlit cigarette. One look at Love and he raised an eyebrow, then took the unlit cigarette out to hold. Had Love been trying to kidnap their precious trump card? "Anoka!" he shouted again. "Let's go before Pia gets mad at you."

"Coming," answered Anoka as she waved bye to Love and ran over to join Ikuto so they could leave.

"Who was that?"

"A nice lady who helped get my balloon down."

"Is that so? You don't see a lot of nice people these days."

"Yeah," Anoka agreed. "Where are we going now?"

"HQ. Pia says the boss just returned. We're gonna meet up with him."

"Beast-san," Anoka whispered. She seemed frightened at the mentioning of him and squeezed Ikuto's hand.

"It'll be fine. You've got us, and besides, the boss won't hurt you. You're special."

∞

"What a cute girl," said Love as she turned around to leave.

"Love!" shouted Takahiko as he popped his face into hers, panting.

"Whoa!" shouted Love as she backed away in alarm. When and how did Takahiko find her? And how many times did he plan on scaring her? "Would you stop that?!"

"Love!"

"What do you want? Stop shouting."

"That was her!" Takahiko pointed a finger to where Ikuto and Anoka had been standing. The moment he saw Anoka from afar, he started shouting to get Love's attention, but she'd been too preoccupied with the balloon.

"Huh?"

"The little girl you were with just now, that was the same girl I met inside the love hotel!"

"What?!" she shouted, spinning around to stop the two who were long gone.

"That's definitely her."

Exactly what kind of twisted joke was this? How could she be so lucky and unlucky at the same time? "But you said she had blue eyes and wore a blue dress. The girl I was with had green eyes and wore a green dress."

"Colored contacts, you fool!"

"Why would a kid wear such a thing?" she asked, twirling to look at him.

"So that people who are chasing her won't recognize her."

"Ah!" Love shouted in realization that she'd been tricked. Anoka, the little girl that Soria had warned them to keep tabs on, Love had let escape with some guy. She couldn't help but sweat a bit. Even Takahiko seemed worried. To make matters worse, they still couldn't contact Aoi. They were doomed if Soria ever got wind of this. Next time, they wouldn't live to see another day.

"You think you can track her down using your magic?"

"If I don't have a possession of hers, I can't."

The two stared at each other and gulped.

"Let's NEVER EVER tell Soria about what happened here today!" they concluded and spun around to leave, pretending they never met Anoka, or let her escape a second time.

25th Lie

ALICE RAN TOWARDS THE FIELDS, barely able to see where she was going from all the tears that clouded her vision. She tripped and fell, only to get back up and continue running. When Poe came into view, she cried harder and yelled with all her might, "Poe!"

At the sound of her voice, he turned, dropping the hoe in his hand to meet her halfway. She looked so frantic. "What's wrong?"

"It's bad!"

"What is?"

"Devastation, he went to the village!"

"What?"

"Granny passed away while you were here. Devastation left to the village."

"He's really planning on dying." Poe took off his straw hat as they ran off to stop Devastation. It took some time before they reached the small town at dusk. Sure enough, Devastation was there, talking to Ms. Hirano who didn't look pleased at his unannounced presence. The entire village was present also. They seemed scared. Devastation, the god they worshipped had never come to them of his own accord and it could only mean a bad omen.

"Devastation!" Poe shouted, breathless from the running.

"Poe-kun, Alice-chan," gasped Ms. Hirano. "I thought you'd left?"

Instead of paying her any attention or replying, Poe was completely fixated on Devastation. "What are you doing here?"

"I told you already," Devastation said. In his trembling hand was Hikaru's worn-out quilt. "I won't return to the Dome with you."

"But-" protested Alice.

Before she could get another word in, Devastation cut her off, "Time's up, Hirano-san. I'm here to end this pitiful life we've been living."

"I object." Ms. Hirano crossed her arms and glared, no longer caring to keep up with her cheerful pretense. After working so hard to get to where she was today, she couldn't give in to Devastation's whims. "How can you suddenly come to this conclusion by yourself without consulting me first?"

"I've already lost what's important to me, and returning with the two behind me is the same as dying. I mind as well end it here on my own accord."

Smirking, Ms. Hirano uncrossed her arms. "So it's true then. Hikaru-chan is still alive."

"*Was.*"

Not shocked by the news, Ms. Hirano eventually shook it off. Hikaru was merely human. One day she would've died. But Ms. Hirano no longer considered herself a normal human being. She had far surpassed that ideal. "What a pity," she said, glancing about. "How about we give you another girl to keep you satisfied?"

"That's right," the villagers shouted, also not able to give up their lives because Devastation no longer wished to live.

Their greed was so apparent, Alice stared in horror. Were these the same people she and Poe had become friends with? Somehow, they no longer seemed like before. These people were more like beasts. Unable to stand aside and listen to them slander Devastation, she erupted, "Stop it!"

Poe turned to look at her in alarm. He'd never seen her lose her cool before, other than the night she pulled her gun on him.

"You think replacing a loved one is possible?! Don't kid yourself!"

Annoyed, Ms. Hirano glared. Alice had no right to interfere. "This only concerns our village and this devil."

"What?"

"Go back to your grand palace with your servant boy."

"That's enough. This will end here," interrupted Devastation. It was as Ms. Hirano had said. This fight against the villagers was his. Even though he was grateful to Alice for defending him, there was no need for her to get attacked either.

"And what makes you think we'll let it end here?" she challenged. "If we kill you and preserve your powers, we can continue living."

Devastation's eyes widened. Ms. Hirano was more cunning than he imagined. Did her desperation for eternal life cause her to secretly research how to implant his powers into one of her own?

"Let's go with that plan," she said, happily laughing. It was the best solution. The powers that Ms. Hirano had always yearned for would finally belong to her. "Everyone, let's kill this devil and live on for eternity!"

"They've all lost it," Poe muttered. The villagers were serious about killing Devastation and keeping his powers to live on. Soon, the situation would get out of control.

Even Devastation himself laughed. When the villagers heard, they stopped.

"What's so damn funny?" snapped Ms. Hirano.

"I'd love to see you try and kill me."

"Then, don't mind if I do."

He grinned and shook his head. It was amazing that humans were such complex creatures, yet at the same time, so simple. Their desire for eternal life had been engrained into their very DNA. "How sad. It's as Hikaru said. Your greed has made you forget that death is inevitable." Devastation raised his right hand into the air as a gold clock made of energy materialized.

"Was that thing always there?" asked Alice.

"I think so. We probably just couldn't see it," answered Poe.

The gold hands on the clock came to a standstill as some sort of barrier gave way and rippled across the air. It could be heard cracking as time came to an end.

"Don't let him destroy us!" shouted Ms. Hirano as they picked up rocks and sticks to attack with. "Kill the devil!"

Tick.

Before anyone knew what was happening, the villagers' running slowed and the hands rapidly spun counter-clockwise until the little hand struck twelve. When the long hand stopped at twelve also, the magic ended as everyone turned to dust.

The kids whose time hadn't yet stopped screamed and backed away. "Monster, monster!" they cried.

Devastation gave a pained smile, remembering the sacrificial children's same reaction. He stared at the kids before him, his sadness replaced with rage. "This is no place for kids such as yourselves. Leave, and never return." Devastation reached a hand out as the kids immediately picked up the stones and sticks the adults had dropped to throw at him, along with curses.

"Stop it!" shouted Alice as she ran forward to protect him.

"It's okay." Devastation turned to smile at her, his forehead bleeding. "I'm already used to this."

"Devastation-"

"Poe," he begged.

"Any-" Poe began, his voice shaking and tears welling in his eyes. There was no way around this situation. He had to face it head-on no matter how hard it was. "Any last words?"

"Just one."

"Then, speak."

"Don't cry."

"Huh?" he said, confused.

With a tender smile, Devastation looked over at Alice who cried again. She couldn't bear to watch as Poe readied himself to kill Devastation. "I can see it. When you find out the truth, you'll be torn in two. That's why, I want to warn you now. Do not break. Hold your head up high. Or else, you'll drown in your own despair and lose Alice."

Poe raised an eyebrow, not understanding Devastation's code. "What are you trying to say?"

"Promise me you won't break so easily."

"I promise," Poe said, hoping to ease his worries.

Nodding, Devastation closed his eyes. Now that he had made peace with himself and the world, he was ready. It was time to give up on this life he'd held for so long. There was no longer anything he feared or yearned for. "*Dar zindagi badi* (In the next life)," he whispered in his native Farsi tongue.

Without a word, Poe snatched the quilt to strangle Devastation with.

Tears quickly flooded his red eyes and spilled as he smiled, making no attempts to break free. He even held onto the quilt while his face turned red. Somewhere far away, he could hear Hikaru's voice. With the last of his energy, he spent it gasping her name before his body became limp and he took his last breath on earth.

Poe let go as Devastation's body hit the ground. His breathing was raspy as the quilt in his hands fell to the ground. Poe hit one knee and threw a hand to his mouth. This was his first time killing a defenseless person, nonetheless, his own kind. It made him sick to the pit of his stomach, like he'd committed a sin.

"Poe," called out Alice.

"I'm fine," he answered too quickly.

"You-"

"I said I'm fine."

Alice stopped objecting to stand beside him. "Okay."

"Let's bury him beside Hikaru-san."

"Yeah," Alice said, nodding. "Does this mean our mission is over?"

Poe looked over, realizing that his Alice he knew had returned. He smiled a sad smile as tears clouded his vision. His arms itched to reach out and hold her, but they had been stained with killing an innocent man. Poe didn't want to touch his beloved with sullied hands. He looked over at Devastation's body and nodded. "Yeah, this is the end."

Alice got down on her knees and draped her arms around Poe. His body was shaking uncontrollably. "This was for the best, right?"

"Yeah," Poe responded, resting his head on her shoulder. If he had forcefully taken Devastation back to the Dome, knowing the deans and teachers, they would torture him into submission. Poe could never forgive himself if he allowed that to happen, especially after coming to understand Devastation. Letting him follow Hikaru was the best choice.

∞

Takahiko and Love exited the elevator to enter the top floor penthouse. Tonight, Franz was leaving Japan and returning to America. They were to escort him out of the hotel. From thereon, the other squadrons would see him back safely to the Golden Palace.

As soon as they approached Franz's hallway, they both stopped. A pretty girl with wavy shoulder length orange hair was standing in the hallway, examining her nails. When she noticed them, she turned to stare without a word of greeting.

"Ah, you two," Nicholas said from behind as the couple turned around. He smiled and motioned to the pretty girl. "Let me introduce you."

"Is that her?" Love asked, already guessing who it was.

"Who is she?" Takahiko asked, clearing his throat and fixing his hair.

"Cat-chan."

"Eh?"

"Takahiko, Love, this is Liz. Liz, Takahiko and Love," Nicholas introduced once they were standing in front of each other.

"EH?!" Takahiko shouted again in astonishment. "So it's really true?! She can morph?!"

"Nice meeting ya," Liz greeted with a wink and made a peace sign.

Takahiko pulled at Love's arm to whisper. "She's really a Life-Kill?"

"Haven't I been saying that from the beginning?"

"But it seemed impossible."

Sighing, Love turned away, boys were foolish creatures. They could never believe until the real thing was staring them in the face. "So," she said, giving Liz a glance over, "you finally decided to show up in your real form, huh?"

Liz hissed, her beautiful cat eyes gleaming while Nicholas chuckled and intervened. "Now, now," he said, clapping his hands to stop the fight. "We're all comrades here. Let's not do this, okay?"

"Yeah, I guess," Love said, turning towards Takahiko who was shamelessly staring at Liz's voluptuous figure and full lips. He was being so obvious about his thoughts, it made Love blush. Was Liz the type all men lusted for? If so, then Love was far from that ideal, with little to no curves. No wonder Soria had insulted her. "Would you knock it off already?"

"She's totally my type. I think I just fell in love at first sight."

"Yeah, yeah, keep dreaming."

"Oh?" Franz said, coming out from his room. He smiled at the four as eight bodyguards exited with him. "You four are already here?"

"Yeah, we are, now let's go," Liz answered, taking the lead.

"And she's feisty," Takahiko said, feeling giddy while Love groaned.

When they reached the front lobby, they made their way out into the cool night. A few black limousines were parked out front along with law enforcement.

"Well, see ya," Love bid and smiled.

"Love," Takahiko growled, elbowing her. She could at least pretend to be sad about this departure.

"What? I'm just bidding him a farewell." Love quickly bowed and stood back up, more cheerful than a while ago. Finally, this mission had come to an end. "See you two as well, Cat-chan and Nicholas-kun."

Franz chuckled and shook his head. He motioned to Nicholas and Liz who hadn't left Takahiko's side. "Actually, you two will be taking these two with you back to the Maroon Dome."

"Eh?!" Love shouted, a little too loud. She couldn't believe that she'd been task with something so bothersome. And why were they even staying behind for? "There's no way in hell!"

"We'll see to it that they safely make it to the Maroon Dome with us." Takahiko elbowed Love again and smiled.

"I don't want to," she growled. "Besides, we were never given any orders to do such a thing."

"Well, uh," said Takahiko. He stopped talking to think about her words. It was true. They'd been given no such orders to escort anyone.

"Oh? Did Dean Kiera and Dean Kosa not tell you that these two would be staying at Maroon for a while? Shall I contact them to verify this information?" offered Franz.

"No!" Takahiko quickly shook his head, wanting nothing more than to settle this quietly. If Dean Kosa were to get a call from the Golden God's representative about Takahiko questioning such a powerful person, his head would go flying. "I mean, no. We get the point. We'll escort them."

"What's with you?" asked Love.

"The dean's really scary."

"You're scared of the dean?"

"Aren't you scared of your dean?"

"No. The one I'm scared of is Oka-sen—I mean, *Umi*-sensei," she corrected and quivered in fear. If Miss Umi had ears that could reach all the way here, Love would have been skinned alive for making such a crucial mistake.

"Don't you think it's about time you leave?" Liz said, impatiently waiting for Franz to leave also.

"Liz," said Nicholas.

"What?" she said innocently. "I really wanna go to Maroon."

"Patience."

"I can't, I really wanna see those two again."

"What two?" Love asked suspiciously.

"Oh, you see," Liz began excitedly. "I met-"

"Liz," Nicholas interrupted, pulling her back and shaking his head. Now wasn't the time to reveal their ulterior motives.

"Okay, okay, I get it." She turned away, pouting and crossing her arms. Nicholas was going to keep her on a tight leash while they were here. If she wanted any fun, she'd have to go at it alone.

"What was that about?" asked Takahiko.

"No idea," answered Love.

"Well then," Franz said, interrupting their conversation. "When I depart, you four will also depart for the Maroon Dome as well. I hope you all get along together from now on."

"Yeah," Takahiko and Love said glumly.

"Sure thing," the other two replied happily. This was their chance to size up the Life-Kills from Maroon and wouldn't let it slip by.

"Try not to start any fights," Franz said, petting Liz on the head.

"Don't touch me so casually," she hissed.

Chuckling, Franz withdrew his hand. Even in human form, Liz was picky about who petted her. "Nicholas, be sure to keep Liz out of trouble."

"I will," Nicholas answered.

"Alright then," Franz said, midway from turning. He couldn't leave like this, not while Love was standing before him. If only he got some one-on-one time with her, he wouldn't need to put her on the on the spot, but it didn't matter anymore. He was pressed for time. "I heard from the dean that there was someone from the Maroon academy who's exceptional."

"Who? Hotaka?" responded Takahiko. "Or Rain?"

"He was obviously talking to me, not you," corrected Love.

"Oh," said Takahiko as he laughed it off.

"Yes, I've heard from Dean Kosa that Rain is very strong, as well as Hotaka," replied Franz.

"So is Kei."

"Taka," hissed Love. She wanted to stop the pointless conversation so Franz would hurry and leave.

"Alright, I'll stop."

"So?" Franz urged, not about to leave until Love gave him a name.

"If you want a name, you'll have to be more specific. They're all tough."

"Who do you believe is the strongest?"

"Well, honestly, I'm scared to death of Yeve."

"Who isn't?" agreed Takahiko.

"Yeve isn't scary," Liz said, coming to her defense.

"How do you even know?"

"Liz," warned Nicholas as she stopped.

"So, who else?" Franz continued.

"Well," Love said, debating. "Umeko—ah, and Jennifer, sometimes."

"But power wise, who?" he specified.

"Power wise, huh? The scariest has to be…Midnight?"

"You had to put that into a question."

"Uh, well," said Love as she scratched her head and wiggled her nose. To be frank, she didn't want to answer Franz's question truthfully. There was nothing about the Maroon Girls' Academy to take interest in, unless of course, he had an ulterior motive. And if by chance he did, she'd deter him. "I'm curious to know. Why do you wish to know for?"

Franz smiled, impressed that Love had caught on. "I want to know how strong she is."

"Well," Love said again, raising an eyebrow at his vague answer. This time, she took a bit more time to think before responding, "It's Midnight, because she's always retained her number one position."

"Oh my, and all this time, no one's been able to usurp her position?"

"No."

"Isn't it time you leave?" interrupted Nicholas. He too had lost all patience and wanted to head to Maroon right away. The suspense of meeting the others was killing him.

"Ah, yes, yes," he answered and smiled at the two again. "Thank you for answering my question and for seeing to it that I was safe while here." Franz bowed and got inside the limousine as the driver drove away.

When he was gone, the four returned to their rooms, packing up to depart for Maroon.

"You lied back there, didn't you?" Takahiko asked.

"Huh?" said Love as she looked over.

"From you girls, isn't Umeko the strongest? I mean, with her poison and all?"

Love stopped halfway from setting her shirt inside her duffel bag and smiled. Even after spending their teenage years together, Takahiko still knew nothing about the girls' abilities and was basing it off on hindsight. Truly, oblivious was bliss. "Yes, yes, how'd you find out I was lying?" she asked and headed towards the bathroom.

"Dummy," he called after her. "Why'd you lie if you know that Umeko is the strongest? Lying to a person with that much power will only get you into trouble."

Now alone in the bathroom, Love placed her hands under the faucet as the water ran. When she finished washing and drying her hands and face, she stared at her reflection in the mirror for a long time.

Her conversation with Franz had resurfaced thanks to Takahiko. Without a doubt, Franz also suspected Love of lying to him too, but had it let it slide, thank goodness. To make it more believable, she should've said Yeve instead given how they all feared her. But when it came to power, that was a different story. "No one knows," Love whispered, reaching out to touch her cold reflection.

Somewhere in her memory, she could hear Yeve threatening them after that horrible incident that changed everything at the girls' academy.

"No one," Yeve said, her back turned to them. Standing next to her as usual, was Soria. It became silent as they stared at the two's backs. It was like looking at two immovable objects. Slowly, Yeve turned to stare at the group. Her eyes never wavered. She enunciated every syllable, hoping to drill the threat into their minds so they never forgot. And indeed, that was exactly what she had done. "No one is to bring up this incident ever again. If I so much as hear a single peep from you girls, you're dead."

Love's clenched fist that rested on the mirror trembled as she threw her free hand over her mouth. When the nausea faded, she lowered her hands and caught sight of the fear from that day reflecting off the mirror.

"Love, let's go!" Takahiko shouted.

"Yeah!" she responded and quickly washed her face before leaving to grab her belongings. Those eyes that had been burned into her memory would soon cast nightmares in her sleep again.

∞

Torches lit the night as it illuminated the two gravestones marked for Devastation and Hikaru. Standing with fresh dirt staining his hands, Poe heaved while Alice stood nearby, watching. Here, in this place, the two lovers would stay united.

Alice turned to look behind. The kids had followed them out into the forest, now that there was no longer an adult figure around. "Should we take them to an orphanage?"

Turning, Poe stared at the kids also before nodding. "That'd be the best solution."

"Then we should get going." Alice walked over to join the kids and crouched to talk with them about bringing them to an orphanage. The kids cried, refusing to part from them.

"The orphanage is the only place that you can go now," said Poe as he approached them, not bothering to clean his hands.

"But," they objected by wailing.

"Where will you be going?" asked a twelve-year-old boy.

"To meet with our deans," answered Poe.

"Then I'm going with you!"

"We will too!" shouted the others.

"Kids," said Alice nicely.

Poe shook his head. He couldn't take on a burdensome task of looking after a group of kids. "We'll take you all to the nearest orphanage we find. After that, we'll depart and that's the end of it. Now let's go," Poe said done with negotiating.

Alice watched him lead the way and stood, ushering the kids along. "Come on. Let's go."

"Your house is big, right?" asked the same boy.

"Well, it's not really our house, but we consider it to be, yes."

"Then why can't you take us with you?"

Alice smiled and shook her head, not wanting to see these kids end up as experiments like herself. If possible, she wanted them to live a normal life without being feared and hated. "That place is no place for kids."

"I'll still follow you."

Alice couldn't help but chuckle at his persistence. "What's your name again?"

"Jacques."

"Jacques huh?"

"My papa is French. So, I'm a halfie."

"Is that so?" Alice smiled and glanced over at Ms. Hirano's son who was still in shock about seeing his mother turn to ashes. Now he was an orphan, with no outlet to target his hatred and revenge.

"I'll grow up to be a strong person," Jacques said, interrupting Alice's thoughts. He reached out to hold her hand and squeezed it with all his might. His mind was made up. He would follow them even if they objected. "When I become strong, I won't need to rely on others."

26th Lie

TOTORI

Remi got down on one knee and touched the trail of blood inside the forest. It had dried as she pulled her hand away and stood. From behind, Noah approached as she shook her head.

"So close," he growled, driving his fist into a tree. "Shit, the dean's gonna have my head for this."

Watching Noah beat himself over this made Remi feel as though she was too calm about the situation, when that was far from the truth. During their first mission they'd failed and needed to be removed. After receiving an earful and getting reassigned to a new mission, the two vowed to succeed at all costs. But that was proving to be harder done than said.

"If Dean Kosa blames you for letting the rebels get away, then I'll also share the same fate," Remi spoke.

Surprised, Noah turned away from the tree towards her.

"After all, I'm your Soulmate. Together we make one." Remi glanced at Noah who continued staring without blinking. Embarrassed, she fidgeted and quickly rambled on again, "It's only right if I receive half your punishment because you know, we're Soulmates and all."

"You're repeating the same thing."

Remi's cheeks flared as she crossed her arms. "I so did not."

"Yes, you did."

"Yeah, well, whatever." Remi uncrossed her arms to stalk away. With their targets gone, she had no need to stay.

"Thanks," said Noah as he chased her to pat on the head. "Your words were comforting."

"What are you talking about? I was just stating the facts about how we're Soulmates. It's not like you're special or anything. So, don't go thinking that I like you or anything. It's just that we're Soulmates."

"You're doing it again."

Remi puffed her cheeks and stormed away again. As a teenager, she'd wanted to be more cool and mature, but still came across as young and immature. It was amazing that Verse who was younger could easily achieve what Remi wanted to be.

Noah watched, unable to contain his smile. He shook his head and chased her again. His worries about letting the rebels flee escaped his mind entirely, thanks to Remi. "Let's return to our car and find the nearest restaurant to eat. After that, let's continue our hunt."

"Alright."

A black crow perched behind tree leaves watched as they joked. It cawed and spread its wings to fly as Noah spun back, catching a glimpse of it.

"What's wrong?"

"I thought I sensed someone's presence."

"You mean those guys are still around?" Remi asked, fully alert. She scanned their surroundings, looking for anything out of the ordinary.

"Don't know," Noah said, shaking his head. His stomach growled as Remi turned to raise an eyebrow. Laughing, Noah linked arms with her so they could leave, forgetting about the enemy. He needed to munch on something that wasn't bread, crackers, and energy bars before he collapsed. "Let's go."

∞

Aoi slicked his red hair to one side and winked, trying to be as charming and seductive as possible. "Hey," he greeted in a sultry tone. "How you doing tonight? Can I buy you a drink?"

When no one responded, he broke down from the pressure.

"Who am I trying to kid? I can't do anything!" he shouted at the mirror.

There was a knock at his inn room as Aoi abruptly stopped crying. He walked out of the bathroom to answer the door, completely composed now.

"Yes?"

"This was sent for you," the worker said, handing over a letter, then left.

Stepping back into the room, Aoi shut the door and locked it. On this island, there was only one inn and one port. There wasn't even a teeny tiny convenience store to buy candy. Nor were there signs that technology had touched this place. The one hundred residents who lived here were scattered about the island, making it the most desolate place Aoi had ever been to. He could only imagine how this island was like during the Godless Ages.

Aoi opened the letter to read its contents.

The meeting is at seven sharp. No exceptions.

"I see." He crumpled the letter the other party had sent and threw it away. Aoi held his composure for some time before losing his cool again. He ran out onto the patio, yelling into the gusts that drowned out his voice, "Soria, where are you?! How could you disappear on me while taking a shower?!"

∞

Remi couldn't believe that while inside their rental car trying to find a place to eat, it decided to break down. With no signal to get ahold of the rental company, they were on their own and had to abandon the car on the countryside roadway. The long walk back to the city would be treacherous, considering last night the forecaster had mentioned a thunderstorm brewing in the horizon.

"I told you we should've taken a bus instead," said Remi.

"I wasn't expecting this to happen," said Noah in defense.

Seeing as how nothing could change the situation, Remi let it go and glanced to the sky, wondering aloud, "I wonder if it'll really rain."

"It will," he answered.

Eyebrows raised, she looked over. "How do you know?"

"From the feel of the atmosphere." They walked for a bit longer until Noah stopped, his stomach rumbling. He sighed, disappointed that he hadn't gotten to eat anything delicious all day. "Let's take a short break. I'm hungry."

Without a reply, Remi sat alongside him and unpacked her bag.

Having grown up with a group of rowdy boys, the silence was killing Noah. He ate his sandwich loudly and smacked his lips together. Even then, Remi didn't bother to ask what was wrong. Scooting nearer, he smiled while she raised an eyebrow, questioning his babyish behavior. "Say, Remi."

"What is it?"

"Doesn't the country air feel nostalgic?"

"Does it really?"

"Why are you so gloomy?"

"Do you need to ask? I didn't get enough sleep last night because you kept tossing and turning and snoring. This morning we had a bagel for breakfast. All day we've been trying to track down our targets. Then, our rental car dies and now here we are, stranded in the middle of nowhere."

"You always have to find something to complain about, don't you?"

"If you think I'm bad, you clearly haven't met Crystal," Remi joked while making herself a sandwich. When she finished, she looked to the orangey-blue sky again where clouds gently floated by. Remi couldn't help but think of Soria every time she saw the sky or water. For an apparent reason, blue was always associated with her.

"Soria!" Remi shouted, running out onto the rooftop in her maroon uniform. She huffed and puffed, while Soria lay on the tiled ground, sleeping. These were the days back at the academy when life was fun and worry-free. "Soria, wake up!"

"Hmm?" she answered and opened her eyes. The sun was so bright she put a forearm to her forehead.

"It's lunchtime. Let's go eat."

"Yeah, sure."

Remi pouted and put her hands on her hips. "Why are you always sleeping on the rooftop anyway? If you don't want to get caught by Tanaka-sensei, you have to find a new sleeping place."

"I like it here though."

"Why?"

"Because the view of the sky is best from here," she responded and reached out to catch the blue sky. "Clear skies are the best. That way we can enjoy the sunshine and see things clearly, the way they're meant to be."

"Hmm?" she answered and took her hands off her hips to glance at the clear skies. A few birds could be seen flying by. The rays of the sun were so bright, Remi had to hold out a hand to block it out as well. Indeed, it was soothing.

"I bet the real sky is even more breathtaking."

Remi pondered on it before smiling and nodding in agreement. "Yep, you're probably right!"

"What are you talking about? I'm *always* right," corrected Soria. She sat up and yawned, ready to eat. "Let's go find Yeve and Verse."

"I already know where they are." Remi smiled proudly, knowing that Soria would ask for the two first thing when she woke up. Which was why, she always kept tabs on where they'd be.

Noah stared at Remi whose mind was elsewhere. If he didn't snap her out of it, she just might never return to reality. "Remi?"

"Clear skies are the best, aren't they?" she spoke.

"Huh? Uh, well, I guess," he answered and nodded. "What's with the random question anyway?"

"A certain friend once asked me that."

Smiling, Noah too glanced at the sky. She was so obvious it wasn't even a challenge. In the years that Noah had known her, he'd mainly seen her stick to the three. "Soria."

"He-he, is it that easy to guess?" Remi scratched her head sheepishly.

"Very," Noah answered, reaching out to nudge her. In the beginning, he'd wondered why the two girls were friends. But after witnessing their friendship, he understood the reason. "Soria seems like the sort of person who will always have your back, no matter what. You chose a good friend."

Remi smiled and nodded proudly. "You couldn't be more right."

There was a pit-pat nearby as the two glanced up. The orangey-blue sky had been cleared away within the blink of an eye as black clouds rolled in and the rainstorm began.

"Shit!" Noah shouted as they quickly packed up to find shelter. He held his pack over his head, trying not to get soaked, although it was useless. The rain was unrelenting as it soaked them. Unable to help himself, Noah burst into laughter. This was the most fun he'd had in a while.

"What's so funny?!" Remi asked, holding her pack over her head also.

"Running in this storm with you!"

Laughing now too, Remi's cheeks heated at his words. Her heart trembled slightly. The boy who had helped lift her spirit when they were ten years old still had this much effect on her. If this kept up, she'd never escape his clutches. "Where are we supposed to go? We haven't come across any house or inn."

"Then we'll have to get creative and hide out under a tree or find a cave."

Remi stopped running to stare at his back in disbelief. "And where are you going to find a cave out here in the countryside?"

"There!" Noah pointed to a hollow tree trunk and turned to grin at her.

"There's no way I'm-"

Not waiting for her to finish, he dashed off to hide inside the hollow trunk. Meanwhile, Remi watched as he got comfy. If she wanted to get out of the rainstorm, she would have to follow his lead.

"I can't believe it." With a groan, Remi ran over to join him. To her amazement, she fit perfectly inside the trunk.

Noah glanced over and smiled. "See? We're safe from the rain now."

Indeed, they'd escaped the rain, but the air was still humid and stuffy. It also didn't help that creepy bugs crawled all around. "I'm still wet. How are you going to solve that?"

"You have a blanket in your backpack. Take off your clothes and wear that," he suggested as Remi blushed. Laughing, Noah turned away while she scowled at him. He was always teasing her. One of these days, she'd have to exact her revenge.

When Noah quieted down, the two sat side by side, listening and watching the rain pound the earth. It was so soothing they laid their heads against each other's.

"Say, Remi," Noah whispered.

"What?"

"How did you come to the Dome?"

Remi raised an eyebrow. His question didn't make any sense. "What do you mean?"

"I mean, how did you find your way to the Dome? Did someone scout you? Kidnap you? Sell you?"

"No, for as long as I can remember, I've always been there. I think I was born there."

"You mean you had no family, friends, pets, or anything outside the Dome?"

Remi dwelled on the question before, answering, "I've never seen the outside world until now."

"Who did you grow up with then? Was it only you?"

Remi smiled. In the beginning that was the case.

She opened the door to the room the dean had told her not to enter, but her curiosity had gotten the best of her. There was nothing inside the room except white cloths that hung from the ceiling. On the other side of the room was an open glass door that allowed the breeze in. Remi let out an awe. She couldn't believe that the teachers were hiding such a simple but breathtaking room. The wind picked up as the cloths swayed. This time she danced along, trying to be as elegant as the cloths. If it was this place, she would have nothing to fear.

"Ha-ha, you're funny. I've never seen anyone dance such a funky dance before," spoke someone.

"Huh?" Remi stopped dancing to twirl around in circles, trying to find the owner of the voice. "Who's there?!"

"You should dance more gracefully." Little Soria appeared from nowhere to pop in front of Remi's face and smile.

"Eh? Who are you?"

"The name's Soria. You?"

"R—Remi."

"Remi, nice," complimented Soria.

"Soria!" called out two other voices.

Remi turned towards the sound of voices and gulped. It was coming from outside the open glass door. Had she been found out? Was the Fashion Posse coming for her again?

"Don't look so scared. It's only Yeve and Verse." Soria smiled and turned to leave. "This place belongs to us. Next time you want to dance here, be sure to ask for permission. Yeve will beat you up if you don't." Soria waved a hand goodbye before running out.

"Wait!" Remi called out, but Soria had disappeared behind the swaying cloths.

Remi hugged her legs and put her chin down on her forearms. The day she met Soria felt like a dream. "I was once alone," she answered. "But after I met Yeve, Soria, and Verse, I was no longer lonely."

"Hmm," Noah said, nodding. "I should've figured that Soria would be in the picture. So then, you four grew up there?"

"There were more."

"Really?"

"Yeah, Umeko, Morgana, Mio, Hanabi, May-"

"That's enough," he interrupted. Five names were enough for Noah to piece two and two together. "Mind as well say, all of them."

Remi glanced up and shook her head. "But they weren't all there. Jennifer, Shayla, Crystal, Midnight, and a few others who didn't survive the experiments came later. They were scouted, I think."

"The same also goes for us."

"Really?"

Noah nodded and smiled, watching the rain fall before him. "Yeah, I'm part of that group. I grew up with my family in the southern islands. After a raid, I lost everything and everyone. One day, out of the blue, a strange man approached me with an offer I couldn't refuse, and so, I went with him not understanding the truth. All I cared about at the time was a place to belong. The strange man who scouted me also brought Hotaka along. That's how we became friends. When we came to the Dome, there were a lot of us. But after the experiments, a lot passed away. Hotaka could've been one of them too. But he was a 'miracle' according to the dean. Then one day..."

"One day what?"

"One day, Hotaka's back started to grow something from the experiments. At first, they were bones, just jutting out, and then, as time went by, they grew feathers. A lot of the boys were creeped out and started calling him a monster, a defect. Even Hotaka himself thought the same."

"It must've been tough on him."

"It was. Every day he thought it'd be better if he died. But you know," said Noah as he reached a hand out to the cold rain. It pelted his palm as he smiled. With a flick, a few drops stopped falling to stay afloat. Noah played with the water for a bit before letting it fall. "King, who was always fourth best to Rain, Kei, and Hotaka, got pissed. He beat anyone who made fun of Hotaka, saying that only he could make fun of Hotaka. He threatened to kill Hotaka too, if Hotaka dared to die before he defeated him." Noah laughed at the memory and withdrew his hand back to his side.

Remi chuckled along, able to picture it.

"He even threatened to kill the others if Hotaka were to commit suicide from their taunts. Tasuku got so scared he cried and wet his pants!"

Remi burst into laughter as she threw her hands to her stomach. Abruptly, she stopped to glance over. "Wait. Who are the two names you just mentioned?"

Too engulfed in his story, Noah didn't seem to hear her question. "Aoi got so mad, he got into a tussle with King. The staff notified the dean and soon everyone was throwing punches, shouting out curses, and throwing food at each other. In the end, only one person remained unscathed."

"Eh? Who?" Remi asked, wanting to know who this untouchable comrade was. Even she had forgotten her previous question.

"Yuudai, that bastard."

"Eh? He sat out the food fight?"

"No, he was involved in it alright. He wrote his name on fourteen of the boys' heads with ketchup. He got the most hits. The rest of us only managed to get five, apart from Rain and Kei who got ten."

Remi raised an eyebrow. "How was he unharmed?"

"I don't know either." Noah shook his head. Even to this day, that answer eluded him. "Every time I ask him how he did it, he'd just laugh and walk away like he's the king of the world."

"I really want to know how he walked away untouched."

"The dean says he knows."

"And he didn't tell you?"

"No." Noah shook it off, yawning now. It'd been a long day. "Wow, reminiscing on the past is tiring."

"It sure is," agreed Remi.

"Say," whispered Noah. "Did anything like that ever happen at the girls' academy?"

"Nope." Remi shook her head and took out her blanket to drape around them. She yawned and placed her head against his shoulder as he placed his head on top of hers. It had been a long day indeed. "Every day we ate, studied, and did our jobs diligently. Nothing chaotic like that ever happened at the girls' academy."

"Hmm, sounds to me like you girls need to lighten up a little and take it easy on life. It's a good thing, you girls met us guys."

All Remi could do was smile and nod.

"Night," Noah mumbled.

"Night," Remi responded. Sleep quickly overcame her and soon she was transported to her childhood.

It was lunchtime as Mio carried her tray of food through the cafeteria, head lowered and eyes to the floor the entire time. Even her blonde hair covered her face, like she was ashamed. She didn't want anyone to look at her plain face. The leader of the Fashion Posse noticed Mio and stood, pushing her from behind as she shrieked and hit the floor. Her tray of food fell and scattered. When Mio looked up and saw who it was, she quivered and quickly averted her gaze.

"You piss me off every time I see your fugly face." The five-year-old Queen Bee of the posse spat and glared down at Mio. With her right leg, she began kicking and insulting a vulnerable Mio who could only cry.

"Stop, please stop," begged Mio.

"Huh? What was that? I didn't hear you."

The other girls in the cafeteria grew silent while watching the commotion. The Queen Bee was at it again, always picking on Mio who couldn't properly defend or retaliate. This was their life at the academy: always living in fear.

"You fugly cow, why are you even alive? Save this world the trouble and kill yourself," said the Queen Bee while her followers laughed and shouted taunts at Mio also. A few even spat on her. Only Jennifer who frowned, stayed out of the bullying.

From behind, someone kicked the Queen Bee by the butt as she fell over.

"Oye, who the fuck?!" she shouted and stood up to glare at Yeve. There were whispers amongst the girls now. Someone was daring to challenge the Queen Bee. It was unthinkable, but it had happened before their eyes. With one glare from her, the cafeteria became quiet again. Everyone knew better than to mess with the Fashion Posse who ran the school. "Was that you who kicked me?"

Yeve smiled with her tray of food in hand. This was her first time joining the ninety-six girls for lunch after an entire school year had passed. She saw no point until last week when the dean forced her hand. If she didn't comply, the dean would torture her with a talk about how useful natural energy was to their lifestyle. In order to avoid that, Yeve forced Soria and Verse to tagalong and eat in the cafeteria with her. Remi who had been to the cafeteria countless times before seemed to be afraid of something. Now Yeve understood why. There was an oppression here.

"Yeah, that was me," admitted Yeve. "My foot slipped when I saw a fat pig standing before me. It was shouting for me to kick its curly-assed tail. So, I did." Yeve chuckled and grabbed her sandwich from the tray to eat.

"What? There was a fat pig with a curly tail around? I didn't see it," said Soria.

"Seriously?" Verse said, glaring over.

"Yeve was joking," Remi said, laughing nervously.

"Oh," Soria said sheepishly and laughed it off.

Meanwhile, the Queen Bee sized Yeve up and sneered. After running this joint for so long, she wasn't about to let a strange girl she'd never met before start a riot. Besides, no one made fun of her and got away with it. This was her town and she was the mayor. Nothing happened here without her knowledge or permission. Everyone knew that and bowed to her authority, never disrespecting her. Since Yeve was new, the Queen Bee would teach her a lesson. "I don't know who you are, but this is my town. You play by my rules. And I'll make you pay for kicking me, ugly cow."

"Oh?" said Yeve. She stopped eating to set her sandwich and tray down on the nearest table. Someone dared to challenge her, again. Obviously, the Queen Bee didn't know who Yeve was either, if she was talking so big like an adult.

"Uh-oh," said the three.

"This is your town? What a sh—sham? because I'm the Empress of the World. So tech…cally speaking, this little town of yours is mine too. So, you should watch the way you run your mouth at me, little piggy."

The cafeteria was buzzing with side talks as the Queen Bee's cheeks flared. If she didn't do something quick, the other girls might think that they could also challenge her. "Let's show her girls!" she commanded to her posse.

"Seems like I have to teach you all some manners too." Yeve dodged their attacks to counter while Verse watched from where she stood. The other girls were screaming and fleeing while others stayed behind to assist the posse.

"I'm not in the mood to fight," Soria said, yawning and walking towards an unoccupied table to sit with Verse and Remi.

"Whoa, you three are actually eating lunch here?" Umeko asked, walking over to join them. She sat with her tray of food and began eating, not caring about the chaos. Most likely it was the Queen Bee going at it with Mio again.

"It's the *four* of us," corrected Remi.

"Then where's Her Highness?"

"Fighting with the Fashion Posse. I think she could use some help."

"Geh, she's already starting a fight?" Umeko said in dread. She shook her head immediately, not wanting anything to do with Yeve. "No thanks."

"If Yeve knew you were here but didn't help, she'll be mad," Verse threatened.

"Y—you wouldn't dare," Umeko stuttered and pointed a finger.

"Try me."

Umeko didn't need to think about it twice. She stood abruptly and stopped eating. "Then, count me in!" she shouted, running over to help Yeve take out the Fashion Posse and other followers.

"Simpleton," Verse said and grinned. She turned to look behind for some time, before turning towards Remi. "Who's that girl?"

Remi glanced over also before answering, "Mio."

"How about you go help Mio, Soria? I think she needs it."

"Oh?" Soria looked over Verse's shoulder, spotting Mio who continued sitting on the floor of the cafeteria. She made no attempts to flee from the fight scene as Soria stood and walked over, offering a hand. With teary, cautious eyes, Mio stared at her goofy smile. There was nothing menacing about her, but Mio couldn't trust anyone. Out of patience, Soria took hold of her hand without consent to stand. "You okay?"

Without a word, Mio nodded.

"You're also a simpleton," Verse said with a smile.

One way or another, the girls inside the cafeteria had gotten involved with the fight that broke out. Only the four stayed out of it. That was the day two groups were formed at the girls' academy. The teachers too got involved with the fight and it wasn't pretty.

After that year, the Fashion Posse never made it through the harsh experiments, except the Queen Bee who died two years later, during a training session.

Remi smiled in her sleep. She had remembered a day where it wasn't the usual, eating, studying, and doing their work diligently. Of course, there was that *other time* too. Once Remi awoke, she would tell Noah about the fight in the cafeteria, but not the other incident. For the other incident, was never to be spoken of again. Yeve had made it clear.

27th Lie

IN AOI'S HANDS were two briefcases. Inside the first was money. In the second were diamonds and files, supplying information about an abandoned warehouse full of weapons in Bangkok.

"I must calm down," he said to his reflection in the mirror. He was dressed in a suit with his hair slicked back. This was no time for his nerves to act up. He had to accomplish the mission with or without Soria. After inhaling and exhaling, he left his room.

As soon as Aoi stepped foot outside the inn, the gust messed up his hair, and his skin prickled. Immediately, he regretted not wearing an Eskimo jacket. There was no point in looking nice if he couldn't maintain his appearance.

While shivering, Aoi made his way to the appointed meeting place. It was a tiny abandoned factory located a few miles away from the port. Once there, he breathed in heavily. A few men noticed him and glanced around, trying to find his missing Soulmate.

"Only you?" asked a girl who came out from within the factory to greet their honored guests. She was wearing a red qipao with her hair pinned up. The freezing wind didn't even seem to bother her whatsoever.

Clearing his voice, Aoi adjusted his suit and turned on his wooing light bulb. He wanted to look as charismatic as possible, though his unkempt hair made him look unprofessional and tired. "Good evening, beautiful lady." Aoi freed one of his hands from the briefcase and took the girl's hand to kiss. "How are you doing tonight? Would you like to go for a drink afterwards?"

"Inside," she instructed without even wavering at Aoi's seduction. She motioned with her head towards the door.

"As you say." Aoi chuckled and let go of her hand as they entered the factory. All the machinery and goods had been taken out, making the factory one huge open room with staircases and landings.

Sitting in the middle of the room was the leader of the group. In his hand was a lit cigar. Standing behind him were his goons. Just a few feet in front of Aoi was an empty table. With a raised eyebrow, he inspected the group while the girl in the qipao left his side. There was no sign of Anoka anywhere.

"Where's the girl?" Aoi asked.

"The goods first," bargained the leader who puffed out some smoke.

"You know," said Aoi as he frowned. "Smoking is bad for your health. While you're smoking, those guys next to you are inhaling the dangerous contents from the smoke. It can lead to cancer, ear infection, and even asthma. Also, there's something called third hand smoking. That's when you start to affect the environment." Aoi rambled like a teacher giving his students a lecture.

"Huh?" they said. The only one who didn't seem dumbfounded was the girl who smiled and laughed.

"Stop that bullshit and let's get down to business!" roared the leader.

"Alright, sheesh, calm your horses." Aoi walked over to the table and set the briefcases down. One of the cronies met him halfway and opened the cases to inspect the genuineness of the money, diamonds, and papers. After verifying the goods, he turned and nodded.

"Now then, where's the girl?"

"There is no girl."

"What–"

The crony withdrew his gun and fired as Aoi quickly dodged, burning the bullet to ashes with his flaming hands.

"As expected of someone from the Maroon Dome," praised the crony. He tossed the two briefcases at the girl who caught it. "Go, Midori."

"Got it," she said, taking the lead.

"Keep him busy, Drake!" shouted the leader.

"I know," he responded, blocking Aoi from chasing.

"Damn you," he growled and gnashed his teeth together. He had been set up from the get-go.

"I'm not letting you leave this place alive." Drake slipped in a red magazine and pulled the trigger.

Flames erupted as it burnt the bullet.

"That's one hot flame." Drake whistled, tossing away his burnt shirt. "In that case, I'll use this one." He took out a blue magazine to slip in and shoot. Instead of one bullet coming out, there were multiples.

"The same trick won't work twice!" Again, flames erupted as it evaporated the water, creating a tiny mist.

"I should be saying that to you," Drake said, pulling the trigger while standing behind Aoi.

∞

"Finally, we've got our hands on a Dome's weapons," the leader laughed from the backseat of the car. They were making their way to the port to leave the island.

"The boss should be happy with this." Midori smiled at the briefcases in her lap. It was about time they started seeing results from this drawn out war. Suddenly, the driver hit the brakes, sending the two in the backseat to jolt forward and hit the chairs.

"What the hell?" snarled Midori. She tilted her head to glance out the front window. Standing in the middle of the road was Soria.

"Who is that?" the leader asked.

"The Soulmate," Midori guessed and grinned. It was too late for Soria to show up now. Drake was probably done annihilating Aoi and would soon join the rest of the team on the ship.

Midori held out her hand as pieces of steel from the car shot out to pierce Soria. Before the attack could land, water bullets that were faster and sharper than blades, cut the steel in halves. "What the-" Midori gasped and gnashed her teeth together. She wouldn't let anyone belittle her and got out.

From behind, the other men in the cars also came out, guns drawn. Not long afterwards, bullets began whizzing across the air. With a swipe, a water saucer sliced at the headlights of the cars, turning the place eerily black.

"Midori!" the leader cried fearfully. He ducked down to the car floor and trembled, wanting off the island. "Kill that thing!"

"I'm not a thing," Soria spoke from outside his car window. The sound of shattering glass joined the roars of the wind as the leader let out one last cry before fading out.

"Damn you!" Midori shouted and attacked at random, not caring that she'd wiped out a few of her own men. All that mattered was injuring Soria.

"You might have to eat more carrots," Soria teased from behind and attacked. "You've been taking such good care of my Soulmate, allow me to return the hospitality."

"No, it's quite alright," Midori refused and stood back up.

"It would be my honor," insisted Soria.

"If you really must," she gave in and grinned.

A red light appeared to her left as Soria turned, barely able to dodge the red bullet that exploded before her, sending her flying. As soon as she got back on her feet, a wall of water shot out to protect her. Sitting beside her were the two briefcases she'd taken from the dead leader.

"Midori!" shouted Drake. He ran over to her side, picking her up in one arm. In the other hand was his gun and a flare that lit the night.

"Soria!" Aoi shouted as he ran towards them, injured. When he saw her, his eyes lit up, glad that she was safe.

"You look like a mess," Soria said, noticing Aoi's shabby clothes.

"I had a hard time."

"I can tell." She walked over to his side while keeping her eyes on Drake and Midori who were also conversing, probably coming up with a plan. "What's that guy's ability?"

"He's like Alice," answered Aoi.

"I see."

"She's strong, Drake," warned Midori.

"I can tell. Not just anyone can keep up with you," he responded and fired his gun.

A water sphere spun around Aoi and Soria to protect. "I know the tricks and limitations to your gun. Someone I know has a similar ability."

Drake grimaced and shot away at the water while Midori used her steel to attack. No matter how good their tag team was, Aoi and Soria's tag team was better. While Soria defended with her fast spinning sphere, allowing nothing to get in, Aoi attacked with his fire.

"She's good alright." Drake smiled and pulled out a new magazine to load. It'd been a long time since he last fought with someone this strong. It took skills and years of training to perfect such a high level that she was displaying. Even now, Soria hadn't lost her concentration.

"We're not getting through," Midori said, wasting energy.

"Let's retreat."

"But Beast-san-"

"He'll understand."

"But we need those weapons."

Drake nodded, knowing that without the weapons, they couldn't change the tides of the war in their favor. However, if they didn't flee, they were guaranteed to die. "I know that," he said. "But there are other ways."

Midori frowned and nodded in defeat. As usual, Drake was the voice of reason. "Water girl," she called out and backed away.

"Me?" Soria asked, raising an eyebrow.

"I'll see you on the battlefield again. And next time, I'll get past your defenses and crush your attacks."

"I can't wait to see you try."

"I won't make you wait too long." Midori summoned for the nearest car's hood as they both hopped on while Drake fired a red bullet.

Aoi jumped forward and held out a hand, fire blasting towards the red bullet to negate its attack. When the explosion died down, Drake and Midori were gone. Only the flare that Drake had left behind lit the night.

"Well, that's that," said Soria as the water surrounding them dispersed, hitting the ground.

After scanning their surroundings, making sure that the two were gone, Aoi swirled around with knitted brows. "You've exhausted your powers."

"I'm perfectly fine."

He glared. Even if her pride didn't allow her to look weak in his presence, he was her Soulmate. If she was to feel the slightest cold coming, he'd do whatever it took to help her recover. "No, you're not!" shouted Aoi. "You're practically forcing yourself to stand! Where the hell have you been anyway?! And how'd you manage to use up so much energy?!"

Soria put a hand to her throbbing head. His yelling wasn't helping. Along the way, she had to stop twice in the ocean to recuperate. Which was why it'd taken longer to reach Aoi than intended. "Love that idiot summoned me to help her. I couldn't get back quicker. So, I had to ride on the ocean water to get here."

"Eh? Is that even possible?"

"Yes, Love has the power to summon."

"No, I mean the part where you're riding on water. Is that possible?"

"Yes, it's-" Soria never finished her sentence before collapsing, already at her limit. It was a good thing Drake and Midori had taken her bait and retreated. If they stayed any longer, Soria wouldn't have been able to keep up. She would've fallen due to exhaustion, leaving only Aoi to fight.

"Whoa!" he shouted, reaching out to catch her on time. The loud thunder above forced Aoi to look up as small droplets of rain fell. That was his cue as he returned his attention to the sleeping Soria in his arms. He put her on his back and grabbed the briefcases along with the flare to return to the inn, so she could recover. Later, he'd contact the deans to report their findings. "Did you know," Aoi whispered while walking. If it weren't for the fact that they had been fighting for their lives just then, this would make for a romantic walk. "I've always liked you, since the moment I saw you catch that blue bird in the forest. That's why, please don't go to a place that I can't reach you."

∞

They were seated inside the cafeteria, eating lunch. It was a lively day just like any other. Suddenly, without warning, Soria jumped across the table they were sitting at, tackling and pinning Wakaba to the floor.

"Soria!" they screamed.

With one knee digging into Wakaba's ribs, and a forearm against her throat, Soria snarled, "Say that again, and I'll rip your windpipe out."

Fear caused Wakaba's body to quiver as her eyes widened from the flames that raged in Soria's eyes that day. She'd been the one to bring out the sinister side to the ever-loving turtle. "Let go!" Wakaba screamed.

"I swear it."

"Soria, that's enough!" the girls shouted frantically.

"Soria!" pleaded Remi as she tried to pry the two girls away from each other.

"Damn it you two!" Verse shouted and rushed over.

"Remi," Noah whispered, gently tapping her shoulder. She opened her eyes from the dream and sat up, hitting her head on the trunk. Yelping, she threw both hands to her aching head, forgetting that they'd spent the night inside a hollow tree trunk. Noah laughed so hard he fell over.

"That wasn't funny."

Doing his best to stop, Noah wiped his tears and sat up, helping her out of the cramped trunk. From above, the sun greeted them warmly. There was no sign that a storm had passed last night, except the sodden ground. "Come on. Let's get going."

"Aren't we gonna eat breakfast at least?" Remi asked, grabbing her bag along with her blanket from within the trunk.

"No."

"Why not?" she asked, folding the blanket.

"I've found them."

"Who?"

"The bad guys," boasted Noah.

"What?" she asked, putting the blanket away to stretch. "Seriously?"

"What can I say? I'm just that good."

Considering that Noah shared the same ability as Soria, Remi had a hunch about his secret. "Does this have anything to do with the rain last night?"

Noah seemed shocked at her guess but grinned. "Now do you see how powerful I am?"

"As I thought, you and Soria can detect people and things when it rains."

"Eh?" Noah said, puffing out his chest, angry that Soria could already manage to do something he had learned just a year ago. "I'm sure I learned it first. I mean, after all, it takes a genius to perfect that kind of skill."

With no need to think it over, Remi shook her head. "Nah, most likely Soria learned it first."

"Oye," he snarled, she wasn't taking his side.

"You know, Soria was one of the few to obtain her powers first and managed to hide it from the staff. I guess that makes her a genius too."

"I wouldn't count on it," he insulted.

"You know," Remi said with a smile. "If Soria were to hear you insult her, she'll drown you."

Noah extended his arm, flicking her on the forehead. He was getting annoyed at Remi for always praising her best friend and no one else. Was her mouth only good for mentioning Soria's name?

"I'm just giving you a friendly warning about not getting on her bad side."

"Well, I heard. Besides, I doubt she can hurt a comrade."

"But she can. This one time-" Remi began and stopped. Her dream flashed before her eyes and her courage to speak vanished. Yeve's words from that day resurfaced. They were to *never* speak of that day, *ever* again.

"What's wrong?" Noah glanced over, worried.

She just smiled and shook it off. "It's nothing."

It was obvious that something had scared her. Though he wanted to know, he didn't dare pry. "After we defeat the bad guys, let's go out and treat ourselves. What do you want for dinner?"

Remi chuckled. "Is that all you can think about?"

"I'm just saying that we'll be fighting the bad guys on an empty stomach. When we finish wiping the floor with them, we'll be hungry. So, choose what you want to eat."

"You're hopeless." Remi shook her head still laughing.

"Fine, I'll decide-"

"A five-star restaurant that serves delicious lamb, I want it medium rare with extra broth. They have to carry a butterscotch cake for dessert and must have white wine. I want there to be violinists playing. After eating dinner, I want to leave and buy some sushi for a late snack. Also, we should get some saké to go with it," interrupted Remi.

Noah stared at her for some time before chuckling. For someone who didn't have an opinion about what to eat for dinner, Remi sure was picky. "You never fail to amaze me."

She blushed and quickly turned away. "Let's just find these bad guys, wipe the floor with them, and go eat an early dinner."

"Wow, I can hear your stomach growling already."

"Not true." Remi's cheeks heated up again. From out of the blue her stomach really did growl, shocking them both.

Again, Noah laughed while she hid her face, wanting to disappear. He reached into his pocket and pulled out an energy bar in offering. "Hope this suffices for now."

"Thanks," she muttered and took it.

"You're welcome."

28th Lie

KYOTO

After successfully managing to pass the first and second initiative tests to become part of the Thunderbolt Gang, Azuma and Shayla sat inside a room, waiting to be questioned by the higher-ups. The room they were in was a cream color. There wasn't much inside except a table and a few sofas. A few recruits were sitting nearby, playing cards.

"I wonder if the preparations for the summer festival has begun," Shayla spoke as Azuma turned to look at her. She had changed drastically to the point where he couldn't recognize her. The once chubby Shayla on the mountaintop with grape-like haircut had transformed into a stunning beauty with a perm. Azuma couldn't find his nerves around her.

Shayla looked over, waiting for a response, but he said nothing while staring at her. "Am I that hated?" she teased and smiled, not realizing how nervous he was around her.

Azuma's heart leapt out of his chest. Even though she had changed, her smile was still the same. It was this smile that made him change the way he viewed girls. "How can I?" he responded with a scowl.

Chuckling, Shayla pointed to the bag of chips sitting beside him. "Can I have some?"

"Sure." Azuma handed the bag over as Shayla took a few pieces.

As soon as she bit into the potato chips, it felt like she was floating on Cloud Nine. "It's been so long."

Azuma raised an eyebrow at her reaction and ended up laughing. "What the," he said at a loss for words. "Why do you look so happy?"

"That's because back at the Dome we couldn't eat this kind of junk food. We were only given our daily nutritious food. More than half the time, Verse would sneak junk food in to me. But when Yeve became my master, I completely cut all junk food from my diet and Verse stopped sneaking them in." Shayla made a face at the bitter memory. Every time she and Verse were found with junk food, they were heavily punished.

The cooks for the girls' academy were strict about their diet too. For breakfast, they were given orange juice, fried eggs, sausage, and a bowl of cereal with milk. For lunch, they were given a serving of yakisoba and chicken with brown rice, and tea. Snacks included two slices of turkey sandwiches and a serving of green salad. For dinner, they were given sushi, sashimi, steamed veggies with rice, and tea to drink again. Even the oil used to prepare the food was nonfat. The only time the girls got to eat junk food was when they snuck it in to their rooms or it was a holiday.

"I wanna go to the festival with everyone." Shayla grabbed another chip from the bag to eat, wondering how the girls were holding up so far on their missions. "I wanna wear a pretty yukata with the girls and play games at the fairground. Afterwards, we can buy some dangos and sit at a secluded place to watch the fireworks."

Azuma smiled in return, eventually nodding in agreement. If they were all together again, it'd be a blast. "Let's do it then. We'll invite everyone and take a day off from work to play."

"Do you think the deans will allow us?"

"We can always persuade them. You know how much they love youthful activities."

Shayla chuckled and nodded, finishing the bag of chips. She licked her fingers as Azuma averted his eyes. Even though she wasn't trying to look sexy doing it, he found it erotic somehow.

"What do you think this surprise third test is?"

"I don't know."

"Hopefully they don't make us kill each other."

Azuma's eyes bulged. Why would she come to such a conclusion? This wasn't a battle royale. The gang would gain nothing by doing such a thing. Then again, Shayla had a point. The best way to test someone's loyalty was by seeing how well they followed orders. "That'll never happen."

"You never know. They could."

Azuma shook it off, refusing to think in such a manner. "Hopefully it's not," he said while Shayla laughed. "Why are you laughing for?"

"You're even more worried than I am."

"That thought never crossed my mind until you mentioned it."

"That's because you don't think."

"What does that mean?"

"Nothing," she said and whistled. Before they could continue with their conversation, the door to the room opened as a girl with strawberry hair walked in. The recruits stood and bowed in greeting.

"Hello, my name is Mina," she greeted.

"Ah-" began Shayla.

Mina flashed her a warning look, silencing Shayla to close her mouth. "Please follow me." She led the way out of the room as the recruits followed without a word. Along the way, she dropped each recruit inside a room before leading the way to the next room.

"You know her?" Azuma whispered once it was only them.

"She was at the dorms, three years ago," explained Shayla.

"What?" he asked in disbelief. "Then why is she here?"

"I don't know. Maybe undercover?"

"Or a traitor."

"Azuma-kun, you're in this room." Mina came to a stop and pointed to an open door.

Azuma gave her a suspicious look but complied and entered. Before disappearing, he turned back to look at Shayla. "You'll be fine, won't you?"

Shayla smiled reassuringly. No matter what happened, she would be fine. While under Yeve's Spartan-like training, Shayla had toughened up. Whatever these people were going to do, it wouldn't be half as bad as what Yeve had done when she threw the chubby Shayla into a creature's lair. After that day, she finally understood the meaning of standing between life and death. "I'll be fine."

Azuma smiled and nodded. "Alright, see you in a bit."

"See you too," bid Shayla. She waved bye to him and left with Mina.

"This way," Mina said, leading the way down the hallway. Once they turned the corner, she spoke, now that it was only the two of them, "Do you remember me?"

"I do."

"Good, because I need your help."

"So, I was right. You're a mole. How long have you been here?"

"Two years."

"Two-" began Shayla as Mina turned to glare. Quickly, Shayla shut her mouth. She couldn't afford to blow Mina's cover.

"Do you want someone to hear?" she hissed, looking about, making sure no one was in the vicinity. "It's a good thing they have no cameras in this place. Or else, they'd see how suspicious you two are."

"They don't?"

"No."

Shayla inspected their surroundings. Sure enough, there were no cameras whatsoever. "So then, why are we here when you're already here?"

"I needed back-up."

"Why for?"

"At first, Dean Kiera believed that I alone was enough to handle the task of bringing this organization down. But things have taken a turn for the worse now that the boss is returning." Mina led the way again as Shayla followed alongside.

"Is the leader really that scary?"

"No."

"Then what seems to be the problem?"

Mina furrowed her brows. Just thinking about it caused her to break into a cold sweat. "It's the doctor, the boss' brother-in-law, that I'm worried about."

"Doctor?"

"That's right." Mina nodded. There was no time to go into details about the doctor. If Shayla really wanted to know, that conversation would have to wait until another time. Right now, she only had time to tell Shayla the basics. "While I'm busy with the boss and doctor, that's where you and Azuma-kun come into play. You'll help destroy the organization."

"Got it."

"When you regroup with Azuma-kun, relay the plan."

Shayla nodded. "Say, Mina-san, why is the boss returning?"

Mina stopped walking abruptly, as did Shayla, who raised an eyebrow. There was no use in lying. The couple would find out the truth one way or another. "You see, Nishikawa-sensei has been working in the shadows with a wealthy man for quite some time now. Their works involved dismembering girls to try and create the right monster to be resurrected from the dead. While he was away on business, he came into possession of something rare, hence the reason for the boss' return."

"What is this thing the doctor got his hands on?" For some reason, Shayla's heart lurched from within. She was almost scared to hear what it was that the doctor was returning with.

"Nishikawa-sensei took a heart from one of our comrades and plans to give it to his dead wife," explained Mina softly.

Shayla's eyes widened. Her heartbeat fastened. Her palms became sweaty. She couldn't believe what she was hearing. It couldn't be true. How? Why? When? Where? But most importantly, "Who?"

"The dean hasn't told me yet."

"Where at least?"

"He was hiding out in Yamagata."

"May and…Kakinouchi-kun."

287

Mina took a few paces forward then stopped outside a closed door. "We're here," she said, ignoring Shayla's look of horror. Mina knocked once as the door slid open. Sitting inside the room were three men.

"We've been waiting," said the middle man as Shayla and Mina both bowed.

"I'll be taking my leave then," Mina said. She slightly bowed at Shayla who bowed in return. While walking around Shayla to leave, she whispered, "Stay cool. You're too easy to read right now. If you blow this interview, you won't be able to assist me in this mission."

Shayla gulped and forced a smile to her face, trying to remain as calm as possible. Mina was right. If she failed here, not only would she jeopardize the mission, but retrieving the heart would also become impossible. *Arata-kun*, she thought worriedly. *How are you going to react to this news?*

∞

Soria opened one eyelid weakly, then the other. She was lying on the cool ground, her head pounding from a blow that made her forehead bleed. The lights were dim. It was stuffy and smelled like dirt along with unwashed bodies. There was a piercing scream as shots echoed throughout the place. Fully alert now, she sat up, only to come face-to-face with a gun barrel. "Eh?"

In that instant, a flowy but thin, red scarf flashed before her eyes.

"Soria!" shouted Aoi's voice as it broke through her nightmare.

She woke up gasping for air as Aoi caught hold of her.

"Whoa, calm down, calm down."

Soria looked around the room, trying to find something out of the norm, but everything was as it should be. The hotel room lavished in expensive, brand-name furniture to paintings. A holographic TV was displayed on the white wall. Doors that opened and closed due to motion sensor, and robotic cleaning mice that did the dirty work were all present. Nothing was untouched by technology. This was her world, yet she kept trying to find something out of place.

"Soria, look at me, look at me!" Aoi pulled her face away from the alien room towards his earthy eyes. "It's okay. I'm here."

"Aoi," she whispered. "I...bad dream...blood...blood..." Soria kept repeating.

"It's okay. It was just a bad dream."

Soria shook her head. The nightmare had felt too real to be fake. Even now, she could vividly recall it and closed her eyes as tears streamed. She had been killed.

Aoi wiped her tears, holding her close. "It was only a dream. It can't hurt you here."

After calming down, Soria could hear the rain tapping against the windowpane. She turned to look, her beloved blue sky nowhere in sight. "Where are we?" she finally asked.

"Back at Nemuro Port," answered Aoi. "While you were asleep, we received a message from the Dome. It says to quickly return. Our third mission is underway."

"Already?" Soria complained, forgetting about her nightmare. She groaned, hating the deans for having a third mission already prepared when she had just finished her second. Were they trying to work them to death?

When Aoi yawned, she finally noticed the bags under his eyes. "Have you been looking after me the entire time?"

"I'm your Soulmate. It's my job." He smiled and crawled under the blanket to take a brief nap before heading out again.

"What are you doing? This is my bed."

"I want to cuddle," Aoi argued as he hugged her.

"Get out. I won't tell you again." Soria held up a fist, ready to hit him.

"Tasuku hates violence. So please, don't be like this when he's around, okay?"

"Huh? Who?" asked Soria. In all the years she had known the guys, she had never heard of anyone by that name. This was her first-time hearing about this person named Tasuku.

Instead of answering her question, Aoi rambled about other things. "Have you ever wondered why we can kill without feeling remorse?"

"Where's this sudden talk coming from?" Soria asked, giving up on trying to get him out of her bed. Had she succeeded, he'd somehow find his way back.

"It's not me who thought this."

"Then who, that person you just mentioned?"

Aoi nodded. "Yeah, Tasuku's a shy person who easily gets scared. He couldn't harm a living thing or even pick up a sharp object in his hands. Even after I helped him train, he couldn't reach his full potential and got taken out from the Soulmate Program to be thrown into the extras."

"So then, his assigned Soulmate is now assigned to someone else?"

"That's right." Aoi nodded and yawned again, his eyes feeling droopy.

Soria reached out to pat his head. This was all she could think of to comfort him after what he'd done for her. "You should go to sleep now."

Fully awake again, Aoi smiled. It had always been his dream for Soria to treat him affectionately. In the past, it felt so far away. Now, it no longer felt like a dream but a reality. He chuckled and closed his eyes to drift off. "Soria," Aoi called out.

"What is it?"

"I want to introduce the two of you one day." He snuggled closer, inhaling her scent. The idea of the two most important people in his life meeting, made him happier than anything else.

"Alright, I'll meet him. Now go to sleep."

"Yeah," he whispered and fell into a deep slumber.

∞

Noah unhooked the straps to his pack and let it slide gently to the ground. They were standing outside an abandoned log house in the middle of a forest. Remi too let her bag down as Noah reached into his pocket, pulling out two navy blue gloves to slip on. She noticed and raised an eyebrow. He caught her look and smiled. "What?" he whispered.

"I thought only Poe and Takahiko wore gloves. Why you too?"

"I always envied how they looked so cool wearing gloves. So, I asked the dean if I could wear them too. He laughed and had the tailor custom make gloves for me."

"Why are you such a jealous-wart?"

"Are we really going to start this, here and now?"

"So, what's the plan?" Remi looked away, grinning. Finally, she had found an opening to make fun of him.

"You lure them out with your flames. When they come running out, I'll entrap them in my water, got it?"

"Got it." Nodding, Remi ran out from hiding to approach the house. She reached for the red orb in her pocket and clasped both hands over it. Soon, fire ignited and shot out, burning the house as a few birds flew off, crying.

"What the hell was that?!" shouted the men as they came running out.

"Gotcha!" shouted Noah. He too came out from hiding as water shot out from underground, entrapping the men inside a water sphere. "Alright!" he rejoiced, giving Remi a high-five.

"Bastards!" shouted the entrapped men. They hit the water to get out, but it was impossible. All they could do was wait for someone to save them.

"Now then," Noah said, clapping his hands, happy to finally catch their targets. Now Dean Kosa had no reason to behead him. "Let's all cooperate and maybe, just maybe, we can all get to go home early. I do the questioning, you do the answering."

"As if."

"Now, now, if you don't cooperate, you'll die."

"Noah, get to the questions," Remi said impatiently while on lookout, in case there were others in hiding.

"Okay, okay." Noah walked over to stand before the water sphere and crossed his arms, his easy-going attitude now replaced with seriousness. "Who's your leader and what are you plotting?"

The men grinned. Even if they were to die, they wouldn't speak.

"I'm trying real hard here to be nice. Don't piss me off, please."

"Damn," they said to each other. "I thought you said you got them off your tail?"

"I thought we lost them too," answered one of the younger guys.

"Oye, oye, I'm talking here!" shouted Noah. The group of men turned to look at him again and smirked this time. "Why are you-"

There was a flash to her right as Remi turned to look. Before she could utter a word, the person in hiding used a blowgun, striking her with a dart coated in some drug. Grunting, Remi dropped her energy orb and fell over.

When Noah heard her hit the ground, he spun around and let his guard down. "Re-" he began as a dart pierced his arm. His head spun until his body felt sluggish and he fell over. The last thing he saw before losing consciousness was a hooded girl and gentleman, walking over to loom above him. In the girl's hand was the blowgun.

The water sphere entrapping the men fell apart as they gasped. "That was a close one," they said, turning to look at the two hooded figures. "Thanks Yana, Kotori."

"It was thanks to Kotori and his animals for informing us." Yana took off her hoodie that concealed her face and bent down, testing Noah's pulse. It was beating normally.

"Is he dead?" the younger gentleman, Kotori asked.

"No." Yana shook her head and stood. She glanced over at Remi and put her blowgun away in her straps.

"Why didn't you kill them?" asked another of the men. "It's dangerous to let them live."

"Holly says not to kill any of them."

"Holly?" they asked in disbelief.

This time Yana nodded. "That's right. She says some of them will join us. Which ones? We're not sure yet until their Awakening approaches." Yana turned her back and left with the men. Their location had been exposed. It was best to put the meeting on hold and flee as far as possible. "Let's go."

∞

With a groan, Noah woke up on the ground rubbing the back of his sore neck. The sky was starting to darken after they'd slept for the entirety of the day. When he remembered what had happened, he took the dart out from his arm and glanced around. Their targets had once again escaped. Lying not far away was Remi as Noah crawled over to scoop her into his arms. "Remi!" he shouted.

"Hmm?" she responded, opening her eyes weakly.

"Thank goodness."

"The bad guys!" she remembered, sitting up too quickly and fell back into his arms, the blood rushing to her head. "What happened to us?"

"I don't know." Noah took out her dart while shaking his head. "Some hooded people attacked us."

"Think you can track them again?"

"Not anymore. I was only able to track them because of luck. Besides, even if we do miraculously catch up to them, they'll be on lookout for us. Heck, they could've even set traps."

"This is the worst," grumbled Remi.

Noah nodded, feeling depressed again. There was no getting out of this one. The dean was really going to have his head.

"But you know, I'm surprised they didn't kill us."

"I'd prefer to be killed. That way, I wouldn't have to go back and feel the dean's wrath."

Remi sat up in his arms, not wanting to think about the deans or the fact that they'd failed their first two missions. "How does drowning our sorrows in dinner sound?" she asked, trying to cheer him up.

Noah looked over, unsure of what to say or think. A cackle escaped his throat as he wiped his teary eyes. Remi was too amazing. She knew exactly how and when to get him out of the slumps. What would he do without her? "Yeah, that sounds great." Noah stood and helped Remi to her feet as she grabbed her energy orb. They walked over to their packs and grabbed it to leave.

Since the walk back to the city would be long, Remi wanted to tell him a story to pass the time. "You know," she began, "I remembered this one time back at the academy when we got into a huge fight."

"Really?"

She nodded, telling him how Yeve had incurred the Fashion Posse's wrath for challenging their authority in the cafeteria. Ever since that day, she became their new target and not Mio.

∞

Seoul, South Korea

Sasuke grumbled while walking beneath the setting sun. All around, people were preparing for the week-long summer festival. Lights were strewn, and paper lanterns hung around stalls. But that was far from Sasuke's thoughts. While heading out to finish their mission, Mio had somehow strayed from his side again. Now he had to find her and give her an earful.

"Mio," he called out, searching every corner and cranny for her. "Seriously, where'd you go?"

∞

Awed, Mio watched as people walked around, wearing traditional hanboks. So, this was how the outside world celebrated holidays and seasons. The air was so festive that she wanted to join the fun. If only the girls were there with her. As soon as Mio realized that she was alone, her smile faded. She'd been doing a good job in keeping her mind focused on her missions. But the fact that the girls weren't with her like usual made the hole in her heart expand.

"No, don't think like that." Mio shook off the blues and forced a smile. She still had Sasuke by her side. That was good enough. "Ah, Sasuke-kun," she remembered and gasped. As soon as she turned around to leave, she bumped into a group of guys.

"Well, hello there, baby girl," they greeted, looking her up and down.

Unsure of what was going on, Mio backed away as two of the guys blocked her in like a rabbit. Were they picking a fight?

"Wanna hang out with us?"

"Hang out?"

"Yeah, you wanna come with us?"

Mio shook her head aggressively. She knew this tactic all too well. The Fashion Posse had used the same line to lure her out to the back of the school, so they could beat her up. Now a grown teenager, Mio wouldn't fall for it. "I'll pass."

"Come on, we'll show you a good time."

"I said no."

"Now, now, don't be like that," the guys said, laughing.

"I'm warning you," Mio said, sizing them up. *Six guys in total, I can take them out if I use my Air Rotation. But in this heavily populated location, I might end up hurting innocent bystanders.*

"Why are you giving us that look, baby girl? We're not bad. Promise. We'll play nice."

"I don't believe you."

"Come on baby girl, if we don't show you any love, no one else will. I mean, look at you," insulted one of the guys. "You're not exactly the pretty or cute type. You're a Plain Jane. No one would want someone like you."

At the insult, Mio's body stopped halfway from attacking. The words they spoke cut her wide open. She could still hear the Queen Bee's insults in her ears, "You fugly girl, do this world a favor and kill yourself."

The group of guys who had transformed into hideous beasts, with claws as sharp as knives, reached out to catch Mio who could only stare. No screams escaped her parted lips as she stood frozen, forgetting about her clear energy orbs.

It was like a nightmare coming to life. After so many years, the ghosts of the Fashion Posse still haunted her.

"What the hell do you think you're doing?" snarled Sasuke. He took hold of the group leader and hit him away.

"What the hell dude?!" shouted the group.

"If you want her, you'll have to get through me." Sasuke glared and lunged forward. Once he finished beating them, he took hold of Mio to drag into the crowd. When they got to a less crowded area, he let go and swirled around. "What the hell were you thinking, getting into that mess?! Why didn't you use your powers?! Are you trying to play a damsel?! And why the hell did you get lost again?!"

Nothing he said processed through Mio's mind as she stood, chest heaving. Usually she would've erupted from his shouting and accusations, but only tears flowed.

"O—oye," he said, alarmed.

Mio sank to her knees and cried, her hair covering her face as she quivered. How long was she supposed to live this way? She thought she had gotten strong enough to confront her ghosts. But they lingered, still trying to make her life hell.

"Mio," whispered Sasuke. He knelt, touching her gently as she flinched and he quickly withdrew his hand.

Not wanting to show any weakness, Mio wiped her eyes and forced a smile. "I'm fine."

"You're anything but fine."

"I'm really fine," Mio repeated as her voice broke. She couldn't lie to anyone, not even herself.

Again, her tears fell as Sasuke squeezed her fragile body that might break at any moment. It was his fault for losing her in the first place. He had no right to get angry. "Why are you pretending to be strong for? There's no need for that. I'm here. I'll protect you."

After a few minutes, Mio dried her tears again and smiled more naturally. Having a Soulmate was convenient in its own way.

Even without her having to say a thing, Sasuke could guess what she was thinking. It was too bad on her behalf that she was assigned to him. "Are you disappointed that I'm not Hotaka?" Sasuke joked and poked her head before helping her stand so they could leave.

Laughing, Mio shook her head. It was amazing that Sasuke could read her like an open book. She had always assumed it was only the girls who could do that. "True, I do like Hotaka-kun, but he likes Midnight-chan. So I won't try to break them apart. Instead, I'll chase after Rain-kun. He's the eldest and most charismatic."

Sasuke couldn't help but snort. That was an impossible feat to accomplish. Rain was too obsessed about defeating Yeve to concern himself with anything else. Mio had a better chance with Sasuke himself or Louis, though he didn't say a word about it. He'd let her figure that out on her own.

∞

After passing the meeting with the higher-ups, Azuma and Shayla became official members of the Thunderbolts. Once the couple met up, she relayed Mina's plan unto Azuma who nodded, saying he'd do what he could to bring down the evil organization. Shayla however, left out the part where one of their comrades had had their heart taken. At this point, there was no need to alarm him. Especially since Mina hadn't gotten information on whose heart it was.

Outside, the wind blew fiercely, keeping her awake as she lay in bed, staring at the dark ceiling. Soon, summer would end, and the endless rain of autumn would be upon them.

Yelling erupted in the hallways as Shayla jumped out of bed and ran over to the door. It slid open as she stepped out in her maple patterned pajamas, wondering what was going on. The other members ran by as she joined them and met Azuma on the way.

"What's going on?" he asked.

"Don't know," Shayla answered, blindly following the crowd. When they reached the entrance, there was a loud commotion.

"Everyone, back away!" ordered Mina as she ran up to the crowd and motioned for them to move. Obediently, they backed away as Mina turned towards the entrance. Two people were making their way through. At the sight, she wavered and gulped.

Doctor Nishikawa was dragging Gon from behind, his wrists and ankles bound. They both looked dirty and exhausted from the long journey. In Doctor Nishikawa's other arm was a metal cooler.

"Nishikawa-sensei," greeted Mina as she walked over to bow.

"Mina-san," greeted the doctor in return. He smiled and looked over at the group who had come out. "Is this a welcome party for me?" he joked.

Mina smiled and stole a quick glance at the group before returning her gaze to Doctor Nishikawa. A simple thing such as fully turning away, she couldn't manage to do while in his presence. It always felt like he was waiting for her to lower her guard so he could dig his hidden claws into her chest and rip out her beating heart. Even as a Life-Kill who shouldn't fear anyone other than the Golden God, Mina genuinely feared the doctor. "Everyone got excited when they saw you." Mina eyed Gon who breathed heavily and raised an eyebrow. "Who's the boy?"

"Hostage," he answered, pushing Gon forward as he tripped and fell over on the ground. "Take him and chain him up." Doctor Nishikawa walked past them and left.

"Stop," Gon instructed, his voice hoarse from all the shouting. His lip was bruised and his forehead bled from Doctor Nishikawa's abuse. Even though Gon was tired and weak, he continued fighting. "Give back the heart."

"Save your energy." Mina knelt, holding Gon who tried to break free from the shackles that prevented him from running.

"Give it back," he kept repeating, then fainted from lack of energy and food. Not once did Doctor Nishikawa turn back to look at them.

"That must be him," whispered Shayla as she watched the doctor leave with the small cooler. Her heart beat faster at the sight of it. She'd been hoping and praying it wasn't true, but it was staring her in the face.

Worried, Azuma also couldn't stop eyeing the cooler. "Shayla," he spoke. "This may sound strange, but that man with the boy-" Azuma took in a deep breath before gulping. "I felt something from the cooler he was carrying—I know, it sounds absurd." Azuma laughed it off as he shook his head. He was starting to sweat uncontrollably. Why did a tiny cooler scare him half to death? "I wonder why."

Shayla stared at him long and hard before answering. She couldn't hide it from him any longer. Azuma already had a hunch. "Arata-kun," she whispered drawing him close to hold still. She tiptoed, putting her lips to his ear so no one else could hear. "Listen and don't freak out."

Azuma nodded, suddenly afraid to speak or even listen.

"That man came from Yamagata. Inside that cooler is a heart."

*May and...*Azuma couldn't even finish his thoughts as his eyes widened. He fought to break free, but Shayla held him back. They both knew what he planned to do, but his feelings ran amok. In order to calm himself, Azuma reached out to squeeze Shayla's arms. She winced but held in her cry by biting her lip until it bled.

"I'm sorry I didn't tell you beforehand," apologized Shayla. "I was hoping it wasn't true, but with that man's appearance, it's been confirmed. He stole a heart. It could be May or...Kakinouchi-kun."

29th Lie

SASUKE AND MIO sat inside a luxurious mansion. Their mission was to find a fourteen-year-old girl with long green hair who had gone missing. She was last seen wearing her school uniform and backpack that had a Doraemon keychain strapped to it. Last week, she had gone to the karaoke club with her friends. After that, she mysteriously disappeared. None of her friends knew what had happened to her upon separating.

The police did their best with the case but couldn't find any clues or evidence of abduction. And so, they ruled it as a frustrated teen who ran away from home.

"Please find my beautiful Anna," begged the mom.

Her husband put his arms around her and held on tightly. "Anna would never run away from home and worry us like this," he agreed.

"Of course," said Sasuke. "We'll do everything we can."

"May I ask you a question?" Mio asked. In her hands was a cup of tea the parents had offered them, but she never once took a sip.

"Yes?" answered the husband.

"I don't mean to offend you in anyway. But I want to know."

"What is it?"

Mio cleared her throat before asking, "Are you sure those kids she hung with were really her friends?"

Mio mind as well have slapped them across the face with that question. "What do you mean by that? Of course they were her friends. They were always together. Sometimes, they'd stay over and study with Anna. How could you ask such a question? We know our daughter. She would never lie to us about those girls being her friends."

Mio nodded, taking a second glance around the perfect house. Rich paintings and lavish furniture filled every single room. Antiques that she could never dream of buying were displayed for visitors to see. Mio could only imagine how the bedrooms looked. Anna was blessed to be born into such a family. She had loving parents and went to a prestigious school for the wealthy. How could Anna or anyone else get sick of this lifestyle? She could have anything she wanted with the snap of her fingers. So why run away from this life? It didn't add up. "There's probably nothing that she couldn't obtain," Mio said, mostly to herself.

"Damn right," answered the husband. He was proud that he could support his family and give them whatever they wanted. He'd worked hard, all for the sake of the two most important women in his life. "If my Anna wanted something, all she had to do was ask and we'd give it to her. She's our only daughter and child. There's nothing that we won't deny her."

"Is that so?"

"Yes, that's so."

"What about simplicity? Could you have given it if she asked?"

Again, the parents were insulted by Mio's questions. Was she really there to help or antagonize them? They weren't sure whose side she was on. "Are you trying to say that she wasn't happy here?"

Sensing the tense atmosphere, Sasuke set his cup down. "Mio," he intervened.

Instead of listening, she rambled on. "No, I'm sure she was happy here." Mio smiled, looking over at the holographic photographs that was set to a loop cycle. In them was the beautiful Anna, smiling without a care in the world. She looked genuinely happy.

"Then what are you trying to imply by asking such questions?"

"I ask because I can see the suffering in her eyes. She was probably scared and confused, not knowing what to do. I bet she was suffocating and wanted someone to save her. But no one was there for her, not even her parents. So, she faked a smile, pretended that her bullies were her friends. You say you could give her anything she wanted, but you couldn't hear her silent cries because you never tried to listen."

"That's enough, young lady!" the husband shouted, standing forcefully. His face turned a beet red as he glared at Mio for provoking them when their daughter was missing. "I will not let you sit here in my house and insult us!"

"Honey," said the wife.

"I'm truly sorry sir," apologized Sasuke. He stood and bowed, not wanting Dean Kosa to hear about how they'd riled up the clients. Turning, he instructed Mio, "Apologize."

"No," she said stubbornly.

"Mio, I said apologize."

"And I said no."

"Young lady, is that any way to treat your employer?!" the husband shouted as his wife stood to try and calm him.

He was speaking to her like she was his own daughter. It was so irritating that Mio jumped to her feet to argue back. "Admit it! You heard her cry every night but ignored it, right?!"

"Mio!" shouted Sasuke as he caught hold of her. "Knock it off!"

"Let go, Sasuke-kun!" She broke free and glared at the two parents, her anger getting the best of her. "What good will your riches do, if you have no one to shower it with?"

It became eerie inside the mansion as no one talked or breathed. All eyes were on Mio.

"All she wanted was a true friend." Mio's lips quivered as she hid it.

"You don't know my daughter. Don't go assuming things."

"I have a feeling that we're the same," Mio whispered and stormed out.

"Mio!" shouted Sasuke. He bowed at the couple, apologized once more, and ran out. Mio was already running down the long driveway of the mansion, wanting to get away as far as possible. "Wait!" He chased her and pulled her back. "What got into you back there?"

"Sasuke-kun," she whispered as tears fell. "She's dead."

"How can you conclude that? We haven't even begun our investigation. And why are you crying?"

"You don't understand." Mio shook her head and broke free, backing away slowly. Her gut feeling told her, Anna was already dead. Someone killed her out of jealousy and cold-blood. "You'll never understand what it feels like to have no one by your side when the world turns its back on you."

"Mio-"

"Those so-called 'friends' either killed her, or she committed suicide."

Sasuke choked on his saliva. He couldn't find his voice. She seemed to be in so much pain and he could do nothing to ease it. "Don't say that."

"I know…" Mio hung her head down low and cried loudly. "I know, because I'd do the same if I was in her position."

∞

The Next Day

Sasuke and Mio were staked out in front of the prestigious academy, waiting for the end of school. Ever since yesterday's confrontation with Anna's parents, Sasuke had been tempted to contact the dean to pull them out. Mio was getting too close to this case. It wasn't normal and called for red flags, but Mio had made her argument. She was going to solve this case with or without the dean's permission, and with or without Sasuke's help.

Unable to leave her high and dry, Sasuke agreed not to contact the dean, but on one condition, Mio was to not lose her cool with Anna's parents again. She agreed, and that was that.

When school came to an end, students flooded through the gates. A few stayed behind for club activities. As soon as they spotted Anna's friends they stalked the posse of flashy teenage girls who laughed and gossiped, heading to their favorite cafes, then to the karaoke club to sing. Afterwards, they went to a top-notch restaurant to eat. Nothing was suspicious about their demeanor or how they went about carrying their daily routines. But that was especially why it was suspicious. The posse had just lost their "friend" and didn't seem to be in mourning.

It made Mio question if the police had properly investigated this case, or if they had been too scared to pass judgement unto the posse of preteen girls. It was such a shame for the girls that Mio had been given the case since she wouldn't give up until judgment was passed.

After the posse disappeared inside the restaurant, the two headed to a nearby street stall to eat also. It'd been an uneventful four hours. "What do you wanna eat?" he asked, nudging her gently and smiling.

"Anything's fine," Mio answered, looking around while seated.

"Alright then," Sasuke said, ordering for them. After finishing, he turned to inspect her again. She was staring at the sky, probably thinking about the case again. "What's wrong?"

"Nothing really." Mio shook her head and reached over to grab her water glass to chug down.

"Are you sure you really wanna go through with this?"

Mio set her half drunken water down and nodded. It was unthinkable to return after coming this far.

"But," Sasuke protested. "You're starting to worry me a little here."

"I'm going to find Anna's body," she said determinedly.

"Like I keep saying, how do you know she's dead? For all we know, she really could have run away from home."

"I know I'm right. And I'm gonna make those nasty girls admit it." When their food came, the two ate, then paid. They thanked the owner and left as Mio threw both fists into the air, smiling. "Okay, let's go!"

Before Sasuke could get a word in, she was already sprinting towards the extravagant restaurant. "That girl," he said, giving chase. After coming to a halt, Mio spun around. The group was also making their way out to return home.

"I've decided just now. I'm going to confront them head-on. Take out your cell phone and record it."

"What?!"

"There's no time to dilly-dally." Mio smiled and ran over to the posse.

"She's really serious." Sasuke fumbled for his phone and hid to record as instructed. Even if they ended up getting nothing at least he tried.

"Yo!" Mio greeted and waved to the posse of girls.

"Uh, hi?" they said, looking her up and down.

Finding herself intimidated, Mio shrank away. When she remembered that she was older by four years, she straightened her back. She wouldn't let their jeers get to her. "Wow. I spot Versace." She pointed a finger to one of their handbags and smiled. These girls were spoiled rotten. Was that why they thought they could get away with just about anything, including murder? Was it because their parents had money and connections? "Isn't that like an out-of-production brand now? How much does it cost anyway?"

"Way too much to tell you," answered the leader who scoffed. Her dyed honey hair glistened in the sun as she crossed her arms. She scrunched her nose, not wanting to breathe the same air as Mio who was way beneath her in terms of class and fashion. In fact, it hurt her pride to be seen talking to a Plain Jane.

"I'd like to know anyway."

"By the looks of you, you probably haven't been properly educated to know numbers," she insulted some more and laughed with her posse.

"What a bunch of nasty girls. Are they sure they're only fourteen?" Sasuke growled, his blood boiling. He was about to come out of hiding to give them a piece of his mind.

Mio simply smiled. She wouldn't break from something like that after going through worse. "I know."

"You know what?"

"I know what you did."

"What did we do?" The leader feigned ignorance while her posse fidgeted, understanding Mio's vague but hidden meaning.

"Let's leave," they suggested.

"We what?" the leader challenged, ignoring her posse's worry. If someone presented her with a challenge, she would accept it, then return it by tenfold.

"You killed an innocent girl named Anna."

For that instant, the leader wavered, but quickly recomposed herself and laughed. She wouldn't let anyone intimidate her, especially a girl she didn't know. Not even the police dared to upset her because of her family name. "Are you stupid? We were friends."

"*Were*," repeated Mio. "That's past tense, you know?"

"What the hell do you want with us?" the leader asked, taking a step forward. She was through with Mio's nonsense and uncrossed her arms. If

Mio wanted to accuse her of something, then she needed to just come out and say it.

"Let me tell you what I know. You pretended to be Anna's friends when really you were bullying her, making her do things, like, oh, let's say, stealing for instance?"

"What an accusation," said Sasuke in disbelief. It was unlike Mio to be exceptionally valiant.

No one spoke as the posse paled. Mio had hit the nail on the head. "Who'd you hear that from?" demanded the leader. "Who told you those damn lies?!"

"I heard it from Anna herself."

The leader glared at Mio before laughing. "Are you like one of those people messed up in the head or something?"

"No." Mio shook her head and crossed her arms against her chest. She had them exactly where she wanted them. All she needed was a confession, and she knew exactly what buttons to push. "I know because I'm Anna."

"Eh?" Sasuke said, unsure of what Mio was playing at.

"What?" gasped the posse.

"You're full of bullshit!" the leader shouted. "I don't believe in that spiritual crap! Now tell me, who told you those lies?!"

"I'm not lying. I really am Anna. And once I tell everyone what you did to me, the cops will have you thrown in jail. Your parents will cry a sea of blood. Compared to what you did to me, that's only half of the hell you'll see. This time, I won't cower down like before. I'll take a stand and fight you with all I have."

"She's really getting into it," said Sasuke.

Clenching her fists tightly, the leader lunged forward to attack. She'd heard enough and wouldn't stand by while some psychotic Plain Jane tried to ruin her perfect life. "Don't fuck with me, bitch!"

"Oye!" Sasuke shouted, no longer caring to film as he ran towards them.

"You say that you're Anna?! You say that you know what we did to you?! Well then, in that case, let's do it all over again! I'll fucking drown you again and again until you're fucking satisfied, bitch! How does that sound, huh?!"

"That's enough!" the posse shouted, trying to pry the leader off Mio. But she had already lost it and was choking Mio, cutting off her air circulation.

"Girls like you should die! You have nothing to show and yet you dare to flaunt around my man?! Over my dead body, whore!"

While bleeding and seeing stars, Mio remembered the cafeteria fight with the Fashion Posse. After causing a ruckus and getting the teachers involved, the groups were forced to clean, then and there. For the rest of the month, their punishment was to clean the bathrooms spotless. Once they were done cleaning the cafeteria they went outside to sit on the bench.

Mio had followed them and was crying nonstop, still apologizing for getting them involved with her fight.

Yeve plugged her ears and rolled her eyes. She had never met anyone who could cry so much before. Maybe this was Mio's hidden ability, to kill people with her wails. "Stop already, you look like an ugly duckling."

"You know," pointed out Soria, "the ugly duckling turns into a beautiful swan in the end."

"Go to hell!" shouted Yeve as she kicked Soria off the bench.

"Ow!" she yelped, falling to the grass and sitting up. "What was that for?! I was just stating the facts! Why are you so mad?!"

"Everything you say, everything you do pisses me off."

"You two," Remi said worriedly while Verse ignored them.

Umeko laid on the grass nearby, cursing at herself for getting involved with the fight. Then again, if she hadn't helped, she'd be in even bigger trouble with Yeve. Either way, it was a lose-lose situation for her. "Was I cursed at birth or something?" Umeko cried.

A fashionable Jennifer walked over and stopped as they suspiciously turned to look. She belonged to the Fashion Posse. "Can I sit?" she asked.

"Sure," answered Verse.

"She's one of the bad guys," Remi whispered.

"I know." She smiled and nodded, motioning for Jennifer to sit while Remi gulped. If Verse's bullying wasn't enough to get Remi to leave their group, then she'd scare her off.

"Thanks," Jennifer said, taking Soria's spot.

"Hey," said a teary-eyed Soria. "That's my spot she took."

"Oh, my bad, I forgot you were there," insulted a smiley Verse.

Jennifer whose uniform had gotten torn while helping the posse during the fight, sighed. "What a day, huh?"

After inspecting her, Yeve replied, "Aren't you part of that girl's posse?"

"I am," she responded and nodded, "but I don't like her. I'm older but she thinks she's better and treats me badly." Happy to have finally gotten out of that group, Jennifer smiled. Their way of doing things never really sat well with her, and when she voiced her opinions, they'd beat her. Now she could become a drifter with no allegiance.

"Waa," cried Mio.

"Ugh, would you stop?" groaned Yeve.

"Ew, boogers!" shouted Soria.

"Go to hell right now!" Yeve kicked her shoe off at Soria who quickly dodged and chuckled.

"Take this!" shouted Verse as she threw her own shoe at Soria and connected. "Turtles-eye!"

"*Bulls*-eye," Shayla corrected while passing by with a pudgy armful of junk food.

One look and Verse's eyes gleamed, forgetting about Soria's existence. "May I have some?"

Shayla stared in return, her own eyes gleaming. Finally, she'd found a comrade who shared a mutual love for food. This was the best day of her life by far. Nodding, Shayla walked over to sit with them as the two girls ate away.

"What the hell am I, a shoe target today?" asked Soria while she lay on the grass staring at the clouds passing overhead. She'd given up on arguing with Yeve and Verse.

"But, t—thanks for saving me," Mio said, wiping her eyes and nose.

"Anytime," answered Umeko who grinned and did a peace sign.

"She was talking to *me*," snapped Yeve.

"Sheesh, how rude."

Standing, Yeve walked over to crouch beside Mio who was sitting on her knees, like she was being punished. "Listen, the next time you get into a sticky spot, beat your way out of it. Don't shrink. If you do, you'll only give them more bullets, got it?"

"It's ammunition," a brainy Love corrected and walked by with a textbook open in her arms.

"Anyways," Yeve said, trying not to get riled up. "You're the oldest. Act like it. Or else I'm going to take it."

"O—okay," Mio stuttered.

"You still have to beat this girl before you can be the oldest," Verse reminded by pointing to Jennifer.

"Shut up, don't remind me," hissed Yeve.

"And that posse's leader," added in Remi.

"Yep, true," Verse agreed, spitting out some crumbs.

"Oh, shut up!" shouted Yeve.

"Not being the oldest really ticks her off, huh?" asked Shayla.

"You wouldn't know half of what I have to go through because of that stupid fact," said Verse with a sigh.

"Clear skies," Soria mumbled in her sleep.

Yeve looked over and groaned. "How the hell did she fall asleep already?" She looked over at Mio who was still sniffling and wiping her eyes. "You wanna know what makes a girl the prettiest? Her smile. See? Like me," Yeve said and smiled.

"Ugh, don't smile. It's creepy," insulted Verse who cringed.

"Shut up," Yeve said, getting into a tussle with Verse. Her patience for the day had reached its max.

Mio broke into a smile and eventually laughed along with the others while Soria slept through their fight. That day she made two vows. The first was to become friends with those girls. The second, to smile for as long as she lived. "Okay, I'll remember that!"

Gasping, Mio took hold of the leader's wrists and twisted it. "Get off me!" she ordered. A gust of wind erupted from her clear pearl bracelet around her wrist. It blew the leader off as she toppled to the other side, landing on her back. "You dare to make fun of me?" Mio challenged. She got to her feet, coughing. "You're one hundred years too late, bitch!"

Scared from the powers that Mio had shown, the rest of the posse backed away and screamed. While they fled from the fight, Mio ran over to beat the leader senseless.

"You want to kill me again? In your fucking dreams! You want to take away my precious smile?! Not on your life! My friends depend on me! They want me to smile so that I can be more beautiful! There's no fucking way I'll let you take away my smile!"

Once Sasuke reached the girls, he yanked Mio off. The leader was lying on the ground, bleeding and unconscious. "Stop!" he instructed.

"Let go! I'm going to kill her! I'll make her pay for hurting me!"

"MIO!" shouted Sasuke. He whisked her around to eye as she stopped struggling. She'd taken her acting too far and could no longer identify the real her. "It's enough. Your head-on attack worked."

Mio smiled faintly and sank to her knees, her body feeling sluggish. The fight was over. "Thank goodness."

"You did good." Sasuke knelt and put both arms around her trembling body. Whether it was from the adrenaline of the fight or fear, he didn't know. All he knew was that he had to comfort her.

"Sasuke-kun," Mio whispered, her forehead placed against his beating chest. It was amazing how being with him could make her feel blessed and cursed.

"What is it?"

She held onto his shirt and cried silently. "Can you promise me, that you'll never betray me? Even if it's a lie, please assure me."

Sasuke held on tightly. It broke his heart to hear her say such words. What had happened in her past before they met? What kind of hell did she live through to make her so fragile? "I won't lie to you. I'll always be with you. This is the truth."

30th Lie

SASUKE CAME OUT from the water depths of the river, gasping for air. He turned to look at Mio who was standing on the banks and shook his head. "She's not down here!"

"But those girls said she was!"

"Maybe they lied to us!"

Mio shook her head in disbelief. "What would they gain by lying to us, after turning themselves in?!"

"By making us look like fools!"

"Search again!"

"Okay." He took another deep breath before diving under.

After the confrontation the day before, the posse of girls turned themselves in, one by one. They were afraid of the repercussions from the Dome after picking a fight with a Life-Kill agent. The only one who refused to admit the truth was the leader. So Sasuke and Mio had to use the evidence they recorded against her. Even then, she still refused to take the blame.

Everyone was shocked beyond words by the outcome. The case was being taken directly to the highest government court, and the families of the posse were going to lose quite a fortune.

Anna's parents were so devastated they didn't know what to say or do.

Afterwards, the Soulmate couple went to the river to try and find Anna's body first, before officers came to join the crime scene and help search.

"She has to be down there," said Mio desperately. After a few minutes Sasuke came back out from under again.

"Still nothing!"

Sirens blared from afar as the two turned their attention towards the main road. Car after car pulled up to the banks of the river. Officers came out in their uniforms and set up a perimeter for the investigation. They quickly changed and joined Sasuke in the water to search.

After hours, they called it a day and left. They would resume the search again the next day when the sun came out and wouldn't rest until her remains were found.

Sasuke sat on the green grass, just outside the yellow taping. Mio sat beside him, staring at the river also. "Mio," he said, breaking through her thoughts. He knew how badly she wanted to find Anna's body, but this was a no-win cause. "We should return now. Our mission is over."

"But we haven't found her body."

"I don't think we'll be able to." Sasuke shook his head and reached into his pocket. In his palm was a necklace with a heart locket he'd found under the dirt of the river. "This was precious to her, remember? When we first talked to her parents they told us that Anna always wore this necklace."

Mio reached out to take the necklace. Anna's parents had indeed told them that. In fact, all the pictures inside the mansion showed Anna always wearing the necklace.

"I think the river creatures got to her first. Or, her body got swept downstream. We won't be able to find her."

"Are you serious?"

Sasuke nodded, disappointed as well. "If she was down there, her body should've been there along with that necklace. But it wasn't."

Mio held the necklace to her trembling lips. They had completed their mission in searching for the truth, but it felt more like they had failed. "Alright then, let's return this back to her parents."

"Yeah, let's," agreed Sasuke. They both stood and left for the luxurious mansion where they had caused an upset. When they reached the mansion gates, Sasuke rung on the doorbell, waiting for an answer.

"Who is it?" answered the sullen husband.

"It's Sasuke from the Maroon Dome," answered Sasuke. The gate immediately opened as the two made walked up the long driveway towards the mansion. Standing at the doorway were the parents. Sasuke and Mio both bowed in greeting.

"Come in." The husband turned his back to enter the mansion, his eyes filled with despair.

Mio reached out and took hold of Sasuke's arm, shaking her head in refusal. She didn't want to stay. The pain in her own heart was already enough. Watching two parents agonize over losing their only daughter would destroy her. Mio just wanted to get this last meeting over with and leave.

"Out here is fine," Sasuke insisted.

The husband turned back to look at the two and nodded. "Alright then." He didn't even have the energy to argue. "What can we help with?"

Sasuke motioned to Mio. Clearing her throat, she walked up the stone steps, holding out the necklace to them. The wife gasped at the sight of it and slowly made her way down. She retrieved the locket necklace and broke down on the stone landing, clutching it to her chest. This was the only thing left of her precious daughter now. Her husband walked over to embrace her, if that could help lessen the pain.

Mio bowed, long and deep before returning to Sasuke's side.

"Sorry we couldn't find her body," apologized Sasuke. He too bowed. "We're sorry to leave halfway through, but the officers will continue looking tomorrow."

"Thank you," the husband said, crying alongside his wife. The two kids had done more than enough. They had brought closure.

"Then, we'll be going now." Sasuke turned to leave, as did Mio.

"Young lady," called out the wife.

"Yes?" answered Mio as she quickly spun back.

"How did you know, when even we didn't know?"

With a weak smile, she shook her head. "I simply guessed. That was all." Again, she bowed at them before leaving with Sasuke.

He glanced down, noticing tears in her eyes. "Mio."

"I'm fine." She smiled and let out a sniffle.

He reached over, messing up her hair. She really did look best when smiling. He wished that she'd never lose that precious smile. "You'll always have me. Even when you find a guy your type and you fall head over heels for him, I'll still stand by your side." Sasuke did his best to smile, reassuring her that she wasn't alone.

Mio stopped walking and took his hand, bringing it to her forehead as tears trickled. He was so understanding, she felt like he was being wasted on her. "Thank you."

"Anytime," Sasuke said, tugging her along. "Come on. Let's get going. The others are waiting for us."

"Yeah," said Mio. She nodded and squeezed his hand as they returned to the hotel to grab their belongings before heading back to the Dome. If only Anna had had a true friend by her side, none of this would've happened.

∞

Hangzhou, China

Hotaka was dressed as a black knight while Midnight was dressed as a red angel. They stood to the side, watching couples and newly acquainted strangers dance the night away. This was supposed to be a joyous mask ball, but the two weren't enjoying themselves whatsoever. Their minds were focused on the secret underground auction that would be hosted in a couple of nights. Only a privileged few were invited to attend. It was their duty to infiltrate the auction, take the goods, and capture everyone involved.

The guests danced, talked, and drank their worries away as the nearby orchestra played a classical by Chopin.

"Oh my," said a man as he walked by and stopped. He was wearing a red and blue magician's costume. When his eyes landed on Midnight's red angel, his eyes widened. Her costume was simple, however it had an eerie glow to it, like she might really spread her wings and fly away. If Midnight had been trying to make an impression amongst the glitz and glamour of the other girls, she had done a good job. "Good evening."

"Good evening," greeted the two in return.

"Are you two not enjoying yourselves?"

"Oh, please don't mistake us for being bored because we're standing here doing nothing. We're actually having a conversation via telepathy," Midnight joked, hoping not to be too suspicious.

The Magician grinned and was soon laughing. Midnight couldn't help but smile also. At least now they were off his radar.

"This must be what they call love at first sight." He reached a hand out and took Midnight's hand to kiss, something she wasn't accustomed to.

Midnight gasped, nearly dropping her champagne glass that was untouched. She couldn't hold her liquor because she'd never drunk before and wasn't about to make a fool of herself.

"Oye," hissed Hotaka.

"Sir Knight, may I borrow your precious Angel for one dance?"

"Don't joke around-"

"Yes. Yes, you may," interrupted Midnight. She forced her champagne glass into Hotaka's hand, giving him no choice, then curtsied to leave with the Magician.

"Is your simple costume a diversion to hide your true beauty?" the Magician asked, leading Midnight out to the dance floor.

"I'm not that beautiful."

"What the hell is she thinking?" Hotaka growled. If she had secretly wanted to dance, she just had to ask. There was no need to dance with a Magician. It was such an insult to Hotaka's pride, he gulped both their drinks.

After the orchestra played a couple of pieces, Hotaka stormed over. He'd had enough of standing on the sidelines watching them dance and laugh the night away. The Magician even had his arm wrapped around Midnight's waist while whispering into her ear.

"That bastard, even I haven't gotten that close to her." Once he was near, he yanked Midnight away from the Magician while they were still talking. Curtly, he spoke, "I'm cutting in."

"Oh, of course," said the Magician. "She is your Angel after all." He bowed, exchanging a knowing smile with Midnight before leaving.

Once he was gone, Midnight glared at Hotaka for interrupting their conversation. "What the hell is with you?" she growled.

"Shut up and dance," ordered Hotaka as he twisted Midnight in a circle.

"What are you-"

"You know, not only am I a good fighter, I'm also a good dancer." When she was facing him again, he placed his hand on her waist and held her hand. The next piece was a little jazzier as they moved quicker to the beat.

"Why are you gloating for? Sheesh, that's the part I hate most about you."

"I wasn't gloating. I was stating the facts."

"It's still called gloating," she snapped and stepped on his feet.

"Ow," he yelped.

"Oops, my bad, I didn't see." She gave him an innocent smile and turned to leave, glad about what she'd done.

Before she could get any further, he caught hold of her hand, drawing her back with such force, she collided into his chest.

"Don't get too chummy."

"I see no problem with that," he answered and moved his feet before Midnight could step on it again. He smiled and twisted her in a circle again.

"You're such an idiot," she insulted. Seeing as how he wouldn't let her go, she mind as well finish the dance and explain the situation. "That man, Robin invited me to the auction, but you just had to come and interrupt us in the middle of our conversation."

"Well, why didn't you say so?" he asked as they took a side-step to match the other couples.

"How could I, when he was standing right in front of us? We'd have blown our cover."

"No use in crying over spilt milk."

Disappointed, Midnight shook her head. Whatever it took, they had to gain access into that underground auction. And the only way to do that was to get invited normally, since they had no idea where its location was or what time it would begin. "Listen," said Midnight, "you can retire to the room first. I'm going to leave with that man for tonight. I'll be back later."

Hotaka couldn't help but raise an eyebrow. Was this her way of getting rid of him, like how she had done so many times at the Dome? "And why would I trust you?"

"Because I'm your Soulmate." Midnight looked him square in the eye, not batting an eyelid.

In that moment, time seemed to have stood still. The world stopped rotating and the sun broke through the dark night. Birds chirped as a rainbow hovered above them. The dance hall had disappeared altogether as they stood on a green hill, overlooking a field of yellow dandelions.

Hotaka's heart squeezed as he smiled. Those were the words he had always wanted to hear. Her parted lips were so enticing, he wanted to reach out and traced them with his fingertips. If it was now, he could pour his heart and soul out without feeling embarrassed afterwards.

"I hate the fact that I'm your Soulmate, but it's the truth. So, it's your choice to trust me or not," Midnight continued.

With a sudden downpour and strike from lightning, Hotaka was forced out from his dream world. A scowl quickly replaced his smile. She had just ruined the moment with her cruel honesty again. Couldn't she try being romantic for a few minutes? It wouldn't kill her.

"So?" she asked.

"I'll wait," he said, his smile returning.

Midnight smiled in return and nodded. Finally, they had compromised. This was the beginning to a great partnership, or so she wanted to believe. "Alright then, don't stay up."

"I-"

"You fret too much." Midnight pulled away from him as the song ended. She curtsied and turned to leave. The Magician, Robin was standing not far away, watching. When she approached him, he smiled and put a hand around her waist once more.

Hotaka glared at Robin from behind his mask and watched the two disappear before heading back to the hotel alone. The mission came first, and he knew she could take care of herself.

∞

Hong Kong

A red boxing glove shot out, hitting Teo clear across the face. His unbalanced body hit the mat of the ring as his head spun. He crawled over to grab the ropes for support and stood. He glanced over at Crystal, pleading for her to throw in the white towel. She blinked back and stared at the white towel in her hand before wiping her sweat with it. It was so hot in the underground arena, she could use a cold-water bottle. Teo stared in disbelief and pointed his blue boxing glove at her. She smiled and gave him thumbs up for encouragement.

"Joo!" he shouted through his mouthpiece.

"Behind!" warned Crystal.

311

Teo turned and was knocked to the mat again by his opponent. He got to his knees, all the while glaring at Crystal who turned away to yawn.

That wretched woman, she wants me dead!

The ringing of a bell sounded as both opponents retreated to their corners. Teo lazily sat on his chair and took out his mouthpiece. His legs felt like Jell-O and his arms felt like they might pop off. Crystal was his trainer and the only support on his team. The opposing team had a coach and three other assistants, wiping his sweat, giving him water, and holding a bucket for him to spit in.

"Are you trying to kill me?" Teo accused.

"Oh my, whatever for?" she asked with an innocent smile. It was her job to assist him in this mission. It would be pointless if he died. Then again, she didn't exactly need him alive either to complete it. "Water?" she offered with a water bottle in hand.

Teo opened his mouth as Crystal poured the water. As soon as it hit his tongue, he ended up spitting it back out. "It's *hot* water! What the hell is wrong with you?!"

"Oh my, no wonder it was so warm in my hands." Crystal laughed and grabbed a towel to roughly wipe his sweat with. Just staring at his face got on her nerves. She still couldn't forgive him for defeating her three years ago. It was because of that incident that Yeve became even harsher towards them.

"Enough!" Teo slapped her hands away as Crystal glared, but eventually smiled. She was enjoying this time to make his life hell for that humiliation.

"My, my, you're so not a happy person." Crystal got out of the ring as the bell rang for the next round. Teo put his mouthpiece back into place and stood to fight his opponent once more. He swung his fist at the opponent who easily parried and countered. Again, Teo's mind raced like crazy. He saw flashes of white light and people in the crowd shouting and throwing their fists in the air. They were like savages, watching a battle royale. His forehead bled as his vision blurred and he fell.

The referee ran over to begin the countdown from ten while Teo lay motionless.

Crystal crossed her arms from the sideline. He was going to toss this match after they came so far. Did he think that she wanted to be here as much as him? No. Crystal would prefer to be anywhere but here, especially since she was so close to her home country, Malaysia. She wanted to return and run down the lanes of the rice paddies. She wanted to feel the sun beat down on her while standing on the highest hill, overlooking her tiny town. But those days couldn't be retrieved. Her tiny town had been decimated when rebels took over. One day, she would return and reclaim that tiny town now that she had powers. Until then, she had to continue accomplishing missions.

Teo lay beneath the sun, smiling with his eyes closed. This was a good dream he was having. In here, he wasn't getting beaten to a pulp and neither was there a sign of Crystal anywhere. "Ah, life's good," he said.

Suddenly, the bright sun disappeared behind the angry gray clouds. Teo sensed the gloomy weather and opened his eyes. He sat up and looked around. Fog was starting to settle in. "What the heck is going on? Where's my happy dream?"

"Teo, if you jeopardize this mission, I swear I'll kill you when you wake up!" shouted Crystal's face from the dark sky.

Fear crawled under Teo's skin, sending goose bumps up his arms. He leapt to his feet and spun around, back inside the ring. The cheers and jeers from the crowd had returned as well. Looking over at Crystal, he tensed. She was smiling, a threatening aura surrounding her.

Did she learn how to be scary from Yeve? he thought and gulped.

"Are you okay?!" shouted the referee who was standing before him.

Teo nodded, wide awake now. How could he not after Crystal menacingly used her powers to enter his mind?

"Let's begin!" shouted the referee as he backed away again.

Teo inhaled and exhaled as he turned around to find his opponent throw a punch. Again, he went down for the hundredth time that night.

Crystal let out a groan and smacked her forehead. This was the worst mission the deans could've given them. At this rate, she was going to fail, and Mio was going to succeed her mission.

After lowering her hand and evening out her breathing, Crystal concentrated on the energy in the room. Once she was able to open her invisible third eye, she smiled and transported out from her body to float in midair. In this astral form, she could hear every minute sound and feel every single person's energy. Every time she was in this form, she always felt exhilarated, like she wanted to fly out of the earth's atmosphere and into space. But today, she had to contain that excitement and flew over to the opponent to enter his mind. Once she had him paralyzed she shouted, "Teo, get your ass up and punch him! Now!"

"Ez fo you ta sayin," he said tiredly and stood up, smacking his opponent who fell like a leaf. "Eh?"

The opponent hit the floor with a loud thud as the shouting from the crowd ceased, everyone shell-shocked. The one who was most surprised at the result was Teo. He backed away, blinking at his opponent he'd just KO'd with a simple slap to the cheek. Was this even planet earth anymore?

"Vito, get up!" shouted the opposing team's manager, but it was no use. Crystal had done something to weaken his psyche.

"Hey, ref, start counting!" demanded an angry Crystal.

"Oh, right," said the referee who forgot his job. He had to get his mind out of the clouds and back into the game. "One," he counted numbly.

"Vito, get up! You can't go down like this!" shouted the manager.

"It's over." Crystal smiled, pleased with her work. When the referee finished the countdown, Teo won the match. The underground room became so eerie they could hear crickets. Teo, still shocked didn't notice Crystal enter the ring behind him.

"You won, now let's get going." Crystal dragged him to the backroom and forced Teo to sit as she grabbed the first aid kit. Not only was she forced to be his manager, she was also forced to be his baby-sitter of all things. She wanted more important missions like taking down evil organizations or infiltrating secret bases, but knew it wasn't possible. It was because Crystal's third eye wasn't strong enough. If only she had trained harder back at the Dome, she'd be on par with the other girls. "Of all people that I had to get paired up with, it just had to be the weakest link," she insulted.

"You," hissed Teo. Ever since they parted from the others, he heard nothing but insults from her. Every chance she got, she would comment on how weak he was.

"I pity myself." Crystal dabbed Teo's cut on the forehead with alcohol as it stung. He let out a yelp and backed away. She didn't even care about hurting him from the harsh dabbing.

"Can't you be nicer?!"

"Would you sit still?" she ordered. Crystal stood from her stool and bent over to dress Teo's wound again. "You could've used your powers."

"My powers are pretty much useless in this kind of situation. Taka, King, or Yuu should be here. Not me. I'm more suited for espionage."

"Yet you easily defeated me during our duel."

"Oye, that's in the past now. Let's drop it," Teo said, not wanting to start a confrontation. He'd feared that the reason Crystal was so bitter towards him was because of that duel. "Besides, it wouldn't be fair to that other guy."

"This is a mission. What would you do if you had lost?"

"I don't know."

"Be happy that I was there."

Teo stared at her and smiled. His hunch had been right when he slapped out Vito. "So, you did use your powers."

"I had to."

"You didn't have to. You chose to."

"Yes, yes, you're right, it's all my fault that you won," she snapped and smacked the Band-Aid on his forehead. After all that she'd done for him, he was going to give her a lecture. This was her thanks for helping.

"Ow," he said, glaring. "Be nicer."

"I've learned my lesson. Next time, I'm letting you die in the ring when someone punches you over and over. You stupid weakling, how dare you lecture me." Crystal grabbed the dirty cotton balls to toss away. She walked over to the closet and tossed Teo's clothes at him. "Get dressed and let's go," she ordered, leaving first.

"What's she so mad about?" Teo smiled and touched his forehead. No matter how sour or rude she was, she was sweeter than she let on. "I knew you'd come to my rescue."

∞

Taipei, Taiwan

Even with a comedy playing on TV, Yuudai was too concentrated on Morgana who sat before the windowsill, sighing. He too sighed and walked over to join her, knowing the reason why she was so lost in thought. Aoi. It was always about Aoi. She was probably worrying about his well-being and whether Soria was picking on him again or not.

Even during their information gathering last night, Morgana didn't care to make small talk. The only time she spoke was when she had questions or concerns. Other than that, she was desperate to finish and return to Aoi.

"Why are you sighing?" asked Yuudai. He lowered his face to her height as she jumped away and shrieked.

"Yuudai!" Morgana snapped.

"What?" he asked innocently.

"Don't do that!"

"It's not my fault you weren't paying attention to your surroundings."

"What do you want?" she asked, composing herself once more to look out the window.

"Thinking of someone?"

"Yeah," she answered and gasped, turning to glare at him. He was always tricking and playing games on her, which was why she was so wary of him. How did he and Aoi even become best friends?

"Gotcha," he said and grinned. It was too easy to fool her. "Who?"

"Aoi-kun," Morgana responded unintentionally. She gasped again and turned to hit Yuudai who swiftly dodged. "Stop making a fool of me!"

"It's not my fault you answer without thinking." Yuudai walked over to the sofa and sat back down. Morgana was once again looking out the window, ignoring him. "Morgana," he spoke softly but she didn't hear. "Morgana," he said loudly this time.

"Huh?" she answered and glanced back. "I won't get tricked this time."

Yuudai shook his head and smiled. "Don't worry. I don't plan on tricking you."

"Then what is it?" Morgana asked, not noticing his sadness.

"Why is Aoi the only one you think about?"

A smile appeared on her face without her realizing it. Whenever she thought about Aoi, an invisible hand would tug at her heart strings. She closed her eyes, her smile still plastered on her face. She would never forget the day she met him in the forest, or when he saved her inside Blair.

As the concrete squares gave way from below, the fear of dying struck Morgana. She didn't want to die yet, not after coming this far. A scream escaped her mouth as she fell to her doom. Knowing Yeve, she would jump in after her. What none of them ever expected was Aoi who jumped from above to rescue her instead. He secured one arm around her waist as they rapidly descended towards the lava. Morgana held onto him with all her might, trembling and crying.

"Don't be afraid," he whispered and smiled. "I'll get us out of here. Trust me." With his free hand, he faced his palm down, using his own fire to combine with the molten lava to blast them up to safety.

The tiny crush that Morgana harbored towards Aoi turned to admiration and love in that moment. He had kept his word and gotten them out of the dangerous situation. Whenever the boys were around—no—even when the boys weren't around, Morgana constantly searched for him, in the wind, in the sky, and in her dreams.

"All those times," she said, returning from her dream world. "All those times at the Dome, he was always so sincere and patient with me. Even when I slowed down the team, he always had my back. Naturally, I fell for him. How could I not? He's so forgiving and loving."

Yuudai stared at her, long and hard. He didn't know what to say. Should he get mad or be happy for her? But how could he be happy when his Soulmate was in love with his best friend? Or was she even in love? Maybe it was infatuation. Or admiration for her savior. Either way, for the first time in Yuudai's life, he made a wish, a terrible and selfish wish.

He wished for Aoi to disappear from the world.

Regretting that wish, Yuudai blinked his tears away. No. He couldn't wish for such a thing like that. Aoi was his childhood friend. They grew up together at the Dome. They were the best of friends amongst the guys other than Shadow and Teo. Besides, Yuudai couldn't be guaranteed that if Aoi were to disappear, Morgana would miraculously stop loving him. She might even chase after his ghost like a madwoman.

Still, that didn't keep Yuudai from seeing Aoi as a rival either. They were also like Hotaka and King and Azuma and Kakinouchi in a sense, except in the battlefield of love.

"Why do you love him so much?"

This time, she blushed until her face was a tomato red. Instead of speaking, Morgana sat still. When she gathered enough courage, she would go to Aoi and confess her feelings. Whether he was to return her affections or not, she promised to always stay by his side.

"You," said Yuudai. He lowered his head and clenched his fists. His wish for Aoi to disappear grew stronger but pushed the thought aside. He would rely on himself to access Morgana's heart, not a silly wish. "I'm your Soulmate. Shouldn't you be more concerned about me?"

"Huh?"

"Forget it," Yuudai said, standing from the sofa. He forced a smile and turned to leave. His anger was seeping out and he didn't want her to see. "I'm gonna buy some food. Want anything?"

"I'm good," she responded as Yuudai left the room. Once he was gone, she turned her attention to the city skyline. It was so beautiful, she wished Aoi was there to enjoy the view with her. "Aoi-kun, I hope you're doing fine."

∞

Yuudai stood inside the elevator, riding it down to the lobby. Small electric currents overflowed from his body that he couldn't keep under control. With a sharp jolt, the elevator stopped moving and the lights died. The red emergency lights came on as the automated voice too came on, assuring him of his rescue.

"At this time, there has been a power outage. Please remain calm. This incident has been reported. Someone will come to your imme-" the voice spoke as Yuudai killed it also, along with the red lights.

No one could save him from this darkness. The only one capable of doing so was his Soulmate who couldn't recognize that he'd also been patiently supporting her since their Dome days. His broken smile caused his tears to trickle. "Please save me," Yuudai begged, clutching his chest.

∞

Doctor Nishikawa came out from within his room neatly groomed and stopped. Standing in the hallway waiting for him was Azuma. The doctor couldn't help but sneer at how cheeky he was for keeping tabs on him the past few days. Was he trying to prove something? If so, then Azuma needed to know that the doctor didn't scare easily.

Azuma blinked and bowed in greeting. He had to yield in this game of stare. There was no other option. "Good evening."

"Same here," said Doctor Nishikawa. He walked around Azuma to leave, without a simple bow. There were things he needed to see to. The minions of his brother-in-law's, he had no interest in.

"Sensei," called back Azuma.

Stopping, Doctor Nishikawa turned back. He could see Azuma's anger seething but didn't seem to care. "What?"

"You're in a rush to go somewhere. May I ask where?" Azuma walked over to block his way again.

Doctor Nishikawa grinned. "Are you challenging me, boy?"

"I'm just asking you a simple question."

"A mere pawn such as yourself has no right to question me."

"I'm not a pawn." Azuma stepped up to the doctor and grabbed him by the collars. Every time he thought about the heart that the doctor stole, his blood boiled.

"Unhand me, boy."

"You-"

"Arata-kun," called out Mina from behind. She walked over briskly as Azuma let go of Doctor Nishikawa. Once she reached their sides, she slapped him. "Show some respect, you ingrate."

Shocked, Azuma's eyes widened. He hadn't been expecting a slap. Then again, he should've seen it coming after confronting Doctor Nishikawa.

"I'm so sorry, sensei," Mina apologized and bowed. "I'll punish him and see to it that this never happens again."

"How about you just dispose of him instead?" Doctor Nishikawa suggested with a sadistic smile.

Mina shuddered. There it was again, the smile that made her think humans were just as dangerous as Life-Kills. "Of course, you're right. I'll see to it myself," she said with a slight bow.

"It was a joke, a joke." He laughed at Mina for taking him so seriously. Then again, he'd never seen her relax around him which was a good thing. "Why are you so scared of me, Mina?"

"I—I-"

"Just make sure you discipline the boy." Doctor Nishikawa glanced at his watch and eyed Azuma once more before leaving. There were things he needed to see to.

Once he was gone, Mina dragged Azuma to where Shayla was waiting inside her room.

"What's going on?" Shayla asked, standing from her seat. Mina had said she'd search for Azuma so they could talk. Now that the two were present, there was a tense atmosphere around them.

"Sit," Mina instructed as Azuma took a seat. If she hadn't come on time, what would he have done or said to Doctor Nishikawa? It would've ruined her two years of staying undercover.

"Uh, so?" Shayla asked again and sat back down, unsure of what to do.

"Don't ever do that again, got it?"

Without a word, Azuma nodded in response.

"Good."

"I'm sorry. I'm still lost," Shayla said, raising a hand.

"You don't need to know." Mina waved it off to deliver the news that Dean Kiera had relayed unto her. It was urgent that the two understood what to do next. "I've received word from the dean. The heart that Nishikawa-sensei stole belongs to May."

Shayla broke down at the news. Meanwhile, Azuma sat, relieved. So, it was May's heart that had been taken, not Kakinouchi's. As quickly as his relief had come, it faded and was replaced with guilt. He shouldn't be happy when Kakinouchi was going through hell from failing to protect his Soulmate.

"The dean wants us to retrieve May's heart and get Gon-kun back home. His father, the chief of police in Yamagata is relying on us for help."

"May," Shayla kept crying.

"Shayla, get ahold of yourself. You won't be able to do anything if you continue crying like that."

Shayla nodded and wiped her eyes. There was a mission she had to carry out and a friend to save. If she couldn't strengthen her heart, she'd end up failing, and that was the last thing she wanted. "I understand."

"Good," said Mina. She looked over at Azuma who was still quiet. "What about you? What's your resolve?"

Looking up, tears filled Azuma's eyes. He quickly wiped them away too, a newfound determination replacing his sadness. "I'll do everything within my power to assist in this mission."

"Good, that's what I wanted to hear." Mina smiled. She liked the unwavering look in both youngster's eyes. "The boss will arrive in two days. You and Azuma-kun start digging for details. Keep your eyes on Nishikawa-sensei. He has a keen sense. Also, don't forget to see to it that Gon-kun is safe at all time. Right now, we have three things to worry about."

"Okay." Shayla nodded again. "You can count on us."

"Alright then, go to sleep. It's already one in the morning." Mina turned her back and left the room. Once out in the hallway, she calmly headed for her room. From the shadows, someone was covertly tailing her, but wasn't doing a good job at it.

31st Lie

"WHAT?!" shouted Naruyuki in disbelief. He choked on his breakfast and coughed as Verse reached over to hit his back. After turning in their reports to the deans, they had been given a quick side-mission before being called back to the Dome for a new urgent mission.

Dark who had been talking, shook his head. He didn't know where to begin. After finishing his second mission, he received news from Gabe that Kakinouchi and May had failed theirs. In the process, her heart had been stolen. "Kakinouchi is in confinement."

"Why?" Verse asked calmly. This was her first-time hearing anything regarding their new mission. A few were already back at the Dome's mansion, awaiting the rest.

"Kakinouchi's lost it. He's attacking everyone and anything he sees. Dean Kosa says he'll do that for the next few days. Once he loses all his energy, he'll stop."

"Do you know what happened on their mission?" asked Naruyuki.

"They were on a case to arrest a doctor who was murdering girls. The doctor somehow kidnapped May and stole her heart. After Gabe-sensei and Umi-sensei examined her body, they put it inside the morgue."

Naruyuki shook his head and lowered his fork. So, even a Life-Kill was vulnerable at times, despite their powers.

"I wonder if the same thing would've happened to me also," Dark said.

"Fool," Naruyuki said, hitting him on the arm. "You're strong. There's no way you would've lost Cammie."

"But you see, I did. Cammie also got captured. That's why I understand how Kakinouchi feels."

It was quiet inside the dining room as Naruyuki glanced at Verse. He also understood that feeling.

Noticing that she was intensely being stared at, Verse glanced over with a raised eyebrow. There were tears in Naruyuki's eyes. "Why are you-"

"Verse," called out Miss Umi as she walked over.

At the sound of her voice, Verse instinctively stood. "Yes?"

"I need your assistance."

"Of course." She excused herself and left with Miss Umi. The two guys exchanged curious glances, wondering what had happened just then.

Naruyuki sat, simply watching as the two disappeared around the corner. He reached for his cup of water and took a drink.

Sensing that something was weighing on Naruyuki's mind, Dark asked, "Did something happen with you also?"

"Do you need to ask?"

"Yes."

"Verse got captured too."

"Wow." Dark whistled and shook his head, feeling embarrassed. "We suck. Did we all fail to protect our Soulmates?"

Naruyuki smiled and shook his head. He could never see Rain, Hotaka, Shadow, along with Yuudai failing in protecting their girls. "Say, you don't suppose Kakinouchi went Berserk, do you?"

"Anything's possible," Dark said with a shrug.

∞

While they walked in silence, Verse kept her gaze straight ahead. She opened her mouth to ask a question, despite knowing the answer. "Why do you need me?"

"Do you have to ask?" redirected Miss Umi. She didn't even glance at Verse, but instead kept leading the way. "Right now, he doesn't seem to be showing any signs of fatigue. If he keeps it up, he'll die."

"And?"

"Just the usual, take away his sadness. He's May's Soulmate. Won't you save him?"

Miss Umi was such a pro at guilt tripping Verse into doing what she wanted, it made her grin. She was nothing more than a tool for them to manipulate and she knew it. Nothing had changed from when she was a child. "I will."

"Good. Keep that in mind."

When they reached the room that Kakinouchi was being imprisoned, they stopped. Miss Umi scanned her card and fingerprint as it took a blood sample. The door slid open as Verse entered the dark confined room alone. Cowering in the corner was Kakinouchi.

She walked over quietly and stopped before him, the door now closed to the room. He looked like a possessed man. "Kakinouchi," she whispered and reached a hand out as he caught her wrist.

Kakinouchi looked up and grinned, his eyes glowing yellow. His wrists were bound by shackles but that didn't stop him from attacking. "Give me your heart!" he shouted, reaching out with his other hand to claw at Verse's chest. Berserk, the room began to ice over.

"Sorry, but I don't plan on dying just yet." Verse dodged his clawing to pin him to the floor, and was whisked away to his inner mind.

The place she stood in was sunny, but a thunderstorm was brewing. Rain fell and lightning struck even though the sun shone. His mind was in shambles after failing to protect May.

Verse walked further into his inner mind. Every staircase she climbed, she passed by a door but it wasn't the one she sought. After walking for some time, a light blue door came into view. Curious, Verse stopped outside it. She was tempted to go inside, but a black door across from it was vying for her attention as well. Debating, Verse ultimately turned away from the light blue door. She had a task to carry out and walked over to the black door. Inside was the cause of his Berserk Mode.

For as long as Verse could remember, she could always tell when the door she was seeking was before her. It wasn't a sixth sense of any kind, but more like a voice calling out from behind it. She twisted the black knob, but it was locked. "I knew it wouldn't be this easy." She jingled with it some more and even tried kicking it down. When she determined that it wouldn't budge, she closed her eyes, conjuring a memory to life.

"Did you call?" a little girl wearing the Maroon girls' academy's summer uniform spoke. Her peach hair and gold eyes sparkled as well as her smile. She was happy to be of service.

"Help me open this door."

"Leave it to me." The little girl walked forward and took hold of the knob to try and open.

"Too bad I can't summon people in real life," Verse complained.

"It's open."

"Thanks, Wakaba."

"No problem." Wakaba smiled and moved aside as Verse twisted the knob. Before she could open the door, Wakaba reached out to take hold of her free hand. "Verse-chan."

"What is it?"

"Is the scar still there?"

Verse winced from the prickle. These memories sure were talkative when she came to this place. "Scars only know how to lighten. They never truly disappear."

"Is that so?" A tear fell from her eyes as she faded into nothing.

Verse looked away from where Wakaba had been standing and pushed the door open. She stepped into the room full of black energy swirls that clung to the walls. Tables, books, toys, and magazines scattered about. She walked over to the sofa and stopped. Sitting in the corner, hugging his legs was Kakinouchi. Cautiously, Verse approached and stopped. "Kakinouchi," she called out.

He twitched from the sound of her voice and looked up, nothing reflected in his soft green eyes. "May," he called out absentmindedly. "Is that you?"

Verse smiled and reached a hand out. "May's not here right now, but she's waiting for you to save her."

"She is?" he asked and blinked, a bit of life returning.

"Yeah, she is. So, come. Let's go."

Kakinouchi smiled and reached out to take Verse's hand. In that instant, the darkness dispersed, and the light returned. From outside, the storm died down. Normalcy had returned.

Kakinouchi's body went limp and the yellow in his eyes disappeared. He slumped over on the floor, eyes closed, no longer Berserk, but instead fast asleep. Verse let go and backed away, gasping for air. She coughed and put a hand to her mouth. Taking her time, she stumbled to her feet, unable to keep her balance. Verse made her way over to the door and pressed the red button but Miss Umi was refusing to open it from the outside. Panic arose in her chest as she pressed repeatedly, wanting to escape. It felt like that time when she'd been imprisoned inside a dark room without Yeve and Soria.

After one whole minute, the door opened as Verse stepped out.

"You did a good job," praised Miss Umi, "again." She was staring at Kakinouchi who was smiling in his sleep.

Without a word, Verse stumbled away, tears in her eyes.

Miss Umi watched her go until she was out of sight, then turned to look at Gabe who stood nearby. Verse had been so intent on leaving she didn't notice him approaching. "Ah, you finally came."

"Why didn't you open the door for Verse?" Gabe snapped and glared.

Chuckling, Miss Umi walked away. Her job here was also done. She had no reason to stay and answer his question. "Go ahead and take back your precious student. I'm returning to the academy to tend to my girls." After rounding the corner out of view, Miss Umi's smile was replaced with cold envy.

After her check-up with Miss Umi, Cammie continued staying inside the infirmary. She didn't want to leave, fearing that she might run into Dark somehow. "Sensei," she said.

"What is it?" answered General Koga who was reading a magazine. She was tasked with overseeing the infirmary while Miss Umi was out tending to Kakinouchi with Gabe.

"When the others return and we regroup, will we go retrieve May's heart?"

General Koga stopped reading her magazine to look up. She thought about it before answering, "We'll have to wait and see. Right now, we have another problem."

"What kind of problem?" she asked, averting her gaze from the window.

Seeing no harm in letting Cammie know ahead of time, General Koga told the truth, "Some of you will have to go save Taiki and Umeko."

"Eh?"

"We haven't been able to contact them for some time now. After sending out spies, we found out that the two idiots have been caught."

"No way, Umeko of all people?"

"That's right."

"I'd understand if it was Soria or Mio, but Umeko?"

"You know, if Soria heard that, she'd drown you." General Koga let out a snort and put a hand to her stomach. They all knew Soria would probably get caught just to get herself out of a third mission.

Cammie gulped and laughed it off but eventually stopped. "Yeah I know. Soria's mighty scary. I still remember when she almost killed Wakaba."

General Koga stopped laughing, remembering as well. "Wakaba," she repeated painfully.

Cammie bit her lower lip. Any conversation pertaining to Wakaba was a taboo subject. Just speaking her name made everyone squirm.

"It's too bad though. If she was still alive today, she'd be strong."

"Yeah, she would've been. She'd be as strong as Hanabi." Cammie turned to look out the window again. It was a beautiful day. Why was she hiding out here when she should be outside enjoying the sunshine? It felt like such a waste. "The day that Soria almost killed Wakaba was because of Verse," she recalled.

"For a kid who mainly kept to herself, you have a pretty good memory," praised General Koga.

"Uh, yeah," Cammie said, embarrassed. Now that she recalled her past, she was the dark and lonesome one who didn't socialize with anyone or participated in anything. She didn't even like being in the presence of the others and didn't want to have friends. All she wanted was to be left alone in the infirmary. After getting to know the girls, she couldn't imagine life without them.

General Koga flipped a page in the magazine and glared. "It was also the day my husband left me."

"Eh? You were once married?"

"Are you trying to insult me here?"

"Ah, no, of course not. I just—I'm sorry," apologized Cammie as she bowed.

General Koga laughed it off and shook her head. "It's okay. That bastard's suffering right now from all the debt his new wife has racked up. Serves him right."

∞

Soria walked down the sidewalk of Nemuro Port with her cell phone in hand. Today they were leaving for Tokyo before heading to the Dome. "Hmm," she said with a frown.

"What's up?" Aoi asked, walking alongside her.

"That was Cammie."

"And?"

"She seemed out of sorts."

"And?"

Soria put her cell phone away to adjust the hat on her head that she had just bought. "She kept apologizing and pleading for me to not drown her. She thinks I'm psychic or something."

"And that's weird, why?"

"The only time the girls apologize to me is when they speaking ill of me," Soria explained and came to an abrupt halt, as did Aoi. Sneering, she whipped out her cell phone, ready to call Cammie and threaten her. "The nerves of that black sheep," she hissed.

"Don't even," Aoi said, snatching her phone to put inside his pocket.

"Hey, give it back!"

"Leave her be. She probably didn't mean it."

"Well, she shouldn't have talked behind my back in the first place."

Aoi thought about it before nodding. "True, but give her a break. She just went through an ordeal with her mission."

Eyebrows raised, Soria asked, "How do you know?"

"Dark told me."

"Of course, should've known." She glanced towards the clear skies and smiled, unable to hide the joy of seeing Yeve and Verse again. Once they were united, she'd talk about all the things she'd encountered.

"But really though," Aoi said, curiously looking over. "Would you really kill her?"

"Hmm, the last time one of the girls dared to say something bad, I-"

"You?"

"I broke the pipes in the cafeteria and almost drowned everyone. Ever since, everyone thinks I'll drown them," Soria said, chuckling.

Aoi laughed as he reached out to pat her head, not noticing that something was wrong with her first example. "Forgive and forget, right?"

Soria smiled. It was easier said than done. That much, she knew.

∞

"What's this?" Mr. Fujiwara questioningly raised an eyebrow. Standing and waiting beside him on the docks was Ms. Tanaka. They had come to welcome Poe and Alice. Instead of just the two, Jacques stood beside Alice, holding her hand tightly.

"This is Jacques-kun," she introduced.

Ms. Tanaka inspected Jacques before raising an eyebrow also. "And why did you bring him here?"

Poe scratched his head. It was a rather difficult story to tell. To make it short, he explained, "The bugger wouldn't stay behind at the orphanage with the others and snuck out to follow us."

"I'm not a little bugger! I'm Jacques!" he corrected.

"Yeah, yeah, whatever." Poe scratched his head again and yawned. "The trip back was tiring as hell. Can I go back to the dorms and sleep?"

"No." Mr. Fujiwara shook his head. "All dorms are off limits to you kids from now on."

"Seriously? Are we departing for our next mission already?"

"No. What I meant was, you'll be staying at the mansion for now. The dorms are for the new students." Mr. Fujiwara gave Jacques a questioningly look, then nodded. Ms. Tanaka seemed to understand and nodded as well.

"Come, I'll take you two back to the mansion. Fujiwara-sensei will take the boy."

"Eh?" said Alice and Jacques in alarm.

Mr. Fujiwara adjusted his glasses and walked over. He bent forward and smiled warmly. "I'll introduce you to some kids your age," he offered. "Maybe you can even become friends."

Jacques backed away, not wanting to part from her.

Alice smiled, squeezing his hand in return. With her free hand, she fixed his hair, knowing they had to eventually part once they reached the Dome, which was why she didn't want to bring him. But another part couldn't bear to leave him at the orphanage either. "Jacques-kun, it's okay. Fujiwara-sensei is a good person."

Jacques stared and let out a sniffle. He understood but was afraid to go to a foreign place alone. How was this any different from staying at the orphanage without her? "Will I see you again, nee-chan?"

"Oye don't act like you're in love with her," Poe snapped and glared.

"Poe," they all said.

"Just saying," he said, not wanting any love rivals, especially a kid.

Alice reached out to embrace Jacques and nodded. "I promise. You'll see me again. I'll come visit you often. Just don't get into fights." Alice let go and chuckled while Jacques cried. Was this what it felt like to have a little brother? "Be a good boy, okay?" she said, wiping his tears.

"Okay." He sniffled and nodded.

Mr. Fujiwara smiled and reached out his hand again. "Come, Jacques. I'm sure Gabe will be happy to get a new addition."

"Okay." Jacques turned and took Mr. Fujiwara's hand. "Bye." He waved to Alice and left.

"Come," instructed Ms. Tanaka. She led the way towards the limousine while the two followed from behind.

"Sensei," Alice said. "Will he become a new student?"

"Of course, he's come all this way with you, it'd be a shame to turn him away. He'll join the other boys at the academy."

Alice grimaced. What she feared most had just come true. Jacques would be put through a series of trials and experiments just like herself, to become a killing machine.

∞

Shayla took a bite out of the apple in her hand. The two were seated out back of the organization's hideout. There wasn't much to do since Mina hadn't given them any further instructions. They were simply to idle about and act like a member of the gang.

"What do you think happened during Kakinouchi and May's mission?" Azuma asked, breaking the silence.

Shayla shrugged. She didn't know, and she didn't want to think about it. "I hope he's fine."

"With the others around, they'll help calm him down."

"Yeah, you're right."

"He's here!" shouted a group as they ran by excitedly. Behind them were other groups as Shayla and Azuma exchanged glances. Everyone was gathering at the entrance gate again. The boss was finally making his entrance. They stood and ran with the others, wanting to see also. Sitting in the driveway were two black limousines. Men in black stood, surrounding it. Even Mina was present, waiting to welcome the boss.

"Here he comes." Shayla held her breath and watched as the door to the limousine slid open.

He swung one leg out then the other, fully clothed in a white tuxedo. On his head sat a white top hat with a white feather. He was holding a white cane and seemed to be in his late forties.

"Welcome back, boss!" the gang greeted in unison and bowed as Shayla and Azuma copied.

"It's good to be back," he greeted and smiled, then waved.

At his gesture, wild cheers erupted. Some pumped their fists into the air. "Yeah, now that the boss is back we'll beat those shitty Bat Angels and win!"

"We'll show them who's the strongest!"

"Sir," said Mina. She walked over and bowed.

"Mina," said the boss. He smiled and opened his arms to hug her. "It's been some time. I take it you're doing fine as well."

"Yes, I am." She smiled and nodded.

"Good, good," he said and laughed.

"Make way," ordered Doctor Nishikawa from behind.

The gang hushed and moved aside as he wheeled a beautiful lady in a wheelchair through. Her shiny gray hair reached her waist as both hands rested on her lap. On her face was a gentle smile.

At the sight of her, Mina held her breath.

"Zena," gasped the boss. Tears quickly welled in his eyes. She still looked the same as before. Doctor Nishikawa had kept his promise. He'd awakened Zena from her slumber. Working with Jin hadn't been in vain.

Doctor Nishikawa smiled and bent down, whispering into his wife's ear.

The beautiful lady looked up and nodded. She stood from the wheelchair with much care and precision. After practicing for the past few days, she was getting better at walking on her own. Slowly, Zena took baby steps to approach the boss before embracing him. "Welcome home, Haj onii-san."

Overwhelmed with emotions, Haj returned her embrace. His beloved little sister was finally back where she belonged. "I'm home," he responded.

Azuma clenched his fists and grinded his teeth together. Doctor Nishikawa was also making his way over to greet Haj. This was the worst possible outcome. So, all those days the doctor had been sneaking off, he'd been assisting Zena with her rehab therapy.

32nd Lie

GABE GRABBED A CIGAR from his pocket to put to his lips. Right when he was about to light it, Miss Umi glared, daring him. Gabe smiled innocently and put the cigar away, knowing better than to smoke in front of her. "I'll uh, wait until I get outside."

"You better," Miss Umi said, closing the file sitting on her lap. They were inside her office, having a meeting. On the screen of her computer were different charts. She'd called Gabe in for an update pertaining the matter of King and Jennifer. "So?"

"King's doing fine. He'll recover in no time."

"And his eye?"

Gabe smiled, thankful that the boys had grown to become so powerful and reliable. Maybe he should resign as the doctor for the boys' academy and be a scout. But if he were to leave, Miss Umi would be lonely. In spite of everything, she was still his main concern. Chuckling, Gabe answered, "Kei was able to get there in a mannerly time to stop the eye from rotting and going blind."

"He's getting stronger."

"Of course, blood is the strongest weapon. But if I may say so, it was because you were quick to react to the situation."

"Stop praising me. It won't get you any points." Miss Umi smiled and took out a cigarette to light.

"Uh," Gabe said, staring in disbelief. She had denied him a cigar to smoke, yet was smoking her own cigarette. It was hypocritical. He wondered if she even realized that. "You should really get Jennifer to rest up. She hasn't left King's side for quite some time now."

Miss Umi smiled and let out a puff. "Jennifer blames herself for what happened. I can't do much about that part. Besides, this'll teach her a lesson or two."

"You're still so evil." Gabe smiled and glanced over at the screen full of charts. Miss Umi was shooting him another glare, but his thoughts wandered elsewhere. "What are you gonna do about your girls? The dean will hold you responsible if anything happens."

Miss Umi puffed out more smoke. She knew the consequences without him having to say a word. "I think I'll be fine for now."

"Umi."

"What?"

"I think this is the one you need to worry about most." Gabe stood and walked over to point a finger to a specific name on the charts.

Miss Umi lowered her hand holding the cigarette. He had read her mind. "I was hoping you wouldn't say that."

"She'll be the one to Awaken on her own." Gabe stared at the files lying on Miss Umi's desk and opened one of them. "And this one will add fuel to the fire," he said, turning to leave. "Well, I'm heading out first."

Miss Umi thanked him for his time and watched him go. When he reached the doorway and paused, she raised an eyebrow, wondering what had stopped him.

"Please be kind to Verse. She already has so many scars. I don't want her racking up anymore." With that, he was gone.

Laughing, Miss Umi put out her cigarette. So, the problem was Verse again. She should've guessed it, it was always about Verse. "Even to this day, he still treasures her the most. Almost makes me jealous how he only thinks about her scars and not mine." Miss Umi turned to stare at the files and closed them. "Now then, what do I do about you two troublemakers?"

∞

In Crystal's hand was a roll of white bandage. She remained silent while wrapping Teo's hands. They were in the backroom, getting ready. This was *the* fight they had been waiting for. In this fight, Teo would be going against the Champ. Whoever won would get to take home the prizes and title as the best fighter.

Though this was a crucial fight they needed to win, Teo was calmly watching TV. Even Crystal was calm.

"So," Teo said, breaking the silence. The past couple of days had been relatively quiet with her. He wondered if she was plotting something sinister again, or if she was genuinely concerned. "Since you can't use your powers this time, how are we going to win?" He looked over.

Crystal frowned. This was her first look of worry, but she shook it off. It was true that neither of them could use their powers. The underground league had taken all measurements to ensure that any Life-Kill who decided to partake would have to rely on their brawns for this last fight. Just the other day, Teo had been issued a mandatory shot to prevent him from using his powers, should he turn out to be a Life-Kill. Even the ring they were fighting in was created by a supposed genius. There was an energy barrier set around it to stop Life-Kills in the crowd from cheating.

"Why do you always have to rely on me?" Crystal asked.

"I just wanted to hear your input."

"Well, I don't have one."

Teo grinned. He flexed his muscles though there was barely anything to show. "In that case, shall I amaze you with my brute strength and win?"

Crystal scoffed and yanked the bandage on tightly. When she finished, she grabbed the gloves to help put on. "Let's go."

"Yeah," said Teo. He slipped his silk hood over his head to follow Crystal out into the hallway. He could already hear the shouts and chants from the audience. Only Crystal was in his corner like usual. The Champ would have many people in his corner, rooting him on. "Say, what would you do if I die in this fight? Will you cry?"

Crystal walked in front, her back to him. "Just concentrate on the fight."

"Seriously, answer the question. What would you do if I died?"

"I'll cremate you and scatter your ashes to the seven seas." She grinned as they walked out into the light of the ring.

"How bitter," said Teo. He smiled and threw his arms into the air. The cheering and booing from the crowd came as the referee inside the ring introduced him for the night. After countless and endless battles, they finally made it to the grand prix.

Teo climbed into the ring with Crystal by his side. He walked into the center, having a short stare down with his opponent. The Champ wasn't as big as the other guys Teo had fought against, but there was a certain air about him that screamed out "Champion."

After the referee explained the rules about wanting a clean fight and the time limit of each round, he had the two butt gloves, then dismissed them to their corners.

"Damn," said Teo as he returned to Crystal's side.

"What?" she asked and took off his robe.

"This guy's tough."

"You can tell by looking?" Crystal glanced at the opponent. The Champ was listening to his coach give a lecture. There was nothing redeeming about him except his height. How did Teo assess him with just one look?

"I bet he can pack a punch. Almost makes me glad this isn't MMA."

"I guess," Crystal said, throwing the white towel over her neck and taking hold of Teo's gloved hands. It was a good thing he couldn't feel how sweaty her palms were.

"So, what's the lecture today?" he joked.

Crystal stared at his sheepish grin. How could he be so calm when she was going out of her mind? With all her might, she squeezed his gloves. "Don't," she whispered.

"Don't lose?"

"Don't *die*. I don't wanna cremate or scatter your ashes any time soon."

"Let's begin!" shouted the referee as Crystal scrambled out.

Teo smiled and slid his mouthpiece into place. Now *she wants to be cute*. He held up his arms, ready to lose. The two opponents met in the center where the referee stood to Teo's left. He raised one hand into the air and brought it down to signal the start of the first round. The bell sounded and soon the audience was in an uproar.

"He's going to lose." Crystal watched anxiously from the sideline. The crowd was getting riled up. It was the defending champion against the rookie who shouldn't have made it so far.

The Champ threw fist after fistful of punches. All Teo could do was dodge. For not being a Life-Kill, the Champ's jabs were quick and accurate, a true athlete to the core.

"Counter!" ordered Crystal.

Teo threw a right jab but missed and stumbled, falling to the floor. The Champ took the opportunity to run over and land a few blows as Teo's head spun. The room was a blur and the light was blinding.

"Teo!" screamed Crystal. Her voice broke through his conscience, forcing him to his feet.

"Are you okay?" the referee asked, looking into his eyes. Teo nodded and wiped his nose with his forearm. It was bleeding. "Begin!"

The Champ wasted no time in walking over and punching Teo again.

∞

As Robin's guest for the underground auction that night, Midnight sat beside him on the second floor of the grand theater, quietly inspecting. The long-awaited day had arrived.

The auction had everything from imported cars, to drugs, to illegal firearms, to children, women, and men. Even if it sickened her how people were being sold off like cattle, she had to sit through it, keeping her cool and not act on impulse. In due time, she would make her move and end it all.

"Do you plan on bidding for anything?" Robin asked, noticing how quiet she'd been all night.

She grinned and nodded. "I am."

"And that would be?"

"Everything?"

Robin raised an eyebrow and chuckled. Midnight was an interesting character and he was smitten by how fearless she was. It had been a good thing that he ran across her at the mask ball. "Don't tell me you're a thief?"

"What if I am?"

Again, he chuckled, taking Midnight's hand to kiss and smile. "The only think you can possibly steal tonight would be my heart."

"That sounds more interesting than this auction," she said, tracing his jawline with her other hand. "How about you and I ditch this place and go back to your hotel room?"

"As much as I'd love to, I have to stay until the end, love." Robin grinned and pecked her on the cheek. "Maybe afterwards," he bargained with a wink.

Midnight giggled, playfully hitting him on the arm.

"Our next bidding piece," the auctioneer spoke from the stage.

Two men brought out a boy about fifteen years of age who was blindfolded and tied up. Though he was already fifteen, his physique resembled that of a twelve-year old's, due to malnutrition and abuse. The boy struggled to get free, but it did him no good while drugged and drowsy.

Midnight stirred. Something about the boy had gotten her worked up. She leaned forward, squinting her eyes to see better. *It couldn't be.*

Robin noticed and leaned forward as well. "What is it?"

"Thought I saw something," answered Midnight. She shook her head and settled back into her chair, thankful that the dimly lit theater hid her tears.

"This boy is our next bidding piece, starting at 250,000 golden dollars," announced the auctioneer.

Soon, the crowd began bidding, higher than the asking price. All the while, Midnight kept her eyes on the boy with unbearable scars on his body.

∞

Hotaka paced inside an alleyway near the underground auction, per Midnight's instructions. It was already midnight. The auction should've begun already. How long was she planning to make him wait?

There was a popping sound from behind as Hotaka cautiously made his way behind the dumpster. Sprouting from the cement was a budding rose.

Soon it grew bigger and bigger until it could eat him whole. The petals unfolded as Hotaka smiled.

"About time," he said, stepping into the center as the petals enclosed around him.

∞

Concerned, Crystal wiped Teo's sweat with a towel. He was breathing irregularly. His lip and forehead were cut from the punches the Champ had thrown. Teo's left eye was starting to swell. Soon, he wouldn't be able to see out from it. It was a good thing that Teo was a Life-Kill. Or else he'd have died from the Champ's blows.

"Just a little more to go," Teo whispered in a rasp.

"Aren't you supposed to be showing me your hidden brute strength?"

Teo chuckled, amazed that she remembered his words. "I have none. It was just a joke. I was never the brute type."

"Teo," said Crystal. The bell rung to indicate the beginning of the next round. There would be two more hellish rounds left until the end.

"I have to go." He did his best to smile and put his mouthpiece in, then stood, walking away.

"It's just a C ranked mission. Don't die for it," she said and climbed out.

Again, Teo went head to head with the Champ, exchanging punches and dodges. Even though Crystal knew the outcome, she continued watching no matter how unbearable it got.

The crowd cheered for the Champ who went in for the kill. Teo was too fatigue to counter or defend properly. He was backed into the ropes when the Champ threw an uppercut and he fell to the floor ring. Every muscle in his body ached. He no longer had any stamina to keep up with the fight. It also didn't help that he couldn't self-heal. Glancing into his corner, he watched as Crystal cried and her shoulders shuddered. She was becoming a blur as he weakly reached a gloved hand out to her. *Don't cry.*

"Don't die, don't die, don't die," she kept chanting.

Teo took hold of the ropes, forcing his legs to stand and turned to look at the Champ. They were both exhausted, waiting for the other to fall first. Surprised at seeing Teo stand back up, the Champ's eyes widened. He had assumed his uppercut would do the magic and win him the match. But Teo was more stubborn than anyone he'd gone against before. The Champ narrowed his brows, wanting to end this fight.

"You're the best, Champ!" cheered the audience. "Beat that chap!"

"Just a little more, Champ! You can win! Just knock him out! The title is all yours baby!" shouted the Champ's coach from the other corner.

Crystal attempted to use her powers, but it was futile. The energy barrier barred her from interfering. Not caring about the consequences, she closed her eyes and concentrated on breaking the barrier. The cheers from the crowd became wilder, something was happening. Crystal opened her eyes, forgetting about dispelling the barrier. Teo was leaning against the ropes, arms covering his face while the Champ pummeled him with punches.

She grinded her teeth so hard together it felt like they would chip. Her fists were clenched so tightly, her nails dug into her dark skin. "That's enough," Crystal said, shaking her head.

They were training in the backroom, getting ready for the match that night. Teo had on his gloves and was punching the hanging punching bag while Crystal sat on the bench, watching.

"So, you're saying you'd die for this mission?" Crystal asked, arms crossed against her chest

"Yeah," answered Teo. Not once did he turn to look at her.

"Why?"

"Orders are absolute."

"What?"

"It's what we were taught. Orders are absolute. Even if it means giving our lives, we must complete our mission."

She shook her head. That was no philosophy to be living by. Whoever had taught them that was crazy.

Teo stopped punching the bag to glance over. He was sweating and panting. "What were you girls taught back at the academy?"

"To survive at any cost."

"Eh? What's with that way of thinking?" He returned to punching the bag again and shook his head. Though they had come from the same Dome, they had been taught to think differently. Why was that? "Weren't you girls taught that we were chosen to change this world? We serve the Golden God and die for him."

"Yes, we were taught about the code that all Life-Kills live by, but we were also taught to survive and return home." Crystal stood and exited, wanting to get some fresh air. This talk was steering towards the emotional side and she couldn't handle it.

When the door closed behind her, Teo stopped hitting the punching bag. He stood, huffing and puffing, a smile forming on his lips. "We'll return home," he whispered. "Together."

Crystal took off the white towel wrapped around her neck to clutch tightly. She didn't want to use it but if it meant saving Teo's life, then she'd throw it in. Crystal glanced at the timer. There was still two minutes left. Although it seemed like such a short time, it felt like an eternity.

The Champ threw another punch as Teo hit the floor once more. His bruised left eye was starting to bleed. Even his lip was in worse condition than a few minutes ago. This time, Teo made no attempts to stand as Crystal held her breath. She watched him lay lifelessly on the floor. Then, he jerked and slowly staggered to his knees and feet. She let out a stifled cry. If he kept it up, he would really die from a concussion. Was completing this mission more important than surviving? Would he really force her into cremating his body and scattering his ashes to the seven seas?

"That's enough!" screamed Crystal. She threw the white towel into the ring as the noisy crowd died down. Like a wild cat, she scrambled into the ring and ran over to catch Teo before he could fall over again. His body was moving all on its own. Crystal wasn't even sure if he was conscious anymore. "That's enough, I said that's enough!"

"Why...?" he said weakly. "...the towel?"

"I told you already, didn't I? No matter what, we have to survive," Crystal answered and cried. She sank to the floor, still holding him. "We have to return home to where the others are. They'll be waiting for us. Even if we fail, it's alright, so long as we have each other."

"Together," he whispered before closing his eyes.

"The match is over! The white towel has been thrown in by the red team!" announced the referee. Soon, everyone was cheering wildly again. The Champ had won.

"You did it!" shouted the Champ's coach and support team.

He smiled at them, but ultimately turned back to look at Teo and Crystal again. No one bothered to help them. There wasn't even a medical team coming out to check his condition. The Champ's support team picked him up and threw him on their shoulders. He threw his gloved fists into the air as the crowd went crazy. Soon, the ring was filled with rowdy fans.

Instead of caring about the commotion, Crystal simply smiled and whispered, "Once we get back, I'll make you some delicious sushi."

From behind, a man in a hooded cloak approached. Moved by Crystal's act of devotion he couldn't stand by and do nothing. "Young miss," he called out as Crystal looked up. He had on dark shades and a scraggly beard. His hair looked so shabby it felt like he hadn't washed it in weeks. The man in the hooded cloak reached into his pocket and withdrew a pink vial. "Take this. Give it to him."

Shocked, Crystal reached out to take the pink vial. "Uh, thank you," she said. "Who are you? Why are you helping me?"

"My name isn't important. As for the reason why, I guess you can say, I understand your feelings. That vial is something I created. It'll return your

boyfriend's strength back in no time. As for his wounds, that depends on him." He chuckled and walked away, disappearing into the rowdy crowd.

"Wait," called out Crystal as she watched him go. "He's not my boyfriend." After a few seconds, she gasped, realizing what the pink vial was. "This is what we came here for," she said and chuckled, looking down at Teo. It was funny how things worked out so well. "It's a bummer we can't bring this vial back to Umi-sensei to test out." Crystal opened the vial and parted Teo's lips, wedging it in. She tilted the vial until the pink liquid disappeared into his mouth.

∞

The rose petals opened as Hotaka stepped out from within, then disappeared where it had come. Hotaka glanced around, taking in his surroundings of the enormous storage room. Whatever Midnight had summoned him there for, he had to quickly find it. Down the hallway, guards were making their rounds. When they rounded the corner and spotted no one, they walked on by.

"What is this room?" Hotaka asked, entering a different room from the storage room. In this room, there were different species of animals. Some came from the depths of the ocean. Others were extinct, while the rest were experimental hybrids. A black wolf nearby sat up when it noticed Hotaka and growled but didn't roar. "So, this is what Midnight sent me here for?"

"Is someone there?" called out a girl. "Please help."

Cautious, Hotaka followed the sound of the voice while concealing himself. When he found the owner of the voice, he stopped. It was a girl encaged inside a water tank. She had a fish's tail and a shark's fin growing from her spinal cord. She wasn't wearing any clothes as her long hair covered her exposed breasts. Gasping, he came out from hiding. At the sight of Hotaka, the mermaid swam to the glass nearest to him and smiled.

"I knew I heard a voice," she said, relieved.

"You…fish…what…" he began, unable to form coherent sentences.

"Experiments," she answered, able to read his expression.

Hotaka quickly touched his back. There were no wings. Relieved, he removed his hand. It was thanks to excessive training that he was able to summon his wings at will. But the poor mermaid wasn't allowed to do so. "You can talk underwater?"

The mermaid nodded, still smiling. "Yes."

"I'll get you out."

"And the others too, please. There are even normal humans here. If you don't save everyone, they'll be mistreated."

Hotaka dwelled on her plea. He was here for a mission and couldn't afford to waste time, but the thought of leaving the mermaid and the others pained him. If he was in their situation, he'd want to be saved as well. Nodding, Hotaka smiled. "I got it. Don't worry. I'll save all of you."

"Thank you so much."

"Don't thank me. Thank the girl upstairs."

"What?"

"Forget it. I'll get you out in a jiffy. Hold on." Hotaka looked about, trying to find a way to climb the water tank so he could break the lock and free the mermaid. When he couldn't find a ladder, he gave up. "Guess I gotta do that," he said. From his back, his shirt fluttered and wings appeared.

The mermaid gasped and shouted in warning, "Run!"

Before Hotaka could get a chance to comprehend the situation, a tranquilizing dart pierced him.

∞

"Are you ready?" asked Robin. They were standing, getting ready to leave for the night. The auction had come to an end. Everything presented had been sold off without a hitch.

"Yeah," Midnight answered as Robin assisted her with her fur jacket.

"So, Miss Thief, are you ready to steal my heart tonight?"

"I'll steal both you and everything here at the auction."

Robin raised an eyebrow while she continued smiling. Midnight was a true mystery, always keeping him on his toes. He couldn't read her like he did most girls. "I highly encourage you to do so."

"Ladies and gentlemen!" the auctioneer shouted, running back onstage with a look of excitement. His microphone was shaking in his hand and his eyes gleamed at what he was about to present.

"Now what?" asked Midnight. "I thought it was over?"

Robin shook his head. "I have no idea either."

"Ladies and gentlemen!" shouted the auctioneer again. "Please do not leave yet! We've just now acquired a new addition to tonight's pieces!"

The crowd began to whisper at this new spontaneous addition. But still, they stayed, wanting to know and see what it was that the auctioneer was so psyched about.

"What the hell is going on?" Robin was clearly upset with the surprise. Everything had an order. He hated it when plans didn't go accordingly.

"Shall we watch?"

"Might as well," answered Robin. They both sat back down with the audience as the auctioneer explained the next bidding piece.

"Tonight, we've shown you some amazing things. But this next piece is unlike anything you've ever witnessed before. It's spectacular beyond words and will blow your mind away. For our newly acquired asset, has wings!"

Midnight perked, so did Robin.

"We will start at ten million!"

The crowd started whispering, disbelieving the auctioneer. A person with wings? It was absurd and had never been done before. "Let us see this winged creature!" they demanded. "For all we know, you could be lying to us!"

The auctioneer sneered at the crowd and motioned for four men to drag Hotaka onstage. He was awakening from his unconscious state.

"Hmm, I feel like I've seen him before," said Robin suspiciously. "From where though?"

How the hell did he get caught? Midnight clutched on tightly to her armrest.

"Make him open his wings," demanded the auctioneer.

The four men nodded and began beating Hotaka. Not once did he let out a pain of cry. And not once did Midnight flinch. "Open your wings!"

"Eat shit," Hotaka snarled.

The four men continued beating him as Midnight rose from her chair, having seen enough. It was time to put an end to this show.

"Show us your magnificent wings if you think you're so superior, boy!" she shouted as everyone turned to look at her, even Hotaka. They were staring at each other like they were strangers meeting for the first time. "Unless, of course, you have none, Earth's Angel!" Midnight taunted and crossed her arms.

"Yeah!" agreed the audience.

Robin looked amongst them and smiled, shaking his head. The crowd was shouting, waiting to see Hotaka's wings. "You sure got 'em riled up."

"It's because I hate liars." Through here, Midnight turned her back to leave. "I'll be returning first."

From the stage, there was a swooshing sound as everyone gasped and Midnight turned back. A pair of snow white wings was fluttering behind Hotaka's back.

"Magnificent," gasped the auctioneer into his microphone. After a moment of silent awe, the room was filled with jabbering.

"Twenty million!" bid a man.

"Fifty!"

"Sixty!" shouted a woman.

"Seventy-five!"

Midnight glared at those bidding. They were acting like savages, trying to get their hands on the last drop of water. "One hundred million!" she shouted as everyone hushed down and turned to look at her again.

The auctioneer stared, taking a few seconds before he remembered his job title. "One—one hundred million, going once, going twice-"

"Two hundred!" shouted Robin.

Midnight turned to look at him, wide-eyed while he smiled.

"Sorry love, but that boy has caught my attention. I can't have you taking him away. I must find out how he obtained those wings. In all my years of experimenting, not once have I seen anyone with wings before."

"What do you mean?"

"I've tried for so long. But all I could do was give fins, tails, ears, extra body parts—never wings. That boy is magnificent. Even if I must dissect him from head to toe, I'll find what it is that was used to give him wings."

From the beginning, she had had a hunch that this auction was setup by none other than Robin. To think he was also the one behind the experimentation was uncalled for. Quickly, she turned to face front and shouted, "Five hundred!"

"Five hundred!" repeated the auctioneer.

"Do you really think you can outbid me? I own this place after all," Robin challenged and stood. "One billion," he said calmly.

"One billion, going once, going twice! Sold to Mr. Robin!"

"You see," said Robin as he leaned over, whispering into her ear. "I'd love to make you into one of my many pieces too."

Midnight grinned, happy that he had disclosed the truth. "Don't dream on it. I've got you surrounded."

"Huh? What are you talking about?"

Laughing, Midnight backed away and climbed onto the ledge. "Watch and you'll see." Tree roots shot out from underground while vines crawled across the walls to block all exits. Flower petals fell from the ceiling, giving her a grand entrance. By this time, the crowd was screaming in fear. A Life-Kill had infiltrated the venue and was amongst them. "Hotaka!" shouted Midnight as she jumped.

"Life-Kill," Robin gasped.

While the four men were in disarray, Hotaka attacked them and flew towards Midnight, catching her before she fell. When he returned to the stage, he set her down. The four men and auctioneer were now entangled in Midnight's vines she had summoned.

"You bitch!" roared Robin. He withdrew a gun from under his jacket and fired at Midnight. Because of his fascination with her, he'd been too blind to see what was before him and got played. A gust of wind, sharper than blades shot out to shred the bullet and cut Robin.

"Lay one hand on her and you can consider yourself dead," threatened Hotaka.

"We should report this to the Dome," Midnight spoke.

"Already did."

"Well, aren't you overly-enthusiastic."

"I came prepared. I wasn't sure on what was going to happen."

"You didn't trust me, did you?"

"Not one bit," he joked and laughed.

"Didn't I say it already? I'm your Soulmate. Start trusting me alright?" Midnight turned to look at the crowd of prisoners who had been caught in her vines, even Robin who cursed. Both she and Hotaka had done a good job in securing the theater and goods. This was another successful mission to file under her name.

Hotaka stared at her, his smile never fading. "I do," he whispered.

33rd Lie

CRYSTAL SAT INSIDE the hospital room while Teo laid in bed, recuperating. It was already six in the morning, but with their failed mission weighing heavily on her mind, she barely got any sleep. A knock at the door broke through her drowsiness as she turned around, rubbing her eyes. Standing at the doorway with a bouquet of white daisies was the Champ.

He held up the bouquet and joked, "Hope he likes daisies."

Crystal smiled and stood, glad that he had a good sense of humor. She needed it. "Thank you," she said, taking the bouquet from him to set inside a vase. After filling it with water, she set it beside the bed table.

"How is he?"

"He'll live."

Relieved, the Champ smiled. "I thought I killed someone again."

Crystal stopped halfway from sitting and looked over. "What?"

"It's nothing." He shook his head and looked around the plain white room. There wasn't much to look at. Then again, this was a hospital. What had he been expecting, rainbow colored walls and painted murals?

"Come closer." Crystal sat on her chair and motioned for the Champ to come closer to the bed. "You're too far away."

"No thank you, I prefer to keep my distance."

"Alright then," she said. "So, why are you here?"

"I came to apologize."

"Why?"

"I gave him a good beating," he said and scratched his head. Though he didn't owe anyone an apology, he had an urge to do so. "I wasn't sure if you'd accept my apology after last night's fight."

A fight was a fight, especially since the title was on the line. She had nothing against him and understood. If it'd been Midnight in the ring, she'd fight for her pride and honor to the end. She wouldn't hand over her number one position to anyone—not even her friends—without a proper fight. "If it's sincere, I'll accept it any day."

"Thanks." The Champ returned the smile and reached into his pocket. He took out a pink vial and held it out. This was all he could give her to ease her mind. "Give this to him. It'll help him recover faster."

Alarmed, Crystal took it with gratitude.

"The winner of the tournament gets a whole briefcase of those. It's to help him recover faster. A supposed genius doctor created it."

"A genius, huh?" repeated Crystal. She smiled again and put the vial away in her pocket. She had a feeling she met that genius just a few hours ago. "Thank you."

"You're welcome." The Champ's cell phone rang as he took it out to silence, not wanting to be disturbed.

"You should get going. I'm sure your fans want to meet you, Champ."

He blushed, looking over at the sleeping Teo again in envy. "I'd prefer to be that guy though."

Crystal perked, her eyes widening. "You prefer to be sleeping in a bed, unconscious? Are you crazy? Isn't it much better to be in your position?"

Shaking his head, the Champ readied himself to leave. The call he had ignored was from his coach. If he didn't go, he'd get an earful later. "All I get are prizes, praises, and a gold title belt. I get no one to stand by my side when I'm exhausted. He's a lucky guy. Let him know that." The Champ waved a hand goodbye and exited.

"What a weird person."

"He was obviously flirting with you," spoke Teo.

"Wah!" shrieked Crystal. She jumped out from her chair and swirled around. "Are you trying to give me a heart attack?!"

Teo opened his eyes and turned to give her an accusing glare. "You can't even tell that he was trying to take you away from me? Even I could tell and I was supposedly unconscious."

"Nothing like that was ever exchanged between him and me."

It was a good thing Crystal was dense. This way, he didn't have to worry about rivals. "What'd he give you?"

"Nothing."

"A love letter?" accused Teo.

"Seriously?"

"Then what is it? Why can't you show me?"

Crystal smacked her forehead. He wasn't going to drop it until she gave in. She reached into her pocket, pulling out the vial the Champ had given her.

Teo sat up, eyes widening. "Isn't that what we came here for?"

"Yep, now we can go back and give it to Umi-sensei."

"Don't you mean Gabe-sensei?"

"No, Umi-sensei."

"Gabe-sensei."

Crystal nodded, giving in again. She didn't want to argue with someone who barely had any strength. "Alright, alright, we'll give it to Gabe-sensei," she said, putting the vial away to sit.

"When should we go back?"

"When you can walk."

"Then, let's leave in a few minutes. I feel better already."

"Hey," Crystal said, glaring at him. He was taking her words seriously. "Just because I said that doesn't mean-"

"But we have to quickly return. Kakinouchi…"

Crystal frowned, knowing the situation Kakinouchi was in. Even she was worried after receiving a call from Dean Kiera to quickly return. But that didn't mean Teo had to act rashly.

"We have to go and lend our support to the others."

"I know." Crystal nodded. That one, she couldn't argue with.

∞

Midnight walked around, inspecting everyone who had been captured. She was trying to find the auctioned boy with unbearable scars. Frantic, she pushed people out of the way. The police were swarming the building on orders from the Dome to imprison anyone who was part of the illegal auction. A few ambulances also came to give aide to the humans who had been captured and abused.

"Who are you trying to find?" Hotaka got in her way, one eyebrow raised. He'd been watching her run around with her head cut off. Whatever she was trying to find, he didn't like how it made her so desperate.

"Someone," Midnight answered.

"Tell me. Maybe I can help."

"A boy, about fifteen, he has a burnt scar on his left chest."

"Kinda specific, aren't you?"

"Did you see him or not?"

"Yeah, he was getting checked by the EMT girl." Hotaka pointed to the third ambulance as Midnight ran off. "Whoa, wait for me." He chased her from behind as they approached the ambulance and stopped. The boy was still there, a blanket wrapped around his scrawny body. He was shivering from the chilly morning.

Midnight fixed her hair, hoping she looked presentable and smiled. "Hi there, I'm-" she greeted in a shaky voice as the boy flinched and cowered, downcasting his eyes. Seeing his reaction to her speak, a floodgate of guilt opened. What kind of hell did he go through while they had been separated? How could she ever help him to heal? "What's your name?"

Instead of speaking, the boy remained silent and refused to look up. He sat and held his shattered body.

"Oye boy, she's talking to you," snapped Hotaka.

Midnight turned, hissing at him for interjecting himself in their emotional reunion.

Ignoring her hiss, Hotaka continued speaking to the boy, "Speak when you're being spoken to."

"That's enough. You're making it worse."

"M—my name is Mere," he answered.

At the sound of his soft voice, Midnight spun away from Hotaka and back to the boy. "Mere," she repeated and quickly wiped the tear that trickled down her cheek.

Hotaka took notice of the warmth in her tone and scowled. She had no need to use such a loving tone with a stranger. Even the way she was looking at the boy got on his nerves. "We have to report back to the Dome, Midnight," Hotaka reminded and grabbed her hand possessively to leave.

"Mid...night," Mere repeated as tears flooded his own eyes. Finally, he looked up as the two made eye contact for the first time. At sixteen, she still looked the same as when they had been kids. He'd expected her to be taller, but she'd received their mother's height genes. It felt so surreal Mere thought he was hallucinating. Or maybe he was dreaming with his eyes open. "Nee...chan...?"

"Huh? Nee-chan?" repeated Hotaka in disbelief. Was the boy going senile? Why was he claiming Midnight as his older sister?

Midnight pulled free from Hotaka's grip to take a step forward. Now that he was properly looking at her, she could finally say what it was that was in her heart. "I've finally acquired the power to protect you."

"What are you talking about?" asked a confused Hotaka.

Unable to blink, Mere stared at Midnight who opened her arms to him. His heart ached and soon the tears trailed down his dirty cheeks. Her words from the past, he could still recall.

"Don't worry." She looked down at him and smiled. they were only five and four years old then, not strong enough to tackle the world on their own. "Nothing will happen to us. Even if we have no parents, we can survive. I'll give you all the things we couldn't have. Trust me. I'll definitely protect you."

This is no dream or hallucination, Mere concluded. This was reality he was seeing. The one thing he had been trying to find had found him instead, and after being separated for so many years, they were finally reunited. "Nee-chan," he whispered, falling into Midnight's embrace. "It's really you."

She smiled and squeezed him with all her might, crying as well. Now that he was in her arms again, she'd never let anyone or anything separate them again. "Sorry, it took me so long."

Hotaka gaped at the two with bulging eyes. He pointed a finger, trying to find his voice but nothing would come out. Finally, he erupted and reached out to break them apart. "What are you doing, Midnight?! Let the boy go!"

"Don't come in-between our sibling love!"

"You can't go around adopting strange kids!"

"He's not a strange kid!"

Mere chuckled at Hotaka's misinterpretation, and suddenly found himself in an interesting position. "Nee-chan," he said, snuggling close to her. "Who's this stranger?"

"You!" Hotaka pointed again and glared. "Stop touching her so casually! Even I haven't done that!"

"Don't say that! It's sounds wrong!" Midnight shouted, her tears ceasing at once. After thinking they could be great partners, Hotaka had reverted to his hateful ways. "People will misunderstand us!"

"Midnight-nee," said Mere as he grinned. "He's scaring me."

"Knock it off you bully!" she screamed.

Hotaka gnashed his teeth together, suddenly getting a bad vibe. The boy claiming to be Mere was going to turn his love life upside down. If he didn't do something fast, he'd regret it for the rest of his life. "I'm gonna cut that runt up into pieces!"

"Come near him and I'll have Umeko poison you!" threatened Midnight as the sun peeked out from the east.

∞

Yuudai groaned and shook his head while standing beside Morgana's bedside. He'd been trying to wake her up for the past ten minutes. "Morgana, come on, wake up. It's morning," he commanded and shook her as she pushed him away.

"Leave me alone."

If he wanted to wake her up, he'd have to come up with a more creative way. At that, a light bulb lit inside his mind. He bent over, cupping his mouth. "Aoi, come wake Morgana for me!"

Clumsily, she sat up and wiped her mouth, for fear of having drool. She rubbed her eyes, and fixed her brown hair to look around. "Where?" Morgana asked desperately. "Where's Aoi-kun?"

"With Soria," answered Yuudai as he ran out, laughing.

"You!" She grabbed her pillow to toss at him, but it ended up hitting the door and falling to the floor.

Yuudai sneered while making his way into the kitchen. "That's what she gets," he said, grabbing two sets of silverware to set on the table. Within a few minutes, an angry Morgana came stalking out in her Wonder Woman pajamas. She put her hands on her hips, then pointed a finger while he sat with a huge grin. "Come eat. I cooked."

"You," said Morgana.

"Breakfast first." He motioned to the second chair as Morgana obediently sat.

"I'll forgive you this once because you made breakfast today."

"What are you talking about? I've been cooking breakfast every day because you're too lazy to wake up and cook."

"No one needs to know that."

"Poor Aoi," Yuudai said, letting out sniffles. He wanted to tease her some more and see what she would say. How could he resist seeing her squirm? It was the highlight of his day. "He'll never get to eat a decent breakfast when he wakes up."

"Don't say that! When we start dating, I'll cook breakfast, even if it means forcing myself to wake up at three."

"No matter how much you dote on him, he doesn't like girls like you."

Choking on her food from the shocking revelation, Morgana grabbed her cup of juice to gulp, then set it down. She took a few deep breaths before asking, "He doesn't like girls like me?"

"Nope," answered Yuudai.

"Then," she said, leaning forward, hoping to get any kind of information out of him. "What's Aoi-kun's type?"

"He already found her and it's Soria," responded Yuudai. He laughed and went back to eating.

"Stop joking with me." Morgana glared some more, refusing to eat.

Giving her no choice, Yuudai grabbed a piece of sausage to force in her mouth as she shrieked. "Why would I lie? I'm telling you the truth. Aoi really does like Soria. You don't think so?"

"No, dey're only bartnerz," Morgana said, her mouth full.

Yuudai let out a muffled laugh and turned away. How could she not know something so simple as that when she was constantly chasing Aoi? Did she not follow who his gaze was always directed at?

"Now what?"

"It's just that you're dead wrong. He's always liked Soria. There's no way in hell he'd let her go." Yuudai shook his head and looked over. Morgana had stopped chewing the sausage he fed her. She was staring at him intently, like she was going to burst into tears. Yuudai's heart lurched in that moment. He smiled and waved off his words. Even if he was telling the truth, he hated how she only showed him sorrow. It didn't make him feel any better. "It was a joke, a joke. He doesn't like Soria. His type is someone like Hana or Hanabi, cute and feminine."

"Eh?"

"You can ask him for the truth when you see him." Yuudai finished his food, ready to leave first. Just then, his phone rang as he stood to go answer it. "Dean," he greeted with a slight bow to the hologram.

"Where are you?" Dean Kosa asked, sitting inside his office.

"Still in Taipei. Why?"

"Either finish your mission by tomorrow night or return by then."

"Why?" Yuudai repeated, suddenly concerned.

"Your next mission is already under way, and it's ranked S."

Morgana stopped eating to swirl around in her chair. Her eyes widened as she rushed over to Yuudai's side to greet the dean also. "Wh—what happened?" she stammered.

"Your comrades are in a heap of trouble and Mina needs back-up. Which is why, you are to return as soon as possible. We need all the help we can lend them, understood?"

"Understood," the two responded as Dean Kosa disconnected.

"Mina," Morgana repeated.

"What?" Yuudai asked, turning to look at her. "You know her?"

"Yeah, I met her once at the Dome."

Yuudai nodded and turned to face front again. If Morgana knew this Mina girl, then their third mission meant serious business. They didn't have the leisure to fool around anymore. It was time to get serious.

"What do you think happened? And who do you think is in trouble?"

"I don't know. But let's finish and hurry back to the Dome."

"Yeah," agreed Morgana.

"Alright, I have the perfect strategy."

"Eh?" said Morgana in alarm. She couldn't believe that Yuudai had already come up with a way to complete their mission in just a few minutes. "It seems I've underestimated you."

Yuudai grinned and crossed his arms in a superior manner. "It's too bad your beloved Aoi-kun isn't a genius like me," he insulted.

Morgana snapped, chasing him around the hotel room with her fist waving in the air, "Stop making fun of Aoi-kun!" After a few minutes of playing cat and mouse, she gave up and bent over, panting for air.

Yuudai who stopped running to stand in the living room, raised an eyebrow. Morgana seemed to be having problems breathing. He couldn't help but smile. "Should I perform CPR?"

"I don't want your lips over mine."

A loud laugh erupted from Yuudai as he turned away, wiping the tears in his eyes. Her rejection caused him more heartache than she could possibly imagine. If he could kiss her just once in this lifetime, he could give his life.

"So, what's your genius plan?" Morgana asked once she caught her breath.

"You're gonna go and apply for a hostess job at the bar," he answered.

"And why would I do something so foolish?"

"Because the bar is for members only and they don't let just anyone in, even for women. Besides, we need a general layout of the place."

"And what about you?"

"You just let me worry about that," he said with a sly grin.

"When do we begin?"

"You go in today to apply. Tomorrow night, we set this plan into motion. Be sure to wear a red one-piece dress, alright? We want our target to take notice of you."

"Are you messing with me again?" she snarled.

"No, I'm not. I'm just letting you know that all men love one pieces on women, even your beloved Aoi-kun."

"Eh?" Morgana quickly blushed and fidgeted with her fingers. If Aoi liked women who wore one pieces, then she would go along with Yuudai's plans. "It seems it can't be helped," she complied.

"Simpleton," muttered Yuudai. "Anyway," he said, clearing his throat, "you lockdown on our target and start flirting with him. Get him to loosen up so he doesn't get suspicious and flee. Once you've gotten him to lower his guard, I'll take it from there and electrocute everyone."

"Why would you do such a thing?"

"I'm sure everyone in that bar is conspiring together. If I don't take them out at once, they'll harm you."

Why did it feel like this was a honey trap? Surely there was another way where they could attack together and bring in the target without having to resort to any of this. Then again, Morgana had no plans of her own, and Yuudai was overly confident about his.

"You got the plan?" he interrupted her thoughts.

"Yeah, and it's stupid. Why do I need you to save me for?"

Yuudai knew she was going to object to his plan, which was why he was ready to play the Aoi card again. "But Morgana, if something were to happen to you, your beloved Aoi-kun would never forgive me." He gave her the saddest puppy-eyed look and let out a sniffle.

"Eh? Well then, in that case, please, do save me." Morgana bowed and stood. If it meant that her well-being would keep Aoi happy, she would allow herself to be saved.

Having had enough of her love sickness, he flicked her forehead as she yelped. Yuudai crossed his arms, shaking his head at her. No matter how many times he said it, Morgana still didn't get the point across her head. "Stop dreaming about Aoi already. He doesn't care nor think about you. In fact, you're not even within his line of sight. Only Soria is." Yuudai turned and stalked away, cursing under his breath.

"What's with you suddenly?!" Morgana rubbed her forehead and clicked her tongue at Yuudai's back. "He's got a rotten personality. If not for his face, he'd have nothing going for him."

34th Lie

MORGANA EXITED the dressing room in her red one-piece. Her hair was curled, and her makeup was done to complement her dress. Even her accessories glittered red. It was as Yuudai had suspected, the members-only bar was swarming with security. It'd been a good thing she followed his orders and stole a copy of the building's blueprint yesterday.

After scanning the dimly lit room and finding her target, a man in his fifties, smoking and drinking near the back, Morgana cleared her throat and walked over. When the group of middle-aged men and young girls in loose dresses noticed her, they stopped laughing. She was making quite an entrance in her red dress. With her most seductive smile, Morgana leaned over, revealing her cleavage. "Good evening," she greeted with a wink.

"Good evening," greeted the men.

"May I join you?"

"Of course," said one of the men. He quickly made room for her, but she ignored him, aiming for the man with the most girls and forced herself in-between them.

"Well hello there, cutie," greeted Morgana.

"Feisty," said the man as he laughed with his buddies. The other girls simply glared at the newbie for trying to bait their big fish away. "Are you new here? I've never seen you before."

"I am."

"I figured. I would remember a beauty such as yourself," he said, touching her chin. "What's your name?"

"Morgan."

"Morgan. What an exquisite name for an exquisite woman," complimented the man. "Would you like a drink?"

"Most definitely," she said and nodded as they ordered another round of shots. As per Yuudai's instructions, Morgana fearlessly drank two shots.

"Whoo!" cheered on the middle-aged men. They clapped their hands impressed, while the other girls intensified their glares. Luring men was a cinch. If only this could work with Aoi.

"You sure are one tough cookie."

"So tell me, what's your name, cutie?" Morgana asked, leaning towards him. She put her index finger on his bulging stomach, running it all over.

"You're very upfront, aren't you?"

"Yes, I am. I hate playing games."

"Why do you want to know for?"

"For tonight, silly," she answered and took hold of his tie to twirl in her fingers. "If you know what I mean," she said with a giggle.

The man laughed and threw his head back. He was starting to like Morgana more and more. A confident woman who could hold her end always got his attention.

"You can't be serious about her," said one of the other girls.

"Like I said before, she's exquisite," he answered, leaning towards Morgana. He put his mouth to her ear to answer the question. "My name-"

"May I call you Boo?" interrupted Morgana.

Again, he laughed. "Call me whatever you like."

"Then, Boo it is."

"Waiter, another round over here!"

Ten minutes into their conversation, Morgana was laughing and giggling uncontrollably. Her cheeks were pink from all the drinking she'd done, and the room was starting to spin a little. She felt full of euphoria, like she was flying without wings.

"So, Morgan, how about we return to my room now?" suggested Boo.

Morgana looked over and pouted. She set her drink down and cupped his chubby face in her hands, shaking both their heads in refusal. "I can't do that Boo."

"Why not?"

"I only wanna go with Aoi-kun."

"Who?"

"I said, it can only be-"

"Ladies and gentlemen!" Yuudai interrupted, standing on top of the bar counter, hands raised into the air. A mask concealed his identity while he wore a cape like a magician. "Tonight, I will show you all a wonderful magical performance!"

"Who's that fool? Get him down. He's ruining my fun," Boo instructed to the guards standing behind him.

"Yes, sir," they answered and bowed to go throw Yuudai out of the bar.

"Seems like it's already begun." Yuudai smiled and snapped both fingers as the lights died, causing everyone to panic. A few seconds later, the lights returned but nothing changed. Nothing was missing, except for Morgana.

Yuudai laughed from where he hid and snapped his fingers again. The lights died once again as the girls screamed and made a run for it.

"Kill that bastard! He's one of *them*!" shouted Boo. He stood and ran for the back exit of the bar with his men. When he made it out, he came face-to-face with Yuudai. "How-"

"That was too easy." Electricity sparked from his hands and struck Boo's men, rendering them motionless. They fell to the ground as the bar's electrical cords sparked and overheated, quickly setting fire. "Come," said Yuudai as he dragged the pudgy Boo away.

"Please, spare me!"

"That's exactly what I'm doing by bringing you to the Dome. If not for that fact, I would've fried you for touching my Soulmate in such a lewd way."

"It can't be," Boo said, quivering. Of all the people to meet, he had to come across Dome Soulmates. And of all places to be imprisoned and tortured, it had to be one of the seven Domes. He would rather face Hades and the fires of the underworld than to be presented to the Golden God at the Golden Palace like a sacrifice. "Then don't spare me! I prefer to die than go with you!"

"Shut up you overgrown pig." Yuudai knocked Boo out and bound his ankles and wrists together before tossing him into the trunk of the car. After shutting the door, he got into the driver's side. Sleeping in the passenger seat was Morgana. "How could you not know that your drink got spiked? Good thing I intervened before you blew our cover." He reached into the backseat and grabbed a blanket to cover her with. Smiling, Yuudai fixed her brown hair. "Sweet dreams," he said, driving off into the smoky night.

∞

Alice hung up her cell phone and smiled in relief. She was sitting in the upstairs lounge room with Verse. More than half of the couples had returned to the mansion. Now, they were just waiting on those who had yet to finish their missions. "Midnight's on her way back."

"That's good to hear."

Alice turned to look at Verse who was eating snacks without a care. "I want an honest answer," she said from out of the blue.

Verse raised an eyebrow, wondering why she was so serious suddenly. "I can't guarantee you anything."

"I heard from Tanaka-sensei that you failed horribly at your mission."

Verse let out a snort and threw a chip into her mouth to chew. It was a given that she'd fail when she hadn't even been serious from the start. "I wouldn't necessarily say that."

"Tell me and I'll decide."

"Well, I let our targets escape after capturing them."

"You failed HORRIBLY," agreed Alice. "Why would you do that?"

Verse looked over and sneered. Alice wouldn't understand her reasons for doing so, but still answered, "I let them go so I could have the joy of catching them again."

"What?"

"I mean, think about it. When you catch a bunny in the wild, you'd want to let it go just to have the thrill of catching it again, right?"

Alice sweat a bit. She couldn't believe the logic behind Verse's failure and shook her head. "And what happened that made your mission so fun you'd want to let them go?"

"I let them capture me and tie me up to make fun of Naruyuki." Verse smiled and reached for the remote to turn on the holographic TV screen.

Unable to help herself, Alice laughed. Every time she thought she had Verse figured out, Verse would give her a run for her money. Standing and stretching, Alice headed out, her stomach growling. "Be back."

"Yeah," Verse said as Love came out from within the bedroom next door.

"Eh? Where's Alice?" asked Love.

"Somewhere."

"Where?"

"Who knows?"

"Geez Verse, it wouldn't kill you to ask." Love scowled and chased after Alice. Hopefully she hadn't gotten far.

"And why should I keep tabs for?" Verse retorted, sliding through channels. After deciding to watch a comedy drama, she dozed off, dreaming about her childhood.

"Wait for me!" shouted a breathless Remi who ran, trying to keep up with the three.

Verse glanced back and let out a frustrated groan. She was tired of having Remi follow them a like a lost puppy. In fact, Verse didn't understand why they had to play with her in the first place. She had a '70's bob-cut hairstyle. It was out of fashion, and she was slow. Everything about her got on Verse's nerves. "Ugh, why is she always tagging along?"

"She's Soria's friend," answered Yeve.

Verse scowled while Soria slowed down to let Remi catch up. Eventually, Yeve slowed her pace too, forcing Verse to stop and wait as well. "I really hate her."

"Verse," called out Miss Umi.

Quickly, Verse awoke to find Miss Umi standing before her. "Sensei," she greeted, standing up to bow and rub her eyes.

"Were you dreaming just now?"

"Not really."

"Don't lie to me."

Verse stared back at Miss Umi who stared intently. There was no use in lying. Miss Umi would beat the truth out of her if necessary. "I did," she answered and yawned.

"Remi?" she guessed.

Verse grinned and nodded. "Is there something I can help you with, sensei?"

Miss Umi nodded, waving at her to follow. "Come. I need to do a quick check-up," she said and took the lead.

"Why am I getting a check-up for?"

"Everyone is."

"Why?"

"To make sure you're not defective."

"Defective?"

"It's a mandatory routine check-up to make sure your brain's not defective."

Still suspicious, Verse decided to leave it as it was. She had a feeling she shouldn't pry because the answers to her questions would only be devastating.

∞

After catching up with Alice, the two went directly to the vending machines downstairs to get some snacks before going on a walk in the gardens. Love reached out to grab the bag of cookies as the tiny door slid open. "I heard you attacked Poe during your mission."

Alice looked over in alarm and eventually nodded. She should've known that it would get out somehow. "I did," she answered guiltily. Love moved as Alice pressed her thumb against the scanner. She punched a red button in front of the Snickers candy bar. A small door slid open as the candy bar popped out for Alice to take.

"What happened?"

"I can't really remember."

Love furrowed her brows, but didn't press for answers. "Want to know what happened with me?"

"What?" she asked as they moved on to get some drinks. Halfway into Love's story, Alice spaced out. The incident back at the village still weighed heavily on her mind. No matter how many times she assured herself that it wasn't something to worry about, her heart would disagree.

"Alice-nee!" called out a faraway voice.

Despite Alice not knowing the owner's voice, she responded and spun around. The hallway was as desolate as a desert.

"…and then I summoned Soria to help me…" Love continued, not noticing how distraught her friend was.

Alice rubbed her forehead and laughed to herself. She felt like she was slowly going insane after returning. When Love moved out of the way, Alice scanned her thumb against the scanner, ready to press the red button in front of the orange drink.

"…did you know that Soria could fly inside a water circle bubble thingamajig? It was pretty amazing…"

Grunting, Alice dropped her snacks and hit her knees.

"Alice!" Love shouted, also dropping her things to kneel. "Are you okay?"

"Just a migraine."

A migraine wouldn't cause someone to drop to their knees. Love scanned the hallway for help, but saw no one else. She was alone on this. "Come on. I'll take you back to your room."

"…and then-" began Naruyuki as he and Dark came into the hallway to get some snacks too. As soon as they spotted the girls, they stopped.

"It hurts!" Alice screamed and cried.

"Shit," Dark said as they ran over. "What happened to her?"

"I don't know," Love replied, still holding Alice. "Suddenly her head started hurting."

"Alice, look at me," commanded Naruyuki as he took hold of her arms. He wasn't a healer for nothing. When she looked up, tears streamed down her face. "Why-"

"Oye you two, why'd you leave me behind for?!" called out Poe as he rounded the corner, yawning. Once his eyes fell on his crying Soulmate, he frantically ran over. "Alice!"

At the sight of him, her blood froze and the hatred from that night resurfaced. "You," she gasped, pushing the others away to withdraw her gun. "Don't come near me!"

Loss for words, Poe halted in his tracks. Again, she was bearing her weapon at him.

From behind, someone knocked her out and caught her. "Dear goodness," complained Miss Umi. "It's one after the other."

Verse stood aside, about as shocked as Poe was. "What was that?"

"She was just overreacting."

"Overreacting my ass!" Verse's fists trembled by her side. She gnashed her teeth together and glared at Miss Umi who was harboring a secret. If it killed Verse, she would get to the bottom of it. "She was obviously trying to kill her Soulmate just now. Why would she do that?"

"This has nothing to do with you!" Miss Umi barked, turning back to hold Verse's gaze. This was the end of their conversation. "Stay out of it."

"What are you hiding?"

"I'm taking Alice with me. Your check-up can wait." Miss Umi picked up Alice and the gun before walking over to stop before Poe. "Forgive her. The drugs still haven't worn off." She did her best to smile and left with Alice dangling over her shoulder.

The hallway became quiet as they watched Miss Umi leave, except Poe. He had his back to them, finding it hard to breathe. Why was this happening again? Deep in her heart, did she secretly hate him?

"What was that about?" asked Dark suspiciously.

"Don't know," answered Love.

Instead of worrying about their conversation, Naruyuki stared at Verse who was still upset. "Verse," he called out.

Without a word, she turned her back to leave.

"Verse!"

"Uh," said Love worriedly. She wasn't sure on how to handle the situation. Suddenly, everything had turned for the worse. What was she supposed to do? Run after her friend? Or comfort the guys? All the choices were horrible. Even Naruyuki was refusing to chase after Verse.

"YO!" Soria greeted, running down the hallway towards them. She was smiling and waving, happy to be reunited again. In her hand was a bag of junk food she'd bought from town. It was for Verse and Shayla to share. "I'M BAAAACK!"

"Soria!" shouted Love in alarm.

"WHERE'S MY WELCOME BACK PAR-" Soria began and stopped, sensing the tense atmosphere. She lowered her arm to her side, her playful attitude vanishing.

"Soria, why'd you leave me behind for?! That's super rude!" Aoi shouted, running towards them. When he sensed how uptight everyone was, he quickly shut his mouth.

"Love, what happened here?" Soria snarled.

Gulping, Love stammered, "Eh? Uh, well uh…"

"Verse better not have been involved."

"Uh, well, she wasn't…kinda."

Without a word, Soria turned and walked out to search for Verse.

"Where are you going?" asked Aoi.

"To shit."

"Didn't you go already?"

"Aoi," snapped the guys.

"Sorry," he apologized, smiling innocently. He'd been hoping to cheer everyone up with a light joke, but it backfired. "So…how's everyone been? Good?"

"Let's go back," they said, leaving one by one.

"What the heck is with this situation?" Aoi grumbled, now the only one standing in the deserted hallway. "I suddenly feel so lost and out of place."

∞

Manila, Philippines

It was a beautiful day with the wind blowing through Hanabi's hair, yet she couldn't seem to stop perspiring. From ahead, Louis was happily reminiscing about his youthful days at the Dome. Hanabi tried her best to listen and engage in the conversation but her mind was elsewhere.

"Ah sorry," apologized a gentleman who bumped into her.

"It's okay." She smiled, shaking it off.

"I'm sorry," he apologized again before running off, late for a date.

Once the stranger was gone, Hanabi threw a hand to her mouth. She stopped following Louis and leaned against a building wall.

"-and then-" Louis chattered, turning to his side where Hanabi was missing. He spun back, worried. "Hanabi?" he called out, rushing over to support her. "What's wrong?"

"I feel like puking."

Louis scanned their surrounding and spotted a café not far away. Without asking, he picked her up and ran towards the café.

"Uh-" Hanabi protested. She hadn't expected him to carry her.

"You need to save your energy." When they reached the café, Louis set her down on a chair beside a table and ran inside the café to order a cup of water. After paying and getting the drink, he ran back out to hand the water to Hanabi. "Here you go."

She smiled and took the cup. "Thanks."

"Anytime," he answered, sitting across from her. "Feeling better?"

"Yeah," answered Hanabi. She sipped her cold water, the color returning to her face. Even her breathing had evened out.

"I knew your powers were strong, but not that strong."

"What?"

"Your powers," repeated Louis as he smiled. It wasn't hard to guess that Hanabi's powers had kicked in at such a time. "It must be strong."

"It's inconvenient."

"But it's strong."

"Why do you say that?"

"Ever since our duel, I've been keeping tabs on you. So, I know how strong you really are."

Hanabi chuckled and took a drink of her water as silence settled in. The rich people surrounding them chatted away, drinking their coffees and eating their muffins without a care in the world.

"What are you thinking about?" Louis asked, interrupting her thoughts.

"It's as you say. My powers are too strong. Sometimes I can't handle it and it completely takes me by surprise." Hanabi turned her cup of water around in circles before pointing to a young couple sitting outside, enjoying the sun. They were on the opposite street. "See them?"

Louis turned to look and nodded. "Yeah, I do." He inspected the couple that was happily joking. The girl had green hair with streaks of purple and wore designer clothing. She was a perfect beauty queen with an even more perfect pearly smile. On her right ring finger was a simple band. The gentleman sitting opposite her wore no designer clothing and wasn't as attractive, but the air surrounding him was calming. His only redeeming quality were his eyes. They were a deep blue, like tanzanite. He too wore a band on his right ring finger. Despite their differences, they complimented each other quite well.

"Do you know how much money that spoiled girl has spent on plastic surgery alone?"

"Eh? You mean she's not natural?"

Hanabi smiled and shook her head. Was a pretty girl always assumed to have been born so perfect? And if she had been born perfect, was it always assumed that she'd gone under the knife? This world was full of contradictions. "She's spent nearly twenty million golden dollars on her looks alone. And don't even get me started on her wardrobe."

"Wow," Louis said with a whistle. He could never imagine spending that much money to fix his imperfections when he could be spending it on more important things.

"That middle-class man is going to die within two months."

"Wait. What?"

Hanabi smiled. Again, she drank her water then set it down. "I bumped into him a while ago and unwillingly saw his past. He's been diagnosed with a heart disease since he was thirteen. The doctors said he wouldn't live past eighteen. Yet he miraculously defied that fate and is now twenty. Just two days ago he fainted and was sent to the hospital. His condition has worsened. His heart is rapidly failing. And as you and I both know, if you don't have money, you can't get a heart transplant. Those couple's rings, he bought with his hard-earned money. Even though he's smiling with her now, he'll die soon, but I guess that's for the best."

It grew quiet amongst them again as Hanabi went back to drinking her water. Suddenly, Louis erupted, "how can you say that it's okay? It's not okay at all. Someone's going to die."

Hanabi stopped drinking to stare at him long and hard. "Why are you getting so emotional? They have nothing to do with you."

"Still, how can you just sit there and say that it's okay for him to die? Don't you think his girlfriend has a right to know?"

"No," she answered flatly.

Louis couldn't believe his ears. Hanabi, whom he thought to be sensitive and caring was saying something so cruel. It was wrong to wish for someone—*anyone* to die. "Why are you like that?"

"How am I like?"

"Sometimes you act so cold, I just don't understand you."

"Neither do I understand you," Hanabi redirected.

"I can't," he said, taking a stand. "I can't sit here and do nothing after hearing what you just said. His girlfriend has a right to know about his condition." Louis turned his back on her and ran towards the young couple, hoping to save them from heartache.

"Louis-" Hanabi called out. She slammed her water cup down and stood to chase him before he made a fool of himself.

"Excuse me!" shouted Louis as he approached the couple and bowed.

"What is it?" responded the healthy looking young man. Up close, there seemed to be nothing wrong with him.

Looks are deceiving. If Hanabi said that he was going to die, then Louis believed it. Hanabi was someone who only spoke the truth. "You may not know me. But I must tell your girlfriend something."

"What?" he asked, confused.

Louis turned towards the pretty rich girl and took hold of her arms. From behind he could hear Hanabi shouting. Any second now, she would come and yank him away. Now was the time to speak or forever hold his peace. "Miss, your-"

It all happened so quickly. One moment Louis was standing before the couple, then the next, he was suddenly standing inside a luxurious sparkly room. Hanging on the pink walls were posters of hunky models. To one side of the bedroom sat a gorgeous makeup vanity, made of oak, where makeup and jewelry boxes sat. Lying on a pink bed with pink draperies with pink pillows was the girlfriend. She was on the phone talking to her friends.

Louis groaned, smacking himself on the forehead. This was the worst timing for his Future Sight to kick in. In the past he used to feel groggy, now as a teenager, he was getting accustomed to the random transportations.

"...he's so pathetic," said the girlfriend. She took the band off her finger and tossed it to the floor, not wanting to be seen wearing something so shabby. With a giggle, she turned onto her back while a stunned Louis recalled Hanabi's words about how the boyfriend had bought the band with his hard-earned money. But she discarded it without remorse.

"Tell me about it, he's so in love with me. I bet if I were to tell him to jump off a cliff, he would. That's how crazy Jabol is about me. I guess poor people really will succumb to anything when in the presence of wealth." Again, she laughed, her friend agreeing from the other end. "Yeah, papa wants me to meet a potential tycoon client's son next Friday. If we hit it off, he wants us to get married by the end of the year."

All the strength in Louis' body drained as he sank to his knees. He couldn't even find it within himself to shout. All he could do was listen to her ridicule the poor dying man. She laughed some more with her friend over the phone, not realizing Louis' invisible presence in the room. Slowly, he crept over to the lonely band on the floor and touched it gently. Like the speed of light, he was whisked back to reality.

"You're scaring me," said the girlfriend.

"Let her go," Jabol said, reaching out to pull Louis away from touching his girlfriend.

"I'm sorry about him," apologized Hanabi. Once she reached their side, she yanked Louis away and gave a wry smile.

"Are you okay, Bora?" asked Jabol.

"Yeah, I'm fine," she answered with a nod. Bora stared at Louis, not appreciating his creepy silent stare. "Are you his girlfriend?" she directed towards Hanabi.

"You can say that."

"You should keep him on a tight leash. Someone might put him down one of these days. He can't go around touching people like me." She dusted her shoulders where Louis had touched and flicked her hair like some diva.

Hanabi's fake smile quickly faded. She lowered herself to Bora's level and hissed, "Now you listen, and you listen well bitch, run that mouth again while in my presence and I'll cut it off."

Bora's eyes widened at the threat. She opened her mouth to retaliate, but Hanabi gave her a daring look saying, "Don't believe me? Try running that mouth a second time. I'm waiting for you to challenge me." Bora decided against it and shut her mouth, suddenly afraid. When she got home, she would get her father to find the couple and dispose of them for crossing her.

"Let's go," Hanabi said, dragging a confused and sad Louis away. Once they were far away enough, she let go. "I can't believe I just threatened someone I didn't even know. Shoot, Yeve's wearing off on me too." Hanabi laughed and shook her head. Remembering that Louis was with her, she glanced back. "And you, I didn't tell you so you could try and be a hero."

Chest heaving, Louis leaned against the building for support. He gasped for air as tears filled his eyes.

"Did your powers kick in too?"

"What else did you not tell me?" he asked, glaring at her.

"Why are you giving me that look for?"

"What else are you hiding?!"

Hanabi's eyes widened at his outburst towards her. Why was he accusing her of wrongdoing when she had done nothing?

"Tell me the rest."

"You already know," Hanabi whispered, able to read his eyes. "Why ask?"

"I want to hear it."

"The moment I sensed her feelings of disgust towards him, it wasn't hard to detect how she only uses people. She's the worst kind of human there is. She made a bet with her friends to date that guy. If they lasted for six months, her friends would have to buy her whatever she wanted." Hanabi narrowed her eyes in on him. Now it was her turn to ask. "What did *you* see?"

Louis looked away and squeezed his eyes shut. If only he hadn't seen that future, everything would've been fine. But would it really have? "Is that why you said it was better for him to just…die?"

"Honestly?"

"Honestly."

"Yes."

"I see." Louis nodded again. This time, he laughed and put a hand to his face. "I guess you're right. It would be better for him to die than to live in agony with that kind of woman."

"What did you see?" demanded Hanabi.

Without a reply, Louis pulled away from the building wall to leave.

"Louis-kun!" called out Hanabi. She attempted to follow, but stopped. He was discharging a strong emotion, causing her to feel nauseous again.

"I wonder if these powers are actually a curse instead of a gift." Louis looked down at his trembling hands, then back at Hanabi who should be following him. Instead, he spotted her still at the same spot, leaning against the building for support. He was the reason that she looked like she might burst into tears. "It's a curse," he concluded to the wind.

35th Lie

WAKANAI, HOKKAIDO

Rain was out in the front, wearing a waiter's uniform, serving customers coffee, tea, and cakes. More than half of them were middle-aged women and girls in high school, hoping to catch a glimpse of the unattainable apple. Every time Rain walked by, they sighed dreamily, wishing he knew their darkest desires that involved him.

Meanwhile, in the back of the small café bakery, Yeve was baking the cakes that Rain was selling.

Before hopping onto a train to Hokkaido, Yeve dropped by a bookstore to buy a few cookbooks. She had to perfect her baking skills, so she could be hired by Heidi, the bakery owner who was their objective.

With her black hair tied into a ponytail, Yeve wore a white chef's uniform and a small white hat, along with an apron. Her hands were covered with white powder after making cream puffs. Walking over to the sink, Yeve washed her hands to begin a velvet cake with whipped cream and strawberry halves to go on top of each slice.

"Wow, you're working so hard," praised Heidi. She entered the backroom and smiled, admiring Yeve's hard work.

"It's my job," answered Yeve. "Everything I do, I do with precision. That's my pride."

"Has anyone told you that you're super uptight?" Heidi chuckled as her jade-like eyes sparkled. She pulled out a stool to sit on and brushed her natural auburn hair out of her eyes. The structure of her face was sharp, showing off her American aspects.

"Break?" asked Yeve as she grabbed three eggs, ready to make her velvet cake from scratch.

"Yeah," answered Heidi. She yawned tiredly and threw her head back to look at the ceiling. When she first opened the bakery shop, she didn't think it'd be so stressful. Now, all she wanted to do was go on a picnic and bask under the sun. "Ah, I'm so jealous."

"Of?"

"I want to be young again and have a handsome boyfriend."

Yeve dropped the egg in her hand as it hit the counter and cracked. "Shoot," she said.

Heidi noticed and smiled. Whenever the topic came anywhere close to Rain, Yeve always acted out of character. "Why are you suddenly so self-conscious? I wasn't talking about you and Rain-kun."

"I'm not dating him." Yeve shook her head to clean the cracked egg. As future Empress, she had to get her emotions under control and not let Heidi jerk her around by the chain.

"Really? Then can I have him?"

"Go ahead."

"It was a joke, a joke Yeve-chan. Sheesh don't get so serious."

"But I am. Go ahead and take Rain away."

Baffled, only incoherent sounds came out from Heidi's mouth. Yeve was taking this joke too far. After calming down, Heidi watched her grab a new egg from the refrigerator to crack into the stainless-steel bowl. She was as composed as before. "May I ask why?"

"He hates me."

"Huh? Why?"

"I don't know, and I don't care."

Heidi glared at Yeve's profile. It was bizarre for the young couple to hate each other and still be together. None of it made sense. Besides, that wasn't how she saw things. Maybe the young couple was just bad at communicating. "Why would you say such a thing? Have you confirmed it yet?"

"No, but I know it."

"How can you possibly know something you haven't confirmed?"

"I just do."

"Is this your way of saying that you hate Rain-kun?"

"I don't know how I feel about him yet."

"Huh?!" Heidi shouted in exasperation and pulled at her hair. Yeve's demeanor and tone was enough to get her worked up. "Then why are you together?"

"Unspeakable circumstances," was all Yeve said.

"Are you sure that's the case?"

"Yes."

"That's not how I see it-" Heidi shook her head and spotted the slightly parted backdoor from the corner of her eye. She couldn't help but smile, wanting to tease them. "Even if you don't know how you feel about him yet, don't you think Rain-kun is handsome though?"

"Hmm," Yeve said, debating.

"Have you seriously never given his chiseled face a glimpse? And what about that body? Or that silky gray hair? Do you even have eyes?"

"FYI, I do. It's just that, in all the years I've known him, I never seriously gave it a second thought. Now that you mention it, I guess he's alright," Yeve answered indifferently, wondering where exactly Heidi was going with this conversation.

Alright? That's all? Heidi pouted and placed her chin on her palms. Yeve was going to be the death of her. "You're too candid. So not cute."

"Like I care what an old woman thinks."

"I am not old," she hissed. "I'm only thirty." Before the two could get any further into their conversation, Rain entered the backroom and bowed.

"Heidi-san," he called out.

"Rain-kun, what is it?" she answered sweetly, wondering when he was going to make his presence known.

"A customer is calling for you."

"Oh," she said, suddenly uninterested. The only time customers asked for the manager was when they had a complaint. As of right then, Heidi didn't want to hear any complaints from anyone. She was still busy trying to break through Yeve's cold exterior. Beneath all that ice, there had to be some hidden warmth. "Tell them I'm not in." Heidi shooed him and turned away.

"He said his name is Sting."

Heidi's face went pale but immediately stood and covered it up with a sweet smile. "I guess I have no choice. Thanks for your hard work, Rain-kun. Yeve-chan, we'll finish our conversation when I return." Heidi quickly left the backroom and went out to the front to greet this mysterious customer while Rain and Yeve quickly exchanged looks but didn't say a word.

The customer who had asked for Heidi was dressed in black clothing and a long black trench coat. He had on a pair of shades and was sitting in a booth isolated in the lonely corner. He was in his late thirties, hoodie over his head, doing his best not to look suspicious, but was attracting more attention than he intended. In his hand was a pack of cigarettes. Since it was illegal to smoke inside the café, he simply held it as a protection charm. When he noticed Heidi, he bowed while sitting.

Heidi quickly sat, slightly bowing also. "Severn, why are you here?"

Severn didn't answer. He simply darted his eyes around the lively café. Rain had returned to help more customers refill their cups. The young kids

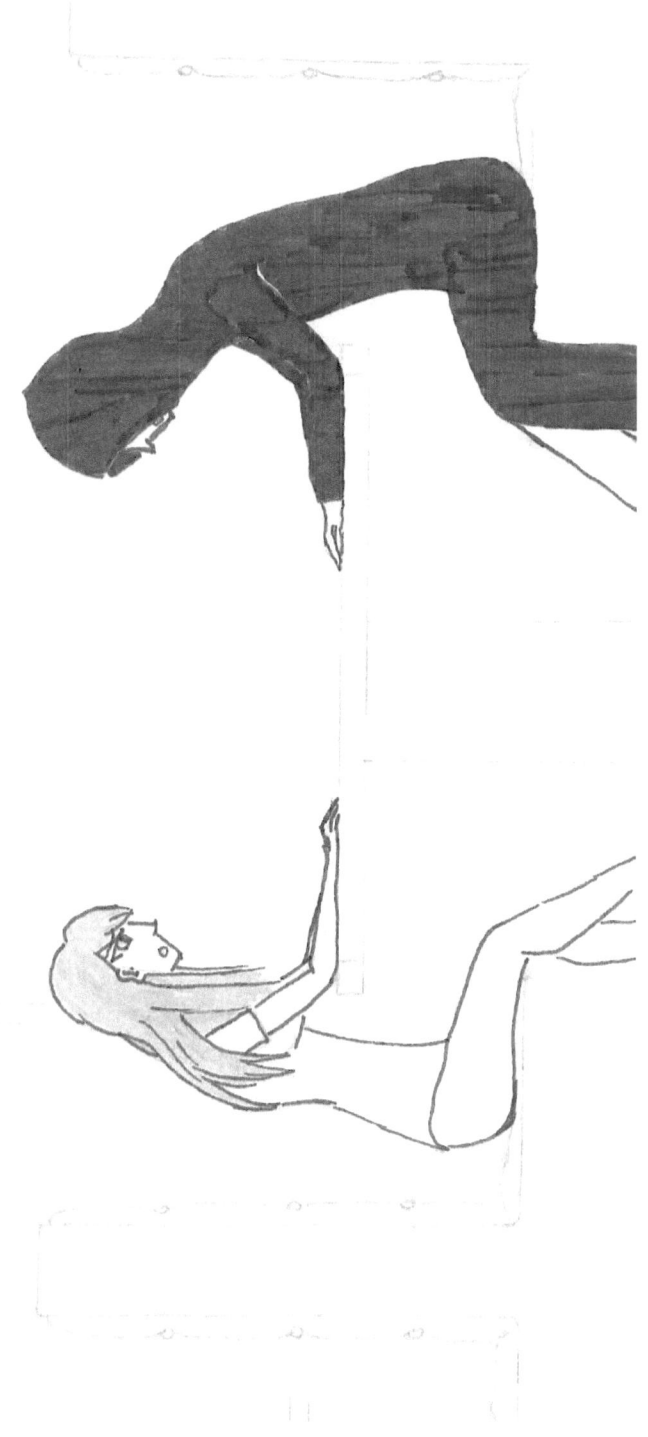

laughed and joked while the adults ate their cakes and talked about life and current events. A few of the women even tried flirting with the uptight Rain who was oblivious.

"Severn," said Heidi.

"You're not safe anymore," he answered, eyeing her behind his glasses.

"What?"

"Michio sent me here to get you because they're on our trail."

"Michio," Heidi repeated, anguish washing over her. She couldn't help but shake her head. Whenever his name came up, nothing good ever followed. Now, after opening her shop for only six months, she already had to leave. "Why must problems always arise when he's in the picture?"

"Heidi-san, please be prepared to leave this place."

"Michio, that wretched man." She put both hands to her face to cry silently. No matter how she cursed him, her love for him never faded. He was all that she thought about. Even her prayers involved him.

"Michio is your husband. He only thinks of your safety."

"Then why did he run from me again? Why is he constantly hiding in the shadows?"

"His job is dangerous. Please try to understand, Heidi-san."

"Of course, I understand."

"Then, the next time I contact you, that'll be when we leave." Severn bowed and stood, exiting the small café. He couldn't stay for too long, lest he wanted Dome Life-Kills and assassins to know his location.

"Have a good day," Rain called after him.

"Oh Michio, what have you gone and done this time?" Still crying, Heidi left for her office as Rain watched on. The sound of bells caught his attention as he quickly averted his gaze to greet new customers entering the café.

In the backroom, Yeve finished her velvet batter and put it inside the oven. After washing her hands at the sink, she noticed Liz, the orange tabby cat lying on the open windowsill. For the past few days, she'd been coming around more often. At first, Yeve was going to dispose of her, but because she never meant any harm, Yeve left her to her own devices and they even became carrot cake pals.

∞

Hanabi walked down the street with a strawberry crepe she'd bought and instantly stopped, taking a few paces back. Kneeling not far away, trying to blend in with his surrounding was Louis. She stalked over, silently kneeling beside him. So, this was where he'd disappeared to when she couldn't find him that morning. Hanabi took a bite out of the crepe before speaking, "Why are you stalking them?"

"Wah!" shouted Louis. He fell forward and turned around to find Hanabi eyeing him. Louis smiled innocently, trying to find an excuse. But his mind was blank.

"So?" she urged.

"I was out on a morning stroll."

"Don't lie to me, Louis-kun."

Unable to look into her piercing gaze, Louis turned away. If he did, he'd blurt out the truth. "I'm really not lying to you."

"So, you're trying to tell me that you were going for a stroll and just happen to come into a rich neighborhood?"

"Yes?"

"The guts of you," she growled.

"Okay, okay, I'm sorry. I've been stalking that wicked wretch called Bora. Forgive me. I didn't plan on it. The next thing I knew my feet were following her." He got on his knees, begging for forgiveness.

"Geez, why are you doing this for? It has nothing to do with you. Let them be. We have a mission to accomplish."

Louis shook his head, now staring into her eyes. He couldn't allow such a good guy like Jabol to suffer. "I don't care about the mission."

"Didn't you say that Fujiwara-sensei said that orders were absolute?"

Louis gulped and nodded. "Indeed, Fujiwara-sensei had said that—but how can I abandon that poor man who's about to die?! He needs my help, Hanabi! Even if orders are absolute, helping others is an absolute as well!"

Hanabi looked into his unwavering eyes. He was serious about getting involved with the two and she could do nothing to stop him. "Fine, do what you want," she said in defeat and stood with her crepe.

"You'll help me then?" he asked and stood also.

"No."

"What a pooper."

"You don't change," she whispered sadly.

"Huh?"

Not wanting to explain her words, she shook it off. "When I'm done with the mission I'll come help you."

"Really? You promise?"

Hanabi winced. She hated that word the most. No one ever kept their promises, and they were only good for their words.

Louis noticed the light in her eyes fade as he reached out to take her hand.

"Don't touch me!" She whipped her hand away, not wanting his touch to linger, especially when he was so emotional.

"S—sorry," he managed to say and forced a smile. Even if he was offended, he wouldn't hold it against her. "I didn't mean to."

"Don't apologize. I overreacted."

"No, you didn't. I know you hate me. I should've been more careful."

"Louis-"

"It's okay," he interrupted. "I'll handle the situation with Jabol. Can you finish the mission on your own?"

Hanabi nodded in response and looked away. She'd unintentionally hurt him and didn't know how to fix it.

"Thank you."

"I'll come help when-"

"No." Louis interrupted yet again, shaking his head. He was determined to go at it alone. "I don't need your help. I'll be fine."

"But-"

"I'll be fine, Hanabi. I don't need you." Louis quickly walked around her and left. Unconsciously, he'd expressed his hurt by taking it out on her.

∞

After an entire day of dealing with the scorching heat, it finally cooled down. Even though Hana was in a place she shouldn't be in, she still came. Like for the past few weeks since Shadow left her, she continued following him like a devoted puppy.

Zara caught sight of Hana first and cursed, tugging at Shadow's shirt sleeve. Since his initiation into their gang, she'd given him the best clothes, discarding his torn ones. Even when she ate the most succulent meals, she shared it with him. Jealous, the other guys in the gang hazed Shadow, hoping he'd leave, but he was stubborn. Just recently they stopped their bullying after Zara caught on.

Annoyed at seeing Hana's face every night, Zara questioned if letting her live had been the best idea. "She's here again, Shadow."

Turning to look, he caught sight of Hana. As soon as she caught them staring, she hid away. Shadow had made it clear to her the day he left, she wasn't important enough.

"Do something about that lovesick puppy or I'll personally see to her."

"There's no need," said Shadow. "I got her." He stood and headed over to where Hana was hiding. Why couldn't the deans send someone to escort her back to the Dome while he wrapped up the mission? Or could it be that they wanted Hana to act as some kind of rival to Zara?

She poked her head out to look again, but ended up bumping her forehead against his chest. "Ah," she said, rubbing her forehead. Hana looked up and smiled when she saw who it was. "Shadow-"

"What are you doing here? I thought I told you to get lost? What do you not understand? Tell me and I'll repeat myself again."

"It's unlike you to be so cruel."

"And you think you know me?"

Hana looked down at her hands, blinking her tears away. They were Soulmates who had spent their pre-teens and teenage years together. There was no way possible that he'd ever hurt her. "Compared to the guys, I don't know you all that well. But compared to the girls, I know you the best."

Shadow's look softened. Any woman in her situation would've left long ago. But not Hana who always believed in him. In order to drive her away, he replaced his warmth with cruelty. He couldn't afford to get caught by Zara, now that he was in her favor. Shadow had to keep up his act until the very end. No matter how much it hurt the two of them, the mission came first. "You don't know anything. Now leave this place before they kill you." He turned his back on her as she pulled him back by the shirt.

"Lie," Hana called. She shook her head, refusing to back down. It was unthinkable that he would leave her for Zara. "You're lying."

"Let go."

"You're lying to me, aren't you? If it's true that you don't care about me, you wouldn't warn me to stay away. Instead, you'd let me come and get myself killed."

"Don't get full of yourself." He broke free and turned to leave just as Zara made her way over. "Shit," he muttered.

"Shadow-"

"Shadow," Zara interrupted, walking over to link arms with him while Hana glared. Zara on the other hand simply smirked. Jealousy was written all over Hana's face, but she wasn't strong enough to issue a challenge. "Still not done shooing the pesky fly away?"

"Just finished," answered Shadow. He draped his arm around her, shooting Hana another warning look. She looked hurt, seeing him hold another woman so close.

"Let's go." Zara smiled and turned to leave.

Hana clenched her fists. If any of the other girls were to be put in her situation, they wouldn't back down. They'd fight regardless if they won or not. She would learn to be strong like them. "Let him go!"

"Huh?" The two turned back as darkness surrounded them.

"I said to let him go!" shouted Hana as she tackled Zara to the ground.

"Hana!" warned Shadow.

"Don't touch him!"

"Bitch," Zara growled as something invisible reached out to hit Hana away in the dark. She screamed, smacking the ground with a loud thud.

"Hana!"

"You," Zara growled as the darkness vanished. Walking over, she hovered over Hana who lay on her side, injured and dizzy. "How dare a pathetic weakling as you oppose me? Come back when you have reinforcements."

"Zara, that's enough," pleaded Shadow.

"What?" Zara turned, noticing the small affection still lingering in his eyes. She laughed in disbelief. How did Shadow get paired with Hana of all girls? It made Zara want to meet the idiots who decided for the two to be a couple. "I see, you still care for the poor girl, huh? Well then, I'll let her live, for now. See if she can survive." With a swift movement, Zara withdrew a dagger from hiding to pierce Hana through the left shoulder.

"Ah!"

"Hana!" Shadow shouted, running over.

Blocking his way, Zara put a hand on his shoulder and squeezed. She hated seeing him worry about someone else and wouldn't stand for it. "Are you sure you want to go to her side?"

"Serve the Golden God, die for the Golden God," Mr. Fujiwara spoke from his memory.

Shadow clenched his fists so tight his knuckles turned white. "I understand."

"Then come," she instructed and left.

"Shadow-kun," Hana pleaded and reached a hand out to him.

Orders…are absolute. He turned his back and walked away, feeling no remorse in abandoning his one and only Soulmate again.

"Shadow-kun, come back." Hana's hand fell to the cement, as did her endless tears. This it made it twice now. The cruelty in his love would bring the end of her one day.

∞

It was rather cool as Yeve stood beneath the starry sky with a piece of freshly baked bread. In her left hand was a transparent cell phone. She was talking to someone while eating. The situation back at the Dome was her new priority. She was to return and assist the others in their next mission.

Yeve nodded and bid the other party a goodbye, "alright, I understand." She hung up and gazed at the stars, smiling. "Clear skies again tonight."

"Who were you talking to? Ex-boyfriend?" accused Heidi. She waltzed out into the open air and smiled.

Yeve looked over and scowled. She took another bite of her bread, pushing Heidi aside to enter the backroom.

Heidi pouted and followed right behind. "Don't you ever smile?"

"Why would I ever show you?" she retorted and took a seat on the stool to finish her remaining bread. She had wanted to eat in peace. Knowing Heidi, it was next to impossible. "It's time to close up."

"Rain-kun is doing that for me."

"I see." Yeve finished her bread, clapped her hands of crumbs, and grabbed her drink to gulp down. It was time to tidy her work space so she could leave for the night.

Heidi leaned against the counter, watching Yeve put the utensils away and wash the dirty dishes. Though she could use the dishwasher, she was doing it old school. It made Heidi smile that she had found the perfect candidate. "Say, Yeve-chan."

"Hmm?" she answered without turning around.

"How does running this shop sound to you?"

Immediately, Yeve stopped her task to glance back. "What did you say?"

"I mean, you're an excellent baker. I bet you could do better than me at running this business and making it boom. So, how about it? Wanna become the new owner?"

Turning away, Yeve asked, "Are you planning to leave somewhere?"

Heidi nodded, but was unable to shake off the blues. No matter how frustrated she got at handling the paperwork and whatnot, she had poured blood, sweat, and tears into the dainty café bakery. It was hard to part from it, but had to be done. "Sadly, I am."

"Where?"

"I can't say." She shook her head and winked. "It's a secret."

"May I ask why at least?"

"My husband, he's in trouble again. I have to go help him."

"What'd he do? Get into trouble with loan sharks?"

Heidi laughed and nodded. That was her first-time hearing Yeve make a joke and it was actually funny. "Yeah, you could say so."

"You know," said Yeve. She finished washing the dishes to dry her hands. "I'm not sure if I'm in any position to say this. But if your husband is that type of man, shouldn't you just leave him? If he's hurt you for this long, he'll just keep doing it. Nothing will change, y'know?"

Heidi thought about it before agreeing, "Yeah, you are right. You're in no position to be saying that to me."

"Sorry."

"But you know, love is crazy. Even if he keeps hurting me, I can't leave."

Barely able to contain her anger, Yeve turned to clear the counter in a hurry. "Why would you continue hurting yourself? That's stupidity and emotional abuse that keeps making you go back, not love."

"Why are you so angry?"

"Because your reason makes no sense."

"Then, what would you do?"

"I'd leave, no doubt."

Heidi smiled and nodded. It was easy for Yeve who hadn't fallen in love to say those words, compared to being in the situation. "Wait until you're actually in my position." Heidi reached out to pat her head.

"Stop doing that," she snapped. "I'm not a puppy."

"I hope and pray that you and Rain-kun make up."

"We're not in a quarrel."

Heidi smiled and nodded. "I know, but it worries me because you two are stubborn. It's important to acknowledge each other if you're going to be soul mates."

"You're in no position to lecture me either."

"Oh my, what a sharp-tongued girl. Your mom must've had her hands full with you," joked Heidi as she laughed.

"I...have no mom."

Immediately, Heidi stopped laughing and frowned. She looked ashamed for having taken her joke too far. "I'm sorry. I didn't know."

"Don't be. I have friends that I consider as family." Yeve looked up and smiled, meaning every word.

So, she can *smile.* A smile crept onto Heidi's face as she wiped her tears. Just when she was starting to break through Yeve's armor, she had to leave. It would be a bitter-sweet departure, but Heidi would remember her cold patisserie chef wherever she went. And if the day ever came where she was allowed to return, Yeve would be the first on her list to meet again. "Just remember that you mustn't fight so much with Rain-kun, okay? You have to compromise to reach your goals."

"Why do you keep blabbering? Go close up the shop," shooed Yeve.

"Yes, yes, Your Highness." She stood and did a mocking curtsy before heading out to the front of the shop, still laughing. Standing just outside was Rain who was smiling and eavesdropping on their conversation. As soon as he spotted Heidi, he bowed with a serious expression. Heidi smiled and returned the bow. Even the handsome indifferent Rain, she would miss dearly. "Did you hear that, Rain-kun? She really is like a high and mighty empress. I hope you're up to the task of trying to keep her happy."

Rain's smile returned as he responded, "I know."

"I wanna stick around and see the progress of your love story."

Blushing, Rain chuckled, chasing the beating in his heart away. There was nothing thrilling to get worked up about. "There is no love story."

"That's what you say. But we'll just have to wait and see."

The door to the back opened as Yeve stepped out, already changed out from her chef's uniform. She raised an eyebrow at the two who were standing around and asked, "What are you two doing?"

"Just talking," Heidi said, winking at Rain. "Goodnight lovebirds." She giggled and walked away to finish locking up for the night.

Yeve shook her head while Rain chuckled. Instead of acting like a thirty-year-old business woman, Heidi was more like a seventeen-year-old side-kick. "Let's go."

"Goodnight," Rain called back. He waved goodbye to Heidi who waved in return as they exited. The walk back to their rented apartment was in silence until Yeve began humming. When she finished, the two glanced up at the stars in unison. "What song was that? It sounded nice."

"A song that Soria used to sing," Yeve answered, hoping that the tune would do its magic and chase away her nagging conscience. But it lingered above her head now like the gallows. With no one else to talk to, she had to settle. "Say, Rain."

"What is it?"

After thinking about it again, she decided to drop her question. It was pointless. "Forget it. Let's get going."

While walking, Rain fell behind as Yeve stopped and spun around, pointing a finger at him, causing him to stop abruptly.

"What are you sulking about?!"

He raised an eyebrow, confused. "I'm not though?"

"Then why are you falling behind?!"

Rain put a hand to his mouth and laughed. If she was worried about him, why not say it directly? Then again, this was Yeve he was dealing with. She had her own way of going about things.

Yeve put her hands on her hips, glaring. Again, her question resurfaced, nagging for his opinion. "Listen up! I have a question to ask you!"

"Um, okay," he said, nodding.

"If you were in Heidi-san's position, what would you do?!"

"Uh, I've been meaning to ask. Why are you shouting? You'll wake up the neighborhood."

"It's because you're too far away! You won't hear me!" It was true. Rain was a good twenty feet away, like he was scared that Yeve might bite him.

"Then, should I close the gap?" he offered and smiled.

It was unlike Rain to act so out of character that Yeve unconsciously took a step back. "What the heck?! That sounded so wrong!"

"See?"

"See what?"

Not bothering to answer, Rain made his way towards her. When he reached her side he gently bonked her on the head and continued on. "What would *you* do?" he asked, returning to the original topic.

"I'd leave that good-for-nothing husband."

"Really?"

"Yes, I would. And you?" she asked again, following from beside him.

While watching the stars twinkle, he agreed with Heidi. Regardless of how many times the woman he loved hurt him, he'd keep returning to her side. "I wouldn't be able to leave my good-for-nothing wife."

"Che," Yeve said, shaking her head. If the mass population also thought the same, she had her work cut out for her. She would need to reeducate them on how not to become brainless sheep. "You know, you're about as crazy as Heidi-san. No wonder you two get along."

"It's because she'd be lonely," Rain explained. He reached a hand out, trying to capture the stars that were forever out of his reach. "If the world was to turn its back on her, she'd have no one. That's why, I'd be that person who would continue walking beside her for eternity."

"Hmph, I don't like your answer." Yeve groaned and fastened her pace, a smile appearing on her face. There was a pinch in her heart as she gasped once. "Isn't that too sad though?" she whispered, her smile fading.

Rain caught hold of her arm as they gazed into each other's eyes. They reflected each other perfectly, even their pain was one and the same. How could two people resemble each other so much? "If you're scared to be alone, should I walk beside you from now on?"

After a few seconds, Yeve broke free. "What's with you suddenly?" she asked, walking away. "We're not in some love drama."

Rain watched her go and raised an eyebrow. "Is it me? Or is it the lighting? But was she blushing?" He laughed and chased after her. After so many years of trying to chip through her defenses, he was suddenly scared to see her core that she hid.

36th Lie

LOUIS WAS ALREADY GONE by the time Hanabi woke up the next morning. She had had a nightmare and was trembling all over. Even her bedsheets were soaked from her sweat.

Sunlight poured through the white shades as Hanabi groggily got out of bed to take a shower and change. When she came back out, she was refreshed. Sitting on the dining table was breakfast and a note.

Here's breakfast. Be back later. —Louis
P.S. We were ordered to return tonight. No exceptions.

Hanabi smiled and pushed the note aside. She lifted the food cover and sat down to eat. Louis was too nice for his own good, which was why he constantly got teased by the guys.

∞

Louis was stalking Bora down the street again while she cheerfully talked on her phone. Today, he vowed to find a solution before returning to the Dome. Turning off her phone, Bora entered a five-star restaurant as Louis followed her in and got a seat for two. The waiter showed him to a table and handed him a menu. He pretended to look through it, but was scanning the place for Bora. When he spotted her, she was sitting at a table on the other side of the restaurant. Sitting across from her was a handsome man—a corporate man to be exact.

Bora was laughing and flirting with him, touching his hand whenever she got the chance. That was probably the man her father wanted her to marry. Louis stood from his chair and made his way to the other side of the room, pretending to bump into them before apologizing.

"It's okay," said the man. He smiled and let it slide. Even Bora smiled, not recognizing Louis. Why would she? His existence meant nothing, even if he'd acted strangely when they first met.

For that instant when Louis ran into them, he had read into their future. They were going to get engaged within a month.

He returned to his original table and took out his phone, pretending to talk to his fiancée who couldn't make it to brunch. Louis apologized to the waiter and left the restaurant, tears in his eyes. "Maybe Hanabi's right. I shouldn't get involved. It has nothing to do with me."

"Excuse me," said someone.

"Oh sorry," apologized Louis. He moved out of the way as Jabol walked by. "Eh?" said Louis as he turned back. "Wait!"

"Huh?" Jabol also turned back to look. "Talking to me?"

Louis stood, debating on whether he should stay involved any longer. In the end, he made up his mind. He had gone all in and couldn't back out anymore. "You may not remember me. But I'm the guy who came up to you and your girlfriend at the café a few days ago."

Jabol thought about it before pointing a finger. "Ah," he said, alarmed.

Louis laughed it off and scratched his head. It was awkward meeting like this again. "I'm sorry if this may seem blunt, but I can't hold it in any longer. Your girlfriend isn't a good person. You should dump her."

The look on Jabol's face hardened. Who was Louis to tell him what to do?

"This is for your own good."

"Who are you again?"

"My name is Louis. I know this sounds absurd, but your girlfriend doesn't care about you. In fact, she's going to marry someone else."

"Listen Mr. Louis, I don't know who you are. But leave my girlfriend alone."

"I'm not doing anything."

"Are you one of her fans?"

Louis snapped, finding it hard to stay patient with Jabol's idiocy. "Her fan? Seriously? I'd prefer to be Yeve's fan than your fake girlfriend's."

"Hey!" Jabol shouted, insulted.

"Listen to me, Jabol-san!" pleaded Louis. "You're going to die in two months! Spend that time with someone who actually loves you! Are you a freaking idiot?! That bitch doesn't care about you!"

Jabol's eyes widened at how Louis knew his name and his condition. No one other than himself and his doctor knew. Instead of feeling shocked, Jabol was overcome with anger as he threw a punch. "Don't call Bora a bitch."

Not expecting a punch, Louis stood and wiped his bloody lip. Even now, Jabol was still defending his wretched girlfriend. How could a man who seemed so intelligent be so stupid? "Why do you waste your time and energy trying to make her happy? She's doesn't see your generosity whatsoever!"

"Go get a life dude," snarled Jabol as he turned around, only to be met with a slap to the face.

"Hanabi," gasped Louis. He couldn't believe that she was there, or that she had slapped Jabol. Even Jabol was shocked.

"Since the idiot behind you is too nice to hit you in return, I'll do it," she said, brushing Jabol and walking over to yank Louis away. Hopefully this entire dragging thing wouldn't become a new routine. "This is why I told you not to get involved."

"But-"

"No buts!"

Louis stopped arguing to allow her to drag him. He glanced back at Jabol whose face was still turned to the side, doing his best not to break down.

"You idiot, you stupid idiot," Hanabi fumed, drawing his attention back to her. "Why must you get involved with every little thing? It has nothing to do with you. Just let it go."

Louis stopped and pulled her back as she turned around, tears in her eyes. Smiling, he reached out to wipe her eyes as she flinched. Why did her tears bring him such joy? "You know I can't. That's not who I am."

Hanabi scowled. "I know and I hate it. Why can't you be more like King?"

"King's too proud." Louis chuckled. Though he was grateful that she had defended him, he couldn't leave like this. It didn't feel right.

"Fine, whatever," she said, letting go of his hand. If this was how he was going to act, then she wouldn't care. "I've got a mission to accomplish anyway. And when the deans ask who did the most work, I'm taking all the credit. I'll tell them that you were too busy trying to play love counselor." She quickly wiped her eyes and walked away.

Laughing, Louis gratefully shouted after her, "Thank you, Hanabi!"

"This is the last time!"

Instead of calling her out on her lie just then, Louis watched her disappear before chasing Jabol who was long gone.

∞

Hana grunted and opened her eyes to the plain, brown colored room. There was only one desk and a lamp beside the bed she was laying on. Panic rose in her chest as she sat up, not remembering how she'd gotten there or where she was.

"Mafuyu-nee, she woke up!" shouted a little boy from the slightly parted doorway.

"She did?" responded a girl's voice. The sound of footsteps echoed in the hallway and after a few seconds the door completely opened. In walked a girl a few years older. Beside her was a little boy. "You're finally up," Mafuyu said and smiled. The little boy reached out to hold his sister's hand, but made sure to stay hidden behind her.

"Where am I?"

"We found you unconscious on the street and brought you here." Mafuyu pulled up a chair and sat down, holding her little brother in her lap. "So, tell me strange girl, why were you at that place? Everyone here knows that part of town is run by Zara and her gang. No one goes there unless they have a dying wish."

"Zara," Hana repeated, the look on her face hardening. She clenched her fists while her usual pigtailed hair was untied and unruly. Just remembering how Shadow chose Zara and the mission over her, made her want to cry all over again. Hana took the blanket off and swung her legs over the side of the bed to bow. "Thank you for your hospitality but I must go now."

"Huh?" said Mafuyu in alarm.

"I have to get Shadow-kun back and knock some sense into him. He can't leave me. I never gave him permission."

"Um," said Mafuyu. "Is this person you're talking about, a servant?"

"Eh? No, he's my Soulmate." Hana quickly shook her head. She hadn't meant for it to come out that way.

"Eh? You're married already? You don't look that old. What are you, about seventeen or so?"

"That's correct."

"Then, I'm older by two years." Mafuyu let her little brother down and stood, pushing Hana to lie back down. Hana was her patient now. She wasn't about to let a patient go running off to their death just yet, no matter how they wished for it. "Don't you dare argue with your elders, missy. Lay in bed until you get better. After you've regained your energy, I'll let you go and have your death wish."

Hana shook her head, trying to fight back. "But I have to go. What if Shadow-kun leaves with that wretched woman? Then I'll lose his trail." Hana put her hands to her eyes and cried from her broken heart. He'd told her that she was his flower under the moon. He couldn't possibly have forgotten that. "I don't want to lose him. I *can't* lose him."

Mafuyu reached out, patting Hana's head in comfort. "I don't know what your situation is, but a man who hurts you is no good."

"He didn't choose to, he was forced to."

"Either way, let him go. He'll only bring you sadness and pain."

"No."

"What a stubborn little missy." Mafuyu sighed, reaching for her little brother's hand so they could let Hana recuperate. "Come Hachi, let's go. The missy needs her rest."

∞

They hadn't yet opened the café bakery for business that morning as Yeve sat in the back, unsure of what to do. Sitting before her was a manila envelope addressed to her in Heidi's handwriting. Yeve didn't need to open it to know it was paperwork of ownership signed over to her. Lying next to the unopen envelope was a pair of keys.

While Yeve considered her options, Rain was leaning against the wall, arms crossed, inspecting her. "I guess this place belongs to you now."

"Rain," she said.

"What is it? Want me to track her down?"

Yeve looked over and snapped, "Stop leaning against the wall like some cool manga character. Stand straight. Or take a seat."

Rain smiled, pushing himself off the wall. He walked over to sit opposite her. His gut feeling had been correct. Yeve hated it when someone, other than herself looked cooler. At least now, she was back to her old self. "What are we going to do? We let Heidi-san get away. Doesn't this mean we failed our mission?"

"Seems so." Yeve smiled, gliding her fingertips over the set of keys.

Rain raised an eyebrow at her carefree attitude. Was she really going to let Heidi slip from their fingers like this? And what about the consequences? "The dean is going to lecture you."

"I'm mentally preparing myself for it." Yeve stood and stretched, trying to find a way out of the situation. In the end, she chuckled. It was impossible to pull this one off. She'd just have to suck it up and deal with Dean Kiera's torturous lecture. Even so, she wasn't scared or intimidated. "Heidi-san will return to this place one day. When she does, that's when we capture her."

"You know what I think?"

"That would be?" Yeve walked over to the sink to wash her hands.

Rain crossed his arms again, watching her every move. Nothing got past his watchful eye. "We had plenty of opportunities to capture her and bring her back to the Dome. Heck, we could've been the first couple to complete our second mission. Why didn't we?"

Yeve moved her hands from beneath the spout to dry as the water stopped. Rain had ruined her mood. Now she no longer felt like baking. "On

381

second thought, let's not open the shop today," she suggested, ignoring his question and taking out her cell phone. The mission was over and done with. She no longer wanted to think about their failure.

"Why?" Rain pressed on.

"Today's our last day here. We should employ some good-natured people and have them run the store for the meanwhile. When I retire from the Dome, I'll come back to run this place."

"With me?" he joked.

"Yes, yes, with you too." Yeve nodded, typing on her holographic screen.

"You've been avoiding my question. Why?"

"Go print some flyers for hiring new employees."

"Yeve," he said sternly.

She turned to look at him. He wouldn't leave until she answered his question. Giving in, Yeve set her phone off to the side. "She's pregnant."

Rain nodded. "I knew that."

"The child in her womb, I don't think it's a normal child."

"I knew that much also. Tell me something I don't know."

"What do you know?" Yeve crossed her arms. If Rain knew all that she knew, why ask such a question?

"Her husband returned for her, so he can monitor the child's development."

"And?"

"That's all I know."

"Then that's all." Yeve uncrossed her arms to grab her phone again.

"You still didn't answer *why*."

Yeve stopped once more and looked up again. For what felt like the thousandth sigh, she pulled her hair into a ponytail. "Why are you so persistent on knowing why?"

"I want to know why you didn't capture her. Even now, given your speed, you can catch up to her and bring her back. But you're not."

"Why didn't *you* capture her?" Yeve redirected.

It was quiet in the backroom as Rain thought long and hard on how to word it. "It's because you looked like you didn't want to capture her, so I didn't. If you didn't look like you wanted to cry each time you saw Heidi-san, I would've gone through with the mission."

"You could have, despite what I wanted."

"And make you cry? Not a chance," said Rain. He shook his head and stood, turning to leave. If he made Yeve cry, the consequences would be dire in the future, since he knew, he'd be the one to suffer the most. "I'll go make some flyers."

"It's because of what you said," Yeve responded, halting Rain who turned back to look at her. "You said, if the world were to turn its back on your wife, you'd be that one person for her. After thinking about it, it made sense. Her husband may be a good-for-nothing man, but his return means that he wants to protect Heidi-san at all costs, despite his mistakes. That's why, I couldn't bring her back to the Dome. I didn't want to separate their family."

Rain smiled and joked, breaking the brief silence, "Wow, you're actually a softy at heart, aren't you?"

Twitching, Yeve grabbed the nearest utensil, a whisk, to threaten him with. "You want me to bake you for the customers to eat?"

Rain laughed and shook his head. "No."

"Then, get going. We've got a long day for interviews."

"Yes, yes," he said, still chuckling, then stopped. "What are we going to write in our report to the deans?"

"Whatever you want. I'll take full responsibility for failing."

"Is that so?"

"Yes."

"Then, how about this?" Rain suggested. He couldn't let his Soulmate take the fall since he was partially to blame for not carrying out orders. "We were intoxicated by the sweet aroma of this place and fell into a deep slumber of peaceful dreams. When we awoke, Heidi-san had already disappeared."

"And suddenly we became the new owners? Oh yeah, that's gonna work Rain."

"And if it does?"

"Then I'll make you a wedding cake."

"I'll take you up on that offer." Rain winked and left.

"He's really serious." Yeve looked shocked, but eventually laughed and shook her head. She was seeing all sorts of sides to Rain these past few months. "Like anyone's going to fall for that farfetched story."

Liz meowed from the open window and took a seat at the ledge as Yeve turned to look. She smiled and walked over to the fridge to grab a leftover piece of carrot cake to give Liz, who meowed at the offer and happily ate.

"Go on, get going. I don't have time to play with you today. I'm mighty busy." Yeve patted her head and returned to her phone to post job recruitments online.

When Liz finished eating and licking her paws, she scampered off to find Nicholas.

"There you are," he said, his thin, red scarf swaying in the light breeze. "Ready to go? I don't want Dean Kosa contacting Dean Campbell about our unauthorized Dome leaves."

Liz meowed in response and rubbed her head against his leg as they disappeared into thin air.

The park was lively that day with families taking a day off to play. Jabol smiled, almost envious. The kids were so carefree, they could play to their heart's content without worrying. It made him want to return to his childhood.

"May I sit?" Louis asked, standing beside him.

Jabol looked up, too engulfed in his thoughts to hear Louis approaching. There was just no escaping him. Nodding, Jabol motioned to the bench.

"Thanks." Louis sat down, breathless. Neither of them spoke as they watched their surroundings. After a few minutes, Louis spoke, "Sorry about the slap. Hanabi got a little worked up."

Jabol shook his head and touched his cheek. It still stung. That was his first time getting slapped. Hopefully, it would be the last as well. "Your girlfriend sure knows how to slap. I wonder how hard she punches."

Both guys laughed at the joke before glancing at the sky.

"I didn't mean to upset you," apologized Louis.

Jabol shook it off, no longer caring. "It's alright. It's as you say anyway. Bora isn't a good person. I've caught her a few times making fun of me to her friends back in Seoul."

Louis looked over, surprised. If Jabol knew, why put up with it?

"I wanted someone to need me," he explained as his lips quivered. "It was the only way to confirm my existence in this world."

"There's other ways to go about it."

"I know, but my time is short."

"You've still got-"

"No." Jabol shook his head and looked down at his unsteady hands. He was unsure if it was due to the fear of dying or being forgotten. "I no longer have weeks or months. The disease is progressing faster than the doctor had anticipated. I probably won't make it past tonight."

"Then why are you here? You should be at the hospital."

"I escaped the hospital before bumping into you."

"But-"

"I don't wanna die inside a hospital. That's why I'm here, in the place I love most, where my grandma used to bring me."

Biting his lip, Louis asked, "Did you tell your girlfriend?"

"No."

"Why not?"

"She'll probably think I'm lying to con her out of money for medical fees." Jabol put a hand to his face and laughed. Even if Bora didn't love him, he genuinely loved her. It was stupid of him to fall for someone so selfish, but he couldn't help it after seeing her cute and loveable sides. Jabol had always wanted to be the one to change her but was incapable of doing so. One day, he hoped that someone more capable would come along to accomplish what he failed to do. "I want to spend my last minutes with her so badly, but I know she'll never come to me of her own free will. She only cares about money and her family status."

"That's why you don't fall for rich girls," warned Louis.

Jabol laughed loudly and nodded in agreement. When his laughter faded, he fidgeted with his sweaty hands. "Tell me. What should I do, Mr. Louis?"

It was quiet as Louis thought about it. Finally, he stood, determined. "I'll bring her to you."

Jabol smiled and shook his head. It was useless. Bora wouldn't come even if a gun was pointed to her head.

"Trust me."

Nodding, Jabol bargained, "Alright then, tonight." If Louis was willing to go this far, he would leave it to a stranger to bring his girlfriend to him, during his last moments. "Thank you. I appreciate it."

"You're welcome." Louis bowed and ran off.

"You won't succeed." Jabol closed his eyes and leaned back in the park bench to nap and wait.

∞

The bullet train came to a halt and soon the doors opened as Severn led the way out with the other passengers behind. "This way," he said as they approached a hooded figure waiting for them outside the station.

"Michio?" called out Heidi.

Michio took his hood off and smiled. He still looked the same as when they met for the first time in America. He hadn't aged at all, though Heidi did. The only thing that changed about him was the length of his hair, his new beard and moustache. Michio held out his arms, welcoming his wife.

Heidi threw both hands to her mouth and cried. She ran over, throwing him into a hug. It'd only been a few months since they parted ways, yet it felt like centuries. "Where did you go? I was so worried."

"I'm sorry. I didn't mean to worry you. It's just that things came up and I had to go into hiding. Anzai, that idiot got greedy and took my vials."

"Anzai?" repeated Heidi in disbelief. She pulled away from his embrace and glared. "You're still working with that buffoon? All he cares about is money, drugs, and women."

"I know. I've already cut all ties with him." Michio nodded and smiled. Like usual, he was being scolded for being a foolish man by his beloved wife. Even so, he wouldn't trade this life for any other. "I heard that Anzai got caught by some Life-Kills sent from Maroon. They're bringing him to the

Dome to interrogate. I had to come get you to safety. It's only a matter of time before they find us."

"It's about this little one here, isn't it?" Heidi asked, touching her stomach. The Dome was after their child, the first ever human and Life-Kill baby to be conceived.

In previous experiments, Dome doctors and scientists tried to make a human woman bear a Life-Kill's child. It ended in tragedy. The unborn child inside the womb ended up killing both itself and the mother. In other experiments, a Life-Kill woman would bear the human child. That too didn't pan out. The embryo was destroyed by the powers of the Life-Kill woman. If the child inside Heidi was to survive, without a doubt, all seven Domes would relentlessly pursue her and the child to the ends of the universe.

"What are we going to do?"

"We're going into hiding."

"Where?" Heidi demanded, tears quickly filling her eyes. She'd seen the ruthlessness of the Domes after living a life on the run with Michio. "Where can we hide? There's no place that the Domes can't get to or find. We won't ever be safe so long as the Golden God lives."

Michio could sense his wife's anguish. She was afraid for her husband and their unborn child who had yet to see the light of day. He cupped Heidi's face as she cried. "You're wrong," he said, assuring her.

"The Dome is actually limited," interrupted Holly as she approached and bowed. "Sorry for the sudden intrusion. My name is Holly. It's a pleasure to finally meet you, Ms. Heidi."

"Who is she?" Heidi asked suspiciously.

Smiling, Michio introduced the two. "This is Holly, an ex-Life-Kill from the Violet Dome. Holly, this is my wife, Heidi."

Again, Holly bowed.

"Holly's with a secret organization who are skilled in hiding from the Domes."

"Severn," said Holly.

"Right," he said and quickly ran off to get the car.

"Where is Severn going?" asked Heidi.

"He's only going to get the car," answered Holly. She took a step forward and stopped, able to sense Heidi's guardedness. Taking no offense, Holly spoke, "I'd like to make a request."

"What kind?"

"May I touch your stomach?"

"Of course not."

"Honey, Holly's an old soul. She won't hurt you," Michio assured, persuading his wife.

Giving in, Heidi nodded. If Michio trusted Holly, she would have no choice, seeing as how they were going to start living together from then on. "Okay."

"Thank you." Holly walked closer and reached out to touch Heidi's slim stomach. She could hear the faint heartbeat of the child inside. He was doing fine as a fetus and smiled, causing Holly to gasp and quickly withdraw. It had come as a shock that the child could already sense its surrounding. Soon, Holly chuckled. The unborn child wouldn't greet death so easily. Neither would he try to hurt his beloved mother. He would grow stronger and protect her from within her womb, until he was born into the sun like a lotus.

"What happened?"

"He likes the scent of red velvet cakes." Holly giggled and smiled, unsure of its significance.

"Red velvet cake?" Michio repeated, confused as well.

Being the only one to understand, Heidi smiled and touched her stomach. "Yeve-chan," she said.

"Who's that?"

Heidi looked up, her hand still placed on her stomach. "I employed an excellent but haughty worker back at the bakery. Her favorite sweet to bake were red velvets. I guess the little one took a liking to it."

"You've also taken a liking to her."

"I sure did." Heidi chuckled and stopped. "Wait. How can the child know so much? It's impossible."

"That child is half Life-Kill. Once he's born into this world, he'll be the first in history who wasn't cloned or modified. His existence is important to the Golden God. If they capture your child, who knows what they could do with the world," explained Holly.

"So then, where are we going?"

"Tokyo," answered Holly. "Shin's excited to meet you after all the stories Michio's told him regarding you. He went all out creating a comfortable room for you."

"Shin?" repeated Heidi.

"He's the protector of the Book."

"Michio-san, Heidi-san, Holly," called out Severn as he pulled up to them while Michio ushered the two over to the black car.

∞

Despite it being time to sleep now that the sky had turned black, Louis was making a ruckus outside the mansion. He was demanding to see Bora, and if she didn't show he wouldn't leave. After an hour of nonstop shouting, she finally went out to see who was causing such a disturbance.

"You, the restaurant guy," remembered Bora.

Louis bowed and stood. At least this time she recognized him, though it didn't make him happy whatsoever. "I know this is sudden. But Jabol-san needs to see you."

"Jabol?"

"That's right."

"And why does he need to see me in the dead of the night?"

"I know it's late, but it's urgent. He's dying and wants to see you."

"He's dying?"

"Yes, he's dying. So please come with me."

Bora stared in disbelief. As if she could believe a stranger who was only good for his words. For all she knew, Louis could be some psychopath using Jabol as bait to lure her out. "I'm not that stupid to follow just anyone."

"Please believe me!" begged Louis.

Bora shook her head and stubbornly crossed her arms. "Jabol's not dying anytime soon. He's healthy as an ox."

"He's not healthy one bit! He's dying! Please trust me and come with me!"

"Leave this place before I call the cops." Bora turned on her heels as Louis managed to snag hold of her. "Ah, let go!"

"Don't fuck with me!" he shouted, pinning her against the concrete wall. Screaming, Bora fought. Only towards her did he find himself cursing. If the guys heard, they'd surely receive heart attacks.

"Rapist, murderer, burglar! Someone, help me!"

Not distraught by her accusations, Louis could only picture Jabol sitting at the park, waiting. He had pinned his hopes on Louis to bring Bora. "Why won't you go to him, in his last hour?! Why won't you go when he loves you?!"

"Get the hell off me!" She lashed out at Louis and ran behind the gates, now safe from harm's way. "I'll make sure that you rot in jail, you psycho!" She turned her back and ran towards the mansion to call the cops.

Louis took hold of the barred gates with both hands and shook it. Tears trailed as he wiped them away furiously. Now wasn't the time to cry. He had to return to the park and sprinted off. If Bora wouldn't stay with Jabol during his last minutes, then Louis would be the one.

∞

Hanabi approached the bench where Jabol lay. The stars were shining brightly but he didn't seem to notice while shivering. Louis was nowhere in sight as she took a seat and whispered, "She's not coming, you knew that, didn't you?"

"Yeah," he answered weakly.

"You're also a fool." She lifted his head off the hard wood to put on her lap. This was the only comfort she could give him.

Jabol smiled faintly in the dark, grateful for her generosity. "Thank you."

"If I had Crystal's power, I'd be able to let you see a beautiful dream."

"What kind of dream would you show me?"

"What kind of dream do you want to see?"

Jabol chuckled and looked to the stars. Soon, he would become one of them. "I want to see a dream where the moon can shine alongside the sun, a dream where the planets are within our view, and sadness no longer exists."

"Is that all?"

"No, there's more."

"Then tell me. Tell me all your dreams."

There were too many dreams inside him, and not enough time to tell them. But he would speak about the most important one. "Show me a love that can transcend time."

Hanabi smiled and fixed his hair, a tear trickling. "I think there's already a love like that. What else do you wish to see?"

"A house overlooking the sea, a picket fence, flowers decorating the yards, a caring wife, filial children, a fluffy cute puppy, and lots of smiles," answered Jabol as his eyes started closing.

"What about the wind?" she asked.

"The wind?"

"Yeah, the wind, the beautiful wind that is never-changing. It'll guide you safely to your destination. When you reawaken, you'll find yourself in your utopian dream."

"I like that. It sounds a lot like heaven."

"Heaven?"

"Yeah, back in the Godless Ages, there were people who once believed in a celestial being called 'God.' He was supposedly the Creator of this planet. He created it in six days and rested on the seventh. After creating His most treasured, Man, He noticed that something was amiss and gave Man, a Woman. From there, that's how we were created."

"My school library has every book known to human history. But I've never heard of that story before."

"You won't be able to find it. It's a Forbidden Book now." Jabol blinked, his vision becoming blurry. Even his body temperature was starting to fall. Shivering, Jabol cried. Death was such a fearful encounter. "It was burnt and considered as witchcraft. All faith and religion were prohibited, and believers were executed. Every statue and place of worship was torn and burnt. Those who survived went into hiding. Even now, they're still being hunted by Life-Kills."

Hanabi's eyes widened at the startling revelation. How was she to perceive this information coming from a dying man? Was it possible? Could what Jabol said be the truth? If it was, were the missions assigned to them now, involving those who had gone into hiding? Were they pursuing those individuals to persecute? Had everything Hanabi been taught a lie?

"That's what my grandma says at least." He chuckled as the pain shot through his body, but he wasn't done talking yet. "Funny, don't you think? If there really is a God from way back then, why is it called 'The Godless Ages?' I've always wondered about that."

The feelings oozing from Jabol brought tears to Hanabi's eyes. She knew, he was telling the truth. It was the knowledge his grandmother had passed down unto him, hoping he could relay to his children. That way, the legends would never die. Little did they know, Jabol wouldn't be able to fulfill that wish. "God," repeated Hanabi.

"Yeah, the utopia we were talking about sounds like heaven. I hope it's real and I hope God's waiting there to welcome me home."

Hanabi held him tightly, his body warmth quickly escaping. She squeezed his trembling hand and whispered, "Without a doubt there'll be someone walking alongside you, holding your hand. You'll never be alone again."

"Thank you." Jabol gasped a few times before he closed his eyes and stopped breathing, a smile on his face. He had taken her words to heart.

Louis came to a slow halt, breathing hard. "Hanabi?"

She turned to look at him, a tear escaping her eye. "I finished the mission early to come stay with him."

"Is that so?" Louis smiled and wiped his eyes. He was always late for the most important things. Hopefully in the future, he wouldn't be late again. "What were his last words?"

"He's in utopia." She smiled painfully and cradled Jabol. "I imagine it to be filled with warmth. In that place, there is no more pain. Just joy."

37th Lie

SHADOW WALKED AROUND the hideout in his black outfit, chosen out by none other than Zara. After receiving word that she wanted to meet him, he'd gone practically everywhere searching for her but still came up empty-handed. Giving up, he returned to his room. When she felt like having her chat, she'd come find him. The moment Shadow turned around the corner, he spotted one of Zara's usual girl groups and asked them about her whereabouts.

"Can't be helped if she's missing. The boss just came back," said the girls.

"The boss?" Shadow repeated and raised an eyebrow. This was his first-time hearing anything regarding the boss. Were the fireworks finally going to begin?

"Yeah, didn't you hear? He came back from his overseas meeting. In a couple of days, we'll leave and rejoin the others at the base to take out the Bat Angels once and for all."

"What's the boss's name?"

The group of girls shook their heads, smiling. It wasn't in their place to say. "Only Zara can tell you, it's part of rules and regulations, or whatever."

"I see." Shadow thanked them and headed back to his room. Once inside, he opened the window so he could sit on the sill and stargaze. Smiling, he wished he had a good novel on-hand.

Out in the hallway, someone knocked on the door, calling out, "Shadow."

He stood to answer the door, wondering what the member wanted. "What is it?"

The girl with braids, held out her hand. Sitting in her palm was a necklace with a tracking device inside. She smiled while Shadow raised an eyebrow, but took it anyway. "Zara says for you to wear it at all times."

"Why?" Shadow examined the necklace like it was some alien artifact.

The girl with braids shrugged. "Don't ask me why. She instructed me to give it to you. So, wear it diligently. She's infatuated with you."

"Don't joke."

"I'm not. This is the first time she's gotten personally involved with someone. Why do you think the other guys are so envious of you? If Zara were to keep tabs on them like she does with you, they'd die from joy."

"That's a little extreme." Shadow shook his head and put the necklace on like a pet.

"What can I say? Those guys must be masochists." She winked at him and turned to leave but stopped. "Ah, that's right. The next time that pretty missy comes around, be sure to drive her away for good."

Shadow raised an eyebrow in questioning.

The girl with braids chuckled at his reaction. "Zara's reached her limit with that pretty missy. If she shows up again, Zara's going to take matters into her own hands. She doesn't like it when others take a liking to what's hers. That's just how she is," the girl with braids explained and turned to leave yet again.

"That Zara, her measurements to keep me in this circle is too extreme."

∞

Hachi cracked the door ajar to the room and poked his head inside. Hana was sitting by the window, glancing out. When she heard the door, she turned to look at him and smiled. "Um," he said shyly.

"Come in." Hana motioned for him, wanting someone to keep her company after having some time to think. She'd been too rash that morning.

Hachi smiled and entered, shutting the door. "How do you do, milady?" he asked and bowed formally.

Hana burst into laughter as Hachi abruptly stood.

"What's wrong, milady?"

Hana wiped her tears from her eyes and walked over to sit at the foot of the bed. It was the first time anyone had addressed her so formally. "My name's Hana. You don't have to speak so formally. I'm not a rich lady like your sister said."

"Oh," he said, smiling sheepishly.

"What's your name?"

"Hachi."

"Hachi-kun, come." Hana motioned for him to sit beside her as he excitedly rushed over. Finally, he could chat with her after spending hours watching her sleep like a princess. Now that she was awake, she was even cuter than those Disney princesses the neighborhood girls were always talking about.

"You have the same eyes as onee-chan."

"Eh?"

"Nee-chan also hates that Zara."

"Why doesn't anyone revolt against her?"

Hachi's smile faded. He quickly shook his head, worried. It was an unthinkable action. "We can't. She and her cronies are too powerful. No one can defeat her. I even heard from the other kids in the hood that she recruited another tough guy, Shadow."

"He's the one you were talking about, right?"

"Yeah," Hana answered and nodded. Now, even Shadow was being feared when he was the sweetest person she knew.

"Don't worry, Hana-nee. I'm sure he'll return to your side once he sees how sincere your feelings are."

Hana smiled, nodding yet again. She quickly wiped her tears and patted Hachi's head. "Thank you for your encouragement, Hachi-kun."

"I don't know what happened but he's an idiot for leaving you for that Zara. He definitely lost a good woman." Hachi chuckled as Hana joined in.

Standing outside the door with a tray of food was Mafuyu. She'd come to deliver Hana's dinner, but decided to postpone it, since the two were chattering away like friends. Smiling, Mafuyu left.

"How many men does Zara have? Do you know, Hachi-kun?"

"No one knows the exact number. Nee-chan says she has too many to keep track of."

"I see." Hana nodded and looked away. Taking Shadow back was going to take a lot of work. She'd need help if she wanted to infiltrate Zara's base. The obstacles in her path was too hard to overcome alone.

"Are you really going back to that death place?"

"Yeah, I have to."

"And you're going to go alone?"

"No. I plan on bringing back-up."

Though she said she would be getting help, Hachi didn't look too convinced. No one had outdueled Zara and lived to tell of it. He only hoped that Hana's reinforcements were an army of men.

"I have trusted friends that are strong." Hana smiled in assurance, knowing exactly who to enlist to ensure her victory.

∞

Yeve awoke inside her ferry room that was bringing them back to the Maroon Dome. Rain was soundly asleep in the next room. Wanting some fresh air, she got up and made her way out to the deck. The wind was unusually fierce that night as her hair swayed in the dark. She walked over to the ledge, peering down at the black water. "Man, what a day," she said and rubbed her forehead. After holding interviews all day long, they were able to find some reliable employees and an assistant manager to run the shop for the meanwhile.

"Hey," called out a voice from beside her.

All the blood in Yeve's veins froze. She kept her gaze down at the water, never turning to acknowledge the owner of the voice. She was suddenly afraid for no apparent reason. The owner of the voice was nothing but an illusion, yet he felt as real as the wind blowing through her hair.

"You know," he said, gently leaning against the railing, his face hidden by darkness.

"Not real, not real," said Yeve. She squeezed her eyes shut and shook her head, but he didn't disappear.

"I love you." He smiled and reached out to brush her cheek gently.

Yeve flung her eyes open at his touch and finally turned to acknowledge him. His classic, messy medium black hair swayed in the breeze. Though she couldn't see his face, she could sense his sadness. His elegant fingers trailed off her cheek while he cried.

"All I wanted was a simple goodbye."

His words caused something within Yeve to rouse from hibernation. She didn't know what it was, but what she did know was she hadn't been worthy of him or his tears. Even now, she still wasn't. So why did he continue crying? With a shaky hand, Yeve reached out through time. Before she could touch him, Rain caught her wrist.

"What's with you?" he asked, interrupting her trance-like state.

Yeve blinked and turned to look at Rain. He had chased the ghost away as she glanced about, trying to find him.

"Yeve," Rain said, worried about her internal battle. This was like that time inside Blair when she started talking to the air before attacking them.

"You look alike."

"Huh?"

Catching on to her words, Yeve laughed it off and pulled her hand free. She suddenly had the urge to hit her knees and cry her heart out. "Did I scare you?" she joked. "Sorry."

Unable to laugh it off, Rain glared. How could she act like nothing had happened? Who did she conjure this time to say that Rain looked like this other person?

"I'm fine. Don't give me that look."

"No, you're not. You-"

"She's finally gone off the rockers," answered Soria who was sitting on a water swan below. The two turned to look, surprised that she had snuck up on them. "If you ask me, I say this whole entire Empress thing has finally gotten to her head."

Yeve glared and pointed, forgetting the ordeal she was just facing. Soria's presence was enough to get her worked up. "If you were here the entire time, say something, damn it!"

Soria pouted, hoping that their reunion would be filled with tears and smiles. Instead, she was met with hostility. "Man, your ugly personality hasn't changed one bit. If this is what I get for coming to welcome you, I'm never doing it again, booger face."

"That's it. You're dead." Yeve climbed over the railings to jump in after her as Rain pulled her back. "Let me go! I'm gonna drown her!"

"I can't drown when I'm a water elemental."

"Then I'll slice and dice you up."

"You may be the Road Runner on land but not on water," she said and zoomed off faster than the ferry, back to the Dome while laughing. "Try catching me now sucker!"

"I'll kill her once we reach dry land," Yeve said with a huff.

It was amazing how Soria could return Yeve to her regular self so quickly. Rain would have to learn from her and chuckled. He could only imagine the look on Yeve's face when she learned that he was receiving lessons from Soria on how to rile her up. From the corner of his eye, he spotted lights and turned to look. "The Dome," Rain said as the Dome came into view. It lit up the night like a lighthouse in the middle of the ocean. They would be reaching its piers soon.

"We're back."

Rain nodded in agreement and smiled. It felt good to be back.

Within minutes, they reached the Dome and got off the ferry. Waiting for them was Mr. Fujiwara and Ms. Tanaka. "Welcome back," greeted the two teachers.

"Yeah," answered the Soulmate couple.

"So, let's go," Yeve said excitedly.

"We have to wait," said Ms. Tanaka.

"For who?" asked the two.

"For them," Mr. Fujiwara answered, pointing to the ocean as they turned to look. Rushing towards them was a water sphere. When it reached the pier, it lifted the two onto the docks and cracked open, falling back into the ocean.

"That was funner than any amusement ride I've ever been on!" Hanabi shouted, fists pumped and eyes twinkling. "Can we do it again? Can we? Can we?"

"Funner isn't a real word," corrected Ms. Tanaka.

"Ugh," Louis groaned before Hanabi could respond. He faltered to one knee and threw a hand to his mouth, turning to puke into the ocean. The five simply stared in disgust. "I feel like puking."

"Can you really say that after you've just puked?" Rain asked.

"Well, anyhow, let's get going." Ms. Tanaka led the way over to the limousine while Mr. Fujiwara assisted Louis.

"That water sphere is the coolest thing Soria's ever created," Hanabi gushed once they were inside the spacious limousine. "It's like being on a roller coaster, except funner and on water."

Yeve shook her head and glanced out the window, trying to spy Soria who was obviously hiding somewhere nearby. "That show-off."

"Are you really one to say that?"

"No one asked for your opinion."

"Funner isn't a real word," Ms. Tanaka corrected again from the front.

Hanabi bit back an argument she couldn't win and rolled her eyes at Yeve who chuckled. They had forgotten what it was like to have Ms. Tanaka around.

Once they reached the mansion, instead of being allowed to rest, the couples were shown to the gold and red theater hall. The mission briefing would begin shortly.

The girls sat on one side while the guys occupied the other side of the theater. As they waited for the teachers and deans, they chatted.

"You're finally back," greeted Crystal once Yeve entered with Hanabi.

"Where else could I go?" Yeve responded while Hanabi smiled and greeted the others.

"Man, still so antisocial as usual."

Love turned towards Alice, asking, "Are you feeling okay now?"

It'd only been a few hours since she woke up and was still feeling the side effects to Miss Umi's drugs. Confused, Alice raised an eyebrow. "Huh? What are you talking about? I feel fine."

"You mean, you don't remember?"

"Oh that, sorry, nervous breakdown," she said giddily and turned away.

Love gave Alice a questioning look and turned around in her seat to stare at Verse. "Tell me you remember."

It was pointless to pursue when Alice obviously wanted to avoid the subject. "I don't really care anymore," Verse said with a sigh. She put a hand to her head and groaned. "I suddenly have a killer headache."

"Should I call Miss Umi for you?" Jennifer offered.

"Not funny," Verse hissed while Jennifer laughed and glanced over to the guys' side. King was as active as ever. There was no longer a need to worry as Jennifer smiled.

"Worry about yourself," Cammie said, noticing her glances.

Jennifer turned and threw Cammie into a hug. It was good to be reunited. She'd missed the girls to death. "Thanks for worrying about me."

Cammie too smiled and returned the hug. "That's what friends are for."

"What happened to your hair?" Hanabi asked, noticing that Jennifer had a new haircut.

"Ah, this," she said and smiled, touching her shoulder length hair. After cutting her luscious locks and returning, Miss Lima had offered to give her a new sleek wavy style. "I cut it."

"Why? It's such a pity. Your hair was so beautiful."

"It couldn't be helped."

"Say," said Midnight who was looking around with a raised eyebrow. Three other girls besides May was missing. "Where's Umeko, Shayla, and Hana?"

Mio finally took notice and looked around too. Shrugging, she answered, "Maybe they're running late."

"No way." Midnight doubtfully shook her head. Umeko was a prompt person and hated late people. There was no way she'd come late to a meeting, especially if it involved an S Class mission.

"Yeah, Umeko wouldn't miss a mission briefing," agreed Jennifer.

While the others were busy talking about the missing girls, Verse joked to Yeve, "I see you made it back in one piece."

"Huh? Want to say that again?" Yeve challenged as the two argued.

"Weird as usual," Midnight and Jennifer said, while Mio smiled. These pointless fights were what she missed most.

"Let's not start a fight," Hanabi pleaded while sitting on Verse's left. "I just returned and I'm in no mood to hear any ruckus right now."

Remi turned in her chair from one row in front to look behind. "Welcome back," she greeted, a little too late.

"Thanks."

"Hey, hey, did you guys hear? Morgana got her drink spiked while on a mission and got groped," Soria joked and sneered, having beaten Yeve and Hanabi back to the theater hall.

"Soria!" Morgana screamed and was out of her seat, cheeks flaring from embarrassment. It was never her intention to get drugged. Neither was she expecting it. If she'd known, she would've done everything within her power to prevent it from occurring. "Nothing like that happened! I never got groped!"

"What are you pooping? Why are you so mad?"

"Because you-" Morgana began and stopped, noticing that everyone's eyes was on her. She glanced over at Aoi who chuckled. "Oh gosh," Morgana said, throwing her hands over her face.

"Your poop is Aoi?" joked Soria as she laughed.

"Soria!" snapped the girls. Even they had heard enough of her vulgarity.

"I hate you girls," Soria complained and clicked her tongue at them.

Yuudai who had been sitting quietly could no longer hold it in and erupted into laughter.

"See? Someone appreciates my jokes."

Verse leaned forward in her chair to glance sideways. She took out a Twinkie from her pocket that Soria had bought and unwrapped it, stuffing it into Soria's mouth. "Eat this and die."

"Whew, that was funny," said Yuudai.

Dark looked over, shaking his head. "Yuu, that's not nice. She's your Soulmate. You should be comforting her."

"Don't wanna," Yuudai murmured and scoffed. It'd be a waste of his efforts. Besides, he was tired of trying and getting rejected. "Why doesn't Aoi comfort her instead?"

"Eh?" Aoi stared at Yuudai who sat beside him, confused.

"I mean she's in love with you. Why don't you comfort her?"

"Oye," snapped King from the front. His arms were crossed and his eyes were closed after having his share of jokes. It was getting rowdy inside the theater hall and he hated it. "Enough with the nonsense."

"Speaking of nonsense," Hotaka said from beside him. He looked over while King ignored him. "I heard you got beaten pretty badly."

At the sudden mentioning of his mission, King opened his eyes and cursed. Kei really did spill the beans. If and when he saw that jealous guy, he'd cut him into pieces. "That bastard."

"So?"

"It was all part of the plan to get inside the laboratory."

"Kei said you'd use that line," Hotaka teased with a smile. Kei had been right. King did lie to make it seem like everything that happened was all part of the plan to finish the mission.

King twitched and glared at Hotaka, then grinned. If this was how they were going to play the game, two could play at it. "I heard your Soulmate adopted a cute little brother. How does it feel to finally be number two?"

"Oye," warned Hotaka as he twitched. Just remembering how Mere clung to Midnight the entire journey back to the Dome was enough for him to tear the entire world apart. "Don't remind me. And also, that damn runt isn't cute. He's a demon."

"Then don't remind me either."

While the two were having a staring contest, Naruyuki shook his head and ate his snacks alone. "Those two will never change."

"They won't," Rain confirmed with a smile. The noise was so nostalgic he could probably fall asleep to it.

"Welcome back kids," Dean Kosa greeted as he walked on stage with Dean Kiera. The teachers stood off to the side as everyone hushed to listen attentively. The meeting was finally beginning. "You've all been gathered here for three important missions regarding your comrades.

"Those that are missing, Shadow, Hana, Taiki, Umeko, Kakinouchi, May, Azuma and Shayla, will be the basis for your next mission. I'll brief you about the kidnapping of Taiki and Umeko first." As soon as Dean Kosa said that one line, the group stared in bewilderment, except a few who knew ahead of time. "You are to find their whereabouts and return them back to the Dome safely, as well as destroy the organization that took them hostage."

"Umeko-san," gasped Naruyuki.

Unable to believe it either, Jennifer shook her head. Her best friend may be a hot-head, but she wasn't a fool who would do something reckless that would result in getting captured. Something serious probably happened.

"The group going to their aide will comprise of Rain, Yeve, Noah, Remi, Sasuke, Mio, Louis, Hanabi, Poe, Alice, Naruyuki and Verse," he announced.

"Why so many?" asked Noah suspiciously.

"The group you'll be going against is called the Bat Angels. They're an evil organization intent on destroying the world with another war. We must prevent that at all costs. Which is why we sent Taiki and Umeko who are one of the strongest amongst you. Their kidnapping only proves that this organization must be stopped. Which is why you'll need all the manpower you can get to accomplish what they failed to do."

Teo rubbed his forehead. It was time for another fight when he'd just finished one. "Here goes another headache."

"As many of you may have heard, May's heart was taken by a psychotic doctor. The second group will go aide Mina, Azuma, and Shayla in retrieving her heart, bringing down the organization, the Thunderbolts, and their leader, Haj, then rescuing the prisoner, Gon Aikawa."

Dean Kiera cleared her throat and took over. "That group will be comprised of, Aoi, Soria, Takahiko, Love, Teo, Crystal, Yuudai, Morgana, Dark, Cammie, and Kakinouchi."

Morgana gasped and threw both hands to her mouth, unable to control her excessive blushing. Just the thought of being on a true mission with Aoi made her squeal. "Me, together on a mission with Aoi-kun? I can't believe it!"

"Have I been cursed?" hissed Yuudai while the guys laughed at Morgana's enthusiasm. The rest of the girls simply rolled their eyes.

Angry at hearing her second mission, Soria glared at Dean Kiera, then turned towards Morgana to speak, "Hey, Aoi-head."

"Don't call me that!"

"I know you like him."

"Eh?!" Morgana gasped and held her breath. Had she been found out?

"I have a great idea. Why don't we trade Soulmates?"

"Eh?!" Aoi shouted, taking a stand. He couldn't believe his ears. "You can't suddenly switch me out for someone else! If the problem was because of our last mission, then I'll prove myself on this next one!"

"Fine, I'll become a lone drifter then."

"You have me! Why would you suggest becoming a drifter?!" Aoi threw his hands to his face and cried. His incompetence had driven away his Soulmate. "In the end, you really do hate me."

"Soria!" screamed Morgana. "Stop hurting Aoi-kun! If you don't stop it this instant, I'm gonna have to kick your ass again!"

"Have you ever bested me in a bout?"

"Argh, you!" She glared at Soria and turned to face Aoi. Her anger faded and she smiled shyly. "Is—is it really okay to swap partners?"

"Kids," hissed the two deans from the stage. They were in the middle of briefing missions and didn't have time for this farce.

Without caring about their anger, Soria raised a hand to ask a question, "Dean, if Morgana wants Aoi, she can have him. I'll take Yuudai. I think we make a better team anyway."

"I second," agreed Yuudai.

Dean Kiera snapped and grabbed the microphone off its stand to scream into, "Your Soulmates are absolute! Now shut up!" she commanded as the kids settled down. "As for you Soria!" she shouted, pointing a finger. It was apparent that Soria was upset with her next mission and was taking it out on Aoi and Morgana. "Your request is denied! You can't have Yuudai! You're forever stuck with Aoi!"

"Damn woman," Soria sputtered.

"Well, if it makes you feel any better, I don't like my mission either," Verse said, trying to comfort her.

Soria looked over and patted Verse's head. "Poor you," she soothed.

"Yes, poor *us*."

"No, just you."

"Uwah, one of these days, I'm really gonna bury you six feet under."

With trembling fists, Aoi glared at his best friend. His pride as a man was damaged beyond repair. "Yuu, were you always a love rival?"

Yuudai looked over and grinned. Finally, they were on the same page and he wouldn't want it any other way. "Haven't we always been?"

"Huh?" Aoi looked genuinely confused. "Since when?"

"A fool like you won't understand its meaning, even in death."

"Stop talking and listen!" Dean Kiera barked, her chest heaving. If they were to interrupt her again, she'd go Berserk. This generation of Life-Kills that sat before her was truly a handful. Every single one of them moved at their own pace and loved fighting. Why couldn't they be like the previous generations and simply obey? Did she have to kill off their personalities and turn them into robots? If so, she had no problem doing it.

Dean Kosa smiled and walked over, pulling Dean Kiera aside. It was time for him to intervene before she really blew a fuse. "I'll finish the briefing," he offered and removed the microphone from her hand. Dean Kosa smiled out at the group, his aura turning black as they flinched. "Kids," he said in his sweetest voice, challenging them to interrupt *him*.

"Crap, there's that scary tone again," Takahiko said and gulped.

"I will now announce the third and final task. The third group will go and assist Shadow and Hana. You are to make sure that Zara doesn't meet up with her boss. That group will be comprised of Hotaka, Midnight, King, and Jennifer. Only you four will go. That'll be more than enough manpower to help Hana."

"Eh, together with him?!" shouted Hotaka and King. They stood from their chairs, pointing fingers and glaring. Were they forever fated to cross paths with one another?

"Wait!" shouted Teo as he stood also. "Why am I not part of that group?! Shadow is my best friend! I should go save him instead of these two dimwits!"

"Who're you calling dimwits?" growled the two while Teo perspired from the landmine he'd triggered.

"If anything, shouldn't *I* be part of that group? Seems like it's comprised of the strongest," Rain said.

"We're strong too," the others growled while Rain ignored them. "He's picking a fight with us again."

"Boys," Dean Kosa said, smiling at the four who were creating another ruckus. "If there's a problem, you're more than welcome to see me personally in my office. Other than that, *sit down*."

The three gulped and obediently sat while Rain was seated to begin with.

"Then, in the morning you set out to your destinations. Get all the rest you can get." The two deans turned and walked out, ending the meeting.

After a few minutes, the group erupted into another argument.

"Why the hell do I have to team up with you?!" King shouted and stood, pointing a finger at Hotaka again. "Jennifer and I are more than enough!"

Hotaka sneered and stood, crossing his arms haughtily. "Are you sure you should be saying that to me when you barely succeeded your mission?"

"You bastard! Shouldn't you be more concerned about that *cute* brother-in-law?"

"For the last time, he's not cute!"

"Shadow!" cried Teo. "Forgive me! I can't save you!"

"Oye, oye, calm down," said Sasuke to the three.

"Why is it you?! Why?!" Aoi demanded and jealously pointed at Yuudai. "Of all the men on this earth, why is it you, my biggest rival and best friend?!"

"I should be asking you that! Why the hell is it you?! You're just an idiot!" shouted Yuudai in return.

"Oye, oye," said Dark as he got in-between them. "Calm it."

Instead of caring about their argument, Naruyuki thought aloud to himself. "How did Umeko-san get captured anyway?"

"How did Taiki get captured?" agreed Takahiko. No matter how he thought about it, he couldn't picture it happening.

Sasuke sighed and gave up on trying to break them apart. It was futile and a waste of his breath. Instead, he sat back and watched the group of guys argue like they were a drama on TV. "Wow, we've all got problems."

"Yeah, tell me about it," agreed Noah.

Not bothering to get involved, Rain stood. The missions had already been assigned. The groups had already been preselected. There was no need to bicker over something they couldn't control. "I'm heading to bed first." He stuffed his hands into his pockets and left with a yawn.

"I'm gonna bail too." Poe stood to follow Rain.

Meanwhile, on the girls' side, they were making their way out of the theater hall.

"Soria," Morgana whined, clinging to Soria's waist. There were tears in her eyes as she sniffled. "Give Aoi-kun to me."

"Let go of me, Morgana."

"If you do, I promise to stop making lies about defeating you."

"If you don't let go of me this instant, I'm gonna poop on you."

"Oh gosh, you're so disgusting!" Even though she said that, Morgana didn't dare let go.

"Why, oh why, must I get stuck with the emo?" Verse asked and left dreadfully. Just thinking about it depressed her.

"I'm gonna try and get some sleep." Cammie bid the others a goodnight and left for her room.

"Those stupid monkeys, why do they act like they're fighting over bananas?" Midnight shook her head. She could still hear the guys shouting as she exited the theater hall. Even though half the guys weren't part of the argument, they had stayed behind to watch.

"Here are two more monkeys," Crystal mumbled as they passed Soria and Morgana who continued their fight in the hallway.

∞

Yeve yawned, wanting nothing more than to rest her head on a pillow, but Miss Umi had called her in to the infirmary. While passing the dining room, she noticed how lively the mansion was. Neither the guys nor girls could sleep, especially since they had things to catch up on. Groaning, Yeve reached the infirmary and entered without a knock. "What's up?" she greeted with another yawn.

"Routine check-up." Miss Umi stood and motioned for Yeve to lie down as she complied. She attached two small white circular patches hooked to machines on Yeve's temples and hit a button. A chart appeared, showing straight and squiggly lines on her computer screen. Miss Umi studied it before turning to take the white patches off. "All done," she said.

"What was that about?" Yeve sat up suspiciously, while Miss Umi sat back down.

Instead of answering, Miss Umi asked her own questions. "Have you been having any headaches?"

"No."

"Migraines?" she continued.

"No." Yeve shook her head again, watching Miss Umi grab a clipboard to check things off one by one.

"Dreams?"

"Kind of."

Miss Umi raised an eyebrow. "What kind?"

"I don't know. They usually disappear when I wake up. Why?"

"I see." She wrote down something this time. When she finished, she asked more questions. "Have you been acting strangely?"

"Like?" Having Miss Umi ask so many unusual questions was out of character, even if she was a "doctor." For as long as Yeve could remember, she was always distant. To start worrying now, Yeve couldn't help but think that something was wrong.

Miss Umi looked up, sensing that Yeve was catching on like usual. No wonder Dean Kiera always had to be cautious around her. Miss Umi rested her hand with the pen on the clipboard to give some examples, "Like seeing things that aren't really there or hearing voices?"

"You mean hallucinations?"

Miss Umi nodded. "Exactly."

"No."

"I see." Miss Umi crossed off something on the list again. She turned towards the monitor screen and smiled at Yeve. "I need to do one more thing."

This time Yeve tensed and frowned. "That would be?"

Miss Umi stood, setting her clipboard facedown. "Don't ask so many questions. Don't you know that curiosity killed the cat?"

"Are you the curious thing that will kill me?"

Miss Umi turned to lead the way and stopped when she heard Yeve's question. She couldn't help but chuckle, almost forgetting what it was like to have such a rebellious student. Amongst the new generation at the academy, not one girl was like Yeve or the other two. In fact, all the new students were proper and obedient, something she wasn't used to after having the three as students for the past eighteen years. "I'm not going to kill you, Yeve."

"I see." Though she still doubted Miss Umi's words, she had no choice in this matter. Miss Umi would perform the check-up one way or another without her consent. "Okay then, proceed."

"Follow me." Miss Umi led the way again as Yeve followed.

∞

Poe yawned while lying inside the infirmary. He wanted to quickly finish this and go to sleep. Knowing the guys who were too excited to sleep, he wouldn't be getting much sleep at all.

"Have you been seeing things or hearing things that aren't really there?" asked Gabe from where he sat.

"None, whatsoever."

Gabe looked over, recording it down on his clipboard before asking, "Nothing?"

Poe frowned before spilling the beans about his conflicting feelings for Alice. Though his gut feeling told him not to fall for her, he couldn't help it. It was as natural as breathing. "Am I weird, sensei?"

Gabe smiled and shut off the computer screen. A deceased student once asked him that same question long ago. Back then he gave an answer that still haunted him to this day. At least this time, he could truthfully speak his mind. "Love just is. You can't expect to understand how it works. It's too complex and doesn't follow any written rules," Gabe said, standing and motioning for Poe to follow. "Come. We've got to do one last check-up."

"Okay." He obediently stood and followed without questioning.

∞

Miss Umi had finished Yeve's check-up an hour ago and was now moving on to Soria who had been procrastinating since her return. "So, nothing unusual?"

After hearing a snore for a response, Miss Umi looked over at the bed where Soria lay. In her hand was a half-eaten banana. Miss Umi had gone to wake her in the middle of the night. In order to keep her awake, Miss Umi had given her a banana to eat. Regardless of what attempts she made, Soria kept falling asleep. Twitching, Miss Umi smacked her awake, "Soria!"

"Ow," Soria said, rubbing her eyes and turning to greet Miss Umi hoarsely, "yo."

"Don't 'yo' me," she hissed. "Why are you sleeping?"

"I'm tired. Can I leave now?" Soria yawned and stared at the banana in her hand. Her eyes widened, not knowing how it'd gotten there.

"Is there anything unusual about your body?" Miss Umi continued, ignoring Soria's curious look at the banana.

"Just that I want to poop suddenly," she answered and took a bite.

"Have you ever considered that it may be the banana?"

Confused, she continued chewing. "What do bananas have anything to do with going to the bathroom?"

"Bananas make you constipated."

"Seriously?!" shouted Soria as she sat up and stopped chewing, her eyes widening again. "I knew it. I knew it was your fault, little banana," she blamed, pointing a finger at the half-eaten banana. She glared this time but still took another bite to finish.

"Soria, be a little more serious here. Have you had any dreams? Or been hearing or seeing anything out of the ordinary?"

After seriously considering the question, she answered, "I do hear something."

Miss Umi raised an eyebrow. "What?"

"The sound of my stomach rumbling, I think I gotta go potty," she answered and bolted.

"Soria!" Miss Umi called back. She shook her head and stared at her blank paper on the clipboard. She glanced at the clock. It was two that morning. Miss Umi tossed her clipboard onto the desk in frustration. She never did know how to handle Soria's ways which were worse than Yeve's. "That girl seriously blows my mind. I so, do not miss her."

38th Lie

IT WAS A LITTLE PAST TWO when Verse left her room, deciding to take a stroll alone. After lying in bed for four hours she couldn't manage to fall asleep. In five hours, they would be leaving for their next mission. Verse scratched her head as she passed Midnight's room just as Midnight came out.

"Oh, Verse," Midnight greeted and smiled. There was someone else who couldn't sleep with all the commotion either. "Wanna walk together?" she offered as Verse walked by without realizing someone was there. "Verse?"

"Huh?" She turned back and finally saw her. "Oh, hey," she greeted.

"What's eating you?" Midnight waltzed over as they headed downstairs.

"Nothing much."

"Yeah, right. Tell me."

Verse looked over and smiled at how nosy the youngest was. "I was just wondering why Naruyuki's so hung up on Umeko."

Midnight grinned, finding something to tease Verse about. "You jealous?"

"No."

Verse answered in such a straightforward manner that Midnight found it more suspicious. If she wasn't jealous, there was nothing to dwell on. "Well," Midnight said, scratching her head, "they are good friends."

"I know," Verse said with a light laugh.

"Why'd you laugh?"

"You should see the look on his face when he talks about her."

"So then, you are jealous."

"I'm not."

Midnight stopped walking, as did Verse. "Why not?" she asked. "Do you have someone else?"

Verse thought about it before shaking her head. "Nope."

"Then let's drop it," Midnight suggested, walking on as Verse followed along. "Every time I talk to you, you make me feel depressed."

Verse couldn't help but laugh. "I so do not."

∞

The guys sat inside the dining room, eating a late snack since none of them could sleep. Hotaka glanced over at Yuudai and Aoi who were sitting away from each other. He hadn't seen them talk since the argument inside the theater hall. "You need to quickly make up with Aoi."

Yuudai looked over and scowled. It made no sense that he had to be the one to apologize. "Never in a million-gazillion years."

"You two are on the same team for helping Azuma. You need to cooperate. For Pete's sake, you're even best friends."

"I'll never cooperate with a nincompoop like him."

Hotaka smiled and shook his head, knowing the reasons for Yuudai's jealousy. In fact, everyone did. The only one who didn't know was Aoi himself and that reason alone was what made Yuudai so frustrated.

"I'm her Soulmate, aren't I? So why won't she look at me? I've tried so many times, only to end up failing. I've never failed like this before," he said, holding his fork so tight his knuckles turned white.

Worried that Yuudai would stab someone with it, Hotaka reached out to take the fork away. When he noticed someone approaching, he looked up and smiled, "Yo, what's up?"

"Uh," said Aoi.

At the sound of his voice, Yuudai snapped his head up and glared away. Aoi was the last person he wanted to see.

"Sorry, Yuu. I shouldn't have overreacted," apologized Aoi. "Instead of blaming you, I should concentrate on how to beat you and make Soria acknowledge me." Aoi smiled, no contempt on his face. He wasn't even upset about the argument anymore. Instead, he was fired up about changing Soria's views on him and wasn't going to admit defeat until he succeeded.

Hotaka smiled as well and nodded. For being such a kid at heart, Aoi was maturing quickly. "Well said."

A smile crept onto Yuudai's face. Aoi forgave and forgot too easily, never holding grudges. This was one of the many reasons why Morgana liked his foolish friend. It was also one of the reasons why Yuudai respected him, though he'd never admit even on his dying breathing. "I'll also work harder so I don't lose to a punk like you. So please, for this next mission, don't get captured and add to our workload. I don't wanna have to save your ass again."

"Don't make up lies!"

"But it's true," Yuudai said with a grin.

"Then, I'll prove you wrong," said Aoi as he walked away.

"Who does he think he is, challenging me like some hotshot? We both know I'll win."

∞

Dean Kiera sat at her desk, going through the reports the girls had submitted. Though it was a little half past two now, she had many things to see to. The girls' reports were still lacking, but she expected that. As time passed however, they'd get better at explaining how they had failed or succeeded a mission and what measurements they took.

Dean Kiera picked up one of the files to skim through before dropping it back down onto her desk. Standing beside her like usual was Miss Lima. Sitting on the desk was a cup of tea to keep Dean Kiera awake, though coffee would be the better choice.

There was a knock at the door as Miss Umi entered alongside Soria. The two bowed and walked over. Miss Umi set down a few more files in her arms.

"It's that time already, huh?" Dean Kiera asked, ignoring Soria's presence.

Miss Umi smiled and nodded. "Yes, it most certainly is."

"So? What brings you here?"

Miss Umi scratched her head. She didn't want to admit that Soria was a handful. But even if she didn't, the dean most likely knew the truth. "She wants to talk about her next mission."

"And what's in it for you?" Dean Kiera asked, already guessing correctly.

"She'll cooperate with me during her check-up."

Chuckling, Dean Kiera shook her head. It was amazing how Soria could practically force anyone's hand without even trying. "Speak."

Soria took a step forward and bowed a second time before standing. "Dean, please switch my next mission with someone else."

Dean Kiera's look hardened. The teams created would ensure the success of the missions. They couldn't go back on their decisions now. "Proposal, denied."

"But-"

"You'll go and retrieve May's heart, along with your team. That's final."

"May-"

"I know you don't like her, and personally, I don't care," Dean Kiera interrupted again, feeling the wrath from Soria's eyes alone. "But orders are final. You'll go. That's the end of that."

408

Growling, Soria spun around to leave. The meeting had been pointless.

Once gone, the dean shook her head. Soria's glare was more intense than Yeve's. Funny how they were so different yet similar. "That girl," she said, now turning her attention to Miss Umi who remained. "How was the pink vial that Michio created? Have you looked into it?"

"Yes, I have."

"And?" Dean Kiera asked, sipping her tea before returning to her paperwork.

Miss Umi grinned. "The serum has no side effects towards us. It heals our body from the inside. The injuries on the outside however, takes time. He made it flawless."

"What about the heart and mind?"

"Can't be healed."

"Stumped by the heart and mind again." Dean Kiera sighed. Were they never to understand the heart and mind's secrets? "Can you recreate the serum?"

Miss Umi shook her head in disappointment. She couldn't recreate something she knew nothing about, especially if it involved the works of Michio. He wasn't called a genius without a reason. "Gabe and I are trying but it's impossible. There's a secret formula."

"Well that's even more reason why we need to retrieve Michio. His intelligence is vital."

"Yes, I agree. If we can get our hands on him, it would highly benefit us."

Dean Kiera nodded and motioned for Miss Lima to pour more tea. "If only Yeve had succeeded her mission, we would already have Michio within our clutches. But no, she let his dear mistress slip away. I was wrong to have sent her instead of Midnight or Umeko."

"I'm sure Yeve was misled."

"I doubt that." Dean Kiera picked up Yeve's report to skim through.

The sweet aroma of the bakery shop made us see an illusion. We quickly fell into a slumber. When we awoke, Miss Heidi was gone.

Dean Kiera chuckled and set the report down. "Does she really think I'll fall for that?" she said and sipped the tea that Miss Lima handed her. What made the report more infuriating was the fact that all Yeve did during her mission, was bake.

"Should I induce the drug on her?"

"Yes, we can't have her Awaken."

Miss Umi bowed and turned to leave.

"Umi-sensei," called back Dean Kiera as she set the teacup down on its saucer.

"Yes?" she answered, turning back.

"Keep a close eye on the other one."

"I have *her* under heavy surveillance."

"Good." Dean Kiera nodded. At least now, she could rest easy if only for a few minutes. Miss Umi bowed her head and exited, leaving the dean to contemplate on things.

∞

The stars continued burning brightly though it was three in the morning. The dew on the grass wet Hanabi's clothes and hair but she didn't bother. The mission was the only thing on her mind as she took the time to calm her soul. Instead of stealing information, she was to save a comrade and infiltrate an organization. It would require her to be at the top of her game.

"Can I join you?" Louis asked, walking over to peer down. He smiled, happy to have finally found her.

Hanabi looked over and nodded in response.

Louis sat and lay beside her, observing the starry sky also. It was so peaceful and calming. No wonder Hanabi chose to stay outside, instead of indoors, where it was noisy. "The stars are beautiful, regardless if they're fake."

"Yeah, they are."

A few seconds of silence passed before Louis spoke again. "You seem kind of down ever since we got back. Is it because of what happened with Jabol-san?"

Hanabi smiled, shaking it off. "I'm fine."

Louis nodded, dropping the topic. He too, didn't want to be reminded of how he'd left Hanabi to finish a mission on her own while he was sticking his nose in another's affair. Turning, Louis reached a hand out.

Hanabi flinched on instinct. "What?"

"Give me your hand."

"Why?"

"I want to see your future."

"I'll pass."

"Why not?"

Her future would be something she decided on. If he didn't allow her this much freedom, then like their past, she could do nothing to change her future again. "I don't need you to look at my future. I know already."

"And how do you know?"

"Because, I've already planned it out."

Louis stared at her for a long time before turning away. He couldn't win. That much he knew. Hanabi was stubborn. If she said she wouldn't do something, she wouldn't do it. It was the same for the guys who refused his request to see their futures too. No matter how curious they were, they

410

wanted the choices of creating it for themselves. "In that case, I won't ask to see your future."

"Yeah, you don't need to."

"Why'd you say it in such a mean way for? Am I not part of that future?" he joked and laughed, but stopped when he noticed Hanabi wasn't joining in. Suddenly, his heart throbbed. "I'm not?" he joked some more.

Hanabi turned to look at him square in the eyes, not blinking. "Do you really want to know the answer to that question?"

Regardless how many times he had to make a joke out of it, he wanted to know. They were Soulmates, bound to each other. He wanted to believe that she'd include him in her future, like how he'd done with her.

Just like the other times, Louis was whisked away towards his Future Sight he couldn't yet control.

He stood inside a café bakery of some sort. It was a place he'd never been to or seen before, but it felt nostalgic for some reason. The shop wasn't a big place, neither was it too small. It was just perfect actually. The ivory colors of the walls gave off a warm homey feel. The chairs and tables felt very in-place. This place, it smelt of sweet cakes. There weren't any customers that day as Louis took his time taking in his surroundings.

Suddenly, the front door to the shop opened as a twenty-one-year-old Louis entered. He watched in alarm and went to examine his older self, since he couldn't interact with others when inside his visions. His twenty-one-year-old self looked so mature, yet filled with a hint of sadness. His eyes seemed so wise, compared to the teenage him, and the kid him. From somewhere in the back, a bell sounded to signal a customer's presence.

"Welcome!" greeted a twenty-one-year-old Hanabi who came out from the backroom, wearing a waitress's uniform. When her eyes fell on him, she stopped walking.

"Hana…bi," whispered Future Louis.

Even the eighteen-year-old Louis who watched the scene unfold was shocked. Hanabi had a shorter hairstyle and emitted the same mature vibe.

"Louis-kun," she gasped but still smiled. Tears welled in her eyes. It felt like ages since they last saw each other. "Welcome to Yoyo's Bakery," she greeted and bowed.

"Eh? Ah, I mean, uh, thank you," Future Louis stuttered and smiled, scratching his head sheepishly. "I didn't know you worked here—I mean, not that I wouldn't have come if I knew. It's just that Rain asked me to come and you know, well, I couldn't really refuse so I came." He reached into his coat and pulled out a postcard for evidence. Indeed, the invitation had been sent from Rain, inviting Louis to the shop.

"I see," she said and smiled. "You don't have to try and justify yourself."

"Ah, yeah," he said softly.

"It's been a long time."

Future Louis did his best to smile, but the pain reached his tear-filled eyes as he bowed. "Indeed, it has."

Although present Louis didn't understand, in his heart there was discomfort. The pair was acting more like strangers than Soulmates.

"Ah, it's really you." At that precise moment, Rain entered the shop too. He had on a trench coat and scarf, like it was cold outside, though it was clearly spring. As soon as the two guys saw each other, they smiled and hugged.

This Rain gave off a calmer aura and even felt like a distinguished business man. His eyes were filled with more life and his laughter was rich. What exactly happened that would make Rain change so much?

"It's been a long time." Future Rain let go and hit Future Louis' arm as the door leading to the back opened.

"Hanabi-" called out Yeve as she came out. Her hair was pinned behind her head while she wore a white pastry chef's uniform. Her apron was covered in powder, like she'd been baking since early morning. There was even a smile on her face. The older Yeve's domineering presence had disappeared altogether. She too had a calm aura.

"Yeve." Future Louis smiled, no longer afraid of her.

"Eh?!" Louis nearly lost his mind. He pointed a finger, unable to believe the absurdity he was witnessing. "I came here to see Yeve-sama?!"

"You," Yeve said, turning her attention to Future Louis.

"Here it comes!" Louis crouched and threw both arms over his head. A threat or lecture was going to come out of her mouth at any second now because his future self had been too casual.

"Welcome."

"Huh?" Louis blinked as the scenery from the unknown future disappeared. Lying beside him on the grass was the eighteen-year-old Hanabi he knew. She continued staring at him with her unwavering eyes. Quickly, Louis turned away. Although he didn't understand what he'd just seen, whatever the future had in store, he would patiently wait. It was his first-time hearing Yeve speak in such a gentle tone. Chuckling to himself, Louis put a hand to his mouth. Maybe, she wasn't so terrible after all.

"What's with you?" Hanabi asked, suspicious of his laughter.

"Nothing." Louis shook his head and smiled at the stars. He was looking forward to what the future had in store for them.

∞

Kakinouchi, who was finally allowed out of his room after going Berserk, headed straight to the morgue where May's body was stored. Once he entered the chilly room, one of the staff turned to look at him and bowed. Kakinouchi also bowed and walked over to where May's body was. He pressed a green button as the drawer slid open.

A puff of cold air arose, keeping her body from decomposing.

May slept like Sleeping Beauty, waiting for her prince to save her. He reached out and held her cold hand, giving it a light squeeze before kissing her forehead. It felt so eerie here, he wanted to quickly take her body out. "I'll be back with your heart. Wait for me."

39th Lie

MINA AND THE COUPLE sat inside Shayla's room, holding a secret meeting about the back-ups that were coming to assist them. "The group will be arriving tonight. Everything's going to be chaotic. So we must move stealthily and accurately, understood?"

Azuma and Shayla nodded and replied, "Understood."

"Then tonight, we bring down this organization before they suspect us any further."

"Isn't this a little too quick?" asked Azuma.

"It is." Mina nodded. She knew what was being asked of them, but it had to be done at all costs. "It'll only be a matter of time before Nishikawa-sensei convinces Haj to eliminate us." Mina dug into her pocket, taking out a piece of paper to hold out. "These are names of the group that will assist us. I need to know their abilities so I can begin assigning groups."

"I wanna see," said Shayla as she glanced over at the names while Azuma unfolded the paper.

"I'll be leading the group to take down the organization. The second group will save Gon and the third group will retrieve May's heart."

"I'm going in that group," volunteered Azuma.

"Arata-kun," protested Shayla.

Azuma pointed a finger to Kakinouchi's name on the paper, ignoring her protest. "I have no doubt he'll go after May's heart. Which is why I have to keep him in check."

After thinking about it, Mina agreed. "Alright," she said, impatient. "Now tell me their abilities."

"Soria," Shayla said pointing to her name. If Yeve couldn't make it, at least they had Soria who was the most unreliable and reliable. "Is a water user. Love is a spell caster. Crystal has a third eye, but her powers are limited. All she can do for now is see as far as ten miles and enter another's mind, though it drains a lot of her energy. Morgana is an ice user, and Cammie can manipulate light into threads."

"And the boys?"

"Aoi, fire, Takahiko has superhuman strength, Teo can speak to animals," answered Azuma.

The two girls stared and raised their eyebrows. They never knew what his powers were until then.

"It's true. He really can."

Chuckling, Shayla shook her head. No wonder Teo had managed to defeat Crystal all those years ago. He had informed the animals to keep tabs on her, in case the day ever came where he needed to use any of her secrets against her for the duel. His surveillance had paid off. Crystal was both afraid and vengeful towards him.

"Continue," urged Mina.

"Yuudai controls lightning—er, manipulates electricity—electric user? —whatever you wanna call it. Dark controls shadows, and last, but not least Kakinouchi, ice user."

Mina tapped her chin, thinking about how to distribute the group.

Shayla stared at Soria's name for a long time before speaking, "May I be the one to split the groups?"

Mina's eyes widened at her request. Leaving a junior to determine the outcome of this mission was reckless. "Absolutely not."

"I can determine who works best with whom."

"Shayla-" she began.

"Trust me. I won't fail in assigning groups."

Mina raised an eyebrow, wondering what had overtaken her suddenly. "And what would you suggest?" she asked, crossing her arms to listen.

Seeing this as a chance to prove her point, Shayla smiled. She'd already considered their powers and personalities, knowing exactly who to pair with whom. "Teo-kun will be part of the group to rescue Gon-kun. With his powers, he'll be able to communicate with the animals and they'll let him know where Gon-kun's being held captive. Takahiko-kun's strong, so he'll be part of that group. Aoi-kun will serve as back-up along with Morgana. She won't allow anything or anyone to hurt him. As for the group taking down the organization, it'll comprise of you and me, along with the exceptional fighters."

"And what about the group retrieving May's heart?"

"Kakinouchi-kun, Arata-kun, and Soria will do."

"And here I was, almost taking you seriously."

"I'm being serious though. Those three will be more than enough."

"Really, that's a reckless plan." Mina shook her head in refusal as Shayla whined once more. She wasn't going to give up until Mina resigned. "Why are you so adamant?"

Shayla smiled and leaned into her chair, recalling how Yeve had whipped her into shape so she'd be on par with Azuma. Even Yeve's diet plan was more brutal than Miss Umi and Jennifer's put together. It made Shayla cry day in and day out until she finally lost all the weight. On top of that, Yeve even made her learn the ways of a tactician, by playing board games, though she never won once against her ruthless master. Right after the end of school days, Yeve would drag Shayla off into the forest to train, regardless if she wanted to or not. Even when she tried to flee, Yeve easily caught her. After thinking about it, she somehow began looking forward to her training more than breakfast, lunch, snack time, and dinner combined. Shayla was who she was because of Yeve.

"Because, my master taught me well, and I know these guys like the back of my hand," answered Shayla.

After a few seconds, Mina gave up. Shayla did have a point. They were schoolmates who knew each other better than Mina did. Just this once, she would go along with her junior's ideas and see how capable Shayla really was. If her plan succeeded, the Dome might've found a diamond in the rough. "Alright, we'll go with your plan. Now get some rest. It'll be a long day." Mina stood and quickly slipped out, trying to avoid detection.

Once she was gone, Azuma turned to stare at Shayla for some time. She fidgeted under his scrutiny as he chuckled. Reaching over, he messed up her hair. She really was a different person compared to when they were younger. "Yeve sure taught you well."

Shayla blushed and smiled. It was Yeve's favorite saying, "Remember the abilities of your comrades and enemies. Engrave it into your soul if you must. When the time calls for that knowledge, you'll be able to assess the situation and deal with it accordingly."

After Azuma finished laughing, he frowned and went to burn the list of names. "I wonder if Kakinouchi will be able to retrieve May's heart when he sees that it's pumping inside another body, a *woman's* body."

"The real question is, will *you* be able to?"

Azuma thought about it while watching the tiny scrap burn before him. "Zena-san is a good person."

Shayla turned away, receiving her answer. Even though Azuma knew that the heart beating inside Zena belonged to May, he was too soft. Knowing everyone else on the list, they too wouldn't be able to take the heart, after seeing what kind of person Zena was, especially Kakinouchi. Only Soria, who detested May would be able to complete this mission.

∞

Having lost count of the days, Umeko hoped that the Dome realized they were missing and would send a team to rescue them soon. Unlike the first day when she had been confined and chained to the room that fed off her life-energy, giving power to the darkness, Umeko stopped trying to self-heal. With what little energy she had, she saved it.

"Still alive, I see." Pia entered the room and walked over to examine Umeko, making sure she wasn't dead yet. They needed the two on the brink of death to use as a bargaining piece to the Maroon Dome for the diamonds and weapons that Drake and Midori had lost.

"You," Umeko growled weakly.

Grinning, Pia stood after confirming that she wasn't dead. It was her job to keep them alive. "Has anyone told you that you don't suit your handsome Soulmate?"

"Oye," said Umeko. She managed to open one eyelid and glare. "Don't even think about it."

"I just now realized something," Pia said in annoyance, "you remind me of a certain weak girl I met not long ago. Like with you, she too didn't suit her Soulmate." Turning to leave, she found Anoka standing in the hallway with a red ball in her hands. "Anoka, what are you doing down here?"

"I wanted to play ball with you."

"Come." Pia walked over to take Anoka's hand as they left.

Umeko let her head drop with a deep sigh and closed her eye. Just talking required strength she barely had. Her body felt like it would break down and never function again. This vulnerability was the worst feeling in the world. "Jennifer, you bastard, you need to come save me, now."

∞

A bouquet of mixed flowers sat in Naruyuki's arm as he walked through the grassy field. It was a beautiful morning with fluffy batches of cloud floating above. Standing beneath a tree's shade with her back to him was Umeko. Down at her feet was a brown Labrador. As soon as the puppy noticed Naruyuki, he barked, causing Umeko to turn and smile.

When Naruyuki reached her, he stopped and whispered, "For you," and held out the bouquet, "my love."

Gasping, he awoke in bed and reached out to the empty air. He breathed heavily and stared at his hand and the ceiling for some time before finally

417

lowering it. Again, he was having that dream. Groaning, Naruyuki sat up and pulled at his untied hair. If Verse had been present again, she'd have given him another accusing look.

"Cheater," accused Dark from where he laid on the sofa.

"Whoa!" Alarmed, Naruyuki spun around. "Don't scare me like that. If you're there, make some noise."

"You're the one who didn't see me lying here to begin with."

Naruyuki turned away, not saying a word. It was true that it was his fault for being absentminded, but Dark had no right to be there in the first place.

"I heard, you know?"

Naruyuki raised an eyebrow, confused and suspicious. "You heard what?"

"I heard you calling out to Umeko."

"I did no such thing. Don't make up lies," Naruyuki said, trying to play it off cool by laughing, but knew it wouldn't work with Dark.

"You can't lie to me. I was right here when you called out her name."

"Don't tell Ver-"

"If your head is filled with thoughts of Umeko, let Verse go. If your heart beats for Verse, then force yourself to think about her until no traces of Umeko is left. If you can't choose, you'll end up being an indecisive man for the rest of your life."

Naruyuki hung his head down low. He knew that without anyone having to tell him. He just couldn't find it within himself to choose. "Why the hell are you here to begin with?"

"Sasuke's snoring."

"That doesn't mean you can come barging into my room."

"How mean," Dark said, turning to pout at Naruyuki. "Be a good friend and let me sleep here for the remaining time until we leave."

"No. Go find a new room. Or sleep in the lounge."

"I'm gonna tell Verse what happened just now."

"Go to sleep."

Dark laughed evilly to settle back onto the sofa. It was his win.

∞

King yawned and entered the dining room to find more than half the guys still awake. Gabe had taken longer than they both expected on his routine check-up. Now King was hungry. He grabbed some food and walked over to sit with Rain. "You seem down."

Without bothering to look over, he answered in a monotonous tone, "Does it really?"

"Whoa, emo much," King concluded, taking a bite out of his crackers. "This is a first."

"Okay."

King glared. It was unlike Rain to be so dejected. "What the hell is wrong with you?"

"Nothing."

"Man, you're really annoying. Keep this up and I'll surpass you."

"We both know you can't beat me even with my eyes closed."

"And here's the hateful Rain I know."

Rain chuckled as King scowled. He shouldn't have said a thing if he knew Rain would revert to his old self so quickly.

"Can I ask you something?"

"Why are you asking? Regardless if I say no, you'll still ask."

Rain looked over and bluntly asked, "Do you hate Jennifer?"

Not expecting that, King choked and reached for his juice to gulp down. He looked over, wide-eyed. "Hate her? I mean, she does talk an awful lot. But to hate her for that? No. I don't."

"Oh," Rain said, slouching over.

"Oye, oye, stop it with that negative aura already," King demanded. He was getting sick and tired of looking at Rain's sad puppy face. "You're the oldest, aren't you? Act like it."

"Is it wrong to hate her?"

King took a bite out of his chili and stopped. "Who? Jennifer?"

"No, you dumbass. I'm talking about Yeve."

"There was no need to resort to name calling." King glared at him but let it slide. This was Rain after all. He moved at his own pace. Getting mad would do King no good. "Why do you hate your own Soulmate?"

Rain clutched on tightly to the spoon in his hand. He glared down at his plate, ready to stab it. "Whenever I see her face, I get this urge to strangle her. But when she smiles—god, when she smiles, it all goes away."

"Hmm," said King. He thought about it before putting the crackers into his chili. "You hate her, you like her, you hate her, you like her. Man, which one are you gonna choose when it comes down to it?"

"I don't know."

"If your hatred for her runs blood deep, will you choose to love her?"

"*If* my hatred for her runs blood deep, I'll kill her."

Wanting to object to his final decision, King decided against it. It wasn't in his place to tell Rain what to do. All he could do was give his support. "Well, there you have it. You've already made your decision." King took a bite out of his chili and glanced over. Rain seemed conflicted even in his own convictions. "You won't regret it, right?"

"No."

"Alright then," said King.

"So tell me, have you finally transformed into a carnivore and taken a bite out of Jennifer yet?" Rain teased as King choked on his food again.

∞

While the girls were watching TV and eating, Morgana had fallen asleep first. She turned onto her side and with a smile, mumbled, "Aoi…kun," as the other girls turned to stare at her.

"She's a stalker even in her dreams," accused Love.

Alice smiled. "She's really in love with him."

"Yeah, but she should remember, Aoi is Soria's Soulmate."

"She remembers." Alice stood to grab a blanket to put over Morgana who continued smiling in her sleep.

Mio yawned and lay down on the floor, cuddling close to Morgana. She closed her eyes, not wanting to be apart from them. "Goodnight."

"Goodnight," said the two.

Love reached out to turn the volume lower before looking in Alice's direction. Catching the look, Alice smiled, able to read her mind. Love had been on her case ever since she returned from the infirmary. If she didn't explain herself now, Love wouldn't stop pestering her.

"Umi-sensei said I had a rebound from my mission with Poe," Alice spoke. "Something-something happened with the electro-something in the air that triggered something in my brain to go haywire. Sorry, I didn't mean to scare you guys. Even I scared myself when I pulled my gun at him."

"Something like that is possible?"

Alice shrugged. She was going to take Miss Umi's explanation at face-value without reading too much into it. "Yeah, I guess." Alice smiled reassuringly. Hopefully nothing like that would happen again.

∞

Midnight was heading towards the eastern wing of the mansion. After meeting up with Verse and getting a quick bite, they parted ways. Now she was on her way to visit Mere who was stationed in the same quarters as the male staff. Even though it was late, she wanted to bid him a goodnight.

From behind, Hotaka reached out and caught hold of her wrist. "Where are you going?" he demanded.

Midnight broke free and scowled. After trying to avoid conflict with him, it proved to be pointless. Now going to see Mere would be harder.

Hotaka scowled in return, knowing the reason why Midnight was out so late. He hated how King just might be right. Instead of worrying about their rivalry, he should be more concerned about Mere whom Midnight was giving her undivided attention to. Even if she pitied him because of the auction, there was no need to pay him a house visit. "He's probably asleep already."

"I'm still going."

"Why?"

"Because I always wish him a good night."

"You *always*?" Hotaka repeated, his expression hardening. "Are you trying to tell me that you know him from way back?"

"Yeah," she said and nodded.

"How so?"

"He's my little brother."

"Yeah, right, little brother," Hotaka said, disbelieving her words.

Having enough of his attitude, Midnight tiptoed to eye him. She poked his chest with her finger and snarled, "Stop talking like that, and stop acting like I'm your property."

"As your Soulmate, I have a right to worry." Hotaka crossed his arms stubbornly. How could Midnight be so unsuspecting towards Mere? For all they knew, this could be part of his plan, to wedge a nail between their relationship. "I think he's a bad guy. You should be more careful."

"Mere is not dangerous." Rolling her eyes, Midnight turned to leave. If anything, Mere was more of a crybaby.

"Oye," Hotaka called out. "You're still going?"

"Yeah, I am."

Not wanting to share her with anyone, Hotaka reached out and yanked her back. He secured one hand around her waist and grabbed her behind the head, forcing his lips on hers. She was his, and he'd remind her that.

Taken by surprise, Midnight let out muffled screams and squeezed her eyes shut. She lifted her arms to push him away, but Hotaka held on firmly. Unable to get away using her strength, she used her powers as vines shot out from beneath. Withdrawing to safety, Hotaka panted while Midnight's chest heaved. She placed a hand to her mouth, disgusted. "What the hell was that?!"

"Letting you know that you belong to me."

Rage flared inside. She had just finished telling him that she wasn't his property. Were his ears good for nothing? "Let me repeat myself. I do NOT belong to you."

"You're my Soulmate. So technically speaking, you do."

That was the last straw as Midnight strode over, slapping him across the face. Even if they were Soulmates, she wouldn't allow him to take advantage of her. "The next time you touch me without my consent, I'll kill you." She turned on her heels, returning to her room. She could no longer meet Mere in her state. He'd suspect something and worry. That was the last thing she wanted. "Bastard," Midnight hissed, wiping her lips obsessively. "That was my first kiss."

∞

After having a piano play-off and wearing themselves out, seeing who knew more compositions from the Godless Ages, Noah and Remi fell asleep on the sofa inside the music room.

Night was slowly coming to an end. Soon, morning would arrive and they would depart.

Verse entered the music room and stopped as the door shut itself. She noticed the couple snuggling and walked over to grab a blanket from the closet. After draping them she made her way to the piano bench to sit. The black and white keys stared back, inviting her to play.

Refusing to give in, Verse glanced out the floor-to-ceiling windows to her left. A soft breeze was rustling the trees outside.

"Verse...?" called out Remi hoarsely. She sat up on the sofa and rubbed her eyes.

"Shh," shushed Verse as she turned around, putting a finger to her lips. Remi nodded and smiled, creeping off the sofa to walk over and sit on the bench beside her.

"Why aren't you asleep?"

"Couldn't," she answered and glanced over at Noah again. He was still sleeping even after Remi left his side. Every time she saw the other couples, there was an itch in her chest that she couldn't get rid of.

"What's wrong?"

"You two are really close, huh?"

"Aren't we all?"

Verse shook her head and turned to look out the window again. She had just noticed. The sky was starting to lighten. "Cammie and I are different from you guys. We have nothing in common with our Soulmates."

"What do you mean?"

"All Naruyuki thinks about is Umeko."

"Are you jealous?" Remi teased and smiled.

Verse chuckled at how similar Remi's thoughts were to Midnight's. Even after trying to force herself to be jealous, Verse didn't feel the slightest hint of anger. Just because they were Soulmates, didn't mean they had to bond on a personal level.

"Verse?"

"That's the weird thing. I'm not jealous or mad. I'm just really envious of you guys for being so close."

Remi seemed startled. There really was no sign of jealousy on Verse's face. Thinking she could tease Verse once and for all, Remi only found herself wanting to assure Verse. "Maybe you should be patient with him."

Verse looked over, confused.

"You never know, one day he might come around and actually see only you. So, you should be patient and wait."

"I don't have patience."

Remi laughed, nodding in agreement. The wind whispered against the window as she turned to look outside also. "But you know, I just have this gut feeling that you should wait. I mean, look at Aoi-kun. Though Soria treats him more like a mischievous pet that needs protection, he patiently waits for her. It takes a lot of devotion, don't you think? One day, Soria will definitely turn to look at him too."

Verse raised an eyebrow and turned to hit one of the piano keys as it let out a high pitch note. "I've been wondering this for some time now, Remi."

"What is it?"

"Are you in love with Soria?"

"Eh?" Remi's eyes widened while Verse laughed. "Geez," she said, shaking her head. "Even now, you're still too much for me."

"But really, why are you so stuck on Soria? It's not like you're sisters or blood related."

Remi grew quiet as her hands trembled. Noticing, Verse reached over to pat her head.

"Forget it. I don't want to upset you. Or else Soria will beat me up again." Verse winked and smiled.

Remi chuckled softly, remembering how Soria had beaten Verse after learning about their fight behind the school. Yeve didn't even bother to intervene and watched. Ever since, Verse stopped picking on Remi altogether, all for Soria's sake. But even after beating Verse, Soria still shared her food like always. That was how they fought and made up. It made Remi envious how the three were so close. Even though she had inserted herself into their world, she wasn't able to stand on the same stage as them.

"You're right. We're not blood related and I might not be as close to her as you and Yeve are, but I consider Soria a sister. She was the first to accept me for me. That's why, I've always tagged along with you three since we were small. I even neglected my healing to force myself to learn how to manipulate energy into fire to complement her. It was never my intention to be a nuisance to you. I just-"

"Enough," interrupted Verse. "I don't want to hear your love confession towards Soria."

"It's not like that."

"If the only person you feel comfortable around is Soria, then stick with her. There's no need to explain yourself until you feel like crying."

Remi pouted. There were indeed tears in her eyes. As usual, whenever she spoke with Verse, it always made her feel like crying. Remi never really understood why that was. "I wasn't going to cry."

"I see the tears in your eyes." Verse hit the piano keys again and stood abruptly while Remi quickly wiped her eyes.

"Where are you going?"

"To sleep."

"It's almost time to leave though."

"I'm still going to sleep." Verse smiled and walked away. Her talk with Remi had unexpectedly calmed her down. "Say," she said, stopping at the open doorway. "I've always wondered about something else too. How far are you willing to follow Soria?"

"What do you mean?"

"If she were to fall into the depths of hell, would you follow her?"

"I don't know what you're trying to get at here. But if it means going down to hell to bring her back, then yes, I'd go."

Verse grinned, already expecting that. "You two are simpletons."

"For you and Yeve, I would also go to hell to bring you back."

Laughing, Verse shook her head. Tears had welled in her eyes but Remi couldn't see. "Fool, even after everything I've done to you, why are you still so nice to me?"

"It's because you and Yeve are Soria's world."

"I don't want to be part of that fool's world." With that, Verse waved and walked out.

"Even if you don't want to, you still are," Remi whispered, watching the door close. "That's why, I'll protect you, for Soria's sake."

"Was she picking on you?" Noah asked hoarsely as Remi turned to look at him. His eyes were still closed, pretending to sleep while eavesdropping on their conversation.

"No. That's just how she is."

"I see," he answered. After a few seconds he asked curiously, "*Are* you in love with Soria?"

Remi laughed at his teasing and shook her head while Noah smiled. She stood from the bench and returned to Noah's side, snuggling close to him again while he put his head on her shoulder. Before dozing off again, Remi made a wish that Verse would hopefully find some closure.

∞

"Following that poop-head down to hell just to save her, who would do such a thing?" Verse mumbled and smiled. She stopped in the hallway and turned to look out the wide window. The moon was visible, and the trees swayed from the breeze. She walked over to place a hand on the cool pane, wondering why she was so content suddenly.

"Let me write you a love song," he offered while standing behind her. Heart thumping, Verse watched as he leaned forward to let out a puff of air, steaming the window. Gently, he placed his elegant index finger on the glass and wrote one single word.

"Promise," read Verse.

Naruyuki who was returning from the dining hall alone noticed Verse standing by the window and approached her. "You're still up too?" he asked.

Verse blinked. Her thoughts that had come alive disappeared after hearing Naruyuki call out to her. She turned to look at him and blinked again. He in return blinked back curiously. Why did it feel like she wasn't really seeing him?

"Verse?"

She ignored his worrisome tone and turned to concentrate on the window again, slowly touching the glass with care.

"What are you looking at?" Naruyuki lowered his gaze to her height and stared out the window. There was nothing outside.

"Promise," she repeated. "I can vaguely remember his promise."

"Who?"

She smiled at the memory of the person standing behind her. His warmth lingered as Verse turned to leave first. "Someone who shines like the sun."

∞

It was past their designated time to depart as the sun was close to noon. Rain yawned and entered the infirmary, having barely slept last night. Before joining the others, he had suddenly received word to do Miss Umi a favor. Unable to object, Rain came at her beck and call.

Sleeping on a bed was Yeve. He glanced over at Miss Umi and Gabe who were playing Poker. "Sensei, I'll tattle," he threatened with another yawn.

"Try, and we'll see how your arm is after the mission," Miss Umi threatened in return.

Rain backed away, fully awake while Gabe laughed.

"Don't ever threaten Umi-sensei. You can't win," Gabe warned and went back to playing the card game.

"Yeah, thanks for the late tip."

Miss Umi pointed to the bed without looking, too concentrated on the cards in her hand. "Wake her up. It's already twelve. You kids need to get going."

"Yeah," he said and nodded, walking over to Yeve's side. She looked so peaceful, it was hard to imagine she was evil.

"Careful with her, she's fragile."

Rain raised another eyebrow. Yeve was anything but fragile. Taking the blanket off, he wanted to ask why she was even in the infirmary to begin with, but decided against it. He didn't want Miss Umi threatening him again. After picking her up in his arms, he bowed his head at the two teachers. "We'll be going now." He turned and walked out.

"Why'd he carry her like some princess for? He could've woken her ass up and let her walk on her own," Miss Umi said with a sigh.

"That's just who he is."

"Softy," she muttered with a grin, "reminds me of a certain *someone*."

"Oye, oye," said Gabe. He smiled, embarrassed about his past. "That was a long time ago when we were still the main characters. Now, we've become the supporting cast for those kids," Gabe joked, grabbing a cigar, then stopped. He looked up at Miss Umi who was still smiling, reminiscing on the past after hearing his statement. "I'm gonna smoke."

"You wanna die?" she threatened and blinked, withdrawing from her dream-like state.

Gabe grinned and put his cigar away. "If only the three of us were still out there, taking on dangerous S ranked missions, this war would've ended long ago."

"Enough. I don't want to hear anymore."

Obeying, Gabe glanced out the window. The sun's rays were shining brightly. He was suddenly overwhelmed with joy and sorrow. Why did life make him want to cry and laugh so badly? "Do you think those kids will make it?"

"They will."

Gabe smiled. Miss Umi had answered too quickly. "You're overconfident."

"I'm not."

"Then, how confident are you when it comes to them Awakening?"

Miss Umi tensed, then turned away. She hated these times the most because she couldn't anticipate anything that was to come. Why couldn't those kids just stay as kids? "That's why you and I are going to create the strongest Life-Kills that won't lose to memories."

"Memories," he repeated. "I wonder if we can truly create a being that will never question us."

"We will, one day." Miss Umi fumbled for another cigarette and put it between her parted lips.

"*He* hated smoking."

She stopped halfway from lighting it and grinned. Nodding, she replied, "I know. Yet he always smoked."

"Is that why you decided to take on that trait, although you hate it too?"

She put the unlit cigarette away, feeling a migraine coming on. "Gabe-"

"I got it, I got it. I'll stop talking now."

It was better to bury a painful past than to constantly live in it. "What about your boys?" she asked.

"Nothing suspicious," he answered proudly.

"Isn't that even more suspicious?"

Gabe stopped smiling to nod. "I thought their dreams would come for them by now. So far, none of them has had any." Gabe frowned. "Now I'm not sure when things will start to get ugly."

40th Lie

RAIN WAS THE LAST to reach the docks. In his arms was a sleeping Yeve as he walked towards the group that was waiting. One look at the two and they raised their eyebrows. He looked like a warrior, carrying his dead beloved home to bury after a brutal war.

"What's up with you two?" asked Teo.

Rain shrugged without much thought. "Yeve's tired and fragile."

"Yeve's anything but fragile," retorted Soria. "She's a butt face."

"Soria," snapped Verse.

"Just kidding," she said innocently.

"What happened to her?" asked Mio worriedly.

"I really don't know," Rain replied truthfully. He shook his head. Miss Umi hadn't told him anything. "I'll carry her for now."

"Just wake her ass up," Soria insisted, so tempted to drown Yeve while she was asleep. "I hate seeing her get carried like some damn princess in a deep slumber."

Verse reached over, smacking Soria over the head. She was getting annoyed herself.

"Let's not do this right now," pleaded Remi.

"So, any lectures?" asked Sasuke.

Not in the mood to make any grand speeches, Rain looked over at Naruyuki. "You do it, Naru. My hands are full."

"Alright then," Naruyuki said, glancing at the group.

King who would usually jump at the chance to give a passionate speech was giving Hotaka and Midnight a disgusting look. She was still mad about the forced kiss and was refusing to look in Hotaka's direction while Jennifer yawned.

Naruyuki shook his head, concerned about the third group. "Soria," he said, glancing in her direction. "Your water spheres."

"Yeah," she said not bothering to obey.

"Get to it," hissed Verse.

"Okay, okay, gosh," complained Soria.

"Don't mess up now," joked Alice.

"The only ones to mess up are you and Morgana."

"Oye!" shouted the two girls while Soria laughed.

"Seriously," Verse said, popping her knuckles. Seventeen years of putting up with Soria had reached its limit.

Still arguing with Soria, Alice could feel Poe's eyes on her, but she didn't dare look his way, afraid that she couldn't repair the damage she'd done.

"Alright everyone, into your groups," demanded Soria as everyone split into three groups. The water from the ocean surrounded the two groups, creating two compact spheres with enough air to breathe. Only Hotaka's group would be taking a ship towards their destination since they had no water elemental.

"Everyone," spoke Naruyuki. "Let's go aide our comrades and return safely with them."

"Yeah," they agreed.

"Let's go, Noah."

"Yeah," he said, blasting his team towards their destination.

"Hold on," Soria said, blasting them across the water surface also.

Once the two groups were gone, Hotaka turned towards the ship that was waiting for the four. "Let's go," he said, leading the way.

The Sea Captain lowered his binoculars and watched in disbelief. The water spheres were moving faster than his advanced binoculars could keep up with. He'd met a few water users in his time, but none of them were this skilled. "We must inform the others."

∞

Bored, Nicholas stood inside Dean Kosa's office, glancing out the window. Even when the cat Liz tried to get his attention, he ignored her. "So, what do we get to do?" asked Nicholas. He looked away from the window to the dean. If he kept his mind busy, he wouldn't be reminded about how the deans refused his request to meet Soria.

"You get to help me with a very important task."

"And that would be?"

"This," he answered, whipping up a poster board. "Ta-dah!"

"Uh," Nicholas said, unsure of what to say. Even Liz stopped purring to raise an eyebrow.

"It's a Golden party for the kids!"

"While the others are out on missions, I'm stuck here with you, decorating for a Golden party?"

"Yep!" shouted Dean Kosa as he nodded. "It's going to be a blast! We'll have snow falling from the sky, and lights will be strewn everywhere! We'll hang mistletoes everywhere—and ooh! Now that the kids are all grown up, they can kiss! That is, if they haven't tried kissing yet—and there's no way in hell they can refuse the kisses under the mistletoes because I won't allow them to!" Dean Kosa swooned in his chair like a lovesick puppy.

While listening, Liz hissed. She wouldn't allow anyone to kiss her Soulmate or Yeve. If anyone dared to pull a fast one on her, she'd scratch and bite them to death.

"Ah, being young is the best," Dean Kosa said, ignoring the hisses. Nothing was going to bring down his good mood.

"Dean, it's still summer," Nicholas reminded.

"I don't care what the real season is! Here at Maroon, we can make it whatever season we want!"

"I can't believe I'm stuck here decorating."

Liz meowed in agreement and turned to look at him. Neither of them wanted to be stuck here when what they really wanted was to see the others in action.

∞

Yeve stirred in her sleep. When she opened her eyes, she saw crystals glittering in the sky. It was so breathtaking she smiled faintly. "Pretty," she whispered.

"Yeve?" said Rain as he looked down at her.

"Rain?"

"Keep sleeping if you're not feeling up to it."

She blinked and looked around. The others were there. Noah had created water chairs, by binding the water molecules tightly until it was practically solid. Everyone was seated, even Rain, who continued holding Yeve. They had set out for their next mission already, "The Rescue," as the deans called it. Yeve did her best to sit up in Rain's arms but found it difficult. "I'm awake now. You can put me down."

"Don't push yourself."

"I'm okay to stand on my own."

"No, you're not," interrupted Verse.

Yeve glared over, still fighting to get free. "I'm heavy. Your arms probably hurt."

"I'm fine," Rain answered truthfully and smiled. "Just stay still."

"Please don't lie, Rain. We all know she's a cow," insulted Verse.

"I'm gonna kill you when I get down," hissed Yeve as the others chuckled. After struggling for a bit more, she gave up and stared at the sky. The water encasing them belonged to Soria. It had her energy written all over it. "It's warm," whispered Yeve.

Rain stared at her, eyes widening. Eventually he smiled, his cheeks flushed. The others noticed but said nothing. He'd realize it one day.

Being the only ones to understand, Verse and Remi didn't bother to correct the misinterpretation between the others and Yeve. It was fun to let them misunderstand her every now and then.

"So," Louis happily spoke up. "Since this is a rescue mission, I think we need a leader."

Remembering something important, Poe held up his hand. "Ah, that person would be me."

"I was volunteering Rain here. Try to take a hint."

"Too bad, the dean already appointed me as leader of this group. I get to make the decisions. If you have any questions or problems, call the dean once we land. He'll tell it to you in full detail."

"Wow," said Alice. She clapped her hands in admiration. "I didn't know you were made leader. Why didn't you tell me?"

Poe looked over and smiled. "I forgot until Louis mentioned it."

"I think Louis-kun needs to take on the role as leader a bit more," Mio said, thinking back to their academy days. Though he seldom was made leader of the teams, when he was, he was effective. Mio liked it best when he was earnest. It made him look mature and cool.

Louis looked over, tears glistening in his eyes. He reached out to take her hands in his own. How was it that Mio, Remi, and Hana were the only ones who could cure his fatigue with a smile alone? Maybe in his past three lives, they had been his former lovers. "Mio-chan," he said. "I love you. Please become my girl."

"Oye," Sasuke and Hanabi hissed while Mio laughed.

"Okay, I see no harm in it," she replied without deliberation.

"As I thought, you've always been the one for me since the beginning," Louis said dreamily.

"Is that so?"

"Mio," snapped Hanabi. "Stop it."

"That's right. Don't play into his delusions. He just might get serious," warned Sasuke.

"I was being serious though!" Louis defended. Again, he was being treated as a fool.

"So was I," Mio answered as their respective Soulmates pried them away from one another.

"Stop! I won't allow anyone to tear us apart again!" cried Louis.

"So, what's the plan?" Rain asked, ignoring the four. Just thinking about getting involved with them gave him a major headache.

"We're gonna have to split into two groups—maybe even three," responded Poe.

"Why three?" asked Noah.

"Because," Poe said, having spent all night thinking about the mission. "We'll need a group to rescue Taiki and Umeko from imprisonment. I'll be part of it of course, along with Naruyuki."

"Me?" asked Naruyuki. He pointed a finger to himself before looking over at Verse who kept her eyes fixated on Poe, waiting to hear the rest of the plan. She wasn't fazed by the fact that Naruyuki would be going to save Umeko, the woman he constantly thought of.

"Yeah you, I'll need you in case Taiki's in bad condition and can't heal. We'll also need Sasuke and Hanabi with us."

"Me?" Hanabi and Sasuke asked as they stopped messing with Louis and Mio who were now somehow hugging.

"That's right." Poe nodded. "If only we had Crystal and her third eye, we'd be able to locate them right away. But since we don't, we'll have to rely on you Hanabi, to find the whereabouts of the organization. Everyone in the retrieval group will protect you at all costs."

"What about me?" Louis asked, raising a hand. He wanted to be of use too if Hanabi was getting such an important task. "I can see the future. Wouldn't using me be much effective?"

"Your powers are random. The visions come and go for you. What if you don't see anything? It'd be a waste of time," explained Poe.

"Well, that was rude. Couldn't you have said it nicer?"

Poe glanced over at Louis who looked like he was about to cry. Sad also, Mio comforted him while Sasuke and Hanabi were at it again, trying to separate them. Poe groaned. His team was filled with troublemakers. "Anyway," he said, returning to the mission briefing. "I'm sure no boss leaves his base unprotected. There'll probably be some powerful guys on guard. I doubt Taiki and Umeko got caught without putting up a fight."

"So, in other words you want the rest of us to take out the organization?" guessed Noah.

Poe knew he was asking a lot out of them, but it was the only plan he could come up with. "Yeah, while the four of us are rescuing the two, the rest of you have to become decoys and attack the base. Keep the enemy busy for as long as possible until we get out. Once we do, I'll contact you to get the hell out of there."

"And how are we going to contact each other? It's not like any of us have psychic powers."

"That's why you've got to come prepared." Poe grinned and grabbed the sack on his back to set before him. He undid the string to toss everyone an earpiece. "We'll keep in contact using these."

"Wow, where'd you get these?" asked Mio.

"Requested them from the dean before leaving. As captain of this team, everyone's safety is my responsibility. Naruyuki already said it. We have to return together."

Everyone smiled, nodding their heads in agreement. Whatever the cost, they'd gladly pay it to stay alive.

"I also forgot to mention," added in Poe. "Yeve and Verse, you two will make up the third group. Your objective is the boss, if he shows himself."

"What?" asked Rain, Naruyuki, and Remi in disbelief.

Instead of caring about their concern over his outrageous order, Poe went on to explain. "When the boss catches on to our infiltration, he'll show himself. Once he does, Verse will be the decoy while Yeve gets him from behind. We all know that once the king is caught, the battle is over."

"What makes you think it's that simple?" Naruyuki asked.

Poe looked over, his eyes steadfast. "You don't trust in the strength of your Soulmate?"

"I do."

"Then let her handle the boss. You just concentrate on saving the two with me."

"Poe-"

"That's final," he challenged.

Angry, Naruyuki turned away. As captain of the team, Poe's words were absolute, even if he was younger.

"Rain, you'll be located on high grounds, taking out anyone who poses a threat. With your accuracy, you should be able to protect us if we're caught in a pinch."

"Understood," Rain answered without arguing.

"Yeve and Verse, don't go dying on me. I'm counting on you two to end this battle in one swift move."

They stared at Poe before exchanging glances and eventually grinning. It was as he said. They knew each other's strengths and weaknesses, better than anyone. Being in a tag-team suited them just fine. "Don't worry. We don't plan on dying anytime soon. Soria would go Berserk if she finds out we died."

Poe smiled and nodded too. "Good," he said, knowing the two girls would come through for him. They were amongst the strongest he had met.

Choosing them to take out the boss had been correct. No one else here was capable, other than Rain, who needed to be on lookout. "When we reach our destination, we run to where Taiki and Umeko were last located." Poe took out a map as Noah created a water table for him to unfold it on. He pointed to the red X and continued, "This is where they were last located before their signals died. If the enemy's stupid enough, hopefully they haven't relocated yet. That's where Hanabi will come into play."

Hanabi nodded, understanding her role perfectly. The first step into getting this mission under way was with how well she performed. This was where she excelled.

While the others listened, Remi fidgeted. She was holding herself back from objecting to Poe's plan of letting the two fight the boss alone. But there was little she could do when not even Naruyuki could change his mind.

Noah noticed her concern and reached a hand out to clasp over hers. She turned to look at him as he smiled. "They'll be fine."

Unable to agree, Remi clasped her free hand over his. She knew how strong they were but had a bad feeling that something terrible was going to happen.

"…well then, remember the plan everyone. Cause as much mischief as possible," Poe said, finishing the briefing.

"Yes, captain," the group responded.

∞

"What's eating you?" asked Zena. She controlled her wheelchair over to where Azuma sat outside, enjoying the sun alone, and smiled.

"Zena-san," Azuma greeted and quickly stood to bow.

"Sit," she said, motioning for him to sit back down on the bench. Azuma obediently sat and looked away as Zena raised an eyebrow. As usual, he was uptight whenever she was around. "Hmm," she said. "I've come to the conclusion that you hate me."

"Eh? Of course not!"

Zena giggled at his reaction. Now it made her want to toy with him some more. "Then why do you always avoid me?"

Azuma gulped. How could he not? He knew what kind of person Zena was and that made things so much worse. She was a beauty with an amazing personality. Her devotion towards her family was something to admire. She was even smart and kind-hearted, the type that Kakinouchi was weak to.

"You never look me in the eyes, Azuma-kun."

Mustering all his courage, he turned to hold her gaze. "I'm looking at you now, right?"

Zena put a hand to her mouth and giggled even louder than before. Azuma's actions and words were so upfront. If she was still a teenager, she might've fallen for his charms. It was too bad that she was married, and he was dating Shayla. "What's with kids these days?"

"But you said-"

"You didn't have to literally stare at me." Zena kept giggling as Azuma turned bright red and looked away. He muttered something under his breath while Zena looked up to the sky where blue clouds lazily rolled by. "Things have changed so much during the time I was asleep. Yet at the same time it hasn't."

"Wh—what do you mean by you fell asleep?"

Zena inhaled deeply, missing the sensation of the wind blowing against her face. Even cats that made her allergies act up, she wouldn't mind having around to pet. "Seven years ago, I was involved in a car accident and had to be kept on life support. I needed a new heart, but the list of donors was so long my husband was worried I'd never get one. While visiting me every day at the hospital, he befriended a young girl who was diagnosed with brain tumor. He told her our story and when she died, she gave her heart to me." Zena smiled and placed one hand against her beating chest gently.

Azuma tensed at the mentioning of May's heart but couldn't retaliate when Zena looked so grateful at having a second chance at life. He couldn't tell her that Doctor Nishikawa had lied about her falling into a coma. She had died and her body had been preserved. The heart inside her chest was never donated, it'd been stolen.

"I'll never forget the girl who gave me this heart. She will forever be in my prayers." A tear trickled down her cheek as she wiped it. "Whoever she is, wherever she is, I hope that she receives nothing but warmth and happiness from now on."

Azuma hung his head down low, no longer looking at the clouds. Right now, he was feeling crummy. The world was too cruel. Of all people, it shouldn't be Zena. She was a good person who didn't deserve to be in this predicament. Soon, he found himself crying.

"What's wrong? Why are you crying also?" Zena chuckled and reached over to soothe him. Azuma was such an emotional boy and that made him endearing. "There, there."

"Zena-san," cried Azuma. "Why aren't you evil?"

"Eh?"

"It'd be so much easier if you were, but you're not."

"Honey," called out Doctor Nishikawa as he walked over to join them. When he saw Azuma crying, he stopped. "What happened?"

Zena turned to smile at her husband. "I was just telling Azuma-kun a sad tale. I didn't think he'd get so emotional," she answered.

Doctor Nishikawa tilted his head at Azuma who wiped his tears and slightly bowed. Clearing his throat, the doctor walked over to stand behind Zena's gray wheelchair. She was getting too close to the recruit. It wasn't a good sign. "Come. Your brother wants to see you."

"Now what does he want?"

"I don't know. You'll have to ask him when you see him." Doctor Nishikawa took hold of the handle bars and pushed her away, not before shooting Azuma a cold glare.

"Azuma-kun!" Zena called back, halting her husband from pushing.

"Yes?" he answered.

"Thank you for listening!" She waved at him and turned to face front again, letting her husband wheel her away.

Azuma waved a hand and watched them leave. He could feel his resolve starting to weaken.

∞

Gabe grabbed a bunch of golden streamers stored away in the closet and tossed them out. He dug in deeper and took out some lights while humming a cheery, festive tune.

"Um, sensei," said Mere. The things Gabe was tossing out had started to pile up until he couldn't see past them. Any more and he'd topple over.

"What is it?" Gabe scrimmaged around, not caring.

"How many more things are you going to grab?"

"Just a few more."

"Uh sensei, you said that fifteen minutes ago."

"Just a few more, hold on a little longer."

"I don't think I can anymore." Mere was struggling as the decorations wobbled, a result from his stick-like arms.

"Put up with it. We have to decorate the place prettily before the others come back from their mission."

Mr. Fujiwara walked by and stopped, returning to join Mere's side. He peered into the closet and cleared his throat. Gabe and the dean were wasting time by decorating. There was no need to go all out for a Golden party. It wasn't like someone was getting married.

Mere looked up and smiled, bowing his head. That was all he could do. "Fujiwara-sensei," he greeted.

"Oh?!" shouted Gabe from within the huge walk-in closet. Finally, reinforcements had come. "Is that you, Raelo-chan?! Help me out here!"

"Call me by my first name again and I'll bury you in there," threatened Mr. Fujiwara.

"I got it, I got it, sheesh."

"What are you two doing anyway?"

"Preparing for the Golden party," answered Mere.

"I see." Mr. Fujiwara nodded and adjusted his glasses. "If you personally ask me, I say, instead of letting the kids slack off and have fun, we should train them some more until they sweat blood and tears."

"Sweat blood and tears?" repeated Mere worriedly.

"Yes."

"Don't scare the poor boy," said Gabe.

"Well, I'll be going then," said Mr. Fujiwara. He grabbed a few things from Mere and walked away briskly. Even if he didn't want to decorate, if the dean gave them orders, he would see that it was done in a timely order.

"There, found it!" shouted Gabe. He came out with a hand saw and stopped, noticing that Mere was carrying half the things he'd thrown out. "Where are the rest?"

"Fujiwara-sensei took some."

Gabe smiled and shook his head. "Despite his cold exterior, he's actually excited about the party."

"He is? I couldn't even tell."

"That's just how he is." Gabe shut the door and led the way. "Right this way m'boy." They walked down the hallway past Miss Umi and a few staff members who had taken May's body out from the morgue. Intrigued, Mere stopped to watch.

"Sensei, who's that girl? Why isn't she on the mission too?"

Gabe stopped to watch as Miss Umi and the staff members disappeared into the surgery ward with May on the stretcher. "That's May. Her heart was stolen."

"Eh?"

"Right now, her Soulmate is out retrieving her heart. Once he returns with it, we'll pop it back where it belongs." Gabe smiled and walked away. "Come along now."

Mere struggled to keep up, fascinated by Gabe's story. "But is it possible for her to stay alive without a heart to pump blood?"

"She's a Life-Kill. It's possible," he answered as they entered the ballroom in the mansion. The two deans were there, instructing the rest of the staff on how to decorate as Gabe's jaw dropped.

"Wow," Mere said in awe. Standing in the middle of the room was a gigantic fifteen-foot Douglas Fir tree, decked out in lights, streamers, and shiny ornaments.

"Dean!" Gabe yelled.

Dean Kosa turned and smiled. "Gabe!" he shouted, excitedly prancing over. The ballroom was exquisitely lit with colorful lights and decorations. "What do you think?"

"I thought we agreed that *I'd* do the decorations this year?"

"Yeah, I thought about it and…I decided against it! So, we went out to the back to cut down the tree! Ha-ha!"

"Wow, this is really amazing," complimented Mere.

In a low growl, Gabe turned his way and smiled innocently.

"Not that I would know, of course," Mere added in and backed away. "I'm uh, gonna go set these things down." He quickly ran off as Gabe turned his attention back to the dean who was directing the staff again.

"And why exactly did you take over the decorations for?"

"Fujiwara-sensei suggested me to," answered Dean Kosa as he walked away, humming.

"Raelo-chan," hissed Gabe. His eyes lit on fire as his fists trembled. After making fun of him, Mr. Fujiwara had backstabbed him.

From behind, Mr. Fujiwara materialized and caught Gabe by the collars to drag away. "Follow me. It's time for your funeral service."

"Just kidding, just kidding!"

"Dean, I'm done putting the lights on the roof," Nicholas said, entering the ballroom with a gun stapler. Right behind him was Liz in cat form. She had refused to morph into human form, for fear that the deans would force her to participate in decorating as well. So, she let Nicholas do all the work while she tagged along.

"Good, good!" shouted the two deans.

"Well, since I'm done, Liz and I are going out for a walk." Nicholas smiled and set the stapler down to leave before they could find more chores for him to do.

"Have fun!" bid Dean Kosa. He waved at Nicholas and turned away, not bothering to ask where their walk was being held. Everyone was too occupied with the party, making sure it would be perfect for when the kids returned.

∞

After hours of carefully staking out Haj's room, Shayla figured out the security routine. When she found an opening, she slipped inside his room and quickly ran over to one of the chairs to sit on. After calming her nerves, she closed her eyes to concentrate. She could feel the ripples in the air as energy swirled around and she finally entered the memory.

Shayla shifted her eyes. She was sitting inside the room, but at a previous time. Haj and Doctor Nishikawa were standing before her as blotchy figures. The memory was so grainy and faint, she could barely make them out. Her powers weren't strong enough to heighten the quality.

"Mina?" Haj asked, stunned.

"That's right." Doctor Nishikawa nodded, a manila envelope in his hand. It was late at night as the two held a rendezvous. Shayla squinted her eyes to see who the sender of the documents was. All she could make out was Jin and Aomori. "It's the only explanation as to how Jin would be taken out so quickly after getting his hands on a Life-Kill. Mina must've tipped her superiors that we were working with him and sent a team to annihilate him."

"Are you sure? I don't want to accuse her blindly."

"No one outside the two of us and Zara knew about Jin. And I've been keeping tabs on Mina."

Haj hit the coffee table with his bare fists as it fell apart, surprising Shayla. For a mere human, he was unusually strong. "To think that Mina would betray me."

"I don't think she was ever on your side to begin with," corrected Doctor Nishikawa.

Thinking of what to do about this sudden information, Haj paced. If what his brother-in-law said was true, then they had to proceed with caution. If Mina found out they were on to her, she'd flee, and they'd lose any lead regarding the Dome's plans. "Capture her and torture her for information, then kill her."

Doctor Nishikawa grinned and nodded. That was exactly what he had wanted Haj to say. If Mina was out of the picture, the heart inside Zena would be safe. "Also, if you permit, may we take out Azuma and Shayla too?"

"Why?"

"My gut tells me that they're part of Mina's team."

"Alright, do as you wish."

Shayla opened her eyes and stood, breathing hard. After regaining her energy, she stealthily escaped the room to find Mina. She had to relay the information she'd just come across. Hopefully it wasn't too late.

∞

Shadow was sitting by himself eating lunch when Zara slid down beside him. She smiled, putting her chin on one palm to admire him. Shadow glanced over, eyebrow raised. It was mighty creepy to be watched while eating, and it had somehow become her bad habit. "What is it?"

"Just marveling in all your goodness," she answered with a wink.

"Where have you been?" he asked, ignoring her sexual comment.

Zara shook her head. There was no reason for her to answer.

"Aren't you the leader of this group? If you keep disappearing each night like how you're constantly doing, the group will fall apart."

Laughing, Zara shook her head to disagree. She wasn't sure if Shadow was concerned or being suspicious. Either way, it made her happy that he too was keeping tabs on her. "You're wrong."

"How so?" He glanced over again. She was still smiling her mysterious smile that he couldn't read.

"Even without me here, the others will act accordingly."

"And how do you monitor that? With this?" He held up the tracking necklace around his neck for her to see. He could feel the wrath of glares coming from the other guys who wanted to be her toy also.

Zara grinned and reached out to trace it. "You're the only one I've ever given this to."

"Why me?"

Zara leaned in closer, whispering into his ear, "It's my special way of marking you."

Shadow pulled back, disgusted. The attraction wasn't mutual whatsoever. He returned to his lunch and finished, ready to leave.

"Shadow," said Zara. She pulled him back by the wrist, not done talking. "Wherever you go, I'll find you."

"Let go. I don't have time for your childish games."

"But you have time for that sickening, childish girl?"

Shadow dropped his tray and swirled back, grabbing her by the throat to slam onto the table. This was his first time treating a girl so forcefully. What was even more, this was his first time feeling such rage. Zara didn't flinch. Nor did she try to break away as Shadow tightened his grip. From the corner of his left eye, he could see the other guys moving in. They weren't going to sit idly by while Shadow hurt Zara. After fuming for a few seconds, he loosened his grip and completely let go. He couldn't lose his cool after coming this far.

Zara reached out to touch his eyepatch and let out a gasp of ecstasy. What kind of power was he hiding? She wanted to see with her own two eyes. "You're still not able to give her up?"

Shadow walked away, not caring about the mess he'd made. If he stayed a second longer, he'd really lose self-control.

Zara smiled and watched him go. "What a vicious man." She rubbed her neck and laughed at the guys who were now surrounding her. "I'm fine," she assured.

"But-"

"I said I'm fine." This time she glared as they bowed and left one by one. From the moment Zara set eyes on Shadow, she knew he was wielding an incredible power. He just didn't know how to use it. Wanting to exploit it, Zara took him in. In fact, she had wanted him to strangle her just then. Only then, would she be able to see what he was capable of. "What must I do to make you show me that power?"

∞

Hana finished tying her hair into two pigtails on either side of her head before straightening her dress. She took one last look in the mirror and smiled. It was time to bid the sister-brother duo a goodbye. They had been more than generous, allowing her to stay for the past few days, but she had overstayed her welcome and needed to leave. There was still a task that she needed to carry out.

Taking a deep breath, Hana calmed her nerves. It was time to face Zara once more and retrieve Shadow.

"Hana-nee," called out Hachi from the doorway.

Hana's smile faded as soon as she saw him. He was shaking all over and held a bloody letter in his hand. "Hachi-kun, what's wrong?" Hana ran over to his side and knelt. Had he gotten injured while playing with the other kids?

"Mafuyu-nee," he whispered and began crying. "She was taken."

"What?"

Hachi held out the letter he found as Hana took it. Quickly, she skimmed its contents. When she was done reading, she threw her arms around him and cried too, neither of them able to stop. Guilt gnawed at Hana. It was because of her that Mafuyu had been kidnapped. If only she had left sooner, Zara wouldn't have targeted the siblings. "Don't you worry about a thing, Hachi-kun. I'll go and save Mafuyu-nee."

"How will you do that? It'll be you against that nasty Zara."

"I'll win somehow. Trust me."

Hachi stared into Hana's twinkling eyes. She was the only person he could put his trust in to bring his sister home. There was no one else he could rely on. Slowly, he nodded and answered, "Okay."

"I'll be back before you know it."

∞

Reaching their destination, the water sphere landed gently on the rubbles of a building and opened. For the first time since they left the Dome that day, the group was finally able to breathe in fresh air. It was a calm night as they looked around. No one was there to greet them, only the flickering lights from up ahead.

Yuudai turned to look at Dark who had been put in charge of the mission and asked, "Is this the correct place?"

"It is." Dark nodded while looking at his 3D map. This was the meeting place Mina had set.

"Then where are those three?" asked Love.

"Over here," Azuma answered. He waved at them and smiled. By his side like usual was Shayla. "Man, is it good to see you again."

Shayla nodded in agreement and smiled too. "We were getting worried for a moment there when you guys didn't show up on time. We thought you weren't going to make it."

"We'd never bail," answered Aoi.

"Yeah," agreed Morgana. "We'll never turn our backs on friends!"

"That's good to hear." Azuma and Shayla walked over, never noticing the water lying on the ground.

Sparks flew from Yuudai's fingertips and landed on the water when the two were close enough, electrocuting them. They never suspected an attack from their comrades. Screaming and convulsing, they fell over, never getting the chance to counter.

"What the-" shouted Aoi and Morgana who turned towards Yuudai with a look of horror.

"They're fakes," Teo explained, pointing a finger at the two bodies that were slowly morphing to their original forms.

"Eh?!" the two shouted in disbelief.

"If that's the case, where's the real Azuma and Shayla?" Cammie asked.

Silently, Dark walked over to examine the two bodies, hoping for a pulse, but there was none. Yuudai hadn't spared them. Standing, Dark returned to his team's side, instructing Soria to surround them inside her water sphere again. "Crystal," he called on.

"Yes?" she answered quickly.

"Can you try to find the three in the city with your third eye?"

"I'll try." Nodding, Crystal turned away, taking in deep breaths to calm her nerves. Once she was settled, she placed both index and middle fingers to her forehead, then closed her eyes. With all the energy she could summon, she opened her third eye and was drifting in the air, trying to find Mina and the two.

"Love," Dark said while Crystal was busy searching.

"Yes?"

"Cast a protection spell."

41st Lie

"DONE!" Love shouted, after finishing her chants. Her protection spell would stay in place until they finished the mission, or until she was killed in battle. Until then, they were practically immune to all melee attacks.

"Done already?" he asked, turning to look at her.

"Yes." Love nodded and grabbed the bracelets that were lying on the spell page to distribute. Once everyone finished putting on their bracelets, she tucked the last three into her pocket. Those were for Mina and the other two when they showed up.

"Good." Dark smiled at the bracelet on his wrist. His team was reliable. At this rate, they would be able to finish their mission quickly.

"Found them!" shouted Crystal. She panted and pointed to somewhere in the city. "They're running towards us."

"Alright," Soria said, blasting them through the air while Teo held onto a worn-out Crystal.

"This is faster than before!" shouted Aoi who was knocked off his feet.

"Then hold on."

"To what?!"

"How would I know?"

They zoomed past cars as pedestrians screamed and pointed to the lightning speed water sphere. Morgana too was knocked off her feet and fell on top of Aoi. "Ah, I—I'm so sorry!" she apologized.

"It's okay." Aoi smiled and shook it off. She had nothing to apologize for. "It's not your fault. It's Soria's fault for going so fast."

Morgana blushed and smiled. It was to be expected that Aoi would understand.

"Uh, Morgana, can you get off me now?"

"Oh, sorry," she said again, but made no attempt to stand.

Yuudai rolled his eyes and reached down, yanking Morgana to her feet. He was getting angry just listening. Exactly why did he have to go through something like this? "You two are nothing but distracting flies."

"Yuudai," she hissed. "That was my chance."

"For what? To get a head-butt and concussion?"

"You-"

"Thanks, Yuu," Aoi interrupted, standing and brushing himself.

As soon as Soria caught sight of Azuma and Shayla, she clapped her hands together. A hand made of water, attached to the water sphere reached out and caught them as they shrieked. They didn't even know what had grabbed them until they turned to find the group.

When Soria was out of the public's eye and had found a deserted alleyway, she landed them safely as the water dispersed.

"Boy am I glad to see you guys!" Shayla shouted, tears in her eyes.

"It's been a while," Azuma greeted with a smile. When he caught Kakinouchi's eyes they both stared each other down. Even after months apart, their rivalry still burned.

"So," Kakinouchi said and smiled. Now *this*, was the Azuma he knew, always challenging him to a game of stare. "What do we do?" Today, he would be the loser.

Azuma smiled victoriously, though it wasn't much.

"Explain to us what's happened. Why were we met by shape-shifting Life-Kills for?" Dark asked as Azuma relayed the message to the group that formed a circle.

∞

The restless cabbie who kept drumming his fingertips on the steering wheel, gulped. He'd programmed his beat-down car to the most dangerous part of the city. The only reason he agreed was because Hotaka had been willing to pay a huge sum that could feed his family for three months.

As soon as they reached their destination, the cabbie pressed a button for the doors to open. The four thanked him and stepped out as Hotaka paid. Like the wind, the cabbie drove away manually.

"Well, he's in a rush," King joked while staring down the deserted street. There was a heaviness to the air as he withdrew his sword. "Why does it feel like we stepped into a zombie apocalypse?"

"Agreed," spoke Hotaka.

"What do we do?" asked Jennifer. She pulled on her accessories as a pair of energy bow and arrows appeared in her hands. Her eyes darted about as well, trying to find any enemy in hiding.

"Let's ask those guys for directions," King suggested, motioning to a group of guys walking their way, smeared in blood. When the other group noticed the four, they stopped.

"What a beautiful color you've got there," complimented Hotaka as he took a step forward. "Mind if I ask where you got that from?"

"Who the fuck are you guys? This is our turf," claimed the leader. He swung his bat onto his shoulder, glaring them down. What was a group of teenagers even doing here in the dead of the night? Did they not know who he was?

"Never mind. Don't answer my first question. I have a more important one. Is there a Zara around here? Mind directing me her way?"

"Zara?" repeated the leader. He scoffed and shook his head. "That psycho bitch? You don't want anything to do with her."

"I'll decide that myself."

"Kid, didn't you hear me? You don't want anything to do with her."

"Just tell me where to find her."

"Really," the leader said, disappointed that his warning was being disregarded. If that was so, he'd do them a favor by ending their lives. It was better to die here than to face Zara.

"Tell me," ordered an impatient Hotaka.

"Alright, but under one condition," he bargained.

"I don't have time-"

With all his strength, the leader threw his metal alloy bat. Eyes locked on, Hotaka side-stepped as the bat flew past him and skidded behind.

"Whoo-hoo," the leader praised, clapping his hands. Even his cronies seemed stunned that Hotaka had been able to dodge the surprise attack. Laughing, the leader nodded in approval. "You're better than you look, kid."

"This bastard," growled Hotaka.

Seeing no point in starting a fight, Midnight crossed her arms. They had a mission to see to. If the leader wasn't willing to tell them Zara's whereabouts, they would just have to go in search of her themselves. "Let's go, Hotaka," she said.

"If he wants a fight, I'll give him one," King said, taking a step forward. He sheathed his broadsword and sneered. His reputation had been damaged after having Kei save him. Hopefully this fight with the leader and his cronies would somehow boost his pride.

"Really?" Midnight groaned.

"Oye little missy, stay out of us men's brawls," said the leader. With no warning signs, vines shot out from beneath to encage them. Frantic, they bumped into each other like caged rats. With only one answer in their heads, they held their breaths.

"If you answer my question, I'll let you live. Where's Zara?"

The leader glared, not wanting to test any Life-Kill, especially ones who wanted Zara. If she was their objective, he'd deliver them to her. "About four miles, east of here, Zara's territory begins there."

"Thank you." Midnight turned and ran. "Let's go!"

"Right behind ya!" shouted Jennifer as she chased her.

"Let's go," said Hotaka as he ran off too.

King glared at them before following. He'd been expecting to participate in the street fight so he could relieve some stress. Now, his anger was boiling again. He couldn't let one failed mission hang over his head for the rest of his life.

The vines slowly undid themselves, letting the group free as they watched the four run off into the night.

"Boss," spoke one of the cronies.

"Tell the others to get underground. Now," he ordered.

"Right!" they shouted and ran off, leaving only one behind.

"Life-Kill versus Life-Kill, this will be an epic battle. Though I wanted to be the one to bring Zara down, if she falls to them tonight, we'll control the entire city."

"They're going to tear this town apart," said the crony.

"That's what monsters are created to do: destroy." The leader turned his back and left with his subject. They had no reason to stay any longer. "Come on. Let's go join the others. I don't wanna get caught in this bloody battle."

∞

Head hanging low, Hanabi stared at the cement while walking down the sidewalk. A group of girls was coming her way, laughing loudly. Counting to ten slowly, Hanabi casually bumped into them and looked up before cowering behind her white hair. "I—I'm so sorry. I-"

"You bitch!" one of the girls shouted, beating Hanabi without warning.

When the group of girls finished hitting, spitting, and slandering her, they walked away, laughing again. They were the feared ladies from the Bat Angels. No one was allowed to touch them without some kind of repercussion, even if it was by accident. Once the girls were gone, Hanabi stood and limped over to where Alice was hiding.

"You okay?" Alice asked, supporting her while she nodded in response.

"Hanabi," Louis called out from the earpiece. He was watching from afar, fists clenched. Sitting opposite him, drinking tea was Mio who gnashed her

446

teeth together. "Are you okay? They didn't hurt you too bad, did they? If they did, tell me, I'll go and-"

"I'm fine," she interrupted.

"So?" Poe asked from his end. Standing beside him was Sasuke who was glaring at Louis.

"They're all from the organization. Any one will do," answered Hanabi.

"Alright then, we'll tail the one wearing purple."

As instructed, the divided group casually stalked the girls to a beauty salon, where they got their nails done. Afterwards, they caught a movie, then ate a late dinner. When they finally split ways, the purple girl headed home instead of the base.

Frustrated, Poe ran a hand through his hair. At this rate, they wouldn't finish their mission until the next day. If he wanted to get anywhere and attack the base in the middle of the night, he had to take measures into his own hands. "Hanabi, come." Poe came out from hiding as Hanabi followed his lead. They were heading in the direction of the purple girl's high-rise apartment.

Casually standing in a circle on the opposite street was Rain, Yeve, Naruyuki, and Verse who ate sweet potatoes. "What are you planning, Poe?" Rain asked.

"This is taking too long." Once he and Hanabi entered the lobby where only one security guard sat behind his desk, Poe walked right up and knocked him out without letting him speak. When Hanabi finished reading his past, Poe propped the guard's body to look like he was napping. They headed towards the elevator and rode it up. Once they were standing in front of an apartment door, Poe opened the lock with the manipulation of his energy rod. Going unnoticed, they slipped into the room as he disabled the security system. He led the way into the living room and came face-to-face with the purple girl. She was in the middle of getting ready for a bath.

As soon as the purple girl saw them, she fought to escape, but quickly fell victim. "Unhand me!"

"Take it easy. We won't hurt you." Poe tied her up with his energy rope and nodded for Hanabi to do her thing.

She waltzed right over and with just one touch, read into the purple girl's past. Gasping, she let go and suddenly felt dizzy.

"You okay?" Poe asked, catching her.

"Did something happen?!" Louis shouted.

"She's fine."

"So?" asked Noah.

"I know," answered Hanabi.

"Then, show us the way," instructed Poe.

"You're also Life-Kills?" the purple girl guessed.

Poe stood, assisting Hanabi. He nodded. That was all the purple girl was getting out of him.

Grinning, she shook her head. It was exactly as Pia had suspected. The Dome had sent reinforcements for the two in captivity. "You can't beat Pia. She's too strong. She even has Anoka with her."

"Who?"

"Here's a piece of advice: run, when you see her." The purple girl laughed as Poe knocked her out with a hit to the back of the head. He retrieved his energy rope and left with Hanabi who led the team to the traditional three-story Japanese home located just outside of town. Trees surrounded the ten acres estate and was heavily guarded. No other house was within sight for miles.

"Looks more like a countryside yakuza organization," stated Louis.

Wiping his sweaty hands against his pants, Poe inhaled. It was time to put his plan into action. "Everyone, in your positions."

"Got it," they answered, splitting away into groups again. When things quieted down, they each reported in.

"Alright," Poe said into his headset. He, Hanabi, Naruyuki, and Sasuke were standing together. The others were in their own sub-groups, waiting for his signal. But before that, he had to talk about something that was nagging at him. "I'm sure you all heard what that girl said back there."

"We sure did," Noah answered.

"I don't know who these Pia or Anoka people are, but if you run across anyone who has that name, or remotely hear someone call out their names, your job is to run away. Got it?"

"Aren't you overreacting?"

"It's better to be cautious than sorry later."

"I saw," Hanabi whispered as Poe turned to look at her. She was trembling. "That Pia girl is strong, so is that Anoka girl."

"There you have it," said Poe. "We don't know their powers. So, do not engage in battle. For now, our objectives are to save Taiki and Umeko, and burn down the base. Now, if the leader is either one of them, then that's a different story."

"Got it," Rain answered. He knelt from where he was hiding, inspecting the base. From this location, he could pinpoint everyone's location, and could assist with his arrows, though the shutters to the house windows were closed. He wouldn't be able to assist Yeve and Verse who would be entering blind.

"Alright, let's go," ordered Poe.

"Right!" they shouted.

Arrows drawn, Rain watched as each group went about their ways to begin the mission.

While a group of guards were making their rounds in the courtyard, Poe and his group sprung out from nowhere. Weapons drawn, the guards tried to fire warning shots. Before they could, Sasuke entangled their hands and stuffed their mouths with vines.

Hanabi ran over to touch one of them, not needing orders. After a few seconds, she let go while the guys finished knocking out the guards.

"Underground basement, west wing, I'm not sure which door. There were a ton, we're just gonna have to bash them all in until we find the one," spoke Hanabi.

"Got it. Thanks," said Poe.

"Yeah," she said, allowing him to lead again.

"Okay guys, go wild out here!"

"Alright, time for fireworks!" shouted Remi. She ran towards the gates, stopping just shy to blast fire from her energy orb. The alarm sounded for intruders as they ran in through.

"We can't let you get all the fun, now can we?!" shouted Mio. She too withdrew her own clear energy orb as wind blast through the air, striking the men running at them.

"Yeve and Verse show us what you've got," said Noah happily.

"Did you need to ask?" Yeve ran past them, heading for the entrance of the house.

"Nah, I just wanted to say it."

Grinning, Yeve withdrew her katana as men and women aimed their firearms. Before any of them could fire, she struck them down. From behind, Verse ran, trying to keep up with Yeve who was already inside the house, taking down more people.

"Her speed fits her perfectly. She can't do anything slowly." Verse bent and grabbed one of the dead men's gun for protection. "I'll be taking this." She ran in through the open doors, dead bodies lying about. The cameras had been taken out as well. Even the shutters to the windows were wide open, allowing Rain eyes on the inside. Grinning, Verse ran off.

∞

One by one, each camera blacked out while Beast sat in his chair, petting his Persian cat. He twirled away from the TVs located behind his desk to face front, his face blazing. The one taking out the cameras were too quick, Beast never got a good glance. "Pia," he growled.

Without a word, Pia stood from the sofa she was sitting on and bowed, leaving to take care of the intruders.

"Rastus," said Beast.

"Yes?" he answered and stood up to bow also.

"Go greet the ones outside."

"Yes." Rastus bowed and walked out calmly.

"To think the Maroon Dome would send in fighters head-on like this, they must be desperate about taking back those two." Beast grinned and reached over, opening the top drawer of his desk to take out a small case of serums. If it was a fight they were looking for, he'd give them one. He refused to lose his base that had taken him years to establish. "Well then, let us go greet them too." He adjusted his suit and stood, walking out of the grand room. Purring from his side was his Persian cat.

∞

The tiled floor cracked open until the poison ivy wrapping the four, opened. Poe ran off first while the three followed from behind, breaking down every door they came across. "Damn it, how many rooms does this damn place have?!"

They ran down the hallway and into a different corridor, still knocking down doors. When the last door came into view, Poe broke off its hinges and glanced inside. Empty.

"Down here!" shouted Naruyuki. He waved at the three to join him as they ran down another corridor.

At the sound of the commotion, Ikuto came to investigate. When he saw the four intruders he came to an abrupt halt. With only himself, he wouldn't be able to do much. "Shit," Ikuto said, turning to flee. From behind, a poisonous thorn pierced him as he yelped and fell.

Poe ran over, grabbing him by the collars. "Where are they?!"

"I'll never tell."

With a scowl, Poe let go of the poisoned Ikuto and motioned for Hanabi as she walked right over to grab Ikuto's hand. Within a few seconds, she let go and stood.

"Taiki-kun's in that room." Hanabi turned and pointed to a room, five doors down. "Umeko's in the next hallway."

"You-" Ikuto gasped, horrified that someone like her actually existed.

"Then, let's go. This guy is useless to us." Poe ran over to the door to break it down. Sure enough, chained inside was Taiki. Relieved that he was alive, Poe ran inside and stopped, his chest suddenly felt heavy. Whatever the dark room was, it was stealing his energy and turning the walls red.

"Shit," Naruyuki said, reaching out to snag Poe. As soon as he was out, the red walls returned to black.

"What the hell was that about?" Sasuke asked, bringing Ikuto along as they stood outside the room, safe from harm.

"It's as you see. Any of your kind that goes in will instantly have their energy stolen. The only one it doesn't affect is Pia," explained Ikuto.

"Poe," called out Naruyuki.

"I'm fine." He coughed violently and knelt as Hanabi bent down to pat his back. Poe wasn't even sure how Taiki and Umeko had managed to survive in such conditions.

"How are we going to get them out?" asked Sasuke.

"I didn't expect this," Poe said, gasping for air. "Can you snatch them from underground?"

"I could try."

"No," Naruyuki said, shaking his head.

"But-"

Without letting Sasuke finish, Naruyuki held up a hand to silence him. He knelt and touched the floor inside the room as the black walls turned red again. When he withdrew his hand, the walls turned black again. Naruyuki inspected the room from where he knelt. Someone had used their energy to create this room. What was more terrifying, another person was involved and had infused explosives into the walls. Unable to help himself, Naruyuki smiled. The combined ability of these mystery people was something to be reckoned with.

"So?" Sasuke asked. "Did you find its weakness?"

"I'll enter first," was all Naruyuki said.

"What?" Poe stood weakly and shook his head in refusal. "Are you crazy? You're our only healer. If I let you go in and if your powers get drained, we're all in deep shit."

"Trust me, Poe."

Ikuto laughed and shook his head at Naruyuki's false bravado. "You're all gonna die here. Pia and Anoka's powers can't be countered. The boss has formed the most powerful group."

"You're wrong," said Naruyuki.

"How so and in which part?"

"The part about those girls' powers being impossible to counter."

"Fine, don't believe me. Try entering. You'll see what I mean when the room explodes and kills us all." Ikuto stopped chuckling to eye Naruyuki's confident back. He winced, able to feel the poison searing through his body. If he could hold on for a bit longer, Pia would soon make her way down to wipe the floor with them.

"I'll take you up on that offer," Naruyuki said, taking a stand. He extended his arm and opened his closed palm as a few flower petals floated inside the room, their vibrant colors lighting the dark. From out of nowhere, the petals burst into millions of tinier petals. They covered the room from wall to wall and floor to ceiling, healing it.

Unable to peel his eyes away from the shiny petals, Ikuto gaped. They were unlike anything he'd seen before. After remembering that these were the bad guys, Ikuto glared, throwing his awe out the window. "There's no one stronger than Pia and Anoka!"

Naruyuki smiled and shook his head. It was easy for Ikuto to assume so because he hadn't met any other Life-Kills.

"Whoa," said Sasuke. His eyes widened as he watched the color of the room change from black to white. When the aura completely changed, Naruyuki stepped inside, unharmed.

"No way," gasped Ikuto.

"See?" Naruyuki turned around and smiled, proudly holding his arms out to his side. He'd found its secret. "All you have to do is negate the powers."

"He was already one step ahead of us," Sasuke said with a grin while Hanabi smiled. "That S.O.B."

"So it seems," agreed Poe as he ran over to break Taiki's chains. There was no time to waste. They had to get to Umeko before any reinforcements came. "Get Umeko!"

"Yeah," said Naruyuki. He and Hanabi rushed off while Poe carried Taiki out. Right behind, Sasuke dragged Ikuto still. They stumbled out and towards Umeko's room where Naruyuki had already negated the darkness.

Once inside, Poe set Taiki down to break Umeko loose from her chains. Meanwhile, Naruyuki assisted in the process of their slow self-heal. Petals swarmed around the couple before pasting itself onto their bodies, a pink aura arising.

Naruyuki placed a hand over Umeko's hand gently as she stirred. It hurt seeing her so vulnerable. If he could trade places with her, he would within a heartbeat. "Umeko-san," he called out.

At the sound of his tender voice, Hanabi flinched and turned away. She was happy to have rescued a friend, yet at the same time, she wasn't either. It was conflicting to watch.

Not bothering with them, Sasuke turned around. The room shook as vines entangled the walls and ceiling where more shining petals were plastered. Thick tree branches coiled itself around the broken doorway to block entry to outsiders.

"Naru...yuki...kun...?" Umeko called out.

"I'm right here," he answered.

"Naru," Umeko whispered and smiled faintly. Through the slit of one eye, she could make out his blurred face and petals. It felt as though he was hugging her tightly in his arms, keeping her safe. Her cold heart warmed, making her want to curl up in his embrace. "You came."

"Always."

Poe and Sasuke exchanged glances, only to end up shaking their heads and turning away. They didn't understand and didn't want to interfere in the reunion.

"Let's get out of here," instructed Poe.

From underground, the earth shook violently as Sasuke concentrated on taking them away.

"Ikuto, you inside?!" shouted Pia's voice from out in the hallway.

"When did she come without us knowing?"

"Pia!" called out Ikuto.

"Sasuke!" demanded Poe.

"I know!"

Pia stared at the tree branches that denied her entry into the room. She sneered at their futile attempt. Something this weak couldn't possibly stop her. Taking the wooden sword off her back, she slashed at the tightly entwined branches. Once they fell, the room that had imprisoned Umeko was gone. All that remained was a large tunnel heading down. "I'll give them one thing though," Pia said putting her sword away. She glanced into the tunnel and jumped in to track them down. "They figured out my trick about the room."

∞

"Guys!" Poe shouted into his earpiece. They were making a run for it after successfully rescuing Taiki and Umeko. "We've rescued the two! Mission accomplished!"

Noah threw both fists into the air, shouting, "Alright!"

Mio turned towards Remi and Alice to high-five. "We did it!"

"Yeah!"

"Remi, burn the building!" instructed Poe. "Yeve and Verse, get out of there! We're done here!"

"Alright," Remi said, nodding.

"Something's not right," whispered Rain. He fired an arrow to save Mio and lowered his bow. He jumped down from his position and ran off. Even without having to be by Yeve's side, he could feel that she'd encountered the boss.

∞

Verse scratched her head and looked at the mess Yeve had caused. The hallways were stained with blood and not a single live person could be spotted. This was the result of her task to hack and cut. With a sigh, Verse stared at the gun she'd picked up. She felt sorry that it was going to rust soon from not having any use.

"Man," Verse said pressing on her earpiece to speak. "Yeve, mission accomplished. Let's go. Didn't you hear Poe? Remi's gonna burn the base. I don't wanna be in here when it burns."

But there came no response.

"Yeve," Rain called out from his end.

Still, no answer.

"Yeve."

There was a choking sound as everyone stopped to listen.

"Yeve," called out Alice worriedly. "Yeve!"

Hanabi stopped running to close her eyes, scanning the area for a strong entity. If Yeve wasn't going to respond, the only way to track her would be through Hanabi's powers. She waited and searched but no one gave off any strong emotion.

"How's it coming?" Sasuke asked as they stopped running also.

Hanabi shook her head. She couldn't feel anything. "Come on, come on," she pleaded.

"Calm down," Louis instructed. "Clear your mind. Breathe. Relax."

In that moment, she almost wanted to argue, but knew it would get her nowhere. After taking a deep breath, Hanabi did as she was told. She calmed down and cleared her mind, then exhaled.

"Now, try again."

After relaxing, Hanabi closed her eyes. Now that she was no longer in a state of desperation and chaos, she could concentrate fully.

Shame.

Hanabi flung her eyes open. It was coming from the east wing. A sense of shame unlike anything she had ever felt before seeped through. Hanabi stared into the night as a waterworks of tears began. She fell to her knees and turned away, puking and trembling.

"Hanabi!" shouted the three guys worriedly.

"What happened?!" demanded Louis.

"R—Rain-kun," Hanabi managed to utter. She threw a hand to her mouth, wanting to scream until her voice box and heart gave out. Even then, she wasn't sure if the feeling would truly disappear.

"What is it?! What's wrong?!" they shouted.

"T—the east wing, Yeve is there."

"What happened to her?" Rain demanded while infiltrating the base through a different entrance.

"Damn," Noah complained as he watched Rastus approach them with more rebels. "It's one after another.

454

While running to Yeve's aide, Verse entered a Victorian styled room and came to a halt. It was as Noah had said. It was one after another. "Hey Rain," she spoke through her earpiece. "Think you can save Yeve on your own?"

"Yeah, but why?"

"I've got my own problem."

"Careful," he said and faded out.

"Yeah, got it."

"Verse, what's wrong?" demanded Naruyuki.

Verse scratched her head, not really in the mood to tell him or anyone else what kind of situation she'd just been thrown into. "You just take care of Umeko. I'll be right out." She killed her end before Naruyuki could get another word in. "Hello there," she greeted with a smile.

Anoka smiled and bowed in her blue dress, a teddy bear in her arms. "Hello."

"My name's Verse. What's yours?"

"Anoka."

Unable to help herself, Verse chuckled. Today was not her day. Of everyone to meet, she had to run into one of the more dangerous ones. "Well, nice meeting you Anoka-chan. What are you doing in this place?"

"I'm here to meet nee-chan."

"And who is your nee-chan?"

"You wouldn't know her."

Verse shrugged, trying to be as cheerful and unthreatening as possible. "I might. Care to tell me her name?"

Anoka opened her mouth to answer but remembered Beast's warning. If she ended up telling the wrong people, they would kidnap her and she'd never get to see her sister again. Biting her lip, Anoka shook her head and turned the other way. "I can't say."

"Nothing bad will happen if you do."

Anoka gave Verse a doubtful look. Her eyes were pinned on the gun in Verse's hand. Noticing, she set it down and held up her hands. If she ran away now, Anoka would suspect her. Since Verse didn't know what the little girl's powers were, she couldn't act rashly.

"I'm not a bad person."

Anoka looked around, still not believing her. "Didn't you kill these men?"

Verse shook her head, answering truthfully, "No. I didn't."

Anoka stared at her some more before smiling again and nodding. "I believe you."

"So, tell me Anoka-chan, who's your nee-chan?"

"Her name is Umi!" Anoka answered proudly, "Umi Oka! But she hates being called by her surname. So, we call her Umi." Her blue eyes twinkled at the mentioning of Miss Umi. "We're not really related, but we grew up together at the academy, so we're practically sisters."

Verse stared in alarm. Was it possible that Anoka was searching for the same Miss Umi working at Maroon? Then again, there were hundreds of people on this planet with the same names. But how many Umi Okas on this earth hated their surname enough to want to be called by their first names only? Verse smiled. She was going to take a chance and bet on the latter. "What are the odds?"

"Huh?"

"You know, Anoka-chan, I actually know her."

Unable to believe her fortune, Anoka cried and ran over, clutching Verse's hand. Finally, she had found someone who could actually help. "Can you take me to Umi-nee then?! Yura—I mean Beast-san said that he would, but he's been dilly-dallying ever since! So, if you know nee-chan, can you take me instead?! We've been separated for a long time! I miss her!"

"Yeah, I'll take you."

"Thank you so much!" Anoka bowed and stood back up. Chuckling, Verse wiped Anoka's tears as her smile faded. She yanked her hand away and frantically scrambled away like Verse had slapped her.

"What's wrong?" Verse asked, reaching out.

"Don't touch me!" Anoka dropped her stuffed animal and hid behind a sofa. Her eyes were wild with fear as Verse stopped halfway from following. "Why?"

"Eh?"

"Why do you have such strange powers?"

Verse's face paled and her hand fell to her side. She couldn't argue. "Ano-"

Screaming and crying all over again, Anoka threw her arms around her body for protection. She couldn't seem to stop her tears as hysteria and panic filled her heaving chest. "You're strange, strange!"

Sensing that she'd strike, Verse lunged forward, hoping to knock her out first. But the tables and chairs from behind, knocked her unconscious.

∞

With her earpiece lost and trampled on, Yeve sat on the dojo floor, wiping her bloody lip. Though it had been a tough task, she managed to slay the Persian cat that transformed into a beast.

Not able to mourn properly, Beast held his precious cat in his arms. Hatred sent tremors through his body as he set the cat down on the floor and rushed at Yeve, able to take her by surprise.

"Not bad," she said, impressed by his speed. Beast was proving to be a formidable foe for not evening being a Life-Kill.

"I could say the same to you. How about joining me? I'll even forgive you for killing my precious Bella."

Yeve laughed and would have to decline. "Sorry to break it to you but I can't join anyone's group. Because you see, I'm gonna rebel against the Golden God and rule the world."

Beast burst into laughter also. He was liking Yeve, more and more. If she were to side with him, they'd be unstoppable. "Too bad, you would make an excellent right-hand man, or in this case, woman."

There was a cut to his left cheek as he stopped laughing to glare. She was still standing before him, katana in her hand. A single drop of blood slid off the blade and fell to the floor as Yeve grinned.

"I'm pretty good, huh?" she boasted.

"You are," agreed Beast. He wiped the blood off his cheek and held up his fists. "It's too bad. I'm better."

"Is that so?" Yeve lifted an eyebrow, motioning for him to attack. "In that case, it's your turn to attack, big guy. I've been the one doing all the work so far. It's not nice to keep a lady waiting."

"I like the look in your eyes. Won't you reconsider?"

Like lightning, she was across the room, injuring Beast who bled. In that moment, his eyes no longer looked the same. Yeve held up her katana in defense position and waited.

Laughing hysterically, Beast grabbed a serum from his pocket. He injected the liquid into his bloodstream before tossing it aside. The previous shot was starting to wear off. If he wanted to defeat Yeve, he had to use the rest of what he had. Even if Beast wasn't a Life-Kill, he could still use their powers, so long as he injected their blood into his body. It was something Pia had taught him through harsh experiments.

"Did you know, I came from an isolated town in the countryside?" Beast said, popping his neck. "In that town, there's a god who could grant youth. I was once his sacrifice, and managed to steal some of his blood before safely escaping to the big city."

"Huh?" Yeve said, confused as to why he was giving her his backstory.

"It's an old tale from my old village about a greedy bunch who would do anything for eternal youth. One day, when I've become this planet's ruler, I'll return to kill them, and drain the rest of that demon's blood for myself."

"Didn't you hear me? The only one fit to rule this planet is me. That's why, you should kneel already!" Yeve ran at Beast, cutting him time and time again. But no matter how much she injured him, he just seemed to recover faster than before. "What the?" gasped Yeve.

"You don't seem to understand. Shall I explain?"

"Don't bother. I'm here to kill you, not talk."

"Devastation could control time."

"Like I said, I'm not here to talk." Again, Yeve ran at him. Right when she was about to cut him, he caught her wrist.

"Gotcha," he said with a smirk.

"Impossible." No one had ever been able to catch her before, let alone see her. She was untouchable.

"Nothing's ever impossible."

Yeve kicked him and broke free as Beast stole her sword. "Just great," she said and stood, weaponless.

"Without this sword, you're nothing."

It was odd how Yeve had thought of Mana just then. Even her heart seemed to ache, but she chased it out and grinned. On the battlefield, such emotions were useless. "Oh? We'll just have to see then." With a snap to her fingers, the hilt of her katana grew spikes, piercing Beast's hand. He yelped, dropping the katana to the floor.

"How'd you do that?"

"It's a secret."

Sneering, Beast placed one foot on the blade of the katana. "If I can't hold it, I'll just step on it."

"Futile," she said and held out her arm as the hilt broke off from the blade. It slid over on its own as Yeve bent down to grab it off the floor. She grinned while Beast stared incredulously. The hilt was materializing a new blade from energy particles. "Like I said, it's a secret." Yeve ran at Beast, ready to deliver the finishing blow, but not before something struck her from behind. She grunted and fell, head spinning.

"Your katana," Anoka said, appearing by Beast's side to point a finger. "It's bleeding."

Sure enough, Yeve's katana was bleeding. She groaned, angry that a kid had been the one to deliver the surprise attack. Standing, Yeve brushed her clothes. With just one look, Anoka had somehow figured out her secret. "Move kid, I don't wanna hurt you."

Anoka turned away to hold Beast's hand. She wanted to leave. The place reeked of death. "Beast-san, can we go to nee-chan now?"

"Not yet Anoka-chan, we still have to beat these bad guys."

"Bad guys?"

"Yes, that's right."

"Just like that strange girl I met in the English room?"

At the mentioning, Yeve's eyes widened at the possibilities. There had been only one person to enter the hideout with her. And if Verse had encountered the child, it was highly unlikely that she'd lose. But if—just *if* she had, then it meant that Yeve needed to leave and find her, wherever she was.

"Yes, like them. If you take out this girl too, we can leave." Beast smiled and patted Anoka's head.

"Then, Anoka-chan will do her best!" she shouted and returned her attention back to Yeve. The look in her eyes hardened.

"You're kidding me," Yeve complained and attempted to flee. From beneath her feet, something beeped. She glanced down, wondering what she'd just triggered. It was a landmine that had mysteriously shown up. "Just my freaking day," said Yeve as it exploded.

42nd Lie

WITH FIVE AGAINST ONE Rastus could only grin. His men he brought along had been wiped out. In due time, he would be next, but didn't dare run from this fight. The five had him surrounded as Rastus inspected the group again. If he wanted a chance at winning, he would have to dispose of the weakest link to lessen their numbers.

Aiming for Mio, Rastus ran at her while Alice fired her gun. Without Rain on high grounds to assist, they had to have each other's backs. Louis ran at Rastus to exchange blows. Remi sent streaks of fire every now and then to assist. In a fit of rage, Rastus went after her while Noah summoned enough energy to encase him inside a water sphere.

"Alice!" he commanded as Alice fired two blue bullets that never stopped moving until it pierced Rastus' heart.

When the fight came to an end, they let out a sigh of relief and smiled wryly. It had taken all five of them to finish him off. They could only imagine how much trouble the boss would be for Yeve and Verse.

From somewhere in the base, an explosion occurred and shook the ground as they screamed and lost their balances. Smoke rose into the sky as the three girls watched in horror. The base was on fire.

"Yeve, Verse!" Remi screamed frantically into her earpiece. Her heart hammered inside her chest as she watched helplessly. "Can you hear me?!"

"What the hell was that?" Poe asked.

"Don't know," Louis answered. "But we're gonna go inside to retrieve them."

"Wait!" Hanabi called out, halting the group from entering the base. "Remi, Mio, listen carefully to what I'm about to say."

"What?"

"I want you, Remi, to set fire to the base."

"Eh?" she gasped, shaking her head. She couldn't add to the fire while knowing Yeve and Verse were still inside. "No."

"What are you planning?" Poe asked.

Not bothering to answer, Hanabi continued persuading the girls. There was no time to waste. They had to listen. "Remi, you have to."

"No."

"Just do as I say!"

"But-"

"I'll explain later! For now, do as I say!"

Reaching out, Alice put a hand on Remi's shoulder and lightly squeezed. She smiled and nodded. It would be okay. They had to believe in Hanabi's plan. She probably knew more than she let on. There was no reason not to trust her.

"Remi," said Noah as she looked up at him. "Do it."

Crying, Remi nodded. She would put her trust in Hanabi too. "Okay."

"Mio, use your wind, expand the fire," Hanabi instructed after getting Remi's consent.

"You're crazy, Hanabi-chan," said Mio. Even she couldn't help but object. Hanabi sounded like a crazed person by putting their friends' lives on the line. Then again, Mio had no plans herself. "But I'll follow your orders."

"Good," said Hanabi. "Burn it all."

∞

Fire erupted from behind as Pia turned back. The flames looked breathtaking in the dark. She couldn't help but smile. "So, Beast-san ended up using the explosives, huh? They must be a tough bunch." She turned, following the trail Poe and the others had left behind.

∞

Naruyuki came to a slow halt as his heart pounded and ached. He set Umeko on the ground as the others turned to look. They were far enough that Pia couldn't catch up unless she had insane speed like Yeve. Fire was blazing from where they had come from. Remi was already burning the base alongside Mio. "Sasuke," Naruyuki said and took a stand.

Looking over, Sasuke answered, "What is it?"

"I'm leaving Umeko-san in your care."

461

"Eh?"

"I'm going back."

"Are you crazy? That girl's on our tail. You should be thankful we got away while we could, carrying these two." Sasuke pointed to Taiki and Umeko who were still unconscious but slowly regaining their energy. Along the way they had dumped Ikuto to deter Pia.

"Naruyuki," called out Poe. He set Taiki down to stand also.

"Verse is in trouble. I can feel it."

"Naruyuki."

"You can't stop me, Poe."

"I wasn't going to."

"Oye, Poe," objected Sasuke. He leapt to his feet, angry that their leader just gave consent to a suicide mission.

"He wants to protect what's important to him. If Mio was in trouble, you'd run back too, wouldn't you?"

Sasuke closed his mouth and looked away, defeated. "Fine," he grumbled.

Poe reached out, hitting Naruyuki on the arm gently. They would part here for the meantime. "Bring her back. We'll be here waiting."

"Yeah," Naruyuki answered and nodded. He ran back towards the smoke rising in the air, never once looking back.

"That guy," Sasuke said, shaking his head.

"He'll get the job done," Poe said confidently.

"I know he will."

Smiling, Hanabi knelt beside Umeko. She had a feeling Naruyuki would return for Verse. After all, it was coursing through his veins.

"Naruyuki-kun," whispered Umeko. The two guys turned to look at her then to each other. Again, they shrugged. It was a complicating issue. While they waited for the others, tears filled Hanabi's eyes that she refused to show. Their love story, how could it be so painstakingly beautiful?

∞

Rain stood inside the wrecked dojo that was quickly rising in smoke. That was his cue to get out but didn't care to do so. On the opposite end of the room was Beast and Anoka. In Rain's hands was his bow and two wooden arrows positioned to kill Beast. Yeve was lying on the floor, unconscious and battered. After Anoka had used her powers to slide one of Pia's explosives beneath Yeve's foot, she fled as fast as possible from the blast, only to have Anoka take her by surprise again.

"If you so much as blink wrongly, I'll strike," threatened Rain.

"You think you can hurt me with that?" challenged Beast.

Rain grinned. "Don't underestimate my bow."

"I think you're overestimating yourself."

"You think so?"

"I know so."

"Then, let's have a shooting warm-up, shall we?"

"Huh?"

"Choose a target for me."

"Are you sure you should be playing around in this fire?"

"Choose," repeated Rain.

Beast grinned and laughed. Rain was too conceited. There was nothing to fear from an archer, especially with the base on fire. "The only thing that scares me is this smoke."

Rain aimed his bow up towards the broken ceiling and shot one of his arrows. It pierced a bat in the smoky sky and came crashing into the broken dojo. Beast watched in disbelief as Rain pointed the second arrow at him again. Rain had shot a bat in the night sky, filled with smoke and fire. "Now do you see? When I choose a target, I never miss."

"You kids," he said, laughing again. "First, the katana girl, now you!"

"Scared?"

"Yes, very," he answered and nodded, his knees buckling. He'd never come across such deadly Life-Kills before. It felt as though each generation got stronger than the previous. The rate at which they were evolving was scary fast and there was no stopping it.

"Then, let me end it here."

Beast picked up Anoka and smiled.

"Even if you use her as a shield, I'll still shoot. I could care less after what she did to my Soulmate."

Beast glared, thinking he could get away with that. However, Rain's eyes never wavered. He would kill Anoka just to get to him. Unwilling to die here, Beast yelled and threw Anoka anyway.

"Ah!" screamed Anoka as Rain reached out and caught hold of her. When he turned to look at Beast, he'd already bolted.

"Damn," said Rain. He looked down at Anoka who was giving him a curious look.

"You and that girl over there, your weapons-"

Rain knocked her out with one hit to the back of the head. She fainted and was sleeping like the dead. He put his bow and arrows away on his back, angry for letting Beast escape.

Flames erupted from the doors, blocking their exit. Soon, the dojo would be engulfed in a sea of fire.

"Should I lend a hand?" offered Nicholas as he appeared by Yeve's side, sitting and smiling with his chin on his palm, not caring about the fire that surrounded him.

"Who are you?" Rain asked, raising an eyebrow.

"A dutiful brother-in-law."

"Rain!" shouted voices from down the hallway. Water blasted into the room as Noah, Louis, and Alice ran inside with wet pieces of cloths covering their noses and mouths.

One look at Yeve and Alice ran over frantically, "Yeve!"

"Oye, let's get out!" shouted Louis.

Rain stared at where Alice was kneeling. Nicholas had disappeared. "Yeah," said Rain. This was no time to worry about where Nicholas had gone. Instead, he had to worry about getting out of the burning base alive.

"Then what are you doing daydreaming for? Let's go!" shouted Noah. He ran over and picked up Yeve.

"Oye," Rain said, walking over to put Anoka in Noah's arms. "You hold the little one. I've got Yeve."

"Is it really necessary to be picky right now?"

"Yes."

"Let's just get out of here!" shouted Louis from the doorway.

"Here, you hold the girl." Noah walked over, handing Anoka over.

"Eh? Why?"

"Are you able to use water?"

"Are you making fun of me?"

"Quiet down. I'm gonna flood our way out of this place," said Noah as he led the way down the burning hallways. Right behind was Alice with her gun in hand. Water erupted from the pipes inside the rooms and flooded their way out. "See?"

"Oh, get a move on it," Louis hissed. Again, his powers were useless.

"Come on guys, let's not argue," said Alice. "We're trying to get out of a burning house here, remember?"

"Oye," said Rain as they ran. "Did you guys by chance come across Verse?"

Noah turned back, shaking his head. So did Louis.

"I hope she got out."

∞

Pia knelt beside Ikuto who lay on the ground, breathing heavily. Soon, he would cease to exist. It was too late to try and take out the poison. Tears filled her eyes as she reached out to cut the vines tying his wrists together. She held his cold hand that trembled from the poison and whispered, "You dummy."

Ikuto opened his eyes and did his best to smile. She had found him. "Sorry. I let them get away."

"That's not important right now."

"Pia," he whispered, doing his best to squeeze her hand.

Pia clasped her free hand over his and squeezed also. It hurt so badly to watch her comrade suffer. He didn't deserve this. If she ever caught the ones who did this, she would give them a slow, torturous death.

"It's enough."

"What?"

"I know that you live to seek vengeance. But I don't want to see you continuing down this lonely road. So, forget about your family status. Forget about your past. And forget about Heita and Misaki. Just live happily. That's the best vengeance in the world." Ikuto smiled sadly and closed his eyes, his breathing stopping and his grip loosening.

The night was silent and still. Nothing dared to make a sound.

"I can't, Ikuto." Pia squeezed his hand one last time. "When I find those two, I'm going to kill them." She grabbed her wooden sword from her back and sliced the ground. It crumbled, creating a hole. Pia pushed Ikuto inside and pushed the fresh dirt over his body. "I hope you rest in peace with your family." Dirt stained, she walked away, tears falling. There was no need to return to the base. Without a doubt, Rastus had been annihilated too. All her comrades had been taken out in one night. Rage overtook her as her fists shook by her side. Now, she was alone again without a place to return to. "You'll pay, Maroon."

∞

The closet was dark and eerie, even so, Wakaba sat inside, crying and hugging her legs. No one bothered to come search for her. For the past few nights she'd been having nightmares. There was always a war raging. When she woke up in tears, no one was there to comfort her. Even when she told the teachers, they waved it off without a care. Miss Umi had promised to make her feel better, but nothing seemed to work. Even the experiments broke her spirit to keep living.

"Hey!" shouted an irritated Verse. She swung the closet door open and popped her head in, glaring. "Shut it!"

The crying Wakaba looked up, too scared to respond or flee. All she could do was stare at her classmate she'd never met before until that day.

"Understood?!"

Slowly, Wakaba nodded.

"What the hell are you doing in here anyway?! You're not the Boogey Man! You're not even scary looking!"

"Uh," began Wakaba.

Verse put her tiny hands on her hips, still staring. Today, she was meeting all sorts of girls. First, there was Mio and the Fashion Posse. Then, there were those who worshipped the posse and those who feared the posse. There was even the chubby Shayla who was hoarding junk food. And now, there was this wannabe closet ghost. How peculiar the rest of the girls were from the three. Why did they even have to associate with the rest for? Damn that dean. "Are you getting bullied too?"

"Eh? No."

"Are you an emo?"

"Eh? No."

"Good, because I hate emo people the most." Verse took her hands off her hips and laughed. "If you're not emo or a monster, then get out of there. You'll really become one."

Obediently, Wakaba crawled out to stand in the bright room with Verse, who shut the closet door.

"Come on," Verse urged, waving at Wakaba to follow.

"Huh?"

"We're gonna go play with Yeve and Soria!" She ran over, caught hold of Wakaba's hand to drag towards the exit as the white cloths swayed. "Geh," Verse let out in dread. She'd forgotten to include one other person. "And Remi, that baby."

"But I don't know you."

"The name's Verse."

"Wakaba."

"Wakaba, hmm, I like you. You're weird and totally emo. But that's cool." Again, Verse laughed and ran down the hallway with her new friend. "Let's go, let's go! I'll introduce you to the others! If that poop-head can have a friend, then so can I!"

From that day forth, Wakaba found a reason for living. Even the experiments she detested became more tolerable. If it was for her best friend, she could do anything.

That was, until that day.

They were seated inside the cafeteria, eating lunch. It was a lively day just like any other.

Wakaba abruptly knocked down her tray of food and stood from the table, slamming her palms down. Soon, all eyes were on the loud commotion as the chattering stopped.

"What's wrong, Wakaba?" asked Remi.

"…hate."

"Huh?"

"…hate."

"Are you okay, Wakaba?" Verse asked, worried also.

"Don't act like you care!"

Still the only one eating, Soria stopped and glanced up while Yeve and Remi were left dumbfounded by Wakaba's viciousness.

"Of course I care. Come on. If you're not feeling okay, I'll take you to Umi-sensei." Verse stood and reached a hand out as Wakaba hit it away.

"Don't touch me with your filthy hands!"

Uncertain of what to do next, Verse forced a smile, but it didn't last long. Her lips trembled, all words leaving her mouth. Was she being thrown away? Or was she being tested? Did having a best friend mean going through hardships like this? If so, how strong was their bond if Wakaba could easily hurt her like this?

"Die, die, die, I hope you all die!"

Suddenly, without warning, Soria jumped across the table they were sitting at, tackling and pinning Wakaba to the floor.

"Soria!" they screamed.

With one knee digging into Wakaba's ribs, and a forearm against her throat, Soria snarled, "Say that again, and I'll rip your windpipe out."

Fear caused Wakaba's body to quiver as her eyes widened from the flames that raged in Soria's eyes that day. She'd been the one to bring out the sinister side to the ever-loving turtle. "Let go!" Wakaba screamed.

"I swear it."

"Soria, that's enough!" the girls shouted frantically.

"Soria!" pleaded Remi as she tried to pry the two girls away from each other.

"Damn it you two!" Verse shouted and rushed over. Once she pried Soria off, she helped Wakaba stand. "Are you okay?"

"Don't touch me!" She slapped Verse's hand again and tried to choke Soria for tackling her. "Let me at her!"

"Stop it!" Verse lashed out, stunning everyone, even Wakaba.

It grew quiet in the cafeteria again as Soria fumed while Remi watched in horror. Yeve simply stood aside, not knowing what to do. How did things get so out of control?

"I don't know what's gotten into you. But apologize."

Wakaba shook her head and cried. "No."

"Wakaba!"

"Why don't any of you remember?" she asked, throwing a hand over her eyes. "Why is it always only me?!" Wakaba turned to look at Umeko and ran out of the cafeteria while everyone watched.

Umeko who sat nearby couldn't blink or look away after Wakaba's accusing glare.

"Umeko?" said Crystal worriedly.

"I'm fine," she answered and smiled.

After that incident, Wakaba avoided the girls altogether. She kept to herself again, no longer wanting to socialize with anyone.

Then, that fateful day arrived.

The day when Verse killed Wakaba.

Darkness was the only thing that existed in the place where Verse was drifting in. There was no light or warmth as she relived her childhood. It was the most frightening and joyous time of her life.

"For you and Yeve, I would also go to hell to bring you back," Remi had said as the recent memory resurfaced. "…It's because you and Yeve are Soria's world."

It'd be easier if she would just hate me. Verse smiled.

But you know that'll never happen, her other conscience answered and chuckled.

"Verse!" called out a voice from far away. It was frantically trying to reach her somewhere in the lonely darkness. "I'm begging you. Don't leave me," he whispered. "If you leave me, I'll chase you. Even if that place is to the depths of the ocean—to the endless universe…even to hell itself, I'll find you and bring you back."

Idiot, you sound like Remi.

"I'll chase you; chase you until you're tired of running. So, come back!"

Managing to open one eyelid for a brief second, Verse shut it. "You…you're loud…Naruyuki."

Relieved, Naruyuki smiled, holding her tightly. "Thank goodness."

The wind howled as they sat amongst the trees, away from the burning base. She could smell wood burning along with blood. "I didn't die, did I?"

"No."

"Oh good, I don't want to be stuck in hell with you."

"Stop joking at a time like this."

Verse cracked a smile. "I thought it was pretty funny."

"Seriously, stop it."

Verse exhaled but ended up coughing.

"Relax, you inhaled a lot of smoke."

"Yeah," she said, fully opening her eyes to see the stars through the smoke. She smiled and reached a hand out to catch them. Instead, Naruyuki took her hand in his.

"You idiot," he snapped.

"Sorry, I took that little girl too lightly."

"You scared me to death," Naruyuki said, burying his face into her long black hair. Just her scent alone drove him crazy. He could only imagine what he'd do if he actually lost her. "Do you know how fast my heart was beating? Do you know how worried I was when I saw you lying on the floor unconscious? I thought I was really gonna have to go down to hell to drag you back."

Verse chuckled as a tear rolled down. Why did that sentence alone cut her wide open? Would he really follow her no matter how far she fell? Or were his words simply just that, words?

"Don't ever do that again."

"I can't guarantee you anything."

"Knock it off with the jokes. It's not the time for it."

"Sorry. That stupid poop-head is rubbing off on me."

Naruyuki finally cracked a smile as Verse chuckled. He lifted his head and brushed her hair out of her face. "Thank you for returning."

"I'll always. I can't die yet. If I do, no one will keep Yeve in check. Soria will become an emo, and Remi will follow me to hell. I don't want that to happen. Even in death, I can't escape that hateful baby."

Chuckling again, Naruyuki squeezed her hand. Now that she was back in his arms, there was nothing to fear. "You promise?"

Tears trickled from her bloodshot eyes as the fading word 'Promise' faded from her sight. However hard she fought to hold it, it refused to stay.

"Hum, hum, hum," the wind sang, trying to soothe her broken soul.

43rd Lie

LIZ SAT ON A TREE BRANCH inside the woods, legs dangling and swinging. She hummed, unable to see the smoke through the treetops, but could smell it. When Beast appeared from the path in front of her, she smiled. "Oh my, you're still alive?"

Coming to a halt, Beast looked up, not expecting anyone to have caught up to him. "Who are you? Are you with the others?"

Liz raised an eyebrow and burst into a cackle. Abruptly, she stopped, no longer amused. "Don't associate me with those weaklings. I'd die if I was from Maroon. Only the Empress do I recognize as strong."

"If you're not part of their group, then move."

"Hmm," Liz said, looking past Beast. "What should we do, Nic?"

"Yes, what indeed," Nicholas agreed from behind Beast.

Alarmed, he spun around. "When did you get there?"

"I've always been here."

"Who are you two?"

"We're from Turquoise."

"Tur—Turquoise," Beast stammered. The reputation of Turquoise was something to fear. To have Soulmates from *that* Dome pursue him, he was almost honored. "You two couldn't possibly be the Soulmates sent here to assist Maroon, are you?"

Liz grinned. "And what if we are?"

Beast smiled. He'd heard the rumors circulating. If they were who he thought they were, he wouldn't live for long. "I heard that you two are as good as the veteran Life-Kills and were dispatched a year early from your peers. The missions given to you have only been ranked A."

"Correction, S."

"S," repeated Beast. He laughed. His luck had run out when he encountered these two.

"Shouldn't you get a move on it, Nic?"

Nicholas smiled and nodded. "You're right. I better get going."

"Where are you going?" asked Beast.

"You're also coming with me." Nicholas took a step forward and disappeared as Beast spun around in circles. When he reappeared, he was standing beside Beast, a hand on his shoulder. "Then, I'll be taking him back to Turquoise first. Dean Campbell will be thrilled."

"Okay, I'll be right here waiting." Liz smiled and waved.

"The 'Man Who Leaps through Space'," gasped Beast.

"That is me." Nicholas grinned, happy to know that his reputation had followed him even to here, then disappeared into thin air with Beast.

Liz swung her legs, humming again. The group dispatched for this mission had finished in a flashy manner. "Franz should be happy with what we've acquired. Now maybe, he can present something worthy to His Highness, our Golden God."

∞

Greeting Yeve when she opened her eyes was the twinkling stars. Her head ached as a nearby fire crackled and popped. On reflex, she sat up, reaching for her katana and stopped. Rain sat nearby, watching while the rest of the team was fast asleep around the campfire.

"It's over," he spoke softly.

"Are you serious?" Yeve asked in disbelief.

Rain smiled at how ambitious she was. "Yeah, I'm serious."

"Damn." Yeve sat back down. She'd missed all the action. "I was so close to defeating that Beast guy too. But that little girl came out from nowhere and delivered a cheap shot. If I ever see her again I'm gonna—ah!" Yeve pointed a finger. Lying not far away was an unconscious Anoka. They'd brought her along as war trophy. "I'm gonna kill that little girl." Yeve grabbed her katana again and stood to strike the sleeping child.

Rain picked up a pebble and tossed it at her head. In a whimper, she turned back to glare at him. "She's a child and she's sleeping."

"Like I care," retorted Yeve. She sheathed her katana and walked over to sit beside him. It was too late to be causing a ruckus when the others were sleeping soundly. "Man, I'm all out of sorts."

"I thought you were gonna kill her?"

"Too lazy."

Rain laughed softly. "Thanks."

"Why are you thanking me?"

"For not killing her."

"I'll kill her when the time is right." Yeve grinned as Rain reached over to nudge her head.

"You can't kill a child."

"If they dare get in my way, I won't show any mercy."

"You're really relentless."

"I'm the Empress after all. I have to be."

"It wasn't a compliment."

"I'm taking it as one," she said, lying down to stargaze. It felt like they were on a camping trip instead of a mission. All that was missing was the rest of the guys and girls, along with s'mores and scary stories. "So, did we succeed?"

"Look for yourself," he said, pointing to Taiki and Umeko who slept closest to the campfire, getting as much warmth as possible. They were wrapped in blankets that Poe had brought along for the mission.

"So," she continued, turning to raise an eyebrow at him. "Why aren't you asleep?"

"I'm taking guard."

"Just you?"

Rain nodded again. "Just myself will do."

"Well, aren't you conceited?" Yeve grinned again and sat back up. She propped her katana in-between her legs to hold like a samurai. "Then, in that case, I'll stay guard with you."

"You don't have to. Sleep if you're still tired."

"I'm fine now," she said with a yawn and closed her eyes.

"Then why are you yawning?"

"Don't mention the minor details."

Again, Rain smiled and reached out to nudge her, but stopped midway. He lowered his hand and looked up to the sky. With her eyes closed, she didn't notice him hesitate. "Let's be brutally honest with one another."

"Hmm?" she answered.

"I hate you."

Yeve opened her eyes to stare at him, then nodded. "Yeah, I had a hunch."

Rain turned to stare as well, neither of them daring to look away. "Since the beginning, I've hated you. I don't think I'm going to stop hating you."

"Yeah, I think I knew that one too." Though Yeve held no animosity towards him, his brutal honesty made her feel much better. This way, there was no need to pretend that they were okay. "It's fine if you hate me. I actually have no opinion of you whatsoever."

Rain nodded, expecting that much out of her. It was just like Yeve to not care even if he was confessing his hatred. "But since we're Soulmates, let's try and get along."

"Didn't see that one coming," she joked and closed her eyes again. After a few minutes of silence, she spoke again. "Say, Rain."

"What is it?"

"Why do you hate me so much?"

"I don't know. Whenever I see your face I get this sudden urge to hurt you. But I can never bring myself to follow through."

"Weird."

"What is?"

"When I see you, I feel like punching you too," she joked again and chuckled alongside him.

"So then, can we start over and be friends?"

"Let's shake on it." Yeve opened her eyes and held out her hand as Rain shook it. "Now we're friends."

"Friends."

"You know…I'm sorry."

It had always been Rain's assumption that Yeve was incapable of apologizing. But she had proven him wrong. Was she always this kind of person? Or was she putting on airs? Or had he neglected to see this part of her? "Why are you apologizing for?"

"You hate me because I dragged you up the mountaintop to get the scroll, right?"

Rain laughed at the distant memory. He couldn't believe that she still remembered. "I forgot."

"Well," said Yeve. If she had done something wrong, she would own up to it. It was one of the many mottos she lived by. "If I did you any wrong in the past, I'll apologize now. I'm sorry. I truly am. These aren't empty words. Believe me, okay?" Yeve held his gaze, meaning every word.

Not hesitating this time, Rain nodded and reached a hand out to place on top of her head. "Yeah, I accept your apology."

"Say, Rain."

"What is it?"

Yeve yawned again, not minding that his hand was still resting on her head. "When the day comes when you remember why you hate me, tell me. I wanna know the reason, so I can correct those mistakes."

"Got it."

"Your hand is surprisingly warm."

"Didn't you say that already?"

"I did?" Yeve asked tiredly.

Rain withdrew his hand, all the while smiling. "Go to sleep."

"But I have to stay guard with you," she protested.

"Don't worry. I'll protect you."

Yeve chuckled and nodded, closing her eyes once more. It was funny, how as a child, she hated being protected and wanted to do everything alone. Now that she was older, being protected wasn't so bad. "Alright, but next time, I get to protect you."

"Deal."

"Aw, how cute," whispered Alice while she eavesdropped on their conversation. With Yeve's yelling, she had woken up.

"Quiet, I'm tired," Verse snapped.

"Okay, sheesh." Alice smiled and quickly fell back asleep on the ground where she laid beside Verse. Hopefully, Yeve hadn't heard them, or else they'd be dead meat the next morning.

∞

When Dark's team reached the base, it was bustling with liveliness. There were two parties going on at once. The first was for Haj's arrival. The second was for Zena and her miraculous awakening.

The team came to a halt, hiding from view. If they were to get caught now, Mina would be immediately executed. The only reason she was alive was so that Haj could interrogate her. Having Azuma and Shayla branded as traitors also didn't help.

After separating into three smaller teams, Dark held his team's gaze. "Let's finish our missions and return safely."

"Yeah," they answered and dispersed.

Before Soria could follow Kakinouchi and Azuma, Shayla reached out to pull her back.

"What is it?" Soria raised an eyebrow, wondering why she was the only one getting stopped.

Shayla leaned over, whispering something. When she backed away, there was a guilty look on her face. "Sorry to put you on the spot, but I can only count on you."

Soria grinned and shrugged it off. It no longer mattered. She just wanted to finish the mission and return to the Dome to rest. "Don't sweat it." She waved a hand to chase after the two impatient guys.

"What was that about?" asked Crystal.

"Let's get going," Dark said as they ran off to start their mission.

Remembering that she had protective charms to distribute, Love reached into her pocket. "Oh no," she said. "I forgot to give one to Azuma."

"Let's hope he'll be fine without it."

Kakinouchi turned back to look at Soria who was jogging slowly. She had no sense of urgency whatsoever. They had to be quick or else they'd get caught. "You're slow," Kakinouchi insulted.

"Shut up," snapped Soria. "It's your fault I'm in a pissy mood."

"What's with you suddenly?" Azuma asked while they ran towards the guest mansion.

"Well gee, let's see. First off, I didn't even wanna be here. Secondly, I hate this mission and you two incompetent fools, along with the deans. Third, I just wanna sleep. Want me to keep going?" she asked and scowled.

The two guys glanced at each other and shrugged. They had no idea why she was angry for when she was fine minutes ago. "Women," they whispered to each other.

"Boys," Soria muttered to herself.

From up ahead, a group ambushed them as they dodged and kept a good distance between each other.

"I was hoping we wouldn't get stopped yet," said Azuma.

"How could we not? Security's so tight around this place," responded Kakinouchi.

"Put your hands up and surrender," ordered the leader of the group.

"Okay." Obediently, Soria held up her hands to surrender, seeing no harm in being taken hostage. It was better than doing as Dean Kiera wanted.

"Why did Shayla recommend you for?" groaned Azuma.

"Shut up and take this." Soria slipped off her charm to toss at Azuma who caught it.

"What's this for?"

"A charm from Love."

"Why are you giving this to me for?"

"Go find that doctor. I'll catch up later."

"Are you serious?" asked Kakinouchi.

Soria glared. Being here in the flesh only made her furious because she couldn't get herself out of it anymore. Things became even worse after knowing that Shayla was counting on her. "Does it look like I'm lying?"

The two guys raised their eyebrows doubtfully.

"Just get lost before I drown you!"

"Yes!" they answered and ran off, suddenly afraid to test her.

"Get them!" instructed the leader as the group fired their weapons, but none of the bullets reached the two Aratas who continued running. "What the-" The leader turned towards Soria who looked bored and angry. They wouldn't get to the two guys unless they took her out first.

It was such a beautiful night. All she wanted to do was sleep beneath it.

"Get her," the leader snarled as his men attacked.

Before they could, water shot out to engulf and choke them. Once they were unconscious, the water spheres gave way, dropping the men to the ground.

"Wowzers, that took the energy out of me. I better catch my breath." Soria let out a long, deep sigh and lay beside the unconscious men. She curled into a tight ball and hummed while staring at the sky.

∞

While running and fighting to save Gon, Morgana suggested, "You know, I think we need a leader."

Taking the opportunity to prove himself, Aoi offered, "Me!"

"I'm not leaving my life in your hands," insulted Teo.

Gasping hurtfully, tears welled inside Morgana's eyes. "What does that mean?"

"Oye, why are *you* the one getting hurt for?"

"If not Aoi-kun, then who else is suitable for that position?"

"Don't tell me you're volunteering yourself, Teo?" Aoi accused.

"No idiot, I'm nominating Takahiko."

"Why Taka?!"

"Because he's the strongest."

"No he's not!"

"Physically," emphasized Teo.

"Well, I could be too," Aoi said in a small voice. He looked away, dejected. It wasn't his fault he didn't have brute strength as a power.

Morgana turned towards Aoi and smiled, trying to cheer him up. "To me, you're the strongest and most handsome."

"Morgana," said Aoi. He turned to look at her and smiled. "Thank you."

"Eh?" She blushed and smiled back. "Y—you're welcome."

Rolling their eyes, Teo and Takahiko just wanted to fall over and die. Being on the same team as these two was going to be a long night.

"Alright then," said Takahiko. He nodded, ready to take on the burdensome job as captain for this sub-group since Dark was no longer present. "Since I'm leader, this is what we'll do, I'll break into the room, grab the boy, you three back me up. I want Aoi in the front, Morgana in the back, and Teo by my side. Keep in contact with your creatures so that we can avoid any surprise attacks."

"Got it," they answered.

∞

Haj entered the room where Mina was being held prisoner. Her eyes were blindfolded, and her wrists and ankles were bound together. Even her mouth was gagged so she couldn't speak. Doctor Nishikawa had injected her with a drug so she couldn't self-heal from the tortures. For now they had stopped, but when they set off for their international base in an hour, the beatings would begin again.

Haj walked over to crouch before her. Though they had allowed Azuma and Shayla to escape, it was alright. They had Mina, the mastermind behind the plot to destroy him. "So, are you ready to tell me what you know?"

Mina let out a muffled cry as Haj reached out to remove her mouth cloth. She gasped for air and smiled. "Don't underestimate those kids," was all she said as Haj put the cloth back over her mouth.

"I'll be back later to torture you myself," he said, standing to leave. As soon as he stepped into the hallway, darkness surrounded him. "What the-" There was clinking from behind as Haj spun around. Someone had slipped past him and was trying to free Mina. He couldn't believe that the Dome already sent out backups. "Men!" he commanded, not able to afford losing Mina. He needed her to spit out information about the Maroon Dome.

"We've taken them out. It was pretty simple actually," responded Dark's voice from somewhere in the shadows.

"Who are you?"

"You should've fled the moment you found out Mina was a traitor."

Haj lashed out at the dark but couldn't hit anyone or anything. All he encountered was the wall. "Damn you!"

From behind, Dark stabbed him through the chest as he gurgled and fell over. Once the darkness faded, the group came into view. They had finished what they came here to do. "Let's go," Dark instructed as they made their way back to the entrance to meet up with the others.

"Wasn't this a little too easy?" Yuudai asked, carrying Mina.

"Let's prepare for an ambush."

∞

The two Aratas finished taking out the men stationed outside Zena's room and entered, finding her seated on her wheelchair before a long mirror. She had on a peach dress and spun around as soon as she saw the boys through the mirror. Just the sight of Kakinouchi made the beating in her heart erratic. Unable to suppress it, Zena placed a hand over her chest. Even so, it didn't stop. She did her best to smile at Kakinouchi and bowed her head. Funny, how her heart would beat for a teenage boy instead of her own husband. Wasn't this *her* heart now? "Is he your friend?" she directed at

Azuma. "Did you invite him to the party too? How come I didn't see you or Shayla-chan there?"

"Eh, uh, well," Azuma stammered, unsure of what to do while Kakinouchi stared at him.

"You actually have a friend other than Shayla-chan. I guess there really is nothing to worry about."

"Eh?"

"Say, what's your name?" she interrupted.

"Uh," Kakinouchi said, unsure of how to respond.

"His name is Arata," answered Azuma.

"Eh? Two Aratas?" she asked and laughed. "Wow, coincidence much?"

"Yeah," said Azuma. He turned to look at Kakinouchi, then away.

Uncertain of what was happening, Kakinouchi glared at Zena. He had to finish his task before Doctor Nishikawa, wherever he was, appeared. "Listen, lady-"

"Please excuse me," Zena interrupted. She let out a sniffle and placed a hand to her cheek that blushed uncontrollably. "I don't know what's overcome me." After wiping her eyes, she smiled sweetly.

"Honey, are you ready to depart-" Doctor Nishikawa began and stopped. He had finished changing into a black tuxedo in the backroom. In his hands was a vintage camera. When he spotted the two boys he stopped in his tracks. He'd been so busy with his attire and packing, he didn't hear them enter. Doctor Nishikawa clutched on tightly to the camera in his hand and gulped. They had wasted too much time with the parties and could no longer escape as planned. Without a doubt, Kakinouchi wouldn't allow him to escape again. Playing it off coolly, the doctor smiled. "Good evening," he greeted.

"Honey, take my photo with the two Arata boys. I want to commemorate this day." Zena wheeled herself over to drag the guys towards the sofa, all the while smiling.

Doctor Nishikawa smiled and nodded. He casually got into place and began snapping pictures of them while a dumbfounded Kakinouchi could only play along. "Smile," he instructed as the two guys obeyed.

"I'm sorry, I never caught your name," spoke Kakinouchi.

"Zena," she answered, smiling at the camera.

"Zena-san," said Kakinouchi. Not once did he take his eyes off Doctor Nishikawa and the camera in his hand. "Would you mind telling me the story about where you got your new heart?"

Zena's smile widened. She didn't mind and enjoyed telling the story.

Once she finished, Doctor Nishikawa smiled. "I'm going to refill the camera." He turned his back, grabbing a new roll of film, but the tears in his eyes made it hard to see what he was doing.

"Zena-san," Kakinouchi said, glaring at the doctor's back. "What would you do if you found out your husband had stolen that heart instead?"

Not once did the doctor turn around. He was keeping his cool and posture before his wife. He couldn't lose it, at least not yet.

Zena who was taken aback by the question quickly shook her head. Again, her heart beat wildly. "Eh? He would never."

"I'm asking hypothetically."

Silence settled in as Zena stared at Kakinouchi's distorted face. She wanted to reach out and comfort him but shook off the feeling. Instead, she turned to her attention to her husband's back. The sight of him made her heart ache. "If he stole this heart from someone," she said, answering the question. "I'd cry my eyes out and curse him even until the day I died."

"Did you hear that…sensei?"

Doctor Nishikawa smiled and nodded. "I heard."

"But I'd still love him regardless," she added in and smiled. While she had been in a coma, her husband had been patiently waiting. Now that they were finally together, she couldn't handle another painful parting. "He's my husband and my world."

Both Azuma and Kakinouchi turned to look at her in alarm. They weren't expecting that last sentence to come out from her mouth.

"I mean, if he was willing to commit such a crime for his wife, doesn't that tell you something? Of course, I'd be sad and disappointed, but I'd still love him, nonetheless. And even if the heart was stolen, I'd apologize and plea the donor to let me live for just one more day. I'd like to see the sunset one last time with my brother and my most beloved. Afterwards, I'll return the heart and go back to sleeping."

Kakinouchi turned away, unable to look at Zena any longer. Why did she have to be the doctor's wife? Of all the women on this planet, why did it have to be her? Retrieving May's heart should've been an easy task. Instead, it became more complicated. Zena was too kind-hearted and lovely, too good for a man like the doctor. "Sensei," called out Kakinouchi.

"What is it?" Doctor Nishikawa answered. He finished refilling the camera with a new film and finally turned to face them.

"You have a good wife."

Doctor Nishikawa nodded, wiping a tear with his pinky. Yes, he knew that. When the world had turned its back on him, Zena had been there for him. With no family, she took him in and gave him a home. The one thing he wanted from this world, he had received from his wife. He would do whatever it took to maintain that happiness, even kill. "Thank you," he said with a genuine smile.

"Kakinouchi," whispered Azuma.

"Why did it have to be this woman?" Kakinouchi asked. "Why couldn't she be evil?"

"I knew you'd say that."

∞

Aoi burned his way through the enemy while Takahiko and Teo followed. On lookout behind was Morgana. If any of the men were to get back up, she was to knock them out again.

The brown mouse running in front of the team stopped in front of a door and sniffed the air before turning to look at them.

"We're there," announced Teo.

Aoi stopped running as Takahiko rushed over to break down the door with a single punch. He kicked it aside and ran in. Chained not far away was Gon. He was so fragile looking, Takahiko was scared to go near him.

"Are you Gon?"

"Who's there?" he answered weakly.

"We're friends of Kakinouchi and May. We're here to rescue you."

"May-san," he said and smiled. "How is she?"

"She's fine." Takahiko smiled and reached over to rip the chains apart. He picked up the fragile boy and ran out of the room. "Recovered the boy. Now, let's get out of here safely and the mission will be completed."

Aoi nodded and backtracked, burning his way through the enemy again. From one of the rooms, someone jumped out to stab him.

"Aoi!" shouted the two guys from behind.

Unsuspecting, Aoi turned on time to find someone pouncing on him.

"Don't you dare hurt Aoi-kun!" Morgana screamed as ice pierced the man who fell over, dead.

"Are you okay?" asked the guys as they ran over.

"Yeah," Aoi answered. He stood with Teo's help while Takahiko was occupied with Gon in his arms. Turning, Aoi smiled at Morgana. He patted her on the head, grateful that she had such a quick reaction. This was something to be expected of Yuudai's Soulmate. "Thanks, Morgana."

"Eh?" she said, blushing like crazy. Protecting him from harm was her duty. "I'll always save you."

"We have no time for your cringy moments," Takahiko said, kicking Aoi to lead the way again.

"Totally," agreed Teo.

"Sorry, let's go," said Aoi as he ran off again. From behind, Morgana created ice walls to prevent any enemy from chasing them.

∞

Kakinouchi groaned and pulled his hair, having no idea why he was going along with taking pictures of the man who stole his Soulmate's heart. It was pointless, and he was only prolonging the mission. The others were probably engaged in combat and needed their assistance. Kakinouchi forcefully lowered the camera in Azuma's hand that Zena had handed him. He glared at the happy couple that didn't deserve to smile after putting others through agony.

Zena's smile faded when she saw his glare. Again, her heart noisily beat. This time, she found it hard to breathe. "What's wrong?"

"Kakinouchi?" Azuma spoke.

"Let's just hurry and end this," he replied.

"How about some milk?" interrupted Doctor Nishikawa. He cheerfully stood from where he sat and walked away from his wife.

"What's with you boys?" she asked and laughed. "Why are you all acting so strangely?"

"How about some warm milk?" he repeated.

"Sure," she said and gave the two boys a concerned look. "Arata-kun?"

"We're fine," Azuma answered with a smile.

She forced a smile and bit back a question. "If you say so."

"That heart doesn't belong to you!" erupted Kakinouchi as Zena jumped from her wheelchair. Even Azuma flinched. Only Doctor Nishikawa stayed calm. "It belongs to my Soulmate!"

It became still like the dead as Zena stared at Kakinouchi, unable to blink. Slowly, she turned to look at her husband's back, her breathing heavy. "Honey?" she whispered. "What's he talking about?"

"Your wife…" Kakinouchi smiled. Even he hated doing this to such a gentle woman. It felt wrong, but it had to be done. "I can understand why you wanted to revive her so badly. She's a devoted person, but that heart belongs to May."

"Honey," Zena said loudly this time.

"I-" Before Kakinouchi could utter another word, Doctor Nishikawa was over within a blink, stabbing each Arata with a needle, dipped in a drug. Love's protection charm was useless against the attack.

Screaming, Zena threw both hands to her mouth and watched in horror.

Doctor Nishikawa stood, hovering above the two while they looked up, dazed. This was the price to pay for taking him so lightly just because he was human. "You say you understand me. Then, in this case, you'll also understand that I'll do whatever needs to be done to keep my paradise."

"What have you done?" gasped Zena.

"I've gotten rid of the pest, that's all."

When Doctor Nishikawa turned and smiled at Zena, she held her breath. Fear struck her from what she saw reflected in his eyes. There wasn't a hint of remorse. It was as if he'd done this hundreds of times before. Zena threw her hands to her mouth again and cried, knowing the reason. It was her fault that he'd turned into a monster.

"It's alright," Doctor Nishikawa assured and wiped his hands on his pants. "Don't get worked up. It's not good for your heart. After I've disposed of their bodies and spoken with Haj, I'll explain everything to you in full detail. But for now, we have to re-locate and-"

Zena let out a grunt as her face distorted in pain. Sticking out of her was a sword made of water that ran blood red. The water blade had missed the heart by a few inches.

"Zena," gasped out Doctor Nishikawa.

Soria stood behind her, holding the water blade's hilt. After catching up to the two, she stayed in hiding, waiting for them to retrieve the heart. The four were so wary of each other, they didn't even notice her entering. As Shayla had said, the two guys were unable to retrieve May's heart while it was beating inside Zena's body.

"You bitch!" yelled Doctor Nishikawa. His tears fell as he grabbed a pen nearby, ready to strike Soria. After meeting and finding out that Jin and he shared a common interest, they sought to create "the Adam of your labours" and failed miserably. Even so, they weren't discouraged. No matter how long it took, Doctor Nishikawa waited patiently. Then, like a falling star, May landed in the palm of his hand. He'd destroy this world before letting anyone take his precious Zena away again. "I'll make you pay!"

"The dead should stay dead." Soria withdrew her sword from Zena's body to slice her head off.

"Zena!" cried Doctor Nishikawa. He ran for her head and picked it up, her blood staining his clothes.

Having killed off her emotions, Soria didn't seem fazed by what she had done. This was a mission, a simple mission. Nothing more. Nothing less. She cut Zena's body open and took out the heart that beat in her hand.

"How dare you!" shouted Doctor Nishikawa as he turned to glare at her.

"If the thought of separation is too hard for you to come to terms with, shall I help relieve your pain?" she offered and pointed her blade at him.

"How dare you hurt my Zena! What has she done to you that you'd kill her in such a crude way?!" Doctor Nishikawa held onto his wife's head and stood, running at Soria. Even if he was to die by her sword, he didn't care, so long as he could be reunited with his wife again. "All I wanted was to grow old with her!"

"Then, do so in the next life where you can live normally." Soria too struck him with one slash. Blood spurt as Doctor Nishikawa hit the floor. Not once did he let go of his wife's severed head.

Soria let go of the water hilt as it gently dissipated into tiny water particles. She turned to look at the two guys who were laying on the floor, breathing heavily. "And here I thought, Aoi needed constant baby-sitting. You two are far worse. I'll stick with what I have."

∞

After saving Mina, as Dark suspected, they ran into an ambush right outside the base and had been engaged in combat ever since. "Oye Yuudai, finish them off with your electricity," demanded Dark as the two stood back-to-back. "Let's not waste any time."

"I'm trying but these bastards won't stay still."

"Just do a sonic boom."

Yuudai looked over and smirked, shaking his head, "I haven't perfected that yet."

"Lame," taunted Dark.

"Shut up. How about you use your shadows instead?"

"The range of this place is too big, I'll be wasting energy."

"Talk about lame."

"Shut up."

"Oye we got the boy and-" shouted Aoi as they came running out only to be met by the army of men. "Not good."

"More fighting?" Morgana asked from behind and came to a halt. She bent over, huffing and puffing. All this running made her want to lie down and take a breather.

"Good, you're here! Come help!" shouted Shayla.

"Hands are full," answered Takahiko.

"I'm not the physical type of fighter," refused Teo.

Casually, Soria walked by with the beating heart in her bloody palm. Floating behind was Kakinouchi and Azuma who were wrapped in water. Without a word, she tossed the heart at Morgana who caught it.

"Ah!" she screamed and dropped it.

"Oye," said Aoi who caught it. "Safe," he said in a sigh of relief.

"Morgana, careful with it," growled Soria. "It took me a long time to get it. Don't you dare waste my efforts, chubs."

"You should've given me a heads-up! And don't call me names!"

"The reason you're even in this group is because you can use ice, along with Kakinouchi, who's useless right now."

"And?" she asked confusedly.

"You might be stupider than Mio."

"Stop making fun of me!"

"Freeze the damn heart until we get back to the Dome," ordered Soria. She turned to stare at the rebels that surrounded them, not intimidated. "Hey, if you all don't wanna drown and die, move."

"Huh?" said Morgana. She froze the heart Aoi was holding inside an iced cube and looked behind. A flood of water was gushing out. "Ah, Soria, you broke the pipes again?!"

"Had to," she said in defense and floated into the air with her water, alongside the two guys. "The rest of you, get up here."

"How do you suppose we do that?!" they shouted.

"Ah, I forgot."

The group bunched together with Mina as the flood washed over them. While underwater, a water sphere was created and raised them to the air to join the three.

"Yuudai, fry 'em," instructed Soria. An opening from the sphere was made as Yuudai stuck one hand out. Electricity zapped across the sky, striking the water below, electrocuting the men who were soaked.

"That's the end of that," said Crystal.

The hole closed in the sphere as they flew off into the night. From behind, they could hear more water pipes breaking, tearing the base down.

Dark smiled and turned to face front. "Mission accomplished."

44th Lie

HANA STALKED towards Zara's group, head held high and back straight. She was even glaring at them. Shadow noticed but turned a blind-eye like usual. Maybe if he treated her like trash, she'd get the hint and leave. "I request an audience with your leader!" demanded Hana.

"Huh?" they all said.

Unable to ignore her, Shadow turned back.

"I said, I request-"

"We heard you loud and clear the first time." The group walked over to where Hana stood and circled her like vultures. Unafraid, she stood her ground while Shadow watched, keeping his distance.

"I won't leave until she comes."

"Why are you so persistent?"

"She's holding someone hostage and I've come to set them free."

Shadow smiled and shook his head. Hana just didn't know when to give up.

"Zara isn't in at the moment, come back another day." One of the guys reached out, pushing her down as she screamed.

The push had been uncalled for as Shadow stood and strode over, standing in-between them. Though he knew this was a bad idea on his behalf, he had to do something. "Let me handle her. The rest of you back down."

"But-"

"Do it," ordered Shadow. The group backed away obediently as he turned his attention towards Hana. It was time to end this once and for all. "Get out of here."

"I'm here to save someone."

"I'm not-"

"It's not you," she interrupted. "Don't get conceited now."

Shadow raised an eyebrow, surprised that Hana wasn't there to take him back. Maybe she'd finally taken the hint. "If it's not me, then who is it?"

"It's a girl."

"A girl?"

"Yes." Hana stood, refusing to back down, even if her opponent was Shadow himself. "Your boss kidnapped one of the girls in town. I'm here to bring her back home."

Shadow glanced around before taking hold of Hana's elbow. He knew this had been a bad idea and dragged her while the others watched.

"What are you doing? Let me go."

"Shh," he shushed, dragging her around the corner, out of view, before pinning her to the wall.

"What are you-"

"Listen closely, Hana."

"No."

"You have to listen to me."

"I don't want to! Now let me-"

"We're both in big trouble!"

Hana stopped struggling to stare at him in bewilderment. Was he really going to confide in her now?

"You know that I was ordered to betray you, right?"

Hana nodded in response. She knew and hated how Shadow went along with the plan so easily. Did he not take her feelings into consideration when leaving?

"I would never hurt you." Smiling, Shadow brushed her hair with his fingertips and let it linger around cheek. He had wanted to do this for a long time now. "Zara probably captured that girl to lure you out, so she could dispose of you once and for all. That's why, we have to leave."

"We?"

"That's right, Zara already found out my real identity."

"Eh?" Hana gasped that their mission had become compromised.

"Please believe me, Hana. We have to get out of here. As for the two siblings, we'll come back to save them later with reinforcements."

Hana thought about it before nodding. "I'll believe you."

"Then, let's-"

"If you were the real Shadow-kun!" Hana slapped his hand away from her neck and gave him a good punch before jumping away to safety. Her knuckles quickly became red as it throbbed. So, this was what it felt like to use her hands for violence. It wasn't a good feeling as Hana gulped, never allowing her eyes to stray from him.

"What was that for, Hana?" Shadow stood and rubbed his jaw. Her punch had been so weak, she never drew blood. What really got to him was the fact that he'd been taken by surprise and couldn't prepare for it.

"I'll only leave once I save the real Shadow-kun and Mafuyu-san!"

"What are you talking about, Hana?! It's me!"

"Enough with your games, Zara! I won't fall for it!"

"You," said Shadow. He stared at her for some time before laughing. So, he'd been found out by the little princess after preparing so meticulously. It only proved that he slipped up somewhere.

Darkness surrounded them as Hana ran at him. She managed to land an attack as Shadow stood unaffected.

"I underestimated you."

"Yeah, you thought you had me fooled."

"I thought I did. I mean, my transformation was flawless. How did you manage to see through it?"

"You mentioned the two siblings. You couldn't have possibly known such a thing unless you were present. Also, Shadow-kun would never leak information about an undercover mission, even to me."

Shadow laughed happily and put a hand to his face. When he withdrew his hand, it belonged to Zara. "I have truly underestimated you, girly."

"You," growled Hana. "Where's Shadow-kun?"

"Ah, Shadow," she repeated. "To think he'd choose a weakling as yourself over me, how infuriating. What's so good about a princess like you anyway? All I see is a bimbo who constantly needs to be saved. So why couldn't he just let you go?"

"Where is Shadow-kun?!"

"I'm gonna do what I should've done since the beginning, and that's to kill you!" Mutating and transforming into a brown owl, Zara turned her head by 360 degrees in the dark. She flapped her wings, aiming for Hana who was standing not far away.

"What the—you can see?!"

"Don't you know? The owl is the king of the night."

"No way." If Zara could see in the dark, then Hana was no match. For now, she would have to flee and find Shadow first.

"Do you really think you can outrun me, girly?"

∞

The foul stench from the room caused Shadow to scrunch his brows and cover his nose with a hand. All the guards posted there were dead. Someone had killed them—someone powerful—and they had done it in the most brutal way possible. He took a step forward and stopped after hearing shuffling from behind. He spun back and caught a glimpse of someone rounding the corner. Right on their tail, Shadow was able to tackle her.

"Let me go! Don't hurt me!" She threw both arms over her head and trembled.

"Who are you?" Shadow demanded, trying to place her face somewhere, but couldn't. "You're not part of the organization."

"My—my name is Mafuyu. I was kidnapped."

"Kidnapped?" he repeated, immediately taking a stand. This was no way to be treating a hostage as he held a hand in offering. "Here."

Suspicious, Mafuyu laid still, not quite sure on what to do. Shadow was clearly part of Zara's gang but was awfully nice. She wasn't sure if this a ruse to get her to lower her defenses or not. "You're not going to kill me?"

"What's the use in that?"

"But those men-"

"I didn't kill them." Shadow shook his head truthfully and motioned to his outstretched hand again. They had to escape before the real murderer returned to the crime scene. "Come on, let's get out of here. It's dangerous."

After deciding that he was genuinely a good man, she reached out to take his hand. He yanked her to stand as they looked down the deserted hallway. "If you didn't kill them, who did?"

"I don't know, but I plan on finding out."

"Excuse me, but what's your name?"

"Shadow."

"Shadow," she repeated, knowing that name from somewhere. "Ah!" shouted Mafuyu. She hit her palm with her hammered fist and turned to smile at him. Now she remembered. "I see, so you're *that* Shadow."

"Huh?"

"You're Hana-chan's boyfriend, right?"

"Hana?" repeated Shadow. "You know Hana?"

"Uh-huh, we found her bleeding on the street and took her in. She's been healing just fine and every day she talks about you to us. She really loves you, you know? You shouldn't hurt her like this."

Unable to help himself, he smiled. Why was Hana talking about him to strangers? What if they were bad people, then what would she do? Then again, this was Hana he was thinking about. She never suspected anyone of being an evil person.

"You know, if you make a girl cry, she'll leave you for a better man." Mafuyu pouted and pointed a finger at him for hurting Hana. It made no sense why men always hurt the women they loved most.

"I understand."

"I bet now that she's all healed up, she'll probably come rescue you."

"How about we meet her halfway?" suggested Shadow.

"Yeah!" Mafuyu answered excitedly. She would be the one to return Shadow back to Hana. That way, Hana would owe her. "Say."

"What is it?"

"Why are you here anyway?"

"I'm here to investigate something."

"You left Hana-chan to come do some undercover work?"

"Yes."

"If I may ask, what would that be?"

"I can't say when even I'm not sure."

∞

The blue energy arrow sliced through the air, missing the owl as Hana bled on the ground. After taking a few hits from Zara and dodging some, she suddenly found herself with little energy to attack with. Even her darkness had vanished long ago.

"So close," Jennifer groaned, appearing with her bow and arrows.

"Girls," Hana called out in astonishment and eventually cried.

"I won't miss this time," reassured Jennifer. She aimed for the owl determinedly and let go as the arrow zapped through the air. Suddenly, the owl disappeared. Standing in its place was a little boy.

"Hachi-kun," Hana gasped, weakly getting to her knees.

"Shit," said Jennifer. The moment she saw him, she lost concentration as the shining blue arrow dispersed into thin air.

"Shape-shifter," guessed Hotaka.

"I see," said Hachi. He touched the particles that were disappearing into the atmosphere and turned his attention to Jennifer. "You manipulate air particles to create your arrows, giving you the ability to have an unlimited amount to fire at will."

Jennifer grinned and lowered her arms to her side. The bow and arrow disappeared while the two accessories jingled on either wrist. "You figured that out from just looking? You're quite a kid," she praised.

"Oye, where's Shadow?" asked King as he looked around.

"Shadow's hands should be full, right about now," answered Hachi.

"Midnight," said Hotaka.

"Huh?" she answered and looked over.

"Can you girls handle the kid?"

With a grin, Midnight popped her neck. "What are you saying? We'll be fine. Just go find Shadow and help him out."

"Alright," Hotaka said and smiled, leaving with King.

"Careful!" shouted King.

"You guys too!" shouted Jennifer in return.

"What else can you do?" asked Hachi. While he was talking and keeping his attention on Jennifer, Midnight walked over to help Hana off the ground.

"You okay?"

"Yeah," answered Hana. She wiped her eyes and smiled. It was nice having back-up, especially these two. "Thanks for coming. I thought I was dead meat for a minute there."

"We could've walked away from this fight if only Jennifer was more accurate."

"I heard that," she snapped.

From out of nowhere, Zara attacked, hoping to take them by surprise, but they dodged and countered. "Not bad," she praised, reverting to her original self.

"She's a tough one," said Jennifer.

"Agreed." Midnight nodded and glanced over at Hana. "Stand back."

"What? Why? This is also my fight!"

"You're injured, right?"

"Uh," said Hana. She put a hand to her chest and shook her head. "No."

"Don't lie. I know that woman hurt you."

This time she remained quiet and slowly nodded.

Sneering, Jennifer popped her neck and knuckles. She was starting to get serious. "You dare to hurt our cute Hana-chan?" Jennifer held out her arms as her bow and arrows reappeared. "I won't forgive you," she said, firing three arrows at once while the earth shook, and vines shot out to cut Zara. They had to quickly finish this fight before the guys returned.

∞

"Oye, Shadow!" shouted King as they ran down the streets, calling out to him.

"Who are you guys?" asked the same group who had pushed Hana. Standing behind them were more men.

"Great," said Hotaka.

King grinned and withdrew his sword to point at the group. Finally, he could fight. "I got these guys. You go on ahead and find Shadow."

"Don't be stupid."

"I'm not being stupid. I'm being serious. I can handle these guys."

"King-"

"If you don't hurry, Shadow's gonna die, wherever he is."

Hotaka turned his back and ran off. He hated it, how King was right again. They couldn't afford to be held up here. "Be careful."

"I'm not dying any time soon. I still gotta defeat you, Rain, and Kei."

Hotaka simply grinned. "The three of us will be waiting."

"I won't make you wait long. The day I become number one is soon."

"Sure it is," Hotaka said, disappearing into the night.

Before Zara's group could chase him, King got in their way and cut a few down. He grinned and pointed his sword at them again. These kinds of mission were more his style, hacking and slashing to get to his objective. Going undercover like the previous one, didn't suit King whatsoever. He had no patience for it. "Didn't I say it already? I'm your opponent, not Hotaka. So, dance with me."

∞

Mafuyu sat on the floor with her back against the wall, staring at Shadow who had lost his eyepatch while fighting. Beneath it was an ominous scarred eye that glowed under the luminescent lights. Shadow turned to look at Mafuyu who quivered. Lying dead on the ground was a group who had attacked them from out of nowhere. "What are you?" she whispered, having never seen a Life-Kill in action before.

"Let's get out of here." Shadow reached down, assisting her so they could escape again as she flinched.

"Don't touch me."

Realizing that she hadn't taken her eyes off his right eye, Shadow shut his right eyelid. Even he was afraid of how it looked. "We have to get out of here. Or do you wish to die?"

Mafuyu shook her head in response.

"Then let's get going," instructed Shadow as he ran off. Mafuyu watched him go, then looked over at the dead bodies. She gulped and chased after him, still afraid.

"Wait for me!" she called out as Shadow glanced back and stopped. A new group was running at her from behind.

"Get down!"

"Eh?" Mafuyu said and turned back to find the men on her tail. A shriek escaped her mouth as she closed her eyes and ducked, throwing both hands over her head. When she opened her eyes and lowered her shaky arms, she found Shadow standing before her, along with six dead men. It only felt like a short while and he'd managed to annihilate them.

"It's good that you're okay." He flashed her a smile as blood gushed out from the gunshot wounds. Without bothering to apply pressure, he turned away to face front again.

"Shadow-"

"Get out of here."

"Huh?"

"I can sense more men coming, so leave," he ordered and winced. Like usual when his right eye saw blood it pounded and acted up like it had a life of its own. Was it trying to search for something—or someone?

Mafuyu stared at him, understanding why Hana had come to love such a man. He would do whatever it took to protect those in front of him. Even when Mafuyu had rejected him a few minutes, he still came to her rescue. "No, I won't allow you to die like this!" she said determinedly and stood, wiping tears away from her eyes as a third group approached around the corner. "I have to bring you back to Hana-chan!"

Hotaka ran past the two, knocking out the men with just one hit each. When he was done, he clapped his hands and turned around.

"Hotaka?" Shadow uttered while in the middle of attacking also. His wounds had healed with the bullets still inside his body. Once back at the Dome, he'd have to ask Gabe to help take them out. After blinking a few times to make sure that his eyes weren't playing tricks on him, Shadow smiled and laughed.

Grinning, Hotaka walked over, noticing that Shadow wasn't wearing his eyepatch like usual. "Look at you, you look horrible," he joked before explaining the situation. "The dean sent us as back-up. Come on. Let's get out of here."

"Yeah," answered Shadow. He nodded and grunted as Hotaka caught hold of him while Mafuyu stood by his side.

Raising an eyebrow, Hotaka glanced at Mafuyu then to Shadow. Why was this girl with him? And why was Hana fighting Zara alone? Exactly what was going on here? "Who is she?"

"Hostage," answered Shadow.

"I see." If she was a hostage, then they would have to rescue her too. "Let's get her out of here then."

"Wait," said Mafuyu. "I have to find my little brother."

"Little brother?"

"Yes, he was kidnapped along with me."

"There they are!" shouted some more men as they ran into the hallway. "Shadow's betrayed Zara! He's siding with the other side! Kill him!"

"First," said Hotaka as the back of his shirt fluttered and a pair of white wings appeared.

Awed, Mafuyu watched. In all her life, she'd been taught that Life-Kills were evil and ugly. But Hotaka was nothing like the rumors. He was magnificent. "Amazing," Mafuyu whispered.

"Let's get the both of you to safety. King and I will come back to find your little brother." Hotaka put his arms around the two and flew up, through the roof and into the night.

"Shoot them!" instructed one of the men as they shot their guns while the rest ran outside to chase the three.

"Wow," said Mafuyu while she looked down below. She could see the entire view of the city as her hair whipped around her face. A hearty laugh came out while she held onto Hotaka. "You're amazing!"

"Thanks," he said and smiled. "Too bad someone else doesn't think so."

"This is the most amazing thing I've ever done!" Mafuyu let out an excited scream and held out one arm to the air, wishing to never descend.

Shadow on the other hand, simply smiled. Everyone who saw Hotaka's wings were always left in awe, while the opposite was applied to his eye.

"Don't bite your tongue." Hotaka flapped his wings as they headed back down to earth. Once they landed, he let go of the two.

"I've got to tell Hachi about this!"

Shadow's left eye widened at her words. Did Mafuyu say Hachi? Why for? Was she also involved? Was this part of the plan to expose Shadow's mission? He turned, forcefully grabbing her by the arm. "Mafuyu-san, how do you know that name?"

"Ow," she winced.

"Shadow," Hotaka said, staring at the two. He wanted to stop his friend from hurting an innocent girl, but didn't want to intervene when he didn't understand the situation.

"How?"

"Hachi's my little brother. He's the one I told you about, the one who got kidnapped along with me."

"Is he blood-related?"

Mafuyu nodded again. What kind of question was that? The day her mother gave birth to Hachi, she was present. She practically raised him after their parents passed away. It was always her and Hachi against the world. "Of course he is." Aware of the look Shadow was giving her, Mafuyu gulped. "Why are you asking?"

"Are you sure he's your brother?!"

"What would I gain from lying?"

Shadow turned to look at Hotaka, frantic now. "We're in trouble."

"Eh?" said the two.

"Hachi-" began Shadow. He gulped also, giving Mafuyu a guilty look like he'd done her wrong. "I don't know how to say this. But Mafuyu-san, your brother, Hachi, he's not who you think he is."

"Eh?" Confused, Mafuyu shook her head and laughed it off. His statement made no sense when she knew everything about Hachi, even about the secrets he kept from her. "Oh, I think I know my own brother."

"He's Zara."

"What?" demanded Hotaka who couldn't believe his ears.

"Yo!" greeted King as he approached them, smiling and waving happily. He had taken out the group all by himself and came to boastfully rub his victory in Hotaka's face. "See? What did I tell ya? I told ya that I'd be able to take them all down." After sensing how tense the atmosphere was, his smile faded. "What's going on here? And who's this girl?"

"King," Hotaka said worriedly. "When the owl transformed into a boy, what did Hana call him again?"

"What?" asked Shadow and Mafuyu in unison. When did such a thing happen?

"Uh, I think she called him, Hachi-kun, if I remember correctly," answered King. "Why? What's wrong?"

"Shit," Hotaka said. His wings reappeared before anyone could say anything. "The girls are in danger! We gotta go back! Now!"

"They'll be fine. There's no way Midnight and Jennifer will lose to a kid."

"Idiot!" Hotaka turned, taking King by surprise. He was losing his cool again when it came to Midnight.

"What's with you?" King asked, glaring at the three who wouldn't go into detail about the situation. "I don't understand, so explain it to me."

"From the way that things sound so far, this Zara, it seems that her ability is similar to someone we once knew. Is that correct, Shadow?" Hotaka turned to look at Shadow who nodded. It was time to tell everything he knew.

"Yeah, I was sent here to keep an eye on Zara. Every night she was always disappearing. I could never keep tabs on her. Then, I stumbled upon something interesting a while back and decided to confirm the truth tonight, but everyone in the room was killed. I couldn't confirm anything and left," explained Shadow.

"Get to the main point," King demanded, still not understanding this Morse code talk.

"Kas."

One word was all it took to make King tremble. It had been a long time since he last heard that name. Kas had died a long time ago when they were children. He never got to meet the girls with them. In fact, he was the last one to die amongst them at the academy. None of the guys knew how or why. All they knew was that he had chosen death over life. It left Dark devastated since they were the best of friends.

Mafuyu who was confused kept looking from one to the other. They had lost her during the conversation. "Excuse me, who or what is Kas? And if Hachi's in danger, shouldn't we get going?"

"Damn," said King. He turned and sprinted while Hotaka took hold of the two again.

"Hold on tight. I'm gonna fly at full speed." Hotaka's wings beat once more as he flew them towards the girls. From down below, King was running as fast as he could. If it was true that Zara also had the same ability as Kas, they were in for a wild ride.

∞

Midnight stood on the petals of a red rose, while encased in clear petals behind her was Hana. Jennifer was running about, firing energy arrows at Zara who dodged and countered. When Midnight finally encased Zara in her cage of vines, she grinned. "Got ya."

Angry at having been caught like a fly, Zara cut away at the vines that only regrew. "Shit, to think I'd lose to two little girls."

"Little girl this," Midnight said, striking her straight through the heart. Zara didn't even attempt to dodge or escape.

"Stop!" shouted Hotaka from above.

"Huh?" The two looked up as Hotaka landed with Shadow and Mafuyu.

"Shadow-kun!" shouted Hana. She pushed the petals away and ran out. The real thing was finally here.

Hotaka ran over, motioning for Midnight to undo her cage. Confused about his worry, she pulled the vines back. Zara's lifeless body fell to the ground as it slowly changed into Hachi's body.

"Hachi," gasped Mafuyu. She threw both hands to her mouth and cried. "Hachi!" she screamed and attempted to run over, but Shadow pulled her back. "Let me go!"

"No," he said, unable to comply.

"Hachi...kun," Hana whispered, halting in her run. Nothing made sense. One moment Zara was Shadow, then she transformed into an owl, then to Hachi, and then back to her normal form. Now she was Hachi again. Who or what exactly was Zara?

"What's going on?" Midnight directed at Hotaka.

King came running up to them and stopped. Hachi's body was lying on the ground, still bleeding.

"Keep away," instructed Hotaka. "No one goes near the body until I give the signal." He turned to look at King and nodded. King too nodded in response as he withdrew his sword. Cautiously, they approached Hachi's unmoving body.

"Hotaka, what's going on?!" demanded Midnight. He was being overly cautious towards a dead corpse.

"I'll explain later. Just keep away."

"You too, Jennifer," King instructed, tightening his sweaty palms over the hilt.

"She's dead," assured Jennifer.

"We don't know that for a fact."

495

"To think we got tricked by her shape-shifting powers," said Hotaka. "We should've known better."

"You can say that again."

"Nee-chan," whispered Hachi. The two guys quickly backed away as Hachi coughed out blood. He turned his head towards his crying sister. Tears trailed as he watched her weep for him. All he wanted was to keep her safe from harm. "Nee-chan," he whispered again and reached out.

"Shit!" King shouted, running over to raise his sword to deliver the finishing blow. They couldn't take any chances.

Mafuyu's eyes widened as she screamed. "Stop it! He's already dying!" Her endless tears fell as she watched helplessly.

"You two!" shouted Jennifer and Midnight in disbelief. "That's overkill!"

"Midnight, escape with the others!" ordered Hotaka. He spun around, reaching a hand out to try and push her away, but she was too far, and he was too late.

"To you, I give my most precious thing," whispered Hachi. King sliced his throat just then as blood gushed out. He took one last gasp and choked on his own blood before dying. King turned around in time to notice that Midnight had hit her knees.

"Fuck."

"Not good," Shadow said, pulling Mafuyu away to safety.

"Midnight!" shouted Jennifer as she ran over.

"Jennifer, stay away from her!" King shouted, running over too.

Right when Midnight lashed at Jennifer, Hana tackled her to the ground.

"Hana," said Jennifer in shock.

"I could sense the darkness in her growing," explained Hana as the two girls stood, unsure of the turn of events.

"His 'will' was given." Hotaka clenched his fists and glared. Midnight was no longer herself.

Getting to her feet, she laughed and flexed her muscles, clenching and unclenching her fists, like it was her first time seeing her own hands. Content with her new avatar, she nodded. "This body will do for now. Though I would've preferred one of the guys." Midnight turned to look at the others and pouted, taunting them. "Aw, you were so close too."

"Get out of her!"

"Oh?" Midnight said, gasping. She threw both hands to her chest, giving Hotaka a surprise look. "Could I be your Soulmate? Is that why you're so angry?"

"Get out."

"Why don't you try forcing me out then?" Midnight taunted with a chuckle. She assessed the group and grinned, backing away. Despite how strong Midnight's powers were, Zara couldn't take the chances. "Until we meet again."

"Like I'll let you leave with Midnight's body."

Watching from a distance, Mafuyu pieced one and one together, after witnessing Midnight's change in demeanor. If they allowed her to leave now, they'd never catch her again. Running past a distracted Shadow and the others, Mafuyu caught of Midnight from behind.

"Mafuyu-san, let go!" shouted Shadow as they ran forward.

"If you're in there, stop it, Hachi!" she screamed and cried, unable to watch him hurt others. "It was because of me, wasn't it? It was because I was weak. I couldn't protect you. That's why you were possessed by Zara, right?"

"Get the hell off me!" Midnight screamed as vines shot out from underground, piercing Mafuyu who finally let go. She let out a grunt and fell to her knees, bleeding. Reaching out, Midnight grabbed her by the jaw. "You're right. It's because you were weak. You couldn't protect your little brother. That's why, I gave him my will to live."

"Ha…chi," she whispered and held out a shaky hand, doing her best to smile. "Let's go home." Tears spilled out as Midnight delivered the finishing blow.

From behind, Shadow caught Midnight as she struggled against the group. After failing to get him off, her eyes turned yellow. The earth shook as tree roots shot out and grabbed the group, tying them to the ground. When she was in control of herself again, she laughed at how useful her new avatar was during Berserk Mode.

"Midnight, fight it!" Hotaka pleaded, unable to lose her like this.

With things the way they were, Shadow opened his right eye he'd been keeping shut. Like the day he dueled Hana at the Dome, his eye could see only in black and white. Above Midnight's head were weird symbols. Instead of one symbol, like with Hana, there were half a dozen. Shadow's eye ached, but he kept it up. He had to decipher what this all meant. What was it about his right eye that he was overlooking?

From Midnight's body, a tiny spirit particle flew out, then another, and another, until millions filled the air.

"What the-"

"Goodbye, dear comrades." Midnight smiled and turned, ready to transform into the owl. She would only be able to hold them down for a few minutes.

"Zara!" Shadow called out as Midnight stopped. She turned back and walked over, allowing only him to freely move.

"Did you call for me, my love?"

"I did," Shadow said, getting to his feet. His eye was glowing brighter than before.

Midnight gasped at the sight, ignoring his threat just then, or about the thought of fleeing. Again, Shadow's right eye kept her hypnotized. She reached out, touching his eye he refused to show anyone. Was Shadow finally going to show his true potential? "I knew it," Midnight whispered and threw him into a hug, tears in her eyes.

"Oye!" shouted the others who could only watch.

"I knew you were the one for me! I was right all along about you being special!" Midnight let go and laughed, now tracing his jawline with her fingertips. "Come with me, Shadow! With both our powers, we can rule the world!"

"I have no intentions of contending for the world with Yeve. Anyone going against her is asking to die." Shadow firmly grabbed Midnight by the shoulder, his eye seeing into the depths of Zara's soul. This was just a small glimpse into the power of his Shinigami's Eye. "Hachi, Midnight, I know you're in there! Fight it!"

"You-" Midnight gasped, trying to break free. She had underestimated his strength. "Let me go!"

Nee-chan, nee-chan, I killed nee-chan, Hachi cried and hugged his legs in the darkness. His sister was dead, and he was the reason. Unable to watch silently, Midnight walked over and reached a hand out to touch his hair, forcing him to look up. She smiled, taking a seat beside him. Hachi's lips trembled as he threw himself into her arms.

"I didn't want to take her will. I really didn't. She just gave it to me."

"It's okay," Midnight kept repeating. She patted his back gently and rocked him. "Tell me, Hachi-kun, how did you meet her?"

Hachi wiped his eyes to explain, "Nee-chan and I were scraping by, trying to find food when we lost each other. That was when I found Zara in a dark alleyway. I thought she might have some money, so I searched through her pockets. She caught my wrist and said, 'I give my most precious thing to you' and then died. When nee-chan found me, I knew something evil was inside me. I tried to tell her so many times but I—I was so scared that she'd hate me or fear me or abandon me. So I kept quiet and let Zara take over. Now nee-chan's dead. I killed her with my own hands." Hachi looked down at his trembling hands to cry all over again.

"Hachi-kun," she whispered and smiled. Midnight cupped his face in her hands, lifting his face to look at her. "I don't believe your nee-chan would fear you. Nor would she abandon you. The one who killed her wasn't you. It was me. My powers killed her."

"But-" objected Hachi as Midnight shook her head to shush him.

"Trust me. I know best since I also have a little brother. I could never fear nor abandon him, no matter what he does."

"You have a little brother too?"

"Yeah, I don't think I'll ever forget the day our abusive master sold him. I thought I would die from losing him, but I continued living. And while living, I came to find out about hope and survival. There was never a day that I didn't use the resources I had to find him. And you know what? When I least expected it, we happened to find each other. That's why, I know that your nee-chan will never hate you. She's probably waiting for you."

"She is?"

"Yes." Midnight nodded and looked behind.

Shadow was standing there, smiling. He walked over to point ahead of them, now taking charge of the situation. "She's over there. Just walk straight, you'll see her."

Hachi wiped his eyes and stood. He debated for some time before taking his first step.

"If you leave Hachi, you'll die, you can't make it out there without me," Zara said from behind and laughed, halting him. "The reason you were able to survive for so long was because of me."

Midnight too stood, urging him to go. "Don't listen to her, Hachi-kun. Just keep walking."

An oppressive air filled the atmosphere as Hachi hugged himself. Zara's presence was suffocating to the point where he couldn't outrun her. It was always like this when he thought about leaving. "Her will is too strong."

"Don't be afraid," Shadow said, whisking the darkness away. Now that he knew the truth, he knew exactly how to counter Zara's powers in this place. "You too, have your own will, Hachi-kun."

It surprised Hachi to hear such a thing as he lifted his head and glanced back. "My own will?"

Shadow nodded. "That's right and it's right here." He pointed a finger to his heart and smiled. "Listen to it and follow it through. It'll lead you to your destination. You'll see, your will is probably much stronger."

"Right here," whispered Hachi. He touched his beating chest where a tiny warmth sparked. That was all the push he needed, as he stood, tall and unwavering. "Thank you, strange onee-san and onii-san!"

"The name is Midnight and Shadow," Midnight corrected with a smile.

"Midnight onee-san, you too, return safely to your little brother." Hachi waved and turned to run. Even with Zara's presence surrounding him, forbidding him to leave, he ran, brimming with hope. Shadow's words had given him the courage to take that giant leap. Hachi too, had his own will that he wanted to see to the end.

"I will," Midnight said, watching him go.

"Hachi, come back!" Zara demanded, strengthening her intimidation. But in this place, she had no jurisdiction over his free will.

"Hachi!" called out Mafuyu's voice.

Tears filled his eyes as a smile overtook him. There was no longer a need to be fearful. Everything would work itself out somehow. "Nee-chan!" he shouted, reaching a hand out.

"Let's go home." Mafuyu caught his hand as they ran off across the bright field and disappeared.

"Damn you Shadow!" Zara threw her hands to her head. Her assumption of his powers had been right, she just never guessed he'd use it against her.

Shadow looked around. With his left eye, he could only see the field. With his right eye, he could see the barren lands where the many fallen humans and Life-Kill souls Zara had overtaken while trying to preserve her life. It was time Shadow set them all free too. "Now, it's your turn, Midnight."

Nodding, Midnight turned to glare at Zara who kept screaming. She could feel her powers waning and wouldn't accept defeat. She was a one-of-a-kind Life-Kill, a secret hybrid from Antarctica. This ability of hers was something that no other Dome knew existed. So, how could Shadow know how to kill her if she was the only one to possess it?

"Now," hissed Midnight. "Get the hell out of my body. Your will has been broken."

"Impossible, impossible!"

"This is *my* body. Get out!"

"No, this is my body now! How dare you reduce me to this kind of state!"

"You've lost, Zara," Shadow answered as each spirit began disintegrating. They too had finally found the fighting spirit to break free from Zara's will.

It looked as though Midnight was possessed as she stood on the street, mouth open wide. Her eyes rolled backwards as the whites showed. No sound came out as colorful spirit particles flew out from her body and floated towards the night sky. Abruptly it felt as though all the strength in Midnight's body vanished as her legs caved in and Shadow caught hold of her. When he touched her arm, she gasped.

"Breathe," instructed Shadow as the others came rushing over. The vines that had bound them to the ground had given way.

Midnight coughed, following Shadow's instructions to breathe. Once her head was out of the clouds, her eyes returned to normal and she blinked a few times, trying to find her voice. "Shadow?"

Relieved that his plan had worked, Shadow smiled. "You're back."

"Midnight!" shouted Hotaka as he ran over to hold her. "Are you okay?"

"Hotaka," she whispered weakly and nodded. "We won."

"Idiot," he said and glared, but eventually smiled. He couldn't lecture her when she'd done such an amazing job in vanquishing Zara from this world. "You did great."

"Yeah," she whispered, closing her eyes to take a nap. The internal fight in her mind had taken its toll, though it seemed like nothing much happened.

"Get some rest. You deserve it."

Jennifer smiled and wiped her eyes, relieved as well. "Waa, I was afraid that we'd lose Midnight to that girl."

King smiled as he poked her head. "Not if I can help it."

"Let's get going. Our fight here is over." Shadow stood and smiled, turning to look at Hana for the first time that night. When she caught his gaze, she crossed her arms and looked away with a pout. Shadow bowed, long and deep before standing back up. "Please forgive me."

Hana uncrossed her arms, throwing him into a tight hug. She let out a wail and buried her face into his chest. All that mattered was that they were together again. "I'll forgive you, as many times as I need to."

Shadow soothed her and apologized once more.

"I seriously thought you had left me."

"How can I do that?" he asked, hugging her in return.

"Geez," Jennifer said, looking over at the two. Even Shadow and Hana were getting chummy. Like Hotaka and Midnight wasn't enough already. "Why do I feel so envious suddenly?"

King turned to look at the two standing behind them, all lovey-dovey and showing too much PDA. There was a sudden spark of rage as he glared and hissed, "Is Shadow now a rival of mine too?"

45th Lie

AFTER ACCOMPLISHING "The Rescue" mission, the kids were allowed to take a break at the mansion for the next few days. When they first returned, Mere freaked out and cried. Hotaka made a big scene, trying to pull the siblings apart, still oblivious to the fact that they were real blood-siblings.

After rescuing Gon, he'd been escorted back home by Dome officials.

Morgana handed the frozen heart over to Miss Umi who quickly left with Gabe to start the surgery. Kakinouchi also left with them to wait outside the operation room. Azuma went to keep him company while they waited together. Shayla dropped in every now and then, bringing food to replenish their bodies. Mina along with Taiki and Umeko had to be put to bed with Miss Lima's assistance. While Anoka was confined to a secret section of the mansion, everyone else simply lazed around after the long trip.

When the deans introduced Nicholas and Liz, Rain didn't seem surprised to see him. He had a feeling they would be meeting again after that brief encounter inside Beast's base. The aura Nicholas had then, didn't belong to an enemy's.

The Golden party was kept a secret. So, all those who knew about it didn't utter a word.

In Dean Kosa's hand was Shadow's report. After reading it, he set the file down. "To think there was someone else who had the same ability," he said, massaging his forehead. It was a good thing they had taken out Zara while they had. If she reunited with Haj, it would've proven to be dangerous. But there was still something troubling the dean. With Zara's power of give-

and-take, what had she given and taken from Midnight when she entered her body? Whatever it was, hopefully it wouldn't come back to bite them.

A knock at the door brought Dean Kosa out of his thoughts as he pressed a button attached to his desk to open it.

Mr. Fujiwara entered and bowed, then stood to speak, "Reporting in about the successful surgery, sir."

Dean Kosa smiled and nodded. "That's good to hear."

"Dean," said Mr. Fujiwara. "About that girl, Zara. Where was she from?"

"Gray."

"Gray?" repeated Mr. Fujiwara in disbelief. "What's a member from the Gray Dome doing here?"

"Partnering up with Haj."

"Speaking of Haj, his body was never discovered, although Dark said he had killed him." Mr. Fujiwara wrinkled his nose. It didn't sit well with him that a dead man could suddenly disappear. "What if he's not dead and tries to seek vengeance on us for interfering?"

"Let him."

"But dean-"

"Let's see how he fares. He couldn't even take on a few kids. What's he going to do when they grow older and become stronger?" Dean Kosa boasted. "At least we obtained something valuable from this mission."

"Shadow's eye."

Nodding, Dean Kosa smiled. "The Shinigami's Eye, as told from Leviathan's myths and legends is finally in our hands."

"You're right." Even Mr. Fujiwara couldn't help but smile. With Shadow's eye, the prestige of Maroon would skyrocket. And one day, they would overcome Turquoise to become the greatest Dome. All that was left to do was set a Limiter on him. It would be stronger than any of the other boys if they wanted to keep him under control. "Dean Kiera wants to have a talk with you," said Mr. Fujiwara. He adjusted his glasses, remembering the other reason he'd come.

"Yes, about that matter," Dean Kosa said. He didn't want to do it, but it was inevitable. It was simply a process that all generations underwent. It was nothing personal. "I'll contact Lima-san in a while to set up a time."

"Understood."

∞

Nicholas made his way to the front yard where Soria was sleeping on the green grass beneath the morning sun. In his hands were two coke cans. One look at her and he smiled. Seeing her up close wasn't good for his heart. But then again, not seeing her was even worse. Quietly, Nicholas walked over while she was unsuspecting of anything and popped his face in front of hers before greeting loudly, "Yo!"

"Huh?" Too lazy to open both eyes, Soria opened only one and found Nicholas a few inches away. Reaching out, she pushed his face away as his red scarf brushed her cheek. "Too close," she mumbled.

"Yo!"

"You're the weird scarf guy with the cat, right? Why are you wearing a scarf in summer? It's hecka hot."

Nicholas pouted and sat beside her. Her first impression of him hadn't been memorable, if that was her name for him. "It's not 'The Weird Scarf Guy with the Cat.' It's Nicholas Triheart. Also, this scarf is precious."

"Triheart, got it."

Nicholas smiled and offered her the can of coke. "Want one?"

Soria opened both eyes this time to stare at the can before taking it. "Sure," she said, unable to refuse the offer. Setting the can beside her, she closed her eyes and went back to napping.

"Can I join you?"

"Aren't you already sitting?"

Nicholas laughed it off and nodded. "I already am, aren't I?" He fell onto his back, the second can still in his hand. The gray sky that he was used to seeing was starting to turn blue. It was amazing what colors he was able to see again with Soria by his side. Now, if only he could keep it this way forever. "I can see why you like it out here."

"You're too talkative."

"I can't help it. Being around you makes me excited."

"And weird," she added in before sitting up to open her drink as it exploded, wetting her.

"Bwa-ha-ha, you actually opened it!" Nicholas rolled around on the grass, laughing. He had successfully tricked her into opening the can, knowing she was probably thirsty. It was so much fun, he laughed 'til his stomach ached.

Not amused, Soria twitched. "Just how old are you?"

"Eighteen," he answered and wiped his eyes that were filled with tears.

"Are you sure you're not eight instead?" she said and threw the can at Nicholas who dodged.

"Sorry, sorry," he apologized and sat up, still chuckling. He watched in wonder as Soria wiped the sticky soda off her face. It made him utterly happy being this close to her. His heart he once believed to have stopped functioning, was beating again. She was the only one who could make him feel like this. "Soria," whispered Nicholas.

"Hmm?" she answered without a care.

"It's okay."

Alarmed by his words, Soria turned to stare at him. "What do you-"

504

Nicholas leaned over, draping an arm over her trembling shoulders. He smiled and squeezed her in his embrace, knowing why she was avoiding everyone else for the past few days. Everything about her, he knew. She couldn't lie to him. Neither could she escape, now that he knew where she would always be. "Don't lie to me. I know you better than you think. The mission you just finished, let it go. Stop dwelling on it. It won't do you any good."

"You," Soria whispered. She pushed him away, suspicious about how he knew all these things. It made no sense, unless he was a mind reader.

Able to read her thoughts, Nicholas shook his head. "I can't read minds."

"Lie," she accused with a pointed finger. "You read my mind just now."

Laughing, Nicholas hooked his finger around hers, refusing to let go. Again, his fuzzy feelings made it feel like flowers would spontaneously bloom around them. "It's because I've known you all my life, that's why I know when something's bothering you."

"I never told you my name. How the hell did you know?"

"My name's Nicholas Triheart. Please don't keep calling me 'you' okay?"

"How, Triheart?" demanded Soria.

Nicholas tapped his chin to think. "Yeve and Verse told me?"

"When?"

"Just now?"

"Every word that comes out of your mouth is a lie."

Nicholas smiled and kept his mouth shut. His lies were easy to spot, but the truth he spoke of though, was harder to decipher. "Even if I lie to you, it's to protect you."

"Soria!" shouted Aoi as he ran out towards them and stopped. In his hands were two cans of grape. When he spotted how close they were to one another, he pointed and shouted, "Ah!" Even their fingers were hooked. "Wh—what are you doing with the foreigner?!"

"Nothing," answered Soria. She withdrew her finger that Nicholas was still holding and stood to leave. It was time to change out from her dirty clothes. "See ya, Triheart."

"Wait, I bought you a drink." Aoi turned, following Soria inside. "And what happened to you? You're all wet."

Soria turned to look at Aoi then at the two grape drinks. "I don't-"

"Soria doesn't like anything grape! It upsets her stomach! Get her a coke instead!" interrupted Nicholas. Again, Soria turned back to look at him suspiciously. He smiled and waved, enjoying this game. "Aren't I right, Soria?"

"How does he know?" Aoi rasped.

As to not raise any questions that she didn't have the answers to, Soria walked away again. Besides, Aoi would just accuse her of lying. "I told him," she lied.

"Eh?!" shouted Aoi as he chased her. "You told the foreigner your likes and dislikes but won't even tell me, your Soulmate?!"

"I hate anything grape." Soria reached out and snatched the drink.

"You don't have to drink it if you don't like it. I'll go buy you a coke instead."

"It's fine."

"It's not fine! You'll get an upset stomach if you drink that!"

Soria opened the grape can to gulp down while Aoi watched in disbelief. She really was going to drink something she disliked. After finishing the drink, Soria groaned. She wasn't feeling well suddenly.

"I told you not to drink it!"

"I'm fine." Soria rushed inside while Aoi followed from behind.

Remaining on the grass, Nicholas smiled, eyes pinned on Soria's back. Regardless if she disliked something, if it was offered to her, she would accept it with gratitude. "Even here, she doesn't change," he said, lying back down to gaze at the sky. Tears trickled as he hid it with his forearm. "Soria Terauchi, I've missed you so much."

∞

"Yeve, Yeve!" shouted a voice from behind while she walked down the hallway with a blueberry muffin in hand. The person behind kept shouting at her to stop but she ignored them, having no obligation to stop for a stranger. "Yeve!" Liz screamed, jumping out to tackle her.

"Whoa!" shouted Yeve. She dropped her muffin as it broke and skidded across the floor. "My muffin," she gasped.

"Didn't you hear me calling out to you?! Why didn't you stop?!"

Yeve twitched, her eyes fixated on her ruined muffin. She didn't even get a chance to eat a crumb. What a waste. "Get off."

"You're so mean. I know you heard me." Liz got off and smiled as Yeve sat up on the floor, glaring.

"You made me drop my muffin. What are you gonna do about it?"

Liz put a finger to her lips and cocked her head to one side to look at the muffin across the floor. She blinked a few times and smiled. "Sorry?"

Yeve reached out, smacking her on the head. "What good does that do me?"

"Ow, I'm really sorry though." Liz pouted and put both hands to her head. All she wanted was to spend quality time with Yeve. Instead, she was receiving a lecture.

"Aren't you that cat who's always with that Nicholas guy?"

"My name is Liz."

"Liz," repeated Yeve. She stood and dusted herself, crossing her arms without caring to offer Liz a hand. All she cared about was carrying out a punishment. "Go buy me a new muffin."

Quickly, Liz stood and saluted her, happy to be of service. "Yes, Your Highness!"

"Hey Yeve," Soria called out while walking by with Aoi. "We're gonna go eat. Wanna come?"

Yeve looked over, wondering when Soria had changed outfits. It was unlike her since she enjoyed lazing around in her pajamas. Yeve opened her mouth to ask, but ultimately shook it off. She didn't care either way. "Yeah, I'll be there." Soria waved a hand and left with Aoi first. Waving a hand, Yeve dismissed Liz. "Another time then," she said, walking away.

Liz stared, jaw hanging open. She was no longer of use, and it was all because of Soria. "That girl's always getting in my way."

∞

Alice entered the infirmary where Miss Umi sat, taking a breather. The surgery had taken three rigorous days to finish. Even though the heart belonged to May, because it had conformed to Zena's body, they had to reintroduce it back to its original body. If they had rushed the surgery, the heart would've bled out once they sewed her up. "Oh, Alice, what's up?" Miss Umi asked in a yawn.

"Sensei," Alice greeted with a bow. "I was wondering if Umeko and Taiki were well enough to join us for lunch."

"Sorry. They're still not awake yet."

Alice nodded, disappointed. "I see."

"Is that all?"

"Hmm? Yeah, that's all."

"I see." This time it was Miss Umi's turn to nod.

"Why?" Alice asked. "Is there supposed to be something else?"

"No." Miss Umi quickly shook her head. "Nothing at all."

"Oh, okay." Alice nodded, but her brows were raised. She bowed and left without further interrogation.

Once Alice was gone Miss Umi averted her gaze from the door to her computer screen. "I better stop getting so worked up around her. She'll start getting suspicious."

"She will," Gabe agreed from his usual hiding spot.

Miss Umi glared at the closet and walked over to open it. Gabe smiled and waved as she dragged him out by the ear. Again, he had the nerves to sneak into her infirmary without permission.

"Ow, ow."

"Now what were you planning?"

"I wanted to scare you. But Alice came in first."

Miss Umi let go and shook her head. "What do you want?" she asked, walking over to sit again, legs crossed. This was something to be expected of Gabe. It was in his nature to be mischievous.

Gabe massaged his ear looked over, then straightened up. "Anoka keeps asking for you."

"I completely forgot," she groaned. A nap sounded so nice, but she was being called upon for everything. If time stopped now, she wouldn't mind. "Out," Miss Umi instructed, shooing him away.

"I can turn the other way," Gabe offered with a grin.

"Not a chance in hell." Miss Umi stood and pushed him out, amazed that he knew what her words meant. After locking the door and quickly changing, she exited to find Gabe gone. "He'll never change." She chuckled and headed towards Anoka's room where she was placed under house arrest. It had been a long time since they last met.

∞

May slowly opened her eyes to a white room. She tried to sit up but her body felt rigid and her limbs wouldn't obey her commands. All she could do was move her fingers. Seconds passed until they turned into minutes. When she was able to lift her head, she realized she was wearing a maroon hospital gown, the same kind Miss Umi made them wear during experiments. Her breathing quickened as she perspired, not wanting to undergo anymore procedures. They hurt too much and she always ended up waking alone.

While she struggled to escape, Kakinouchi walked in through the door with a bouquet just then. He saw and ran over, frantic. "Whoa, hey there."

"I have to get out of here," she said, crying silently. "If I don't, Umi-sensei's going to perform more experiments on me."

She looked so lost and confused, he didn't know how to comfort her.

"Help me out of here."

"It's okay," Kakinouchi assured, cupping her face in his hands. Nothing bad would happen to her again. He'd make sure of it. "Umi-sensei won't be doing any experiments. You're safe. Trust me."

Gulping, May nodded, trusting him. After calming down, her breathing returned to normal, and her heartbeat slowed. "Why are we here?"

"You don't remember?"

May scrunched her brows, recalling how they constantly argued during their mission. She remembered Chief Aikawa and Detective Shige—even meeting Gon and talking with him before getting abducted. The next thing she knew, she was lying under a bright light. Doctor Nishikawa was there, wearing a surgical mask. He had finished sedating her to pick up a scalpel in his gloved hand.

"Your heart is mine," he claimed and dug the scalpel into her flesh.

May gasped as her body jerked, reliving that nightmare. He had operated on her before the sedatives fully kicked in. "Ah!"

"May!" shouted Kakinouchi as he held her down. "Get ahold of yourself!"

She gasped one last time before touching her chest where her heart was beating. There were no scars from the surgery after self-healing. She stared at Kakinouchi who smiled in relief. Enraged, May sat up, pushing him away. How dare he smile after what happened?

"Oye," said Kakinouchi in alarm. "What was that for?"

"You let him take my heart!" she accused.

Even though he wanted to tell her it was partially her fault for going along with Aikawa's plan, he lost his voice. Instead of blaming him, she should be happy about being awake and reuniting. But as always, she could only find fault with him.

"You're not fit to be my Soulmate!"

The door to the white room opened as Azuma, Shayla, and Jennifer entered, bearing gifts. They had come to check-up on her only to find her conscious and blaming Kakinouchi for her situation. Lying on the floor was his bouquet he had brought along.

"Get out," demanded May. "I don't want to see your face! I don't need a Soulmate like you!"

Shayla was across the room within a flash, slapping May with all her might. The room seemed to echo as Jennifer gasped. May's face remained turned, her cheek red.

"You ungrateful bitch!" Shayla shouted as her balled fists trembled, wanting to punch May this time. It surprised her that she'd be so consumed by bitterness towards one of her friends. "Kakinouchi-kun's been by your side the entire time! He held your hand even when you were presumed dead! He never stopped believing that you'd come back! He even risked his life to retrieve your heart! Can't you show him a bit of gratitude?!"

"Shayla, stop," pleaded Kakinouchi.

"I will NOT stop until I've torn her into shreds."

"Jennifer, help me."

"Ah," Jennifer said, nodding. She set her things down and ran over to calm Shayla, who refused to stop. With no other alternatives, Jennifer had to force her out of the room.

"Let me go, Jen! I'll show her who's boss!"

"Shayla, come on. May just woke up."

"Oh, don't try to defend her for being a bitch!"

"Well, she's probably still in shock from the ordeal."

"Shock?! Oh please, the one in shock is me!"

"Okay, okay," Jennifer said, not allowed to say a thing without having Shayla turn it back on her somehow.

Once the two exited, it became silent in the room again. Kakinouchi turned towards May, giving his best smile. "You're right." He nodded. "I failed. I let Nishikawa-sensei take your heart." Kakinouchi bowed for a long time as Azuma watched in disbelief. He had no reason to apologize when he had done nothing wrong. Everyone had been informed about May's selfish decision to be used as bait. "I'm sorry." Kakinouchi stood and picked the bouquet off the floor to place on the drawer before exiting. Not once did he turn to acknowledge Azuma.

"What?" May snapped once it was only them. "You wanna hit me too?"

Azuma grinned at her nasty attitude, also tempted to slap her. Instead, he dropped his gifts to the floor. May didn't deserve his sympathy. In fact, she didn't deserve a single thing from anyone. She was self-centered, the kind Azuma hated most. He shook his head and was soon laughing.

May turned her head to look at him. "What's so damn funny?"

"It's true that Arata couldn't protect you. But you know, it's not entirely his fault. We all heard about how you ran off and got yourself caught. Now suddenly, you wanna blame Arata for your own shortcomings. Some nerves you've got there, lady."

May grinned and turned away. It didn't matter if he was right, or that she was in the wrong. All that mattered was that Kakinouchi was her Soulmate. It was his job to protect her. And he had failed.

"You know what else? You are right. You do need a new Soulmate, because Arata's too good for you—no, in fact, you don't deserve a Soulmate whatsoever, since you're not worthy of anyone." With that, Azuma walked out.

When she was alone again, May threw both hands to her face and cried. Shayla and Azuma were right. May was ungrateful. It was her fault that she had been thrown into this predicament. Kakinouchi had objected to Aikawa's plans, but she wouldn't listen. The part that broke her was what Azuma had said. May didn't deserve Kakinouchi as a Soulmate, even though she had come to desire him.

∞

They were sitting inside the dining hall eating and chatting. The girls were sitting together and the guys were sitting together. Shayla was still fuming about what had happened a few minutes ago.

"Should I go knock some sense into her?" offered Love.

"I've already done that."

Love popped her knuckles and grinned. "It doesn't hurt to beat her a second time."

"Yeah, I agree. We should really put her in her place," spoke Crystal.

"Let's stop talking about May," Hanabi said, quivering from where she sat. It was unbearable to listen to.

"Why not? She's being a total bitch after waking up."

Hanabi stood, slamming her palms down onto the table. She didn't want to hear another word about May.

"Hanabi," said Jennifer worriedly.

"Hey," Yeve said, looking up. She had stopped eating to set her fork down. All this talk about May was getting on her nerves as well. "Everyone needs to shut it. I'm getting a real huge migraine right now."

Hanabi hung her head down low, her hands still shaking. "Sorry," she apologized and quickly left.

"Hanabi!" called out Louis as he chased after her, forgetting his food.

"I wonder what's wrong with her," said Morgana.

Alice watched Louis chase Hanabi and turned to face front. She shook her head, worried too. "Her powers probably acted up again."

"What a disastrous lunch," said Cammie.

Verse nodded in agreement and stood, wanting some time alone. "See ya." She pushed her chair back to leave with her empty plate.

Liz came, happily waltzing over to stand next to the girls' table. In her hand was a plate of food. "Hey, hey, can I sit with you girls?"

"Uh-" answered Cammie as she looked up.

Without waiting for a proper reply, Liz shouted, "Thanks!" and quickly sat in Verse's chair beside Yeve, afraid that someone might beat her to it. "Ah, we meet again, Yeve. What a coincidence. This must be a small world!"

Soria picked at the olives on her plate and didn't bother to look over, but still responded to Liz's comment, "It's obviously called STALKING."

Liz glared over and hissed. Why was Soria answering when no one had been speaking to her? "I heard that."

"Oh," Soria said, finally looking over. "Wow, we meet again, what a small world."

"Why you-"

"Cat-chan," Love interrupted and set some cheese on Liz's plate to stop the argument from escalating. "Eat this and behave, okay?"

"Don't call me that." Liz glanced at Love's offering and scoffed. "And just so you know, cats don't eat cheese, mice do."

"I thought cats ate everything?" Mio asked as Liz hissed again.

"Should we get you some carrot cake and milk then?" offered Yeve.

Liz's eyes twinkled at the offer. A smile quickly overcame her. She nodded, forgetting about Soria's presence. Yeve was finally acknowledging her. "You really will?"

"Can't you tell a joke when you hear one?" asked Midnight.

"Well, I'm leaving too." Yeve stood and walked away with her tray. Her appetite had vanished, though she'd been starving minutes ago.

"I'll go with you too!" offered Liz. If Yeve wasn't going to stay, then she had no reason to either. Liz grabbed her untouched food and stood, eyeing Soria who played with her olives again. She stooped over to whisper. This would only be between them.

Wondering what they were secretly conversing about, Remi raised an eyebrow and set her fork down. Even the other girls looked suspicious. "What are you two whispering about?"

"Understood?" Liz said, ignoring Remi's question and pulling away.

Soria smiled and nodded. "Sure, if you say so."

Liz's cheeks heated as she glared. She hated how Soria took her words lightly. "I'm going to enjoy shredding you to pieces."

"I'm game any day. Just tell me when," accepted Soria.

"Soria," objected Remi. Though she didn't know what they were arguing about, she didn't like the tone that Soria was using. Neither did she like how Liz was provoking her best friend.

Liz grinned and whispered once more. "I'll show you I'm much stronger than you, Soria Terauchi." Liz turned away, but stopped. "Oh my," she gasped with an exaggerated, shocked expression. "I'm so sorry. I'd forgotten. Here, you're just called plain ole, '*Soria*.' My bad." She grinned and skipped away, winning for once.

Terauchi. Soria Terauchi. Soria's eyes widened and shook as she stood from her chair. The room suddenly started spinning as she held onto the table for support. That couldn't be right. It just couldn't. Maybe Liz was messing with her again. But if that was true, why did that last name fit in so well with her first name? "Hey!" Soria called back.

"What happened?" Remi asked.

"Cat!"

The pipes behind the walls of the room started shaking as Liz stopped to glance back, eyebrows raised. She was nearly out the door and didn't have time to deal with Soria's tantrum when Yeve was getting further away.

"Don't think you can say something like that and walk out on me!"

"Hmph," let out Liz as she exited without a care.

"You dare have the guts to ignore me?" Soria turned, leaving her plate of half-finished food behind.

"Soria!" called out Remi.

"Don't follow me!" Soria swirled back and glared. "I'll deal with that cat alone." With that, she walked out as Aoi came running over.

"What just happened?" he asked.

"Don't know," Crystal answered, shaking her head.

"Damn it," he said, running out after her.

"Aoi-kun!" Morgana called out, standing to chase him as Cammie held her back.

"Don't chase him, Morgana."

"But-"

"Morgana," warned Midnight. She looked up, shaking her head. None of them were in a position to deal with the situation accordingly, and could only sit back and watch.

46th Lie

RAIN MADE HIS WAY out of the mansion to go on a midnight stroll. Not a minute longer, Nicholas came sprinting out from behind. He jumped down the stone steps and ran off in such a hurry he didn't notice Rain. After getting a head start, Nicholas stopped and glanced back, finally aware that he'd passed someone.

"Rain," said Nicholas desperately as he ran back. "Do you know where Liz is?"

Having no reason to know where she was when he had no business with her, Rain raised an eyebrow and shrugged for an answer.

"I can't find her."

With a sighing, he slowly descended the steps, hating how he knew where she was. "Follow me."

"So, you do know. I knew you were lying."

"How so?"

"No one goes out taking midnight walks like this."

"Some people still do."

"You of all people probably don't."

Rain looked over with a grin. "You think you've got me all figured out, don't you?"

"Kinda."

"If you want to find that cat girl, shut up and just follow me." Rain walked by, hands in his pockets. He was curious about the real reason why the two Soulmates from Turquoise was there, but never questioned. As they walked in silence to a closed off area where pets were kept, sure enough, Yeve and Liz came into view.

As soon as Nicholas' eyes fell on Liz's back, he ran into the pen. His uncontrollable anger seethed as he yanked her to her feet.

"Ow, Nic, you're hurting me."

Without answering, he dragged her off as the two left behind watched.

Yeve stood from where she knelt, a white bunny in her hand slept soundly despite the commotion. She walked over to Rain's side and raised an eyebrow. "What was that about?"

"I don't know." Rain shook his head, not bothered. It wasn't his problem to deal with. Thank goodness. He turned, raising an eyebrow at her. "What are you still doing out here? It's already nighttime."

"I know." Yeve returned to the cage and stooped down to put the bunny back inside. She locked the door and stood up to stretch. "But the cat girl wouldn't let me return to the mansion to sleep. She kept saying that she was homesick and wanted me to keep her company because Soria was coming for her head. Supposedly, I was the only one who could save her."

"Huh?"

Yeve shook her head in frustration. "I don't quite get it either, but Soria really did show up, fuming. Good thing Aoi showed up too."

"What a complicated life you live."

"You just figured that out?"

"It was a joke." In a light chuckle he nudged her, half expecting her to punch his arm, but she did nothing. "You should go to sleep. I heard we're having a meeting tomorrow."

"Ugh, again?" Yeve complained, suddenly finding herself worn out. She left the pen with Rain and locked the gate before heading towards the mansion. "By the way, why are you out here?"

"Taking a stroll."

"Do I need to be your bodyguard?"

"No. You look tired. Go to bed before you collapse on the ground. I refuse to carry you a second time."

"Che," she let out. "I don't plan on letting you either."

This time he laughed and strayed from the path they were on. "Goodnight."

"You know, on second thought, I'm coming with you."

"You don't have to. I'm just gonna walk and think."

"Then, I'll walk and think with you. After all, two heads are better than one."

Rain shook his head and smiled. Regardless of what he said, she wasn't going to listen. It'd be easier if he just went along with her whims. "Alright, this way," he said, leading the way through to the back.

"Why are we going this way?"

"If we don't, that cat will stalk you down again."

"She's not really stalking me," denied Yeve.

"Oh, she's stalking you alright."

"You have no sense of sincerity."

Rain chuckled and looked up to the moonless sky. All he could see were the stars. However, whether he could see the moon or not, he knew it was always there, just like the sun.

"You look sad."

"Do I really?"

Yeve nodded in response and stuffed her hands into her pockets. It almost looked like Rain wanted to cry. Maybe, it had been a bad idea for her to follow him after all. She should've let him be, but he looked like he needed someone to talk to. "You know, if it's about something that I can help with, I'll do what I can."

Smiling, Rain reached out to pat her head. "Thanks, I'll remember that."

"Yep, anytime."

"Here, let's take a break," he said, taking a seat.

Instead of sitting, Yeve stood, now crossing her arms. They had barely gotten anywhere, yet he was already suggesting to take a break. "Are you serious?" she asked, watching him lay down. "You're already stopping to rest?"

Through negotiating, Rain motioned for her to sit as well.

Yeve gave a deep sigh and eventually gave in. She unhooked her katana to lay beside him. The night was cool and calming as she closed her eyes.

"You're one to talk," he laughed.

"It's because you stopped."

After his laughter faded, he wiped his eyes. He hadn't laughed that hard, yet the tears came anyway. "You think the meeting tomorrow is going to be about another mission?"

Another mission was the last thing she wanted to hear about. "I could use a vacation to Hawaii right about now."

Rain chuckled, as an owl hooted from nearby, halting him. The trees rustled as minutes passed between them. All he could hear was the wind and his own heartbeat. "Can I ask you something?" He turned to look at Yeve and noticed that she was fast asleep.

Shaking his head, he sighed. She should've returned like how he instructed. But watching her sleep so vulnerably by his side brought so much peace to his mind. If only he could keep her this way forever. "I wanted to ask, back on the ferry, who were you trying to catch? I know Soria interrupted us to bail you out."

Even though he waited for an answer, Yeve remained silent.

"You'll tell me who that person is, won't you?" Rain reached out to touch her but stopped. Instead, he put his hand to his mouth as tears formed again. "Why do you make me so sad?"

∞

"Nicholas!" Liz screamed, breaking free. She rubbed her wrist that ached and glared at him for not caring that he'd hurt her. As soon as Liz saw his own glare, her eyes softened. She knew that look anywhere. "Why are you giving me that accusing look for?"

"That's because I *am* accusing you," he responded coldly.

"Why? What did I do to you?"

"It's about what you did to Soria. Not me."

Of course she'd be the reason. She was always the reason. Liz should've seen it coming. It was because of *her* that Nicholas laughed without a twinkle in his eyes. Liz laughed and shrugged, crossing her arms. She'd done nothing wrong. "I didn't say much. I just told her that Yeve's closer to me than her."

"Liz," Nicholas snarled in warning.

"Soria wasn't even fazed by my words," she said, seeing no point in getting angry. "She even challenged me. Gosh, that's so like her."

Nicholas smiled, expecting nothing less of Soria. "Then," he said, his smile fading, "what'd you say to rile her up?"

Liz grinned and uncrossed her arms. "I called her by full name."

Anger swept over him as he roared, "Liz!" Nicholas reached out, grabbing her by the throat to choke. The fact that she was his Soulmate, he no longer cared for. Liz had hurt Soria, that was all that mattered.

"Nicholas," she gasped, trying to pry his fingers loose. "You're…hurting me!" With all her might, Liz scratched his hand as it bled.

Wincing, Nicholas quickly let go, he'd lost control for a moment.

"What are you doing? Trying to kill your Soulmate?!" she accused and coughed, the whites of her eyes red.

"I'm sorry," he apologized.

"If you're so worried about her, you better go find her. She might lose control again."

"Don't keep pushing her. She's not the same."

Liz smiled and lowered her hands, tiptoeing to eye him. "I know. And I don't care, because I've always hated her." She shouldered him and stormed away, tears in her eyes. Again, he had that look on his face like nothing else mattered in the world except Soria.

47th Lie

LOST IN THOUGHT, Umeko sat in bed, gazing out the window while Taiki remained asleep. Alice entered the infirmary and stopped. Startled, she called out in a whisper, but Umeko didn't seem to hear. Concerned, Alice walked over, placing a hand on her shoulder. At her touch, Umeko retreated from her thoughts.

"Alice," she greeted with a smile as they hugged. It felt like centuries since they last saw each other. "It's good to see you again."

"Yeah, same here," answered Alice. When they pulled away, she took a seat on a nearby chair and smiled as well. It was good to have the hot-blooded Umeko back, but there was a disturbance in the air as Alice frowned. "What's wrong? You seem kind of down."

"Do I really?"

"Yeah, you are. Are you okay?"

Umeko wore her best smile and chuckled. "I'm fine."

"Umeko," Alice said doubtfully. Umeko was a horrible liar. She was even worse than Mio and Hana at telling lies.

Umeko looked down at her hands. How was she to explain to Alice in order to not sound insane or delusional?

"Tell me. Don't bottle it up. It's not good for you."

"I...I keep hearing a voice."

"A voice?"

Umeko nodded and fidgeted with her fingers. Even now, his voice still resonated in her ears. At first, she ignored it, but after waking, his voice only grew stronger. She could no longer pretend that it had no effect on her whatsoever. Everywhere she looked, everywhere she went, she expected to see him. He was important to her, that much she knew. Umeko took in a deep breath before disclosing the owner's identity, "I think that voice belongs to Naruyuki-kun."

"Eh?"

Umeko threw a hand to her face, laughing and crying altogether. "I know. It sounds insane, but it's true."

"Does Taiki know?"

Umeko shook her head and turned to look at Alice. How could she tell her own Soulmate something that even she didn't understand? The reason she had confided in Alice was because she wanted someone to hear her out. She wanted someone to confirm that she wasn't going crazy and that it was okay for her to feel this way. "It started after our parting and I didn't think much of it until recently."

Alice nodded, reaching out to hold Umeko's gloved hands in comfort, though it did nothing to soothe her pain. "But you have to remember, Naruyuki belongs to Verse. I think you should just forget about that voice."

"You really think so?"

"It's for the best. Or else you'll end up hurting yourself."

Umeko sat, mulling over Alice's words. It was true that Naruyuki didn't belong to her. And though she wasn't that close to Verse, they were still comrades. Even if it hurt, Umeko had to let go. If Jennifer was there, she would also agree with Alice. In fact, if it was any of the other girls that Umeko had confided in, they would've said the same thing. But the thought of abandoning the voice caused her to breathe unevenly. "Yeah," she whispered, scratching at her chest. "You're right."

Only able to squeeze her hand, Alice could see that Umeko was wavering in her resolve. She couldn't forget no matter what Alice suggested.

Awake in bed, but with his eyes closed, Taiki clenched his fists and pretended to still be asleep. He had plan on scaring them both by sitting up and shouting, "BOO!" but could no longer find the strength after hearing Umeko's confession about the voice.

∞

The hands on the clock nearby ticked as Teo and Naruyuki sat inside the guys' lounge room, playing Poker. It was getting later but none of the others bothered to return to sleep. At this rate, they were going to wake up late tomorrow for the meeting and receive another lecture from Mr. Fujiwara.

"You think we should go find them?" Teo asked.

Naruyuki shook his head, inspecting the cards in his hands. "They'll come when they feel like it."

"What if something happens to them?" Teo set down three cards and picked up three new ones from the deck.

"We're not their caretaker." Naruyuki set down one card and picked up a new one.

"Good point."

"Then again, it wouldn't hurt to check-up on those babies."

"Yeah, I was thinking the same thing," agreed Teo. He set down his full-house and smiled.

"You," said Naruyuki in disbelief.

"I win."

"Damn," he said in dread. Losing to Teo was unimaginable. It also hurt his pride. "One more round, then we can leave."

"Alright, if you wanna keep losing to me." Teo grinned while Naruyuki snarled and reshuffled. When he was done, he dealt five cards each and set the rest of the deck in the middle.

"Poker?" Yuudai asked, entering the room with a loud yawn. He waltzed over to glance at Teo's hand and whistled. "Nice."

"You can't trick me," Naruyuki said, setting down two cards to pick two from the deck. He smiled at his hand and lowered it. "I heard from Taka that you conspired with Poe last time to win. I'm not so gullible to fold."

"Alright, don't believe me then." Yuudai shrugged as Teo set down two cards and picked up two. Suspicious, Naruyuki raised an eyebrow. When Teo saw the cards he'd drawn, he laughed and showed his hand. Four of a kind.

"What the-" Naruyuki began and hung his head down low. While he moped, the other two laughed and high-five. This was what he got for taking Yuudai the trickster lightly.

"You need to work on your skills some more. Or else you'll end up losing in a real gamble."

"Yeah, yeah," said Naruyuki. He stood up and stretched as Teo did also. Right when they were about to leave, the others made their way in, laughing and yawning. Their efforts were in vain.

"Never mind, forget it, seems like we don't have to anymore," said Teo.

Naruyuki smiled, inspecting the group. He raised an eyebrow. A few of them were missing. "Where are Rain, Aoi, and Hotaka?"

"Hotaka's with his adorable brother-in-law," King joked and grinned.

Dark looked over and smiled. "Are you still pissed?"

"I'm not pissed."

Noah chuckled. "Don't pick on him. He's just jealous because he can't be lovey-dovey with Jennifer."

"For the last time, I'm not jealous!"

"Guys," Shadow said with a yawn and walked over. Covering his eye was a new colored eyepatch. "Let's stop and go to sleep. I'm tired as hell."

"As for you," King said, turning to point a finger at Shadow. "I won't lose to you either."

Shadow stopped dead in his tracks, glancing around before pointing a finger to himself. "Are you talking to me?"

"Yeah you, you, Rain, Hotaka, and Kei, all four of you. I won't lose to any of you." He turned and stormed off to bed, annoyed. Aoi had been right when he said *everyone* loved Shadow.

"That was random," said Sasuke. "What'd you do to him?"

"I have no clue," answered Shadow.

Kakinouchi also followed behind King to sleep without a word to anyone. The rest simply watched. It'd been a rough day for him.

Azuma glared as he watched the door close. "Damn that May."

"He's still down about what she said, huh?" said Noah.

"I don't think he's ever going to get over it." Azuma shook his head and stalked off to bed too. Just thinking about May got him worked up again.

Louis stood, worrying all by himself. He looked from one to the other. They were too calm. "How should we help them?"

Yuudai looked over and threw him into a headlock, "Oh, no, you don't. Every time you attempt to help someone, you create a bigger mess. Just sit and watch. Those two will be fine on their own."

"I do not make a mess of things. Also, there's nothing wrong in wanting to help those in need."

"You're right. There's nothing wrong with that logic. However, when *you* become involved, *everything* goes wrong."

"Oye, what does that mean?"

"Guys," interrupted Takahiko who was rubbing his forehead tiredly. "It's getting late for an argument."

Yuudai nodded and yawned. "If anyone sees Aoi returning, tell him not to make a racket. If he wakes me up, I'm gonna electrocute his ass." Yuudai dragged Louis with him and waved while heading off to bed also.

"Oye, why are you dragging me with you too?!"

"If I don't, you'll do something bothersome like usual."

"I do not!"

"Night," Takahiko bid and took off his headband. He ran a hand through his hair and left with the others while Poe and Naruyuki remained.

"You're gonna wait?" asked Naruyuki.

Poe nodded, making himself comfortable on the white sectional sofa. He couldn't sleep until he confirmed the safety of the three missing guys. "You can go on ahead and go to sleep too."

"In that case, I'll keep you company," Naruyuki offered and took a seat on the love sofa.

Poe smiled and closed his eyes. "You don't have to."

"I insist."

"Alright, knock yourself out then." After a few minutes, Poe asked, "Why are you really here?"

"I wanted to stay with you."

"Anyone can see that's a lie."

"It's not a total lie." Naruyuki smiled.

Again, it was silent. "What's eating you?"

It took some time before Naruyuki finally spoke up. He had to confide in someone before he burst from within. Keeping this information to himself was proving to be too much to handle. "From us guys, who do you think is closest to Verse?"

Poe opened his eyes and turned to look at Naruyuki. He raised an eyebrow, suspicious at the question. "Shouldn't that be *you*?"

"Other than me."

Thinking, Poe settled back into his sofa. Because Verse constantly hung out with Yeve, the rest of the guys were too scared to approach her, even to say hi. "There's no one else."

"Hmm," groaned Naruyuki.

"Why are you asking for? What's the meaning behind it?"

"Then, let me ask you a different question. From us guys, who shines most like the sun?"

"Louis?"

"Not a chance in hell."

Poe simply laughed at Naruyuki's strong objection. "Then, Aoi?"

"I highly doubt it."

"If you won't tell me the whole truth, don't bother asking my opinion."

"Verse said in a dreamlike state, that she remembered someone's promise and that this person shone like the sun."

Naruyuki was so obvious Poe couldn't help but laugh. This other guy that Verse had mentioned got him so worked up his face even distorted. "You're jealous, aren't you? Wow, I never thought the day would come where you'd get jealous."

"Shut up."

"Sorry," apologized Poe as he wiped the tears from his eyes. "I just never expected to see this side of you. You should let Verse see it. She'll laugh and cry and might even fall for you instead."

Groaning, Naruyuki turned away, not appreciating Poe's rude joke. "I knew I shouldn't have asked."

"Then why did you?"

"Because I—ah!" shouted Naruyuki. He sat up so quickly it alerted even Poe who sprung up.

"What is it?"

"It could be that Hei guy," he snarled. "I knew something was suspicious."

"Huh?" said Poe confusedly.

"Next time I see that guy, I won't show him any mercy." Naruyuki was going off in his own world while Poe raised an eyebrow.

"Uh, okay, weird," he said, lying back to ponder on the question. Since Poe didn't know who this Hei person was, he would be excluded. However, when it came down to comparing someone to the sun, only one person came to mind. "Taiyou."

Naruyuki stopped ranting to look over, a stone-cold expression on his face. In the end, he laughed it off. "Nah, no way, Verse has never met Taiyou before."

"You're right." Poe nodded and smiled. Naruyuki was going on about Hei again. Though Verse and Taiyou had never met before, Poe couldn't wave the impossibility away. Initially, he dropped it. Getting Taiyou mixed up in this ordeal wasn't the best choice, given his past with Naruyuki.

∞

Hotaka and Midnight were in the kitchen cleaning up after dinner. While making her way to visit Mere, she found May wandering aimlessly in the hallway like a ghost. Nearly losing her mind, Midnight was able to get herself under control. She gave May a good scolding before suggesting her to tagalong. When Hotaka saw them, he inserted himself into the picture. After making it to the staff's wing and eating dinner with them, the Soulmate couple was ordered to clean while the staff retired to bed first.

Glancing over, Hotaka asked, "Are you sure you shouldn't be returning?"

Midnight simply shook her head. "The girls are probably fast asleep. They won't even notice I'm missing."

"I still think you should get some rest. We have to wake up early for a meeting with the deans."

"I know."

"Then we should go."

"If you want to go so badly, you can go alone."

Hotaka quickly scowled. "I can't leave you here in the lion's den."

Midnight rolled her eyes and turned towards him. It was getting really old. "For the last time, this isn't the lion's den."

"It is. You just don't know it." He threw his arm around her, darting his eyes around. Mere was nowhere to be seen, but he wasn't about to let his guard down. "I must protect the little lamb."

"Let me go." Midnight elbowed him and walked away. Hotaka was right behind as they entered the living room. When she couldn't find Mere, she scratched her head. It was indeed late. She wanted to bid him a goodnight and leave. "Where did Mere go?"

"Didn't you hear him?"

"No. What'd he say?" she asked, turning to look at him.

"He said he was going to show May around."

If that was case, she'd watch some TV and wait for him to return. Midnight took a seat on the sofa and instructed the TV to turn on as Hotaka sat beside her to watch the news.

"...attack on the London Bridge this afternoon," reported the newscaster woman.

"Hmm," Midnight said, frowning.

Instead of paying the news any attention, Hotaka continued staring at her before calling her name.

"What is it?" she asked while watching the news intently.

"I'm sorry."

"Huh?" She finally peeled her eyes away from the TV and over to him.

"I'm sorry for what I did. I'll reflect on it. So, forgive me."

Midnight raised an eyebrow, confused. "What are you talking about?"

With a click to his tongue, Hotaka scowled. Was his kiss so insignificant that she'd forget it so easily, when he was racking his brains over it? For some reason, it really got him going. If she was willing to forget, he had no problem reminding her. "I'm talking about the kiss."

Midnight groaned, having temporarily erased it from memory until he mentioned it. Now that she remembered how her first kiss had been forcefully stolen, she wiped her lips. It had always been her dream to kiss the man she would spend the rest of her life with on a romantic beach. "Let's just put it behind us."

"Put it behind," Hotaka repeated in disbelief.

Midnight turned away to watch the news again. They showed a man standing on the London Bridge, holding a girl captive. He was laughing and crying all at once. In his hand was a gun. Suddenly, the man shot the girl then turned the gun on himself. They both fell into the river as Midnight watched in horror. Hotaka quickly shot out his hand to cover her eyes.

"I'm not a kid," she said, pulling away and standing.

"Where are you going?"

"To grab a drink of water, then return with May."

Why was she pretending to be strong for, when they both knew she couldn't stomach what she'd just witnessed? Standing, Hotaka turned off the TV before following her.

∞

May sat on the steps just outside the entrance to the east wing of the mansion. She stared at her feet while Mere walked over, a blanket in his arms. Gently, he draped it around her and smiled. May looked up and smiled, thanking him as he sat.

"You're welcome," he said as May returned to her thoughts. "What's wrong?"

"I think I overdid it this morning."

Mere raised an eyebrow, confused. "What did you do?"

"I said some mean things to Kakinouchi-kun."

"What did you say?"

May buried her face into her forearms and shook her head. Every time she remembered, shame washed over her. "It's already done and over with."

"May-san," said Mere. He reached out, patting her back gently. "I think it's okay."

"No, it's not."

"You're his Soulmate after all. I highly doubt he hates you."

Tears welled in her eyes. Mere was wrong. It was because Kakinouchi was her Soulmate that he put up with her. If it wasn't for that, he would've abandoned her ages ago. Heck, she wouldn't be surprised if he'd gone to Dean Kosa to request for a new Soulmate. "You don't understand, Mere. I said some things that I can't ever take back."

Mere stared at her tear-stained face before shaking his head. "I still think it's okay."

"You say that because you weren't there."

Mere nodded in agreement. It was true that he didn't know the full story. However, he had a positive outlook on the situation. "All you have to do is apologize."

May laughed at his suggestion. Her pride would never allow her to do something shameful like that. "It's useless."

"Just apologize and see where things go from there."

"I can't. I hate apologizing."

Mere chuckled at her stubbornness and hugged his legs. Even if May knew she was wrong, she refused to take blame, regardless of her possibly losing something or someone precious in the process. "If you don't apologize May-san, nothing will ever change. Don't you think it's sad to let this misunderstanding stay with him forever? He'll probably think you hate him when really you don't."

May remained quiet. She hated the idea of being hated. Of everyone, she didn't want Kakinouchi and Yeve to hate her. It was the recognition of those two that she sought.

"Kakinouchi-san seems like a good person. He'll understand." Mere turned to look at her and smiled again. Living here for a few days had made him more observant of his surroundings. He quickly wanted May to stop wallowing in self-pity. "You should apologize and prove to everyone that you're fit to be his Soulmate."

May wiped her eyes and sniffled. Mere was making more sense than she did to herself. "Thanks."

"You're welcome."

"You know," May said, taking a good look at him. "You're really handsome, Mere. I wouldn't mind if you were mine."

"Eh?" he said, turning pink.

From behind, Midnight kicked May who shrieked. She had her arms crossed, not enjoying May's dirty joke. No girl with romantic feelings would ever be allowed to get within a mile of her precious little brother, for as long as she lived. "He's off limits. Go find your own man, stupid wannabe-ghost."

Seeing this as a chance to get rid of the runt once and for all, Hotaka smiled and crouched beside May. He gave her a thumbs-ups for encouragement and gave his permission, "Take him to a galaxy far, far away."

"If you two think I'm joking around, try me."

"It was a joke, a joke," May said, laughing it off.

"I wasn't," said Hotaka.

"Whatever, we're heading back. Mere, get inside and go to sleep," instructed Midnight.

Mere nodded and stood, giving her a hug while sticking a tongue out at Hotaka for making fun of him. "Goodnight, nee-chan." Mere kissed Midnight's cheek and quickly ran inside. That was his payback.

"That cheeky brat," Hotaka hissed.

Midnight glared at May who was still sitting on the steps with the blanket over her. "I'm warning you now, May. Don't you dare try seducing my cute little brother. I'll kill you."

"I know, I know." May nodded and stood to leave with them. "Oh?" she said, remembering. "Mere's blanket."

Reaching over, Midnight snatched it. "I'll return it tomorrow."

"No, no, I will," insisted May. "I was the one-"

"You really have a death wish, don't you?"

"No, no, be my guest and return it for me."

"That cheeky brat," Hotaka hissed. Now Mere was even making Midnight run errands for him.

∞

Soria lay, floating atop the stream out back. Though the water rushed downstream, she remained in the same place, staring up at the sky. Aoi sat on the banks where it was dry, chin on his palm, watching her. Water

526

butterflies danced all around as two water dragons glided elegantly by, never straying far from the caster.

"Soria?" Aoi called out. It was getting late. They had been there the entire afternoon and evening.

"Hmm?" she answered.

"Let's go back. Aren't you cold?"

"Not really."

"Well, I'm cold." He rubbed his hands together to get any kind of heat and breathed warm air onto his frozen fingers.

"Why don't you create a campfire?"

Not finding her joke funny, Aoi stood and blasted a streak of fire. The attack took her completely by surprise as she fell into the water and stumbled out, gasping for air. Meanwhile Aoi smiled, happy to have finally gotten her attention.

"What was that for?"

"To get you to look at me."

Soria glared, angry that he nearly killed her from the shock. Eventually, she smiled and reached a hand out to him who was far away. The water beneath made up for the distance and slowly took a leaf out of his hair. "How'd you get a leaf in your hair anyway?"

Not expecting that, Aoi touched his red hair and blushed. "Thanks."

"No problem." Soria shook it off and turned to look at the stars again. After leaving the mansion to find Liz, she found her clinging to Yeve. Before a nasty fight could break out, Aoi showed up, dragging her away. Ever since, she never returned to the mansion, for fear that she wouldn't be able to control her anger again. "Thank you," whispered Soria.

In that instant, the world became brighter. Or maybe it was coming to an end. Without blinking, Aoi stared at her profile until they stung from the dryness. He blinked and wiped his tears, a smile plastering his face. She was unfair to him without even knowing it. But no matter what, he'd always return to her. "What for?"

Instead of answering, the water below her erupted into millions of butterflies. Aoi watched in awe as the butterflies surrounded him, high up and down low. He reached a hand out to touch them but they flew away. Soria laughed while Aoi glared at her for teasing him.

"You know," he said, placing his hands on his hips. "You're amazing, Soria. You must've been a genius in your previous life."

"I think so too."

"Geez, how conceited."

"You think I'm bad? Yeve's worse than me."

"I bet." The two chuckled until the silence settled in. After a few minutes, Aoi's look softened and he asked, "What really happened back there?"

Without a response, Soria laid on the water surface again, wishing to burn the memory from existence. The water below rumbled without her realizing it. Even the water butterflies and dragons seemed to have lost their elegance.

"Why won't you tell me?"

"Even I don't understand."

Unable to silently watch any longer, Aoi waded into the freezing river. His body shivered but he ignored it and grabbed Soria's wrist, forcing her to lose concentration a second time. The water butterflies and dragons fell from the sky as it sprinkled down on them. Like usual, Soria kept him at bay from her true feelings. During times like these, she should rely on him. "Come. We're leaving."

"I still want to stay though."

"For what?!" he demanded. "There's nothing here!"

"Why are you so angry?"

"Because you won't confide in me about that despair in your eyes!"

"What despair?" Soria laughed and shook it off. "I have no despair."

Aoi choked on his words. Even though she laughed and smiled before him, her eyes were hollow and drained. How could she lie straight to his face? "Stop bottling your feelings in! If something's bothering you, tell me!" he shouted, taking hold of her shoulders to squeeze. "Why won't you trust me?"

"I do."

"No, you don't! You've never!"

"I'm being serious though."

"Liar."

"I'm serious."

"You're such an amazing liar." He laughed and let go, feeling so tired suddenly. How long were they going to keep playing this cat-and-mouse game? "Fine, stay for as long as you like." He waded out as Soria watched him go. Not once did he glance back.

"Shouldn't you at least hear him out?" Nicholas asked from hiding, once Aoi was gone.

"Who's there?"

"From this afternoon," he answered softly.

"Triheart," Soria said with a grin. "Why are you here?"

"I'm sorry that Liz upset you."

Laughing, Soria shook it off. She had no one to blame but herself. "Your Soulmate has a sharp tongue. Even her outer appearance is sharp. I shouldn't have let her get under my skin like that."

Nicholas smiled and looked up to the sky. Like with Aoi, he could also sense how tense she was. "What's wrong?"

Refusing to answer, Soria stood silently. If she wasn't willing to tell Aoi, what made him think she'd tell him?

"Is it about your name?"

Although Soria shouldn't be surprised that Nicholas knew, she still was. "Today, for the first time in my life, I was called by full name. When I realized that I never had a last name while growing up, I became enraged. You see, only Hotaka, the two Aratas, Noah, Jennifer, Crystal, Shayla, and Midnight have last names. So, why did your Soulmate give me a last name for?"

Nicholas remained silent, cursing Liz and her big mouth in his head. If it could cause a disturbance in Soria's passive demeanor, she would use it to her advantage. Closing his eyes, he responded, "A name is only a name."

"No. A name is what your parents give you."

Nicholas nodded again and came out from hiding so she could see him. Tears clouded his eyes and glistened in the dark. He wanted to run over and hug her with all his might. It took everything he had to control that urge. He didn't want to scare her after only meeting a few days ago. "That's just like you." He smiled and took a seat on the ground, chin on his palm like how Aoi had done. "You're too soft. Isn't that why you hesitated when you struck Ms. Zena?"

Soria flinched from where she stood. Tears found their way to her eyes. Why did Nicholas know these things without her having to say a word? How did he know what it was that she hid inside her heart? Who exactly was he?

"Choose me, Soria. If you do, you won't have to dwell on the past that keeps haunting you. You can start anew with me. That much, I can promise."

Soria glanced over, still standing in the water. For an apparent reason, she couldn't look away. "Why do you look at me like that?"

"Like what?"

"Like you've just reunited with me."

Unable to hold back, Nicholas' tears spilled out at her words. He reached a trembling hand out, trying to touch the woman he loved, but as usual, she evaded him like a dream. "That's because I have."

48th Lie

A LIGHT BREEZE blew past the group as they stopped before a hedge maze, located out to the back of the mansion. It extended far beyond the eye could see and was at least fifteen feet tall.

After being forced to wake up from the staff that early morning, they assembled inside the theater hall to be briefed by the deans for another mission. When Dean Kosa had finished explaining, he instructed Nicholas and Liz to lead the group to the maze.

Now that they were standing before it, they gaped, never knowing or expecting that such a thing existed. Or did the deans impulsively create it for today?

Nicholas turned to smile at the group and pointed to behind him. It was as Dean Kosa had said, this next mission was as easy as pie. "You gotta make it out to the other end of the labyrinth with your Soulmate. Whoever comes out first is the leader. Whoever comes out last is the loser. It's that simple."

"The only rule is, no using your powers. You must solely rely on each other and your brains," Liz explained.

"To ensure that you guys don't use your powers, you have to wear these bracelets." Nicholas distributed maroon bracelets as the group put them on. Once they finished putting on the bracelets, Nicholas continued with his explanation. "The bracelet will nullify your powers so that you can't use it to get out of the maze."

Mio turned the bracelet around on her wrist, amazed that something so small could wield so much power.

"That's all," said Nicholas. "Please make your way in."

"Ooh, and, no time limit! Just make it out before you starve to death! Happy hunting!" shouted Liz. She waved a hand and moved aside. "Do your best, Yeve! Come out as number one! I'll be waiting for you on the other side!"

Yeve smiled wryly. "Uh, yeah," she mumbled while Rain chuckled.

"I'll see you on the other side too, handsome swordsman," Liz said, giving King a quick peck.

"What the?!" shouted Jennifer in alarm.

"Good luck everyone," bid Nicholas. He walked past them, not bothered that his Soulmate had just kissed another man on the cheek. While they walked away from the chaos that Liz created, Nicholas stopped before Soria. He smiled again and messed up her bed head. "Try to rank in the top five. That way, we can be together."

"You!" Aoi shouted, pointing a finger at Nicholas who laughed and walked on by. "That guy's being too friendly with you, Soria!" Aoi threw her into a hug, refusing to let go.

"I don't like shouting," she said and yawned.

"Hmph," Liz said, flicking her hair to run after Nicholas.

"It sure sucks to be Yeve, Soria, and Jennifer," Verse said, scratching her head. Not that she cared about their troubles anyway. If she had that much drama in her life, she'd dispose of the problem first before fleeing far, far away. It sounded like the most practical way. Maybe she should suggest it to them but decided to keep it to herself instead.

King popped his knuckles, getting ready for a bout. Now that he and Jennifer had finished arguing, it was time to get serious about this next mission. "Jennifer," he said.

"Huh?" she answered, still skeptical about Liz's peck on his cheek.

"Are you a fast runner?"

"I guess."

"Well then Hotaka, you can eat my dust! Jennifer, let's win this competition! Considering that Yeve can't use her powers too, this is a piece of cake! Rain won't be able to defeat me!" King took hold of Jennifer's wrist to drag into the maze, laughing. He was already picturing himself as the victor.

"Who does that troll think he is, making fun of me just because I can't use my powers? I can defeat him even with my eyes closed," Yeve retorted while Rain laughed wholeheartedly.

Midnight crossed her arms, watching as the two disappeared behind the tall bushes. "He's as enthusiastic as ever."

"And he needs to change it," added in Hotaka.

Midnight smiled and uncrossed her arms, heading towards the entrance of the maze also. It was time to get serious too. Knowing Yeve, she would probably come out as number one in this mission, regardless if she could use her powers or not. "His enthusiasm is what makes him fun to be around. He doesn't give up easily and it starts to grow on you."

Hotaka glared and followed. She was awfully cheery when talking about King. In fact, she was always praising the other guys, but never Hotaka himself. "I can be like that too!"

"Why are you suddenly shouting?"

Louis pumped his fists into the air, shouting as Hotaka and Midnight disappeared also. "Let's go everyone! Let's go!" Laughing, he ran into the maze excitedly.

"Uh, he forgot you," Noah said, turning to look at Hanabi.

"It's okay. I can track him down," she assured.

"No using powers," reminded Hana.

Hanabi smacked her forehead with her palm and groaned, already forgetting what Nicholas and Liz had finished explaining. Waving a hand goodbye, Hanabi rushed off to chase Louis who'd probably get lost and add to her workload.

"Alright, let's do this," said Taiki as he ran ahead too.

"Yeah, I've been left out of all the fun lately!" agreed Umeko as she ran after him.

"Well, that's our cue." Rain smiled at the rest as they entered the maze.

∞

Sitting at the exit way, sipping tea, eating sweets, and playing a game of chess was Dean Kosa and Dean Kiera. A patio set had been brought out especially for that day while they waited to see who would make it out first. The umbrella was unfolded, blocking out the sun's glares. The teachers too were present, giving the kids from the academies the day off to relax. Only Miss Umi who was with Anoka wasn't present.

While sitting beside Nicholas under the tree's cool shade, Mere put his chin down on his palm and stared at the three exit ways to the maze. The suspense of waiting was killing him. "I hope Midnight-nee makes it out first."

Ms. Tanaka nodded, having no doubts. "I'm sure she will."

Even Mr. Fujiwara nodded in agreement. "I'm sure Hotaka will also."

"Although I wouldn't mind if May-san came out first," Mere added in and blushed.

"Eh?" they all said, turning to look at him.

∞

The aisles to the maze was so wide, five people could walk side by side without bumping into each other. The bushes were neatly trimmed as Azuma and Shayla walked in silence. Every now and then she'd glance his way, but he never met her gaze and was in a trance-like state.

"Talk to me," she said, reaching out to stop him. Blinking, Azuma looked over as Shayla squeezed his arm. "Don't worry me so much."

There was so much concern in her eyes that he reached out to squeeze her in his arm. How could he be so fortunate to have her as his Soulmate? He wouldn't dare trade her for the riches of the world. "I'm okay now."

"Don't you dare lie to me."

Azuma chuckled and shook his head. "I'm not lying. If I keep worrying about Kakinouchi, I'll only end up worrying you more."

"Darn right," she agreed.

"Come on. Let's get out of here," he said, taking hold of her hand to lead the way.

Shayla stared at him for some time before nodding in defeat. Even if she were to pry, Azuma wouldn't give in. She would have to be the one to lose. "Kakinouchi-kun will be okay."

Azuma tightened his hold on her hand. He nodded. Shayla had seen right through him as usual.

"This morning I saw May talking to herself in the mirror. She kept repeating the same word. Guess what it was?"

"Sorry?"

Shayla nodded. The question had been too easy to answer. She should've worded it differently. Then again, however she phrased it, he would've guessed correctly. "They'll be fine without us meddling. May will apologize and if she doesn't, my master will teach her a lesson or two, just like how she disciplined Umeko."

Azuma shuddered. Yeve really was a handful. It amazed him that Rain was still sane. Then again, Rain was mentally tough. From the guys, he was most capable of keeping up with her, in terms of ability and personality. They thought so alike. It was a no-brainer as to why the deans paired them up.

"It's a beautiful day, isn't it?" Shayla asked, switching topics.

Indeed, the blue sky was so beautiful it made Azuma feel crummy for being gloomy. "Thank you."

Shayla looked over, bashful from the sudden thanks. "Why suddenly?"

"I realized just now that I'm not half as strong as you. It's because I have you that I haven't broken down yet. So, I wanted to thank-you for being my Soulmate."

"Aw geez, you're making me blush!" Shayla reached out and hit him on the arm, chuckling and blushing.

Azuma turned to look at her again and smiled. She had the same look as that day when he found her inside the forest. He reached out and messed up her hair. "I'm the luckiest man alive."

"Stop it," said Shayla. Her smile brightened more than before, and her heart felt fuzzy and ticklish.

"I'm really serious. I must've done something right to have you."

"Geez, you womanizer," she accused as Azuma laughed and denied it.

∞

For as long as Hanabi could remember, she'd always had poor stamina. Fighting was never her forte. Which was why, she preferred espionage missions. Louis suddenly leaving her behind made things only worse on her behalf. Hanabi's chest heaved after running for a few minutes. She leaned against the tall bushes for support, wanting to puke. "I feel like forfeiting."

"Hanabi!" Louis shouted from behind and jumped out, throwing his arms around her as they fell over.

"Ah!" she shrieked, hitting her head on the ground.

"I'm so glad I found you!" Louis snuggled close to her and let out a sniffle, still lying on top of her. "I was so scared when I realized that I was all alone! Don't ever leave me again, Hanabi!"

"You were the one who left me," she reminded.

"Oh? You are right. I did, didn't I?"

"Get off. You're heavy." Hanabi pushed Louis away by the face as he whimpered. Once she got him off, she stood, rubbing her aching head. Hopefully she hadn't received a concussion. When Hanabi noticed that Louis was making no attempts to stand, she held out a hand.

"Thanks," he said, taking her hand to stand. After dusting his pants, he smiled. "Now that we're together again, how about we get out of this maze and become leader, huh?"

"I highly doubt that's going to happen."

"Don't say that. You never know unless you try."

"Don't set your goals too high. You might fall into depression if you can't achieve them."

Louis gasped, insulted. He stopped walking to fall on his hands and knees. It felt like the world had come to a standstill and a spotlight beamed down on him. Off in the distance he could hear a sad tune being played. "Are you trying to say that my powers are pathetic?"

Hanabi stopped to glance back, not expecting him to insult himself. "Who said your powers are pathetic? Your powers are strong. Once you learn to control it, you might become a wanted man. All your enemies will worry about you and ignore your comrades because you're more of a threat."

"Then, in other words you have faith in me?"

Hanabi smiled and turned away, placing a hand over her mouth. His tears trailed down his cheeks, making him look like an abandoned puppy that had

534

just been saved. It was too cute that Hanabi couldn't hold in her laughter. She returned to his side and soothed him. Suddenly, it felt like she'd been transported back to that day on the cliff when they were ten years old.

∞

"This is such a pain in the ass," Poe complained to the blue clouds that floated by. Sitting next to him making a crown out of daisies was Alice. They had decided to take a quick break as he glanced over and sat up on the green grass. "Whatcha doing?"

"Huh?" she answered and turned to look at him.

Poe pointed to the crown of daisies that she was holding. Not responding until she had finished making the second crown, Alice placed it on top of his head. After seeing how silly it looked on Poe, she laughed.

"It doesn't suit you. Maybe I should give it to Naruyuki instead."

"Oye," Poe hissed, then smiled. It was true anyway. Flowers didn't suit him. "What's this for anyway?" He touched the crown of daisies and watched as she placed the first crown on top of her own head.

"Our halos," answered Alice. She stood up and twirled in a circle then struck a pose. "Cute?"

"Very," he answered and stood as she laughed. "You seem different from usual."

"How so?"

"You never used to smile this often."

Shocked, Alice turned to look at him. Was he serious? Or was he joking around? "I always smile."

"I still think something's unusual about you."

"It must be you." Alice playfully hit him on the arm and ran off, laughing. "Come on, let's leave this maze behind! I wanna show the girls our new halos!"

"Yeah," agreed Poe as he chased her from behind.

Out of the blue, sadness washed over Alice as she ran with all her might to escape it. From behind, Poe quickened his pace to catch up. "I actually think you're right. There might be something wrong with me."

Poe caught her from behind as she twirled to look at him. "What'd you say just now?"

"I said, if you're too slow we won't ever make it out."

Poe frowned, never doubting her words. "In that case, leave it to me, the Great Detective Poe." He laughed proudly as Alice joined in. In this short amount of peace, he would treasure it. Who knew how long Alice would keep smiling for him?

∞

Midnight yawned while walking down the green aisles. Hotaka turned to look at her and shook his head. She wasn't even trying to make small talk with him. Without a doubt, the others were lively chattering away. Hotaka walked on ahead and stooped down as Midnight walked by, yawning again.

"Oye," said Hotaka as he ran over to block her way. "Didn't you see me?"

Midnight raised an eyebrow. "Yeah, I see you."

"I meant a while ago."

"Huh?"

"I was stooping so that you could get on my back."

"Huh?" Midnight raised her other eyebrow, then snapped her fingers in realization. "Ah, were you offering me a piggy-back ride?"

"No duh, what did you think I was doing?"

"I don't know, pooping?"

Hotaka twitched. "Why would I go to the restroom out here in a maze of all places?"

"I don't know, because Soria's weird like that?"

"What does Soria have anything to do with us?!"

Midnight shrugged. "How would I know? I just wanna get out of here." She pushed him aside and turned around the corner. "Ouch!"

"Midnight!" shouted Hotaka as he ran after her and stopped. She had gotten herself entangled in one of the bushy vines.

"Ouch, ouch," she said, trying to break free.

Hotaka tried to hold back his laughter as Midnight glared.

"Help me, damn it."

"Okay, okay," he said, helping.

Once she was free, she glared at the vines that snagged at her hair. She'd been too careless, thinking that nothing could hurt her here. "Damn, I just got a taste of my own powers."

"You dummy," Hotaka said, still chuckling.

"It's not funny," she snapped as they headed towards the straightaway path. She was blushing from having been caught in such an embarrassing situation. Up ahead, there were no longer any forks in the path.

"You didn't get enough sleep last night, did you?"

"I did."

"Liar, then why are you yawning?"

"I'm just bored."

Bored? As in, she didn't find him entertaining? As in, Louis, King, and Aoi more to her liking? As in…she wanted to leave him? Suddenly, Hotaka was reminded of their previous mission. Even though Zara had taken over her body, the look she gave Shadow was filled with desire. To prevent himself from starting an argument, he continued with their original topic. "I knew we should've returned sooner to bed."

"And I'm telling you, it's because I'm bored that I'm yawning."

"What does being bored have anything to do with yawning?"

"You don't know?" Midnight asked and raised an eyebrow. "You yawn only when you're tired or bored."

"Lie," accused Hotaka who couldn't admit or believe that he was a boring person. In this world, he was one of the most charismatic men. Just ask any girl, they would agree.

"It's already been clinically proven."

"Lies again."

"Ah!" shouted Midnight. She stopped walking as they reached the end of the long path, and put a hand to her bare neck.

"What is it?"

"I think while I was entangled in the vines, it snatched my necklace!"

His anger quickly diminished. Midnight was more of a klutz than he thought. "Are you serious?"

"Yes, I'm serious!" she shouted, running back. She couldn't afford to lose the necklace that the dean had given her. She'd never hear the end of it from Miss Umi and Ms. Tanaka. In fact, she might even get punished like Yeve and Soria. Just thinking about it made Midnight shudder. Now wasn't the time for punishments or lectures. She wanted to spend this limited time making as much memories as possible with the girls before they were forced to go separate ways for missions again. "Damn those vines, I'll show them who their master is!"

"Seriously?!" shouted Hotaka as he chased after her.

∞

"YOU KIDS!" Ms. Tanaka roared, stumbling upon the group comprised of Rain, Yeve, Aoi, Soria, Naruyuki, Verse, Sasuke, Mio, Yuudai, Morgana, Teo, Crystal, Dark, and Cammie. They were lazing around, eating a picnic beside the stone water fountain. The group immediately stopped what they were doing to look at Ms. Tanaka and Mr. Fujiwara whose faces distorted.

"Uh," they said, unsure of how to get themselves out of the situation.

Ms. Tanaka pointed a finger, continuing to shout, "I knew something was suspicious!"

"I'm disappointed in you kids," added in Mr. Fujiwara. He shook his head, unable to believe that Ms. Tanaka's hunch had been correct. While at the end of the maze waiting, she kept saying that there were a few of the kids who were slacking off. She wouldn't let it go until the deans agreed and sent them to investigate.

Now here they were, witnessing the worst possible scenario.

A woman's intuition was a scary thing.

"We didn't mean to," said Morgana in defense. The group had stumbled upon the fountain in the middle of the maze and decided to take a break. It was that simple. It wasn't like they had planned it or anything.

Ms. Tanaka glared some more before pointing solely at Soria who choked on her bread. "Soria," she accused. From them all, Soria was the likely candidate for causing trouble and slacking off. This laid-back atmosphere had her name written all over it.

Verse reached over to hit Soria's back. "Take it easy, take it easy."

"But sensei, it wasn't me! Seriously, it wasn't me this time!" Soria shouted in defense.

"Then who was it?"

"Uh," they said turning to their right where Takahiko and Love were coming towards them with some berries. As soon as Love saw the teachers, she stopped skipping and humming to gasp, "sensei."

"So, it was you Love," growled Ms. Tanaka. She grinned and popped her knuckles. "The nerves you have for slacking off on such an important mission. Has it been too long since you graduated? Should I remind you how I punish disobedient students?"

"No, I remember! Please don't punish me!"

"Did you use your powers?"

Love held up her right wrist where the maroon bracelet was, as proof.

"Then how do you explain all this food?" asked Mr. Fujiwara.

"I packed it all." Love held up her backpack and smiled nervously. There was no way she was getting out of this mess.

Mr. Fujiwara inspected the pack from where he stood. He couldn't help but raise an eyebrow. "No matter how you look at it, Tanaka-sensei, it's impossible."

"I'm no longer amazed at what these kids can and cannot do anymore."

"See? Told you it wasn't me," said Soria who continued eating.

"You kids," Mr. Fujiwara said, returning to the topic at hand. "You do realize that you're not allowed to work together, right?"

The group stared at each other, then to the two teachers again.

"Triheart and Liz left that part out," answered Yuudai.

"Those two," said Mr. Fujiwara as he shook his head and adjusted his glasses. How could they leave out the most important part of this mission? "Well, now you know. You're to rely solely on your Soulmate."

"Now you tell us when we're already together," said Dark.

"What are you gonna do sensei, make us start from the beginning?" joked Aoi as he laughed and stopped. The two teachers weren't joining in. "You can't be serious!"

"Yes," they answered in unison.

"But we're already halfway into the maze!" objected Naruyuki.

"Too bad," said Ms. Tanaka.

"Oh, come on, sensei," the girls whined, tired of the walk.

"Stop whining. It won't make a difference."

Mr. Fujiwara snapped his fingers as the maze split in half from the right where Takahiko and Love had come from. "Follow the path out, it'll lead you back to the beginning. When you re-enter, split up. If you don't heed my instructions, you'll be writing me a 200-page essay on grass."

"Aw man," they complained and stood up to leave their picnic.

"I wanted some berries though," whined Mio.

"Damn," Yeve said, pulling at her hair. She should've grabbed Rain and made a run for it as soon as she saw the two teachers. "Can't believe I have to restart."

Noticing that Aoi was depressed, Morgana smiled, wanting to cheer him up. A smile suited him best. "Don't feel down, Aoi-kun. We'll make it out together. I won't leave you behind."

"Thanks. You're so sweet."

Blushing, Morgana nodded and turned away.

Yuudai rolled his eyes, coming in-between them. Just how slow-witted could his own Soulmate be? "We're required to split."

Recalling Ms. Tanaka's words, Morgana gasped. Now she was the one who was depressed.

"Damn," Verse grumbled to the sky. "I knew we shouldn't have joined them in that stupid picnic."

Naruyuki couldn't help but chuckle. "I told you we should get a move on it, remember? But you wanted to stay and eat."

"I was hungry. Are you saying it's my fault we got caught?"

"Eh? No way. That's not what I was trying to imply."

Finding herself low on energy to argue, Verse rubbed her growling stomach. "I only ate one measly piece of bread."

"Really, that stomach of yours still amazes me even now."

"Verse and Shayla are my little piggies, didn't you know that?" Soria insulted as Verse chased her down the pathway, cursing.

"Those two," Yeve said with a shake to the head while the others laughed.

49th Lie

KING RAN AHEAD, SMILING. Jennifer was trailing behind, huffing and puffing. She opened her mouth to yell at him to slow down but only wheezes came out. King hadn't allowed her to take a moment's rest. It also didn't help that the bracelet was preventing her from stealing any energy.

"Ooh!" shouted King. He could see the exit way. Once he was out of the maze, he threw his fists into the air to celebrate. The breeze picked up as his spiky hair swayed. "We did it!"

Jennifer ran out to join him as she fell over on the grass, panting. The two deans were still sitting, eating soufflé and drinking Earl Grey tea. Miss Lima was standing next to Dean Kiera. Gabe too was present as he stood by Dean Kosa's side. Sitting not far from them were Nicholas, Liz, and Mere who were also waiting. As soon as they spotted the two at the right exit, they smiled and waved. "You two finally made it out."

Instead of worrying about their congratulatory words, King desperately tried to find Rain or Hotaka. When he confirmed that they were nowhere to be found, he celebrated. "Whoo-hoo! First place!"

"You…" Jennifer said, breathlessly looking up at him. "…didn't have to run so fast…my legs…feel like…they'll fall off…any second…"

"I beat those two! Now I'm the leader!"

"I'm about to die here…be more worried about me," she hissed.

"Eat my dust!" King laughed, still ignoring Jennifer's beaten state.

"Whatever…I don't care anymore."

"Congrats on making it out," Mere said, walking over with a cold-water bottle he took from the cooler. He knelt beside her and smiled.

"Thanks."

"Come on." Mere helped her to stand as he handed her the bottle.

"Thanks," she said again and took the cold-water bottle as they walked over to join Nicholas and Liz beneath the tree's shade.

"Hah, I win, I win, I win!" shouted King in a sing-song voice. He was even doing a light dance to show his victory.

Meanwhile, Liz stood and walked over. When King saw her, he gulped and stopped dancing. Jennifer who was sitting with Mere raised an eyebrow. "I knew you'd make it out," said Liz. She leaned over to kiss him on the other cheek. "This is my congratulatory gift to you."

"You two!" screamed Jennifer. She stood on her Bambi-like legs and wobbled over, grabbing King by the collars to shake while ignoring Liz who smiled nearby. "I knew something was going on between you two."

"Eh?!" shouted King in disbelief. He shook his head. How could that be true? He didn't even know Liz existed until the deans introduced them. "There's nothing! I swear!"

"Aw," Liz said, blushing. "Don't you remember the time you picked me up into your arms and I kissed your lips?"

"Huh?!"

"King, you," hissed Jennifer.

"I never did such a thing! Believe me!"

Right on cue, Hotaka came out from the middle exit with Midnight beside him. She was fixing her necklace around her neck, not even giving King a glance. Hotaka on the other hand raised an eyebrow at the situation. "What's going on here? Did I miss something?"

King swirled around at the sound of Hotaka's voice and forgot about his ordeal with the girls. He quickly ran over, grinning and pointing a finger in Hotaka's face. "I finally beat you and proved that I'm the superior one! Now bow before your king!"

Midnight looked up after hearing his words and raised an eyebrow. "Uh," she said in protest.

"Are you an idiot?" interrupted Hotaka. "I came out already."

"Huh?" King said.

"Really?" asked Jennifer in disbelief. Even her anger had diminished.

Mere smiled and nodded. "They did."

"They did," confirmed Liz as she skipped over to sit with Nicholas again.

Jennifer plopped back down. She had wasted her energy running just to come out in second place.

King crossed his arms and grinned. This was probably a tactic's of Hotaka's to get under his skin. With no proof, King wouldn't believe them. "Then, why weren't you out here?"

"Midnight lost her necklace, so we turned back."

"Don't joke with me!" Losing his cool again, King threw a punch as Hotaka easily parried, grabbing his arm to pin behind his back. "Let go you bastard!"

Shaking her head, Midnight walked over to join Jennifer and the others. This quarrel had nothing to do with her and she wanted no part in it. "I'll leave you two lovebirds alone."

The two guys turned towards her and glared, shouting in unison, "Not funny!"

Dean Kosa laughed and sipped his tea, not worried about their quarrel either. "Oh, what I would do to be young again."

"Agreed, they're so lively," said Dean Kiera.

"Ah, youth," they said in unison.

"Dean!" King shouted. He was going to whine his way to the number one spot. "It's not fair! Hotaka should be out here waiting for the rest of us! Or else it shouldn't count!"

"Face it, you'll never win me," said Hotaka. He let go to join the others as well. Mere was fussing about Midnight's ruined hair while she explained how the vines had attacked her.

"Not fair, I came out first!" King kept shouting.

∞

Hana trailed from behind Shadow, looking about. The birds they heard chirping at the entrance of the maze vanished. Even the rustling made by the wind couldn't be heard here. It felt like the end of the world. "It's really quiet, isn't it?"

Shadow glanced back. She was lagging further behind than when they first entered. He was starting to think that she hadn't completely forgiven him for abandoning her. And if that was the case, he would somehow find a way to get her to acknowledge him again. "Hana," he called back.

"What is it?" She stopped looking around to look at him.

"Keep up or else you'll get lost." Shadow held out a hand as Hana walked over, not bothering to take his hand. At least he got his answer.

"Do you think the others got out already?"

He shook his head and followed. "I doubt it."

"Then why haven't we run into any of them yet?"

"I don't know. Maybe the maze is bigger than we thought."

"Probably."

"So," Shadow said, trying to make small talk. "What do you think the purpose of this mission is?"

Hana shook her head. "I don't know. But it's not like-"

"Really?!" shouted Morgana's voice from ahead. "You heard Aoi-kun's voice from over here?!" She came running past them with Yuudai who led the way. She was squealing and blushing at the thought of seeing Aoi again.

"Yes, yes, he's this way, follow me." Yuudai rolled his eyes in annoyance and noticed Shadow and Hana. He smiled and waved a hand in greeting before disappearing behind the bushes.

"See ya, Hana," Morgana bid and waved a hand.

"Wait!" Hana called out. Since they had met up, they could keep each other company. "We can go together!"

Morgana glanced back while Yuudai continued walking. As much as she wanted to travel with Hana, it was impossible. "Tanaka-sensei says that we can't work together. We can only travel with our Soulmates." Morgana waved again to chase Yuudai.

"What was that all about?"

Shadow walked over to join her side, arms crossed. He was just as lost as she was. "I don't know. But when did she speak with Tanaka-sensei?"

"Hmm," Hana said, tapping her chin. She was thinking back as well. It was Nicholas and Liz who had explained the rules to them. Even the two deans didn't bother to explain a thing, yet somehow Morgana knew. "Maybe something happened while we were separated?"

"Could be."

"Then-" Hana began as her stomach growled. Embarrassed, she blushed and laughed it off, putting a hand over her stomach. "Don't mind me."

"Seems like we gotta find our way out before we really do starve to death." Shadow laughed and bent down, picking her up with one arm.

"Ah!" she shrieked in alarm. "What are you doing?"

"Carrying you, since obviously you have no more stamina."

Hana pouted for being an inconvenience. If this kept up, she'd get abandoned again. "I can still walk. Let me down. I'll prove it."

"Why are you suddenly so stubborn?"

"Because," Hana whispered, wanting to get stronger for him. If she could, they'd never part again, but knew that this was the extent of her powers. She was a failed experiment that would one day be replaced. Until then, she wanted to remain by his side. "Shadow-kun," she spoke, gently draping her arms around him. "We're good now, right?"

"Always," he answered.

∞

"There!" shouted Taiki. He pointed to the exit way and ran with Umeko right beside him. After being rendered useless in their second mission, and having been saved, they were finally going to redeem themselves, no matter how insignificant it was.

"How do you know?" Umeko asked suspiciously. "It could be a trap."

"No, this is it. Because I definitely smell Earl Grey!"

"What a weird nose you have. You can smell tea from this far away?"

"Yep," said Taiki as he wrinkled his nose and smiled.

"Why?!" shouted King's angry voice from up ahead.

"Shut up, you're loud!" responded Hotaka's voice.

"Wow," Umeko said, shocked. Taiki's nose was better than she'd given him credit for. Perhaps, he'd been a dog in his previous life. "This really is the exit."

"Didn't I say so already?"

Umeko turned to look at him and smiled. "I guess I should trust you more then."

"That's right." Taiki nodded as the scent of the tea grew stronger. A light breeze wafted by as the ending of the straightaway neared. Soon, they would reach the other side. "Umeko."

"Hmm?" she answered, not turning to look at him.

"Let me remind you, I too can save a life, not just Naruyuki."

Umeko blinked, confused at his implication.

"I just wanted to remind you," he said, never deterring from the path he ran on. Hopefully one day, he'd be rewarded for his perseverance.

"You made it!" shouted Jennifer. She was waving at the two who had come running out of the maze without realizing it. They came to a slow halt and smiled. Unconscious on the ground beside Jennifer was King.

"Yo," greeted Hotaka as he waved and smiled.

Taiki stared at King then to Hotaka, asking, "What'd you do to him this time?"

"He was pissing me off."

"You still didn't have to lose your temper," said Midnight.

"No fighting," Mere pleaded and hugged her. There was enough fighting going on as it was. He didn't want his sister getting involved.

"Sorry. I won't."

Losing his temper again, Hotaka turned and kicked Mere. "How many times do I have to tell you? Don't cling to her like that."

"Ow," Mere whimpered, letting out a few sniffles. His sister's Soulmate had just kicked him when he was trying to help.

"Hotaka!" shouted Midnight as they got into a big brawl.

"Wow," Umeko said, laughing. A lot of interesting things had happened while she was gone. It created a void in her heart when she realized that she couldn't share the same memories as the group who had spent time together without her.

"Remember," whispered Taiki as Umeko looked over.

"We did it!" shouted Yuudai as they all turned to look. He and Morgana had also made it out of the maze, just right behind Taiki and Umeko. His maze skills were phenomenal. Even after having to start from the beginning, he beat the rest who didn't have to restart.

Morgana faltered to her knees and threw a hand to her mouth. She felt like puking from the nonstop running but didn't want to repulse Aoi. And so, she shakily fixed her hair and panted, desperately searching for Aoi who wasn't there. There wasn't a single sign that he had exited. "Eh? Wait. Where's Aoi-kun?"

The group who had come out glanced at each other and shrugged. "Aoi never came out."

"Eh?!" shouted Morgana in disbelief. She had been tricked and glared up at Yuudai. "You lied to me!"

Proud that he had deceived her into believing him, Yuudai grinned. It wasn't his fault she was gullible. "Had to," he said with an evil chuckle. "I'm truly a damn genius. Please call me Genius from now on everyone."

"Like hell," answered Hotaka and Taiki.

"You devil!" Morgana shouted, hitting Yuudai's leg with her puny fists.

"I had to, or else you wouldn't follow me."

Determined to find Aoi, Morgana attempted to return to the maze. Already able to guess what she was thinking, Yuudai caught hold of her to drag away. "No! Let me go!" she screamed.

"There's no way I'm chasing you into that damn maze."

"But I have to go find Aoi-kun! He needs me!"

∞

Aoi stared and gulped. He was standing before a dead end in the path he had chosen. "I think we're lost." Aoi turned to look at Soria, tears in his eyes. Instantly, those tears got vacuumed back where they came from. Soria was trudging along, yawning without a care. "Soria!" he fumed.

Coming to a complete halt, Soria stopped yawning. "What? What happened? Why are you yelling? Are we under attack?"

"We're not under attack! We're lost! Be more concerned!"

After thinking for a few seconds Soria offered, "Then, should I use my powers?"

"We'll get disqualified!"

Shrugging, Soria responded, "So what?"

"So what?" Aoi repeated in disbelief. How could his Soulmate be so carefree? If she didn't take this mission seriously, they could end up being the laughing stock. Just the thought of losing made Aoi cry silently. He let out a few sniffles and wiped his eyes, hating the thought of dying from starvation while inside the maze.

Defeated, Soria walked over to soothe him. She didn't understand why he got depressed each time he thought about his ranking amongst the guys. It wasn't as if that determined a person's value. But because he cared so much, she'd help him out. "How about this," she suggested. "We backtrack. Once we cross a fork in the path, you can choose which way to go. The next fork we come across, I'll choose. We keep taking turns and eventually we get out."

"Ooh, good idea," agreed Aoi. His eyes lit up like lanterns at the suggestion. It was so genius, he wondered why he hadn't come up with that idea first.

"Simpleton."

"Just like you," said Verse as she walked by.

"Huh?!" shouted Soria as she swirled to glare at Verse, but only caught sight of her hand waving bye before it disappeared around the green corner.

"See ya," Naruyuki bid.

"Let's go!" shouted Aoi as he dragged Soria off.

"Whoa!" she shouted, alarmed at his new determination.

∞

Crystal stalked down the path, glaring and grumbling to herself. Keeping his distance, Teo walked from behind. Crystal was like a ticking time bomb and he couldn't read when she'd erupt. Abruptly, she halted, as did Teo. How long was this pathetic maze going to keep her imprisoned? It was already noon. She was getting tired and hungry after not getting the chance to eat Love's bentos. Inhaling deeply, she raised her face to the sky and shouted, "Get me out of here!"

"Don't worry. We'll find our way out eventually. And even if we don't, I'm sure the dean will send in help," he assured.

Crystal gave him a look of disbelief and walked over as Teo took a few steps back. Reaching out, she caught him by the shirt collar. Teo was too laid-back about this mission. There was more to it than just escaping a maze. "Do you really think those two deans will send out a search party to look for us if we don't make it out on our own?"

"Uh," Teo said, thinking. Eventually he shook his head. "I have no hope."

"I thought so."

"Oh?"

"What is it?"

Teo pointed a finger behind her as Crystal turned back. No one was there. "I thought I saw someone walk by, through that aisle."

"You did? Who?"

"I don't know. They were too quick. Should we check it out?"

"No!"

Jumping at her sudden shout, Teo threw both hands over his ears. He had gotten a fright just then. "What's gotten into you?"

"I don't wanna go!"

"Why are you freaking out for?"

Crystal clung to his arm, refusing to let go. It felt like someone was watching them as her hairs stood on end. "It could be a ghost."

Teo stared at her long and hard. He wasn't amused by her joke. It was too childish. Besides, he didn't believe in ghosts. If Crystal was trying to scare him, it wouldn't work.

"I bet it's a ghost haunting this maze."

Teo blinked and eventually laughed. She wasn't trying to scare him. Neither was she trying to make a joke out of what he'd seen. Crystal was genuinely saying it out of fright. Seeing this vulnerable side to her made him want to be her knight in shining armor. "Are you scared of ghosts?"

Just because he found her weakness again, she wouldn't allow him to make fun of her. "Ghosts are no laughing matter."

"Crystal, there are no such things as ghosts."

"Yes, there are."

"How do you know?"

"When we were kids, we had a sleep-over inside the school gym. All the girls were gathered together. We stayed up all night telling stories. When it was Verse's turn, she told the scariest ghost story of all time. Even to this day, I still have nightmares."

"And?"

Crystal gulped at the faint memory and shuddered. "Remi cried so hard that the teachers heard, and they came to investigate. After finding out that it was Verse, they gave her a good scolding. It was the second time she had created a commotion with her ghost stories. They even lectured Mio, that as eldest she had to know when to stop the stories from getting out of hand. But Mio was scared stiff she couldn't even move."

Unable to stop himself, Teo erupted in laughter and fell over on the grass, both hands to his stomach.

"You insensitive jerk," she said, watching him laugh at her misery.

"I'm sorry. I'm sorry." He stopped rolling to sit up on the ground, wiping his eyes. "What happened next?"

Crossing her arms in dissatisfaction, Crystal turned away. She wasn't going to tell him the rest of the story if he was going to act this way.

Standing, Teo patted her. "I'm sorry. Really, I am. Continue."

She looked over, inspecting him. He seemed genuinely sorry as she continued with her story, "In the middle of the night when we all fell asleep,

I woke up to someone moaning and groaning. When I looked over, I saw the ghost by the doorway. She had her hands to her stomach like this-" Crystal imitated the ghost by walking and groaning "-and the scariest part was what the ghost said. 'Bathroom, bathroom, I will go to the bathroom and murder anyone who dares enter.' After hearing that, I refused to use the bathroom on the first floor, ever again!"

Again, Teo fell back to the ground, rolling in circles. The story was more comical than it was scary.

"It's not funny!"

"But you see. It is!"

"You really are a jerk!"

Teo stopped laughing again to lay still. He took a few minutes to himself before sitting up and smiling. Now that he had recomposed himself again, he could assess Crystal's story to assure her that ghosts didn't exist. "Don't you think the ghost was one of you girls?"

"Not possible."

"Well, I think it's possible and I think Soria's the culprit."

Crystal shook her head, absolute that the ghost wasn't one of them. "It couldn't be Soria. When I looked over she was still sleeping."

"I'm betting my money on her. She's always talking about poop. If not her, then your eyes were playing tricks on you."

"Why aren't you taking me seriously? There really are ghosts. There are the vengeful ones, kind ones, and lost ones."

Teo stood and shook his head. "There are no ghosts. Period."

"I beg to differ."

"Come on, let's get real. Even if there are, they're all in here." He pointed a finger to his head and grinned while Crystal glanced around again.

There was no sign of a breeze or a single soul inside the maze. It was so creepy, her skin prickled. She wanted to get out ASAP and rejoin the others where she knew it would be noisy. "Watch, one day you'll see, there really are ghosts."

∞

Remi put her hands behind her head while the two walked, trying to find their way out. The sun was high into the sky, indicating it was already noon, and yet they hadn't managed to find a sign of the exit. In fact, they hadn't come across any of the other couples yet. "You think the others made it out?"

Noah shrugged. "I hope not. If we happen to be the last ones out I'm gonna cry my pretty eyes out."

Remi turned to look at him and raised an eyebrow. "Pretty eyes?"

"Yes, pretty eyes. Don't you see these round pretty eyes?" Noah stepped closer for Remi to get a better look at his blue eyes. Indeed, they were pretty with long lashes.

She lowered her arms and laughed, pushing him away. "Okay, okay, I get it."

"I don't want to be the last. I don't want to be the last."

"That won't help. You're not a spell caster."

"I can still wish."

"So," said Remi as they resumed their walk again. "What do you think this mission really is?"

"Well," Noah said, thinking. It was true that this mission was too easy. There had to be more to it than just getting out from within a maze. The deans always had a hidden motive to everything that was assigned. "Maybe it's a test to see if we're compatible as Soulmates."

Remi stopped to cross her arms. What Noah said made no sense. "Why would the deans do that?"

"How would I know? It was just a suggestion."

"It's a ridiculous suggestion." She uncrossed her arms to quietly walk alongside him. Every now and then she'd turn to look at him without a word. His suggestion was weighing heavily on her mind now.

"What?" he asked, catching her looks.

"I won't forget you."

"Huh?"

"If what you say is true, and if the deans say we're not compatible, and decide to separate us, I won't forget you. All the good and bad times, even the misunderstood times, I'll keep them with me forever. I don't...want to forget you."

Noah's eyes widened and eventually his look softened. He didn't want Remi to see how glad he was to hear those words. "That'll never happen. We'll always be together."

50th Lie

.

EVER SINCE SPLITTING from the others, neither Kakinouchi nor May bothered to acknowledge each other. At the rate they were going, they'd never make it out, whether it was together or alone.

After getting her nerves under control, May inhaled and opened her mouth to apologize but nothing came out. Quickly, she shut her mouth, not wanting to look foolish. "Damn," she muttered.

"Did you say something?" Kakinouchi turned to look back.

"No."

Without a word, he turned to face front as May bit her lip. She was doing the exact opposite of what she wanted. *Why did I have to sound so pissed? I'm not even pissed,* she thought, *now he probably really hates me.*

"I think we're walking around in circles." Kakinouchi stopped walking to examine their surroundings. He remembered the clipping he made in the hedge beside him.

"Can't you do better?" As soon as those words left her mouth she felt like falling over and dying. *Forgive me, Mere! I'm a coward!*

"Sorry," apologized Kakinouchi as he led the way down a different path.

"Don't apologize. I don't need it." *I did it again! Damn myself!*

Reaching his breaking point, Kakinouchi stopped walking, as did May. It was so tiring to be the only trying. "You know, I've been doing a lot of thinking."

May crossed her arms, looking at his back, still stubborn. "About?"

"I think we should tell the deans to split us up. I'm sure there are others who don't want to be partnered together. So, we should change Soulmates."

"Eh?" May gasped, her arms falling to her side. She hadn't seen that blow coming.

"Yeah, I think that's the best solution." Kakinouchi nodded at his conclusion. After thinking all last night, this was the best he could come up with. It was better to go their own ways.

"Are you serious?"

"Yeah, I'm serious."

"Well," she said looking away smugly, "since you put it that way, I guess there's no helping it. We'll have to tell the deans then."

The entire time Kakinouchi spoke, his smile never left his face. She had easily agreed without putting up resistance. This was the extent of her dislike towards him. Kakinouchi turned around to bow.

"What are you doing?" she asked, her breath caught.

"Thank you for everything." Kakinouchi stood. His forced smile still plastered on his face. "Goodbye." Turning on his heels, Kakinouchi left while she watched him go.

Mere's words from last night reran in her mind. She had to apologize, or else nothing would change. If the hurt stayed with him forever, she'd never be able to forgive herself.

May reached a hand out to stop Kakinouchi, but he rounded the corner and disappeared. Gasping from the sudden emptiness that appeared in her heart, she sank to her knees and cried. He had easily left her behind without turning back to see how she was coping without him. How could she make things better? What was she supposed to do to get Kakinouchi back? Was this really the end? The only man she wanted to be with, how could she let walk away so easily?

Yeve, who had come across the scene and was eavesdropping came out from hiding. She ran a hand through her hair and watched as May cried. "Geez, what the hell?" she groaned.

There was no need to turn around to see who the owner of the voice was as May sniffled. "Now isn't the time to make fun of me."

"If you have the time to cry, shouldn't you stop him?"

"But he already left."

Yeve crossed her arms and kicked May's head gently from behind. She was tired of hearing excuses, and tired of listening to people cry. It was a headache, always having to play the counselor to the girls' problems.

"Ow," she whimpered.

"So what?"

"I don't have the courage to stop him."

"Sometimes you have to swallow your pride to keep what's most precious."

May sniffled again and finally glanced back. Yeve was grinning the same grin as when they were little. It was this grin that scared May half to death, yet at the same time, made her respect Yeve. "What's most precious?"

"That's right." Yeve knelt and pointed to where Kakinouchi had been. Slowly, May turned to follow her gaze. "Swallow that pride to keep what you desire."

"What I desire..."

"Go."

May wiped her eyes and nodded, determined now. "I'll go apologize."

"Be nice to him now. If you're not, I'll be the one to kick your ass. And I won't be as nice as Shayla was."

May stood and ran off, turning back to smile, brighter than the sun. "Thank you, Yeve! I love you!" she shouted and disappeared to find Kakinouchi.

"Geez, she's just like Mio."

"People either love you or hate you," Rain joked from behind.

Yeve turned to scowl at him, not appreciating his joke. She walked over, gently hitting him on the arm before smiling. "Let's get going."

"You sure know how to give a speech."

"It's just pretty words to make her chase Kakinouchi. There's no special meaning."

"They were pretty words alright," he agreed as they walked away.

"To think those two idiots still haven't gotten out yet, when we had to restart from the beginning, I pity them."

"I'm sure they didn't get out because they didn't want to."

Yeve nodded, knowing that much. It was because Kakinouchi and May didn't know how to communicate. That was why they were constantly bickering and getting into unnecessary trouble when it could easily be avoided.

"Say, would you do the same?"

"Do what?"

"Would you run after me like that if I were to leave?"

"Hell no." Yeve shook her head. "I'd probably see you off with a smile and replace you. After all, I have bigger issues to worry about than you leaving."

"Oye," he said, reaching out to nudge her head harder than usual. Her words had hurt more than he'd like to admit. "So, you won't chase me if I walk out on you? You won't sacrifice your pride to stop me and won't consider me as the most precious thing to you?"

"No." Yeve shook her head truthfully. There were other people who were more precious to her than her own Soulmate.

"You answer too quickly to questions. Think about it a bit more."

"I already said no."

"You," said Rain as he threw her into a headlock and smiled. "If I'm not the most precious to you, then who is, huh? Who is it that you'd give your life for?" Though he asked, he knew the answer.

"Soria and Verse."

"I knew it."

"If you knew, why ask?" She smiled as Rain reached over to cover her eyes. "Hey," Yeve said, alarmed, and tried to pull away but he held on tightly, not allowing her to see his sadness. "What's gotten into you suddenly?"

"Did you know?" whispered Rain as he rested his chin on top of her head. "In your eyes, there's always a face reflecting back."

"Huh? Isn't that your own reflection?" she asked, no longer resisting.

"No. It's not me." Rain shook his head and closed his eyes, afraid that the face would appear before him. "At first, I thought it was Soria and Verse. After getting a good look, it's someone else entirely. That's why, when you said that I wasn't precious, I thought you would say that person's name."

After a moment of silence, Yeve finally spoke, "have you ever thought maybe it's your own vision?"

"Huh?"

"Don't you think it's your own reflection that's being reflected back in my eyes?"

Rain tensed, unable to answer. She was sharp as usual.

"Who is it that *you* keep seeing?"

He quickly let go and turned his back to lead the way. The conversation had become intense and Rain didn't like it. If they started down this road, he wouldn't be able to stop until one of them cried blood. "Come on. I think we're getting close to the exit already."

"Rain!" Yeve called out.

"Sorry, I didn't mean to stir up any trouble. Let's get going. I don't want to be the last couple." He turned back to fake a smile at Yeve who could no longer pry at his desperation to flee.

∞

Dark and Cammie who also made it out sat with the group, talking and joking. They were the sixth couple to exit behind Louis and Hanabi. King who had woken up from his unconscious state was picking yet another fight with Hotaka. An annoyed Jennifer tried to pry him away with Louis' help. Meanwhile, Yuudai plugged his ear, not wanting to hear the two guys and Morgana who was sulking about Aoi again. Midnight however, didn't care about the commotion and was talking to Mere, Nicholas, and Liz.

When Mr. Fujiwara and Ms. Tanaka returned, they were surprised to see Yuudai already at the exit. The group seemed suspicious about why the two teachers were so angry, but they wouldn't spill the beans and headed straight towards the deans to whisper. In the end, the deans laughed and said, "ah, youth." Miss Lima stood silently, pouring Jasmine tea this time and smiled. Already prepared on a tiny table nearby was two small plates of dark chocolate Earl Grey truffles that was to be served with the tea.

When Hanabi noticed Cammie hugging her legs and staring at the three exits, she scooted closer. Cammie was reverting to her old ways from when they were children. "What's up?" Hanabi casually asked.

Cammie glanced over and smiled. "Nothing much."

"Then why are you staring so intently at the maze?"

Shaking her head in response, Cammie turned to look at the exit again, just wanting to be left alone.

Able to sense that, Hanabi scooted away to hit Louis on the back. He coughed and glared at her for hitting him so hard. Laughing, she apologized.

Dark looked over at Cammie and caught Hanabi's gaze. She smiled encouragingly, then went back to talking to the others. Dark stood and walked over to sit beside Cammie who didn't move or even turn to look at him. "What's up?" he asked, making small talk.

Cammie shook her head, not a word came out from her lips.

"Who are you waiting for?"

"Yeve and the others," she answered softly.

Dark smiled and nodded. She had finally spoken, if only a few words. He leaned back to look at the sky, wondering what to say to keep her talking. "Who do you think will come out next?"

Cammie thought about it and laughed. She put a hand to her mouth as Dark watched in bewilderment. It wasn't every day that he got to see her laugh. Even as kids, her smiles were reserved only for the girls.

"Soria?" Dark joked.

Cammie laughed louder and shook her head. She turned, hitting him on the arm, not realizing what she'd done. "Soria would probably turn this mission into a game. She's not coming out next."

Dark couldn't stop smiling. He had made a joke, and she had laughed. In that moment, his breath and heart was stolen again. This was the closest he'd ever felt to her. What would happen if he were to get closer? Wanting to know the answer, Dark plotted his every move slowly. This way, she wouldn't be able to detect it until it was too late to find an escape route. "Then, who?"

"Hmm," Cammie said, smiling to the sky. "Probably Shadow and Hana."

"I agree with you on that one."

"You know, I never knew this, but you're quite a funny guy."

"You just now figured that out?" he joked some more and posed.

Cammie laughed silently. By this time, the five girls were staring at them. It was rare for Cammie to be laughing so much. They glanced at each other and smiled. It was a great change. Cammie needed to make friends, even if that new friend was her Soulmate.

"If you ever want to laugh, come to me." Dark reached out and nudged her head softly. "I'll always find a way."

In that moment, something inside Cammie swayed. She reached out to snag Dark's hand and squeezed it. A fire ignited. Rage. Passion. Hate. Not even she was sure on which one. Her hands began shaking from the confusion, and even tears welled in her eyes. "Stay like this for a while."

"Cammie?" said Dark worriedly.

"Just a little while," she whispered.

Ms. Tanaka adjusted her glasses that sat upon her nose and glanced at the two. Even Gabe and Mr. Fujiwara observed, though they didn't intervene.

∞

After Yeve's speech, May ran after Kakinouchi with all her might to apologize. In the process, she got herself lost and was now spinning in circles, panting. "Kakinouchi-kun!" she shouted desperately into the quiet maze. "I know you're out there! Can you hear me?!"

When silence met her a second time, May sunk to her knees, breathing hard. The tears started at the corner of her eyes and quickly streamed. Not bothering to wipe them, she sniffled and was soon wailing. She had lost him all because she couldn't be honest.

"May?" called out Kakinouchi from behind. He had heard someone crying and came to check it out. "What's wrong?" Swiftly, he ran over to her side and knelt, looking for any wound. "What happened?"

May stared at him, unable to believe her luck. Now she wouldn't be an embarrassment to Yeve.

"Why are you staying quiet? Tell me what happened."

"I—I sprained my ankle," she lied and wiped her tears.

"Why didn't you call sooner?"

"You left me behind."

Kakinouchi opened his mouth to counter but nothing came out. He had no right when he really had left her behind. "Sorry," he apologized.

May smiled and let out another loud sniffle. She reached a hand out to pat his head while he stared back, surprised at her tiny affection. "Th—thanks for finding me."

Kakinouchi lifted her hand off his head. Though he wanted to smile and laugh, he couldn't do so. May's emotions were unpredictable, and he never knew when it'd change. "It was nothing. I was actually just getting out of here," he answered, turning his back to her. "Get on."

"Eh? I'm heavy though."

"Are you doubting my strength?"

The two grinned at each other as May stretched her arms but stopped. "No," she declined.

Kakinouchi turned around, surprised again, then glared. Here it was again, her inconsistent behavior. "An injured person is in no position to object. Just get on my back and stop arguing with me for once."

"No," she repeated and crossed her arms haughtily.

"May, would you-"

"I won't get on the back of some stranger. I'll only let my Soulmate save me and carry me off to safety."

Kakinouchi opened his mouth to shout but stopped. She was refusing to look at him. Slowly, he smiled and shook his head. Not only was she stubborn, she was incredibly cunning. "What do you want from me?"

More tears filled her eyes as she cleared her throat, afraid that her trembling voice would give away her true feelings. "I don't want anything," she said, her voice trembling anyway. "I'm just waiting for Dean Kiera to come find me, along with my Soulmate."

"And who exactly is your Soulmate?"

"W—won't you reprise that title?"

She was being so truthful it left Kakinouchi dumbfounded. What exactly was happening? Did something possess her when he left? Why was she suddenly so gentle towards him?

"There's no such thing as resigning from being a Soulmate. A Soulmate is supposed to remain by your side forever, even until the end of time." May turned to look at him, her expression softening. The tears remained as she bowed her head down low, begging. "That's why, won't you return to my side?"

"Come on. Get on. Let's go," Kakinouchi whispered.

"I know I'm being selfish, but please, return to me."

"Give me your arms."

"You won't-"

"How can I refuse when you're trying so hard to stop me?" he interrupted.

May looked up, tears streaming. She smiled a broken smile and stretched out her arms, wrapping them around his neck as he stood and walked. His back was so warm, she placed her head against it, inhaling his cologne. "I'm sorry," she whispered.

Kakinouchi stopped in his tracks as time froze. A smile played its way across his lips as he started walking again. This time, he looked up to the sky. Suddenly, everything seemed bright and weightless.

May tightened her hold around him, afraid to lose him again. "I never meant to hurt you." Her voice trembled as she continued to finish the rest of her apology. "I just don't know how to act around you. So I end up saying bad things. It's like, you bring the best and worst out of me. Can you forgive me?"

"I forgive you."

May held in her cries and sniffles, though a few escaped. Her shoulders shuddered. Kakinouchi was being wasted on her. He deserved someone better. But because May was selfish, she couldn't let him go, not now, not ever. He belonged to her for as long as she lived. "I'll try to be a good person from now on. I'll also do my best as your Soulmate. So please, don't say things like you'll leave me again. If you do, I'll go Berserk."

Kakinouchi laughed at her exaggeration while she chuckled and wiped her eyes. "I'll see to it that you keep your promise about being good."

$$\infty$$

"Ah!" Mio shouted as the two rounded the corner. She stopped walking to point a finger as Sasuke followed her gaze. Walking twenty feet ahead of them was Naruyuki and Verse who were conversing and approaching the exit also. Just a few more paces and they would get out first.

"We can't let them exit before us," Sasuke said, leading the charge against their enemy. When they were close enough they let out war cries.

"What the-" began Naruyuki as he turned around to find Sasuke tackling him.

Verse too turned to find Mio charging at her like a bull. Pointing a finger, she dared Mio, who didn't seem afraid at her ominous glare. "Mio, don't you-"

The four of them came flying out from within the maze's third exit and landed on the grass as the group stared in bewilderment. More than two-thirds of them had made it out. They glanced at one another and shrugged. Instead of walking over to help, they simply watched.

Sasuke and Mio stood, giving each other a high-five and laughing. "We did it!" they shouted, hugging this time. "After all that we've gone through to get here!"

"Sasuke," hissed Naruyuki.

"I'm gonna kill you, Mio," threatened Verse.

"Yay!" they screamed, ignoring the two.

Finally making his way over, Noah held up a finger, informing them, "Technically speaking, Naruyuki and Verse came out first, so why are you two celebrating?"

"Eh?" gasped Sasuke and Mio. "How so?" they demanded.

"Think about it. If you two had run past them to come out first, you'd be ahead. But you tackled them, which technically means, their backs passed the line before your heads did."

Sasuke and Mio stared at each other, their jaws hanging. Hearing the truth from Noah left them traumatized. They fell over on the grass, writhing and crying. "I never thought of it that way before!" shouted Sasuke. "I'm LAST, AGAIN?!" shouted Mio. They rolled around, clutching their chests like they were taking their last breaths on earth. They crawled towards each other and hugged, still crying. "Such fools we are!"

"Uh," Crystal said, walking over and smiling. "You're not the last ones."

"Eh?" Sasuke and Mio sat up, their tears suddenly ceased. "We're not?"

"Nope," answered the rest from beneath the tree as they shook their heads.

"Then who is?" the two asked suspiciously. They weren't going to fall for any tricks.

Naruyuki dusted himself and glared at Sasuke. Even he could tell who was dead last. "Obviously, can't you tell?"

The couple stared at those who had come out, naming everyone. Soon, their eyes lit up. Kakinouchi and May still hadn't come out. They turned to look at each other and rejoiced once more.

"I'm not last!" shouted Mio.

"Yippee!" celebrated Sasuke.

"I think being around Mio has made Sasuke stupid," insulted Love.

Poe laughed nervously, unable to help but agree. No matter how rude it sounded, it was true. "Somehow, strangely, I agree."

"They're a stupid couple," Verse said.

"Yep," agreed Naruyuki as the two walked over to join the others.

"Wow, after a thousand years," Umeko greeted with a grin.

"Not funny," Naruyuki said, reaching over to throw her into a light headlock. Verse smiled and shook her head at them. It was like returning to their preteen years. Taiki too turned to look but didn't smile. He glanced at the smiling Verse and walked over to her side.

"Aren't you the least bit concerned?" he asked.

Verse turned, giving him a side-glance. "Am I supposed to?"

Taiki stuffed his hands into his pockets and nodded. He hated how he was the only one worrying about how close Naruyuki and Umeko were. Then again, he knew the truth and Verse didn't. "You should be. But seeing you like this makes me feel like I don't trust Umeko enough."

"Do you?"

"I do."

"Then why are you so worried?"

"It's Naruyuki that I don't trust."

Verse raised an eyebrow, confused. "Isn't he your friend? You should trust him too."

"Not when it comes to this."

"To what?"

"If you can't see it for yourself, then forget it," answered Taiki as he shook his head.

"What are you two whispering about?" Naruyuki turned to glance at them, wondering what Taiki was whispering to Verse about. Still in his headlock was Umeko.

"Naruyuki-kun, let me go! Let me go!" Umeko laughed and tried to get free, though she wasn't putting up much of a fight.

"Just discussing the weather," Verse lied and smiled.

Naruyuki scrunched his brows but dropped it. "I see," he said, letting go of Umeko.

"Geez, my hair is all messed up now."

"Sorry," he apologized and reached out to ruffle her hair. "I know how much your hair means to you."

"Damn right," she said as they shared another laugh.

"Do you still trust him now?" asked Taiki.

Verse thought for a minute before giving her response, "he can play around with as many women as he wants. All I care about is that he gets my back during missions."

Smiling, Taiki shook his head. Verse sounded like a faithful wife while he sounded like a jealous husband. This talk was making him look bad. "You sound too cool. I yield."

"So," said Takahiko.

"So what?" answered Sasuke.

"Not you."

"You didn't have to be so rude."

"What took you two so long?"

"Mio got lost," Sasuke answered again.

"You didn't have to tell them!" she screamed and bit him as he laughed. "That tickles!"

"Stupid couple," the group muttered.

Takahiko looked over, eyeing Naruyuki. "Why'd you two take so long?"

Naruyuki could only smile. The reason was quite foolish but he wouldn't lie. "Verse got hungry and made us go back to the abandoned picnic to grab the bentos that Love had packed."

"Ah!" Love shouted, finally remembering what she had forgotten after coming out from the maze: her bentos. "It slipped my mind!"

"Don't worry. Verse ate it all. Not a single crumb was left behind."

"Eh?!" shouted everyone.

Verse glared at Naruyuki and sat down. "Hey, don't make me sound like a pig."

"You are," he joked and laughed.

"I told you she was my little piggy," Soria joked as the girls fought.

"Wait," Shayla snapped and turned to glare at Verse. "What bentos that Love packed? When did this happen? And where's my share?"

"Ah, I ate your share for you because I was afraid that Yeve might beat you again for eating too much," she explained, halting her fight with Soria.

"Aw, you're too kind!" The two hugged it out while the others stared. Shayla was too simpleminded, and Verse was too cunning. They were surprised Verse hadn't devoured Shayla by now.

Remi stood, glaring at Verse. "Wait a minute here," she said. "You guys-"

"-had a picnic without us?!" interrupted King.

Rain simply shrugged, seeing nothing to get upset about. "What does it matter?"

"You guys left us out! That's what!"

"Oh, don't cry, we'll hold another picnic," said Dark.

Shadow turned towards Teo, eyebrows raised. "Were you there too?"

Sheepishly, Teo laughed it off. "Tee-hee, I got caught, did I?"

"You guys really did such a thing?"

Teo smiled proudly and nodded. Taking that rest near the fountain was the best thing he'd done all day. "Yep," Teo answered.

"Then, next time, let's hold a picnic with everyone."

"Okay, deal."

While listening, Jennifer trembled in envy and jumped to her feet, pointing a finger at them. They had taken a leisurely rest and gotten to eat Love's bentos while King had been working her to death. There was no justice in that. Not to mention, King and Liz were having an affair of some sort behind her back. "Not fair, not fair, not fair! Who was part of it?!"

All those who went held up their hands as Jennifer groaned, more frustrated than before. At least half of them had been present at the maze picnic. "Even you Morgana, and you happened to come out in fourth place?!"

"Ehe," Morgana laughed sheepishly. "Technically speaking, Yuudai was the one to lead us out, not me."

"It doesn't matter!"

"If I had known, I'd have wanted to join too. It was probably a lot of fun," stated Midnight.

"I bet," agreed Mere.

Hotaka turned to look at her when he heard and glared at the group. He stood, following Jennifer's lead by pointing and shouting, "How dare you guys hold a picnic without us?! We wanted to join too!"

"Why are you mad?" asked the group. "You weren't even mad a while ago."

"Well, I am now—no, in fact, I'm super furious at you guys!"

"You are one sad little guy," Rain insulted. "Why do you keep having mood swings for?"

"Ah, youth," said the two deans as they chuckled.

"Fools," Liz said, sitting beside Yeve, arm linked with King.

To hide her jealousy, Jennifer smiled, though her aura grew more sinister with each passing second.

"Would you let me go already?" King growled, feeling Jennifer's wrath.

"Don't wanna," Liz answered.

"Ah," said Kakinouchi as he exited the maze and stopped. "Yo," he greeted and smiled.

Waving in greeting, May smiled also. When she realized how many of them there was, she began counting heads. Slowly, her smile faded, the stone-cold truth slapping her. "Wait a minute here."

Catching on, even Kakinouchi seemed astonished. "Eh? Are we perhaps the last couple?"

"That can't be!" shouted May. She jumped down from Kakinouchi's back and ran over to point a finger at Mio. Of all people, she had lost to Mio the idiot. It was unthinkable. "Mio made it out before me?!"

Mio grinned and did a peace sign. "He-he, I ain't the loser no more."

"How did that happen?!"

"Don't take it to heart," said Hana.

Seeing her so energetic, Kakinouchi walked over, pointing a finger at her feet. "May," he said.

Turning towards him, she clung to his arm. At the start of the mission, she'd assumed that they'd be the second last couple. But to come out dead last, the thought never crossed her mind. "Kakinouchi-kun, why are you so calm?! Erupt! Do something! Say something!"

"I do have one thing to say. Your ankle is fine."

Abruptly, May stopped shouting and let go of his arm. Her supposedly sprained ankle had miraculously healed, and she could now stand perfectly on two feet.

"Huh?" said everyone in confusion.

Playing it off until the end, May suddenly fell over, holding her ankle. "Ow, oh my gosh, it hurts like hell! I think I'm gonna die!" She stole a glance at Kakinouchi who crossed his arms, not buying her act. Gulping, she stood, attempting to run, but not before Kakinouchi caught her shirt.

"You lied about twisting your ankle?"

"Why are you mad about that?! That's nothing! Get mad about us being last! *Dead last!*"

Exchanging glances, Azuma and Shayla shared a laugh. Kakinouchi and May had made-up somehow and they had a hunch about who was behind it. There really was nothing to worry about after all.

"Yoo-hoo, uh-huh, yeah, chicka-boom-boom," sang Sasuke and Mio as they clapped their hands and shook their butts.

Soria scowled and shook her head. "What a disgusting dance."

"Yoo-hoo, uh-huh, yeah, chicka-boom-boom," Aoi sang and shook his butt too. When he noticed Soria glaring, he stopped to sit back down, smiling innocently.

"Disgrace."

Sitting beside her, Nicholas smiled and laughed. "You actually want to dance too, don't you?"

"How did you know?" Soria gasped.

"You're too easy to read."

While the kids were busy arguing and joking, running about, chasing each other, the two deans were taking a stand from their chairs. It was time to return to the mansion.

"Now then, let's go announce the results," said Dean Kosa.

51st Lie

AGAIN, THEY WERE SEATED inside the theater hall, awaiting the deans. While the others complained about being back, Rain glanced about, his suspicions returning. The entire staff was present, as well as Nicholas, Liz, and Mere who had been called to attend the ceremony. This was too extreme for accomplishing a measly maze mission.

Once Dean Kosa and Dean Kiera appeared, the chattering amongst them stopped. He fixed his suit jacket, awfully well-dressed for an assembly, and walked over to stand before the microphone. Even Dean Kiera and the others wore extravagant attire. "Your mission today wasn't just to determine how well you cooperated and communicated with your Soulmate," announced Dean Kosa. "It was also to decide on your positions."

"Positions?" repeated the group.

"Correct. Your first three missions were supposed to decide your rankings. We wanted to see your trust in one another, but because of unforeseen circumstances, your third missions were assigned hastily. However, it did give us great insight into your relationship as Soulmates. And so, these are the results of your ranking."

"Wait, you ranked us according to how we came out?" asked Sasuke in disbelief.

Dean Kosa chuckled and nodded. "That seems to be the case."

"Isn't that unfair? If we'd known, we'd have taken it seriously."

"Were you not?"

"Eh? Well-" began Sasuke as he averted his gaze. He couldn't confess that he'd been serious, but still came out second last. His results wouldn't differ even if he tried a tad-bit harder.

"We will now call you upon your ranks. Once you hear your names, come onstage and stand in that order."

"That means…" May gasped. "I'm last!"

Mio who sat not far away gasped also and cried. This was the best day of her life. She could relive this moment forever. "Finally, I'm not ranked last amongst us girls."

"Congrats." Hana smiled and soothed Mio who cried on her shoulder.

"Damn it. If I knew, I would've ran my ass off in that maze," said May. She held up her trembling fists, tears streaming down her face too. So, this was how the deans wanted to test them, by giving out useless missions that played a bigger role. And she'd failed it.

"Does ranking really matter that much?" asked Poe.

"Yes," snapped King.

"You know," Yuudai said, glancing over at Louis. "I've been meaning to ask, was Hanabi the one behind your success at coming out?"

"So what if she was?"

Snorting at how good his guess was, Yuudai sneered. "Loser."

"We will start from the last spot," Dean Kiera said, ignoring that the kids were having their own side conversations.

"No, no, no," cried May.

Kakinouchi turned to look at Azuma and glared. "Azuma," he hissed.

Grinning, he let out a cackled laugh. It felt amazing not being last but felt better besting his rival once and for all. "I always knew you were the weaker one of us."

"I'm gonna dethrone your ass."

"I'm looking forward to it."

"Kakinouchi and May, in last," announced Dean Kiera as the two stood and sulked onstage. Next in line came Sasuke and Mio, Naruyuki and Verse, Teo and Crystal, Azuma and Shayla, Noah and Remi, Aoi and Soria, Rain and Yeve, Takahiko and Love, Poe and Alice, Shadow and Hana, Dark and Cammie, Louis and Hanabi, Yuudai and Morgana, Taiki and Umeko, King and Jennifer, and in first place, Hotaka and Midnight.

Once they were standing on stage, the two deans smiled.

"Well, this sucks, if I knew we were getting ranked, I would've tried harder," said Takahiko.

Yeve nodded. "Yeah, tell me about it."

"Would you really have tried?" Love asked, her eyebrow raised in doubt. She knew Yeve was a liar when it came to taking missions seriously, unless her life was on the line.

"Fat chance," Yeve snorted, shaking her head this time. "Being number one as a couple isn't my goal." She grinned. "It's to-"

"-take over the world. We know," Love interrupted and rolled her eyes. If only she could receive a golden coin for every time she heard that tiring line.

"Did you just roll your eyes at me?"

"What? No. Of course not. Why would I ever? I highly revere you, Your Highness." Love hastily curtsied to appease her, not wanting to become a lowly chess piece.

"I thought so."

Rain who stood between the girls scowled and flexed his muscles. "These results don't prove anything."

"Are you sure? You seem super pissed to me," Aoi said, glancing over.

"No," he snapped.

"Liar."

"You know if you'd been a bit serious, you could've ranked in the top five and kicked Louis off," Dark directed as Shadow smiled and shook his head. He had no intentions of ranking in the top five—or ten. If he'd known, he would've fallen further behind.

"Nah, I'm good."

"Oye I'm standing right here, I can hear you loud and clear," hissed Louis.

"My bad, I forgot you had ears," Dark responded as the two got into an unnecessary tussle.

"Stop, stop," commanded Shadow as he tried to break them apart.

"Kids," Dean Kiera said in her sweetest tone as the fighting ceased immediately. Her aura was turning black as they tested her again. Once they quieted down, her black aura disappeared. "And to celebrate your promotion to 'Angels' we're throwing you a Golden party."

"Angels?" they repeated, "Golden party?"

"No wonder the dean rejected my proposal to join the summer festival," Shayla grumbled. "She already had this party planned out."

"You were but inexperienced children when you ventured out into the real world. Now that you've proven to us, your superiors, that you've matured, you become 'Angels' to protect our God."

"Well, let's not waste time and begin the Golden party!" Dean Kosa shouted excitedly. He wanted the kids to see his decorations.

"Dean," Soria said, yawning. She was uninterested in the entire ordeal. "I don't really care about being an Angel or the party. I just want to sleep. I'm tired from all the missions."

"Soria-chan," Dean Kiera said sweetly. Her aura was turning black again, though Soria ignored it. "No one's getting out of this Golden party.

Everyone's going to attend. The tailors have even custom-made you ladies an evening gown."

"You sure have a lot of free time on your hands to waste, dean."

Dean Kiera twitched, angry that Soria wasn't scared by her black aura she was releasing. "Ah," she said with a snap to her fingers. "Yeve, submit to me a 200-page essay on what you find attractive about your Soulmate by tomorrow morning, as Soria's punishment."

Rain raised an eyebrow and glanced over at Yeve, whose eyes widened in horror. He wanted to know what she would write in that report.

Without warning, Yeve pushed Aoi aside, forcefully grabbing Soria, who was yawning by the collars. "You stupid poop-turtle, you're going, and you're wearing the damn dress, got it?"

"Okay," Soria said with a nod.

Dean Kiera smiled victoriously, her eyes gleamed from having Yeve take her bait. All she wanted to do now was stand on a hilltop and laugh at the top of her lungs. "Then, off you ladies go! Tanaka-sensei, if you would please!"

"Yes, dean," she responded and bowed. "Girls," she instructed as they each came down from the stage to follow her. Meanwhile, Mr. Fujiwara was instructed to take the guys with him. Once the girls reached Ms. Tanaka's side, she wasted no time in grabbing Soria's collar to drag away.

"Eh? Wait a minute. Sensei, why am I the only one getting dragged?!"

"If I take my eyes off you for one second, you'll run off to who-knows-where. And I'm in no mood to chase you."

"You're just being biased now, sensei!"

"I wonder why they're holding a Golden party for. It's only summer," said Umeko.

"Beats me," answered Jennifer as she shook her head.

"It's kind of suspicious though, isn't it?"

"It sure is," agreed Midnight.

∞

King sat on the sofa, adjusting his black bow tie. It was irritating his neck as the rest of the guys lounged around, already dressed in their suits for the night. A few had on ties while others had bow ties. Some even wore vests with no overcoat. They were all well-groomed to attend a ball for royalty. "Sensei," King said, glancing out the window where it was snowing.

"What is it?" answered Gabe.

"Why is there a Golden party being held in summer for? And why is it suddenly snowing outside?"

Gabe smiled and fixed Hotaka's tie. "You're good to go."

"Thank you, sensei." Hotaka stepped down to join the others who were already dressed.

"Sensei," said King again. He was being ignored all because of Hotaka.

"I'll answer that question," said Mr. Fujiwara as he entered the room with a well-groomed Nicholas and Mere.

"Wow," Sasuke said with a whistle. "You two are looking good."

Mere smiled and slightly bowed. "Thank you."

"You guys look..." Nicholas began and scanned the room full of guys. He sneered but quickly replaced it with an innocent smile. "...decent," he finished off.

"Is he picking a fight?" snarled Noah.

"He most definitely is," Aoi said, popping his knuckles.

"So?" King urged, ignoring the others to fixate on Mr. Fujiwara.

"You boys won't be spending the upcoming holidays together. That's why this party was arranged."

Unaffected, Nicholas took a seat nearby and crossed his legs. Meanwhile, Mere stood, looking a little unrest from the direction the conversation was taking. The rest of the guys were stunned beyond words. They could only stare at Mr. Fujiwara and Gabe without blinking.

"Now that you've been promoted to Angels, your missions will become more difficult," continued Mr. Fujiwara. "Ranks one through five will be leaving tomorrow morning to see to international affairs with Nicholas and Liz, while the rest of you will remain in Asia."

"Let me guess, our next mission has already been decided," said Teo.

"That's correct," Gabe answered, not sugarcoating anything.

∞

Mio sat silently on her chair, staring at her hands. Her nails had been polished especially for the party. Her hair had been elegantly curled and tied with hair accessories. Ms. Tanaka had just exited after explaining that they'd be separated for a very long time. No one knew when they would reunite again. It could be weeks, months, or maybe even years. Tonight, was the last time they'd get to spend as a unity.

As merry as she could, Mio stood from her chair and smiled. "Come on girls. Let's make lots of memories tonight. Even if we get separated again, we'll always be okay, because we have each other in our hearts."

Hana wiped her nose with a tissue. She nodded and forced a smile, trying not to cry too. "Yeah," she agreed. "Let's joyously celebrate."

"Hana," said Crystal.

"Wh—what is it?"

"You're already crying and the night hasn't even begun."

Indeed, Hana's tears were streaming, ruining her foundation. "What are you saying Crystal? You're crying too."

"No I'm not." Crystal had her back turned to them and was crying silently, her nose running as she wiped it with a tissue.

Yeve stared at the girls and stood in her orange evening gown. Her hair was pinned extravagantly as the jewelry chosen by the staff glittered like the sun. They'd done a good job in making her appear like an empress. Turning towards the top five ranking girls, Yeve smiled, proud that they'd be attending to international affairs. If it was them, she had nothing to worry about. "Jennifer, you're the oldest out of the five, take care of them."

Jennifer turned to look at Yeve and grinned. She nodded and dabbed at the corners of her eyes with a tissue, not wanting to smear her makeup. "I know that without you saying it."

"It's a good thing that it's you five who are going. If it was Mio, who knows what will happen," she joked as the girls laughed, except Mio.

"I'm very strong, FYI," she defended. "I'm no longer in last place."

Yeve laughed and patted Mio's head in comfort while May snarled from where she sat. This would be her last instructions to ranks one thru five, until they met again. "Be careful and remember to return in one piece. We'll be here waiting, no matter how long it takes." Yeve walked out as the door opened and closed behind her.

"She's so mean to me, yet she's always there to save me. It makes me…" Mio burst into tears as the girls turned to look at her. "Waa, I don't want to separate again!"

Wiping her eyes, Hanabi walked over to hand Mio a tissue before hugging her.

"Don't you dare cry too, Hanabi," warned Love.

"Why? Are you going to cry too?"

"Of course not!" answered Love. She turned away and quickly wiped her eyes, smearing her liner. "Shit."

"This room has become so…emo," Soria complained with a groan. "Emos, I hate emos the most. Ugh, emos."

"Why are you being so rude? Are you constipated or what?" asked Verse.

"Don't kill the mood you two," snarled Midnight.

"Emo," concluded the two in unison.

"You two," said Shayla as she stood up to shoo them. "Out."

"Hey, wait," objected Soria as the door opened. "I'm not done talking. I need to bid them farewell."

"You can bid them farewell tomorrow morning when they leave."

"I can't, I'll be too busy sleeping."

"Soria, you stupid poop-head, be nice and wake up to send us off!" Morgana shouted after her before the door completely closed.

Verse stared at the closed door, then to Soria. Shayla had locked them out, preventing them from entering. "Look at what you did. I got kicked out along with you."

"Yeah, sure it's my fault." Soria scratched her head as they headed towards the ballroom.

"I hate emos too," Verse said, walking alongside her.

Meanwhile, inside the room, the girls were talking, crying, and laughing about the future and past.

"We should get going," reminded Cammie.

"Yeah," agreed Morgana. "Before the teachers come for us."

They all stood, touched up their makeup, then left the room. When they entered the ballroom, the guys were already there waiting. The three who were always together stood near the concession table, eating. Nicholas and Liz were also chatting with them while Aoi cursed and glared from his end. The first song of the night came on as no one bothered to dance.

Louis held a cup of punch in his hand and looked around. The girls were off to one side and the guys on the other. It felt like their pre-teen years had returned, when they used to be awkward and cautious around each other. But it was different now. They were comrades and needed to occupy the empty dance floor. For their last night together, they needed to celebrate their promotion to Angels. "What a boring party," complained Louis.

"Then make it lively," suggested Noah.

"I think I will."

"Then go."

"I am." Louis walked over to the stage and tapped on the microphone. He cleared his throat into it as everyone turned to look.

"What's he doing now?" King asked suspiciously.

"Don't know," Rain answered in his tailcoat tuxedo and slicked back hair. "But I don't like it."

"Excuse me, everyone," Louis spoke into the microphone. They were all staring, waiting for him to continue. "Mio-chan, Remi-chan, and Hana-chan...I love you!"

"Soulmate-san, get that idiot down!" demanded the guys as Hanabi strode over to drag Louis offstage by the ear.

"No matter where I am, I'll always come back to you!" Louis shouted, blowing kisses at the girls who stared in disbelief. "So, don't let your hearts stray from me because my heart will always be where you are!"

"I feel sorry for poor Hanabi," said Umeko.

"I love you!" Louis shouted again as Hanabi pinched his ear harder. "Ow!"

"How the hell was that supposed to liven up the party?" asked Noah. He shook his head in disappointment, knowing better than to rely on Louis. If he wanted something done, he had to do it himself. Noah strode over to the microphone and stopped.

"Not you too!" complained Dark.

"I'm not gonna say or do anything stupid!" he shouted in defense as everyone laughed. After recomposing himself, he cleared his throat and spoke again, "Anyway, let's play a game to liven up this party, shall we?" he suggested. "I'm going to have Teo turn the lights off manually. Within a minute, you scramble across the room and grab the person you wish to dance with."

"What kind of icebreaker game is this?" asked Kakinouchi.

"Alright then, game begins when the lights go off." Noah smiled and motioned for Teo to walk across the room to where the light switch was.

Once there, Teo put a finger on the OFF button and turned to look at the group. No one looked willing to participate. He couldn't help but smile wryly.

"One," counted Noah. "Two. Three!" he shouted as Teo switched the lights off.

"Nee-chan!" shouted Mere as he ran towards Midnight. If no one was willing to start the dance segment of the party, then he would do it.

At the thought of Mere, clinging to Midnight, Hotaka twitched. He wouldn't lose to Mere in a battle if it meant dancing with Midnight. "I'm participating."

King stopped drinking his punch, surprised at Hotaka's determination. "Eh? You are?"

"I won't lose." Hotaka sprinted off at random as King set his drink down.

"Oh, I see! This is a battle of speed in the dark! How genius, Noah! In that case, I'm participating too!"

"That's not what this is!" Noah responded.

The only sounds in the dark belonged to Hotaka, King, and Mere, running to the other side where the girls stood silently.

From the stage, Teo could hear Noah sighing into the microphone. His idea had failed. At this rate, this would be the most depressing Golden party in history. After thinking, Teo grinned evilly. He knew exactly what trick to use to force the girls to participate. He inhaled deeply and shouted at the top of his lungs, "IT'S A GHOOOOST!"

"Ah!" screamed Mio.

"Where, where?!" demanded Crystal.

"IT'S ON YOUR SIDE, GIRLS!"

"Ah!" the rest screamed as chaos ensued. They took off running towards the guys' side, trying to escape the ghost that only Teo could miraculously see.

"Whoa, oye, calm down!" shouted Poe.

"Ouch!" yelped Aoi.

"Save me!" pleaded Remi.

"Don't let it catch me! Don't let it catch me!" shrieked Love.

"He-he," Teo laughed evilly. From out of the blue, someone collided into him and screamed. "Ow!" shouted Teo as they fell.

"What the hell is going on?!" shouted Sasuke.

"Ah!" Mio screamed again. "The ghost's a pervert! It touched my chest, it touched my chest!"

"Y—you damn ghost, I won't let you get the best of me this time!" shouted Shayla. "I—I'm not the same chubby cowardly kid with the grape-like haircut, who loves sweets and junk food and meat, that you remember from the past!" At that precise moment, something touched Shayla's forearm as she let out a piercing scream. "Kyaa!"

"I think everyone's lost it," said Midnight calmly. Suddenly, something yanked her dress as she screamed and threw a punch.

Hana who could see perfectly well in the dark smiled nervously as Shadow calmly made his way over to her side. His eyepatch had been taken off, allowing him to see. Though he didn't want to use his eye for something trivial like this, it was inevitable. "Everyone's really panicking," said Hana.

"It's really amusing," said Shadow.

"Teo, open the lights!" demanded Takahiko.

"Yeah, okay, give me a minute!"

"Now!" shouted everyone.

"Geez," Dark said, walking towards Teo who was trying to sit up on the floor. The person who collided into him wouldn't get off. Once the lights were back on, everyone blinked and let their eyes adjust. On the floor, everyone was entangled.

"Whoa," said Aoi as he turned to look at Morgana who was squeezing his hand.

"A—Aoi-kun!" Morgana gasped, not realizing that he was the one she ran into. It was a coincidence—no— "This is our fate," she said, dreamily clasping her hands together. Petals fell as the universe spun around them. Even birds appeared and chirped a lovely tune, as naked cupids flew by, giggling. "For us to always meet like this, what more could it mean, other than to tell us that we were destined for one another?"

"Huh?"

Flabbergasted, Yuudai sat nearby with his mouth hanging open. "How the flipping hell did that happen?"

"Who knows?" answered Remi. The two turned to look at each other and backed away immediately. This was the most awkward pairing. "Whoa," they said.

"What the hell is this?" asked Yeve. She grabbed the orange cat off her lap as Liz meowed, trying to lick her face. Not interested, Yeve tossed her aside without hesitating. "Don't even think it. I'll never let a cat steal my first kiss."

Liz meowed again and trotted over to rub her head against Yeve's forearm, not caring that she'd been treated so cruelly.

"That's called stalking alright," concluded Rain as he knelt beside her.

"She's just being overfriendly."

"Who are you trying to kid?"

"Myself," Yeve answered, burying her face in her hands. "So please don't take away the only sanity I have left."

Rain laughed and helped her to stand. "Sorry Cat-chan, but I'm going to dance with her."

Liz glared and hissed, not hiding her dislike towards him.

"Midnight," said Jennifer as she loomed over King's unconscious body.

"I—I'm sorry Jennifer. I didn't know it was him. I seriously thought it was the ghost," apologized Midnight as she bowed over and over. Though she tried to stay strong, the fear of the ghost ultimately won. Damn that Verse for scaring her ages ago. Now, she'd have to sleep with a nightlight on again.

"I thought you didn't believe in ghosts?"

"I—I don't!"

Standing aside, Hotaka and Mere laughed at King for having grabbed the wrong girl and paying the price. It was the highlight of their day.

"Forget it, he's unconscious." Jennifer scratched her head and sighed. There was no other choice but to bail. "Guess I'll take him back to his room."

"What about the party?"

"You guys enjoy it." Bending, Jennifer grabbed King by the collar, not bothering to carry him or call the teachers for help. She simply dragged him like a sack of potatoes, ready to be sold at the market. "Goodnight and enjoy!" She waved to the others and left with King.

During the chaos, May had been the one to ram into Teo while fleeing. Disappointed that her partner wasn't Kakinouchi, she scowled. "So, are we supposed to dance with the one we caught hold of?"

"I guess," Teo answered, wanting his partner to be anyone other than May also. The look on her face made him want to slap it off. No wonder Shayla had gotten angry and lost it.

"Yeah, I guess too."

"Yeah, I guess so."

"They're all depressed about their dance partners," spoke Hana. She put a hand to her mouth and giggled. This game had truly been amusing.

"They have no one to blame but themselves," Shadow said, putting his eyepatch back on. "Besides, who believes in ghosts anyway?"

"Can you really blame us? Back then, we were still young and naive."

Shadow glanced over and smiled. "Let me guess, you were one of those who believed?"

With an embarrassed laugh, Hana nodded. As a child, she'd been too naïve. It was a wonder why the Fashion Posse never bullied her either. "Verse's ghost stories were notorious and super scary."

Chuckling, he held out a hand, no longer wanting to talk about ghosts. Unlike the other guys, he would ask the one he wanted to dance with, to dance. "May I?"

Hana blushed, taking his hand to step out onto the dance floor first.

"Look at those two," Louis said, spiteful that Shadow was the only one enjoying a lovey-dovey relationship. He also wanted to cuddle with a girl and have her fawn over him. But Hanabi hated skin contact unless she was the one instigating it.

"So, are we gonna dance or what?" Dark asked, scratching his head.

"What's with the attitude?" snapped Verse.

"I wasn't giving you attitude. I was just saying."

"And I'm just saying too."

The two shared a glare before turning away. "This isn't gonna work out. I can just tell."

"I second."

Shayla stood and brushed her purple dress. She turned towards her partner and reached a hand out with a warm smile. "Let's join Shadow-kun and Hana too, Kakinouchi-kun."

Smiling, Kakinouchi nodded. It almost made him jealous how Azuma had such a compassionate Soulmate. He took her hand to stand as they approached the dance floor just as the next song was beginning. "I can see why Azuma is so head over heels for you."

Shayla laughed and blushed at his compliment. "I see that you're also a womanizer," she teased as they danced to the music.

"I'm not though," he denied as they shared a laugh.

What were the odds that Azuma's rival was dancing with his Soulmate? Did it mean that he and Kakinouchi were interconnected no matter what? With a shaky fist, Azuma watched them dance and laugh with tears in his eyes. It made him want to go on a rampage that Kakinouchi had beaten him to dancing with Shayla first.

"Shall we?" Alice interrupted.

Turning, Azuma smiled. He'd worry later about his questions and concerns. For now, he had a dance to get to. "Yeah, let's," he said, taking the lead out to the dance floor.

"How did Alice wind up with Azuma?" asked Poe in disbelief.

"I don't know. But let's dance." Mio took hold of Poe's hand to drag out to the floor. She wasn't about to lose the opportunity to mingle with the other guys, especially Rain.

"We all got mixed up," said Sasuke.

"We sure did," Yuudai agreed from nearby.

"Shall we dance?" Morgana asked shyly. She held out a hand and blushed, never wanting this night to end. This would be her first dance with Aoi. Hopefully, it wouldn't be the last.

"Uh well," said Aoi as he turned to glance at Soria who yawned. When she caught his gaze, she smiled and gave him thumbs-up for encouragement. Smiling in return, Aoi watched as Nicholas who hadn't left her side all night took her hand to drag onto the dance floor. Surprised, she tripped, but Nicholas didn't seem to care as Aoi groaned.

"What's wrong, Aoi-kun?"

"It's nothing. Let's go," Aoi said, leading Morgana out to join the others. Soria was his Soulmate. He'd have plenty of other chances to dance with her.

"Shall we?" asked Mere as he held out his hand to Midnight.

"Oye," Hotaka said, slapping his hand away. "Isn't there someone else you'd prefer to dance with?"

"Wh—what are you talking about?" Mere stammered, trying not to let Hotaka's teasing get to him.

"How about you go take May from Teo?"

"There's no one else for me other than nee-chan."

Mere couldn't hide his emotions whatsoever. Midnight prayed he never had to play a bluffing game where his life was on the line. Smiling, she urged him, "This is the only time I'm allowing you to dance with a girl. So, take the opportunity and go ask May. Once the song is over, I'm taking you back."

"But I want to dance with you."

"We can dance anytime."

"But you'll be leaving soon."

"So will May." Midnight reached over to poke his forehead, tears in their eyes. Neither of them liked the idea of her traveling overseas while he stayed behind. "I'll come back and have my dance with you. Don't worry."

Mere nodded. He knew Midnight was strong and could take care of herself. It was the idea of having to part again that really tore him inside. If he could, he would want her to stay forever.

"I promise to return." She hugged him and kissed his head, then gently pushed him. "Now, go."

"Okay." Mere turned and ran off to intrude on Teo's dance with May.

"He's growing up so fast before my eyes."

"Now that I've gotten rid of the runt, shall we dance?" Hotaka beamed and held out his hand.

"Do we have to? I'm not really in the mood."

"Too bad," said Hotaka as he dragged her out onto the dance floor.

"Geez," she said laughing and shaking her head. "You just never listen, do you?"

"What can I say? I do what I want." Hotaka smiled and twirled Midnight in a circle before placing his hands on her hips. "Remember our first dance?"

Midnight groaned. If she could, she wanted to permanently delete it from her memories too. "It was a disaster."

"It wasn't a disaster. You just weren't cooperating with me then. That's why tonight, I'm requesting for you to trust me."

Laughing, Midnight nodded. Since this was their last night with the others, she would be obedient and give in.

∞

The black sparrow flew into the room and landed on its perch. Hooked to its leg was a note as Miss Lima who was the only one inside walked over to take it. She skimmed the contents and whistled for the sparrow to leave as it flapped its wings to fly out the open window. Miss Lima folded up the note and left the room to find the two deans sitting in the game room, playing chess while the kids made a ruckus in the next room. Instead of intervening they seemed to be enjoying it.

"Dean," called out Miss Lima as she bowed at the two.

"What is it?" answered Dean Kiera.

"Word from the other three. They've finished their mission and are returning to the Dome."

Dean Kosa smiled and moved his bishop diagonally by three spaces, claiming Dean Kiera's queen. "I knew they wouldn't have any complications."

"Me too." Dean Kiera smiled and moved her rook five spaces up. "Checkmate."

"What? Now hold on there. I wasn't looking when you moved. You could've cheated," he accused.

"You know I don't cheat." Dean Kiera chuckled and leaned back into her chair, watching Dean Kosa fret. Without him around, she'd have no one to tease. "So then, what are we going to do about those three? I must say, they've proven their worth without a Soulmate."

Instead of replying, Dean Kosa was still inspecting the board, wondering how he lost when Dean Kiera clearly lost her queen. Had he somehow fallen into her trap like usual?

"Do you think we need to request for an overseas transfer?"

With that, Dean Kosa glanced over and smiled. "You read my mind."

Jennifer brought King to his room and even put him to bed, fixing the blanket over him. "I can't believe you grabbed Midnight and was knocked out senseless." She laughed and shook her head.

Outside, the snow continued descending, fitting in perfectly with the theme of the Golden party. Jennifer walked over to the window and pushed it open. The cool wind blew in as the flakes melted against her face. She wanted to throw on a jacket, a woolen hat, mittens, and a scarf to play in the snow with everyone. After they were done throwing snowballs at each other, they could create snowmen and drink hot cocoa. Only then would they really be celebrating the season.

"The snow's really beautiful, don't you think so?" Jennifer turned to look at him, but he was soundly asleep.

Shutting the window, she made her way back to his bedside and took a seat. Jennifer reached out to brush his hair, admiring his features. "Forgive me for giving my first kiss away to Jin. It was never my intention to kiss anyone but you. So, don't you dare go cheating on me with that cat." She smiled and placed a kiss on his forehead before leaving.

After a while, King opened his eyes. His cheeks were a flushed color. He hadn't been expecting such a sudden kiss or confession. Though it wasn't on the lips, the forehead made him just as nervous. Turning towards the window, King watched the snow glide silently past the window. He wasn't sure if it was the theme of the holiday or not, but he felt like falling in love. "As if I'd choose a cat over you, fool."

52nd Lie

WHEN THE SONG ENDED, everyone switched partners for the next dance, then took a break to grab some snacks and drinks. Now that the awkwardness had settled down, Umeko slipped out of the ballroom and out into the snowy night. She huffed as a puff of white air rose into the night. "I keep forgetting this sky isn't real."

"But it feels real," Naruyuki spoke from behind as Umeko whisked around to find him smiling at her. He too had slipped out of the ballroom to get some air. His long white hair that was usually pulled into a ponytail had been let loose. It swirled all around as Umeko held her breath. He looked so divine and beautiful, she found herself tearing up at the sight of him. "Come," he said, grabbing her silky gloved hand to lead towards the back courtyard.

Smiling, Umeko followed.

Once they reached the back, they sat in silence and watched the snow.

"Nervous?" Naruyuki asked after a few minutes.

Umeko stared at him for some time before nodding. "Very," she responded. This was her first time to leave Asia. She wasn't sure on what to expect. Would the outside world welcome her, or shun her? She was scared, never having been this far away from the girls before. If she became homesick and failed her missions, she'd be a disappointment to them. After all, she'd be working with other Life-Kills from other Domes, another first.

Naruyuki squeezed her hand that he hadn't let go of. It made Umeko blush as she squirmed. Something as simple as holding hands could make her heart beat this fast. "Let me engrave your touch in my memory."

"What a romantic you are," she whispered and smiled.

"I wonder whose fault it is." He chuckled. Even without her saying a word, he could feel her insecurities. "No matter how far you are from us, remember that everyone's got your back. There's nothing to fear. You'll do just fine, Umeko-san."

Her tears trickled as she placed her forehead against his arm. "Naruyuki-kun," whispered Umeko. The sound of his voice resonating through her ears was soothing. Only him did she not want to part from. "Can you say my name again? This time, without any honorifics."

"Why are you crying?" he asked, worried that he somehow upset her. "I'm sorry if I hurt you."

"You did nothing." Umeko shook her head and chuckled. His sincerity only added to the ever-growing list of reasons why she loved him.

Love. Was that really true? Was this feeling love?

"What's on your mind?" Naruyuki asked, breaking into her thoughts.

"I'm just really happy I got to meet you," she answered, not wanting to confess the entire truth until she confirmed this feeling. "I wanted to talk to you at least once before leaving."

Naruyuki nudged her head and laughed. "What are you talking about? Even if we don't get to talk before you leave, once you return, we can always talk then."

Umeko nodded in agreement. "Yeah, you're right." There was nothing to worry about. Once she returned, she'd force him to stay up all night talking about nonsense. Instantly, her smile faded when she recalled Alice's words. Naruyuki was Verse's Soulmate. It was better to let him go than hang on and hurt everyone involved. Umeko had even agreed to let go too. But how could she when he robbed her of her thoughts? This feeling, she wanted to nurture it and see what it brought her, whether it be pain or joy.

"What's wrong?" he asked, sensing her new sadness. He fixed her hair, making her heart jump.

"Just thinking of you."

Naruyuki's eyes widened at how direct she was and laughed. "Thank you for thinking of me."

"I've always." Umeko draped her arms around him, listening to his beating heart. He was so warm, and everything she dreamt he'd be. If only time could freeze so she didn't have to part from him again.

Smiling, Naruyuki draped his arms around her, wishing that nothing would harm her while overseas. "Umeko," he whispered.

Her smile widened and her heart jumped again. He had listened to her plea. "What is it?"

"Be safe."

Taiki who also snuck away happened to see Naruyuki dragging Umeko. Wondering what they were up to, he secretly tailed them and watched as they sat outside in the snow, talking and hugging. No matter how much he wanted to interfere, he was afraid. And so, he stuffed his hands into his pockets and walked away. "Am I the only one feeling insecure?"

After sneaking out with Hanabi, Louis also happened to witness the scene and was now fretting alone. Meanwhile, Hanabi had her back turned towards the three, uninterested. "Wh—what should we do? This looks bad. Taiki saw Naruyuki and Umeko together. I mean—it's not a bad thing. We're all comrades after all. Hugging is no big deal. It's just that, the way they're looking at each other-"

"Let's not talk about it," Hanabi interrupted.

"But if this keeps up, Taiki will misunderstand."

Hanabi rubbed her forehead, feeling a migraine coming on. If any of them were to cry, they should be crying tears of happiness. But everything was turning out to be hectic. "Don't even think about interfering."

"But we gotta help them reconcile before leaving overseas."

"You know, in a sense, I'm happy that we'll be leaving before you can do something meddlesome."

"Don't say that. I just want to help them."

"Louis-kun," Hanabi said, resting her hand on his shoulder. "Sometimes meddling in others' affairs only worsens things. You gotta stand back and see how they work it out for themselves. You can't always be there to give a helping hand."

"But-"

"Promise me you won't do anything before we leave. If you do, I'm gonna drown you in the ocean tomorrow."

Louis gulped. After dwelling on Hanabi's words, he nodded in agreement. He would see how the situation progressed before getting involved. "Alright, fine, I won't interfere."

"Good," she said turning to look at Naruyuki and Umeko. Taiki was gone, yet the emotions from them lingered in the air, making Hanabi nauseous.

∞

While Morgana rambled on about how sad she was to leave overseas without Aoi, he was busy glancing around the room, not quite listening. After Soria had finished dancing with Nicholas, she danced with Louis next. Wanting to be next, Aoi tried to get away from Morgana who incessantly asked him to dance each time, ignoring Yuudai's attempts. Unable to refuse, Aoi kept dancing with her, never allowed to dance with Soria. Now that the group had decided to take a break, a few of them snuck out to escape the last dance. Soria was amongst them.

"…but I'll quickly finish my mission and come back to you Aoi-kun," said Morgana as she blushed.

Aoi set down the cup of punch he was holding and smiled at Morgana. "Excuse me." Briskly, he turned and walked away, already guessing who had kidnapped Soria.

"Eh? Aoi-kun?"

"I'll be back." Aoi turned back to smile and held up a finger. "Give me a minute."

"Okay." Morgana nodded and smiled back, waiting for his return.

Ready to bail also, Cammie walked by with a cup of punch in her hands. She took a sip then spoke, "You do realize he won't be coming back, right?"

Morgana turned and gasped. "Don't say that."

"Actually, I take it back. He'll return…with Soria." Cammie laughed and walked away, waving a hand farewell. It was midnight and she wanted to get some shut eye.

"That was so not funny." Morgana turned to look at Aoi and noticed that he was missing. "Eh? You're kidding me." She ran over to where he'd been and scanned the ballroom. While she was preoccupied, Aoi had slipped out from under her nose.

"Who are you looking for?" asked Shayla as she walked by.

"Aoi-kun."

"I saw him leaving just now," Shayla said, pointing a finger to the door.

Morgana turned to take hold of Shayla's shoulders and squeezed. "With whom?" she demanded.

"Uh, by himself. Who else?"

"Why'd he leave for?"

"I don't know."

"Do you know where he went?"

"Again, I don't know. It's not like I asked."

"Geez, Shayla," whined Morgana.

"Don't blame me. I didn't do anything wrong. If you wanted to keep tabs on him, you shouldn't have let him out of your sight."

"Wouldn't that be stalking?"

"Look at Cat-chan," reminded Shayla. She let out a sniffle and fake cried. "My poor master, she'll never be able to get rid of that cat."

"Aoi-kun, I'll definitely find you," Morgana said, running out of the ballroom.

"Verse was right about her being a stalker."

"Wait! Not you too, Morgana!" Teo shouted after her. More than half of the group had escaped. "Where the hell is everyone going when the last dance is coming up next? We gotta go to sleep after this!"

"Are you gonna shout all night long, or dance with me?" Crystal asked, holding a hand out.

"I'll dance," Teo replied, taking her hand to join the remaining ones.

∞

Rain, Poe, and Azuma sat outside on the stone steps, taking in a breath of air. They had left the party for a good ten minutes already, joking beneath the snowfall.

"Ready to go inside?" asked Azuma.

"Nah, I wanna stay a bit longer," answered Rain.

"We all know you wanna get back to Shayla," Poe teased.

Blushing and glaring, Azuma got into a tussle with him while Rain watched and laughed. "Ah, Alice," he said, pointing a finger.

"Why are you saying Alice's name for?"

"Look." Azuma pointed as the three guys turned to look. Sure enough, Alice and Hana were sneaking out to the forest.

"What are they doing?"

Able to sense his worry, Rain pushed Poe to leave. "Go."

"Yeah," he said, chasing after the girls.

"And he was making fun of me a while ago," grumbled Azuma. He dusted the snow off his tuxedo and stood, turning to look at Rain. "You sure you don't wanna head back inside?"

"I'm sure."

"Is something bothering you?"

Rain shook his head, refusing to yield. "Am I ever bothered by anything?"

"True." Smiling, Azuma turned to take his leave first. He wanted to have the last dance with Shayla. "Don't stay out for too long. You'll catch a cold."

Once Rain was alone, he smiled to the falling snow that showed no signs of letting up any time soon. The mission maze was still weighing heavily on his mind. If he had tried harder, he would be able to travel with the others. Then again, if he was gone, he'd worry about those who were left behind. It was a no-win situation. They were bound to part at one point in time. "I wonder how long we'll remain separated this time," Rain whispered into the night.

"You think too much; don't you think?" Dark plopped down beside him and smiled.

Rain turned to look at him, so lost in thought, he didn't hear Dark approaching. "What are you doing out here? I thought you were inside dancing."

"I wanted some fresh air."

"Liar."

"I'm not lying."

Rain grinned, guessing the problem, "Cammie?"

Dark grinned in return and hit Rain on the arm. There was no use in denying it when he'd detected the problem.

"So, what's wrong?"

Dark's grin faded. In its place was sadness. He didn't understand why he was hated when he was nothing but good to Cammie. Even when he racked his brains over the reason, he couldn't come up with one. It wasn't like they had a feud as kids. Neither did he wrong her. Yet, she seemed to despise his existence. "She's been avoiding me all night and won't dance with me. So, she retired to bed early."

"Why didn't she want to dance?"

"Beats me." Dark shrugged and turned his gaze away from the sky.

"You wanted to dance with her at least once, right?"

"Not really."

"Who are you trying to kid? I can see how depressed you are."

"I'm not the type to get depressed," he replied and stood up to stretch. It was getting late. He didn't want to talk about Cammie anymore. It really was starting to depress him. Dark turned his back and waved a hand. "Well, I got my breath of fresh air."

"Dark," called back Rain.

"What is it? I want to sleep."

With a wild guess, Rain asked, "When she looks at you, does it feel like there's someone reflected in her eyes?"

Dark's eyes widened as he spun around. "How'd you know?"

Rain smiled and looked away. "It's the same here."

"Yeve?"

Rain nodded, returning the problem back to Dark. "If it's bothering you, you should confront her. That's the best choice."

"Why don't you take your own advice?" Dark teased and grinned, as did Rain. "Don't stay out here for too long. You'll catch a cold." He stuffed his hands into his pockets and walked away.

"I've already confronted her," Rain whispered.

"You're the eldest. You shouldn't worry them like this," spoke the ghost with beautiful long white hair that reached her waist. Her green eyes sparkled in the snow. Even her simple yellow dress made her light up in the dark. She placed her back against his. It was extra warm as she propped her arms on her raised knees. "The snow's so beautiful."

Even though her presence was sudden, he felt no apprehension and didn't try to shake her off. Instead, he smiled and watched as the snow landed on his face. "It's fake," he replied.

"It's still beautiful." She held out both elegant hands, trying to catch the falling snow. When they melted on her palms, she stood and walked past him, her hair swaying gently. Unable to take his eyes off her, Rain held his breath and watched as she carefully imprinted her footprints into the flawless snow. After a few paces, she spun back and smiled. "This year, let's build an igloo. How about it?"

"Sure, anything you want," he replied, his heart filling with a warmth he never knew existed until then.

"You're too passive. Why do you always agree so easily?" She pouted and eventually laughed. "But that's just like you."

"I'm not passive."

She blew some air into the sky and watched her breath disappear. Being near him felt so fulfilling. "You can't lie to me. I'll always spot your lies."

"You're also a bad liar," he redirected.

"No wonder we suit each other."

With a chuckle, Rain nodded. "You're right."

"Who're you talking to?" Yeve asked, plopping beside him. She turned, giving him a curious look.

The ghost standing before Rain had vanished. Surprised, he turned to look at Yeve and blinked a few times, making sure she was real.

"Hello? Are you still in there?" Yeve asked, waving her hand in front of his face.

He blinked again and smiled. "I'm still here."

"Hmm," she said doubtfully and pursed her lips to inspect him. "You're lying to me. But I won't nag."

"I'm not lying." He reached out, gently nudging her before turning towards the untouched snow. The footprints he had ingrained into his mind was long gone now. It was nothing more than a painful memory.

"You're a horrible liar. Don't even start with me."

Rain's eyes widened at her words, then softened. This was unfair.

"You know," said Yeve. She stood and walked towards the undisturbed snow in the front courtyard, her gown trailing behind. She hadn't noticed the change in his demeanor. "When winter comes and it really snows in the outside world, let's build a snowman!"

With a nod, tears filled Rain's eyes. "And how big do you want to build it?"

"I don't know. One that reaches the sky?"

"That's impossible."

She turned back to look at him and grinned. The snow stuck to her black hair like petals. "Nothing's ever impossible."

"How about an igloo instead?" he suggested.

"Igloo?"

"Yeah, how about it?"

"Hmm," said Yeve. She thought about it before eventually nodding. "That doesn't sound bad. Alright, an igloo it is then. One that suits an Empress."

Rain laughed. Like usual, Yeve was going at her own pace. From behind, the hauntingly beautiful ghost returned.

"Isn't that a little cruel, Rain?" she asked before disappearing again. Rain turned to look behind. No one was there. He shook it off and turned to face front where Yeve was throwing snow into the air, smiling. For an odd reason, he suddenly felt cold and alone.

∞

Yuudai sat atop the mansion rooftop watching Aoi run around the estate, shouting for Soria. Every now and then he'd trip and fall. Groaning, Yuudai smacked his forehead, wishing he had befriended someone else when they were kids. His good reputation was being damaged because of Aoi's klutzy personality. "Why is it you?" Yuudai muttered and laid down on the tiles.

"Aoi-kun!" Morgana shouted from down below.

At the sound of her voice, Yuudai tensed and closed his eyes. He was tired of being an onlooker. It only brought him pain, knowing that she was chasing his best friend, who was searching for his Soulmate, who had been kidnapped by Nicholas, who was being chased by a vengeful cat. Their love hexagon was so bizarre and theatrical that Yuudai had to laugh and cry. When he finished laughing, all that remained was sorrow.

53rd Lie

AFTER LEAVING THE GUYS BEHIND, Poe chased the two girls into the forest. When he spotted their crouched forms, he came to a halt. They were intensely observing two white, deer-like creatures dig for food beneath the snow-covered ground. When the mother creature found some rootlings, she gave it to her young. As soon as the young ate the rootlings, its horns began glowing a magical white.

Never encountered something so majestic before, Poe stared in awe. He'd always assumed that the creatures living inside the Dome were hideous predators. He never imagined that such harmless and striking creatures like this existed. "Wow," gasped out Poe.

At the sound of his gasp, the mother leapt forward. With a shake to her head, some sort of white glitter appeared and the two vanished. Even the way they fled from danger was beautiful.

Wondering who had ruined the show, the two girls turned to find Poe.

"What was that?" he asked, ignoring their shocked look that now turned into death glares. "I've never-"

"You scared them away!" shouted Alice as she stormed over.

"Eh?"

"Aw, it was just getting to the good part too," whined Hana as she took a stand also. It wasn't every day that she got angry. But she was genuinely upset with Poe.

"Wait a minute. It wasn't my fault."

"Yes, it was," blamed Alice.

"I'm really not at—okay, fine, I am," he admitted, knowing that he was the cause for the creatures to flee. "But how can you blame me? It was my first time seeing them. I was mesmerized. What were they anyway?"

"They're Snow Scorees."

"Have you never seen them before?" Hana raised an eyebrow and was no longer upset. Instead, she was more amused.

Poe shook his head in response.

"Are you serious?" asked Alice.

"Does it look like I'm joking?"

Chuckling, Hana walked over to join them. Now that the Snow Scorees were gone, there was no need for her to stay any longer. She would allow the two Soulmates to have some time alone together. "Well, I'm heading back. You two take your time." Hana winked and ran off giggling, while Alice glared at her hidden meaning.

"Snow Scorees, I've never seen anything like them before," Poe said, still in awe.

Shaking her head, Alice pulled him to go. The night was getting late. The five couples were going to get up early and leave tomorrow. They needed to wake up on time to send them off. "Let's go too."

"Wait. What about the creatures?"

"They won't be returning."

"But what if-"

"Trust me."

Not arguing, Poe allowed her to half-drag him. "How did you find them to begin with?" he asked, wanting to get as much information as he could, so he could gloat about it to the guys later.

"You're really serious, aren't you?"

"Like I said, does it look like I'm joking?" Poe poked Alice's head as she laughed. "So?"

"Well, the story goes like this: when we were still kids, our dean once told us a story about some elusive magical creatures that only came out during the winter nights. We never believed her because we were never able to ascertain the creature's existence. One winter night, a beautiful girl saw a snow creature standing outside the courtyard from her dorm room. She went out to greet this magnificent creature and somehow befriended it. The entire staff, and even her friends were stunned that the snow creature would show itself.

"Many times, the beautiful girl's friends tried to befriend the snow creatures, but none of them ever succeeded. It was as if the snow creatures only wanted that beautiful girl as their friend. So, every winter when it snowed, the snow creatures would come out to play with her and her friends. If the beautiful girl wasn't present, the snow creatures wouldn't appear."

"Is that beautiful girl Hana?" guessed Poe.

Alice laughed again, shaking her head this time. Was Hana someone who invoked the guys' protective instinct? "Nope, she's someone...you boys don't know." There was sadness in her tone as Poe poked her again. The sadness disappeared at once as Alice's smile returned.

"Who was she then?"

"Her name was Wynter."

"Wynter," repeated Poe. "Beautiful name."

"I know, right?" Alice agreed, puffing air into the dark sky. "Like her name, Wynter was a real beauty. She had long white hair and beautiful green eyes that sparkled every time she stood beneath the sun."

"Was she really that much of a beauty?"

"If she was still alive, you boys wouldn't be able to stop gawking at her. She'd probably steal all your hearts with her smile alone. I bet Louis would even propose to her. She's a genuine femme fatale."

"I see. Is that why you and Hana came out here? To find the creatures?"

"That's right."

"Is there something else?" Poe asked, able to read Alice's expressions correctly. There was something else weighing on her mind.

"I can't hide anything from you, can I?"

"You can try. You probably won't succeed."

Laughing, Alice shook her head. "Ever since Wynter's death, the Snow Scorees seemed to vanish altogether. Even when we went in search of them, we couldn't find them."

"And since it's snowing tonight, you and Hana decided to try your luck."

"Yeah," she said.

"Sorry. I ruined a joyous once-in-a-lifetime chance for you."

"You sure did."

"You didn't have to agree." Poe let out a disheartened sigh after hearing Alice's story. If only he hadn't followed them.

Sensing that he was troubled, Alice pinched him.

Wincing, Poe looked down at her. "What was that for?"

"Don't beat yourself over it. Hana and I are happy that we got to see them at least once by ourselves, without needing Wynter."

Without another word, they walked back in silence. When the courtyard of the mansion started to near, Poe gathered all his courage to ask, "Do you hate me, Alice?"

"Eh?" she said in alarm. "That was out of the blue."

"Do you?"

"Why would I hate you for?"

"Just a gut feeling."

"Should I?"

"I don't know. You tell me. You've been acting strange since our second mission."

Alice did her best to smile, tightening her hold around his arm. Even she knew that she was acting strange. But there was no answer she could give that would ease his insecurity. All she could do was apologize for her rude behavior. It was unacceptable as his Soulmate. "About that…I'm sorry."

Poe smiled, able to hear Louis' voice shouting from the mansion. Hotaka could also be heard, shouting at him to stop shouting. The party was probably over if those two were out in the hallway. "Don't worry about it anymore. It's all in the past now."

"Yeah," Alice said, nodding.

∞

The five couples, along with Liz, stood on the pier of the Dome. Once they boarded the ship and sailed out to the mainland, they would be going separate ways to their next missions. The deans and teachers weren't present since they had academies to run. This send-off would only involve the kids.

"Where's that Triheart?" Yuudai growled. Nicholas was the only one not present. And without him, they couldn't leave.

"Beats me," Taiki answered.

"Cat-chan, where's your lover?" Love asked.

Liz glared her way and hissed, arms linked with Yeve. She didn't even want to think about Nicholas at this point. His not being by her side, meant that she was of no importance to him.

"What's your problem anyway?"

"Shut up. You're annoying."

Gasping, Love pointed a finger. She had just been told to keep quiet by a cat. Before Love could get a word in, Takahiko threw a hand over her mouth to drag behind the group.

"Please don't start anything," he said.

"Really, what's taking him?" agreed King. Even he was getting annoyed.

A car zoomed towards them from the tunnelway and parked as Nicholas scrambled out. "Sorry!" he apologized while smiling and adjusting his scarf that the wind was swaying. On his back was a bag. "Hope I didn't keep you all waiting for too long."

"You have no respect for time," Aoi insulted.

"I don't want to hear that coming from you," Nicholas retorted as he walked over to join the others.

"You-"

"Knock it off," Dark said, pulling him back.

"But he-"

"Well," Rain said with a smile. He didn't even care about the commotion being created before departure. Just like that day, inside Leviathan's lair, they had come to another fork in the road. But unlike that time, they could no longer travel as a team. "All of you, take care."

"Of course," the guys answered and smiled.

Jennifer nodded. There was no need to get emotional. They would meet again. This was just a temporary parting. Once the others were ready to receive international missions also, they'd be reunited. Even though Jennifer knew this, she couldn't help feeling overwhelmed. "You girls take care too."

Midnight glanced amongst the others. She recounted and scowled. One girl was missing like usual. "Soria didn't make it?"

"You know her, she's still sleeping," answered Yeve as she yawned. Even though she was tired, she still came out, not wanting to miss their departure.

"How can such a girl survive for this long?" Hissing, Liz shook her head while Yeve poked her. "Swowwy," she apologized in an innocent, childish tone.

Morgana crossed her arms and scowled as well. "Didn't I tell her last night to make it for our send-off? Sheesh, does she not care that we're leaving faraway? That dang poop-head, I'll show her when I return."

"I'm sure she cares," Hana said in Soria's defense.

"Then why is she still sleeping? She should force herself to wake up and bid us a farewell."

"Morgana," pleaded Cammie. "You know how Soria's like."

"That's what makes me frustrated." Morgana glared into the air, wondering how she could rile up Soria once and for all.

Aoi smiled and stepped forward, not wanting his Soulmate to be ridiculed or misunderstood. "Morgana," he said as she blushed. "I'll bid you farewell in Soria's stead. So please, let her off this once." Aoi bowed and stood. "Please take care of yourself while abroad."

"Eh? Oh, uh, no, it's not like that. I don't usually badmouth Soria like this. I'm always praising her."

"Lies," called out the girls.

"Shut up." Morgana glared at them while they grinned. She hadn't meant to upset Aoi. Quickly, she bowed in return and stood back up, coyly playing with the ends of her brown hair. Getting the chance to talk to him one last time was more than enough. "Thank you. You take care too, Aoi-kun."

"Thanks, I will. Just remember to come back safely."

Morgana nodded, her smile brightening. Hearing Aoi say those words made her more determined than ever to return to where he'd be.

"Say, Aoi," Nicholas spoke as an idea came to his head. It was rather genius, so he had to say it. "Since Morgana clearly wants to be your Soulmate, I'll gladly take your position as Soria's Soulmate."

"Huh?!" shouted Aoi, Yuudai, and Morgana.

"Nicholas!" Liz shouted, blushing furiously. He was belittling her before her face.

"Would you stop it with that already?" growled Yuudai. He crossed his arms, not amused.

"Yeah, what Yuu says. Stop joking around," agreed Aoi.

"Eh, well, I wouldn't-" Before Morgana could finish her sentence, Umeko elbowed her to shut up. Yeve was losing her patience with them. "Aha-ha, that's right. It wasn't a very nice joke."

"You guys," Yeve snarled. She hadn't woken up early to hear such a pointless argument take place. "What's so good about that damn poop-head anyway?"

"What Yeve says," Liz agreed.

"Well-" began Nicholas and Aoi.

"It's a rhetorical question!" Yeve erupted. "All of you, just leave already!"

"Evil as always," Midnight said.

"But I was really-" began Nicholas.

"So," Teo interrupted, stopping him from speaking another word. Once Yeve got going, no one would be spared. And he didn't want to get caught up in it. "You guys take care while we're not there to back you up."

"Yeah, come back in one piece," agreed Noah.

"You guys take care too while we're away," King bid. "I don't want to receive word while overseas that any of you died on a mission."

Scowling, Kakinouchi crossed his arms and grinned, taking this time to insult King. "Who the hell do you think you are, Second? The one who should do the worrying is us. We don't want to hear that you got captured and tortured again."

King twitched and turned to glare. "Huh? I don't want to hear that coming from someone who went Berserk."

"You," Kakinouchi hissed as the two got into a brawl.

Azuma watched, not amused. "What the hell? Do they think they're still eight?"

"Let them, it's their way of showing their brotherly love," joked Naruyuki. He laughed and turned to find Louis staring, tears in his eyes. "What the-" He backed away, creeped out. "You've been staring at me and Kakinouchi the entire time, even while inside the car."

"NaruNaru!" shouted Louis as he ran over to hug him. He let out a few sniffles, then turned to give Kakinouchi a puppy look.

"What?" demanded Kakinouchi who had finished his fight with King. Even he didn't want to get caught up in Louis' business before they parted. It would only end in disaster.

"NaruNaru, be sure not to do anything stupid while I'm gone!"

"Louis, get the hell off me," ordered Naruyuki. "Also, don't give me weird nicknames."

"Do you hear me? Don't do anything stupid!"

"You're really annoying."

"Kakichi, be sure to take care of Nono, alright?!" Louis sobbed, reaching out to hold Noah's hand. If he had known that he'd be separated from these three, he wouldn't have ranked in fifth place. "Don't let any harm befall him."

"Let go," Noah ordered, slapping Louis' wrist away. He was confused as to why he was now getting involved, involuntarily.

"Mio-chan," Louis said, turning his attention to Mio now.

"What do you want with her?" Sasuke demanded.

"I'll come back for you, I promise!" He threw her into a tight embrace and cried. He couldn't picture the next few months or years without her. It was because she was always there to cheer him on that he could continue. "I love you the most!"

Tearing up, Mio returned his hug. From all the guys, Louis was the one she didn't want to part from most. "Me too."

"Both of you, knock it off!" Sasuke shouted, trying to pry them apart again. How long were they going to play this charade?

"When I return, we'll get married!" cried Louis.

"Okay," answered Mio.

"Really, someone, stop him," begged Taiki. "I'm already out of energy just thinking of stopping him."

That was her cue as Hanabi walked over to drag Louis towards the ship first. If she didn't stop him now, he'd never stop crying. To save herself the headache, she'd intervene. "With me, right now," she demanded. Hanabi turned back, waving a hand goodbye and smiled. "Bye-bye!"

"Bye!" bid the group.

"Wait!" Louis shouted, not done talking and turned back, still crying. "NaruNaru, Kakichi, remember what I said! Don't you dare ignore my warnings! Nono, take care of yourself while I'm gone! Don't you dare get into any brawls without Kakichi by your side! My lovely three angels, wait for me!"

"That was weird," said Dark.

"He's always been a weirdo since we were kids. You can't expect him to suddenly change," said Noah.

"You can say that again," agreed Azuma.

"I'm going to miss Louis-kun the most," Mio said, sniffling.

"Please. Fall for anyone but him," denied Sasuke.

"Attention, attention," the captain spoke from the speakers of the ship as the group turned to listen. "This is your captain speaking. At this time, Soulmate couples ranks one thru five, please board the ship with Turquoise's

Nicholas and Liz. The ship will be departing shortly. Once again, Soulmate couples ranks one thru five, along with Turquoise's Nicholas and Liz, please board at this time. The ship will be departing shortly. Thank you."

"Well," Hotaka said, smiling, "seems like we gotta go."

"Yeah," Shadow said, nodding. "Take care."

"Bye!" they shouted to one another and waved.

"See you soon!" shouted the girls.

"Take care!"

Heading towards the ship to join Louis and Hanabi, the five couples walked away.

"Take care of Soria until I return for her!" Nicholas shouted and smiled, waving a hand back.

"Don't ever return!" Aoi roared.

"Take care, nee-chan!" shouted Mere. He was frantically waving his hand, tears in his eyes. "I'll be right here waiting!"

Midnight walked up the slope, smiling and waving in response. "I'll be back before you know it!"

"Aw," Jennifer said, watching Mere hold back his tears. She also wanted someone to send her off and welcome her back too. "Mere is such a cutie. It makes me want to have a brother too."

King looked over, then down at Mere, wondering aloud, "Why are you always envious of others?"

"I'm not," she snapped.

"At least I get to be with you, King!" Liz shouted, hugging him from behind.

Jennifer gave him an accusing look while King shook his head profusely. He had to clear the misunderstanding or else his love life would end before it could even begin.

"It's not what you think!" he shouted, trying to break free. "Let me go, cat woman!"

"Don't wanna!"

"King, you two-time jerk!" accused Jennifer.

"For the last time, nothing's going on!"

While the couple along with Liz argued, Yeve stood on the docks, smiling like it was the best day of her life. Finally, Liz would no longer be around to cause her trouble.

"You should see the look on your face." Rain stood beside her, chuckling. Yeve who was usually good at hiding her emotions was showing it for the world to see.

"Can't help it."

"Hotaka!" called out Mere who was now crying, unable to hold back his tears. Midnight was leaving before his eyes again.

Glancing back down, Hotaka raised an eyebrow, wondering what he wanted. A horn blared, indicating that they were ready to depart.

"I don't like you! You remind me of a horrible person!"

Hotaka twitched, ready to take off his shoe to throw at Mere for picking a fight. "Damn runt," he hissed. "Don't think I won't jump down!"

Walking over, Taiki leaned against the railings and smiled. "You're not supposed to say that to your Soulmate's little brother, Hotaka."

"Like I care."

"But because you're Midnight-nee's Soulmate, I'll put my trust in you! Bring her back to me, safe and sound! If she so much as receives just one tiny scratch, I'm going to tell the dean to pardon you as nee-chan's Soulmate! So, if you don't want that to happen, take care of her! I'll never forgive you if you don't!"

Hotaka grinned, not expecting Mere to say such a thing. "You don't have to give me such a serious speech! Who do you think I am?! So long as I'm here, Midnight doesn't need to worry about a thing!"

"Good," Mere whispered. The ship was starting to sail out across the ocean floor as he waved again, tears continuing to stream. He really couldn't handle this abrupt departure after all. "Take care!"

"Bye guys!" they shouted to one another and waved one last time.

Once they drifted far away enough, Nicholas and Liz left to their cabins, leaving the ten to stand on the deck.

"Well," Taiki said, turning to leave also. "Anyone up for breakfast?"

Umeko nodded. "I am."

One by one, they left until it was only Louis and Hanabi.

Louis leaned against the railings, watching the Dome shrink into the horizon, until it completely disappeared. Because their first few missions had been relatively close to each other, he didn't worry. Now that they were being sent overseas, he was worried to death. The futures he foresaw as a child and pre-teen resurfaced. No matter what Louis did, he couldn't shake it off. If only Naruyuki and Noah could be by his side, he'd have nothing to worry about. Especially since he didn't know when those futures he had foreseen would take place. "I hope those three take what I said to heart."

Hanabi looked over and smiled. "They'll be fine."

Louis turned to hold her gaze. Hanabi was as cool as ice. It was unfair that she never got anxious when their powers were complements. Was it because their views on life were different? "Aren't you worried?"

"No." Though she said that, it was a lie. Her heart felt like it was heading towards the biggest storm of the century.

∞

594

Once the group returned to the mansion, Miss Lima took them into a meeting room to brief about their next missions. She went around the room, handing each person a file.

"I knew this was going to happen once the others left," complained Teo. Crystal nodded. "Tell me about it."

Upon opening her file and reading its contents, May groaned. "Ugh, you're kidding me, right?"

"Kidding about what?" asked Miss Lima.

"You want me to find a missing cat in Tokyo?" May held up the file in her hand for Miss Lima to see. It was ridiculous that she had been given such a simple task.

"Too easy," agreed Kakinouchi.

"The dean was the one who assigned the missions," explained Miss Lima. She shook it off, having no need to listen to them whine. Her only task was to hand out the files. "If you have any questions or concerns, you can go to the dean."

May stuffed the file back into its folder and crumpled it. "I will."

Kakinouchi looked over at Sasuke who was carefully rereading his file. "What's taking you so long?"

"My next mission requires me to be attentive."

"Huh? Why?"

"I have to go undercover."

"Eh?" May said, glancing over. "That should've been *my* mission!"

"He-he," Mio laughed, giving May a peace sign. Finally, she was being taken seriously. "I guess the dean has finally recognized my true talents."

"You have no talents."

"Sure, Seventeen," taunted Mio. She put a hand to her mouth and laughed. Soon, she and May were brawling while their Soulmates intervened, pulling them apart.

Soria who had been forced awake by Verse sat inside the room, legs perched. In her hand was the file Miss Lima had finished distributing. "Why do I keep traveling up north?" she complained and yawned.

"Where are you going?" asked Hana.

Before Soria could answer, Aoi jumped to his feet and threw his hands into the air excitedly. "Oh yeah, here I come, Alaska!"

"Are you serious?!" the guys shouted, blowing steam. Why was Aoi also getting the chance to travel outside of Asia?

"Why is he going but not me?!" Noah also stood and pointed to Aoi, demanding an explanation for this absurdity. It was clear that the deans had assigned missions based on couples and success on previous cases.

"Like I said," Miss Lima said, still not caring. "If you have any problems, you may go to the deans. Complaining to me won't get you anywhere."

Aoi sighed dreamily, already picturing the snowy mountains and beautiful coastal ranges. It was the most romantic getaway. This time for certain, he was going to find time a way to take Soria on a date, whether she wanted to or not. "I wonder what I should pack."

"Hey," Soria said, holding up her file. "Anyone wanna trade?"

"Me!" volunteered Remi and Mio as they raised their hands.

Just as the dean had suspected, Soria was trying to get out of her mission. Because of that, she'd given Miss Lima special permission to hit Soria and anyone who tried trading missions with her. Following through, Miss Lima walked over to smack the three girls over on the head. "No trading missions. What's been given is final. If you have a problem, go to the deans." She walked back to the front and stopped, turning to look at the group sitting before her. "You are to report back to your rooms, prepare for your missions, grab any last-minute items you need, and set out quickly."

"Are you serious?" asked Verse.

"Please make haste," she added in and motioned to the door as the group stood to exit.

Once they were out in the hallway, Shayla held out her arms to halt them. She had something important to announce. "Wait!" she shouted, while the others raised their eyebrows. "Since we couldn't attend the summer festival, let's go to the autumn festival instead."

"Huh?"

"There's going to be another festival held in a couple of months to celebrate the fall season. Let's go together. There's going to be tons of games and lots of fireworks. I wanted to go with everyone during the summer festival, but the dean rejected my proposal. Even though the others are gone, we can still go. Or if a couple of months is pushing it, we can attend the winter festival instead."

"Ah," Azuma said, remembering. During their second mission, Shayla couldn't stop talking about the festival. Now that the madness from "The Rescue" had died down, they could relax by having fun. He turned to smile at the others and nodded. "Yeah, let's go."

"Sure," the others agreed, seeing nothing wrong with it.

"The festival," Mio said dreamily.

"Hmm," Yeve said, scratching her head. "I don't really wanna."

"Yeah," agreed Verse. "Too much hassle."

"I would prefer to spend that time sleeping instead," Soria said with a nod also.

Shayla glared at the three. She should've guessed that it would be these three who would object to her plans. If she didn't think of something fast, they were going to ruin this second attempt for her. "Master," Shayla said, holding up her index finger. A thought had occurred to her just then. She was one hundred percent sure it would work. "Didn't you hear me? I said that there's going to be tons of games."

"So?" Yeve asked without a care.

"Oh?" Shayla lowered her hand to cross her arms. "I see how it is. You're afraid that if you challenge those humans at the fair, you'd lose for sure." Shayla unfolded her arms and shook her head. "Of course, even the *Great Empress* would have her own weaknesses."

Yeve twitched, her aura turning a foul color as everyone backed away. Shayla was taking a big risk. "Oh? You dare to sully me?" she challenged and pointed a finger at Shayla. "Bring it on, you stupid disciple! I'll show you that I, future Empress of the World, have no weaknesses!"

Shayla grinned, having won this fight.

"Simpleton," Verse said.

"Oh, Verse," Shayla said, smiling innocently. "There's going to be tons of food. And I heard they're cheap. I really wanted to pig out with you."

"I'm going."

Naruyuki looked over, sweating a bit. Verse had been won over more easily than Yeve. "I can't believe you."

"You should've seen that one coming," said Cammie.

"I did," said Remi.

"You three, shut up," hissed Verse.

"So, how about it?" Shayla insisted.

"I still want to sleep," Soria responded.

Shayla glared, thinking she had dealt with all the obstacles. Clearly, there was still one left on her path to happiness, and it was the biggest one. Again, Shayla crossed her arms to take on the challenge. "I guess the future Empress has no hold on her loyal subjects."

"Soria," growled Yeve.

"Eh?!" shouted Soria. She couldn't believe that Yeve would fall victim to Shayla's tricks. "You can't be serious!"

Laughing victoriously, Shayla grinned at Soria who glared in return. This was a challenge that Soria wouldn't back down from, given how Shayla had incited her fury.

"You damn chubby grape head," hissed Soria. "I'll remember this day."

"Don't call me that! I'm no longer that person!"

"Sure you're not. We all know that deep down you haven't changed, my little purple piggy."

"Waa, death to you, Soria!"

"How can a chubby grape head kill me when she died years ago? All I see in her place is a shallow skinny wannabe-Yeve." Soria laughed evilly and walked away. She may have lost the battle, but she surely won the war.

"You're so cruel!"

"There, there," Azuma soothed as he patted her back. "Don't take what she said to heart. It was just a joke."

"No, it wasn't! Soria's always serious! When is she never serious?!"

"Yeve," Verse pleaded, tired of hearing her eating buddy cry. "Do something about your pupil."

"Come on," Yeve said, dragging Shayla away from Azuma.

"B—but master, Soria was making fun of me again. How can I not get hurt from her words?"

"I know. I heard. I'll deal with her later."

Azuma chuckled. He couldn't believe that Shayla's strategy had resulted in a success. In the process, she'd been delivered an unexpected blow.

"Wow," Kakinouchi said with a whistle. He'd never seen Soria so serious before. "Was Soria always so relentless?"

"You haven't seen anything yet," Takahiko said.

"What does that mean?"

"Soria's always been this way," Crystal answered while May nodded in agreement.

"So, we're all good now?" Verse asked, wanting to leave too.

"Yeah, we're good to go," Rain answered.

"Where do we meet up?" asked Poe.

"First, I gotta ask for permission," reminded Azuma.

"Then, once you do, let us know."

"Will do."

"What if we can't finish our missions on time?" asked Mio.

May grinned. Now was her turn to taunt Mio. "Oh my, what's wrong Mio? Didn't you say you had *real* talent? There's no need to fret. Or could it be that you have no faith in this so-called *'talent'* of yours? Is the time limit too short? Do we need to extend it by two years for you to finish your mission?"

"O—of course not! I'll show up on time! You just watch!"

"We'll just have to see then."

"May," said Kakinouchi as he shook his head. She was back to her unforgiving sadistic ways.

"If Azuma can get permission from the deans, we'll meet in Harajuku," Rain said to the group. "For the meanwhile, let's just concentrate on returning in one piece to attend this festival."

www.ingramcontent.com/pod-product-compliance
Lightning Source LLC
Chambersburg PA
CBHW022232020726
47496CB00004B/863